The Order
of the
Albatross

Or

Prometheus Undone

J. Clark Hallvin

Published in the United States by MacGuffin Books.

ISBN: 0615785093
ISBN-13: 978-0615785097

CONTENTS

The Order of the Albatross

Or

Prometheus Undone

On the 17th of June [30 June N.S.], around 9 o'clock in the morning, an unusual natural occurrence was observed. In the North Karelinski village, 200 kilometers north of Kirensk [southeast of the Tunguska basin], the peasants saw high above the horizon to the northwest a strangely bright cylindrical heavenly body, which for 10 minutes moved downwards. The weather was hot and dry, and the sky was cloudless with only a small dark cloud observed in the object's general direction. As the object neared the earth it seemed to smudge, becoming a giant billow of black smoke accompanied by a loud booming, as if large stones were falling or artillery firing. All the buildings shook. At the same time the cloud emitted flames of uncertain shapes. All villagers were stricken with panic and took to the streets. Women cried, thinking it was the end of the world.

The newspaper *Sibir*
Irkutsk, Russia
July 1908

This excerpt was taken from a yellowed newspaper clipping found between the pages of Grey's original manuscript. The article was in Russian and accompanied by a note, an English translation written in a woman's hand.

Ah! well a-day! what evil looks
Had I from old and young!
Instead of the cross, the Albatross
About my neck was hung.

Samuel Taylor Coleridge
"The Rime of the Ancient Mariner"

1: GUTTER DAYS

I will always remember my greatest performance as if it were yesterday, for never before has the fate of the world depended on so few, Yours Truly among them.

No doubt, Dear Reader, you interpret such a claim as gross exaggeration. How, you ask, could a former Vaudevillian have played a pivotal role in saving the world?

I know it sounds far-fetched, and there is no shortage of those willing to declare, "Don't believe a word of it! Prometheus Grey is a rogue, a reprobate, an inveterate liar!" Nevertheless, I maintain that what follows is true, faithfully recorded to the best of my ability, and embellished only where necessary. As proof of my integrity I offer this: recording my adventure profits me nothing. In fact, quite the opposite. By telling this story I jeopardize my life and livelihood. Why, then, would I document something that puts me in danger? The answer is simple.

Love.

And spite.

And knowledge! For mine is a tale the world must know in case such evil should rise again. So, like my namesake, the great titan who stole fire from the gods for the sake of Man, consider this my gift to the world, for the facts are no less incendiary.

Since circumstances are so dire, I will go one step further to prove my integrity. I will point out that over the course of my life I have played a variety of roles, most of which are reflected in the account that follows. In it I serve as the hero, but on occasion I also come across as a bit of a scoundrel. No matter how I am portrayed, I must confess the role I ultimately fulfilled—the one Fate reserved for me, and which I was born to play—was that of The Fool.

But it is not unheard of for The Fool to take center stage, to beguile the

1

audience, and to steal the show.

My story begins in New York City, February 1908. I had by that time been in dire straits for no less than a year. My financial situation had forced me out of my palatial Brooklyn apartment and into the foulest gutters of the Bronx, where my daily bread was replaced with whatever scraps I could muster. The usual fare was whatever diseased meat the urchins happened to be selling. I never asked, but looking back there is no question it was something unwholesome, perhaps the flesh of a mangy dog or cat, or worse, sewer rat, served on a wooden skewer. But beggars can't be choosers, as the saying goes, so I ate to stay alive.

I remember with crystalline clarity the moment I decided I could no longer bear such an ignominious life. Whatever creature I had just eaten had not been properly cleaned, and as I plucked bits of oily fur from my tongue, I decided the time had come to take revenge upon the man responsible for my misery. And before the police could clap me in irons and throw me in jail (perhaps the only fate worse than New York's gutters) I intended to go one step further and snuff out my own light.

As chance would have it, I had awakened that morning to an unpleasant surprise, and it was this that put such wicked thoughts in my head. The nighttime breeze had carried some trash into the alley where I slept, depositing it gently in front of my nose. When I opened my eyes I found myself face-to-face with a tattered and stained handbill bearing the name of my nemesis in large, bold letters. I tried to recoil, but after sleeping on cobblestones I was too stiff to move. So I took it slowly, and after a minute I managed to prop up against a wall and, with great loathing, read the advertisement.

It announced a series of performances by my enemy at the Byzantium Theater on Broadway. The engagement was to run daily during the evening matinee.

The news, and Fate's flaunting of it, infuriated me. Had I not been tormented enough? Had I not already fallen as low as Man can fall? To taunt me with my enemy's success while I lay in the gutter was intolerable. I decided to illustrate the full measure of my contempt by retreating to a more private recess of the alley, where I put the paper to an unwholesome-yet-appropriate use at the conclusion of a particularly loose bowel movement.

After that small victory I felt better for a while and thought I had put the matter to rest. I dug into my pockets and came up with four pennies, the last remnants of my once modest fortune. I then made my way to the street, where I spotted a rascally-looking boy selling skewers of meat. I would have preferred to save my money for rotgut, but four cents would get me no booze, so decided instead to blow it on a last supper, as it were.

It was the first time in months hunger had triumphed over thirst, probably as a result of my inadvertent sobriety. When I had fallen asleep I had been well sloshed, and I had expected to experience some degree of lingering inebriation the following day. However I must have slept longer than intended, because I was as sober as a tea-totaler.

Battling the stiffness in my joints I shambled up to the boy, who seemed a little unnerved. By the look in his eyes I thought he might bolt, but when he heard the jingle of coins in my hand he found his courage and offered me a spit. I sadly surrendered my last pennies, accepted the horrible looking meal, and retreated back across the street into the alley.

I collapsed in my familiar spot and, against better judgment, began to feast. The meat was overcooked, covered in a palpable layer of ash, likely to hide its true nature. But my hunger convinced me to pay no heed.

As I lounged upon the cobbles the advertisement again popped into my head. The name it bore—the very name I had spent the last year trying to forget—stood out in my mind as boldly as the letters in which it had been printed. I began humming to myself as a distraction, instinctively choosing a cheery tune remembered from my civilized days: Beethoven's *Ode to Joy*. But despite the *Ode* in my ears, the taste of ash in my mouth, a throbbing headache, and a pain in my posterior from sitting on inhospitable stones, the name persisted. I simply could not shake it. And the longer it occupied my thoughts, the more agitated I became. Rage that had been long suppressed began to boil up to the surface.

The sun was approaching its noon apex when I finally had my epiphany. The combination of that damnable name and the taste of burnt sewer-meat made my hands shake and my stomach churn. I rolled onto my side to ease my release, and as I lay there retching I finally had a vision of revenge. It was a mad, self-destructive idea, yet the more I pondered it, the better I felt. It seemed so fitting and right that within seconds I had convinced myself it was the only course of action left to me.

As my stomach settled I struggled to my feet and rummaged through piles of trash until I found the offensive paper. It was smeared with filth (my own, admittedly) but the words could still be made out: Byzantium Theater, Nightly, 27 January – 1 February. With a start I realized the final performance was that very day. I had no time to waste.

I strode from the alley I had for so long, and so reluctantly, called home. After more than a year living on the streets and waiting for death, my life—or what remained of it—again had purpose. Therefore I took it as a good omen when a block later I passed the boy who had sold me my vile breakfast. Without warning I rushed him, seizing him by the scruff of the neck. Before he knew what was happening I had given him a good thrashing and taken off down the street. I was well beyond the reach of John Law by the time I heard the familiar tweet of his whistle.

Unfortunately, I had a considerable journey ahead of me. I was in the Bronx, and the Byzantium Theater was located on Broadway. I was some distance from the splendor of that marvelous venue, and since I was penniless a carriage or trolley was out of the question. I would have to make the

3

journey on foot, and it would take me the remainder of the day.

The day passed uneventfully, aside from the shocked expressions I garnered from passersby. Judging by their faces, I must have appeared more destitute and deranged than even I imagined. I had been wearing the same set of clothes for almost a year, and though I hid them beneath a tattered overcoat, my entire ensemble must have reeked of the street.

As I passed a shop with a large glass window, I got a glimpse of my reflection and was mortified. My hair was greasy and in a state of disarray. Beneath that were eyes set in circles so dark they seemed to be staring out of the abyss. My complexion was so pale and unhealthy as to be green, and my jaw was a garden of tangled whiskers. I could not recall the last time I had seen my reflection—perhaps it too had been a year—but I had never suspected I looked so awful. The humiliation was too much. I pulled my ragged coat closed to shield myself from gawkers and pressed on.

By sunset I was walking along Broadway. Marquees blazed with electric lights, and the sidewalks were as crowded with people as the street was with traffic. The hustle and bustle threw my thoughts into disarray. I was overjoyed to return to the avenue of my hey-day, but I did not let my elation distract from my mission. As I elbowed my way through the throng, I could not help but wonder how many of them had once been part of my audience, and how surprised they would be if they recognized me now.

The only challenge remaining was to find the Byzantium. I knew it well enough. I had performed there on occasion. Now, however, that seemed like a lifetime ago, and picking out the correct theater was like trying to conjure up my earliest childhood memory. But I knew if it were before me I would recognize it, so I continued to weave my way through the crowd.

Within minutes I found it. Lamps burned brightly all around, illuminating the faces of those on the sidewalk. I presumed the crowd was there to see the very performance I intended to crash, and as I crossed the street I smiled to myself over the surprise they would soon receive.

By then I had authored a complete plan in my head. From my days working the theater I recalled a rear door with a transom, and above that a series of windows leading to upper offices, any of which I could enter with ease. My plan, therefore, went like this: once inside I would climb into the rafters above the stage, hidden from the crowd by the proscenium arch, and lie in wait. When my nemesis appeared I would anticipate the opportune moment—preferably the climax of one of his tricks—to dive headfirst toward him, plummeting thirty feet to the stage, simultaneously crushing him and breaking my own neck. It was a near perfect plan. The only flaw was that as the projectile, I would not live long enough to relish his demise.

But Fate, who has so often intervened in my life, had other plans. As I pressed through the crowd toward the theater, I noticed the doors were shut tight. Then my eyes fell upon the billboard, which advertised another performance entirely, a show featuring some fool with tamed doves.

I was flabbergasted. As I stared in disbelief, I noticed a corner of the poster was peeling off, revealing a glimpse of another beneath. I grabbed the loose corner and tore the poster from the board, uncovering the advertisement I had expected.

"What's this?" I cried. I was merely voicing my confusion, not expecting anyone to answer, but I drew the attention of a man standing nearby who had witnessed my assault on the sign.

"Miscreant!" he said, shaking his umbrella at me. "What do you think you're doing? Leave that alone, and get away from there before I call the police!"

"Where is he?" I cried, pointing at the poster. "He's supposed to be here!"

The man frowned and glanced at the signboard, tilting his head back to look through the spectacles at the end of his nose.

"Who, Houdini?" he said. "Look there. His engagement ran through February first. Today is the second. You missed it, you drunken fool."

I was too shocked to react to his insult, too outraged by yet another mockery of Fate. The fickle harlot seemed unable to make up her mind about what to do with me.

The cruel twist unhinged me. After a year of misery I had finally acted decisively, in a way that would both satisfy my need for vengeance and bring an end to my deplorable life, only to be mocked by a faded and weatherworn poster flapping gently in the breeze. I stared at it for a long time, as if by will or denial I could turn back the clock to the day before. But alas, capricious Fate had robbed me of revenge. The anger ebbed out of me, and in flowed further humiliation.

Thus robbed of purpose I wandered aimlessly down the street. I paid no heed to where I was going. I followed whatever sidewalk or avenue my feet fell upon. Eventually the sounds and spectacle of Broadway were left far behind. I have no recollection of what neighborhoods I wandered, or for how long. I was so crestfallen that I could have wandered through the gates of Hell without noticing.

At some point during my trek I stumbled into a vagabonds' alley, for I remember figures slumped against walls, snoring loudly, half buried in trash for warmth against the winter chill. The stench of garbage and offal was overpowering. I was about to collapse among them for the night when I kicked something that clattered across the cobbles: a bottle of rotgut, three quarters full. Its owner had fallen asleep, the bottle slipping from his grimy fingers.

I looked around in the darkness wondering if anyone had noticed, but no one stirred. The snoring continued unperturbed. As if escaping from a den of sleeping lions, I picked up the bottle and stole out of the alley.

I made my way to a nearby streetlamp, where I held up the bottle in admiration, like a father celebrating a newborn son. It gleamed in the light, the dark liquor within glowing with the promise of escape. I uncorked it and took a long draught that instantly warmed me to my toes.

"Well, then," I said quietly. "I cannot endure this any longer. I shall drink

5

until all feeling leaves my body, and then I shall jump from a very high rooftop and conclude the tragedy my life has become."

I set off along the sidewalk once again, taking occasional swigs from the bottle. I still had no destination, but somehow it seemed better to be moving than to collapse in a reeking alley. I walked and drank for longer than I can recall, and as the bottle emptied so did my senses. From then on, all I can offer are snatches of memory that may, or may not, have been reality.

I remember a good deal of weaving and staggering; the panicked face of a woman; a gaudy red velvet parlor, perhaps a bordello, and being ejected by a man built like an icebox; a seemingly endless carriage ride (how this came about I have no clue, for I was penniless); a fall resulting in a shattered bottle; watching the liquor disappear between thirsty cobblestones; and haphazardly scaling the exterior of a building, presumably to attain a height from which to leap to my doom.

At that point memory failed me entirely, and I have no idea how many hours or days passed before I regained my senses. When I awoke—apparently I had been too inebriated to carry out my suicidal plan—I was lying on my back, staring at a cloudless, star-speckled evening sky. My head ached, but not as much as I expected after such a bender.

I sat up and took in my surroundings. I was on a flat rooftop with a raised ledge. I climbed to my feet and approached the edge, which afforded me a commanding view of the neighborhood. Judging from the clean stone facades of surrounding buildings, I determined I was in a well-to-do area. I looked around until I found the river, and gauging my distance and location I guessed I had crossed into Manhattan.

As I wondered at the events that had brought me there, I noticed a light nearby, emanating from a glass protuberance in the roof: a skylight. As the roof was otherwise flat and uninteresting, that knee-high crystal pyramid acted as a magnet for my curiosity. I approached it and heard the sounds of muffled music and conversation. Crouching, I peered through into a large living room, filled with guests dressed in evening finery, all laughing and sipping champagne from delicate glasses.

There were perhaps ten couples milling about while a handful danced to music from a phonograph. The dancers twirled gracefully, and when the music stopped everyone applauded. It was the kind of social I had been born to attend, the kind to which I had once received regular invitations. If I were to walk into that room now—even if I wore a tuxedo and did not reek of whiskey and filth—the party would come to a standstill. My reputation alone would bring it to a screeching halt. The guests would all be astonished. They would slowly turn their shocked expressions to their hostess as if to ask, "What on earth is *he* doing here?"

Then again, perhaps I presumed too much. I preferred to believe they would have remembered me upon sight. After all, I had been the premier spiritualist among their ilk for several years, and before that I had been an accomplished and celebrated escape artist. After my fall from grace, however,

I had been forsaken rather quickly. Since then no one had offered me consolation or even the pretense of sympathy.

I watched the party below, transfixed; and as I observed it a strange thing happened. The magic of the spectacle began to fade and was replaced by a steadily growing anger that took me completely by surprise. Without intending to, I suddenly found myself scowling down at them, sneering at their pretentious ways, and thinking they needed to be taught a lesson. And who better to teach them than the one they—or their kind, at any rate—had ostracized?

I crept along the ledge and inspected the walls below for windows I might find accessible. It did not take long to find one I could easily reach from above, and lowering myself to it I set to work.

It was a tricky business. The maneuver required me to suspend myself by one hand while working on the window with the other. Fortunately, as a result of my liquid diet, I had become so light that my neglected muscles were able to hold out. The rest of the task was child's play. Window locks are simple mechanisms—little more than an inconvenience for one as versed in locks as I—and this one happened to be only partially latched. By placing my free hand against the glass pane I was able to sufficiently disturb the frame until the latch disengaged. Within seconds I was inside.

I found myself in a dark room with a tiled floor, and immediately in front of me I could feel the cold, hard porcelain of a cistern. With outstretched hands I moved further inside until I found a wall, then felt my way along it to the door. I opened it slowly and stepped into the darkness beyond. By chance I had chosen the right window through which to climb. It belonged to the master bathroom, and I now found myself standing in an expansive bedroom.

Darkness prevented me from a complete survey, but the glow of streetlamps outside provided enough light to see that it was lavishly furnished. I stood for a moment in awe of the shadowy splendor. Then the sound of the music downstairs reminded me of my intent and its urgency.

I crept to the bed and rummaged through the nightstands, where I found a gold watch and a frail studded silver necklace, both of which I pocketed. Next I crossed to a bureau and quietly ransacked its drawers, coming up with a few bank notes. Looking around the room I noticed several other items of value—vases, statuettes and the like—but nothing I could hope to carry while scaling a building. So, reluctantly, I made my way back to the bathroom, through the window, and onto the roof.

Once up top I strolled to the skylight to glance at the party one last time. The celebration continued without pause. No one was wise to the fact I had been in the house. I smirked at the thought, basking in my skillful accomplishment. Then I found a drainpipe, slid down to the ground, and headed back toward the Bronx.

Considering how bad my luck had been of late, this series of events put me in good spirits. In fact, you could say I was inebriated by my success, for looking back I cannot remember much more of that evening, even though I was stone sober. I only know that I did not further imbibe.

I walked the streets well into the early morning. Eventually I found myself in Central Park, and I fell asleep on a bench. My next memory is being jabbed in the ribs with a billy club, and opening my eyes to find a patrolman standing over me. As a rule I avoided trouble, so I pretended to move on until the officer was out of sight. I then found another bench and collapsed.

I pulled out my spoils from the night before. I first counted the bank notes and discovered I had managed to come away with close to twenty dollars—a veritable windfall for someone in my wretched state. Next I produced the timepiece. It was an admirable piece of jewelry. I wound it and flipped it open to make sure it was running, and inside the lid I noticed the inscription: *God gives us the time we need.* I scoffed at its optimism and continued my inspection. I dug deep in my pocket and fished out the necklace. When I examined it I gasped, for I had expected it to be a piece of costume jewelry. On the contrary, it was a genuine treasure. The chain itself was woven from a spider's silver thread, and the studs spaced along its length were tiny white diamonds. I had no idea of the item's value, but I knew it was worth a small fortune.

Later that morning I began my search for a buyer, which itself turned out to be more complicated than expected. I needed only visit a few saloons to locate the class of persons who indulged in such illicit business. Time and again, however, as I worked up my courage to approach one of them, I had the uneasy feeling it would be a mistake. Somehow I knew that if I revealed the pilfered treasures, I would be killed before I saw a penny. Finally, I decided my life was more important than recouping my fortune in one fell swoop, and I abandoned the idea of fencing it.

As I walked slowly along the sidewalk I could not help chuckling to myself over the irony. I had in my possession an item quite possibly worth more money than I had made in my lifetime, yet I was unable to turn it into cash for a simple cup of coffee.

Still, I had twenty dollars in my pocket, and that was enough for a new start—the first step toward a new life and regaining my dignity. I found a small shop that made decent, if not stylish, clothes and purchased a new suit. I then visited a public bath where I cleaned, shaved, and donned the suit to become a new man.

My complexion and generally poor state of health still made me look suspect, and there was only one fix for that. By late morning I was sitting down to a hearty meal of steak and eggs in the first reputable-looking restaurant I could find. As I feasted I realized I had become civilized again. No one would have guessed that just hours earlier I had been the filthiest wretch in the city.

After my meal I stood on the street corner, puffing a ten-cent cigar as I wound the timepiece and set it to the correct hour. Those simple pleasures exhilarated me, and I vowed I would never return to the streets. I would do whatever it took to wear clean clothes, eat palatable food, and sleep in a bed every night. I would sooner commit murder than return to a life of misery.

2: THE GHOST

Here begins the chapter of my life in which I was known as the Ghost of Manhattan. The moniker arose from the fact that no one, not a single witness, ever laid eyes on me, nor did I leave a trace of evidence in any place I thieved. I have the press to thank for the name, for it was the newspapers that so christened me. When my burglaries of New York's aristocrats stymied the police, the papers said only a ghost could come and go at will and leave no trace. Thus "The Ghost" was born.

I must admit the name flattered me. As a performer it appealed to my sense of showmanship. It was precisely the sort of gimmick a shrewd entertainer might employ to entice people to his show. It also amused me due to its unintended irony. In the latter half of my professional career—prior to Houdini's betrayal—I had largely abandoned feats of escape in favor of occult services. As a spiritualist I routinely communed with the dead, allowing the bereaved to communicate with their dearly departed for a nominal fee. It was all farce, but it entertained and eased the suffering of my clients, which made it all worthwhile. Now, the man who had once communed with ghosts became a Ghost—a wonderful twist!

But I am getting ahead of myself. After cleaning up and purchasing a new suit, I found an apartment for rent in Harlem, just a few minutes' walk from Central Park. The landlady, Mrs _____, was a shrewd, bespectacled septuagenarian whose entire character could be summed up by her stained apron and her perpetual scowl of suspicion and disapproval. She turned a deaf ear to any haggling over rent, and in the end I succumbed to her demands for a sparely furnished, one room apartment. Then she showed me to the door of my new residence, handed me the key, and shuffled away without showing the slightest hint of welcome.

Once established in a normal, albeit parsimoniously, furnished home, I sat at the small table by my only window and pondered my future. My face, name, and reputation were anathema. No degree of self-reinvention would have enabled me to resurrect my stage career, and venturing back into the arena of occult services was out of the question. I briefly considered legitimate, everyday employment as a possibility, but I could see no appreciable future in it.

As I pondered these things I absentmindedly reached into my pocket and produced the stolen necklace, fondling its tiny diamonds as a priest does the rosary. As I gazed upon its beauty an idea dawned on me. The answer was so simple I had overlooked it. I would become a professional thief.

It made perfect sense. The skills I had honed throughout my career—stealth, climbing, lock-picking, trickery—naturally mirrored those of thieves. The criminal element offered the most reward and required the least effort. And I had a fortune to rebuild, for mine had been wrongfully taken from me. Yes, I had misled people with my spiritualism, but that hardly justified the court's decision to seize my assets, divide the money among my clients, and leave me penniless. One could argue that high society was to blame for my misfortune. Where were New York's aristocrats when I stood so wrongfully accused? Did anyone come to my defense? Did anyone offer me aid or solace? No, not one of them took pity on me. So just as I had been robbed of my livelihood, I would now reclaim my fortune from those who abandoned me. Houdini may have been the engineer of my demise, but the city's elite were no less culpable.

Thus the decision was made and my new career chosen. I became a thief.

Strangely, thieving gave me new purpose and direction. I once again had a reason to get up, get dressed, and go out every day. A day without performing some task in service of that ignoble art felt like a day wasted. As I had no office, club, or other social engagements to attend, pilfering became my full-time obsession. Planning larcenies exercised my intellect; scaling apartment buildings tested me physically; and defeating locks each night kept my mechanical skills finely honed. It felt so wonderful to be working again that I forgot I was breaking the law.

While I had a very real fortune to rebuild, it was the *act* of theft, rather than greed, that drove me to such industrious criminal heights. In less than a month I plundered no fewer than two dozen homes of the well-to-do, each time displaying the same acrobatic mastery and understated flair as I had on that first ill-fated evening. And thanks to the newspapers—in particular the *American* and the *Evening Journal*—the reputation of The Ghost quickly flourished. I once again became the talk of the town.

As I made my way nightly across rooftops to rummage through the drawers of New York's elite, I initially sought only cash, or baubles that would turn a quick dollar. Soon, however, I began to take whatever items caught my eye. Mostly these amounted to items of jewelry, extravagant pieces that would prove almost impossible to fence. But I was making enough money from selling lesser items that I did not care. Even when money had ceased to be a problem, I felt compelled to continue.

Greed for wealth ceased to be my prime motive. Instead, a different sort of greed had taken hold: a hunger for thrill and infamy. I began to steal simply to maintain my reputation, to ensure my name stayed in the papers. There were many instances when I had no need for money at all, but I nevertheless risked life and limb to make off with some lady's precious items. In this way I ensured I was never far from the thoughts of my public. My philosophy was, if more than a few days passed in which the papers failed to print an article about my escapades, then the city was deserving—nay, *in need of*—another performance. So I tried to swipe something valuable almost nightly, and in so doing I kept The Ghost's fame and notoriety alive.

But alas, there were considerable flaws in my machinations, followed by one resounding stroke of bad luck. The main flaw was that in addition to stealing far more than I needed, I also foolishly kept most of the ill-gotten goods. It was not out of avarice; rather it happened as pure coincidence. After each burglary I made my way back home and thoughtlessly deposited my booty in a dresser drawer. This went on for several months, and by the time John Law caught me the drawer was so brimming with gold, silver, and gems, it would have made Long John Silver drool with avarice.

Bad luck came at the height of my criminal fame, when I came under suspicion of murder. To this day I have no explanation for it, but here are the facts as I know them.

I had embarked upon my nightly adventure to keep alive The Ghost's reputation. At midnight I donned my traditional black suit and cap, climbed from my window to the rooftop, and began winding my way toward the homes of the wealthy. Earlier in the day I had cased a mansion that I intended to add to The Ghost's list of exploits. Upon reaching it I quickly exploited its window ledges, drain pipes and gutters to make my way to its roof. At the top I discovered a rooftop garden, which I crept through and found a door leading into the house. Once inside I went straight for the master bedroom. As I slowly opened the door I heard the quiet sigh of someone breathing. I peered in and saw the unmistakable silhouette of a woman on the bed. Not to be denied, I crept in and headed toward the jewelry box on the dressing table. I opened it and with knowing fingers felt through the contents until I came across what I sought. Without need for further inspection I scooped the items up, stuffed them into my pockets, and made my escape.

It was a flawless performance, and another mysterious bit of thievery would have been chalked up to the Ghost, if not for what happened next.

The following morning I awoke with a sniffle and decided to break with my daily routine. I slept later than usual, and it was almost eleven o'clock before I dressed and went in search of a copy of the *American*. A block away I found a boy hawking papers. I eagerly purchased one but was disappointed to find no article on the Ghost therein. I supposed the crime had been discovered too late to make the morning edition, so I headed to a nearby cafe for brunch before heading home.

When I arrived back at my building I ran into the landlady on the stairs. I greeted her as I passed, but her only reply was the usual scowl, accompanied by a suspicious glare. I was somewhat nonplussed because, as far as I knew, I had given her no reason to suspect me of anything. But she always struck me as a funny old bird, lacking in common sense and social graces, so I gave her no further thought. I returned to my apartment and spent the remainder of the day perusing the paper while warming myself in the sliver of sunlight that pierced my window.

The next day I again broke with routine. Still feeling sluggish I slept late into the morning and awoke feeling much better. When I rose I again went in search of a paper. This time I was so certain there would be an article on The Ghost I postponed looking for it. Instead I folded the paper under one arm and headed to the local cafe. During my meal, I overheard talk at the next table about a tragic crime. Apparently two nights before a woman had been murdered, and it was causing quite a hubbub because she had been one of the city's most charitable philanthropists. She was beloved by all, and the police were giving the case their utmost attention.

After my meal I headed home, and along the way decided to see if I had made the front page. I unfolded the paper and was met by the headline concerning the murdered woman. It was not what I wanted to see, but since it was the story of the day I read on—and the more I read, the more uneasy I became.

The article was written more in the fashion of an editorial than reportage. It began by decrying the horrible murder of such an angelic woman, and only after a lengthy diatribe did it deliver the details of the crime. The house in question had been accessed through a door upon the roof. The perpetrator was then believed to have made his way downstairs to the bedroom of the victim, where he found the woman fast asleep. The murderer had then, in an unprovoked and bloodthirsty manner, plunged a knife into her heart before making off with her jewelry. There was no sign of struggle, or that the woman had caught the criminal in the act of stealing. It appeared the perpetrator had murdered the woman in cold blood while she slept.

As I read the story I came to a standstill. A chill ran through me and I stood aghast. Could this have been the same house I had robbed? The odds made it seem unlikely, but it sounded very much like the same mansion. I read on to the article's final, damning line: "Police have no suspects as yet, though the method of entry is remarkably similar to the style of the infamous Ghost. While officials would not comment on any connection between The Ghost and the murder, New Yorkers would be wise to take extra care when locking up at night."

I felt as if a knife had been thrust into *my* heart! The Ghost was no murderer. I wanted to storm into the offices of the *American* and punch the author squarely in the face. But for all of my righteous indignation, I was still overwhelmed by a growing fear that the police would blame The Ghost for the atrocity. The murder of such a beloved public figure would require a speedy resolution, and since the only evidence pointed to a Ghost gone mad, I knew my days were numbered. I resolved to leave the city immediately, to cash in the items I still possessed, and to find a house in the country where I could live out the remainder of my life in anonymity.

I should have known something was amiss when I approached my building and spied two policemen on opposite corners of my block. I should have turned around at once and never returned. But I gained courage from the impossibility that police could have so quickly linked the Ghost back to me. So I held my chin high, walked past the nearest officer and up to the front door. I felt the eyes of both constables on my back as I climbed the steps, so I quickly let myself in. But putting the door between the police and myself offered only a brief moment of relief. As I began to climb the stairs I met another half dozen officers, a bearded gentleman in a tweed suit, and my scowling landlady.

"That's him!" the shrew cried, pointing at me with a trembling, arthritic finger. "He's the one!"

"I beg your pardon," I replied, shooting a confused look at everyone in attendance. But that was all I could muster. My thoughts were far too frantic to come up with anything to say.

"Mr Grey, is it?" said a mustachioed officer. "You're under arrest."

Two men immediately stepped behind me and placed my hands in cuffs. I gave no resistance. My nerves were so frayed that my vision began to go dark around the edges.

"On what charges?" I demanded. I meant to sound indignant, but even to my ears I sounded frightened.

"We're still putting that together," the officer replied. "But for starters we'll say possession of stolen property, and suspicion of burglary and murder."

As he spoke, another officer came down the stairs carrying the treasure drawer from my dresser. Mrs ___ gawked as the loot was paraded past her.

"Well, well! What have we here?" the constable said, eyeing the passing jewels. "That's quite a collection, Mr Grey. Or should I call you Mr *Ghost*?"

There was not much to be said after that. In fact, I do not believe I said anything for a long time. All my energy was spent on staying conscious. Several times I felt my knees giving away, and if not for the officers holding my arms I would have tumbled down the stairs. The officer in charge continued speaking, but by then all I could hear was the sound of blood rushing. The darkness at edge of my vision crept further inward. Finally, I accepted that extrication was impossible, and I surrendered to fear and fainted dead away.

3: THE TOMBS

I awoke in abyssal darkness. If not for the rough stone floor beneath me I would have thought I was afloat in space. In reality I was alone in a black, windowless cell. I remained motionless for a few minutes as my head cleared and my eyes adjusted. It turned out the cell was not pitch black after all; the soft glow of a nearby bulb seeped inside from a small window in the door.

I climbed to my feet and surveyed the room in the light available. The cell was simple, as most cells are. The walls were of rough stone, and the door was a slab of solid iron containing a small, square window at eye level. The furnishings were hardly worth mentioning: a mattress stuffed with an insufficient amount of straw, and two buckets of water, presumably one for drinking and bathing, the other for evacuation. I was revolted to find the reek from both buckets identical, making it impossible to distinguish between them. But at the moment it did not really matter, because, once again, I was at the end of my rope.

I felt as if I were already in the grave, forsaken and alone. It was only when I heard a cough outside my door that I realized a guard stood nearby. When my head felt clear enough I staggered to the door. As I peered through the window I found the guard, bouncing on his toes to pass the time.

"Excuse me," I said feebly.

The guard's rhythmic toe-bouncing suddenly stopped.

"Finally awake, eh?" he said. "You just missed your visitors. Lucky for you."

"Visitors?" I asked.

He chuckled to himself and shook his head.

"Your *visitors*," he replied, sparing no sarcasm, "were four men sent down to question you, though by the look of them they had more in mind than questions."

It took a moment for his meaning to sink in. I gasped.

"But not to worry, at least for now," he continued. "You were still passed out, and they thought pounding on you in such a state would be awful pathetic. They said they'd come back later and take care of business, as it were."

I made a mental note: there was no shame in fainting, or pretending to faint. It might save me from a savage beating.

"Where am I?"

"The Manhattan House of Detention," the guard said.

"The Tombs?" I gasped.

The name was fitting. A place for the dead, or those like me, who soon would be. After my first demise I had become rather familiar with trial law. In spite of my innocence, I knew the circumstances would suffice to convince a jury I had murdered that poor woman. I had never felt so hopelessly cornered and doomed. I felt the cold grip of oblivion tightening around me. I would have again collapsed had the guard not spoken and brought me to my senses.

"And before you go getting ideas, you've got nothing but stone, metal, and a hundred cops between you and freedom. So don't be entertaining ideas of escape."

For anyone else the suggestion of escape would have been ludicrous, but given my talents and reputation, the warning made sense.

"You needn't worry about that," I said. "Even if I were to get free, where would I go? I trust the news is spreading like wildfire."

"I don't know about that," the guard said, rubbing his chin. "But after what you did, you'll definitely make the papers."

"You've heard the story, then?" I asked.

"I have," he said. "They say you're The Ghost, and a murderer to boot."

"I'm innocent of *that*," I said indignantly.

"I must say, I'm shocked you would do such a thing," he continued, as if he had not heard me. "I'll admit that many of us were entertained by your antics. You were a mystery, and having you about made life more interesting. Everyone dreamed of catching you, but we also got a private laugh when jewelry went missing from some rich lady's collection. But with this murder business you went too far."

"I didn't murder anyone!" I protested. "I don't know what happened to her. As God is my witness, I've never killed a soul!"

The guard clicked his tongue and shook his head.

"Well, that's not how it looks," he said. "If I were you, I'd be making my peace, just in case."

His words only reinforced what I already knew—that I was on an inescapable path to Judgment—but hearing it voiced was like a knife in my heart. It stole the breath from me. I slowly doubled over and collapsed on the moldy mattress. All I could do was await the next turn of events, which sounded like it would be a beating within an inch of my life.

Surprisingly, the beating never came. Whenever I heard movement in the corridor I would feign sleep, just in case, but no one ever opened my cell

18

door. I began to think I had been forgotten by all but my guards, who routinely changed several times a day. The only noise I heard came from the moans and cries of distant prisoners, and the occasional whistling or shuffling of the guards. I tried to get the date and time from one sentinel, but he proved to be particularly surly and threatened to crack my skull if I did not shut up.

After what felt like several days, something wholly unexpected occurred. I heard the sound of many feet approaching, and believing it to be the delivery of an overdue pummeling, I immediately collapsed on the floor as if I were too weak to stand. Someone turned a key in the lock, the door swung open, and two officers came in and hoisted me to my feet. When I feigned unconsciousness they began slapping my face and jabbing my ribs until I came around.

I expected it was only a taste of what was to come, but to my surprise they instead led me out of the cell, through a labyrinthine series of dark corridors, and up some stairs. We passed through several more locked doors and corridors, and my surroundings began to look more civilized. Stone and steel were replaced with wood and plaster. By the time we reached our destination my surroundings resembled any other office building, the exception being the ubiquitous police presence.

I was deposited in a room containing only a table and several chairs. My hands were again cuffed, and then without explanation I was left to contemplate the first sunlight I had seen in days as it streamed in through a high, barred window.

Several minutes passed before anyone returned. When the door finally opened, four men entered: two guards armed with billy clubs, and two gentlemen in suits. The first man was an older, heavy-set official, or at least I judged him to be. The other gentleman put me in mind of a professor: he wore spectacles, a short beard, and a brown tweed suit. Beneath one arm he clutched a small leather satchel. Suddenly I recognized him—he had accompanied the police when I was arrested.

After closing the door behind them, one officer pointed his club at a chair and I obediently took a seat. He then took a spot behind my chair while the other stood guard on the door. As they took their positions I again feared the overdue beating was now at hand. But as I waited for the club to come down on my head, the portly man spoke.

"I understand you're Prometheus Grey, the former entertainer," he said. "The escape artist and spiritualist fraud."

"Yes," I reluctantly replied.

"Do you know why you're here?" he asked.

"I believe I'm here for a variety of reasons, not the least of which is the murder of an innocent woman," I said. "But sir, I'm innocent. I've never harmed another soul. I've never even raised a hand in anger. I wouldn't dream of such a thing."

The man frowned and raised a hand to cease my pleading.

"Do you know who I am?" he asked.

"No."

"I'm Commissioner Bingham," he said importantly. "I'm not a judge or lawyer, so you need not plead your innocence to me. I'm only interested in facts, and right now the facts lead me to believe you committed murder."

I opened my mouth to protest, but the commissioner's stern look silenced me.

"For a moment let's entertain the idea of your innocence," he said. "Even if you're innocent of murder, the matter of your burglaries remains. We're still trying to trace all of the stolen items we found in your apartment, but sufficient evidence already exists to identify you as the one the papers call The Ghost."

Here he shot a glance at the scholarly-looking gentleman as if to make a point, but the man seemed unmoved. He gazed stoically at the commissioner for a second before returning his eyes to me.

"To that I must plead guilty," I said. "I was The Ghost, but only because I fell on hard times. I am not a criminal at heart."

"Mr Grey," he said with an annoyed sigh, "I won't tell you again. This is not a court, so pleading has no place here. I want only the facts."

"Very well, sir."

"As for your hard times and getting by," he said, "I'd say you had far more ill-gotten wealth than one needs to simply *get by*. But that's not why I'm here. Do you know this man?"

He nodded at his companion, who looked at me coldly, almost disdainfully.

"No," I said.

The commissioner stiffened and placed his hands behind his back, looking perturbed by my answer. He looked back and forth between the gentleman and me several times, as if expecting to see some hint of expression that would suggest otherwise. After a long pause he sighed in greater exasperation and nodded to the guard behind me. I winced expecting a blow, but instead the officer pushed my chair toward the table and set my cuffed hands upon it.

"Get on with it," the commissioner said.

The tweed-suited gentleman stepped forward. He removed the satchel from beneath his arm, unbound the leather ties that secured it, and laid out the contents: a thin leather-bound book, a series of loose papers, an inkbottle, and a small sponge. He arranged a clean piece of paper in front of me, opened the inkbottle, and applied the ink to the sponge. Next, taking my hands in his, he lightly applied the sponge to my fingertips.

I watched in fascination as these events transpired. He performed these duties without once looking me in the eye or speaking to me, as if my hands were the only part of me in the room. After applying ink to each finger, he gave them a quick inspection and gently pressed them against a sheet of paper with a slight rolling motion. I was curious, but not surprised, that each application left a print, and I wondered at the meaning. He repeated the ritual until there were ten black prints on the page. When he was done he straightened, wiped his hands with a kerchief, and presented the paper to the commissioner.

The commissioner turned and walked to the window, where he donned his own spectacles and held up the paper to the light. It took him only a few seconds to scrutinize the man's work.

"And what does this prove?" he asked quietly.

The tweed gentleman returned to the table and began shuffling through his papers until he found a single page, which, from the brief glance I caught, seemed to display another series of prints. He took the page and the leather-bound book to the commissioner, and the two turned their backs on me and talked in hushed tones. I watched as the commissioner closely examined both pages while his companion made reference to the notebook, pointing between the papers and his notes as if assiduously trying to make a point. While they carried on their quiet discussion, I examined the face of the guard by the door. I looked for some clue as to what was happening, but the only thing I gleaned from his expression was his complete disinterest in the proceedings.

"Very well," the commissioner said at last.

Both men turned to face me once again, regarding me in silence. I had the distinct feeling some fateful decision was being reached.

"Sir, I just want to say—" I began.

"What of the thefts?" the commissioner said, addressing the tweed gentleman.

"Consider the matter resolved," the man said, albeit quietly as if it was not intended for my ears. "I will handle the details."

The commissioner scowled. He was clearly not pleased with the outcome of whatever was transpiring. He glared at the man, who returned his gaze with perfect stoicism. It was only then I realized the two were not colleagues at all, that they stood on opposite sides of an issue involving me.

Finally, the commissioner shot a disparaging glance at me before nodding to the guards, who at once leapt into action. Before I could comment, they hoisted me from the chair and ushered me away.

I was too bewildered to speak, but it was just as well. The guards soon had me back in my cell where I had time and solitude to wonder about what had happened. I had not been beaten, so I was inclined to think the interrogation had gone well. Without further explication, however, I had no way of knowing what had just transpired. I had the vague feeling I had somehow been exonerated, but I could not tell how, or why. I collapsed on the mattress and stared into the darkness, wondering about the identity of the tweed man, what interest he had in me, and what would happen next.

I did not have to wait long. A few hours later I was again ushered by two guards through winding corridors and upstairs into the light of the administrative offices. This time, however, I was led up another flight of stairs to a plush office, where I was again deposited in a chair, this time before the desk of another important-looking man. He was attended by a younger gentleman and engaged in signing several papers. When he was finished he handed them to the younger man who hurried out of the office.

"Grey, is it?" he said, ordering the contents of his desk without looking at me.

"Yes, sir."

"I'm Deputy Commissioner Faurot," he said. "It looks like today is your lucky day. You're being released."

"I am?" Though I had already deduced something was afoot, I had not expected I would be set free.

"Yes," he replied. "An unusual course of events has happened today. The commissioner and I don't exactly understand how you fit into them, but suffice it to say they resulted in clearing your name, for murder anyway."

"That's wonderful!" I exclaimed. I was unable to contain myself. Tears began to well in my eyes. I half rose from my chair to embrace him, but a guard forced me back down.

"As for your other crimes," he continued, "the burglaries and stolen property are a different matter. I may not have the authority to convict you, but based on the evidence I'm quite sure you're guilty. Therefore what I do now, I do reluctantly."

He nodded at a guard. The man approached the desk and accepted a slip of paper.

"That's the address," Faurot said. "Make sure he gets there."

The guard nodded and returned to my side.

"I don't understand," I said. "Am I not free? Where am I going?"

Faurot fixed me with a steely gaze.

"You're a very lucky man, Mr Grey. You must have friends in high places. But mark my words, I know your type. You've already started down a path of crime, and one crime leads to another. No matter how refined you come across, you're a criminal at heart. I don't know what the future holds for you, but know this: you've slipped the noose this time. From now on, you'd better walk the straight and narrow. One false move in my city and I'll make sure you never see the light of day again."

I stared blankly at him, not knowing what to say.

"Take him away," Faurot said.

The guards grabbed me by the scruff of my neck and hoisted me from the chair. As they ushered me to the door, Faurot made one last comment.

"You're not getting off scot-free. You're being remanded into the custody of your benefactor, who will be responsible for you."

"Benefactor?" I said. "Who—?"

But the guards had me out the door before I could get an answer. Since I was being set free, more or less, I complied with their manhandling if only to hasten my departure. But my cooperation did not stop them from lifting me by my arms, carrying me down the stairs, out the door, and roughly tossing me into an awaiting paddy wagon. Passersby stared at the spectacle, and I was suddenly keenly aware of how awful I must have appeared. Then the door slammed shut behind me and the wagon lurched forward.

I stumbled to one of the narrow benches along the interior and sat down. As we rolled along I attempted to straighten my clothes and brush my hair, to make myself look presentable, but the effort was wasted. Several days in a dungeon had me looking like a dreg.

I gave up hope of looking respectable, at least until I could bathe and get a new set of clothes. Instead my thoughts returned to the phenomenon of my exoneration and freedom. In spite of my crimes, in spite of the damning circumstances surrounding the murder, I had "slipped the noose," to use Faurot's words. By grace or good fortune I had cheated an evil fate. I looked out the barred window set in the wagon's rear door. As the Tombs receded I almost laughed. Yet another miraculous escape by the inimitable Prometheus Grey!

4: EMANCIPATION

As the carriage wound its way through the city I briefly considered calling upon my considerable skills to pick the lock, jump out, and disappear into an alley. The more I considered the situation, however, the less escape seemed desirable. I was a penniless wretch. I could easily escape, but what would I be escaping to, or from? Besides, my curiosity had gotten the better of me. Who would go to such lengths to clear my name and set me free? I had many influential admirers from my early days in show business, and more than a few respectable women had been infatuated with me. I had always assumed my occult chicanery had killed off those sentiments. Perhaps I had been wrong all along. So it was that my curiosity held me in check, and I did not try to escape.

Toward the end of my journey it began to rain. I edged closer to the wagon door just to feel a few drops on my face. After the Tombs I wanted desperately to wash all trace and memory of it away. As I scrubbed my face with a cuff, the carriage came to a halt. I waited patiently for the driver to climb down from his perch, walk to the back and open the door. When it swung open I was met with a look of annoyance that told me my erstwhile chauffer did not much care for me. I thought I would smooth things over by thanking him for his service, but before I could get any words out my eyes fell on our destination.

The wagon stood in front of an old townhouse that was in need of some repair. Weeds were plentiful in the small garden, paint was peeling from the eaves, and the windows looked as if they had not been washed in years. My eyes traveled the expanse of that sad estate and came to rest on the door, or rather upon the weathered oval sign that dangled above it from a wrought-iron curlicue. The sign bore the crude silhouette of a bird, and beneath that the inscription *Corona Ornithological Society, Est. 1877*.

"Bird watchers?" I asked.

"Just move it," the officer replied, motioning toward the door with one hand and shoving me with the other.

I was more perplexed than before. I was quite sure I had never been to that forlorn residence. I had no idea whom I would find inside.

"Are you sure this is the correct address?" I asked as we approached the door. But the officer would not lower himself to speak to me. It was clear that in his eyes I was still a criminal.

At the door he reached past me and rapped loudly. Nothing happened for a long time. He sighed and rapped again, this time longer and louder. Shortly after the second barrage the door swung open to reveal a young woman in a blue dress and white apron. The smell of sumptuous foods cooking wafted out behind her and immediately banished all my fears. She smiled and stepped aside as if we were expected.

"Good afternoon," she said with a smile. "Come in, please, Mr Grey."

I stepped inside without hesitation and turned to see if the officer would follow. He remained on the step.

"He's all yours then," he said. "I'll be outside with the wagon."

Before the maid could reply he turned and strode back toward the vehicle.

The door closed and I briefly tore my mind away from the delicious fragrances to inspect the interior. The foyer was lit by a regal but dusty chandelier and contained a coat rack, an umbrella stand, and a small table beneath a hanging mirror, all of which looked newer and in better condition than the house they occupied.

The girl must have read my expression.

"Forgive the mess," she said, as if my approval mattered. "We've only just moved in. There's still much to be done. This way, please."

She set off down the hallway and I dutifully followed. As I passed the mirror I was again reminded of my appearance. I wanted desperately to bathe, shave, and change clothes before meeting my benefactor, but alas, there was nothing I could do. I was at the mercy of my unknown savior and his staff.

We passed several doorways, and a cursory glance into each gave credence to the girl's story. The rooms were sparely furnished and in some disarray as items were in the process of being unpacked. We turned left and passed through a room destined to be a study, continuing on through another hallway. There the girl stopped outside another door, looked me up and down, and chose her words carefully.

"We'll be serving supper shortly. Perhaps you'd like to clean up?"

"I would like nothing more," I said. "Except perhaps a taste of the wonderful meal I smelled the moment you opened the door."

I took my time cleaning up, inasmuch as my ravenous hunger would allow me. I was able to clean my face and hands sufficiently, but the ablutions did nothing for my unshaven chin and stained clothes. All I could do was sigh at myself in the mirror and press on.

The girl led me back to the main hallway and deeper into the house to the dining room. The furnishings here were also spare, but some care had been taken to make sure the room was ready to receive guests. It contained a large table around which ten could easily dine, covered with a pristine white tablecloth. As I examined my surroundings the girl spoke.

"Please make yourself comfortable. Mr Cross will be with you shortly."

She then left the room, closing the door behind her. I listened for the sound of a key turning in the lock, but none came. The girl, and presumably everyone else in the house, trusted me to not run off. Of course running off was out of the question, at least until I could get a good meal, meet this Mr Cross, and discover his interest in me.

Cross—the name was unfamiliar to me. Still, it was entirely possible I had at some point in my career met or entertained him. Before I became, or took on the persona of, a medium, I routinely performed acts of escape in both public and private venues. In my time I had performed before tens of thousands of New Yorkers by my reckoning, so if Cross was a native of the city it was probable he had seen me. However, that did not explain his interest in me.

A few minutes later the door opened and my host stepped in. I faced a man with dark, well-oiled hair, trimmed mustache, and clothed in an immaculate dark blue suit. He stopped midway between the door and the table, rubbing his hands together as he looked me over with a courteous smile.

"Mr Grey," he said. "Welcome. I'm sorry if I kept you waiting."

"Not at all," I replied, shaking his hand. "Prometheus Grey, at your service. And if you're the one responsible for clearing my name and setting me free, I owe you considerable service indeed."

"I am glad you think so," he replied with a wide grin. "I'm George Cross. We've never met, but I know you from your performances years ago."

There was my explanation: Cross was an admirer from my heyday. I would have preferred my savior to be a wealthy widow, or the daughter, recently come of age, of an influential aristocrat. But a man in a maelstrom will cling to any flotsam in his moment of need. Cross would suffice.

No sooner had we made introductions than the young maid appeared in the door and announced dinner was ready. Cross and I stepped aside and watched as the girl and an older, heavier, and similarly dressed woman began carrying in dishes and arranging them on the table. Once the table was set the servants disappeared back into the kitchen, and Cross motioned for me to be seated. When we were both in place he poured me a glass of wine, which I eagerly accepted.

"So you're a fan from my Vaudeville days?" I inquired. I quickly drained half of my glass and attacked the food before me. "Pray tell, which of my performances did you see?"

"In truth, I only saw you perform twice," he said. "Once by complete coincidence."

I was a bit surprised by his response. It seemed odd that a fan with only a superficial knowledge should take such interest in me.

"Very well, which ones were they?"

"The first was at the Hammerstein in 1902. You managed to escape from a series of handcuffs and chains that were progressively more difficult. You invited members of the audience to fasten and inspect them to ensure you were adequately bound. In each case the audience was confident you would not escape, but you made short work of your bindings every time. It was remarkable. It seemed almost superhuman."

I smiled and raised a glass to him.

"And the second occasion?"

"Coney Island, 1904. I witnessed you dangling upside down from the Ferris wheel in a straightjacket. I didn't see the entire event, but I arrived in time to see you escape, shimmy back up the rope, and throw handfuls of Ferris wheel tickets over the crowd like confetti."

"I remember!" I exclaimed in a moment of reverie. "That was the only time I performed that particular escape. What the audience didn't know was that all my wriggling had inadvertently loosened the knots around my ankles, and I came within seconds of falling to my death. After that I decided such life-threatening stunts were no longer worthwhile."

Cross nodded in understanding. "I think the most interesting thing about your performances was your invocation of the spirits, calling upon the ghosts of former conjurers and magicians to aid in your escapes."

"My shtick," I admitted with a chuckle. "All good entertainers have a way to hook the crowd."

"An interesting choice," he said, looking at me knowingly. "Especially since it directly contrasts with the style of another prominent artist. I'm referring to Houdini, of course."

I froze in mid mastication. The mention of the name filled my mouth with bile. I drained my wineglass to wash it away.

"Forgive me," Cross said, refilling my glass. "After your escapes, what happened next?"

Though he did not let on, I was sure he already knew the answer, because the rest of New York certainly did. But I supposed he wanted to hear my version, so I played along.

"As I said, I decided my life was too precious to risk on such stunts. I needed another way to entertain, and since my profession already lent itself to mystery I chose to explore its occult possibilities. As you must know, spiritualism has been a popular distraction of the aristocracy for decades. I gradually replaced grandiose public performances with private séances. It turned out to be very profitable. I would have been a fool to pass up the opportunity."

"I admire your enterprising nature," Cross replied. "But you must admit your spiritualist practice was exploitive. There's a difference between entertaining a public audience, and entering people's homes to prey on their misfortunes."

"On the contrary," I said. "As a performer, what do I care of the venue?

Whether on the stage or sitting in the parlor of a Manhattanite, my job was to perform. What could be better than a supernatural performance that gives hope to the bereaved?"

"Hope?" Cross asked dispassionately. "False hope, perhaps, since you weren't actually communing with the dead."

I began to feel hot under the collar. The conversation had taken an ugly turn. Cross did not seem to be one of my devotees at all. At that moment I decided, in spite of what he had done for me—which still was not clear—I did not like him. I also realized that he still had not explained his interest in me.

"We could argue the finer points all night," I said, helping myself to another glass of wine. "Now, I'd like to hear more plainly why you went to such lengths to clear my name and get me out of jail."

"Of course," he said. "A full explanation is overdue. I ask only that you be patient. All, or at least most, will become clear."

I continued to eat, watching him expectantly.

"I'll begin by revealing what I know of you," he said. "Please, if my information is at any point erroneous, feel free to correct it."

I nodded. He lowered his head in thought for a moment before continuing.

"Saint Louis, 1885. At the age of nineteen you convinced Hieronymous Mangle, of the Mangle Brothers Marvelous & Magical Midwest Roadshow, to hire you based on a trick you had conceived, called The Devil's Extra-Dimensional Wardrobe. The trick involved you hiding in a large wardrobe in such a way that no one could find you. People from the audience were invited to inspect the wardrobe, but no matter how thorough and time-consuming their inspection, no one ever succeeded. Then, once everyone had returned to their seats, you would exit the wardrobe as if you had been standing just inside the door all along. It was, and remains, your greatest trick."

"Right enough," I said, smiling at the memory.

"It secured you a permanent position in the Mangle Brothers show, and you toured with them for three years. During that time you honed and expanded your talents to such a degree that you became almost impossible to contain. Ropes, chains, boxes, cages—nothing could hold you. Eventually your travels brought you to New York, where you found an endless audience and opportunities in Vaudeville. You left the circus and made the city your new home. The rest of your professional career is of course well known. You spent the next fifteen years perfecting your art, performing solely in and around New York, an unorthodox move that limited your exposure and cost you widespread fame. Nevertheless, you enjoyed a successful career. It's ironic that your adherence to the occult, the invocation of the spirits in your acts, both contributed to your success and led to your downfall."

"Yes, ironic" I said bitterly. I was in no mood for an objective review of my undoing, but Cross pressed on.

"It was unquestionably the spiritualism in your act that drew a wider audience and eventually gave you a foothold among the more superstitious members of New York's elite. As we already covered, while the spiritualist angle may have offered a safer career, you took it too far. You hoodwinked the bereaved, and though you may have given them some brief comfort, in the end your act was pure trickery."

"I suppose that's one way to look at it," I said stiffly.

"It was then that you crossed paths with Houdini."

There it was—the name I had come to despise more than any other. I felt my face reddening with shame and humiliation.

"You realize," I said defiantly, "that's not his real name."

I spoke as if revealing some weakness in his character. Cross was apathetic.

"Yes, I'm aware of it," he said, waving a hand dismissively. "As chance would have it, Houdini turned out to be a true believer in spiritualism, so much that he undertook to expose fraudulent mystics and mediums. You, unfortunately, were his first target."

Cross knew my history too well. I bit my tongue, leaned back in my chair, and folded my arms. There was no getting around it. I was about to relive my ultimate humiliation.

By 1904 I had become quite popular throughout New York for my spiritual services, so it was only natural that Houdini targeted me first. His betrayal of a fellow performer, however, was absolutely despicable. A true gentleman and colleague would have warned me, not ambushed me. When he disguised himself as an aging widow who had need of my services, I was completely beguiled. I wondered why he (or in this case, *she*, as he went by the name Mrs Esther Periwinkle) had offered me such an exorbitant fee (twice my going rate), but it was such a generous amount that I leapt at it without any questions.

I met Mrs Periwinkle at what I presumed to be her home on the East Side. I knocked on the door and was met by a shrunken little woman who was so hunched over she could not even look me in the eyes. The way she walked, half stooped over with a hand bracing her back, was so exaggerated I dismissed the possibility that it was pantomime. No self-respecting performer would dare be accused of such a horrible act.

She led me through a dark and musty living room, already completely shut off from daylight by heavy curtains, to a small alcove containing a tea table and two chairs. The only light came from a single burning candle atop the table. As I seated myself she drew a final velvet curtain across the nook's entrance. Judging by the arrangement she was no stranger to séances, or at least to preconceptions of them. I did not require such arcane privacy, but since most people assume communion with the dead must be performed in blackness, I played along.

When she sat down across from me I noticed a visible trace of moustache on her upper lip, but I attributed it to her Methuselaen age. I grasped her hands, which were strangely firm, closed my eyes, and began to speak in voices of the dead. As with all my performances I wanted to give the old bird her money's worth, so I feigned a few mistaken identities before I presented her husband. When I finally got around to him I spoke in gentle, loving tones and offered words to succor the bereaved.

Looking back, I should have suspected something was amiss when she began asking me very peculiar questions—about relatives, living and dead; about misplaced heirlooms; and especially about her own identity—absurd questions like, "I just don't feel as if I'm myself today, so who might I be?"

I thought she was senile. Now, of course, I realize Houdini was toying with me, having fun at my expense. But at the time my only concern was to comfort a distressed soul, collect payment, and be on my way. So I brushed her questions aside and instead talked at length about how her dear husband would always be near, watching over her, and waiting until the day they would be reunited in the Hereafter.

At the conclusion of the séance she seemed to choke back tears. She excused herself and exited the alcove, drawing the velvet curtain closed behind. I took advantage of the respite to mop perspiration from my brow with a handkerchief, as the alcove had become hot and stuffy. The old widow had certainly made me earn my keep that day, with her strange questions that almost seemed like attempts to catch me in deceit. A lesser man would have undoubtedly stumbled, but I was sure I had pulled it off.

As I waited for her to return with payment, I thought I heard the scuffling of feet. I took the sound to be the old woman returning, but the shuffling went on longer than seemed reasonable or necessary. I was becoming sweaty and impatient. I decided I could take no more and reached for the curtain, but in the same moment it leapt away from my hand.

The curtain was thrown back, and I was immediately blinded by a flash of light. I threw up my arms to shield my eyes, stumbling back and knocking over my chair in the process. As spots faded from my eyes, I realized I had been photographed. When I could see again, I stood before a host of reporters and policemen, all flanking a smirking Houdini. I was arrested, taken before a judge, and warned against further schemes. And to eliminate the possibility of continued spiritualism, the story of my downfall—complete with the humiliating photograph—ran in all the local papers. My reputation and career were destroyed.

Now, Dear Reader, you understand precisely and completely why I held Houdini in the highest contempt.

"After the demise of your career," Cross continued, "you disappeared so completely it was as if you had vanished into the Devil's Extra-Dimensional

Wardrobe for good. I had a difficult time tracking you down. After a year with no sign, I thought you had either met some foul end or left the city. Then the Ghost burglaries began, and I suspected you were the culprit."

"Why?" I asked.

"When the burglaries persisted for several months, and when the police failed to produce a single clue, I began to suspect someone unusual, perhaps a magician or escape artist, was responsible."

"Why did you suspect me and not some master criminal?" I asked.

"The city has no shortage of criminals," Cross said. "But none of them possess the mental and physical dexterity needed to pull off burglaries as spotless as yours."

Cross proved to be somewhat clever and insightful after all. My bitter ruminations of Houdini began to fade.

"What about the murder?" I asked. "How can you be sure I'm innocent?"

"The gentleman who arranged your release is in my employ," Cross said. "If anyone could find you and prove your innocence, I knew he could. Beyond that, I had only a gut feeling. From what I knew of you, you didn't strike me as the type."

"You seem to have an answer for everything," I said. "But tell me, how is it you know so much about me? More to the point, why do you take such an interest?"

A tight-lipped grin spread across his face. He stood up from the table and slowly paced the room.

"Before I answer those questions, it's time I revealed something about myself," he said.

I crossed my arms and gazed at him expectantly.

"I work for the government," he said. "Specifically, I serve the President of the United States."

"Really?" I said dubiously. "In what capacity?"

"The utmost secretive," he replied.

I thought on it for a moment. As audacious as it sounded, it would explain his influence and ability to get me out of jail.

"Do you have some credentials?" I asked.

"They do not issue credentials for the sort of work I do," he replied. "In fact, you would be hard pressed to find a member of government who would acknowledge me."

"I see," I said skeptically. "What is it you want from me?"

He paused for dramatic effect. "America requires your service, Mr Grey. I want to recruit you as a secret agent."

I stared at him incredulously. While I was a man of many talents, I could not fathom what use the government would have of me, or what the job of *secret agent* encompassed. I took a moment to go over the scant possibilities before surrendering to bewilderment.

"I don't understand," I confessed.

"Nor should you," Cross replied. "It's not an advertised line of work. It's extremely rare, and so secretive I can't yet reveal the details to you. But here is what I can tell you. You are a man of unique talents, and the nation has need of them. Do you accept the position?"

I stared at him blankly. Slowly, I began to chuckle and shake my head.

"Surely you don't expect me to leap at such a mysterious offer," I said. "I have no idea what the work entails. How can I possibly accept?"

"Because the alternative is that I hand you back over to the police," Cross replied, "to face the burglary charges they have against you."

My smile faded. I had no desire to return to jail. Still, deep down I struggled with the offer. There was something about Cross I did not like, his smugness perhaps, or the fact that he was giving me an ultimatum. I wanted to reject him simply out of spite. Succumbing to such extortion was only slightly less distasteful than taking my chances with the legal system.

"Also," Cross continued, "I should mention that you will be compensated for your service. If you accept, you will receive an annual pension of ten thousand dollars for the remainder of your life."

My indignation and resentment immediately began to ebb.

"In that case," I said, rising from my chair, "it is my patriotic duty to accept."

He shot me a knowing grin before turning and calling for the servants. The two women I had seen before returned.

"Mrs McMurtey," he said, addressing the older woman, "please inform the officer outside that his services will no longer be needed."

"Yes, sir," she said, and disappeared.

"Ms Abigail, Mr Grey will be remaining with us. Please show him to his room."

"Yes, sir," the young woman said.

As I crossed the room, Cross beamed at me.

"I'm glad you will be joining us," he said. "Get a good night's sleep. Tomorrow our work begins."

I followed the girl upstairs to the room arranged for me. Although the rest of the house seemed to be in disarray, my room was organized and decorated quite nicely. I was especially impressed with the bed, which was large, made up with virginal white sheets, and softer than anything I had experienced in recent memory. After surveying it I turned to the girl, Abigail, and wondered if perhaps she would sweeten the deal. But before I could address her she said goodnight and closed the door. As I stood alone in the middle of the room I again realized I was in dire need of a bath. But the wine had made me drowsy, and I climbed into bed, clothes and all. The last thing I remembered before falling into an impenetrable slumber was the sound of rain against the window, and thinking, "A pension! Well played, you old devil!"

5: THE PUGILIST

I awoke the next morning to a knock at my door. As I rolled over to answer I realized I was still in my dingy clothing from the night before. Mortified I jumped up and began tearing the filthy rags from my body. When I did not answer the knocks were repeated, followed by the voice of Abigail.

"Mr Grey? Are you awake?"

"Almost," I said, groggily, still too confused to craft an appropriate response.

My answer must have confused her, because I heard footsteps as if she had begun to walk away. As I shed my last bit of clothing and stood exposed in the middle of the room, I heard her backtrack and knock again.

"You're awake, then?" she called.

To my horror the doorknob began to turn. In a moment of panic I leapt for the bed and dove beneath the covers. The door opened slowly, and she tentatively stuck her head in.

"May I come in?" she asked.

"By all means," I replied, pulling the covers up to my chin.

She entered the room carrying a tray, upon which I spotted a breakfast of eggs and bacon. As she stepped forward she spotted the pile of clothes on the floor. She paused and gave me a funny look. At that moment we both blushed and she began to back toward the door.

"I was just bringing you some breakfast," she said. "I can come back."

"No," I said, sitting up. "That won't be necessary."

When she saw my bare chest she blushed even more. While I too was made nervous by the fact that only a sheet hid my nakedness, the smell of the food was enough to make me risk embarrassment.

"I'm sorry to have disturbed you," she said. "But it's nearly nine, and Mr Cross said he needs you downstairs by ten."

"It's nine already?" I asked. I finally registered the light streaming in through the window.

"Yes, sir," she said, awkwardly placing the breakfast tray upon my lap. She then stepped back and stood by with her hands clasped before her. "That's why I decided to bring up your breakfast. Mr Cross expected to see you at the table this morning, but you were still fast asleep. Rather than wake you he said I should let you rest, as this may be a long day for you."

"A long day, you say?" I had no idea what Cross had in store. I gnawed on a piece of bacon and eyed the girl. "What, pray tell, will I be doing?"

"Well," she began. I could tell she was trying to choose her words carefully. "I think I'll leave that for Mr Cross to explain. I really don't know much about his business. My job is just to get you fed, dressed, and downstairs by ten."

I surmised she was lying. Such is the way with servants. They pretend to know nothing, but they see and hear all. She probably knew more about Cross than he knew about me. I had hoped the girl might confide in me, make me feel as if I had an ally in the house, but Cross had secured her loyalty.

"I get the impression I'll be staying here for a while," I said. "What's your name?"

I had already heard her name, and she certainly knew mine, but proper introductions had never occurred.

"Abigail," she said.

"A pleasure, Abigail," I said. And with a flourish of my hand and the bacon it held, "Prometheus Grey, at your service."

I thought this turn of social standing quite witty, and I hoped Abigail might see the humor in it and be at ease. But the only effect it produced was a more noticeable blush, and a curt conclusion to our conversation.

"A pleasure, sir," she replied. "When you're done with breakfast, just leave the tray and I'll collect it later. The bathroom is at the end of the hall, and the wardrobe has some clothes you can use until we get you fitted. Please be mindful of the time and come downstairs by ten. If there's anything else you need, just pull the sash and it will ring a bell."

She pointed to a slender length of satin cloth hanging beside the bedpost.

"All right," I said. "Ten o'clock. Thank you."

She gave me a slight nod and turned to leave the room. As she turned, however, her eyes lingered for perhaps a second longer than expected. It was just enough to suggest that deep down she wanted to stay and say more. By the time I had interpreted the look, however, she was gone.

I took my time preparing that morning. I leisurely ate my breakfast in bed while listening to the sounds of birds in the park across the street. After breakfast I inspected the wardrobe and found it well stocked with respectable suits that would adequately fit me. I was in no rush as I dressed, savoring the crispness and clean smell of the clothing. When I was done I stepped from my room in time to meet Mrs McMurtey coming up the stairs.

"Ah!" she exclaimed. "I was just coming to fetch you. I'm glad to see you're dressed. It's almost ten. You can wait for Mr Cross in the study."

I went downstairs a few minutes before ten o'clock and found the women had put quite a dent in the unpacking. As I meandered to the study I noted that most of the boxes I had seen the night before were gone, and everything was neatly arranged. The large bookshelves, which had been empty the day before, were fully stocked, and the floor had been swept of loose packing straw. The study was organized and ready for business.

I seated myself in an upholstered chair and awaited the arrival of my employer. I noticed the desk was already in use, its surface cluttered with papers and the like. A letter opener sat atop an opened envelope, acting as a paperweight. I innocently picked it up and toyed with it. As I leaned over to replace it, I suddenly felt mischievous. After a quick glance over my shoulder I picked up the opened letter. The envelope bore only the identity of the addressee, "Mr George Cross", which meant it had been delivered by courier rather than by mail. I opened it, removed the single sheet of paper, and read its contents.

21 January, 1908

Mr Cross,

Thank you for your visit, and your invitation. Regrettably, I must decline. I am not the sort who seeks adventure beyond overcoming those obstacles that block scientific discovery. If my work is to benefit the nation, my achievements must be made in the laboratory.

While I will not be able to join you, I am writing to inform you of someone who might be of interest. I am hosting a guest whose identity I am not at liberty to divulge. However if you will pay another visit to Wardenclyffe, I will make introductions.

Forgive me if I am being mysterious. I assure you that, given your endeavor, you will find this acquaintance most interesting.

Confidentially,
N. T.

As I refolded the letter, I heard the sound of a horse. A glance out the study window showed a coach coming to a halt in front of the house. At the same moment the hall clock began to chime ten. I fumbled to insert the letter into its envelope and return it to its spot on the desk. I heard the door open, followed by Mrs McMurtey greeting the arrival. As the clock continued to chime, I took my seat and acted nonchalant.

Soon footsteps approached. I expected to see only Cross, and I was surprised to find him accompanied by another gentleman—none other than the bearded gentleman in tweed, the one who had argued for my release from jail. Cross noted my surprise.

"Mr Grey, I take it you recognize this gentleman?"

"Yes," I replied, smiling at the man to show my appreciation. He returned only a steady gaze.

"This is Mr Dietrich," Cross said. "He's one of us, another who has enlisted with our cause."

"Prometheus Grey," I said, extending my hand.

"Meyer Dietrich," he replied, grasping my hand only long enough for a single shake.

"Thank you," I replied. I could not recall shaking the hand of someone less interested in making my acquaintance. But if Cross noticed tension between us, he sidestepped it by pressing on with business.

"Please have a seat," he said, taking his spot behind the desk. "We have some items to discuss. I see Mrs McMurtey and Abigail have been busy this morning. Excellent! One less item to worry about. With the house in order we can focus on more important business."

"I look forward to it," I said. "Our conversation last night left off at a critical juncture. I still have no idea why you've enlisted me."

I shot a glance at Dietrich, but I could read nothing in him.

"I'm afraid the answer to that question must wait a while longer," Cross said. "I have another appointment soon. But I didn't want to leave without introducing you two. You see, Mr Dietrich has been in my employ for some time, and he is capable of answering many questions you would ask me. Keep in mind, though, that he is not likely to answer anything regarding the specifics of our mission."

"If that's the case, what business do we have to discuss?" I asked. "It seems the two of you are set against telling me anything."

Cross leaned forward, placing his folded hands on the desk.

"I have a job for the two of you," he said.

"What is it?" Dietrich asked, suddenly interested.

"There is another we must try to enlist," Cross said. "I need you to visit him. He will be vital to our mission."

I was becoming annoyed by repeated vague references to *our mission*.

"I don't see what help I can be," I said. "How can I possibly recruit someone when I don't even know what we'll be doing?"

"Mr Dietrich will do most of the talking," Cross replied. "As for you, Mr Grey, I'm not sending you for a specific purpose. Instead, I'm sending you because you have a remarkable ability to adapt, and a propensity for turning situations to your advantage. Should any trouble arise, I hope that some of your luck will rub off on Mr Dietrich."

38

I straightened in my chair, feeling somewhat dignified by Cross's response. His words echoed truth, except perhaps for the part about luck. I had never considered myself a lucky man. A glance at Dietrich revealed he did not like the suggestion that he might depend on me for anything, certainly not his well-being.

"And what trouble might we run into?" I asked.

Cross shrugged.

"You're going to make a legitimate business proposition. No trouble should come of it. Nevertheless, it's in our best interest to expect the unexpected. From now on, you will both benefit by making a practice of working together."

"Very well," Dietrich replied stiffly.

"So, who are we going to recruit?" I asked.

Cross shuffled through the papers on his desk and produced a slip of paper, which he handed to Dietrich.

"The gentleman's name is William Irish," he said. "I think you'll find him working as a dockhand at the harbor. He's a large man, very distinguishable. If you're unable to track him down—"

My mind wandered as Cross went on talking. The name sounded familiar to me. I was sure I had seen or heard it before, and I had the strange feeling the context in which I encountered it was less than favorable.

Dietrich, on the other hand, was unconcerned.

"I'll see to it," he said, pocketing the slip of paper.

"Thank you," Cross said, glancing at his watch. "Now I must cut our meeting short. I mustn't be late for my next appointment. I've already arranged a cab for you. It should be here shortly."

Dietrich and I followed him to the front door, where he bid us a final farewell before jumping into his private coach and riding away.

That left Dietrich and I standing together in the foyer in awkward silence. I was normally quite adept at conversation, but faced with a man who did not appear to like me, I was at a loss. We regarded each other in silence for an uncomfortably long moment that was finally, and thankfully, interrupted by the arrival of our cab.

"It's time to go," he said.

He proceeded to the vehicle without hesitation, as if he had a clear understanding of all our mission entailed. Still baffled, I hurried after him, fearing he might leave me behind.

As the carriage rolled along, Dietrich offered nothing to help pass the time. Instead he seemed content to scowl out the window at pedestrians. From the fierce look in his eyes I got the impression he was forever scrutinizing everything around him, and his dour expression suggested he saw little of which he approved.

Under normal circumstances, if I found myself in the company of such

39

irritable or impassive personalities, my habit was to move in the opposite direction, to seek out more lively fare. Trapped in a cab with Dietrich, however, my options were limited.

"Cross is a mysterious fellow," I said, thinking if I leapt into the middle of a nonexistent dialogue it might alleviate the awkwardness. "Recruiting people with 'special talents', as he puts it."

Dietrich nodded without taking his eyes from the window. Over the traffic I thought I heard a noncommittal grunt of acknowledgment. Having drawn him out, I seized the opportunity to engage.

"Since you were able to clear my name and arrange my release," I said, "I suppose I owe you thanks. So, thank you."

"You're welcome," he replied without looking at me.

"Since you handled my case," I went on, "I take it you know much about me, such as what talents I possess."

"Yes," he replied.

"Then you have me at a disadvantage," I said. "If you don't mind my asking, what are yours?"

He continued to stare out the window. After a long pause I thought he had chosen to ignore me. I was beginning to craft a biting remark about respect and common courtesy when finally he spoke up.

"I have a keen mind, a perfect memory," he replied. "I am also experienced in investigation."

"Well, that explains a great deal," I said with a laugh. My amusement finally drew his attention from the window.

"It explains what, exactly?" he asked defensively.

"It explains why you were able to clear me of the murder charge," I said. "When I first saw you, I didn't know what to make of you. Now it all makes sense. As a detective, you were able to find proof of my innocence."

"I did not say I was a detective," he corrected. "I merely said I have experience in investigation."

"Oh," I said. "I thought they were the same."

He regarded me for a moment before dispelling my misinterpretation with a curt shake of his head. He then returned his attention to the window. But I was not going to let the conversation stop there.

"What evidence did you find?" I asked.

He closed his eyes briefly and worked his jaw as if I were a pestering child.

"Fingerprints," he replied.

"What?"

"Fingerprints," he repeated. "It's a system of classification developed by the British decades ago. Only recently has it come into practice in America. When we touch objects, we unknowingly leave behind prints from our hands and fingers. These prints are unique to every person. By examining the prints on an object, we can determine those who last touched or held it."

"Fascinating," I said, examining the complex swirls on my fingertips.

"In your case," he went on, "the murder weapon, a knife, was left behind.

The knife had a handle of finished wood, smooth enough to hold a print. Mr Cross arranged with the commissioner that I should examine the weapon. The commissioner agreed, knowing only that I employed the latest method of criminal identification. However, he believed I would provide more evidence to build the case *against* you, not prove your innocence."

"I can imagine his consternation when you did otherwise," I said.

"There's no need to imagine it," Dietrich said. "You witnessed it. He was greatly displeased. He did not approve of dropping the murder charge against you. For him, it was more important to have a suspect in custody, to show the police were successful at catching criminals, to reassure the public, and ultimately to maintain the image of competency."

We rode in silence for a time as I reflected on his words.

"It's ironic that you and I should find ourselves part of a common endeavor," I said, "even if I have no idea what our endeavor is."

I paused, hoping Dietrich might take the bait and give me some detail on that for which Cross recruited us. He did not.

"There's you, an investigator, who dedicates his life to the pursuit of facts," I said, "and me, an entertainer, whose career is built on deception. It's hard to imagine a more unlikely duo, unless you were paired with a criminal."

"Precisely," Dietrich interjected.

I stared at him, not grasping his point. He noted the blankness in my gaze.

"You *are* a criminal," he said, matter-of-factly. "You are a fraud and a thief. You should have faced the burglary charges. But because I believe in our mission, I followed Cross's instructions and made an argument for your release. Now, I must live with my decision."

I was speechless. He did not appear to be living with it very well.

"Let's be clear," he continued. "I cleared you of murder, but it was Cross who pulled strings to set you free. Though we are working together, you should know that I find your membership anathema to the spirit of our mission."

If I had had any idea of what our mission involved, I might have been insulted. My ignorance aside, it was clear Dietrich was in a foul mood, and I was not going to offer myself up as a target for it.

"So much for idle conversation," I muttered.

The cab rattled on. Dietrich and I stared out opposite windows for the remainder of the trip.

I smelled the harbor long before I saw it. At first it made itself known by a cool, salty breeze, but as it grew nearer, other unpleasant odors wove themselves into the olfactory tapestry. I discerned the smells of smoke, rotting wood, and rusting metals, overlaid with the stench of dead fish and seagull droppings. When the breeze kicked up, it carried the odors away, but when it died down the stench immediately settled around us. As the cab made its way down toward the water, I heard the harbor's sounds: the incessant squawking of gulls, the rumble and clang of machinery, the occasional bellow of a steamship approaching port. By the time we came to a halt all these sensations were omnipresent, now mingled with the chatter and shuffle of an endless parade of travelers and stevedores.

The cab stopped a stone's throw from the harbormaster's office. Dietrich and I fittingly exited the carriage by opposite doors. This had the result of placing the carriage between us, alleviating some of the discomfiture I was still experiencing after his tirade. But it also created a problem when the crowd flowed around the obstacle, making it impossible for me to get around the carriage or to be heard above the din. I had the not-entirely-irrational feeling Dietrich might abandon me, which at that moment I would not have minded. But before the possibility could play out, the driver snapped the reins, the cab pulled away, and I stood facing my simmering companion.

In spite of his secret knowledge of our mission, and his alleged higher intellect, Dietrich at that moment seemed as clueless as I was. We each turned slowly, completing circles to take in our surroundings. When we once again faced each other, he could not meet my eyes for more than a second without becoming noticeably agitated. He started to fidget, his hands patting his pockets as if looking for something, while he looked around as if expecting to spot some clue that would lead us to William Irish. After a few moments of juxtaposition, the crowd flowing around us like a river, I decided to be the bigger man, to attempt to bridge the chasm between us.

"It might help if you tell me what you know about the fellow," I said. "I can't help you if I know nothing about him."

He looked at me as if I had doused him with a cold bucket of water. After his outburst in the cab he must have thought he had shut me up for good.

"William Irish is employed here as a dockworker," he said. "He's also a known pugilist."

"Pugilist?" I asked. "He's a boxer?"

"In the crudest sense," Dietrich replied.

It took me a moment to decipher his meaning.

"A prizefighter?"

"Yes," he replied.

Suddenly I realized why the name seemed familiar. Years ago I recalled hearing rumor of a man who was coming up through the prizefighting circuit. He was supposedly so brutal and unstoppable that the legitimate boxing circuit expelled him. He was then relegated to bare-knuckles prizefighting, where he savagely demolished all his opponents, some even dying as a result. Soon, no fighter would get into the ring with him, and he became a spectacle, a sort of circus freak, or so I had heard. Then he disappeared.

William Irish, alternately known as Will, or Bill, Irish. But at the height of his success he was best known by a more vulgar moniker.

"*Black Irish?*" I exclaimed.

Dietrich suddenly became hostile again.

"Quiet, you fool!" he hissed, striding the few paces that separated us.

"Why on earth do we need him?" I asked.

"Fortune favors the prepared," Dietrich said. "It will be advantageous to have a fighter along. Irish should prove an effective deterrent."

"A deterrent to what?" I asked, louder than intended.

"Keep your voice down!" Dietrich replied. "Don't advertise our business."

I stared at him, wondering what conceivable cat I might have let out of the bag. The people passing us by took no notice of us whatsoever.

"If we can't even say his name, then how do you expect to find him?" I scoffed.

Dietrich had no response. I watched in amusement as his eyes cast about for some clue to point us in the right direction. It was then that I recognized his Achilles heel.

"I think I know my purpose here," I said. "In spite of your keen mind—not to mention your brutal honesty—you're somewhat lacking in social graces."

"Ridiculous," he replied.

He returned to searching the crowd with his eyes, more frantically than before. I began to fear he might do something absurd to extricate himself, simply to prove me wrong. He bent his right arm at the elbow and unconsciously flexed his fingers. I had the uncomfortable feeling he was about to randomly seize and interrogate someone from the crowd.

"Excuse me," I said, stepping between him and a passerby. The stranger was an older man, even older than Dietrich, dressed in grimy worker's clothes. By the lunch pail in his hand he looked to be on his way home. "Are you familiar with a gentleman by the name of Bill Irish?"

"You talking about that Black Irish fellow?" he asked.

"Why, yes," I replied. "I think the man we're looking for once went by that sobriquet."

The man gave me a funny look, then gave the same to Dietrich. I could not tell what he was thinking. Either he was trying to decide if helping us would be worth his while, or he was trying to figure out the meaning of *sobriquet*. To help him out, I reached for my wallet.

"Forgive me," I said. "I'm probably wasting your lunch hour, or causing you to miss the train home. Let me compensate you."

As I reached into my wallet I realized I had no money. Everything had been taken from me in the Tombs. A pension might be forthcoming, but I had yet to see a penny.

"Oh, dear," I said. "I seem to have forgotten to stock up. Mr Dietrich, would you mind compensating this kind gentleman? I'm good for it."

I shot him a wink. He stiffened and fired back a look of disapproval. But given the awkwardness of the situation he acquiesced. He reached into his pocket and produced a dollar, which I immediately snatched and pressed into the stranger's hand. The compensation banished the man's reservations.

"Thanks," he said, nodding down the dock in a southerly direction. "He works down that way, at the far end."

The dock extended almost as far as the eye could see. I looked at him expectantly, hoping for more, but that was all he seemed to know. I thanked him again for his help and sent him merrily on his way.

I turned to Dietrich, who was apoplectic. I relished the fact I had so deftly handled the situation, and I was more than a little pleased that I had forced him to sacrifice a dollar. But as he glowered at me I decided to avoid any public unpleasantness. I quickly set off down the dock, and he grudgingly followed.

We spent half an hour working our way down the dock, weaving through people coming and going. As we made our way, the ships began to look less regal and more worn. Soon we had left the luxury liners far behind, and only cargo ships and rust buckets lay ahead. On our inland side the buildings followed the same pattern. The whitewashed structures closest to the harbormaster gave way to vast, dark warehouses that looked in need of maintenance.

At intervals I asked for assistance locating Irish, and each time we were sent further down the dock. This produced two converse effects. The further we walked, the more people seemed to know of Irish and his whereabouts. Eventually a man who looked as if he had lost a bout with scurvy directed us to a ship only a couple hundred yards away. At the same time, however, I steadily became aware that Dietrich and I were out of our element: we had crossed the threshold of polite society and entered the strange and grim land of the mariner—a realm where bulging arms, scars, tattoos, and missing teeth were trademarks, and distrust of the landlubber was ubiquitous. Troglodytic dockhands glared at us as we passed.

Finally we reached our objective, a large black cargo steamer that was fighting a losing battle against barnacles and rust. Dozens of men could be seen engaged in repairs along its length, welding, riveting, and scraping.

We inquired with the foreman, a salty old grouch who was more interested in smoking his pipe than helping us.

"What do you need Irish for?" he asked. "He break the law?"

"No," Dietrich said. "We are not police. We are here on business. *Private* business."

The man frowned as he looked us up and down, but perhaps fearing we were men of import he finally gave in. He grudgingly led us up the gangplank, across the deck, then down a staircase and through a bewildering series of dark passages, delving ever deeper into the bowels of the ship. When at length he opened a hatch, we found ourselves in a wide cargo hold, lit only by a broad shaft of sunlight pouring through the open deck doors above. The hold was full of all sorts of crates and barrels, and a crew of men that was systematically removing them from the ship. As Dietrich and I took in the scene, a large palette appeared in the opening above and was slowly lowered into the hold by a deck crane. As we watched it descend, men came forward to load it, a lumbering creature among them. Even before the foreman pointed him out, it was obvious which man was Black Irish.

Our guide stepped forward and we followed. Irish made an immediate impression, even from far away. He looked to be the size of three men, and by the ease with which he manhandled crates and barrels, he was as strong as an ox, maybe even a team of them. As we approached, the man grew to a size that seemed even more improbable. It was not so much his height that impressed us, because he stood little over six feet tall. Rather, it was his massive build. From a distance he resembled more a rectangular slab of stone than a man.

While Irish's size immediately impressed me from afar, up close his appearance gave me reason to reappraise him. Beneath the brim of his flat cap his face was similarly broad, containing two beady eyes beneath a prominent brow, a lump of misshapen clay for a nose, and beneath them a jaw so prominent it suggested a primeval underbite. He had removed his shirt to perform his labor so that his suspenders dangled at his sides, leaving him in a grimy and sweat-stained undershirt from which protruded arms the size of tree trunks. However, he was old, or at any rate older than I had imagined him. The stubble on his shorn head was a mix of auburn and grey, as were the whiskers on his unshaven chin. And though he possessed great size and strength, he moved rather slowly, suggesting a grizzled weariness. He reminded me of an old circus elephant, a beast grown too slow and clumsy to perform tricks, but still used for physical labors.

Regardless of these observations I was keenly aware that under no circumstance did I want to be on Irish's bad side. No matter how haggard he looked, a single punch from one of his huge fists would flatten me.

"Irish!" the foreman called. "Someone's here to see you."

Irish paused, a large crate still in his arms. He looked Dietrich and me up and down.

"What do they want?" he replied.

"Mr Irish," Dietrich said, suddenly stepping forward. "I'm Meyer Dietrich, and my companion is Mr Grey. We have a proposition that you may find interesting."

The foreman shot us an unfriendly look.

"Proposition?" he said. "You never said anything about a proposition. You got the nerve to come here and steal a man from me?"

Dietrich rounded on the man, a scathing rebuke upon his lips, but I adeptly defused the situation before he got us into trouble. I hooked one of the foreman's arms and began guiding him back the way we had come.

The man at first resisted, taken aback that I would lay a hand on him. And he was especially perturbed that I was pulling him away from a conversation he would no doubt like to overhear. However I eloquently persuaded him to walk with me.

"You misunderstand," I said in a hushed tone. "This is prizefighting business."

As we stepped through the hatch I glanced back at Dietrich. I was pleased to see he had already pulled Irish aside for discussion.

At the mention of prizefighting, the foreman became intrigued.

"Yeah?" he said. "What's that mean to me?"

"If he is willing to step back into the ring," I said, "even for a limited engagement, there is much money to be made."

The man's eyes glittered.

"Really?"

I was able to coax him along with promises of fees and percentages should Irish fight, and still more profits if Irish were to win. By the time we were back on deck I had him fully onboard with our phony cause. I then turned around and headed back toward the hold, laughing to myself at the man's fatuity.

As I attempted to retrace my steps I was at first confident I could find my way back to Dietrich. But I must have made a wrong turn somewhere, because I soon found myself in a series of tunnels that looked completely unfamiliar. I foolishly continued along those strange and stifling passages, perhaps longer than I should have, thinking I would eventually find my way. Finally I admitted I was lost, and I was relieved when I suddenly heard voices.

They came from further down the passage, and I headed toward them. As I walked they became more distinct, or at least clear enough to know they belonged to men, and I prepared myself for the embarrassing explanation I would have to provide. I was perhaps too relieved to find help, otherwise I would have been more cautious. But in my haste I found the hatch and stepped through without hesitation.

I found myself faced with an unexpected tableau. The walls of the room were lined with grease-smeared machinery and dripping pipes, and in the center of the room two strange men sat upon the floor. One man, the older of the two, was a scraggily greybeard wearing the tattered remnants of a black suit and a half-crushed stovepipe hat. Between his incoherent cackles he took long swigs from a tin flask. His companion, a scruffy younger man wearing a derby and a coat that looked like it was fashioned from sackcloth, sat with closed eyes as he held a lit match over the bowl of a rustic pipe. As I watched, he exhaled a cloud of acrid blue smoke from his nostrils.

I froze, unsure of what I had stumbled into. Presently I realized I had discovered a pair of vagabonds, a drunkard and possibly an opium addict, who had taken up residence in a remote part of the ship. I considered them little cause for alarm, because I myself was a trespasser on the ship. They, however, did not infer the same about me. To them I was an intruder, a threat to their merrymaking, and possibly the sort who would report their illicit behavior to the police.

I backed toward the entrance hoping to depart, but the greybeard noticed me and bellowed something indecipherable. The younger man suddenly opened his heavy-lidded eyes and leapt into action. Before I could react he dropped his pipe, sprang to his feet, and pinned me to the wall.

"Who are you?" he snarled, his breath like brimstone.

I watched over his shoulder as the greybeard struggled to his feet. I stammered in an attempt to come up with a response, but nothing intelligible came out.

"Is he a cop?" the old one asked, squinting at me. He had an unsteady, maniacal look in his eyes.

The youth placed a strong forearm across my throat, forcing my head back against the wall while his free hand searched my pockets. He quickly found my billfold and passed it to the old drunk. I thought they would be relieved to learn I was not affiliated with John Law, but the fact that it was empty only frustrated them more.

"There's nothing in it," the drunk said, hurling it to the floor. He then brought his face within inches of mine and eyeballed me.

"He ain't talking neither," the ruffian said. "He ain't saying who he is."

"Then what the hell's he doing here?" the old man demanded, taking a step back.

"What are we going to do with him?" the youth asked.

The old drunk staggered forward to inspect me again. This time his nose grazed my cheek as his bleary eyes rolled around in his head trying to focus. I endured another bout of his mephitic breath before he raised a hand and wagged a finger as if an idea had come to him. He staggered to a back corner of the room where he swayed for a moment, regained his balance, and rummaged through a dark and stained carpetbag, muttering to himself all the while.

I was mostly interested in what the drunkard was up to, but my eyes kept drifting back to the face of the man pinning me. Judging by his eyes he seemed to be struggling against sleep, though his grip was still like iron. At one point he seemed to have drifted off, standing with his arm still across my neck, only to suddenly awaken with a start, applying more pressure to my throat than before. A moment later the old drunk cackled to himself, and he slowly turned to reveal a long, dirty straight razor.

Even before the appearance of the razor I had concluded the two meant my undoing, and I knew if I wanted to survive I must take advantage of the slightest opportunity. As the maniacal old man staggered forward, the youth's eyes closed and his head sagged again. Seizing the moment I shoved my opponent away, causing him to sprawl backward into his elder companion.

For a moment they were immobilized, the sleepy youth supine in a state of shock, the greybeard pinned beneath him. In that instant I leapt through the hatch and ran at breakneck speed through the maze of corridors. As I ran I tried to look ahead and choose the path that offered the best chance for survival, but I was moving too fast. Ideas flickered through my head faster than I could acknowledge them. I had been reduced to an animal, acting purely on survival instinct to escape the predators at my heels.

And they were indeed at my heels. Before I had reached the end of the first corridor I heard several shouts, followed by footsteps as both men hastened in pursuit. As I ran I tried my best to recognize places I had passed on my way down, so that I might find my way back to Dietrich, or up onto deck. But too often I remembered some vaguely familiar feature only after I had passed it, and with those ne'er-do-wells giving chase I could not halt or go back.

I do not know how long I ran, desperately weaving my way through the bowels of the ship, but soon I started to run out of steam. My chest and legs started to ache, and I slowed down appreciably. Expecting to feel hands clamp down on my shoulders at any second, I ducked into the next available hatch, hoping to find a place to hide. But the hatch I chose, or which Fate chose for me, was an empty galley. All the cabinets and counters were affixed to the walls, leaving the middle of the room bare. As I spun around helplessly gasping for air, my pursuers caught up to me.

They entered the room cautiously, their breathing as ragged as mine. The young one now seemed entirely awake, and the old one looked as if he had come completely unhinged. His eyes were wilder than before, and a string of spittle dangled from his lower lip and entangled itself in his long, filthy beard. I backed away as they separated to circle me. The old one blocked the door, still wielding the razor. Fearing he might leap at me and cut my throat, I kept my eyes on him. But then I realized the youth was trying maneuver into my blind spot.

"Now we're going to make a pretty mess of you," the greybeard rasped.

Suddenly the senselessness of it all came rushing to me. The situation was completely outrageous. I had done nothing more than make a wrong turn, and instantly I had two mortal enemies. But why? What threat did I pose to them? It was completely absurd!

"Wait!" I exclaimed, raising my hands. "Just hold a moment!"

My words, however, acted like a trigger. No sooner had I uttered the last syllable when the youth leapt onto my back, wrapping his arms around me. The old man grinned, raised the razor above his head, and charged. I closed my eyes, anticipating the icy sharpness of the razor on my neck. I was done for.

Or so I thought. Since I had closed my eyes, I did not see the beginnings of what happened next. I heard the shuffle of feet followed by a shriek. I assumed the old maniac was charging, and in a last-ditch effort I kicked at the space in front of me to keep him away. To my surprise the blow never came. As I opened my eyes to investigate, the addict released me and I fell to the floor.

The sight before my eyes was like an artist's rendition of an ancient hero doing battle. Towering above me stood Black Irish. With one outstretched arm he held the greybeard aloft by his razor hand, and with the other he repeatedly pummeled the old man's exposed ribs like a punching bag. In the space of a few seconds he landed three crushing blows. I watched as the drunkard's face repeated a horrible series of spasms similar to a fish out of water gasping for breath.

It was then that the addict foolishly entered the fray, or at least intended to. Seeing his companion so abused he charged, leaping over me in the process. But Irish seemed to expect this, and in the same moment released the drunkard, who collapsed in a heap beside me, and swung his fist round to meet the younger man's face. I can only liken the blow to being hit in the face by a steam engine. It was so powerful it hurled the man back across the room, where he slammed into a wall and collapsed.

The battle was over in five seconds, maybe less. The old drunk lay gasping on the floor while his young companion sat slumped against the wall, exhibiting no signs of life. As I marveled I heard a sound at the hatch. I turned to see Dietrich enter the room. At first he looked at me accusingly, as if I had been up to some mischief. Then he swept the room with his eyes and he seemed to understand. He bent and helped me to my feet.

"Thank you," I said, straightening my clothes. "Thank you both."

"What happened to you?" Dietrich demanded. "We've been looking for you for ten minutes."

"I got lost and came across these two. I don't know why they attacked."

"A drunk and an addict," Dietrich said, demonstrating his uncanny ability to instantly absorb details. "I've encountered their like before. Logic does not play into their decisions."

As Dietrich turned his attention to the fallen, I turned to Irish, who seemed not the least put off by events.

"I suppose a proper introduction is in order," I said, extending my hand. "Prometheus Grey."

He accepted my hand, but he seemed more interested in Dietrich and his examination of the vagabonds.

"Bill Irish," he simply said.

"Yes," I said. "Black Irish. Your reputation precedes you."

He looked me over with his small, dark eyes, and I felt an uncontrollable chill. For a split second I thought the brute might pick me up by the neck and throttle me. But before I could dwell on it further, Dietrich spoke up.

"This man is barely breathing," he said, indicating the youth. "I think he might be dying."

Irish nudged the gasping drunk with a booted toe.

"So might this one," he said.

"We must get them medical attention at once," Dietrich said.

Irish looked at him impassively. He showed no trace of thought or emotion, but I could tell what was going through his head. Personally, I was of the opinion we should leave the vagabonds there, and get away while we could. Dietrich, however, was still a prisoner of his scrupulous morals.

"Before we do that," I said, raising a tentative finger, "let's consider the consequences. If we call for a doctor, the police will get involved, which will bring us unwanted attention. If we're to maintain a low profile, I think we should avoid such entanglements."

"We are not animals," Dietrich stated, emphatically. "I will not simply abandon these men to die. It would be criminal and inhumane."

As I tried to find a way around his convictions, Irish offered a simple solution.

"I'll handle it," he said. "No need getting your hands dirty. After you're gone, I'll tell the foreman these two came at me. He'll understand and send for a doctor."

It sounded like a perfectly good plan to me. It would allow Dietrich and I to extricate ourselves, and result in medical attention for the bums. Irish would remain somewhat entangled, but his story made sense and should clear him of any crime. With no testimony to the contrary—except that of the bums, who, if they lived, no one would believe—everything would be fine.

Dietrich took a minute to mull it over. He was clearly at odds with any sort of deception, but even he could not argue the logic of it. Under the circumstances, Irish's plan offered the best solution.

"All right," he said. "But you must be quick. I think that one has a punctured lung."

Dietrich pointed at the old drunk, who at that moment coughed up a modicum of blood.

"I'll be quick." Irish reassured him with a grin.

Dietrich finally seemed satisfied, and together we exited the galley and began weaving our way out of the ship. His memory of the tunnels proved far better than mine. He was able to guide us to the deck without a single misstep. As we descended the gangplank and set foot on solid ground, I realized that in the excitement I had forgotten the purpose of our visit.

"By the way, what did Irish say?" I asked.

"About what?" Dietrich asked.

"About joining us," I said.

"He is onboard," Dietrich replied. "He will join us at the house tomorrow."

"Good show," I said, trying to be complimentary.

I gave him a congratulatory slap on the back, a gesture he did not much appreciate. But I did not let his attitude put me off. I acknowledged the fundamental differences between us, but after that incident I somehow felt closer to him. And though he would sooner be skinned alive than acknowledge it, I suspected he felt it, too.

6: THE PRINCESS

After recruiting Irish the remainder of the day was uneventful. Dietrich and I returned to the house expecting to give a full account of our journey and encounters to Cross, but he did not return until late in the afternoon. So Dietrich and I spent our time separately, each engaged in his own pursuits. He spent most of his time in the study, poring over books while sipping coffee. I spent my time in the living room with the newspaper, catching up on current events. Occasionally one of the servants would wander through performing their household duties. I successfully engaged them in a few brief exchanges.

My conversations with the ladies proved more interesting than I anticipated. From them I learned several facts about the ladies themselves. For instance, Mrs McMurtey revealed that her husband worked in construction, they had four children, and they lived in the South Bronx. I smiled and nodded politely as she disclosed the quotidian details of her life.

Abigail was more interesting. I learned she lived in an apartment in Harlem, and she was being courted by a young man who worked as a grocer. But she rarely got to see him, because of the demands of her job. She arose every morning at five o'clock in order to complete the long trek to Corona Park on foot (from which I inferred she could not afford other transportation). Sometimes she was kept so busy, she did not return home until ten at night. She remarked that such long days made it difficult to maintain a relationship, but she followed up by saying she was happy to have her job.

I marveled at these revelations, thoroughly impressed by her work ethic, yet outraged that this semi-attractive young woman was forced to walk several miles to and from work each day, alone and in the dark. In spite of her protests, I vowed I would take the matter up with Cross the next time I saw him.

The most surprising item I learned from her was that Cross did not reside at the Corona Park residence. While the servants maintained it in the manner of a middle-class house, it was in fact nobody's home. The only people who had so far spent a night in the house were Dietrich and I. Each night after concluding his business, Cross waited at the curb for a coach which promptly arrived at 9 o'clock and carried him away to places unknown.

Around four o'clock Abigail and Mrs McMurtey began preparing supper, and at the stroke of five, just as food was being brought to the table, Cross returned. The women rushed to greet him, and Dietrich followed close behind. I could not see what all the fuss was about, and I remained at the dinner table. Eventually Cross and Dietrich found their chairs, dinner was served, and Dietrich launched into his report.

"Mr Irish has joined our cause," he said.

"Excellent!" Cross exclaimed. "If he is still the man I remember, he should prove an excellent deterrent to trouble."

"That's an understatement," I muttered into my wineglass.

Dietrich bristled, but Cross found my statement amusing.

"He's quite an imposing individual, isn't he?" he said.

I nodded and gave Dietrich a questioning look as I took another sip of wine.

"You should know," Dietrich began, "there was an ... incident."

Cross sat back as Dietrich recounted our encounter with the vagabonds. He did not once interrupt. Instead he allowed Dietrich to provide all the details on his own, which Dietrich did in a thorough manner. At the conclusion Cross returned to his meal, seemingly unconcerned.

"If Mr Irish does not turn up tomorrow, I suppose we'll know his plan did not work," he said. "If he is unable to join us, we may need to alter our plans. But let's hope it doesn't come to that. Presuming Mr Irish avoids legal entanglements, what time can we expect him?"

"By nine," Dietrich replied.

"Perfect," Cross said, rising from the table. "I have one parting request of you. I ask that you both be downstairs by nine to meet Mr Irish, and be prepared to depart by ten. We have one more member to recruit."

"Really?" I said. "Who's next?"

Cross gave me a tight-lipped smile.

"You'll find out tomorrow," he said "Goodnight, gentlemen."

He then secluded himself in his study for the rest of the evening.

For Dietrich and I the rest of the evening passed quietly. He found another book in which to bury his nose, and I stepped out for a walk. I needed only cross the street to find myself in a park. The sun had already sunk beyond the horizon of buildings, and the sky was rapidly darkening. It was still early February and quite cold. I stuffed my hands in my pockets and followed a path around its perimeter. The park was small so my jaunt was brief, but by the time I completed the circuit the cold was gnawing at me and I headed for the house. As I reached the steps, the door opened and out stepped Abigail.

"What a surprise!" I said. "Fancy a walk around the park?"

"Oh, no, thank you," she said. "My day is over, and I still have a long walk home."

I looked up at the night sky and shook my head.

"It's inexcusable that Cross allows you to walk alone through the city at night," I said. "And I'm going to tell him as much, the next chance I get."

"That's very kind of you," she said. "You are a true gentleman."

I gave a mock bow and was rewarded with a giggle.

"But now I must go," she said. "Good night."

And off she went, alone on a five-mile trek through New York's darkest and most dangerous streets. I watched after her as long as I could, until she blended with the shadows. Then with a sigh I went inside.

In the foyer I found Mrs McMurtey, who was herself preparing to depart. Dietrich stood nearby, thanking her for her service and wishing her a good night. I did not feel like exchanging pleasantries, so I gave them a courteous nod and climbed the stairs to my room. I left my door ajar in the event I might pick up some scrap of conversation that would give me a clue to our business. I then propped myself up on the bed and thumbed through the newspaper.

By nine my chin was touching my chest, and I would have been out for the night if I had not been awakened by noises in the foyer. I looked out my window in time to see Cross climb into his coach and drive off. A moment later Dietrich ascended the stairs.

"Finally calling it a night, then?" I said.

He looked up in surprise and stiffened.

"Yes," he said. "Good night."

"What were you and Cross up to?" I asked. "Did I miss something important?"

"Just tying up some loose ends," he replied. "Nothing to concern you. Good night."

"Memorable day we had," I said. "Quite a harrowing experience with the hoodlums on that ship. I suppose I should thank my lucky stars that you and Irish came along when you did."

"I suppose," he said, continuing down the hallway. "It's getting late, and Cross needs us ready by nine tomorrow."

"I'll be the first one up," I said.

He nodded and continued on his way. I poked my head out and watched as he walked to a door at the end of the hall.

"So that's you?" I said. "I was beginning to wonder if I was the only person living here."

"Yes, this is my room," he said.

"It's nice to finally know at least one of my neighbors," I said, jovially. "As for the other bedrooms, I presume one's for Irish, when he arrives. And the other?"

"For our fourth," he said, stepping into his room.

"All of us under one roof," I called after him. "Except for Cross. Where do you suppose he goes at night?"

"Home," Dietrich replied. "Good night."

Before I could get in another word, he closed his door. As I stood pondering, I heard the unmistakable sound of a key turning in the lock.

I awoke the next morning to a knock at my door. I felt strangely fatigued and chose to ignore the intrusion by placing the pillow over my head. But the knocking persisted, and soon I heard the door open, followed by a tentative voice.

"Mr Grey? It's after eight-thirty."

Slowly I registered the voice as Abigail's. Though every fiber of my being resisted, I rolled over and pulled the pillow from my head. I must have looked comical because she placed a hand over her mouth to stifle a giggle.

"Time to get up," she said. "The others are already downstairs. Mr Cross asked that I remind you of your appointment."

"Appointment?" I said groggily.

"Yes," she said. "I think someone's coming by the house today, to meet you."

"Ah," I said. "Mr Irish. Yes, tell them I'll be down shortly."

She nodded and closed the door. I reluctantly rolled out of bed, donned a robe, and staggered down the hall to the bathroom. By the time I completed my ablutions I felt thoroughly awake. After dressing in a smart grey suit, I headed downstairs and found Cross and Dietrich standing in the hall. Just as I greeted them the bell rang, and Abigail hurried past us to the door. When she opened it she gasped and stepped back in awe, clearly shocked at the size of the caller.

Irish stepped inside, practically filling the foyer. He wore clothes so similar to those of the day before that I was sure he had not changed. The only difference in his appearance was a dark woolen longshoreman's coat wrapped around his ox-like shoulders.

"Welcome," Dietrich said, stepping forward. "Allow me to introduce our employer, Mr George Cross."

Irish shook hands, but his face showed little emotion.

"And here we have the ladies of the house," Dietrich continued, "Mrs McMurtey and Ms Abigail."

Irish gave them a nod.

"And Mr Grey you already know," Dietrich said.

I was about to offer him my hand when Cross interjected.

"This way, please," Cross said, indicating Irish should follow.

They started down the hall. Dietrich followed, and I fell in behind him. When we reached the study, Dietrich stopped unexpectedly and tried to close

54

the door, causing me to run headlong into him. He gave me a strange look, as if I were the last person he expected to see, and he froze in the doorway. I had to shoulder him out of the way to get inside.

Cross waited until the door was closed and we were all seated.

"Mr Irish," he began, "I know this must seem suspicious, hiring you as a bodyguard for an unknown expedition. All the more reason to thank you for accepting the job."

"The pay's right," Irish replied simply.

"Good," Cross said. "But even though I sought you out for protection, I want to make clear that restraint will also be required."

"Restraint!" I said. "You should have seen the short work he made of those vagabonds yesterday!"

Cross looked at me sidelong.

"All I ask," he went on, "is that you exercise discretion. Your reputation, and certainly your stature, will draw enough attention. In the work ahead, undue attention will jeopardize our mission."

At mention of our mission I perked up, hoping some details might follow. But at that moment a knock came at the door, and the servants entered with a tray containing coffee. They took a few minutes to serve us, then disappeared. By the time they left the room, talk of our mission seemed to have been forgotten by everyone but me.

"Now," Cross said, "if you'll indulge me, I'll bring you up to date on our status. Forgive me if I do so quickly, because we have an important appointment to attend this morning."

Cross said nothing more about our cause, and instead began to recount all the mundane details leading up to that moment. When I realized I was not going to learn anything new, I quickly lost interest and excused myself.

Since I had not yet eaten I decided to scare up some food. I headed to the kitchen and found the servants. Abigail was washing dishes, and Mrs McMurtey was seconds from tossing a pair of leftover crepes into the trash. Before they toppled into the bin I leapt forward and relieved her of the plate. I then found a spot along the kitchen counter and began to eat. Mrs McMurtey stood motionless for a moment, looking me up and down. Then, shaking her head to herself, she went about her business.

"Mm," I said after a couple bites. "Quite good. My compliments to the chef."

"Mrs McMurtey made them," Abigail said over her shoulder. "She's a wonderful cook, much better than me."

I smiled at Mrs McMurtey to show my appreciation.

"I'm about finished here," she said to Abigail. "I'm going to start upstairs."

The splenetic maid swiftly departed, leaving only Abigail and me in the kitchen. I listened to the clink and clatter of the dishes as she continued her work. When I finished off the last bite of crepe, I rolled up my sleeves, took my plate to the sink, and thrust my hands into the soapy water. Abigail was beside herself in disbelief.

"What are you doing? Let me do it."

"Nonsense," I said. "It's just one plate. Besides, I'm not a freeloader. I can pitch in and do my share now and then."

She looked me in the eyes, still incredulous. I pretended to ignore her and finished scrubbing and rinsing the plate. When I set it aside to dry, I looked up to find she was still looking at me appraisingly. In that moment I sensed something between us. I held her stare and smiled. My position at the sink placed us in close proximity, with only inches separating us. She filled my vision, and I took in the details of her face. I noted her dark eyes and lashes, the almost imperceptible array of freckles across her nose, the loose strands of hair across her brow—all elements that contributed to her vague beauty.

I have never fancied myself a poet, so forgive me if what I say is banal, but we shared a moment that seemed endless. As we regarded one another, I began to feel as if the natural conclusion to the moment was a passionate embrace. It did not seem prudent, nor could I reasonably justify it, but it felt inexorable. As I leaned toward her, however, something must have interrupted her thoughts. Suddenly she blushed and withdrew her hands from the sink. I watched, disappointed yet amused, as she hurried from the kitchen, drying her hands on her apron as she went.

At ten o'clock the door to the study opened and the others came out. I was sitting by a window in the living room perusing the paper.

"Mr Grey, it's time to go," Cross said.

"Go?" I asked, feigning surprise. "Oh, yes, this mysterious appointment. All right, let's get to it."

I joined them in the foyer, but before we moved Dietrich emphatically cleared his throat and gained Cross's attention. He nodded at Irish, and Cross took his meaning.

"Mr Irish," Cross said, "I hope you won't take offense, but there's no hiding the fact that you've led, shall we say, an adventurous life that has left you rough around the edges."

Irish looked at him warily.

"Perhaps you'll allow us to smooth some of them out," Cross replied.

He called to Mrs McMurtey, who quickly appeared at the top of the stairs.

"Would you mind showing Mr Irish his room, and perhaps pulling out the brown suit for him?" he said.

"Yes, sir," the matron replied. "This way, Mr Irish."

Irish, who clearly had not been consulted about any of this, gave us an annoyed look. Why he looked at me I have no idea, for I had played no part in it. But in the end he must have considered it a small bruise to his dignity, because he lumbered up the stairs.

In a relatively short time he returned wearing a brown suit that on anyone else would have been nondescript, but on him created the impression of a gorilla banker. He, or more likely Mrs McMurtey, had even washed the grime from his face.

"Splendid!" Cross said, inspecting him top to bottom.

Dietrich also nodded in approval.

"Thanks," Irish said grudgingly. "I'm surprised you got the fit right. But I don't see the need."

"I'll explain along the way," Cross said, ushering us out the door.

As if on cue our transportation rolled up in front of the house. The coach came to a stop, and the driver climbed down and opened the door. We all climbed in, and once everyone was settled the coachman climbed back to his perch, slapped the reins against the horses' backsides, and we were off.

"So, where are we going?" I asked.

"Shoreham," Cross replied.

"Isn't that a distant reach of Long Island?" I said. "It will take all day to get there by coach."

"Correct," Cross said, "which is why we'll be taking the train. There is a station only minutes away."

Fifteen minutes later we came to a stop in front of the station. We climbed out and followed Cross inside. He purchased the tickets, doled them out, and we made our way to the platform. The train was already waiting, and we boarded straight away. Soon it let out a piercing whistle, and shortly thereafter we were jolted as it went into motion. Once the great engine was up to speed I tried to make conversation.

"Shoreham," I said. "It's a bit out of the way, and a strange place to find a recruit."

"Perhaps," Cross said, "but when we arrive I think you will have a better understanding."

"Shoreham," I said again, rubbing my chin and looking into the distance. "Why does that ring a bell?"

Cross gave me a questioning look, clearly interested to see what I knew of the place. Dietrich watched me as well, but Irish stared out the window as if none of it had any bearing on him.

"Aha!" I exclaimed at last, striking a fist on one knee. "The scientist, Tesla, has a lab there. Something to do with experiments in electricity."

Cross smiled and nodded, clearly impressed I had made the connection.

"Very good, Mr Grey," he said. "The place is called Wardenclyffe, and it is, in fact, our destination."

Irish turned from the window and shot me a look that said he was impressed by my guesswork. Dietrich looked at me suspiciously, as if he had figured out I had gone through Cross's mail. He also appeared unsurprised by any of it, as if we were discussing the plot of a book he had already read. It was clear he knew more about our business than he let on.

"But it's not Tesla we are hoping to recruit," Cross continued. "He would be a valuable member of our team, but he is devoted solely to his work. He would never abandon it. Instead we are going to meet one of his guests, someone who could be of even greater assistance."

Cross had my attention. Even Dietrich suddenly appeared interested, and I realized in this matter he was in the dark, too. Cross paused, trying to pick words that would, as usual, reveal as little as possible.

"If you're going to speak in riddles, don't bother," I said.

"The time has come for me to speak more plainly," he conceded. "We are going to meet Tesla, who will introduce us to the person I hope to recruit. This person—a lady, and I mean *lady* in the truest sense—is someone of the highest character and dignity. It will serve us well to make a good impression."

We all stared at him, shocked to hear a woman might be joining us. None of us knew what our mission would entail, but we knew it was potentially dangerous work. The idea that a woman would be among us was both fascinating and appalling.

"A lady, you say?" Irish said, suddenly taking an interest.

"Yes," Cross replied.

I found myself in the grip of an internal conflict. On one hand, after the hard times I had endured of late, I looked forward to a woman's company, even if it was strictly business. On the other, inviting a woman on our quest perilous violated my gentlemanly instincts, no matter what capabilities she possessed. A glance at Dietrich's dour expression revealed he and I finally agreed on something.

"Mr Cross," he said in a confidential tone, "I had no idea you intended to invite a woman. Given the risk, I don't think it's appropriate."

Cross considered it and turned to Irish.

"What do you think?"

"All the same to me," the brute replied.

Next Cross looked at me. Apparently my opinion would be the tie-breaker.

"Since we're already racing toward Shoreham," I said, "we might as well meet her before making our decision."

No one disagreed.

"Very well," Cross said. "You will meet her. But know this: I've already met her and extended an invitation. She has tentatively agreed to join us."

"Then why are we going to interview her?" I asked.

"We won't be interviewing her," Cross said. "She will be interviewing you."

That surprise shut us up, and since Cross would offer no more details, we sat in silence for the remainder of the trip. It was not until the whistle blew to announce our approach to Shoreham that I finally broke the silence.

"What's her name?" I asked.

"Katherine Alexander," he said. "*Ms* Alexander, to you and me."

Outside the station Cross signaled for us to gather around. He then turned and pointed at a large tower silhouetted against the sky, perhaps a mile distant.

"Wardenclyffe," he said. "Our destination."

Without further explanation he set off toward the overwhelming object. As we walked I examined the tower more closely. I estimated it stood about two hundred feet in height and consisted of a complex latticework of steel-reinforced wooden beams. The beams had been assembled in an octagonal shape, wide at the base and narrow at its apex. Atop the supports sat a broad platform, and arching over it was the skeleton of a dome. At first I thought it was a local attraction, an observation tower built for tourists. But given the remoteness and drab landscape of Shoreham, I soon concluded there would be little to observe, even from that lofty height.

As we drew nearer I pulled my eyes away from the spectacle and examined the building at its feet. The structure stood in the midst of a large cleared lot and consisted of a single story, broad enough to encompass a great many offices and laboratories. However it seemed strangely quiet, the only sign of its inhabitance being an idle horse and buggy parked to one side, and the occasional sounds of light construction nearby.

"This is where Tesla does his work," Cross said. "You will meet him shortly. He is a gentleman, but he may seem standoffish. Like many men of genius he has his quirks, so don't interpret his eccentricities as rudeness."

As we approached the building the door opened, and out stepped a well-dressed young man who more resembled a clerk than a servant of science.

"Welcome back, Mr Cross," he said. "Mr Tesla is expecting you. He's currently performing an inspection of the tunnel complex. Follow me, please."

Before Cross could reply the young man turned and led us into the building. We followed him straight through and out the back door, heading directly for the strange tower. At its base—in the very midst of its superstructure—milled a handful of men dressed in work clothes, all staring downward. As we neared I realized the ground beneath the tower was hollow, that a great vertical shaft had been delved into the earth. The wall of the shaft was lined with cement, and attached to it was a ladder that disappeared into the darkness below.

As we approached the men took notice, but they paid us little heed, because echoing up from the shaft came the sound of voices. One voice in particular stood out and seemed to be issuing a litany of instructions.

Soon someone below called out, and the idle men began cranking a large winch, raising something from the darkness below. As they reeled in the rope, the voices below grew steadily nearer. Soon a railed wooden platform came into sight containing two men: one wore clothes similar to the other workers, but the other wore a spotless white lab coat over a dark grey suit.

When the platform came level with the ground, both men dismounted and walked toward us, though neither paid us any attention. Instead, the gentleman continued to converse with the workman while removing his lab coat, which he then absently extended in one hand to our young guide. Once the gentleman felt assured the foremen understood his instructions, he turned to us.

"Gentlemen," Cross said, "meet Professor Tesla."

"Mr Cross," Tesla said, striding forward. But instead of offering his hand he stopped several feet away, stood very straight, and clasped his hands behind his back. "It's good to see you again. These gentlemen must be the ones you told me about."

Tesla quickly scanned the lot of us, and except for the extra second that his eyes lingered on the spectacle of Irish, he seemed politely unimpressed.

"Allow me to introduce my companions," Cross said, gesturing at us in turn. "Mr Dietrich, Mr Irish, and Mr Grey."

In lieu of a handshake, Tesla directed a courteous nod at each of us.

"It is my pleasure to meet you," he said. "Now, let's return to my office."

And without further pleasantries he strode deliberately back to the building with us chasing after him.

Tesla led us to a large laboratory within the building. Judging by all the tables laden with blueprints, tools, and mechanical apparatuses, a great project was underway. But in spite of its suggested magnitude, the laboratory boasted only a meager staff. Whatever Tesla was working on, he had a lot of work ahead.

Once inside, he crossed to a desk in a corner of the room and took up a position behind it. But he did not seem to need it, at least not for its intended purpose, because he neither sat down nor retrieved anything from it. Instead, he seemed to use it solely for the purpose of placing a physical barrier between us. There were no chairs for guests, so we stood before him expectantly.

"This is a remarkable place," I said. "I've read of it in the papers. But I must admit, I don't entirely understand its purpose."

"Nor should you," he said. "The Wardenclyffe facility is entirely unique, as will be the experiments I conduct here once it is complete."

"What kind of experiments?" Irish asked.

"In world telegraphy," he said. "I have developed methods to transmit telegraphic messages, and perhaps later electricity itself, through the very air we breathe."

As he spoke I watched Irish's face. It was obvious he had no idea what Tesla was talking about.

"Fascinating," I said on his behalf.

"I've followed your work for some time," Dietrich chimed in. "If your experiments are successful, they will change the world."

"As they should," Tesla replied. "And for the better. There will come a time when the great truth, accidentally revealed and experimentally confirmed, is fully recognized. Everyone will know that this planet, with all its appalling immensity, is to electric currents no more than a small metal ball.

When it is shown that a telegraphic message, as secret and pure as thought, can be transmitted over any distance, and that the energy of a waterfall may be harnessed to supply light, heat, or motive power, humanity will be like an anthill stirred up with a stick."

Dietrich nodded in approval of Tesla's vision. I, on the other hand, remained skeptical.

"Fascinating," I repeated, this time less enthusiastically. But it was enough to awaken Tesla from his dream.

"Now to business," he said. "Mr Cross, have you explained to your companions why they are here?"

"I've explained they are to meet Ms Alexander," Cross replied. "But that is all."

"Then I shall provide a brief summary, and tell you all I am able," Tesla said. "Ms Alexander came to me several months ago. She hails from Europe, though her precise origin and history I am not at liberty to discuss. I mention this only to avoid awkwardness during your introduction. It is natural to ask questions of a new acquaintance, but do not press her for details of her life. She is a woman of the highest quality, and she deserves gentlemanly treatment. I recommend you address her formally, not by her name. Lastly, you must maintain your distance. Although it is considered polite and customary, she will not offer you her hand. Do not approach her or attempt to take it. Do you understand?"

We all nodded, though we were baffled by these arcane, last minute instructions.

"Good," Tesla said. "Follow me."

He led us through the lab and down the hall, stopping outside a closed door. He paused for a moment to look each of us in the eyes before throwing it open and ushering us into the room.

The room was an office, probably Tesla's, and contained a desk and numerous bookshelves. The only incongruous element was a small tea table which had been set near the window. Near it stood a gaunt old woman in a plain dark dress with wiry hair and suspicious eyes. In her shadow, gazing out the window, sat the most angelic creature I had ever seen.

The moment is forever burned into my memory. From where we entered she sat in statuesque profile, back straight, chin slightly raised toward the sun. She was fair, but beautifully so, more pristine than pale, with long golden curls pinned up and back from her face. She wore a dress of virginal white that glowed in the sunlight, along with small white gloves made all the more fascinating because they were outmoded by decades.

We filed in and lined up as if assembling for inspection. The young lady turned to us with a smile as bright as the sun.

"Madame," Tesla said. "Mr Cross has returned, this time with company. Gentlemen, may I present Ms Katherine Alexander, and Irena, who is in her employ."

The young woman smiled and rose from her chair. She took one step forward, closely shadowed by her servant, but neither came any closer.

"Thank you, Mr Tesla," she said. "Who have you brought with you, Mr Cross?"

"Allow me to introduce my associates," Cross replied. "This is Meyer Dietrich, whom I told you about."

Dietrich greeted her stiffly, with a nod and a forced smile.

"Mr Dietrich," she said, "I understand you are an investigator. That must be fascinating and challenging work."

"Yes, I suppose," he replied, trying to remain aloof, but the young woman's warmth and charm had caught him off guard. "But don't read too much into it. I have a knack for it, that's all. I am no hero."

"A worthy pursuit, nonetheless," she replied. Her eyes moved to Irish.

"William Irish," Cross said next, indicating the giant.

Contrary to my expectations, she looked up into his broad granite face with the same magical smile, without the slightest hint of intimidation.

"I do not follow sports," she said, "but I understand you are a prizefighter of some renown. From your size I do not doubt it. You must be exceptionally capable."

"Yeah, I suppose," Irish muttered. He was either unable or unwilling to say more. Ms Alexander graciously filled the silence.

"I understand your purpose is to provide us protection. Hopefully it will not be necessary, but now that I have seen you, I have the feeling no one will bother us."

Irish shuffled his feet and straightened his jacket. If his complexion had not been so ruddy I would have sworn that he was blushing.

"And finally," Cross said, "we have Mr Prometheus Grey, a former escape artist, among other things."

As the lady's eyes met mine I forgot myself, along with Tesla's simple instructions. I had waited so anxiously for my introduction, and I wanted so desperately to make a good impression, that I instinctively stepped forward to take her hand. I did not complete more than a step, however, before she gasped and recoiled. In an instant her cronish chaperone, Irena, stepped between us and glared at me menacingly. I froze, baffled and mortified, before quickly stepping back in line.

"Pardon me," I said. "It's a pleasure."

My *faux pas* averted, the old maid slowly stepped aside and Ms Alexander noticeably relaxed. As more proof of her inherent grace, the young lady recovered almost instantly, pressing on as if nothing awkward had happened.

"Mr Grey, I find you the most mysterious of all," she said. "I cannot imagine what Mr Cross suspects we might face to require someone of your unique talents."

At that moment I wanted nothing more than to answer the question for her, if for no other reason than to prolong our conversation. But I, too, had no idea what lay ahead that might call upon my distinctive capabilities.

"I think of Mr Grey as our contingency plan," Cross explained. "Whereas

Mr Dietrich and Mr Irish will provide specific services, Mr Grey provides us with flexibility."

Ms Alexander thought about it for a moment.

"A wise precaution, and a wise choice," she acknowledged. "In that light I cannot think of anyone better suited for the task."

By now her smile had returned, and with introductions complete she took a moment to look each of us in the eyes again, finally stopping on Cross.

"Thank you for coming today," she said. "You have my deepest gratitude for making so long a journey for such a brief meeting."

"Think nothing of it," Cross replied.

Suddenly, inexplicably, it seemed as if our appointment had come to an abrupt end. As Dietrich, Irish, and I looked bewilderedly at one another, Cross began to shoo us from the room. Tesla then ushered us out of the office, down the corridor, and out of the building.

"That's it?" I exclaimed. "We came all this way for simple introductions?"

We were back in Wardenclyffe's front lot. Dietrich, Irish and I were standing near the road, out of earshot. Closer to the building, Tesla and Cross were conversing.

"Hardly seemed worth it," Irish agreed.

Dietrich looked at us, then turned to regard Cross and Tesla.

"She was enchanting," he said. "But I agree. It was impractical, and I don't know what we gained from it. She seemed to already know about us, but I still have no idea what she offers."

"Indeed," I said. "She was enchanting."

We stood there grumbling and awaiting Cross for some time. Eventually Tesla returned to his lab to pursue his world-changing work, and Cross joined us and began herding us back to the station.

"I've never questioned your judgment," Dietrich said as we walked along. "But I don't understand what this was about. What does Ms Alexander provide that will enable us to better perform our mission?"

Cross regarded him with some surprise. Perhaps he would have expected such talk from Irish or me, but he had not expected it from Dietrich.

"Ms Alexander speaks five languages," he said. "She also possesses a keen intellect, and it never hurts to have another clever person on one's side."

Dietrich frowned and surveyed the surrounding countryside.

"I'm not opposed to having a fourth member," he said. "But a woman will weaken the integrity of our group. They are a distraction. By no fault of their own, perhaps, but their very presence works to undo the judgment of men."

Irish and I chuckled.

"I'll tell you what she can *undo*—" he began.

Cross immediately raised a hand in protest.

"Please," he said.

"And I renew my argument from before," Dietrich continued. "It is unconscionable to take a woman along when we face certain danger."

My ears suddenly perked up.

"Certain danger?" I asked.

But by then Cross had suffered enough questions.

"Gentlemen," he said, "believe me when I say Ms Alexander possesses many qualities that could prove beneficial to our cause. However, the discussion is premature. You met her and made your impressions. It now falls to her to decide if she wishes to join. Whatever the outcome, Tesla will send a telegraph as soon as she decides."

We spoke little while waiting at the Shoreham station. I was ready with more questions, but Cross avoided them by purchasing a newspaper and finding a lonely bench on which to read it. And Dietrich seemed self-absorbed, wandering off and leaving Irish and me alone on the platform. I tried several times to engage Irish in conversation—about politics, debauchery, anything—but since he considered monosyllables sufficient to uphold his end, I eventually gave up and wandered around aimlessly until the train arrived.

We arrived back at Corona Park just after sunset. We were all famished, and God bless Mrs McMurtey and Abigail, who, following their servants' instincts, had timed dinner to be ready by the stroke of five. As we opened the door they were pulling food out of the oven. I was prepared to sing their praises when Abigail presented an envelope to Cross.

"This came by messenger just before you arrived," she said.

Cross opened the envelope, removed the letter, and read in silence.

"Well done, gentlemen," he said, cracking a smile. "You must have made a good impression. Ms Alexander will join us tomorrow morning."

The frown I had grown so accustomed to seeing on Dietrich's face suddenly deepened. Irish made no comment and followed his nose into the dining room, where he pulled out a chair, sat down, and began helping himself to the food. Mrs McMurtey gasped and shooed the others in behind him, leaving me alone in the foyer.

The lady would join us—my heart soared!

7: MACHINATIONS

The next day I awoke before sunrise. I felt inexplicably restless so I arose, dressed, and made a round of Corona Park. I took the same route as I had before, walking the perimeter in a counter-clockwise direction as I wondered about the events of recent days. It all seemed so improbable, and though I still did not know the details of the mission ahead, it was beginning to sound like a deadly business. Dietrich's words at Wardenclyffe—I distinctly had heard him reference *certain danger*—had not slipped my mind. In spite of my trepidation I could not shake the feeling that I was on the threshold of something grand, that I was being presented an opportunity for greatness and renown far exceeding any I had previously achieved or imagined. And to share the company of a woman like Ms Alexander along the way … well, that would make the job all the more enjoyable.

Ah, Ms Alexander! I thought I had outgrown such boyish infatuation, but the sensations I experienced were undeniable. From the moment I had laid eyes on her I felt like I was back in the schoolyard. Standing there beside Cross, Dietrich, and Irish, I felt the urgent need to win her attention. In my time I had enjoyed my share of women—my Vaudevillian days had proven especially rewarding—but they all paled in comparison. Ms Alexander was undeniably the most perfect embodiment of feminine beauty and grace I had ever encountered.

As I rounded the park the sun peeked over the horizon. As I made the final turn into the home stretch, I found myself almost face-to-face with Abigail, who was on her way to the house. I was not yet in the mood for conversation—all I wanted from her at that moment was breakfast—but our fateful collocation made ignoring her impossible. When I saw her face light up with surprise and recognition, I knew I was destined for a dialogue.

"Good morning!" she said. "What are you doing up and out so early?"

"Just getting some exercise," I said. "The morning air is bracing."

"I agree," she said. "After my walk to work I always feel invigorated."

We fell in side by side. Abigail walked faster than I preferred. After all, I was out for a stroll, not a race. But it would have been rude to fall behind so I kept her pace. After our greeting an awkward silence fell. It did not bother me much, but I could tell by her sidelong glances that it made her uncomfortable. I forced out some obligatory small talk about the weather to distract her. Still, I sensed she was anxious. When we reached the house she smiled, hung her coat, and hurried off to the kitchen. I seated myself in the living room and awaited the breakfast I had so eagerly anticipated.

Mrs McMurtey arrived a short while later, and soon the aromas of coffee, bacon, and fresh bread began to permeate the air. Not long thereafter I heard the sounds of bedsprings and heavy feet on the floor indicating Irish was up. I did not hear a sound from Dietrich until he came down the stairs, already washed and fully dressed in his tweed suit. When he spotted me he hesitated and shot me a suspicious look, which I acknowledged with a nod and a smile. He disappeared into the kitchen, returned with a cup of coffee and the morning paper, and seated himself in the chair opposite me.

"What's on the agenda today?" I asked. "A journey to the Oklahoma Territory in search of a retired gunfighter?"

He looked up from his paper and regarded me impassively. I expected a chuckle, a scowl, or any sort of emotion for that matter, but all I got was a stoic gaze.

"Is that a jest? Honestly, you don't seem to take anything seriously."

"What do you mean?" I replied, completely baffled.

"Or more likely you just don't pay attention," he said, his predictable frown returning. "Mr Cross went over today's schedule at dinner last night. Granted, you seemed to be daydreaming most of the time, but since listening requires so little effort, I thought even you were capable of it."

I half smiled at his poor attempt at humor. Dietrich stared at me a few seconds longer, probably waiting for more of a response to his jibe. When none came he rolled his eyes and continued.

"Ms Alexander will arrive later this morning. At that time Cross will reveal to everyone the reason for our recruitment, and the details of our mission. As he repeatedly emphasized last night, today will be your final opportunity to resign. If for any reason you do not think you have the mettle to follow through, you should leave today."

"And what of the stipend?" I asked.

"Forfeiture," he said. "Yet another point made quite clear last night."

He returned to his paper, and I contemplated his words. Considering my situation, dropping out of Cross's little troupe did not offer me much promise.

"Dietrich—" I began.

"*Mr* Dietrich, if you please," he interrupted.

"Fine," I said. "*Mr* Dietrich, yesterday at Wardenclyffe you mentioned we are going into certain danger. What do you know?"

He was about to reply when the perfectly timed convergence of Irish rumbling down the stairs, Cross at the front door, and Mrs McMurtey and Abigail hurrying from the kitchen, cut our conversation short.

"Good morning everyone," Cross said. "Is breakfast ready?"

"Yes, sir," Mrs McMurtey said. "We're about to bring it now."

"Wonderful," he said, sounding chipper. "Gentlemen, care to join me at the table?"

He headed into the dining room, followed by the others. Annoyed by the interruption, I chose to protest by remaining where I was until I finished my coffee.

Little was discussed at breakfast. Irish spent most of the time shoveling food into his mouth. When he was done, he leaned back in his chair and favored us with a series of wet and poorly concealed belches. Dietrich, Cross, and I dined in a more civilized manner, which is to say we took our time. We had barely taken our first bites when Irish arose from the table and announced he was going outside for a smoke. We spent the rest of the meal in silence. By the time the hall clock struck nine-thirty, we had finished and gone to our separate corners of the house. Cross was in his study, Irish had returned to his room for a nap, and Dietrich and I quietly sat in the living room awaiting the main event of the day.

As I stared out the window I began to nod, and as a result I almost missed the arrival of the much anticipated coach. Just as my chin touched my chest I awoke and glanced out the window to see it coming to a stop at the end of the walk. I jumped up and shrugged into my jacket, as I felt it was important to make a good impression. Dietrich noticed and went to inform Cross that our final member had arrived.

"Lend a hand and fetch Mr Irish, would you?" he said as he headed for the study.

I watched from the living room window as Ms Alexander exited the carriage. The driver opened the door and offered her a hand, which she politely declined. She stepped down, followed by her scowling servant, taking a moment to look up and down the block, across the street at Corona Park, and finally at the house. From that distance I could not read her expression, but I suddenly felt ashamed to be associated with such a dilapidated place. She then thanked the driver and disappeared from my view. A moment later a knock came at the door. I stepped into the foyer just as Cross and Dietrich arrived.

"Where's Mr Irish?" Dietrich asked.

I shook my head and shrugged. Cross opened the door and stepped aside.

"Ms Alexander, welcome, and thank you for joining us," he said.

The lady entered, followed by the crone Irena who was clearly prepared to fend off any advances. I noticed that Ms Alexander once again wore a dress that covered her entirety, to include little gloves on her delicate hands. She was far too young to be influenced by Victorian ideals and fashion, yet she went to extraordinary lengths to keep them alive.

"Thank you," she said. She looked at Dietrich and me. "It is a pleasure to see you again."

"The pleasure is ours," I said.

This time I resisted the urge to take her hand, instead executing a slight bow at the waist. As I performed this maneuver, Mrs McMurtey and Abigail approached from the kitchen. Cross introduced them in turn before sending Abigail in search of Irish, and Mrs McMurtey to prepare refreshments.

"Please, do not trouble yourselves," Ms Alexander said.

"Not at all," Cross said. "Mrs McMurtey will make coffee and tea, Abigail will get Mr Irish, and then we'll get down to business."

A moment later Abigail returned with a lumbering Irish, who gave our new arrivals a grunt and a nod in greeting. Unlike the rest of us he had neglected to put on his coat, appearing instead with shirtsleeves rolled up to his elbows, exposing massive, ham-like forearms. Ms Alexander's eyes flickered over them, but she otherwise revealed no interest or fascination. We then removed to the study, where Cross took a position behind his desk while the rest of us scattered to the sofa and chairs. Irena followed in the footsteps of Ms Alexander, until Dietrich politely banished her to another room on the grounds that our discussion would be confidential. But before Irena moved a muscle she looked to Ms Alexander, who nodded her approval. Only then did the old maid stalk out. Then the doors were shut and locked, and Cross took his place behind the desk and launched into his presentation.

"It's time to discuss the reason you are here. First, I'll begin with a brief introduction of myself. As I've told each of you, I'm under the employ of the government. I've been assigned the responsibility of recruiting those unique and useful to its cause. However, I do not hold an official title. I was appointed in secret by the President himself. While I've been given the authority to act on America's behalf, you will not find anyone who will publicly acknowledge it."

"I came by this position on accident. I consider myself an academic, a historian of sorts, but the plain truth is I formerly held a position at the Library of Congress. When I began there in 1881, I never dreamed I would be chosen for the office I now hold. I expected my life would play out in normal librarian fashion, spent in academic pursuits surrounded by stacks of books. That suddenly changed one day when I came across this."

Cross turned to a shelf behind his desk and produced a tattered leatherbound book.

"I discovered it while processing new books into the archive," he said, handing it to Ms Alexander.

"*Ordo Ab Chao*," she read aloud, "by Brother Iscariot."

"The Latin translation is *Order from Chaos*," Dietrich offered. "As for the author, his name is obviously a pseudonym, with its own nefarious meaning."

We watched as Ms Alexander opened it and flipped through the pages.

"The text is German," she said. "What is it about?"

"That is a story in itself," Cross said. "While working in the Library, I found it among thousands of books awaiting categorization. I did not know a word of Latin or German, so I had no idea what it said. But something about it seemed sinister, so I took it to the translation office for inspection. When, three days later, a pale and jittery man returned it to me wearing a look of horror, I knew something was amiss. I set aside my other tasks and dove into the text, soon discovering it was some anarchist's unholy doctrine. It is divided into thirteen chapters, each one outlining one aspect to a much larger plan."

"What plan?" Irish said.

Cross paused for effect.

"To master all laws, religions, and governments of the world in order to enslave Mankind," he said.

We sat in silence and absorbed the outlandish premise. Tedium finally got the better of me.

"So some madman wrote a book about ruling the world," I said. "How did he propose to go about it?"

"I have read the book," Dietrich interjected. "It is divided into thirteen precepts, each of which provides strategic instruction to achieve desired effects. If achieved, the combined effects would throw civilization into chaos, allowing secret societies to profit and rule from the shadows."

I arched an eyebrow. Ms Alexander began to read aloud from the table of contents.

"Assassination. Controlled Starvation. Germ Warfare. International Conflict...."

"Manipulation of the Exchange. Arousal of Ethnic Prejudices, et cetera," Cross continued. "These are but a few of the insidious practices employed by the Illuminati to enslave us."

"Illuminati?" Irish said. "What's that?"

"*They*," Cross replied, "are the enemy."

"Once I discovered the purpose of *Ordo Ab Chao*," Cross went on, "I knew something needed to be done. But I was at a loss of what action to take. My first thought was to go straight to the police, but then I realized their scope was much too limited to deal with something like this. That left me with a predicament. What organization could I turn to that could handle a problem of certainly national, and likely international, scale? I needed ponder it only a short time before I had my answer. I immediately departed the Library and hurried along Pennsylvania Avenue until I arrived at the Department of Treasury.

"Inside I identified myself to the staff, and after a series of brief interviews I found myself in the office of the Secretary himself. I explained about the book and what it contained, but the Secretary seemed rather at a loss as to why I would seek him out. The only reply I could muster was this: 'Sir, while this may not seem a clear cut case of jurisdiction, the Secret Service falls under your department. I can think of no matter more deserving of secret scrutiny.' He must have seen the wisdom in my recommendation, because he took the book and said he would look into it. I then went on my way, satisfied that I had done right, and convinced that was the end of my involvement.

"I couldn't have been more mistaken. Within the week two men paid me a visit at the Library. They identified themselves as Secret Service men, and they insisted that I accompany them to a meeting. I was apprehensive, but I agreed and followed them to a waiting cab. I presumed we were going to Treasury, but as we approached we did not stop. Instead we rolled right past and around the corner to the White House. The men escorted me inside and deposited me before none other than President Roosevelt.

"By that time I was flummoxed. I would sooner have expected to find myself on the moon than standing before the President. He thanked me for taking action, because he too was a man of action. He then prompted me for my story, and I related what little I had learned since finding the book. When I was done, he surprised me by asking for my opinion on a course of action. Specifically, he desired to know if I thought the matter deserved further investigation, or if the text was an anachronism of revolutionary thinking. I sensed he was testing me, and I gave him my honest opinion. I replied that such inflammatory ideas were surely worth investigating.

"Roosevelt eyed me shrewdly before saying that he thought the same. He then revealed that the book had been discovered more than a decade earlier, and that he was already aware of the threat it represented. This made me feel rather foolish, as if I had wasted his time. He must have sensed my embarrassment because he quickly launched into a detailed explanation.

"The book had been discovered and brought to the attention of the government as early as 1851. The President at the time, Fillmore, was a rabid enemy of secret societies of any sort, and he sent forth federal marshals to hunt down the source of these ideas. They began by investigating the Freemasons, and from there tracked the ideas back to a radical European group which had split off from the Masonic Lodge more than a century earlier. This new group called itself the Order of the Perfectibilists, and later the Ancient and Illumined Seers of Bavaria. By the mid-nineteenth century, however, they had renamed themselves the Illuminati.

"In 1776, the Illuminati were created by a Bavarian named Adam Weishaupt, known to his followers as Brother Spartacus. By all accounts Weishaupt was an intellectual—a lawyer, professor, and philosopher—but he was also infatuated with mysticism and secrecy. In Weishaupt these qualities commingled to create a radical world view, one in which he imagined Mankind would benefit from the complete dissolution of organized government and religion. It was a heretical belief, and unsurprisingly it got him into trouble. In 1784 the Bavarian government intercepted some of his writings, proclaimed them seditious, and outlawed the Illuminati. Weishaupt fled to the nearby duchy of Saxe-Gotha-Altenburg and befriended a duke to ensure his political protection. There, he continued to promulgate his ideas until 1811, when he either died or disappeared. Little was heard of the Illuminati for the next forty years, until *Ordo Ab Chao* first appeared.

"The author, known only as Brother Iscariot, clearly meant for it to be kept secret. In the book he espoused principles very similar to Weishaupt's, yet he came to a very different conclusion. Where Weishaupt sought to obliterate institutions of power, Iscariot sought to exploit them, to secretly control them, by pitting one against the other if necessary, to amass wealth and power."

Cross paused to let us absorb the Machiavellian intricacies of such a sinister scheme. To me, it still seemed far-fetched.

"It's absolutely evil," I said. "But so far you've only presented us a book containing twisted ideas. How do you know the Illuminati still exist?"

"An apt question," Cross admitted. "It brings me at last to Roosevelt's most disturbing revelation. The investigations begun by President Fillmore continue even today. Over the years they uncovered many shocking truths, namely that the Illuminati had a hand in almost every American calamity over the last fifty years. The secession of the confederate states. The assassination of Lincoln. The Exchange panics in '73 and '93. The sinking of the *Maine* and our war with Spain. The assassinations of Garfield and McKinley. And these are only the instances we know about, and only those threats against the United States. Who can say what other evils they have worked undetected elsewhere in the world?"

His eyes came to rest on Ms Alexander as he spoke these last words.

"What does it have to do with us?" Irish asked.

"At last to the reason you are here," Cross said. "At the conclusion of my meeting with the President, to my great surprise he gave me a special commission and appointed me as Agent-in-Charge of investigating, and eliminating, the Illuminati threat. At first I objected, but he insisted based on what he deemed my commendable judgment and patriotism. Besides, I was already *in the know*, as he put it, and he had a good feeling about me. His only stipulation was that I recruit similarly wise, remarkable, and reliable persons to assist me, and that our business be kept secret.

Again he paused, this time looking at us expectantly.

"So, there you have it," he said. "If you accept, your mission is to pursue the Illuminati to their source, and to do everything in your power to stop them, once and for all."

The room fell silent. Ms Alexander, Irish and I stared into the distance as we tried to envision the scope and implications of our charge. To put a stop to something, someone, or in this case to an entire organization, once and for all, suggested a conflict that could only be resolved through bloodshed.

Suddenly I understood Dietrich's statement from the day before. If we were to face off against men bent on ruling the world, certain danger was an understatement.

Cross stood with hands folded in front of him, looking at us patiently. Dietrich's head was bowed and his eyes closed as if in deep thought.

"That explains the generous stipend," I mumbled.

"Consider it reward for doing the nation, and the world, a great service," Cross said. "If you succeed, it will be the least we can do to show our gratitude. To succeed will require your collective intellect, strength, and subtlety. It will also require anonymity for as long as you can maintain it. If you are discovered, they will no doubt attempt to neutralize you."

I gulped. The scenario I had imagined involved us hunting the enemy. I had not considered the enemy might end up hunting us.

"Are you trying to talk us out if it now?" Irish asked. He had a grim smile on his face that showed nothing in the story had shaken him. I marveled at the man, finding him simultaneously admirable, reassuring, and unsettling.

"By no means," Cross replied. "I did not dedicate a year of my life to seek out the perfect candidates only to scare you off. Rather, it's important that you understand *everything*, to include the inherent danger of the situation, before you commit to it."

"Thank you for your thoughtfulness," Ms Alexander said. "But you need not wait on my account. The Illuminati are a threat to all, and I will gladly help."

I had sensed she was a determined young woman, but I had not expected her to be so deliberate. It was a strange quality to find in so beautiful and delicate a creature. As I admired her, Irish spoke up.

"Count me in," he said.

Cross smiled at them both before sweeping his eyes across Dietrich and me.

"As you already know, I too am committed," Dietrich said.

I had expected nothing less. It was obvious Dietrich had signed on some time ago. So Cross's questioning gaze was really intended for me. I was the only holdout.

As I returned his stare I intended to tell him I would need to sleep on it, part in seriousness, part for dramatic effect, and part to vex him. But I was keenly aware of all the eyes upon me, and I felt obligated to answer now. As a performer, one would expect such pressure to have had little effect on me. However I suddenly felt as if I were in a shrinking box, that all sides were closing in, and the only way to escape was to acquiesce.

"Yes, of course," I said, startled by my own voice. "I'm in."

I spent the remainder of the day sitting in the living room, staring out the front window at the park across the street, staring without seeing for my mind was preoccupied. I wondered about our undertaking, and the excitement and risk it posed. I tried to imagine what specific dangers lay ahead, and began counting off all the ways in which I might soon meet my end.

It was a strange line of thought for me. I had never really feared death before, not even when my performances had me bound and submerged in water, or wrapped in a straightjacket while dangling upside down from a perilous height. I was always aware that I *could* die, but death, especially a violent one, had seemed a foreign concept. It was like a war that one hears about on the opposite side of the world, a danger so distant it could never conceivably find its way to my door; and while news of it is terrible, the pang of despair one feels for the faceless masses caught up in it is only a passing sensation that is forgotten a moment later.

The difference between that sensation and the one I experienced was that mine refused to pass. Instead it lingered and held me prisoner for hours on end. It was so powerful it put me in an almost catatonic state. When I finally came out of that dreadful paralysis, I could not recall anything that that occurred for the past several hours. When I glanced at the window the combined effects of the parlor lights and the dusk sky caused it to function as a dark mirror, in which I saw a dim and disturbed reflection of myself.

Dinner passed much the same way, but rather than being preoccupied with morbid thoughts I was simply numb. Perhaps hours of unconsciously grappling with mortality had worn out my faculties. I was distantly aware of everyone at the table. I heard conversations going on around me, but nothing registered until Ms Alexander announced she was leaving.

"What?" I asked, coming back to my senses. "I thought we were all staying here?"

Everyone looked at me.

"She already explained she has other arrangements," Dietrich said. "She will meet us tomorrow at the dock."

"The dock?" I asked.

"Yes," he said impatiently. "At noon. We will board the ship together."

He turned to Cross, shook his head, and dropped his napkin on the table in a gesture of exasperation. Cross took it all in without comment.

"Thank you, Mr Grey, for taking an interest," Ms Alexander said graciously. "I have other plans for the evening. But do not fear, we will have plenty of time to become acquainted in the days ahead."

I still was not sure what she was talking about, or why we would be meeting at the dock, but I decided not to pursue it under Dietrich's derisive gaze.

"Before you go I have one more item," Cross said. "Earlier I failed to mention that my duties require me to stay here, to receive your reports and communicate them to the President."

This was news to all, but no one objected or appeared surprised. For my part, I was happy to leave Cross behind. For some indecipherable reason he rubbed me the wrong way.

"Therefore," Cross continued, "we should establish who will be in charge.

I've chosen Mr Dietrich to direct you in my absence."

No one was surprised, but the news annoyed me since Dietrich had thus far proven a testy character. I anticipated a difficult journey ahead.

"Now I must depart as well," Cross said suddenly. "Good evening everyone. Ms Alexander, my coach is at your disposal."

They departed, and I returned to my spot in the living room and watched them go. It had been a very strange day, and I had not yet entirely escaped the odd mood that had come over me. I suddenly felt an irrational need to be outside, to go to the end of the sidewalk and watch the coach until it had passed out of sight. I jumped up, grabbed my coat, and hurried out the door.

By the time I reached the street it had passed from sight, but I could still hear the horses' hooves as they pulled it toward downtown. I followed in their wake at a leisurely pace, wondering what might pass as conversation between the two. Before I had walked half a block, all evidence of the coach was gone. I stopped and stared into the night. The cold evening air was bracing. I was beginning to feel my senses returning when I heard someone approaching from behind.

"Good night, Mr Grey," came a clear voice. It was Abigail beginning her long, solitary walk home.

"Is it that time already?" I said.

In the dim light of a streetlamp I saw her smile. Encouraged, I jogged a few steps until I was at her side.

"What are you doing?" she asked.

"I thought I would accompany you," I said, "at least part of the way."

Her face passed into shadow and I could not see her expression, but she continued to look at me, probably impressed that I was willing to escort her. She nodded, quickly coming to terms with the fact that I was not going to be shaken off.

We walked for a long time in silence, and we were both completely comfortable with it. Then, predictably, she broke the spell.

"Mr Cross said you're leaving tomorrow," she said.

"Yes, that's what I hear. Did he tell you where we're going?"

"No," she said. "Where?"

I laughed at her misinterpretation of my question. I decided it was better not to reveal my ignorance.

"I'm afraid I'm not at liberty to discuss it," I said.

"Oh," she said. She became quiet again.

"My, this is a long haul," I said a few minutes later. "We must have walked a mile already."

"Not quite yet," she said. "But it is a long walk. I appreciate the company, but you really don't have to do this, Mr Grey."

"Nonsense," I said. "It's a pleasure. Besides, with you gone for the night, what are my alternatives? I'll tell you: the surly company of Irish, or the stuffiness of Dietrich. I'd rather walk to Hoboken barefoot, in three feet of snow."

"Mr Grey!" She drew back with a look of mock offense.

"Oh, stop it," I said. "You know I'm right. You don't have to admit it, but deep down you know they're about as fun as a case of the gout."

She burst into girlish laughter, and as we passed a streetlamp I noted a brightness in her eyes I had not seen before. We continued walking, and our conversation continued along the same line. Occasionally I introduced a new subject only to follow with a witty and insightful remark that pushed the bounds of impropriety. Each time I received the same look of mock horror, and on occasion she pretended to be so offended that she would stop dead in her tracks and refuse to take another step until I retracted.

This exchange went on for a long time, even longer than I realized. But as long as she was willing to play the game I carried on. At some point we ended up walking arm in arm. It must have happened gradually and naturally, because I was completely unaware of it until I looked down and saw her practically leaning on my shoulder.

But soon her enthusiasm began to fizzle. Where earlier she had been quick to laugh and encourage the scoundrel in me, now her mood quickly cooled. I then knew we were near her apartment, and she was preoccupied with finding a way to disengage and say goodnight.

As we approached a building on our right—a tenement by the look of it— she slowed her pace and I knew our trip was at an end. She released my arm and clutched her bag with both hands.

"I don't know what to say," she said, avoiding my eyes. "I'm so sorry to have dragged you so far."

"This is your building, I take it?" I asked, trying not to show my disappointment.

"Yes."

"It certainly is a long way from Corona Park," I said. "I'm amazed you walk this distance twice a day, and in the dark. Mark my words, I'm going to talk to Cross about this and see if we can get you a room in the house."

"Thank you, Mr Grey, but that's not necessary," she said.

"Please, call me Prometheus," I said. "I know we've only known each other a few days, but in that time I've come to know you better than I've known anyone in years."

She thought about it for a moment, and I saw a hint of her smile reappear.

"All right, then," she said. "Prometheus."

Speaking my name transformed her smile to a giggle.

"Well, good night, Prometheus," she said.

She turned to climb the stairs to her door. I pulled the watch from my pocket.

"Holy Mother, it's almost eleven!" I exclaimed. "If I walk, I won't get back until well after midnight. I suppose I'll have to catch a cab. Do they come around these parts often?"

She stopped half way up the steps and hesitantly turned. We both knew the answer.

"I'm afraid we don't see many cabs around here at this time of night."

"Oh," I said, looking at my watch again. "That's unfortunate."

"I'm so sorry, Prometheus," she said. "I never intended to lead you this far from home."

"Don't give it another thought," I said. "It was entirely my doing. And it was a pleasure, especially considering this may be my last opportunity."

"Your last opportunity for what?" she asked.

"To spend time with you," I said. "As you know, we ship out tomorrow, and, well, I don't want to alarm you, but then I'm probably not revealing anything you haven't already figured out. Our business, the mission we'll be on, is likely to be dangerous. In fact, the phrase *certain danger* has been thrown about quite a lot—"

"Really?" she exclaimed.

"—And none of us really knows what to expect. But don't be alarmed. It's not as if we were press-ganged into service. We're undertaking the mission voluntarily. So if anything happens to us, we have only ourselves to blame."

"Mr Cross doesn't discuss business around us," Abigail said. "I had no idea you would be in danger."

"*Certain* danger," I said with a nod. "But we'll make the best of it."

She took one step toward me, but she remained several steps above. She looked as if she was in absolute torment. She alternated between looking at me and down the street. I suspected she was praying a stray cab would come around the corner and resolve the situation for her, but no such luck.

I let her struggle for a minute. I would have allowed her all the time in the world, so she could reach the conclusion without any prodding from me, if the hour had not been so late, and the temperature so cold.

"Abigail," I said finally. "I don't want to put you in an awkward position, and if I am, please say so and I'll be on my way. But I don't think this situation is an accident."

She looked at me, a little unnerved.

"What do you mean?"

"Neither of us intended to find ourselves in this predicament," I replied, "but Fate has placed us here for a reason. I don't mean to embarrass you by speaking of it so plainly, but yesterday morning, didn't we share a moment in the kitchen? While washing dishes I felt something between us, and I think you did, too."

She opened her mouth but said nothing. She wanted so desperately to confess what she obviously felt, but propriety lay across her path like a landslide. I inspected my watch again.

"It's eleven o'clock, and I'm five miles from home without a ride," I said. I glanced up and down the street. "Everyone is in bed, or at least indoors. No one is here to see, so you don't need to worry about what others might think. Say the word and I will gladly stay."

She stood frozen, wracked with indecision. I watched as she opened and closed her mouth, each time unable to commit. Soon I began to feel guilty for placing the girl in such an awkward position, and I was ready to give up and start the long walk home. I snapped my watch shut and half turned to walk away.

"Come in," she said unexpectedly.

It was little more than a whisper, but it was all I needed to hear. I followed her up the steps. She fumbled with her key at the door, but soon we were inside and climbing up three flights of stairs. I followed her through a gauntlet of tight, poorly lit hallways to her apartment. More fumbling of keys and then we were inside.

Her home was little more than a kitchen and a bedroom, and even more depressing inside than out. Clothes dangled from lines strung across the room, forming a makeshift curtain around her bed—useful for shielding one's eyes from the sad reality that pressed in on all sides.

As soon as the door latched behind us, I gently placed my hands on her arms and guided her toward the bed. She moved willingly, if a little rigidly. As I drew her toward me, she hesitated.

"What about Jonas?" she whispered.

"Who?"

"My fiancé," she said, laying her head on my chest.

I hesitated. While I had no qualms over sleeping with an uncommitted woman, a fiancé complicated the matter.

"Has he given you a ring?"

"No."

"Has he proposed?"

"No."

"Has he openly professed his love, or made clear that, at some undetermined point in the future, he plans to make you his own?"

"He's hinted at it, but … no."

I sighed with relief.

"In that case, my dear, he's no fiancé."

After a few awkward minutes she began to warm up, and though reservations still haunted her, I was able to coax from her lithe frame a satisfying performance. We soon found a mutually satisfying rhythm and the repetition became like a mantra. Inasmuch as possible, I used it to concentrate, to help prolong the moment. While my body celebrated earthly pleasures, my mind wandered through time and space, and I unexpectedly experienced a moment of divine abstraction.

Then, suddenly, I found myself surrounded by an inky blackness. Strange images began flying through my head, some flights of fancy, others nightmarish in depiction. I saw the death of Houdini; Cross looking down upon me in Judgment; Irish engulfed in fire; Dietrich laid upon his deathbed; and Ms Alexander … Ms Alexander in her little white gloves ... Ms Alexander in *nothing but* her little white gloves …

8: ENTANGLEMENTS

I experienced a nightmare in which I was being strangled by a serpent. I awoke to find myself entwined in Abigail's arms. The sun was not yet up, and the apartment was still cloaked in darkness. I remained still as long as I could stand it to avoid waking her, but restlessness finally overcame me. I tossed and turned until she let go. Then I slipped from the bed, feeling my way around the room to collect my clothes. In the darkness I stumbled into some hanging clothes, causing me to flail about wildly as one does after walking face first through a spider's web. I stubbed my toe on something heavy and stifled a cry. Hopping on one foot, I managed to collect my entire ensemble. As I donned my rumpled clothes, I heard a stirring from the bed and froze like a frightened rabbit.

"Jonas?"

"Back to sleep, my dear," I whispered

She moaned in reply. Within seconds she was again lightly snoring, and I crept to the door and let myself out.

Since it was so early the walk back to Corona Park was long and quiet, giving me ample time to reflect. I again found myself wondering what I had gotten myself into—what dangers lay ahead—but finding the matter disturbing I instead turned my thoughts to Ms Alexander.

I still knew almost nothing about her besides the fact that she was not American, which made her involvement all the more intriguing. Her origin, and her presence and purpose at Wardenclyffe, remained a mystery. Both Cross and Tesla clearly held her in high esteem, which meant she was a person of some importance. I surmised she was probably wealthy, which would explain Tesla's interest. (He was rumored to be short on funding.) But Cross's interest was vague. Aside from multi-lingual beauty, I could not determine what capability she added to our company.

Then there was the curious matter of her Victorian fashion, and her ever-

79

present gloves. During our time spent together so far, she had never removed them. I supposed they fit with her apparent aversion to physical contact, but I was not wholly convinced this provided a full explanation. For the remainder of my walk home I wondered what horrible abuse she had sustained that made her so phobic of touching, or being touched.

I arrived back at our headquarters before the sun had broken the horizon, and I gladly climbed into bed to get some sleep before breakfast. When the smell of bacon reached me I arose and went to the table to find Cross and Dietrich being served by Mrs McMurtey. To my relief, Abigail was notably absent. As I sat down, Cross passed me an envelope.

"What's this?" I asked.

"Your traveling papers, and a ticket," he said.

I opened the envelope and inspected the documents. My passport appeared to be accurate, more or less, with the exception of my profession, which it listed simply, generically, and insultingly, as *clerk*. I frowned at the unspectacular fictional career to which I had been assigned. But my mind was taken off the matter when I read the destination on the ticket.

"London?" I exclaimed.

Cross and Dietrich both stared at me. Cross smiled, though somewhat painfully. Dietrich only shook his head.

"Yes," Cross said. "And in order to make your ship we must depart by ten. In the meantime, please do me the favor of waking up Mr Irish."

As I headed to Irish's room, I kicked myself for not thinking ahead. I had been so distracted over the last twelve hours that I had not thought about preparing for the trip. At Irish's door I pounded several times. The door never opened, but I heard the creak of bedsprings.

"What?"

"We depart in an hour," I said. "We're on a ship to London."

He muttered something in response, but it was drowned out by his bedsprings. I had the distinct feeling he had rolled over and gone back to sleep, but that was none of my concern at the moment. I had packing to do.

Back in my room I grabbed a steamer trunk from the corner, filled it with the wardrobe Cross had provided, and carried it downstairs. As I maneuvered it into the hall, Mrs McMurtey stepped from the kitchen.

"No sign of Abigail yet?" I asked.

"No," she replied. "It's not like her to be late. She must be ill."

At nine forty-five we assembled at the door, with the exception of Irish who had not yet shown himself. Cross was becoming impatient and was about to head upstairs when Irish came lumbering down. He was back in his old clothes and carrying his worn carpetbag.

"There is a perfectly good steamer trunk in your room," Cross said. "And I see you've returned to your old clothes. Are the suits I provided not to your satisfaction?"

"They're fine," Irish said. "But these will do."

Before Cross could further complain a coach pulled up outside, and we hauled out our luggage and loaded it up. As I hefted my trunk aboard I spied a figure, almost two blocks distant, hurrying toward us. Even before I could make out any details I knew it was Abigail. I was relieved to see she was not in fact ill, but I still had no desire to see her. I was not in the mood for a public display of emotion, so I quickly climbed in behind the others, rapped my knuckles against the ceiling, and we were off.

The dock was choked with traffic. Our driver had to slow to a crawl to keep the horses from trampling pedestrians. The beasts managed to carve a path for us, and soon our coach rolled up alongside a long line of others near a large steamship, the name *S.S. Minnetonka* emblazoned on its bow. On the dock travelers were excitedly saying their goodbyes, and on the deck passengers had already begun lining up along the rail in preparation for departure.

We exited the coach and removed our bags. I spotted Ms Alexander less than a stone's throw away. I was disappointed to see her servant and chaperone, Irena, still accompanying her. But in the same instant I noticed several young men casting glances at our shapely companion, and in that moment I was relieved that Irena's stern looks kept them at bay.

"Ms Alexander!" I called out, waving like a schoolboy. She smiled and inconspicuously waved back.

We hauled our luggage over and added it to hers, which consisted of no less than three steamer trunks—more than Dietrich, Irish, and I had combined. But if anyone noticed, they made no comment on her feminine inability to travel lightly.

Cross waved down a steward and had the bags taken aboard. He then took advantage of his last chance to address us in person. He eyed passersby suspiciously and motioned for us to take a step closer.

"Friends," he said in a low voice, "before you go I want to thank you one last time for the sacrifice you are making. I would also remind you that the less others know about your business, the greater your chance for success. I recommend you trust no one you don't already know, or are not referred to by a trusted source. We are on the trail of the enemy, and he is so far oblivious. A single slip could give you away. If the enemy learns of your endeavor, he will act to stop you. I know it all sounds foreboding, and I don't mean to alarm you. But please be cautious, and suspicious, of everyone from this day forth."

At the end of his speech no one spoke. I think we had expected more of a pep talk. But in the next moment Cross was smiling again and spreading his arms as if he intended to gather us together for a hug.

"Farewell!" he said. "Enjoy your trip, and be careful!"

I think the display was more for onlookers, any one of whom could have been Illuminati agents. But a quick scan of the crowd told me they took no interest in us. They were preoccupied with saying their own goodbyes and boarding the ship.

Ms Alexander stepped aside with Irena. They exchanged words in low voices. Though I feigned interest in whatever Cross was saying to us, I was really trying to overhear the exchange between the women. But they must have switched to a different language, because the few scraps I picked up were incomprehensible. With sidelong glances I watched as the stern old woman suddenly softened, and both women fought back tears. One drop escaped Ms Alexander and slowly traced its way down her cheek. The old woman moved her hand as if to catch it. But then she caught herself and jerked it back, clasping it with the other to resist the temptation.

As Dietrich finished a confidential exchange with Cross, the women completed theirs, and Ms Alexander led the way onto the ship. The gangplank deposited us on the main deck, and once aboard we followed stewards to our quarters. It was here that we temporarily parted company with Ms Alexander. Her billeting had her in a room on the upper promenade, whereas the rest of us descended into the bowels of the ship. We descended stairs to the saloon deck, an expansive and elaborately decorated room that put me in mind of a Vaudeville theater, with a high ceiling, paneled walls, and allegorical figures burnt into the woodwork. The room was filled with chairs and sofas upholstered in red satin damask, making the place seem bright and cheery.

Our staterooms, however, were neither bright nor cheery, though some effort had been made to dress them up. The rooms existed in a sort of organized cluster on one side of the ship. Those lucky enough to receive a cabin against the outer bulkhead had a window, or porthole, that let in light and could be opened for fresh air. The remaining rooms were built inward and across the hall, which meant they amounted to stuffy steel boxes the size of a walk-in closet. This is where we were assigned. In spite of the limited space they had somehow managed to fit in bunk beds, a sink, and a sofa, making the tiny space too cramped for two adults to inhabit comfortably. But the most unexpected and unwelcome surprise came when the steward led Irish to one room and pointed Dietrich and I to another.

Perhaps I had expected too much from Cross, but considering that we were working for the government, and, as Cross said, that we were putting ourselves in harm's way, I had expected better accommodations, even private rooms. Doubling us up, and trapping me with Dietrich, was like a cruel practical joke.

Given the frown that appeared on Dietrich's face, he was similarly displeased. We stood at the threshold and stared at the confined space, neither of us willing to take the first step. But then other passengers began to pile up behind us in the corridor and we were forced inside. I entered and inspected the beds to discover the bottom bunk sat on an unforgiving metal plate, whereas the top bunk was suspended on springs.

"I suspect you've got a few years on me, old man," I said. "You probably don't want to leap up into bed every night. I'll take the top bunk, if you don't object."

He nodded and turned in place to examine the room. After completing a full rotation he faced me again. The confines of the room made us uncomfortably close, with less than two feet between us. We stared at each other for a moment in silence before simultaneously arriving at the same conclusion.

"Care for a walk around the deck?" I asked.

"A fine idea," he replied.

We gathered with everyone else on the main promenade to watch as the ship set sail. There we found Irish already leaning on the rail, but Ms Alexander was nowhere in sight. I had the feeling she was cloistered in her cabin. We fell in alongside our colossal companion and watched the spectacle. Soon the ship blasted its horn and began to slowly pull away from the dock. The crowd, both aboard ship and dockside, whipped itself into a frenzy of cheering and waving. People at the rail threw confetti over those below. Everyone on land and sea was in high spirits. It even put me in a festive mood. For a moment I forgot our mission and our dismal quarters entirely, and I fancied myself a tourist like everyone else.

"Excuse me, gentlemen."

We turned to find a steward had come up behind us. He extended a note to Dietrich, who accepted it and read aloud.

"Gentlemen, I am staying in suite No. 1 on the promenade. Please join me at one o'clock so we may discuss our business in private."

Dietrich fished a coin from his pocket and gave it to the steward, who then hurried off.

"We have our first meeting within the hour," he announced. "Please be prompt as I have news to share with all."

He then turned and walked off without another word, leaving Irish and I to shrug at one another. With an hour to kill we both went back to leaning on the rail.

"Strange that he is our captain, yet the lady sets our schedule," I said.

Irish replied with a grunt and a nod.

"I'm beginning to wonder who's really in charge," I added.

But Irish had said all he would on the subject. I went back to watching New York recede into the distance.

At the designated hour Irish and I found Ms Alexander's suite, with she and Dietrich already awaiting us therein. Her rooms were palatial compared to the cramped and squalid staterooms to which we had been consigned. The suite consisted of the sitting room, a separate bedroom, and a private bath. I took all this in within seconds of entering, and in the same amount of time I went through a series of emotions ranging from wonder (I had no idea that such elegant rooms existed onboard), to indignation (that I had not been assigned similar accommodations), to resentment (that Cross would hold one of us in such high esteem above the others), to acceptance (after a moment of gazing upon Ms Alexander's regal beauty, I agreed she was worth every penny).

We seated ourselves around the room. Ms Alexander occupied one small sofa, and Irish and I squeezed onto the other. Dietrich, our de facto leader, stood so he could look down on us.

"As you know, I have been working with Mr Cross on this endeavor for some time, hence my taking the reins in his absence," he said. "I hope this does not offend anyone. I hope I have your full commitment, and that we will work together flawlessly."

I shifted in my seat. I was not fond of taking orders, but I reluctantly accepted the situation. I glanced at Irish and read in his face that he did not care one way or another who claimed to be in charge. He was like an ox in a field: he could easily pull a plow, but until yoked he would do as he pleased.

"I think I speak for everyone," Ms Alexander said, "when I say you have our unwavering support. Mr Cross made everything clear. Gentlemen, do you agree?"

I nodded. If those words had come from anyone else I would have thought them audacious. But coming from her they sounded so inarguable that I willingly accepted them.

"Sure," Irish said in a bemused tone. "Unwavering."

Dietrich nodded appreciatively at Ms Alexander.

"As we are now underway," he continued, "allow me to recapitulate our purpose. Among the many details of Mr Cross's exposition, you will recall this whole business began with Adam Weishaupt, and his Order of Perfectibilists, which ostensibly grew from Freemasonry. Given this fact, I have determined the most reliable way to track down the Illuminati is to go back to their source, to seek help from the eldest of Freemasonry's chief institutions. To this end I have established correspondence with a gentleman Mason in London. Our contact's name is Mr Edward Ensley."

"Are we then to assume he knows our purpose?" Ms Alexander asked.

"No," Dietrich said. "So far my written inquiries have been academic. He believes I am writing a book. I informed him of our visit and he has agreed to meet us."

"Thank you," Ms Alexander said. "At last I understand the purpose of going to London. Is there anything else you can tell us, to better prepare us for the work ahead?"

"I'm afraid not," Dietrich said. "Until now, I admit Mr Cross and I explained only what needed explaining, and nothing more. It was a precaution should anyone decide to bail out. But since everyone is now committed, I have revealed everything. From here on we must improvise."

The word caused me to perk up.

"Improvisation? Excellent! As a performer I'm no stranger to it. In fact, more than once, one of my escapes went awry, forcing me to think and act quickly in order to save my neck— "

"There is one more item I failed to mention," Dietrich said suddenly. "I believe dinner is served at four o'clock. Ms Alexander, will you do us the honor of joining us?"

"Thank you," she said. "But tonight I shall dine in my cabin. I do not enjoy crowds."

Disappointed, I decided to press the issue.

"But if our only exposure to you is in such brief snippets, how will we ever get to know you?"

The lady, who was normally the model of poise, blushed slightly.

"You flatter me, Mr Grey. However, we still have far to go and much time to get acquainted. Please do not consider my decline an insult. I am simply not up to being sociable this evening."

"Of course," Dietrich said, nodding to her and glaring at me. "When you are ready we will be delighted to have you."

She smiled appreciatively. Dietrich's sycophantic manners seemed to smooth any feathers I had ruffled.

"In that case, gentlemen, thank you for coming. I am sure we will see each other again soon."

She smiled at us from her seat, her words making it clear our meeting was at an end. After she had so graciously resisted my persistence I thought it best to leave without another word, though I wanted nothing more than to stay there with her, in silence if necessary. But Dietrich and Irish began shuffling toward the door, so I obediently followed.

The journey to London took eight days to complete. For the most part everyone kept to themselves, though I managed to establish a routine that allowed me to get better acquainted with Irish and Ms Alexander.

I found Irish's favorite haunt our very first night at sea. I had seen several men coming and going aft of the upper promenade, and I decided to investigate. I climbed the stairs and discovered a location known as "the smoking room," which, as far as I could tell, was nothing more than a place for men to escape their wives and bask in tobacco and liquor. As I entered I spied Irish sitting at a bar, downing a mug of beer. I casually wandered over, feigned surprise, and seated myself on the stool beside him.

To my surprise, Irish turned out to be easy company, especially over drinks. He did not talk much, or at all, really. Instead he sipped his beer, intermittently drew on a rolled cigarette, and repeatedly said *you don't say* in response to my Vaudevillian tales. It became our routine. We passed every evening that way, often until late into night.

In the case of Ms Alexander, it took some effort but I eventually managed to penetrate her defenses. Contrary to her reassurance that we would soon get to know one another, she never once joined us in the dining room while aboard the *Minnetonka*. Instead she remained cloistered in her rooms, except on those rare occasions that she ventured onto the promenade. But even then she never went more than a few feet to the nearest rail. On two occasions while making my own rounds I spotted her and wanted to approach, but I knew if I approached she would withdraw to her room. So instead I took up a position behind a lifeboat and spied on her.

She seemed content to stand there alone, staring out to sea. In those moments I wished I had a painter's hand, or the equipment and skill of a photographer, so I could forever capture her in quiet repose. But each of those divine moments was fleeting, because inevitably other passengers would happen by, and she would get unnerved and retreat like a frightened doe. I say *unnerved*, but she never seemed frantic or worried. In fact, it was quite the opposite. Whenever others seemed on a course of intercept, she would turn her back, casually take a few steps in the opposite direction, pause to gaze a moment longer at the sea, then casually lower her eyes as if in thought and step through the doorway.

By our third day I had had enough of it. No matter how luxurious her rooms, the thought of her wasting away in them was more than I could bear. I decided to impose upon her. Around one o'clock I knocked on her door. She called out and seemed hesitant to open it. When she heard my voice, however, she dared to crack it the space of a few inches.

"It's a beautiful day at sea," I said. "Care to join me for a stroll?"

I could tell the idea pleased her, but she was oppressed by whatever burden she carried that forbade her to be sociable.

"Thank you," she said. "I appreciate the invitation, but I think I will remain indoors today."

I had expected rejection, and I was prepared with a follow-up.

"Pardon me for saying so, but you've already spent the last two days alone in your cabin. So don't pretend like staying in today is an exception to your routine."

Her jaw dropped and her eyes went wide. She was not accustomed to someone of my bearing. I had her off guard, and I pressed my advantage.

"I'm sorry if I'm being rude, but the truth is I—*we*—are all worried about you. It's not healthy to stay cooped up. You would put our minds at ease if you would join us for dinner, or at least join me for a stroll."

She remained a statue for several seconds, staring at me like no other woman had before. My confidence began to melt away. I suddenly felt like a child who had just sassed his mother. It was a ridiculous sensation because I was many years her senior, yet everything about her suggested she possessed more refinement than I had ever known. I sensed a rebuke coming, and I was summoning an apology when she finally spoke.

"Thank you for your concern," she said. "But I do not feel like going out today. However, since you are worried, and since I do not want to offend anyone, I will meet you half way. Please, come in and join me for tea."

She opened the door and I stepped inside. She then turned and led me a table where a tray sat complete with a teapot and, conveniently, two cups and saucers. She indicated for me to sit on one sofa, and she took the other. As I sat awkwardly holding the dainty cup, she regarded me and took a deep breath.

"What shall we talk about?" she said.

I had not expected our conversation to start so bluntly. I stammered for a moment, trying to come up with a clever topic. Failing that, I decided to simply pursue the natural questions on my mind.

"You already know something about me," I said. "You, however, remain a mystery. I would very much like to learn more about you."

She drew another deep breath.

"Where shall I begin?" she asked.

"I detect an accent in your speech, but I can't identify it."

"Yes," she said. "My accent is disguised, though unintentionally so. When I was nine I departed my homeland for an education in Paris. Over the following years I traveled to many countries, learning what I could of their languages and customs. As a consequence, my time spent traveling did much to obscure my identity, at least on the surface. If my accent is unrecognizable, it is because I seldom speak in my native tongue."

"It sounds like you've seen more of the world in your travels than most will see in a lifetime," I said. "But if you've dropped any clues to your accent, I've missed them entirely."

She laughed at my confusion.

"I have not dropped any yet," she said. "I am Russian."

"Fascinating!" I said, to keep her at ease and talking. "I've never met anyone from Russia, at least that I know of. What's it like?"

The topic turned out to be one upon which she was happy to elaborate, and it sustained our conversation for almost an hour. Occasionally I interjected a question to keep her going, but she required little prompting from me to soliloquize about her homeland. She told me about the founding of Moscow and Saint Petersburg, the grandiose castles and cathedrals, the unruly Cossacks, the great Siberian *taiga*, and the numerous tribes one could find from East to West. But the entirety of Russia's history, culture, and peoples was too much for me to absorb, and midway into her speech I gave up trying to comprehend it all. Instead I was satisfied to look into her eyes and listen to her voice, which by the end of our visit had taken on a mild huskiness. At length she covered her mouth and cleared her throat.

"Forgive me," she said, pressing a gloved hand to her perfect breast. "I think that is the longest I have spoken in years. You should not have allowed me to carry on."

"On the contrary!" I said. "It was a pleasure to hear you speak, especially on such an intriguing subject. Russia is so far away, I never gave it any thought. I see now what I've been missing."

She placed her hands in her lap and smiled, and somehow her smile seemed warmer than before. Not that her earlier smiles lacked sincerity, but she suddenly radiated a glow I had not previously witnessed. It was as if everything until that moment had been polite, and I had finally scratched the surface of the real Ms Katherine Alexander.

"Thank you for stopping by," she said at length. "I enjoyed your company. As a man of the stage you make an exemplary audience. But now I think my voice needs a rest."

She needed say no more. I had basked in her glow far longer than any mortal deserved, and certainly longer than I had expected when I knocked on her door.

"The pleasure was all mine. Thank you for tolerating me." I stood and made for the door. "Would you mind if I visited you again? Say, same time tomorrow?"

She regarded me as an adult regards a child who has ignorantly asked an impertinent question. She hesitated only for a moment.

"That would be nice," she said.

"In that case, I look forward to our next visit. Good afternoon!"

My chest swelled as I closed her door behind me. I felt invigorated, as if I had just overcome a great obstacle. I felt like Jason of legend, who, after taming fire-breathing bulls, defeating an army of stone warriors and a sleepless dragon, had finally laid claim to the Golden Fleece. I completed a half dozen circuits around the deck before I had worked off enough energy to sit still.

As much as I enjoyed my nightly visits to the saloon to carouse with Irish, and my daily tea times with Ms Alexander (which became the highlight of every day aboard ship), neither of them granted me insight into their lives. Irish said little and was content to sip his beer as I regaled him with tales of Vaudeville. Ms Alexander, however, spoke lots, and on a variety of subjects, but none of them revealed anything telling about her private life, or her past. The real surprise came on our seventh day at sea, when Dietrich revealed an unexpected and staggering amount about himself to me.

It occurred as the conclusion to a chain of events that began on our second day at sea. I had found Irish in the smoking room the night before, and I had sidled up to him at the bar. When he realized he had company, he leaned back and gave me an unwelcome look. But since we were partners, at least in the interim, I decided to not be put off, to get to know him one way or another. It took only a few rounds of drinks at my expense to break the ice, and thereafter he was more amicable. After a few hours of drinking I made my way back to my stateroom and fell asleep until noon the next day.

This pattern repeated for the next five days, with Irish and I keeping the bartender employed until late into the night. Consequently I was sleeping until noon each day, rising just in time to clean up and make my daily visit with Ms Alexander. So I saw little of Dietrich, only crossing paths with him in the dining hall at supper. But this unspoken arrangement suited both of us, because Dietrich was a solitary man, content to pass each day alone in intellectual pursuits.

On our sixth night, however, I did not imbibe as much, nor did I stay up into the wee hours of the morning. When Dietrich arose for his daily routine the sounds awoke me, and I was unable to fall back asleep. But I did not arise. Instead I laid still, listening to his movements, and found myself wondering how I would spend my day, and he his. This roused my curiosity, and for lack of better entertainment I decided to find out what he did each day.

I feigned sleep until I heard the door close behind him. Then I rolled out of bed, quickly dressed (easily accomplished since I had fallen asleep in all but my coat and shoes) and took off in pursuit. I did it all with such haste that I was out the door and on his tail before he had reached the stairs.

I followed him to the dining hall, where he cordially greeted other passengers before secluding himself at an empty table, where he stuck his nose in a book while breakfasting on coffee and a Danish. After forty-five minutes he closed his book and departed; ascended the stairs to the promenade deck and made several circuits; paused to gaze over the shoulder of an artist painting a woman's portrait; continued on his way; stopped along the rail to breathe deeply of the salty mist thrown up by the bow; spent another minute coughing it back into the wind; and then proceeded to the nearest stairwell leading to the upper promenade. From there he took a series of corridors to a door in which was set a large glass window bearing in white, smoky letters the word *LIBRARY*.

It came as a surprise. I had assumed the forward section of the upper promenade was reserved, so I had never investigated it. I casually edged up to the door and looked inside. The room was large and decorative, boasting several bookcases, upholstered chairs and sofas. It was also bright, owing to a large skylight of ornate glass in the ceiling. I watched discreetly as Dietrich made his way across the room, nodded politely to the other occupants—all women—claimed a chair in one corner, and stuck his nose back in his book.

The room contained perhaps a dozen women, only half of whom were actually reading. The rest were engaged in hushed conversation, which judging by their expressions was devoted to feminine mischief. It was this latter group, the gossipers, who noticed me standing outside and shot me disparaging looks. They must have seen me as an intruder on their privacy, or perhaps as a predatory bachelor, because soon all but two departed, taking with them their suddenly chilly air.

As the door closed behind them Dietrich looked up and caught a glimpse of me. I resisted the urge to run and hide. He had caught me, and in that moment the best way to allay his suspicions was to charge in as if I had come on an errand of my own. As I entered he stuck his nose back in his book.

The remaining women noticed me, each looking up and smiling warily. I meandered about the room for a few seconds, stopping to scan the books on the shelves—all romances by the look of them—before gasping and pretending to notice Dietrich for the first time. But he did not reciprocate. He continued to ignore me, so I occupied the chair nearest his and stared at him until his shoulders sagged and he lowered his book.

"What?" he demanded.

"You salty dog!" I whispered, leaning forward and slapping him on the knee. "So this is where you've been spending your days. I must say, you've been playing a clever game, and with some toothsome pawns."

I glanced at the remaining two women. They pretended to ignore us, but it was a ludicrous charade. Dietrich sighed.

"For your information," he hissed, "I come here to read."

"Of course," I said, shooting him a wink.

He rolled his eyes, but before he could protest further the women surrendered to the idea that their sanctum was under siege. They quietly stood and exited the room. As soon as the door closed behind them, Dietrich abandoned his reserve.

"What are you doing here?" he said. "Don't pretend you came here to read."

"I was merely exploring when I happened to see you. I thought I'd say hello. I apologize for running off your quarry—"

"For the last time, I come here to read!" he said angrily.

"Really?" I said. "Are you reading a romance of some sort?"

He shook his head in frustration. I cocked my head to one side to get a better look at the cover of his book.

"*An Essay on the Principle of Population*," I said. "If that's a romance, it must be a poorly written one."

He closed his eyes and breathed deeply, as if he could wish me away. He could not.

"Calm down," I said. "I'm just having fun with you. I know it's a serious work, though by the sound of it a romance would be more entertaining."

"I am not seeking entertainment, but fulfillment," he said. "I am trying to prepare myself for the work ahead by better understanding our foe. Are you at all familiar with the theories of Malthus?"

I gazed at the ceiling for a moment before shaking my head.

"Malthus's theory suggests the world's population is growing at a rate that exceeds its ability to produce food. Does that problem sound familiar?"

"Should it?" I asked.

"*Ordo Ab Chao*, Chapter Three," he said, bristling as he quoted from memory. "*While Man is inherently weak of character and prone to vice, there are yet simpler ways to turn him against his neighbor. Deprive him of his most essential needs, food and water, and he will fight his neighbor for them, tooth and nail.*"

"Ugh!" I said. "Have you memorized that infernal book?"

"Is your mind a sieve?" he said, throwing up his hands. "I have explained to you how my mind works. I cannot help but remember it perfectly, and in every detail!"

"Ah, yes," I said. "Your memory is infallible."

"Yes," he said. "Now, do you understand the relevance of Malthusian theory?"

"I suppose," I said. "People need food. The more population grows, the more food is needed."

"A simple explanation, but you have the idea," he grudgingly admitted.

"But it all sounds too ridiculous to be taken seriously," I said. "It's not something *we* have to worry about at any rate."

He closed his eyes and rubbed his temples. Apparently I had just ceded some intellectual territory.

"You are short-sighted," he said, "not to mention naïve. Fortunately, at least one of us takes this business seriously."

"Sir, you offend me," I said. "I take our endeavor every bit as seriously as you. If these Illuminati are real then they must be stopped. But until I encounter Brother Iscariot, or an Illuminati agent, or some other genuine proof, I will continue to think this is a wild goose chase."

"What of *Ordo Ab Chao*?" he asked. "Someone authored it. Is that not proof enough? What of the word of the President?"

I was taken aback by his zeal, and shocked that he would so readily accept everything Cross had said at face value. Not that I disbelieved Cross, but I required proof before I would acknowledge a conspiracy. But on this occasion I held my tongue to keep peace between us. Dietrich, however, would not be deterred.

"Confound it, Grey," he said. "If you don't believe any of it, why in blazes are you here?"

My motive was nothing more than the stipend, but I realized Dietrich was too idealistic to appreciate honesty.

"I suppose a debt of gratitude," I said. "When my future looked bleak, you proved my innocence and freed me from jail. Look, if you think the Illuminati pose a real threat then I will follow you to the gates of Hell to oppose them. But until then I consider our voyage a long overdue holiday."

I slouched in my chair and clasped my hands behind my head to drive my point home. Then an idea popped into my head.

"By the way, now that I've discovered where you've been spending your time, do you know where I've spent my evenings?"

"By the smell of liquor and smoke you bring into our room every night, I would guess the smoking room."

"Exactly!" I exclaimed. "Irish and I have met there every night since we came aboard, and we're getting along famously. Tonight is our last night aboard, and I insist that you join us."

"No, thank you," he said, opening his book and trying to read—as if that indicated his final word on the subject. But now I was the one who would not be deterred.

"Nonsense," I replied. "I'll come collect you after dinner. I won't allow you to sit alone in our room tonight, or to sleep, until you've joined Irish and me for a drink."

I stood and looked down at him. He tried to protest, but I cut him off.

"If you wish to be a gentleman about it," I said, straightening my tie, "you could save me the trouble of seeking you out and simply come to the smoking room around eight. But as I said, it doesn't really matter. If you're not there, I'll find you."

I walked away, whistling cheerfully as I went. Outside on the promenade I laughed aloud, for I had hatched a clever plan.

If clever equates to simple then my plan was nothing less than brilliant; and since it was so brilliant I knew it would not fail. My plan, simply put, was to get Dietrich to relax so he might actually enjoy himself and speak more freely, allowing me to learn more about him. In order to transport him to that nigh unimaginable state, I planned on getting him positively sloshed.

And by and large my plan worked to perfection, though like a cur one stoops to pet on the street, it bit me in the end. But otherwise everything went smoothly. At eight fifteen Dietrich had not yet shown up. I was about to go roust him from our room, or begin our gentlemen's game of hide-and-seek, when he entered the smoking room.

He stopped short inside the door and looked around with unease. When he saw the room contained only Irish, me, and another few gentlemen sitting nearby, he seemed somewhat reassured. I do not know what he thought he would find, but judging by his nervousness I think he expected us to be sloshing mugs around while belting out drinking songs. But the crowd was not that sort. The room, and the mood, was usually very reserved, and that night was no exception.

I motioned him over to our spot at the bar. By then Irish and I had already downed a few and were on our way to having a good time. Of course Irish was less affected owing to his large size, but the smile that spread across his face upon the arrival of our stick-in-the-mud companion revealed the beer had put him in a sociable mood.

"Welcome aboard, captain!" he said, clapping Dietrich on the shoulder.

Dietrich stumbled under the weight of that beefy limb. He shot out a hand to stabilize himself against the bar.

"Never thought I'd see the day," Irish continued. "What'll you have?"

The bartender, a spindly man with black bands wrapped around his shirtsleeves, watched with some amusement. He had become accustomed to seeing Irish and I every night. The first night he had seemed wary, probably intimidated by Irish's size. But we had never caused a commotion above a hearty laugh, and he had warmed up to us quickly. He now looked at Dietrich expectantly.

"Brandy, please," Dietrich said. He made a gesture with thumb and forefinger to indicate he wanted a sip and nothing more.

The bartender poured a drink and slid a rather full glass across the bar with a wink.

"Your friend, Mr Grey, is picking up the tab," he said.

Dietrich eyed the glass, and me, before accepting it.

"Gentlemen, charge your glasses," I said, raising mine. "I propose a toast to remember this moment."

"What's the occasion?" Dietrich asked.

"The wholly remarkable occasion of prying you away from your books and out of your room, like a New Englander pries an oyster from its shell. Truly, I have never encountered a more stubborn clam!"

Irish and I had a good laugh. Dietrich made no sound, but I saw the corners of his mouth twitch as if fighting off a grin. Irish and I clinked our mugs and sought out Dietrich's snifter.

"Drink up, old man," I said, tapping his glass.

He took a miniscule sip. I could see I had much work ahead of me.

"So," said Irish. "This one tells me you've been spending your days in the library?"

"Yes," Dietrich said.

"I hear the library has quite a selection," he said with a mischievous grin.

Dietrich reflected on it for a moment.

"Not especially," he said. "The books are old, and almost exclusively romances."

Irish looked at him with mixed emotion. His mouth was frozen in a grin, but his brow was furrowed in disbelief.

"What're you talking about?" he said. "I'm talking about the ladies."

Dietrich colored a bit.

"Smart move, staking your territory there," Irish said. "I would've never thought of it. And here we are at journey's end, with no more time to try."

I chuckled to myself. Dietrich shot me an annoyed look. I pointed at the still brimming glass in his hand.

"Drink up! You still have a long way to go."

He looked down at his glass and sighed. I sensed he wanted nothing more than to escape, but manners prevented it. Reluctantly he took a somewhat larger draught of his brandy.

I slapped Irish on the back.

"Now, Irish"—during our carousing I had taken to calling him as such—"don't harass Mr Dietrich. He's a man with a lot on his mind, no pun intended, and more responsibility than we've realized. After all, Cross put him in charge, and it now falls on him to guide us."

"True enough," Irish said, and he again raised his glass. "Here's to you."

Dietrich was mollified by this toast. We all touched glasses and took a large drink. Even Dietrich took a larger gulp than before.

"Thank you," he said.

We turned and leaned on the bar then, and a moment of silence passed. Fearing I might lose him, I launched into one of my stories to keep him engaged.

"Where were we? Oh yes, when you walked in I was talking about the time I performed an escape of my own invention, called 'The Ineludible Pyre'. Perhaps you've heard of it. No? No matter. It was unquestionably the most clever, and certainly the most dangerous, escape of my career, which is why I only performed it once to a capacity crowd. It involved me being hooded, restrained in a straightjacket, packed in a casket, the empty spaces of which were filled with sawdust, and inserted into an active crematorium ..."

As I spoke my mind was more focused on Dietrich than on my story, but my presentation of the tale did not suffer. I had told it many times and could recite it while solving algebra. It was quite easy for me to rattle it off in abundant detail and dramatic fashion, while noting Dietrich's every sip of brandy, which, as my story went on, became more frequent. And when that story was complete I moved on to another, and another, with a watchful eye constantly on his glass—each time it reached one third, I signaled the barkeep with a finger aside my nose, and the glass was refilled. And due to my vigilance my plan paid off, for an hour later Dietrich could barely stand.

I had not informed Irish of my plan for fear that he would unwittingly betray it. So he was not in-the-know, and he was surprised and disappointed when I roused Dietrich from his drunken stupor and helped him back to our cabin. But our departure did not change Irish's plans for the evening. He stayed put on his barstool, hefting his glass and engaging the barkeeper in conversation.

Though inebriated, Dietrich was not so far gone that he could not manage himself. Aside from a bleariness in his eyes and a slackness in his posture, he was still himself, but more affable. I had an easy time getting him back to the room and into his bunk. Once he was settled I sat down on the sofa across from him, drew a deep breath, and began my interrogation.

9: THE PANTOLOGIST

What follows is the story I wrought from Meyer Dietrich onboard the *Minnetonka* as our transatlantic journey drew to a close. My methods were perhaps unscrupulous, but if I was expected to follow the man anywhere, especially to my doom, I needed to better understand him. During our very first *tete-a-tete* he had treated me with restrained hostility, and though we had since grown closer, we were still far from brothers-in-arms.

I will not bore you by describing the scene in our stateroom that night. Suffice it to say my questions began innocently and gradually gained more significance, with the effect that I eased Dietrich into a narrative that soon required no further prompting. I had only to sit back, listen, and suffer through his annoyingly detailed account. Several times I felt myself drifting off to sleep, and subsequently awaking with a start, so I cannot be sure I did not at some point lose consciousness. Nevertheless, the account does not suffer from it. If there are gaps or inconsistencies in his tale, they were left by Dietrich, not Yours Truly. I stand by my version wholeheartedly.

What I have documented in the following pages is the story of Dietrich's life, memorized to the best of my ability, and regurgitated many years later. Given his attitude toward me you might wonder why I have bothered to recount it at all. I will not at this time reveal my motive, but I assure you that by the end all will become apparent. For now, suffice it to say he earned it.

Meyer Dietrich was eight years old when he first recognized his unique mental ability to perfectly memorize and recall every detail of an experience. It was 1864, and he was living with his mother and father on the outskirts of Bonn. It was late Sunday morning, and he was sitting cross-legged on the floor of his pastor's house with several of his peers. Light streamed in through the window of the front room. The pastor's wife, a snowy-haired

95

woman, was delivering a catechism on the Ten Commandments. At the end of the hour she sat back in her chair and scanned their faces.

"Now, who would like to try and recite the Commandments, and what they mean to us?" she asked.

As the woman looked for volunteers, all eyes avoided hers except for Meyer's.

"Meyer, why don't you give it a try?"

"Just the first one?" Meyer asked.

The old woman smiled.

"Try as many as you can," she said kindly.

He stared at her and contemplated his options. Even at that young age he knew his memory was better than others. For this reason learning had always been easy for him, because all he witnessed or experienced was forever accessible to him. But he had never revealed his ability to anyone, least of all to an adult. He had the vague feeling it would change everything; and though he would be happy to receive praise, he wondered if the ensuing change was one he would enjoy.

As he pondered the situation the clock on the mantle ticked away, and the expression on the face of the pastor's wife began to look doubtful. She straightened and was about to call on another child when Meyer spoke up.

"Thou shalt have no other gods. This means we should fear, love, and trust in God above all things. Thou shalt not take the name of the Lord, thy God, in vain. This means we should fear and love God that we may not curse, swear, use witchcraft, lie, or deceive by His name, but call upon it in every trouble, pray, praise, and give thanks. Thou shalt sanctify the holy-day. This means we should fear and love God that we may not despise preaching and His Word, but hold it sacred, and gladly hear and learn it. Thou shalt honor thy father and thy mother. This means we should fear and love God that we may not despise nor anger our parents and masters, but give them honor, serve, obey, and hold them in love and esteem. Thou shalt not kill. This means we should fear and love God that we may not hurt nor harm our neighbor in his body, but help and befriend him in every bodily need…."

And so on, until he had repeated every commandment, and flawlessly regurgitated every word of the lesson.

As soon as class ended the woman excused herself, retreated to another room of the house, and returned with her husband. Upon request, Meyer repeated his performance as perfectly as before. When he was done, the pastor laid a hand on his shoulder.

"God has given you a wonderful gift." He said. "You should use it for the greater glory of Him, and to help your fellow man. Do you think you can do that?"

"Yes, sir," Meyer said, though he had no idea how he might go about it.

Word quickly spread, and the remainder of the day was spent with neighbors subjecting him to all manner of unscientific puzzles, hastily designed to test the limits of Meyer's memory. But no matter what they threw at him, he recalled it perfectly.

Meyer's parents were also proud, because their son showed promise in an area in which they had never excelled. Neither of them had finished their schooling, because in their respective youths each had been called upon to help support their families. Meyer's mother, Claudia, had only one marketable skill—sewing—and became a seamstress. His father, Josef, lacked marketable skills of any sort. But by virtue of his breeding he was the rugged type, the kind of man more inclined to *doing* than *thinking*. In other words, he was a man of few marbles, but he had an inclination to act—sometimes impulsively—which made him ideal for military service. He enlisted in the Prussian Army, and in less than a decade attained the rank of *Feldwebel*, or Sergeant Major, whose role was to motivate the troops as they faced cannonades and withering musket fire.

Claudia and Josef never complained about their meager lot in life, but like most parents they wanted a better life for their son. So when the pastor brought Meyer home and explained what Meyer had done, Claudia and Josef were ecstatic. They both dropped to their knees, hugging him long and hard, because their prayers had been answered. They were convinced that he was, or would be, a genius. And that made Meyer special, which meant, ergo, that God must have a special plan for him.

Like all of God's chosen, Meyer had a lifelong series of trials and tribulations to overcome before he would embark on his greatest endeavor. Nothing quite so dramatic as being called upon to perform, or become, a human sacrifice, but events no less tormenting.

Meyer's earliest difficulties came only days after the revelation of his natural talent. He attended school with the same children who sat beside him on the pastor's living room floor. Initially his peers were impressed by his ability, but the more praise and attention he garnered, the more they began to envy him. Soon envy gave way to resentment, and it was not long before cruel names were invoked, and blows exchanged, or more precisely received, because Meyer was too meek to raise a fist in reply.

At first he hid his schoolyard scrapes from his parents, ashamed of what they might think of him. Eventually a boy blackened his eye, and there was no hiding it. Meyer walked to the supper table that night as if he were going to the gallows. And the events that followed were as unpleasant as he had expected, only in a different way. Once his parents wrung the story out of him, his mother broke down and wept, which made Meyer do the same. And his father became angry and indignant. He paced and ranted, directing his fury at the ceiling, not at Meyer. But the boy did not understand the difference. All he knew was that he had brought misery into their home.

To his surprise, however, in the next moment his parents were on their knees hugging him, and then his father took him into the yard to teach him to fight. Meyer imitated his father's moves, and at the conclusion of the lesson they both felt better and believed Meyer would be able to defend himself. But whatever quality Josef possessed that made him a man of action was lacking in Meyer. In each subsequent encounter Meyer was no more effective than a punching bag. He hid this fact from his parents, and always led them to believe he had given as good as he had received.

He was deeply ashamed of not fighting back, but it was beyond his control. He simply could not bring himself to look another boy in the eye and strike him. He tried to understand it, but it required incisive self-analysis, and he was, after all, still a boy. In the end he decided it must be God's intent, that the Lord had instilled in him that rare ability to literally turn the other cheek. Deep down, however, he knew he was deceiving himself, that it was an excuse for cowardice.

Any of this information would have caused ongoing weeping and consternation in the Dietrich household, so he kept it to himself. Any time he sensed a beating—he actually developed a sixth sense for them—he learned to drop to the ground and curl up in a ball. When he performed this cowardly maneuver, it always resulted in one of two outcomes: either the bully would take it as a triumph of wills, kick some dirt in his face, and walk away; or the beating would occur as intended. On those occasions when the bully followed through, Meyer's trademark fœtal defense afforded him a good deal of protection, especially for his face, so he no longer bore the tell-tale signs of a pummeling.

Thus life went on in a seemingly normal fashion for the Dietrichs. As far as they knew, Meyer had overcome his problems. And it satisfied Meyer to know his parents had peace of mind. He would gladly suffer a beating every day rather than shame or disappoint them.

And after Meyer accepted this fate, all seemed well, or as well as could be expected under such circumstances. Two years passed, during which he took (and hid) his lumps. He was ten years old before he suffered his next unique trial.

In the summer of 1866 great tragedy befell the Dietrich family. Prussia went to war with Austria, and Josef's unit was called up at once. A messenger arrived at their door and presented him with papers. He was literally standing in their living room one second, and gone the next.

What followed was exceedingly strange and inexplicable, though Claudia would always insist it had something to do with Josef's departure. The following Sunday morning as they sat in church listening to the sermon, Meyer suddenly fell over in his mother's lap. She thought he had fallen asleep, and in front of the pastor. Mortified, she tried to wake him. Then she noticed his eyes were still open, and no matter how she tried to rouse him, the boy would not respond. She became frantic, and her excitement spread throughout the church. Everyone rushed forward at once to help. The town doctor was among them, and once he penetrated the wall of gawkers he swept the boy up and carried him out.

Claudia followed the doctor to his office. He placed the boy on a table and produced a small bottle of smelling salts, waving them under Meyer's nose with no effect. He opened a drawer and produced a small needle, which he used to poke the boy's fingers and toes. When done with the needle he stood back and rubbed his chin for a moment, then began clapping his hands in front of the boy's face while calling his name. But none of it had any effect. Meyer remained catatonic.

The doctor's limits had been exceeded, and the best he could speculate was that a mysterious brain peculiarity had rendered the boy suddenly insensible. He had no prognosis to offer whatsoever. Claudia became hysterical. It took some time to convince her that it might be just a phase, and that he might come out of it at any moment. Eventually the doctor calmed her down. He explained that Meyer appeared healthy in every other respect, and that—maybe—he would come through it, given time.

Six weeks later, as Claudia stood in the kitchen making soup (the only food she could give her insensible son), a letter arrived informing her that Josef had been killed. It was accompanied by a small wooden case containing a Maltese cross of pure gold, emblazoned with the Prussian royal cipher: the Golden Military Merit Cross. The news devastated her. For the next three months Claudia may as well have been the household idiot, because she quite literally lost her mind. She did not become hysterical, but instead wandered around in a daze. She still performed her essential duties, most notably those tasks that involved taking care of Meyer, but all in a stupor, as if her mind was gone and her body was repeating habits to which it had grown accustomed.

The locals understood Claudia was in mourning, and that she was still reeling from the tragedy that had befallen her son. But soon they began to question her ability to rebound, which led to questions about her sanity, and her ability to care for the boy. They asked the question of the pastor and the doctor, and after several closed-door meetings they agreed the only answer was to pray for the Dietrich family's recovery—but in the meantime they would also send them to an asylum where they could be cared for properly.

In spite of the town's good intentions, God seemed to have a different plan in mind. A neighbor woman took pity on Claudia, and one night went to the Dietrich house and rapped on the door until Claudia roused from her torpor.

"The town has decided to commit you and your son," she said. "You must come to your senses and start behaving normally, before it is too late!"

Claudia stared at the woman in silence before answering.

"I have lost my husband, and my son sleeps as if dead," she said. "Nothing will change until I get my son back."

"Then you must flee," the woman said. "The doctor is going tomorrow to make arrangements at the asylum. You must go at once!"

She produced a small bundle of money wrapped in a handkerchief and pressed it into Claudia's hands. Until that moment Claudia had reacted to the woman as if in a dream, but the contact suddenly sparked something in her. She rose above her misery long enough to realize the woman was right. The asylum was nothing more than a jail, a place to send the tragically distraught, to put them out of sight and out of mind. If she wanted Meyer to have hope, she must take him far away.

She thanked the woman and closed the door. An hour later she had assembled two bundles of clothes, placed them—and Meyer—in the back of a dilapidated cart, hitched it to an old mule, and rode out of town forever.

When Claudia left town she had no true destination other than *away*. God must have been guiding her, because she met with no danger or resistance. In fact, there was little worth mentioning about her trip except that she—a lone woman, in a fragile state of mind, with an invalid son, in a rickety cart, pulled by a decrepit mule—miraculously managed to travel from Bonn to Antwerp, about one hundred and fifty miles, in seven days. Also, as chance would have it, an archaic treaty had passed away in recent years, reopening Antwerp's ports along the Scheldt River to a bustle of trade. Claudia needed only step out over water to land on a riverboat that would take her to the North Sea. Until then she had not imagined traveling so far, but when the moment arrived it felt right. For a small fee she was able to buy passage for herself (but not Meyer, as the boat captain considered him more akin to baggage). They made it to Vlissingen, and from there Claudia spent the last of her money on passage aboard a trade ship to London.

During her travels a small part of her rational mind had been working out a problem, which was simply *where do we stop?* Initially she had wanted only to escape the crazy house, and she had given no thought to where she and Meyer would next call home. As she traveled through strange new territories, she became convinced that as different as these new lands were, they offered nothing different from Bonn. Upon arrival in London, her hopes were further dashed, for never before had she seen such a crowded, sooty, factory-ridden city. So she resolved to go further still, to go as far west as possible, to cross the Atlantic for rumored opportunities in America. There she hoped to make a new life for them both.

There were many ships plying the seas back and forth between England and America, so Claudia would not have had much difficulty finding one headed west. What is interesting, however—and what Meyer Dietrich conveniently overlooked during his narration—was how a penniless Claudia managed to secure passage for herself and her burdensome boy upon a steamship making a trans-Atlantic voyage. (To me the answer is obvious, but I will leave this riddle to the reader's fertile imagination.) Suffice it to say Claudia again performed another miracle, and by the onset of 1867 she and Meyer had arrived in New York.

Naturally, Meyer was oblivious to it all, riding along in his catatonic state. In London his mother had sold the mule and cart and procured a wicker wheelchair, in which he unwittingly spent his days. During their ocean voyage Claudia spent most of her time wheeling him in a slow and endless circuit of the deck.

While crossing the Atlantic, Claudia finally shed the remnants of her delirium. From the moment they had set out across the ocean she had started to feel better, and by the time they pulled into New York harbor she felt like herself again. But new trepidations would soon arise.

The dock swarmed with people, so many, in fact, it did not look like it could accommodate another boatload. But that did not matter to the newly arrived immigrants, who coursed around her like the waters of a rushing river, sweeping her and Meyer up along the way and depositing them into the most diverse sea of humanity imaginable.

Most of the throng was white-skinned like her, but from their mouths came so many distinctly different sounds that she thought America must be the crossroads of the world. There were plenty of swarthy-skinned people, too—Italians, Hungarians, Greeks, Sicilians, a variety of gypsies from across Europe, and who knew what else. There were even contingents of blacks moving about freely. It was too much for a simple Prussian Protestant to absorb.

She stood on the dock bewildered, not knowing where to go or what to do next. She had thought she would follow the crowd, but it was so chaotic there was no flow to it. She was about to pick something out above, like a distinctive building, and make her way toward it—anything to get out of the throng—when she felt a gentle hand on her arm, accompanied by a familiar voice in her ear.

"You look lost. May I help you?"

In actuality, the voice was not at all familiar, but the language was. The speaker was a fellow German, and his accent further revealed he was Prussian, or had been at one time. Claudia spun around to find a gentleman smiling at her sympathetically. She did not know what to make of the cut of his suit—the fit seemed baggier than anything a self-respecting Prussian would wear—but she reminded herself that she was in a strange new land. No matter how frumpy the man appeared in his ill-fitting suit, both he and it were clean, which made him stand out in this crowd.

Claudia almost wept. It had been weeks since she had spoken to anyone (other than an insensible Meyer) in German. The man seemed to understand at once.

"There, there. I understand. You speak only German. Ah, and I see your son is ill. How unfortunate for you! I'm with Tammany Hall. If you will come with me, I can help you find a place to stay, with fellow Germans who will aid you in your time of need."

For Claudia, this was beyond belief. To set foot on the soil of a new land and within minutes be welcomed and looked after by such a caring person was inconceivable. She clung to him like a stone in a rushing river.

"Excuse me," she said, as they made their way into the heart of the city. "What is Tammany Hall?"

"Why, my dear, I'm glad you asked!"

The stranger deposited her with not one, but four, German families, all living in the basement of a tenement. He introduced her to the inhabitants, then pressed a few dollars into her hand, said "Remember to vote with Tammany!" and disappeared from her life.

His abrupt departure notwithstanding, Claudia was thrilled to be in the company of other Germans, and to have a couple dollars in her hand to boot. The other families seemed less enthusiastic, because what little space they possessed had suddenly dwindled. However they were all in the same situation, having only recently emigrated, so with a collective sigh they took in Claudia and Meyer and cared for them the best they could.

It was then that the "Christmas Miracle" occurred, as Claudia would refer to it forever after. It happened on Christmas Day, 1867. The residents of the basement lacked the means to celebrate with gifts or a fancy meal, so instead they sat in a group and listened as the eldest of the tribe read from the Bible. Then, in the midst of discussion, someone spoke.

"Where am I?"

It was a voice that none of the children or their parents recognized. As they looked around for its owner, their eyes habitually skipped over Meyer in his wheelchair. But Claudia recognized it. She dove at her son and hugged him, and in the next instant was on her knees weeping and thanking God while squeezing Meyer's hands.

And, eventually, she answered his question.

"America. We're in America."

Claudia was so overjoyed to have her son back, she totally forgot about all the misery Meyer had missed. It was not until he asked for his father that that she remembered. Then it all came rushing back to her. She dreaded the explanation, but there was no way around it. She explained how Josef had died heroically in Germany's civil war, and as she spoke she watched his eyes brim with tears. But nary a tear fell. It seemed to her as if Meyer had suddenly mastered himself and willed them away. Impressed by this unexpected maturity, she dried her own eyes, went to her things, and dug out from her meager possessions a small case. She then presented it to Meyer, and said, "Merry Christmas."

Meyer accepted the gift with feeble hands. He opened the case and removed Josef's posthumously awarded medal.

"Your father's Military Merit Cross," she said. "He would have wanted you to have it, and to keep it as our family's last surviving heirloom."

Though it was difficult for Claudia not to seize and hold him prisoner in her arms for the rest of his life, she resisted the urge and sat down quietly beside him. Meyer held the medal in silence. By the time he looked up he had quietly resolved to do whatever he must to take care of his mother, and to make his father proud.

Meyer may have escaped catatonia, but his awakening brought with it another strange affliction, or obsession, that appeared within days of his recovery. On his third day of consciousness he looked up at Claudia from his wheelchair, and spoke in an imperative tone.

"Mother," he said, "I must read."

Claudia did not at that time comprehend the gravity of the statement. But she understood that being confined to a wheelchair was tedious, and he would probably be there for some time, at least until he built up his strength. He would need something to do, and to learn.

"I'm sorry," she said. "Remember, this is America. All its books are in English. But wait! We have a German Bible. You can read this for now."

Meyer accepted the Bible and thumbed through its many pages as if inspecting it. It created in Claudia an uneasy feeling, as if he were scrutinizing it.

"This will be fine, for now," he said. "But if we are to live in America, we must learn English."

"Yes," she said. "I have already started learning what I can, here and there. And when the men of the family return home at the end of the day, they tell us of the new words and phrases they picked up."

"I have heard them speak about what they learned," he said, "but it is too little and too slow. I hear the other children already speaking in words the adults do not understand."

"They go to the neighborhood school," she said.

"Then I must go as well."

Claudia firmly objected to this on the grounds that Meyer needed to become stronger before she would let him out of her sight. Meyer tried several tacks, but Claudia blocked each one. Finally, he had a desperate idea.

"If you will not let me go to school, then at least take me out of the house. Take me for a walk along the streets, or to the market, or anywhere there are people other than the ones who live in this house."

Claudia agreed, and for the next several weeks she took Meyer along on errands. It was somewhat difficult navigating crowded sidewalks with a boy whose muscles had almost atrophied, but he needed the exercise for a full recovery, and she enjoyed the company. After all, she was still rejoicing at his return. What she did not know, and what Meyer did not tell her, was that he was less interested in her than in the many strangers—and the conversations—that surrounded them.

Meyer's plan came to fruition soon enough, in no small part due to his unique memory. Every conversation he overheard taught him something new. Early on he may not have understood the English vocabulary, but he was able to comprehend many meanings through context. And over time he was able to compile in his memory an experiential vocabulary and grammar that enabled him to speak, read, and write in almost perfect English.

By spring of 1868 he was finally able to move about on his own.

"Mother, now that I'm well I must get out and learn."

Claudia was still apprehensive about sending him to school.

"Summer is almost here," she said. "There is so time left this year. I think it will be better if you wait until next year."

"I do not need school," he said. "Books will suffice."

Suddenly Claudia looked sad.

"We do not have the money for books," she said.

"I know," Meyer said.

He slowly reached into his pocket and pulled out a clunky gold object, which he reluctantly held in the palm of his hand. "We could sell this."

"Your father's medal?" Claudia exclaimed. "Never! How could you even think of such a thing?"

Meyer hung his head and returned the medal to his pocket. Claudia felt simultaneously dismayed that he would consider pawning his father's decoration, and ashamed of her inability to provide the simplest academic necessities. After she calmed herself, she decided to do whatever necessary to provide him with the books he so desperately desired.

And again we came to an awkward junction in the tale, because Dietrich either did not know how his mother suddenly began to acquire money; or he knew and chose to obfuscate about it; or perhaps he knew but had convinced himself otherwise. In any case, Claudia, whose ability as a seamstress was not in great demand, began working *somewhere* at night that soon provided her with enough money to procure for her son a variety of books.

At first Claudia brought home dime novels, but Meyer would polish them off within a day and ask for more. So she began buying larger books with many pages—textbooks, anthologies, random encyclopedias—anything that would keep his omnivorous mind occupied.

She attributed Meyer's hunger for knowledge to the time he had lost to his extended stupefaction. She thought perhaps he was trying to make up for lost time, to catch up with other children his age. But very quickly she realized the voracity of his reading bordered on obsessive, and she became concerned. She had no idea why, or what there was to be concerned about, since reading seemed a harmless pursuit. Still, she had an uneasy feeling that his insatiable intellectual appetite was becoming a problem.

If she had asked Meyer for an explanation, he would have explained that his mind was like a great empty crater fed by a trickle of water, meandering to it from some lofty height far, far away. Eventually, perhaps over hundreds or thousands of years, the tiny rivulet would entirely fill the concavity, but in the meantime the wait was intolerable. If Meyer did not keep his mind engaged— if his intellect was not consuming something during his waking moments—he felt as if he might literally go insane.

But given the problems his brain had already caused them, Meyer wisely chose not to share this similitude. And fortunately, Claudia never asked him for an explanation. After narrowly escaping the asylum, the answer would have frightened her to death.

Meyer, however, understood it instinctively and perfectly, as if filling his voracious mind were no less a necessity than food and water. Furthermore, he knew the remedy as well as he knew his own name—he needed to read and learn. Constantly. In every waking moment that he was not otherwise occupied, he needed to have his nose in a book. The more he read, the less the empty spaces of his mind haunted him, and the sooner those uncanny recesses would be filled.

Claudia's ambiguous nocturnal industry eventually earned them enough money to move out of the basement and into an actual apartment upstairs. This afforded them their own private space while keeping them near their adopted German friends and family, though due to his bookishness Meyer's interaction with them was almost nonexistent. Nevertheless, they lived in harmony for several long, quiet years, with Claudia dutifully plying her trade until late at night, while Meyer sat at home reading newspapers, almanacs, encyclopedia, or anything else of substance.

One night in 1873, when Meyer was but seventeen, Claudia did not come home. Since she had never confided in him where she went at night, he had no idea where to look for her. He let another day pass, hoping she would return, before he took any action. When another night passed and morning came with no sign, he went in search of a police officer, and found one walking his beat on an adjacent street. Meyer stated his problem. The officer escorted him to the station and turned him over to another, who took his report and sent him home.

Within days Meyer was summoned to the police station again, and from there taken to the morgue. He was led to a cold, tiled room containing several tables. One table contained a body covered with a sheet. The officer pulled back the shroud, exposing nothing below the chin. It was Claudia. Meyer nodded, which was sufficient for the officer.

"What happened?" Meyer asked distantly.

"Strangled," the officer replied.

Meyer did not ask where they had found her, or what she had been doing. None of it mattered, because whatever she had been involved in, he knew it was for him. He expected, even wanted, tears to fill his eyes, but the moment was too surreal. The officer raised his eyebrows in admiration of Meyer's self-control and drew the sheet over the body.

They departed for the police station. The officer assured him they would do their best to capture the murderer, but Meyer was skeptical. He did not voice his doubt, but instead kept his thoughts to himself until he had completed his business at the station. Then he exited and quietly sat on the steps. He sat for an hour in contemplation, wondering about life without his mother, and his future. He thought of his father and the golden cross he had received for his heroic wartime sacrifice; and he thought of his mother and all she had sacrificed for him. It did not take him long to reach a decision on how to proceed. He arose, went back into the station, and signed up to become a New York City police officer.

Police training did not go well for him. Academically he did fine—given his flawless mind, he only needed to peruse his lessons to perfectly and eternally commit them to memory. He could rattle off laws, statutes, and regulations at the drop of a hat. And his mental faculties also served him well in practical applications—his memorization of crime scenes enabled him to write immaculate reports, and to recognize overlooked clues long after the scene had been cleared away. But no matter how intellectually superior he was to his fellow cadets, his perfect mind could not make up for his frail stature and hesitancy. Years of bookishness and inactivity had robbed him of strength and wind, and he came in last on every physical trial. When faced with a situation that required him to act quickly and demonstrably—i.e., without thinking—he froze like a hunted rabbit. Even before his training was complete he was dropped from the class.

Once again Meyer found himself sitting on the steps to the station, this time lamenting his aborted career as a policeman. He had been convinced this was the path for him, a way to honor his parents, and to protect the weak and unsuspecting as they sought to make their way in this callous world. He was crestfallen that it was not to be.

There was one man, however, who saw in Meyer a spark of promise, and a hint of opportunity. Thomas Byrnes was a young Irishman with the robust moustache of a man twice his age. He was the department's brightest star, a man of considerable wit and determination, who was not afraid to take drastic action to get the job done.

During idle moments Byrnes had on occasion dropped by the training room. While the cadets underwent physical trials he had witnessed several of Meyer's humiliations, and like the rest he had been quite entertained by them. But he also had noted Meyer's keen mind, and a clever man himself, he recognized an opportunity that would benefit everyone—Meyer, the department, the city, and of course, himself.

Byrnes found Meyer seated on the steps with head hanging between his knees. He sidled up without a word, lit a pipe, and casually puffed as if oblivious to Meyer's presence. Meyer noticed him and expected to be run off, so he was surprised when Byrnes finally spoke.

"Let's go have a talk," Byrnes said.

He followed Byrnes to a nearby coffee house, where they sat down at a table and Byrnes treated him to a cup. As Meyer drank he expected some kind of consolation, some gentle but encouraging words to succor him in his moment of rejection. But the look in Byrnes' eye was more calculating than sympathetic.

"You're a good lad, wanting to join the police," Byrnes said at length. "It tells me a lot about your character. But as the instructors said, you're just not cut out to wear the uniform."

Meyer had hoped this meeting might presage a second chance. He dropped his chin to his chest.

"Hold on now, that doesn't mean the police don't have a use for you. I'm a captain, see? And an inspector to boot, all after only six years in the Department, mind you. I've a natural instinct for the work, and I suppose that makes it my calling. What do you reckon is your calling?"

"I thought it was police work," Meyer said with a shrug. "But apparently I'm not cut out for it, even though I have a mind and a memory like no other. I thought the police might put me to good use, but it doesn't seem to matter without the ability to swing a club."

As soon as the words escaped him, Meyer colored, realizing he had just disparaged the very institution to which he had aspired, and to which Byrnes belonged. But Byrnes laughed.

"Swinging a club is important if you're walking a beat," he said. He then leaned over the table on his elbows and spoke in a low, conspiratorial tone. "But what if I were to say you can help the police *without* wearing the badge? What would you say if I were to offer you a job, say, as my *private* investigator?"

Meyer was instantly curious.

"What does that mean?" he asked, bewildered yet hopeful.

"It means that when I have a tough case, I'll call on you," Byrnes explained. "You come out, look everything over, then we put our heads together and solve it. You and me together. What do you think?"

On this rare occasion Meyer did not have to think at all.

"That sounds perfect!" he exclaimed. He felt like his life was back on track, and a clear path lay before him. Then he hesitated.

"But if I'm not employed by the Department, how will I be paid?"

"You let me handle that," Byrnes said. "For now, I'll pay you out of my own pocket, on a case-by-case basis."

Meyer's enthusiasm began to ebb. Byrnes was better off than him—after all, the man had a paying job, considerable status, and a promising future—but even Meyer knew officers did not make that much. Still, he was reticent to call Byrnes' finances into question, so he voiced his financial concern in a different way.

"Case by case?" he said with a frown. "It doesn't sound like steady work."

Byrnes smiled broadly.

"This is New York City. Believe me, sonny, the work will be steady."

"And that is how I made my living for the past twenty-two years," Dietrich said, removing his spectacles and rubbing his eyes. "I worked for Byrnes. I was not an officer, but I assisted in his investigations. I was on the periphery of every scene, absorbing the details that would enable him to make arrests. As a result, his career skyrocketed."

Dietrich stared at the ceiling of our cabin for a moment in troubled silence, and I hoped he had reached the end of his tale. I was by then exhausted.

"Byrnes was correct," he continued. "There was never a shortage of work. You would not believe it, Grey—the horrible things people do to one another. I would not believe it had I not seen it again and again. For my service Byrnes paid me well, so well, in fact, I fooled myself into believing everything was all right. Then in '95 it all came crashing down. Byrnes was charged with corruption and removed. The humiliation of it! That I—a man of such keen observation and memory, who had guided Byrnes in solving hundreds of crimes—had been working for a criminal all along. And do you know what is strange? He was removed by the very man for whom we now work!"

I furrowed my brow.

"Cross?"

"No, you fool, Roosevelt! He was on the Board of Police Commissioners in '95. It was he who sacked Byrnes."

"Ah," I yawned. "What a strange coincidence."

"But the cruelest irony," he continued, "is that I spent twenty-two years in Byrnes' employ, trying to do some good, when in fact I was working for a villain."

He rolled his head toward me and squinted.

"How does one compensate, Grey? How does one make up for twenty-two years of complicity in vice and corruption? Would *another* twenty-two years of good deeds make up for it? Or would it take a lifetime? Or is it possible to redeem oneself with one single, shining act?"

It was with this question hanging in the air that our exchange ended. Dietrich closed his eyes as if to ponder it, and a moment later the spectacles slipped from his fingers and clattered on the floor. I placed them on the sink, turned off the lamp, and collapsed on my own bunk, pleased with my accomplishment.

10: THE U.G.L.E.

London was a dreary place, even in springtime. I had heard it existed in a perpetual nimbus of fog, but I had taken it as hyperbole.

We arrived around seven o'clock in the morning before a gauzy wall that soon enveloped the ship, limiting visibility to less than a tenth of mile. Nevertheless, it quickly became apparent we were near a hub of civilization. Like forlorn behemoths, ships and foghorns bellowed morosely to one another. I felt myself go slightly off balance, and I knew we had reduced our speed to avoid collision.

As the *Minnetonka* maneuvered its way up the Thames and pulled into port, everyone emerged on deck to witness the docking; even Dietrich, after our late night interview, had managed to rise in time. Ms Alexander, who after our daily tea times had grown closer to me than the rest, stood by my side, as much interested in the proximity of our fellow passengers as in the hazy view of land.

The fog was so dense, however, that I started to doubt the city's presence. Much of the shore remained obscured to us. The further up the Thames we progressed, the thicker the fog became. The ship slowed to a crawl. Eventually we started to favor the starboard side, drifting closer to shore until it came hazily into view. The ship pulled alongside the dock, and we watched shadows flit through the fog as dockhands worked to moor us. We had hoped to watch this spectacle unfold against the background of the city, but London offered only a drab grey canvas.

"This is dreadful," I muttered. "I'm amazed we haven't collided with anything."

"I encountered this before, several years ago when passing through London on my way to America," Ms Alexander said, waving a hand in front of her face in a vain attempt to disperse the mist. "But it was not as bad, and the odor was less quarrelsome."

"Yes," I said, taking a whiff. "The air does have an unclean quality. What causes it, I wonder?"

Dietrich began to cough into his fist. One could hardly blame him. Even my chest felt tight, as if pea soup were invading my lungs.

"Pardon me," he said when he had recovered. He removed a handkerchief and held it over his mouth a moment before continuing. "The odor you detect is part industry, part burning coal. The fog traps the coal-smoke and they commingle, which results in this foul concoction."

We made our way to the gangplank. A large crowd had gathered before it, everyone in polite competition to be the first off the ship. As we approached, Ms Alexander hesitated. Remembering her social anxiety I slowed my pace and cleared my throat. Dietrich and Irish looked back.

"There's no need to hurry," I said. "Why don't we pause and enjoy the view?"

Irish looked at me as if I were an idiot. Fog obscured every direction.

"What view?" he said.

Dietrich, on the other hand, understood instantly.

"Why not?" he said. "No need to jockey for position in this crowd. We still have time to make our scheduled appointment. And if we miss it, I know where to find Mr Ensley."

"Where's that?" I asked.

"The United Grand Lodge of England," he replied.

As we stood back and waited for the crowd to thin, Dietrich, the perennial didact, edified us on the history behind the United Grand Lodge of England, or U.G.L.E. It was, unsurprisingly, the first and oldest Masonic Grand Lodge in the world. It dated back to 1717 when its founders saw the need to somehow corral the numerous Masonic lodges springing up. Britain, Scotland and Ireland each had their own Grand Lodge, thus the *United* Grand Lodge was created to encompass them all. The purpose of creating such a hierarchy was, ostensibly, to ensure continuity in Masonic tradition, and to keep fellow Masons from wandering too far from the fold. These efforts notwithstanding, an array of self-styled lodges continued to crop up, based upon, and espousing, Masonic practices.

"So," Dietrich said, "while the U.G.L.E. was created to unify the brotherhood, nonaffiliated lodges continued to exist, coming and going throughout the last hundred years."

"And what is the exact nature of a nonaffiliated lodge?" Ms Alexander asked.

"It depends on each lodge," Dietrich replied. "Many are kith and kin to the original brotherhood, and they peacefully coexist. But there are some, shall we say, eccentric lodges, with which no traditional Mason would associate."

I was about to ask him to elaborate when Irish interrupted.

"How do you know so much about this?" he said, eyeing Dietrich suspiciously.

"It was the subject of my correspondence with Mr Ensley," he replied. "He is a Masonic historian within the U.G.L.E."

Irish rubbed his chin and nodded, but he still had a reflective look. He was as suspicious of this business with the Masons as me. Then he gestured at the few remaining passengers descending the gangplank.

"Looks like the crowd has cleared."

"Then let's be on our way," Dietrich said.

We descended the gangplank into the fog below and presently reached the steadfastness of the dock. At first I suffered a slight vertiginous sensation; apparently after seven days at sea I had become accustomed to the motion of the ship. It took me a few seconds to shake off my sea legs, but soon *terra firma* felt like home again.

Dietrich walked with purpose, leading us through the customs house with negligible hindrance. It almost seemed as if the attendants were expecting us. I interpreted it to mean Dietrich had made arrangements, greasing the skids as the saying goes. I shot him a suggestive look.

"Mr Ensley has already paved the way for us," he said. "I have done nothing felonious, if that is what you are thinking."

"The thought never crossed my mind," I replied.

Within minutes we cleared customs while our fellow travelers still stood in a long line. The customs men deposited our considerable luggage by the curb, where the drivers of several hackney cabs eyed our bags, and us, with interest. Dietrich sized them up and hired three to accommodate us. Our bags were quickly loaded and we followed suit.

"The Hotel Metropole," Dietrich said so all could hear.

He won the honor of sharing a cab with Ms Alexander that day. Meanwhile, Irish and I each climbed into one of the remaining cabs to ensure the drivers did not abscond with our belongings.

As our cabs rattled along London's convoluted streets, I tried my best to get a feel for the city, but the fog confounded me. It rendered the people as shadows and the buildings as monolithic grey masses. It was so thick I could not even get a sense of direction from the sun. If by some misfortune I had fallen out of the cab, I would have been completely lost.

We were fortunate, then, that our drivers did not lead us astray. They knew the twists and turns of London's streets like the backs of their grubby hands, fog notwithstanding. As we trundled along I could tell by the sound of the riverboats off to my left that we were roughly following the north bank of the river. Thirty minutes later we pulled up in front of the Hotel Metropole, a large wedge-shaped building that pointed to the Thames.

The cabbies unloaded our belongings, Dietrich paid them, and they disappeared into the fog. Then bellboys appeared, and before we said a word they started piling our trunks and bags onto handcarts and wheeling them into the lobby. We followed them inside, signed for our rooms, stowed our belongings, and reconvened downstairs.

We sat around a small table in the café, a cup and saucer in front of each of us. The café itself was a spacious room with ten tables, only two others of which were occupied at the moment. Since there were so few patrons we had almost the entire place to ourselves, so we had chosen a spot before a large picture window looking onto Whitehall Place. The view continued to be dismal, but the window afforded us a good deal of diffused light.

"It is now ten o'clock," Dietrich said. "Mr Ensley should meet us here at eleven."

He absently wound his watch as he explained our agenda for the day.

"But before he arrives I would like to remind everyone that in my correspondence I never mentioned any traveling companions, because at that time I did not know with whom I might be allied. So when Mr Ensley arrives he may be put off by your presence."

"You want us to make ourselves scarce?" asked Irish.

"That won't be necessary," Dietrich replied. "At least not yet. I want to introduce you all to him. After that I will do the talking. But I ask that you remain attentive to his disposition."

"In other words, improvisation may be in order," I said.

"Exactly. If he seems like he is hedging, please find a reason to excuse yourselves so I can speak with him privately. Ms Alexander, if you don't mind, I would like you to take command in such a situation."

"Of course," she said.

"Mr Irish, Mr Grey, you need only follow Ms Alexander's lead. If she departs, please accompany her."

Irish and I nodded.

"Now that our roles are clear, we may sit back and enjoy our tea," Dietrich said.

As far as I could tell Irish and I did not have roles at all. I did not like being put aside, but I was quite pleased at the idea of sticking by Ms Alexander.

We conversed pleasantly while waiting for Mr Ensley to arrive, and as we sat and sipped it occurred to me that it was the first socially pleasant occasion we had all shared. Aboard the *Minnetonka*, Ms Alexander had declined all invitations to leave her cabin, but this time she had not attempted to be reclusive. Instead she seemed almost at ease, happy to wile away the minutes at our cozy little table. I surmised it was because the café was secluded and rather empty at the moment. Whatever the reason, it was pleasing to see her so relaxed as she listened with polite interest to Dietrich's ramblings about London's history.

The hour passed quickly, more quickly than I would have preferred under the circumstances. But soon I noticed movement out of the corner of my eye, and I turned to see a man in a dark suit questioning the café attendant. He held a bowler in one hand and an umbrella in the other. He was of average height and build, and his hair was dark except for a touch of grey in his generous sideburns. He approached our table and we arose to greet him.

"Pardon me," he said. "I'm looking for Meyer Dietrich."

"That is me," said Dietrich, extending his hand. "Mr Ensley, good to finally meet you."

"The pleasure is mine," he said. He then took in the rest of us. "Who do we have here?"

Dietrich went round the table introducing us. After each introduction Mr Ensley exclaimed how wonderful it was to make our acquaintance, or found some other way to compliment each of us. When he came to Ms Alexander, he extended his hand expecting hers. Instead, he found himself facing a wall of Irish, who had superimposed himself between them. It was so unexpected it took all of us by surprise. Mr Ensley withdrew his hand and shot Irish a baffled look, which Irish completely ignored. Dietrich, who I anticipated would become apologetic, instead sidestepped the affront by pretending it had not occurred. He took Ensley by the arm, guided him to a chair, and immediately engaged him in conversation as if nothing awkward had happened.

We all suffered through several minutes of banal conversation, discussing our voyage and our first impressions of London, before Dietrich finally got around to business.

"Pardon me if I am now blunt," he said, "but I would like to discuss the subject of our correspondence. Specifically, I am interested in the history of your fraternity."

Ensley's eyes flickered, but he maintained a pleasant smile.

"Of course," he said.

He glanced at the rest of us, then over his shoulder at the others taking tea nearby. Without saying a word he made clear that Freemasonry was not a subject normally discussed over tea.

"I will answer your questions, if I can," he said.

"As I mentioned in my letters, I am much interested in the history of your organization," Dietrich said. "You wrote that it dates back to the late fourteenth century."

"Correct," Ensley said. "The oldest known lodge dates to the sixteenth century, but we possess documents from as early as 1390."

"And since that time," Dietrich continued, "the brotherhood has flourished, spreading the world over, resulting in great diversity."

"Again, correct. As members of our noble institution moved abroad, some fell by the wayside while others stood up new lodges. This has been a source of satisfaction and frustration for us. We are pleased to find others so willing to create new lodges and edify their brethren on our tenets of charity, social responsibility, and community leadership, but the truth is we have lost track of them. Today there are hundreds, perhaps thousands, of lodges the world over who do not fall under our jurisdiction, and which have broken with our strict traditions."

"Really?" Dietrich said, feigning surprise. "Then how is it they are able to call themselves Masons?"

Mr Ensley stiffened and his smile wavered. He glanced over his shoulder again to see if anyone had overheard. At first I did not understand what had affected his mood, but then I realized it was the first time the word *Masons* had been mentioned.

"They simply *do*," Mr Ensley replied. "They do not ask permission, nor do they seek our approval. Hence they may engage in all sorts of inappropriate pursuits, tarnishing our name and reputation. But I think maybe this conversation is not appropriate for this location—"

"Forgive me," Dietrich said, realizing his *faux pas*. "That was impolitic of me."

Ensley relaxed somewhat, but he still looked uncomfortable. He half smiled and nodded while adjusting himself in his chair.

"How does the brotherhood then associate with these rogue lodges?" Dietrich asked.

"We don't. They are irregulars, and our members are forbidden to associate with them."

"So you have no idea how many there are, where they are, or what goes on within them?" Dietrich asked.

Here Ensley's good humor returned somewhat. The trace of a smile began at the corners of his mouth.

"We may not be in the loop, but neither are we in the dark."

"Ah," Dietrich replied, knowingly.

As I sat and watched I suddenly realized Dietrich was not as rigidly mechanical of mind as I had thought. He was attempting to guide discussion toward the topic of renegade Masons and the Illuminati, but he seemed hesitant. Each time he discovered an inroad, it was as if he took a few steps down it and then turned back. While it pleased me to see him trying to improvise, it was a painfully clumsy effort that started to wear on my patience. I listened for another few minutes as he tip-toed around the subject, but finally I could take it no more.

"I have a question," I said, breaking the imposed vow of silence.

Dietrich and Ensley both looked at me in surprise. They had monopolized the conversation to such an extent that they seemed to have forgotten I was there.

"Yes," Ensley said.

"I've heard of a group that supposedly split off from—"

I caught myself before *Masons* came out. I was quite unused to talking in so many euphemisms.

"—the brotherhood," I said with a wink. "They're very mysterious, but perhaps you know something about them. Are you familiar with the Illuminati?"

Everyone froze. It was as if a viper had suddenly appeared in the middle of our table and was ready to strike the next person who dared breathe. In the seconds of silence that followed I made a quick sweep of my companions. Dietrich was a portrait of disbelief and fury. Ms Alexander also wore a look of disbelief, but in general she looked more mortified than angry. Irish, however, only looked confused, his brow furrowed and his mouth half opened.

As I analyzed their expressions I realized I had again crossed the invisible line between polite conversation and the taboo. But by then there was nothing to be done, so I feigned nonchalance by dropping a few lumps of sugar in my tea and stirring it patiently while awaiting an answer.

Dietrich inhaled sharply, and I could tell he was about to prostrate himself and apologize on my behalf. But Ensley interrupted him.

"Yes, Mr Grey. I have heard of them, or the myth of them anyway. I know they existed more than a century ago in Bavaria, but they died out shortly thereafter. Today, they are only kept alive in rumors spread by the paranoid—"

Here he turned his head and darted his eyes around the room before continuing in a lowered voice.

"—and the Anti-Mason movement."

My companions began to breathe again, and to fidget in their chairs.

"But this is not a topic for a place such as this," he continued. "I hope you will forgive me if I am the one who is now blunt. Mr Dietrich, perhaps I misinterpreted the purpose of your correspondence. I presumed you were writing a book that would help demystify the brotherhood, but I think I have misread you entirely. Is Mr Grey's topic what you really came to discuss?"

Dietrich opened his mouth to respond, only to be cut off a second time.

"Gentlemen," Ms Alexander said, rising from her seat. "I hope you will forgive me, but the café is quite warm. I would like to step outside and get some air. Mr Irish, *Mr Grey*, would you care to accompany me?"

"Sure thing," Irish replied, standing up from the table.

I much wanted to hear Dietrich's response to Ensley, but I could not pass up Ms Alexander's invitation.

"Absolutely," I said, and I arose and followed her outside. There, I received an unexpected and unpleasant surprise.

"What was the meaning of your outburst?" Ms Alexander demanded.

It caught me off guard. I stammered as I attempted to explain, and to come to terms with being rebuked by so young a woman.

"Yeah, what the hell was that all about?" Irish chimed in.

Ms Alexander now rounded on him.

"Mr Irish, please. I do not care for such language."

Irish stared at her baffled, looking much as he had after my outburst. Ms Alexander came back to me.

"Mr Dietrich was doing quite well on his own," she said. "Our instructions were to let him do the talking, as Mr Ensley is his contact, not ours. Our only role was to sit quietly, to listen, and to learn."

As she reviewed the rules, I vaguely recalled Dietrich saying something along those lines.

"Yes, but he was taking forever to make his point," I said petulantly. "Someone needed to ask the questions that really matter."

"It is not yours to decide how the interview should proceed," she said. "Mr Dietrich is our captain. He knows more about this business than any of us. If we are to have any hope for success, we must unite and support him."

I opened my mouth to reply, to say something scathing about Dietrich and the situation that would make her see things my way, or at least feel ashamed about chastising me. But nothing came to mind. It was probably for the best, because I did not enjoy being on her bad side. Instead I clenched my teeth and turned away to master myself.

"Fine," I said. "I'll apologize."

I turned back around to Ms Alexander's steely gaze. She still looked at me sternly, but I detected a slight softening in her eyes.

"An apology will do, for starters," she said. "Please refrain from future outbursts."

We waited outside the hotel in silence. I was angry and ashamed and did not feel like talking, and I suspect Irish was still puzzling over his own reprimand. Eventually he wandered away and sullenly smoked a cigarette on the corner.

After my offense I expected to see Ensley indignantly depart at any moment, but he did not appear for at least a quarter of an hour. We were all getting tired of standing around by then. Even Ms Alexander, whose grace and poise were impeccable, began to shift from one foot to the other like a bored child. I was about to recommend we go back inside when Ensley appeared. He donned his bowler, tipped it with a courteous smile, and went on his way.

We made our way inside and found Dietrich in the lobby. He was back to his usual stoic self, though when he saw me he frowned. Ms Alexander quickly intervened.

"The matter has been handled," she said quietly. "Now, what happened with Mr Ensley?"

"In spite of the unpleasantness, I think I managed to salvage the situation," Dietrich said. "But first I had to confess that while I find Freemasonry a fascinating topic, I was not writing a book, and I apologized if I had led him to believe otherwise. He seemed to appreciate my forthrightness and my apology. I next explained Mr Grey's comments as ignorance, a mix of rumor with bits of information he had pieced together from me."

"And he accepted your explanation?" she asked.

"Eventually," Dietrich said. "But first I had to dissemble."

"You lied?" I said.

"No," he said testily. "Your outburst put me in an awkward position. I had to think quickly. If I'd had more time I would have found another way, but the circumstances were beyond my control."

"What did you tell him?" Ms Alexander asked.

"The truth," he said matter-of-factly.

There was a moment of silence as we absorbed this statement.

"You told him of our endeavor?" she said in disbelief.

"Yes and no," he replied. "Yes, I told him we are investigating the Illuminati. No, I did not reveal our ultimate purpose. But he has no doubt surmised our interest is not purely academic. Anyway, we roused his curiosity enough to win another meeting."

"Oh?" Ms Alexander said, looking hopeful.

"Tonight," he said. "Nine o'clock, at Freemason Hall."

"In that case, well played, old man!" I said, clapping him on the shoulder.

He absorbed the blow as if made of stone.

"And," he said, "he asked that I bring *you* along."

"Me?" I asked, placing a hand on my chest.

"Yes."

"Only Mr Grey?" Ms Alexander asked.

"Yes."

"Why?" we asked in unison.

"I have no idea," Dietrich said, bristling. "But let's hope your next performance is better than the one you gave today."

After our morning meeting we returned to our rooms. I had thought I might do some sightseeing, but when the view from my window looked as if it were filled with smoke I concluded there was not much point. So I stayed in my room until shortly after noon, when we met downstairs in the café again for lunch.

I was pleased to see Ms Alexander had again ventured out. It appeared that in spite of her phobia she was more willing to risk social interaction on land than at sea, perhaps because it afforded her more opportunities to maneuver. And she repeated the performance again at supper, when we met in the hotel lobby at seven and walked to a nearby restaurant. She was a bit more anxious that time, owing to being out and about, but she managed it, and to the joy of all. There is nothing like the company of an exceptional woman in public. I wished only that she would take my arm, but I knew it was out of the question.

As it turned out, I came to realize that *I* was the main reason she had ventured out with us. At both lunch and supper she waited for lulls in the conversation to engage me and offer advice on how to comport myself at my next meeting. At first I found it charming, because I was flattered to have her attention, but it eventually became annoying to have such a young woman telling me how to behave. In order to avoid offending her I ordered several strong drinks, and by the end of the second I was back to my initial state of simply enjoying her company. By eight-thirty she could have slapped me in the face and I would have cherished the contact.

Eight-thirty, coincidentally, is when Dietrich announced it was time for us to take our leave and head to Freemason Hall. We stood, excused ourselves, and accepted the good wishes of our companions. As I attempted to disentangle myself from the surrounding chairs, Ms Alexander whispered some final tidbit of wisdom to me. But in my condition I could make no sense of it, so I smiled, nodded, and followed Dietrich outside.

Dietrich, too, was full of advice for me as we made our way to our appointment, but the effects of liquor still buoyed my spirit, and I was able to tune much of it out. After two blocks I asked if we were going to get a hackney cab, but he explained we were only a few minutes away by foot. When I asked how he knew where to go, he explained he had looked at a map earlier in the day, which of course meant that now the pattern of London was now and forever committed to his memory.

As we walked through the dank and pervasive fog, I felt droplets of water gathering on my face. The coolness started to revive me and clear my head. I very much wanted another drink to sustain my good mood, but there was none to be had, and Dietrich would not have allowed a quick stop at a pub. So we stayed on course and at ten minutes to nine found ourselves standing outside Freemason Hall.

The hall was a large structure set in the middle of the block along Great Queen Street. The façade, constructed in the classical style and replete with a portico of several arches and columns, stretched away to our left and right. It reminded me of a government building back home, ominous and sullen.

We came to a halt outside the large, wooden doors. Dietrich placed a hand on the brass handle and paused.

"You're clear on your role?"

"Oh, yes, of course," I said. I did not have the faintest idea what he was talking about, but I was sure it involved me speaking as little as possible.

He nodded once, cleared his throat, and opened the door.

Whereas the exterior attempted to overwhelm with gravity, the interior attempted the same with grandiosity. The foyer was broad and covered in tiles of black and white marble. Classical influences were still present, mainly in the columns that lined the walls and the intricate frieze above, which at a glance depicted a variety of mythical Greek figures. The foyer opened into a lobby that continued the same motif, and there, standing in the middle of the room, hands clasped behind his back and a smile on his face, patiently stood Mr

Ensley.

"Welcome," he said, stepping forward and shaking our hands for the second time that day. "Welcome to Freemason Hall. I trust you had no difficulty finding us?"

"None at all," replied Dietrich. "A quick walk from our hotel."

"Indeed," Ensley said. "Well, down to business. I asked you to come here tonight because there is much about Freemasonry that, while not secret, we nonetheless prefer to keep confidential. The café of your hotel was not a good place to continue such discussion. Also, as you are no doubt aware, Masons are looked upon by some with suspicion. Yet another reason we prefer to discuss our business in these halls."

"We understand completely," Dietrich said. "We are sorry if we put you in a compromising position."

Ensley waved a hand dismissively. He turned and began slowly strolling toward a pair of large doors at the far end of the lobby.

"That is behind us now," he said. "Please don't give it further thought. But now I would like to hear more about this investigation of yours, Mr Dietrich, which strangely has led you to us with questions about the Illuminati."

"There is not much more to tell," Dietrich said. "I am currently involved in an investigation in which a certain book was found containing references to the Illuminati, and some radical ideas for societal change. It is probably insignificant, but I have a duty to look into the matter."

We came to the large doors and Ensley opened them, ushering us inside. We passed into a large room that resembled a cross between a sanctuary and a theater. The floor was lined with pews on the left and right, and the ceiling was high, arched, and lined with balconies. At the head of the room a lectern stood upon a dais. The temple, as it was called, was decked out in gold and royal blue.

"And what is the title of this book?" Ensley asked.

Dietrich hesitated, then concluded it was of minor significance.

"*Ordo Ab Chao.*"

Ensley looked at him but said nothing. It was plain Dietrich had surprised him.

"Am I to understand you have this book in your possession?" Ensley asked.

"In a manner of speaking," Dietrich said. "It is back in New York."

"Have you read it?" Ensley asked.

Again Dietrich paused to consider his response.

"Yes, I have read it."

"So you know something of the Illuminati after all," Ensley said. "More than you led me to believe."

"Yes," Dietrich said. "Again, I apologize. As an investigator it is my habit not to reveal what I know until a decisive moment."

As we strolled down the center aisle I had been preoccupied with the temple's grandeur. It came as a surprise when I noticed another gentleman standing with his back to us at the far end of the room. He seemed to be staring into the space beyond, as if in thought. Otherwise, the sanctuary was entirely empty, and the voluminous space echoed our discussion. There could be no doubt he was hearing every word.

"And you chose to come to us," Ensley said. "Why?"

"To be honest, I have no other leads," Dietrich replied. "I hoped the U.G.L.E., the most venerable of Masonic institutions, might be able to tell me something about it, and its author. The Illuminati rose under Weishaupt, who we know began as a Mason."

"Yes," Ensley said. "But this is all history. I fail to see how any of this could be relevant today."

Dietrich sighed.

"Regrettably, I am not at liberty to discuss the details."

"I see," Ensley said, sounding unconvinced. "But it might be more expedient if you tell me what information you are seeking."

"Anything and everything about the Illuminati," Dietrich said. He really was not very good at conversation, much less interrogation. "But ultimately I wish to discover if you know of any present-day adherents."

At that moment a new voice chimed in—a strong and resonant voice that resounded throughout the hall with great presence. We all looked up and realized it had come from the man on the dais.

"If you are able to find modern adherents of that sect, you will have succeeded where the Masons have for a century failed."

The man turned to face us. He was tall and trim, and dignified, with graying hair and a robust but neatly-waxed moustache that turned sharply up at the ends. He wore a well-fitted dark suit, and over it his Masonic trappings: a necklace made from blue ribbon, from which dangled a golden insignia of the square and compass, and an intricately embroidered apron, all in blue and gold. Most notably, he wore a long, highly-polished sabre at his hip.

He looked down on us with keen eyes. I felt like a fieldmouse beneath the piercing gaze of a hawk.

"Gentlemen," Mr Ensley said. "I present the Grand Master of the United Grand Lodge of England, His Royal Highness, Prince Arthur, Duke of Connaught, Strathearn, and Earl of Sussex."

Dietrich and I were stricken dumb. Neither of us had anticipated a meeting with anyone other than Ensley. We were not mentally prepared to interrogate the Mason's Grand Master, much less a member of the Royal Family. We glanced between one another and Ensley for some clue of how to proceed. But Ensley was no help. In fact, I think he delighted in watching us squirm, probably his little way of exacting revenge after learning of our deception.

Prince Arthur, on the other hand, was like a statue. He stared at us, hands clasped behind his back, patiently awaiting a conclusion to our stammerings.

Eventually Ensley must have felt vindicated, because he spoke up and saved us from ourselves.

"Your Highness, these are the gentlemen I told you about, Mr Meyer Dietrich, with whom I have corresponded for several months, and his traveling companion, Mr Grey."

Prince Arthur nodded to each of us in turn. We each executed a half bow.

"It's an honor to meet you," Dietrich said. "I hope you will excuse our poor manners. This is most unexpected."

"Do not worry yourselves," Prince Arthur said. "I may descend from the Royal line, but as the Queen's fourth son, the throne was never in my future. I made my career as a military man, and that is how I think of myself."

Dietrich and I nodded appreciatively. But even though the Prince had let us off the hook, he continued to look down his nose at us.

"We were just discussing the purpose of their visit," Ensley interjected.

"Yes, I heard," the Prince said. "It intrigues me that you have come to us for information. Most consider the Illuminati extinct. And even during their time they were not part of any Masonic brotherhood."

"True," Dietrich said, recovering. "But they were founded by Adam Weishaupt, who was himself a Mason, for a time."

"And a Bavarian," the Prince said. "The United Grand Lodge has no jurisdiction over, or direct affiliation with, lodges outside the United Kingdom."

"Yes," Dietrich agreed.

"Then why come to us?"

"It seemed wise," Dietrich replied. "Germany might be the more logical place to start, but we had no leads there."

"And random inquiries would arouse suspicion," the Prince said.

"Precisely."

"If the Illuminati still exist, that is," the Prince said.

"I hoped the Masons might be able to direct us," Dietrich said, "to any contacts, native or foreign, who might enlighten us."

"A vain hope," the Prince said. "The Illuminati are conspirators of a bygone era. Today, most Masons dismiss them outright."

"Most?" Dietrich asked.

"There are a few who believe the Illuminati never perished," the Prince said. "They believe the sect went into hiding and continues to influence world affairs to this day."

"If that is true, I share the concern of the few," Dietrich said.

"But these Masons are a mere fraction," the Prince said, "a vast minority among the many who scoff at such ideas."

"A dangerous attitude if the threat were to prove real," Dietrich replied.

"Yes," the Prince agreed. "Unfortunately, some of the believers are of such lofty position that they cannot speak publicly on the subject. To do so would be a suicide of reputation."

"I begin to understand the complexity of the situation," Dietrich said, "both within the brotherhood and the nation. It is a tricky business."

"It is," the Prince replied.

Dietrich clasped his hands behind his back and stared at the floor. It was apparent he was pursuing a line of thought, which under other circumstances would have been nothing unusual. But his silence dragged on for an uncomfortable amount of time, and it struck me as terribly rude to indulge in a flight of intellectual fancy, altogether ignoring the Prince. I began to edge toward him, hoping to bring him out of his meditation. Suddenly he raised a finger.

"However, if an outside party were to investigate the matter and provide its findings, that would allow *the few* to find out if their concerns are justified or unwarranted."

Prince Arthur considered it for a moment.

"Yes. That would be a mutually beneficial arrangement."

"*The few* would reap the benefits of such an inquiry with little risk," Dietrich said.

"Little risk?" queried the Prince.

"Forgive me," Dietrich said. "No risk."

Prince Arthur held Dietrich with his steely gaze for a long time, as if looking into his soul. And, suddenly, I had the strange feeling he could see into our souls, and that he knew everything we knew, and everything about us and our mission, in spite of all Dietrich's double-talk. A chill ran down my spine.

"Mr Ensley," the Prince said.

"Sir?"

"Whom do we know who might possess such esoteric knowledge?"

Ensley thought on it, but his furrowed brow revealed he was stymied.

"I'm afraid I can think of no reputable person who might possess such information."

"Disreputable, then," the Prince said.

Ensley thought on it a moment longer.

"I can think of no one," he said finally. But in the next instant he brightened. "On second thought, there is *you know who.*"

The prince regarded him strangely. It was the only time during our encounter that I detected even the slightest crack in his patrician façade. For a moment he looked puzzled. Then his eyes flickered before rolling in their sockets.

"Surely there is someone else."

"Regrettably, I can think of no other," Ensley replied.

The Prince frowned and thought it over. Finally, he sighed and looked at Dietrich.

"There might be one who can help you, but I am loathe to send you to him. I cannot vouch for his veracity."

"If he might be of help, we will gladly meet him," Dietrich said eagerly.

"Very well," the Prince said. "Mr Ensley will arrange it."

"Of course," Ensley said with a half bow. "At once."

We sensed it was time to go. Dietrich and I followed Ensley's example, each bowing slightly at the waist. But as we turned to depart, Prince Arthur spoke.

"Mr Dietrich, you guarantee anonymity?"

"I do," Dietrich said.

Prince Arthur casually placed a hand on the hilt of his saber.

"Let's hope so," he said.

Dietrich and I stood in the lobby while Ensley rummaged through his office for information on our next contact. Since we had a moment alone I took the opportunity to compliment him on his handling of the situation.

"Well played!" I said. "I'm not sure what happened in there, but you played the Prince like a fiddle."

Dietrich was taken aback.

"I did no such thing," he said. "If anything it was the Masons who played us today."

"How's that?"

"Come now," he said, looking at me in disbelief. "The Prince's presence here tonight was no coincidence. Everything was arranged, otherwise it would not have gone so smoothly."

I still was not following what he was saying—or not saying, as it were.

"I'm sorry, but I don't have the knack for this double-talk and second-guessing," I said. "What are you talking about?"

He smirked and studied me for a moment, as if he thought I was joking. His smirk faded once he realized I was tragically ignorant. He glanced at the doorway through which Ensley had disappeared before continuing.

"Very well," he said. "After our meeting this afternoon, Mr Ensley obviously reported to the Prince, who secretly believes the Illuminati still exist. But the Prince cannot admit this because it would make him a laughingstock, and he would lose credibility. Rather than risk exposing himself as a paranoiac, he struck a deal with us to investigate the matter for him. All he asks is that we keep his name out of it, and that we report back to him with our findings."

I reflected on our meeting and could not recall any of these points being discussed. But my bafflement became secondary as a larger concern surfaced.

"So now we're working for the President *and* the Royal Family? Isn't that a conflict of interests? What would Cross say, or for that matter Roosevelt?"

"A moot point," Dietrich replied. "We revealed nothing they would not have surmised from the nature of our questions."

"Ah."

It was finally starting to make sense, so I was happy to let it drop. But Dietrich was still wound up.

"We have been exceptionally lucky today," he said, sounding uncharacteristically jubilant.

"How so?"

"Our first, and greatest, stroke of luck came when my letters, sent blindly to the U.G.L.E., found their way to Mr Ensley," he explained. "He is clearly a believer in the Illuminati, and a stalwart supporter of the Prince."

"And why is that lucky?"

"You heard the Prince," he replied. "There are but a few who would have taken the matter seriously. If my letters had found someone other than Ensley, we would not be standing here right now."

I mulled it over.

"If that was our first stroke, then what was the second?"

"Oddly, I think it was your outburst at our meeting this afternoon," Dietrich replied.

"Really?" I stood a little straighter and smoothed my lapels.

"Yes," Dietrich said. "Until that moment Mr Ensley and I were involved in a game, each trying to determine the other's true mind. Eventually I would have got around to revealing our real interest, but only after easing into it. But I think your bluntness paid off, because he got from you what he did not expect to get from me."

"And that is?"

"A straight answer," Dietrich said. "By asking him so plainly about the Illuminati, you accelerated events. Ensley came straight back here and informed the Prince, who immediately took an interest in us."

"In that case, I'm glad to have been of service."

Dietrich shot me a look that was half warning, half amusement.

"Remember, it was luck," he said. "Please do not *impose* your luck on us again without warning."

I grinned and executed a mock bow. Then a final question came to mind.

"Neither the Prince nor Ensley ever asked me a thing. I wonder why they requested my presence?"

Dietrich turned away, looking again for a sign of Ensley. He did not seem prepared to answer, which was fine since my question had been rhetorical. But then he began to fidget as if pressured, and at last he turned to me.

"Again, you may credit your bluntness," he said. "I think they wanted you here in case I proved intractable. Ensley hoped you might blurt out something revealing."

"So, my role tonight was to play The Fool."

Dietrich looked away and said nothing. A moment later Ensley returned, walking at a quick pace.

"I apologize for the wait," he said. "But this was a contact I never thought I would call upon. It took me some time to find it. I hope it proves useful to you."

He handed Dietrich a small card with some printing on it. Dietrich accepted and stared at it.

"This man is a Mason?"

"An irregular," Ensley replied. "He fancies himself a Mason, but none of the *several* lodges to which he belongs are recognized by the U.G.L.E. In fact, it is due to his mystical quest, his desire to unlock all of life's mysteries, that I think he might be able to help you. He has traveled to diverse parts of the world in his pursuit of the occult, and he has made many questionable and sordid acquaintances."

"I see," Dietrich said.

"But when you meet him, don't be fooled by his strange manners," Ensley said. "For all his ridiculous eccentricities he is quite intelligent. Devilishly so, in fact."

Dietrich nodded and sank into thought. I was about to inquire about this mysterious person when Ensley distracted me.

"By the way, Mr Grey, what is it you do back in America?"

Always an enjoyable question to answer! I pondered my possible responses. I decided in this case to go with the most glamorous.

"I'm a Vaudeville performer in New York."

"Vaudeville?" Ensley said, for the first time seeming genuinely interested in me. "In what capacity?"

I stood up a little straighter.

"I'm an escape artist."

"Really?" he exclaimed. "How fascinating! What an exciting profession it must be. I hear Harry Houdini is also from New York. Do you know him?"

I gritted my teeth against the torrent of expletives that came rushing forth. I then organized my expression to mimic a smile. Dietrich—bless him—came to my rescue.

"Thank you, Mr Ensley," he said. "But it is getting late and we must be going. I promise a discreet report on anything we find in the course of our inquiry."

He hooked his arm through mine, spun me around, and led me from the hall. Outside I thanked him, and I eventually got around to asking him whom we were going to meet next. But he did not answer. Instead, he passed me the small card. I had to wait until we passed beneath the next streetlamp to make it out, and even then the fog did its best to interfere with the deciphering. However, I finally managed to catch enough light to make out the writing.

Mr Aleister Crowley
21 Warwick Road, London

11: THE WICKEDEST MAN IN THE WORLD

I never fully appreciated the labyrinth of London until the fog lifted the next day, and we went in search of Crowley's residence. Once we got away from the center of the city and its many distinguished buildings, we were faced with a maze of row houses, block after block of tall thin structures that went on without end. Our driver seemed to know where he was going, but London was so confusing he could have driven us around in circles and we would have been none the wiser.

"Who is this Crowley gentleman we are going to see?" Ms Alexander asked.

When Dietrich and I had returned from our meeting with Prince Arthur the night before, it was too late to summon everyone to a meeting. Instead we waited until morning, and Dietrich gave our account over breakfast. Irish was bored by our tale, but Ms Alexander found it fascinating. She was particularly interested when we mentioned Prince Arthur, and she insisted that we describe everything about him in painstaking detail. I must confess it irritated me to be called upon to describe another man to her, so I let Dietrich do most of the talking.

By the time Crowley's name came up we were climbing into a coach. I had never heard of him. Fortunately Dietrich had already acquired some knowledge of the man.

"He is an odd fellow by all accounts. He began his career as a poet of some ability, though his primary interest now lies in cosmic mysteries. He has made it his life's ambition to get at *all* truths, especially those that are hidden."

"Hence his fascination with the Masons," I said.

"Yes," Dietrich said. "In order to peer into all corners of existence, he has also invested a great deal of energy in exploring the occult."

"The occult?" Ms Alexander exclaimed. Her tone and expression revealed that she found the idea deeply disturbing.

"Yes," Dietrich said, not noticing her discomfiture. "In fact, he has written several texts on the subject."

"He sounds sinister," Ms Alexander said. "And this occult business makes me uneasy. I hope you will not mind if I wait outside while you interview him."

Dietrich looked at her with a small amount of surprise.

"Oh," he said. "Of course. Hopefully it will not take long to get the information we seek."

We eventually pulled up in front of a row of houses like any other and picked out number twenty-one. Dietrich, Irish and I dismounted the coach and started for the door. Half way up the walk Dietrich stopped and turned to Irish.

"You wish to accompany us?" he asked.

"Well, yeah," Irish said. "I didn't come all this way for nothing."

"I understand," Dietrich said. "But I wonder if this is the best time."

"What do you mean?" Irish asked.

"You are very imposing," Dietrich explained. "Crowley does not know we are coming. I worry the sight of you might disturb him, making him less cooperative."

Irish thought about it. I could see in the way his eyes darted around he was looking for a logical and well-reasoned argument that would allow him to continue. But there was simply no denying the fact that he was huge, and he would probably alarm anyone at whose door he unexpectedly knocked. Finally he accepted it. He sighed and his great shoulders sagged.

"Yeah, alright," he said.

"Not to worry," I said, clapping him on the shoulder. "Your time will come."

He stalked back to the coach and leaned against it, rolling a cigarette and moping.

"So it's you and me again, eh?" I said cheerfully. Dietrich and I may not have been boon companions, but I appreciated the fact that he had no objection to my company.

"So it would seem," he said quietly. "Though if you want to wait in the cab, I have no objection."

"No, I'm fine," I said. "Besides, Crowley sounds like a real character. I'm curious to meet him."

Dietrich nodded and we proceeded up the walk. He rapped at the door and we waited.

"Have you already worked out what to say?" I asked.

"I have imagined several scenarios," he said. "But if Crowley is as colorful as his reputation suggests…"

We waited a full minute and received no response to repeated knockings. But we were sure we heard a clattering sound emanating from somewhere within. Dietrich knocked again with greater insistence. In the silence that followed we again heard a commotion, this time accompanied by an eerie moan that made the hair stand up on the back of my neck. I began to wonder if Crowley had not gone too far in his occult practices and summoned an apparition. Dietrich, on the other hand, frowned and knocked harder than before. At the end of this series the door finally opened with an eerie creak.

The creature that opened the door almost made me turn tail and run. I first thought it was some morose spirit, as pale and bedraggled as it was. It almost seemed to hover before us, framed against the utter darkness beyond, its loose-fitting lace nightgown billowing as if stirred by an otherworldly breeze. But Dietrich did not flee, so I steeled myself against the chilling effect. And I was glad I did, because after a second glance I realized the ghostly figure was actually a young woman, delicate in feature and as pale as a corpse. Whatever feminine allure she possessed, however, was overwhelmed by her more disturbing qualities: her long, dark and unkempt hair; her wide, dark-circled, staring eyes; and her thin, bone-white hands, one of which she raised and pointed right at me.

"You are not my husband!" she exclaimed. "Has he sent you to torment me, to put me away in some asylum? By Horus, I will not go! Lay a hand on me and you will be cursed!"

The combination of her deathly appearance and her unholy curse caused me to take a step back. But while I was transfixed by her accusatory finger, Dietrich looked to her other hand, half concealed as it was by her generous gown. Then the girl collapsed forward into his arms, followed immediately by the sound of breaking glass. I looked down to find a bottle shattered on the stoop.

"Help me with her," Dietrich said.

Together we struggled to lift her and keep her away from the shards at our feet. But in spite of her slight frame she was unnaturally heavy, and neither of us was accustomed to managing such dead weight. I grabbed her legs and we haphazardly succeeded in lifting her off the ground, but then I twisted her in such a way that almost wrenched her out Dietrich's hands. She would have spilled to the ground if Irish had not been watching and quickly rushed to our aid. In one scoop he had her safely cradled in his arms.

"Bring her inside," Dietrich said.

Dietrich and Irish disappeared into the darkness of the house, but I was hesitant to enter. After all our talk of the occult, combined with the blackness within, I feared something evil might be lurking inside. Then Dietrich began to pull heavy curtains back from the windows, and the interior became brighter as a sullen light seeped inside.

The interior was much as one would expect to find in an old London home. The spaces were small but quaintly furnished, and aside from the heavy curtains the house's formal décor was the standard fare. In fact, the whole scene struck me as rather unremarkable for the home of an occultist, and in that respect I was disappointed. As for the informal decorations, they were ubiquitous and abundant. Every flat surface contained a variety of empty liquor bottles, and the flattest surface in the house—the floor—was strewn with them. One could hardly take a step without inadvertently sending one clattering across the floor.

"I guess that explains the noises," I said, sidling up beside Dietrich and Irish.

The two men were standing over the unconscious woman, whom Irish had deposited on a chaise lounge in the living room. Dietrich bent over her and felt her forehead, her cheeks, and then took her hands.

"She is inebriated, and very cold," he said. "She probably passed out on the floor."

I found a decorative blanket—embroidered with an ancient Egyptian figure, a man with a falcon's head—and placed it over her. Dietrich stooped to examine the bottles.

"She is clearly an alcoholic."

"A prodigious one at that," I said, admiring the quantity and variety.

"Would you dispose of them, before one of us breaks his neck?" Dietrich asked.

While Irish and I collected bottles, Dietrich continued to rub the young woman's hands in an attempt to wake her. Eventually she started to come around, but she only repeated her previous performance.

"Release me, worm! You know not whom you touch. I am a high priestess of Nuit, Goddess of Death and the Eternal Night Sky, Queen of Space. Retreat, before Shezmu, Lord of Blood and Slaughterer of Souls, carries you to Hell!"

She rolled away from Dietrich and again became insensible.

"I hope those are empty curses," I said, "because they are beginning to pile up around us."

Dietrich actually chuckled. A moment later Irish returned.

"I checked through the house," he said. No one else is here."

Dietrich rubbed his chin and studied the woman.

"If I were to guess, I'd say Crowley left some time ago, and this woman is his estranged wife," he said.

"What now?" Irish asked.

"We wait," Dietrich said. "Let her sleep off some of it. Maybe we can get a sensible word out of her then."

He seated himself in an armchair next to the woman, and Irish and I shrugged and went off on our own errands. Irish went to the kitchen and began rummaging for food, and I returned to the coach to update Ms Alexander.

"Crowley is gone," I said. "Dietrich believes for good. The young lady inside is drunk out of her mind. We're waiting for her to regain enough sense to speak to us intelligently."

"I see," she said with a small sigh.

"We may be here a while," I said. "You might want to come inside."

She glanced at the house.

"No, thank you. I will wait here."

I glanced at the driver, who was politely pretending not to listen.

"He is no doubt charging us," I said. "Are you sure you don't want to come inside?"

Ms Alexander leaned her head out the window.

"We may be here for some time. I intend to wait here. You need not worry about the fare. I will pay for your time."

The driver leaned over, looked down at her, and tipped his hat.

"Much appreciated, Miss," he said.

"There, it is taken care of," she said, leveling her eyes at me.

I sighed.

"If it was our earlier mention of the occult that makes you uneasy, we've been through the house and found nothing unusual about it."

"Perhaps not," she replied. "But just as a haunted house may look normal, it can possess an altogether different feel. And there is a feeling about this place that makes me uncomfortable. I will wait here."

I thought her misgivings were all imagined. But there was no point arguing with a determined woman, so I spent the next half hour wandering between the coach and the house, checking on the status of both women, keeping one entertained and awaiting the awakening of the other.

When Mrs Crowley finally awoke she was a different person. For the first time she did not rouse from her soporific slumber spewing archaic curses. Instead, she replaced them with such an uncontrollable and disconsolate wailing that I feared she would bring the police. Dietrich tried his best to quiet her, but as we were strangers she was not much interested in what we had to say. Soon Irish joined in, holding her down for fear she might hurt herself, which only caused her caterwauling to intensify as if we were holding her down for a branding. Without consulting anyone Dietrich concluded our only recourse was to gag her, and he was in the process of pressing a handkerchief over her mouth when a voice came from behind.

"Gentlemen, what is going on in here?"

We were all shocked to find Ms Alexander standing in the archway to the living room. Apparently Mrs Crowley's incessant howling had generated enough curiosity that our lady finally had overcome her fear of evil spirits. And to her eyes we must have made an interesting tableau, with Irish holding the grieving woman down, Dietrich holding a handkerchief over her mouth, and me, hopping around the periphery unsure of what to do.

"Mr Irish, release her!" she commanded. "Mr Dietrich, I hope you intend to offer her that handkerchief to dry her tears. And Mr Grey, make yourself useful and get her something to drink."

We all followed her orders to the letter. Dietrich and Irish both stepped aside, and surprisingly the woman, who had been thrashing against our best efforts to comfort her, simply rolled over on her side and sobbed. Ms Alexander calmly approached her, and though I could read in her face the discomfort she felt, she seated herself at the woman's side.

"Mr Grey, a drink?" she reminded me.

I hurried off to the kitchen. As I absentmindedly prepared a drink, I marveled over her ability to so effortlessly gain control of the situation. I was leaving the kitchen when I realized I had poured a glass of gin, probably not the best panacea for a forlorn alcoholic. I quickly downed it myself, refilled the glass with water, and headed back to the living room.

During my absence nothing more had transpired, though the woman seemed to have calmed down a bit. She still wept, but her emotion now took the form of a lot of sniffling, and wiping of her eyes and nose with Dietrich's handkerchief. Ms Alexander still sat poised at her side.

"Here's the water," I said.

Ms Alexander set it on a small table nearby. She then placed a gentle hand on the woman's shoulder.

"My dear, what's your name?" she asked.

The woman half turned to face us.

"Rose," she said. "Rose Crowley. Who are you?"

"My name is Katherine Alexander, and these gentlemen are my friends. We came here to see Mr Crowley, but I take it he is not here."

"No," she said, her weeping intensifying for a moment. "He doesn't live here. We've separated."

"I am sorry to hear that," Ms Alexander replied. "Is there any way we can help?"

Dietrich, Irish and I looked at each other. We did not know what she had in mind, but the idea of taking a side in the Crowleys' marital dispute was not on our agenda. Dietrich bravely took it upon himself to intervene.

"Pardon me, but this is not what we came for—"

"Gentlemen," Ms Alexander cut him off. "Please do us the courtesy of waiting elsewhere."

It was as if a door had been slammed in Dietrich's face. He merely looked at us, shrugged, and went in search of somewhere to wait it out. Neither Irish nor I was willing to earn her scorn so we dutifully followed.

We sat in silence around the table in the dining room. Occasionally I overheard small bits of conversation interspersed with bouts of weeping. Half an hour passed before Ms Alexander appeared in the doorway.

"What's going on?" I asked.

"I am awaiting Mrs Crowley to finish a letter," she said.

"What sort of letter?" Dietrich asked.

"The personal sort," she replied. "I asked if there was anything we could do to help. She asked that we convey a letter to Mr Crowley."

"Mr Crowley?" Dietrich said, becoming more interested. "Where is he?"

"He moved to Paris several months ago."

"Paris?" Dietrich said, rubbing his chin and descending into thought.

"Yes," Ms Alexander replied. "He is at 50 Rue Vavin."

"Paris," he repeated. "I guess there is no way around it."

"Don't sound so disappointed," I said. "I'm sure there are worse places to go. Of course I've never been there, but I hear it's remarkable."

"It is wonderful," Ms Alexander confirmed. "Perhaps one of the most beautiful places on Earth. I lived there for some time. I for one will welcome it after gloomy London."

"When do we leave?" Irish asked.

"We have no further business here," Dietrich replied. "We will leave as soon as I can make arrangements."

He craned his neck to look past Ms Alexander into the living room.

"How much longer before she's done with that letter?" he asked.

Ms Alexander arched an eyebrow.

"As long as she requires," she said evenly.

"I must say, I was both thankful and surprised when you intervened," I said. "In the cab you seemed set against coming in here."

"Some instincts are more powerful than others," she replied. "My spiritual instinct told me I should have nothing to do with this house or its inhabitants, but no woman could in good conscience ignore another's cries of agony."

"Really?"

"Yes," she said. "Now excuse me while I check on Mrs Crowley."

She returned to the living room. Since the rest of us had no further purpose in the house, we stood and marched outside to wait by the coach. Soon Ms Alexander followed, quietly closing the door behind her.

"I convinced her to call a doctor, to have someone check on her state of health," she said.

"She'll probably be back at the bottle within the hour," I said.

Ms Alexander shot me an unpleasant look.

"There is no need for such callousness," she said. "I for one will pray she overcomes her demons."

"Of course," I said. "I only meant that in her condition—"

But she did not wait to hear the rest. At her approach the driver leapt down and opened the door. She politely declined his help and climbed in. The rest of us followed, and once aboard the driver clicked his tongue and snapped the reigns. I watched out the window as the morose house of Crowley passed out of sight.

The same afternoon Dietrich wired Cross about our plans and arranged our travel to Paris for the following day. First we would take a train to the coast, then travel by ferry to the continent, then board another train for the City of Lights. The entire trip would take one day.

I heaved a sigh at the thought of another day consumed with travel. We had arrived in London only two days before, and only after a week at sea. No matter how dreary London might be, it was a relief to stay put for a while, and to have a room to call one's own. But as Dietrich pointed out, there was no way around it. We needed to talk with Crowley, so it was time to move on.

The train ride to the coast was so brief that it hardly warrants mentioning. The part that was worth mentioning, however, was that as we approached the ocean the air cleared and the English countryside was laid out before us. It was like stepping from night into day. We were all dazzled by sunlight and rolling green hills. And we were especially thankful when, as the ferry set off across the channel for Calais, we were able to look back on the strange majesty of Dover's bone-white cliffs.

We landed in Calais around noon, and from there everything became hectic. The ferry docked fifteen minutes behind schedule, and we had a train to catch. We had to compete with all the other passengers for the cabs and coaches in waiting, but Dietrich eventually managed to secure one for us. By then we were so far behind schedule we feared we would not make our train. Slipping the driver a few extra francs did wonders to get us back on schedule. We made the train to Paris with only minutes to spare.

It was during this leg of our journey that I realized Ms Alexander had literally grown closer to us, or at least to me. It did not occur to me until I was sitting beside her on the train, almost elbow to elbow, and she showed no trace of concern, no obvious fear of proximity. This was a marked improvement of her behavior since our introduction.

We arrived in Paris in late afternoon, and once we had collected our bags and ourselves, Dietrich deferred to Ms Alexander since she was the only one among us who spoke French. This delighted her because it gave her an excuse to practice a language that had gone neglected for some time. But no matter how long it had gone unused, once dusted off she spoke as fluently as any of the natives. And of course her beauty and manners had porters, cab drivers, and clerks leaping over one another to attend us. We made it to our hotel, the Plaza Athénée, in record time, and we were enjoying dinner in the hotel restaurant as the sun began to set.

"What is next, Mr Dietrich?" Ms Alexander inquired.

"I'm glad you asked," he said. "Because I have a very aggressive plan which begins this very night. I learned from the *maître d'* that Crowley's address is no more than a short cab ride from here."

"Back to work," I said, "and so soon after arriving. I had hoped we would have a chance to recuperate."

I read the same sentiment in the expressions of Irish and Ms Alexander. Dietrich must have seen the same, because he somewhat relented.

"On second thought, I will only need the assistance of one of you," he said. "Mr Grey will suffice."

"Me?" I said. "Why?"

He glanced at Ms Alexander, then back at me.

"Because of your knowledge of spiritualism," he said in a low voice.

Out of the corner of my eye I saw Ms Alexander look inquisitively my way.

"Ah, of course," I replied. "Say no more."

And I was sincere—I wanted him to say no more on the subject. My capitalistic venture into spiritualism was the source of my downfall and shame. And considering Ms Alexander's devout Christian faith, and her apparent disdain of the occult, I did not want to reveal that piece of my past.

"So you will accompany me, then?" Dietrich asked.

"Absolutely," I cried, more to get off the subject than out of genuine desire.

We finished our dinner, and I could tell Ms Alexander was itching to ask me questions. And she tried, too. But each time I either interrupted her or changed the subject to prevent a precipitous fall from her grace.

Dietrich hailed a cab outside the hotel. As we were climbing into it, Ms Alexander hurried out to see us off. By the way she scurried, I half expected her to throw her arms around my neck and hug me. Then I noticed something in her hand, which she began waving as she crossed the sidewalk.

"The letter," she said, holding out an envelope. "From Mrs Crowley. Please deliver it."

I accepted it even as Dietrich gave the address to the driver. We were off before either of us could say another word.

The cab headed in a southerly direction from the Plaza Athénée and soon crossed the River Seine, which was busy with all manner of boats coming and going. We crossed by means of the Pont Alexander III bridge, the most exquisitely detailed structure for crossing water I had ever witnessed. In America, especially in New York, bridges impressed by magnitude and scale, but in Paris they seemed as ornate as the finest works of art. At least that is how the Pont Alexander III bridge appeared, with its gilded cherubs, sylphs, and winged horses dancing atop massive stone socles. To add to the spectacle, as we crossed the bridge we glanced out our right window and received an impressive view of the Eiffel Tower silhouetted against the darkening sky.

"I can understand why Crowley gave up London for Paris," I said, marveling at the view. "Though London's murky atmosphere seemed better suited for witchcraft."

"That reminds me," Dietrich said. "I apologize if I put you in an awkward position at dinner. I did not want to go into detail about that part of your career. While I do not approve of your past, I did not want to use it to pollute your present, if you follow me."

"I follow," I said. "Thanks, and I appreciate your candor, inasmuch as you were able to be candid about it. But judging by the look Ms Alexander gave me, I think the cat is out of the bag. I will have to deliver an account sooner or later."

Dietrich nodded and went back to looking out the window. I was a trifle irritated at him for jeopardizing my relationship with her, but I could tell he was genuinely sorry to have put me on the spot. And that made an impression on me since, over the last few days, I had felt a kinship with him, as if we were finally becoming friends.

We came to a halt in front of a large, tiered building of white stone. Dietrich paid our fare and we stepped inside, finding ourselves in an expansive courtyard overlooked by apartments. As we took the place in, thin, scratchy music wafted down to us from a phonograph somewhere above.

"Not what I expected," I said. "Which one's Crowley's?"

Before Dietrich could give it any thought we received our answer. A spectacle of a man happened to descend the stairs. He was young but paunchy, and deathly pale with unnaturally black hair that matched his casual suit. Upon his face he wore an expression of such smug superiority, it was as if he owned all of Paris. Somehow, I knew this grim fop would know Crowley.

"Pardon me," I said, forgetting that French was the language of the realm. "Can you direct us to the apartment of Mr Aleister Crowley?"

The man stopped several steps above, though his musky perfume continued to waft down over us. The fumes caused Dietrich to choke, which elicited a smirk from the eerie young man.

"And you are?" he asked in a French accent.

"Americans," I said. "Prometheus Grey, and my colleague is Mr Dietrich."

He eyed Dietrich suspiciously.

"You, sir, look like a policeman."

"I'm not a policeman," Dietrich replied coldly.

"Then what are you?" he inquired archly.

"Students!" I said, grasping the first idea that came to mind. "We wish to learn the mysteries of the universe."

"Ah!" the fop said, casually placing one hand in a coat pocket as if posing for a portrait. "Then you've come to penetrate the darkness? If so, I hope you find your lesson as stimulating as I found mine."

I looked at him expectantly, but he only smirked in reply. In fact, he did not look as if he intended to tell us anything. He filled the silence by producing a long, thin cigarette and tapping it lightly against its case. Then a voice came down from above.

"Who is it, Laurent?"

A man in a black satin dressing gown stared at us from a landing several tiers up.

The younger man inclined his head but kept his eyes on us.

"They're here for you," he said. "They say they're students."

"Students? That can't be. I have no more lessons for another hour."

An awkwardness settled over us. I was sure we had roused their suspicions. Then the man above called out.

"Send them up and I'll get to the bottom of it," he said, and he disappeared from the rail.

The one called Laurent grinned at us wickedly.

"Number six-six-six," he said with a wink. He then departed, though the pungency of his cologne clung to us for several more minutes.

We climbed the stairs to the sixth floor and followed the walkway around until we came to what should have been apartment sixty-six, but someone had mischievously scrawled an additional "6" upon the door. I was instantly thankful Ms Alexander had not accompanied us. I shuddered to imagine her reaction at this mockery. Dietrich knocked, a voice called out "Come!", and we let ourselves in.

We walked into the most bizarre domicile I had ever encountered. The apartment was simply furnished but elaborately decorated with all manner of occult paraphernalia. The walls were adorned with an assortment of paintings and sketches depicting Egyptian drawings, astrological and other mythical symbols. The whole house appeared to function as a library, as every wall contained a shelf of some sort populated with a variety of dusty tomes. And scattered throughout in an orderly manner were a variety of suggestive knick-knacks: colored potion bottles, half-burnt candles, Tarot cards, a pair of jewel-handled daggers, manacles. The remaining surfaces of the room were home to Crowley's many papers—uncountable letters and perverse sketches littered the desk and tables. In fact, the only clear surface seemed to be a chessboard atop a small table by the window, the pieces neatly arranged in their starting positions. But of course even this had been altered to reflect Crowley's personality—the black pieces were modeled after demons and devils, and the white after morose and arabesque Christian saints.

And in the midst of it all sat our host. He had thinning dark hair that he wore combed back. He was thin of limb but round in the belly, which made him look rather like a caricature. Of peculiar interest, however, was that the man, whom we had seen only moments before looking disheveled in a dressing gown, had magically cleaned up and donned a suit. He sat in a high-backed chair, his rapt attention upon an ancient-looking tome in one hand. He looked as if he had been there for hours in deep, contemplative thought.

"Mr Crowley, I presume?" asked Dietrich.

Crowley raised a hand to halt the interruption. He continued to gaze into the book for a long, uncomfortable time before finally regarding us with exaggerated disinterest.

"Yes?" he said.

"I am Mr Dietrich, and this is my partner, Mr Grey—"

"Ah, yes," he said, snapping the book closed. "The *students*." He crossed his legs and leaned on one hand.

"Er, yes," Dietrich replied. "We are students, in a sense."

"In a sense?" Crowley asked, arching an eyebrow.

"Yes," Dietrich replied. "Though not in the capacity you might presume."

"And what might I presume?" Crowley asked waspishly.

"That we are students of the occult," Dietrich explained. "We are seekers of mysteries, but the mysteries that interest us are those of Man."

"The mysteries of Man are inexorably tangled in the occult," Crowley said. He glanced out the window briefly, then whipped his head back to us. "To deny it is to embrace ignorance."

"Perhaps, but—"

Crowley tossed up a hand.

"I abhor ignorance," he said, "especially of a willful nature. And it would be willfully ignorant of me to continue this meeting without a better explanation of who you are, and why you are here."

Dietrich hesitated. He was not used to being toyed with.

"We are from New York—" he began.

"Yes, Americans," Crowley said, idly rotating a wrist round and round. "Your speech gave that much away."

"—and we are seeking information on the Masons."

Crowley froze, his hand in mid flourish.

"The Masons?"

"Yes," Dietrich said. "I am involved in a matter that is intertwined in their history. I hoped you might be able to answer some questions for me."

Crowley gripped the arms of his chair and drew back like a snake about to strike.

"How dare you ask me to betray the brotherhood!" he hissed.

"I'm not asking you to betray anyone," Dietrich insisted.

But Crowley would not allow his indignation to be assuaged.

"I achieved Grand Master status only after much study, sacrifice, and swearing of oaths. Do you think I would betray that trust? Do you presume I would divulge the Brotherhood's secrets at the drop of a hat?"

"No—" Dietrich said.

"Wait!" Crowley exclaimed. "It is true that I am a Mason, and a Grand Master privy to their deepest secrets. But *who* told *you*? Who *betrayed* me?"

Here I witnessed a most memorable occasion. Dietrich was speechless. It was clear he had never encountered anyone as clever and dramatic as Crowley. As he tried to choose a new path of inquiry, he began to stammer. Sheer nonsensical noise began to erupt from his lips as if awkwardness could be staved off simply by filling the silence.

I winced. It was like witnessing a runaway wagon, loaded with fine and irreplaceable crystal, lose its wheels one at a time. It was such an unpleasant experience that even Crowley, who had at first grinned wickedly at the consternation he had caused, soon scowled in annoyance.

While this transpired I had an epiphany. Crowley was not as offended as he pretended to be. His sinister smiles, provocative words, and paranoid accusations were all part of a grand spectacle, a phenomenon to which I, as a man of the stage, was no stranger. In that moment he became transparent to me. At heart he too was a performer, and opportunity—any encounter that allowed him to shock or confound—was his stage.

"Sir," I said stepping forward, "no one has betrayed you, at least not to us."

His scowl slowly faded. He began to look interested again.

"Allow me to introduce myself," I said. "I'm—"

"Mr Grey," he said. "Yes, I know. *He* said as much."

"True," I said. "But Mr Dietrich didn't tell you *what* I am."

"And what exactly are you?"

I hesitated to add suspense. I could tell I had piqued his curiosity, even though he tried not to show it.

"Prometheus Grey, escape artist, spiritualist, and magician, at your service," I said with a bow.

He eyed me in silence. I could tell he had not expected me to be so surprising and prolific.

"Prometheus Grey?" he said, narrowing his eyes. "Never heard of you."

"Perhaps not," I said with a chuckle, "but I'm well known in New York, and not without cause. I'm a man of many talents."

"So it would seem by your many titles," Crowley said, folding his hands and leaning forward slightly. "Tell me, what sort of magic do you practice?"

"The magic of escape, mainly," I said, "because I have a knack for it. But it does not preclude a fascination with, and active interest in, other forms."

Crowley studied me for a moment as if considering his next move. I felt as if I were sitting at his chessboard.

"You speak rather obtusely of magic," he said. "Tell me, are you familiar with *sex magick*?"

Dietrich and I exchanged nervous glances.

"Er, no—"

Unexpectedly, he turned his attention back to Dietrich.

"What is it you want from me?" he said pointedly.

"We wish to know …"

Dietrich inexplicably trailed off into silence. I regarded him, wondering what tactic he was employing, but when he met my eyes I saw he was flummoxed.

"You wish to know what?" Crowley demanded impatiently. "Now is the time to speak plainly, to put aside the verbal jousting and be clear. If you want me to help you in any way, be forthright with me now!"

I knew then that we would not be able to delude him. We had come to him blindly and stupidly, believing through the strength of our convictions that we could pry answers out of him. But he was too clever.

And Dietrich knew it, too. He looked at me desperately. I shrugged in response. He cleared his throat and took a moment to collect himself.

"Mr Crowley, we wish to know about the Illuminati," he said.

Crowley's eyes flickered.

"Why?" he asked.

"That is a private matter," Dietrich said, gradually regaining his composure. "We seek answers that can only come from a member of that cult, if it still exists today. We were told that if there is a Mason alive who possesses such knowledge, it would be you. So we have come to you hoping you will help us. If you won't, please inform us directly. We have no time for foolish games."

A long, uncomfortable silence followed in which Crowley simply glared. When he finally spoke I expected him to throw us out. After all, to him we were nothing more than an imposition.

"Your question, then, concerns the Illuminati, *not* the Masons," he said. "Why take such a winding path?"

"Because it is a sensitive matter, and we are strangers," Dietrich replied. "We could not predict how the subject would be received."

Crowley nodded almost imperceptibly. He took several more seconds to study us in silence.

"In truth, what you are after is not *what* I know about the Illuminati, but *whom* I know that are members."

"Correct," Dietrich said.

Crowley shifted in his seat, recrossed his legs, and glanced at the clock on the wall.

"Very well," he said with a smirk. "The first question is simple enough, and I shall answer it directly."

"We appreciate it," Dietrich said, looking surprised.

"What I know of the Illuminati comes from a book, a pernicious little treatise entitled *Ordo Ab Chao*."

"We, too, have read this book," Dietrich said.

"Then you know it proposes a plan to dominate the entire strata of society," Crowley said. "Though I think it rather misses the mark."

"The mark?" asked Dietrich.

"Yes," Crowley replied. "It equates power with wealth. The mark it so widely misses is that wealth is finite and temporal. True power can only be attained through societies like the Silver Star, which are dedicated to uncovering mystical truths, the *Arcanum Arcanorum*, the Secret of Secrets, and through spiritual means such as my Thelema, which empowers mind and soul."

Dietrich and I looked at one another, wondering what clues we were missing.

"That aside," Crowley continued, "in this respect we are on equal footing, for I know nothing more about the Illuminati."

"I see," Dietrich said, frowning.

Crowley raised a hand.

"But wait! I have yet to answer your second question."

We looked at him expectantly, for it seemed we might actually come away from this absurd meeting with something useful.

"Yes?"

"Before I answer," Crowley said, leaning back comfortably in his chair, "there is something I want in return. I require a service."

"What service?" Dietrich asked.

"The details are inconsequential," Crowley said dismissively. "No harm will come from it. Do you accept my terms?"

Again we looked at one another, and seeing no other way forward we shrugged.

"Very well," Dietrich said reluctantly.

"Good," Crowley said with a grin. "In that case, Mr Dietrich, we will bid you a good evening. Mr Grey, you will remain here with me."

Our jaws dropped. Before we could reply, Crowley sprang from his chair, seized Dietrich by the arm, and guided him to the door.

"You needn't worry about Mr Grey," he said, pushing Dietrich out. "I'll see to it he gets home safely."

Before the door closed I caught one last glimpse of Dietrich, his face frozen in an expression of shock and apology. Then the door slammed shut and he was gone. Crowley and I were alone.

"Now then, Prometheus," he said, relishing the moment. "Let's get down to business!"

Until that moment I had only experienced genuine fear twice in my life. The first time was the day Houdini had me arrested. I had thought I was going to jail, but after my character had been thoroughly assassinated, the judge seemed content to release me. The next incident was of course my second arrest, upon suspicion of murdering a New York socialite. My isolation with Crowley, however, made both seem inconsequential.

He laced an arm through mine and led me to a picture window overlooking a small arboreal square. We gazed down as couples idly strolled among the trees along lamplit walkways. The juxtaposition was not lost upon me. I would have much preferred to be one of those men, to have any woman, no matter how homely, upon my arm in Crowley's stead. But I did not have long to entertain such thoughts, because true to his word, he was all about business.

"I sense a bond between us, Prometheus," he said. "I believe we are kindred spirits, and I believe you sense it, too."

I gulped in response.

"Further, I believe it is more than mere fate that has brought us together this night."

He spun me around to face him, grabbing me by the shoulders. Not knowing what to expect I winced and closed my eyes. When he hesitated, I slowly opened them to find an expression of dismay.

"Are you ill?" he asked.

"Er, no, I—"

"Then stop acting so absurdly and pay attention," he said. "Tonight I require a performance."

A puzzled look crossed my face. To me, *performance* meant demonstrating my talents as an escapologist, or perhaps a spiritualist. Uttered by Crowley, however, the word took on a more sinister meaning.

"I am involved in an intricate stratagem in which your assistance may prove invaluable," he explained. "I find myself in a lover's triangle. I know a young man, a pupil, who in his confused state desperately and foolishly desires a young woman. But the third member of our triad, the *desiree*, if you will, has no lasting interest in him. She is willing to lay with him, but to her he is nothing more than a distraction. Besides, she is quite brilliant and exquisite, and far too worldly for this boy to master. And, coincidentally, the girl is a dalliance of mine, and married to another. So the young man has no lasting hope with her."

"I see," I lied.

"As mentor it is my role to awaken and edify, particularly in the case of this ignorant boy," Crowley continued. "He has somewhat unwittingly cast his lot with an arch crowd, a group that possesses far more guile than he imagines. If he is to survive, I must hasten his initiation into worldly and spiritual maturity. I have devised a series of lessons for him, intended, for lack of a better method, *to shock* him into these realizations, to accelerate his education, so that he will be able to run with the wolves, as the saying goes, rather than be consumed by them."

Crowley's dark eyes probed mine. I tried to look astute, but I had no idea how I fit into this scenario.

"What do you want from me?" I asked.

He smiled and wrapped an arm around me.

"My protégé will be here within the hour," he said. "In the meantime, look—the femme fatale approaches!"

He flung out an arm and pointed at the square below. I followed the line of his finger to a walkway. There, walking toward us, was a young woman in an emerald dress, her face obscured by the brim of a hat perched atop her head. I could tell nothing more about her from that lofty distance, but by the shape of her I anticipated a very attractive creature.

Crowley suddenly disappeared from my side and swept into an adjoining room. I did not follow, but I took one step that I might see inside. It was a bedroom, and he seemed to be straightening it by collecting discarded clothing from the floor.

I returned my attention to the window, hoping to get another look at the approaching girl, but she had passed from sight. A moment later Crowley was again at my side, now bearing a decanter and a glass filled with a greenish liquor.

"Here," he said, pushing the glass into my hands. "I sense you will need this."

I was never one to refuse a drink, and certainly not in a situation as strange as this. I finished it off in one large draught, which made Crowley's eyes dance with delight. A moment later a knock came at the door. Crowley clapped me on the shoulder, winked, and hurried to it.

He opened it to reveal a vision, a woman of such beauty that for an instant I forgot Ms Alexander entirely. The woman in green had a pale oval face adorned with such classical features that she seemed more art than human. Her perfect visage was framed by honey-brown hair that glistened in the dim lights of Crowley's apartment. As she entered she moved with an almost cat-like grace.

"Welcome, my dear," Crowley said, taking her hand and grandiosely planting his lips on it.

The girl smiled, and in response kissed him lightly on the cheek. She then looked at me, eyebrows raised.

"Mr Prometheus Grey," Crowley said. "Allow me to introduce a dear friend, Mrs Euphemia Lamb."

I began to feel very warm, but I could not tell if it was in response to the drink or the girl's intoxicating presence.

"Mrs Lamb," I said with a courteous nod. "A pleasure to meet you."

She regarded me for a moment, inspecting me up and down. She then looked at Crowley, who gave her a devilish grin. This seemed to be all the encouragement she required, because she immediately came forward and took me by the hand.

"A pleasure to meet you, Prometheus," she said. "But please, you must call me Euphemia."

The warmth within me continued to grow. Perspiration began to form on my brow.

"Absolutely," I said. "Euphemia."

"And where have you been hiding this one, Aleister?" she asked. "I consider it an affront that you have not introduced us before."

"I was not hiding him at all, my dear" Crowley said. "He is a *very* recent acquaintance, but be assured that he is one of us. We are kindred spirits, he and I."

This seemed to make an impression on her. She looked up into my eyes with admiration.

"I take it our plans for the evening have changed?" she said.

"They have, my dear, and for the better, I think," Crowley said. "This will drive the lesson home, more-so than I had planned."

"Then the lesson will be more interesting for both of us," she said. "Shall we get to it?"

Crowley glanced at the clock.

"At once," he replied.

I still had not deciphered the meaning of their exchange. I was feeling so warm I found it difficult to concentrate at all. A mild dizziness had come over me, accompanied by numbness. I felt untethered, as if I were afloat between worlds. I must confess that I enjoyed it. But before I could comment, Euphemia took me by the arm and led me to the adjoining room. There she shut the door, seated me on the bed, and began to disrobe.

Under normal circumstances I might have objected, at least long enough to ask for an explanation, but the situation felt inexplicably *right*. I recalled Crowley's earlier words, about how Fate had brought us together. Everything happening was simply *meant to be*.

Euphemia undressed casually, occasionally changing her pose, moving from one graceful motion to the next. When she was down to corset and stockings, she placed her hands on my shoulders and looked into my eyes for what seemed many minutes. Then, suddenly and with wicked mirth, she pushed me back onto the bed and fell on top of me.

What followed was an almost dreamlike ordeal, prolonged and euphoric. The scene alternated between moments of slow lasciviousness and primal animalistic passion. It seemed without end, and indeed I hoped as much. If this was the life Crowley offered, I was prepared to pledge myself as a loyal disciple.

As I wallowed in pleasure I thought I heard something, sounds that came neither from Euphemia, me, nor the loudly squeaking bed. But in my euphoric state I eagerly dismissed them and surrendered to Euphemia's delightful performance. The sounds, however, persisted, continuing to weave their way through her cries of joy and gasps of pleasure. Finally, I tore my eyes from the vixen bouncing on top of me and searched the room for the source. I suddenly realized the door was half opened, and framed in that space was Crowley, and another young man I had never seen before. He was boyish, with thick curly brown hair, clear blue eyes, and a head that seemed too large for his slight frame.

Slowly my senses began to return. As my mind rose above the waves of ecstasy I vaguely recalled Crowley mentioning a triangle, one corner of which was occupied by a naïve young man who was hopelessly infatuated with an exquisite young woman—the same girl who happened to be astride me at that very moment.

Suddenly I sobered. Not entirely, but enough to separate a part of my mind from earthly pleasure, and to discern the young man was weeping. And looming over him was Crowley, positively beaming as he whispered into the boy's ear.

"You see, Victor?" he hissed. "She is beyond you, and in more ways than one. Even if she took you, you could never hold her. She is wanton! You must put her out of your mind and take solace in your studies. I can show you the way, if you will let me into your heart!"

A chill ran through me, and I became instantly self-conscious. I grabbed Euphemia by the waist in attempt to stop her, but she instead took encouragement and cried out in delight. At the sound of her pleasure the young man broke and began to sob uncontrollably. I watched Crowley's hand creep up to the boy's shoulder. He pressed his lips to the boy's ear.

"Wait in the garden," he said.

The young man lowered his head and backed out of the doorway. A moment later I heard the distant sound of a door closing.

"What's happening?" I managed.

Crowley sauntered into the room and seated himself on the edge of the bed. Coincidentally, Euphemia at that moment exhausted herself and came to an abrupt but dreamy halt. She took a moment to catch her breath. Then, as if I were not even there, she turned to Crowley.

"Does this conclude the lesson?" she asked.

Crowley reached out and stroked her hair.

"It does," he replied. "I believe young Victor will now prove an apt student. Thank you, my dear."

He leaned over and lightly kissed her on the lips. He then stood and looked down at me.

"And thank *you*, Prometheus!" he said loudly. "You may get dressed. I'll await you in the parlor."

He left us alone and closed the door. Euphemia disentangled herself from me and collected her clothes. I suddenly felt ashamed and covered myself with a sheet, which I hid under while speechlessly watching her dress. During this time she seemed completely unaware, or uninterested, in me. She went about her business and, once adorned, met my gaze.

"It was nice to meet you, Prometheus," she said. "I hope we meet again."

Then, without another word, she departed.

I laid there for several minutes as reality settled in. The effects of the liquor had faded, and now I marveled in full realization of what had transpired. Presently the door swung open and Crowley looked down at me in annoyance.

"Get up!" he demanded. "This is no hotel for vagabonds. I thought you would be dressed already. Quickly now, Victor is waiting."

I obediently leapt out of bed and hurriedly dressed. In the parlor I found Crowley gazing out the window into the square, slowly sipping a dark liquid from a glass.

"What drink is that?" I asked as I adjusted my tie.

"This?" he said, languidly swirling the drink in his hand. "A potion of sorts I discovered in Cairo. You performed a great service for me this evening. Now I am obliged to answer your final question."

"Ah, good," I said.

But Crowley said nothing. Instead, he stared at me, his lips twitching with impatience.

"Are you going to ask or not?" he said finally.

"Oh," I said, but after the events of the evening I had completely forgotten the point of it. I looked around for a clue that might take me back to our earlier conversation. Crowley sighed in exasperation.

"Clearly your memory requires some assistance," he said. "The remaining question was this: whom do I know that is a member of the Illuminati."

"Ah!" I said. "Yes, that was it. So, whom do you know that is a member of the Illuminati?"

A smile slowly formed at the corners of his mouth.

"No one," he replied.

I was stricken dumb. Crowley tried not to laugh, though he was amused and very self-satisfied.

"What?" I said.

"No one," he repeated. "I know *no one* that is a member of the Illuminati."

I stared at him in disbelief. If I had been a man inclined toward violence I would have struck him.

"No one?" I exclaimed. "If you don't know anyone then what was this all about?"

"Do you jest?" he replied. "You were instrumental in banishing young Victor's love for Euphemia. It was you who finally broke his resolve. I could not have done it so effectively."

"That's not what I meant!" I said. "I played a part in this debauched scenario in return for information, not to be tricked."

He raised his chin defiantly.

"You asked a question, and I answered it truthfully. If you don't care for my answer, that is beyond my concern."

I was fed up with his games. I headed for the door. I was half way through it when he called to me.

"Wait!"

I turned to find him staring at the floor, eyes closed, one hand raised.

"You must learn to apply your mind to the problem at hand," he said. "My answer may be insufficient for your purposes, but even now there is an answer before you. Will you storm off without finding it?"

I had an urge to leave, to slam the door behind me and let that be my answer. I felt that every moment I remained in his presence I risked being tricked into another of his games.

"What answer?" I demanded.

He raised an eyebrow.

"You asked what I knew of the Illuminati, to which I replied I know nothing, no more than what I read in *Ordo Ab Chao*. You then asked whom I know among the Illuminati, to which I truthfully answered no one. The question you have so far failed to ask may very well provide the answer you seek."

"What are you talking about?"

"The question you should be asking, dear Prometheus, is *how* I came by the *Ordo Ab Chao*."

I considered it. I feared that if I asked I would find myself wandering in another maze of deception. I shuddered to think of what immoral exercise he might next require. But I also dreaded returning to my companions empty-handed, so I played along.

"Okay. How did you come by the *Ordo Ab Chao*?"

Crowley grinned with mischievous delight.

"Victor gave it to me," he said.

"Victor?" I said. "You mean the young man who was just here?"

"The same," Crowley said as he strode to the door. "He's down in the garden. Good luck getting the answers you seek from him."

I was speechless.

"Oh, and when you're done with him, please send him up," Crowley said. And with that he shut the door in my face.

I did not move for some time. Instead I stood atop the stairs trying to muster up the courage to face the youth whose romantic dreams I had so irrevocably shattered.

"Pardon me. Victor, is it?"

Night had fallen and the garden square was dark except for the hazy light from nearby lamps. The young man sat despondently on a bench beneath a tree, his chin upon his chest. At the sound of my voice he looked up. The faint light was enough to reveal his tears had dried. Upon seeing me I expected him to rise up, to beat impotently against my chest with his fists, to vent his anger and frustration. And given my role in the injustice perpetrated against him I was prepared to stand there and suffer it. (He was gawky and spindly of limb, so I was not concerned about serious injury.)

Victor, however, did not meet me with anger. Instead he wore an expression of sheer weariness and defeat, which made me feel even worse.

"Yes," he said. "Who are you?"

"Oh," I said, surprised. "Perhaps you don't recognize me in the dark. I was the one you saw upstairs—"

"I recognize your face," he said sharply. "What's your name?"

"Sorry," I said. "Prometheus Grey."

I extended a hand, but he looked away. Awkwardly, I seated myself beside him.

"I meant it when I said I was sorry," I continued. "I did not plan for this. When I arrived to visit Crowley, I had no idea Euphemia would also be there, or that events would proceed the way they did. I also had no idea who you

149

were, or that you were in love with her. I would never have done such a thing had I known the injury it would cause."

I was not entirely truthful on that point. Euphemia's beauty was so disarming, I suspected I would have fallen prey to her charms even if she had arrived wearing a potato sack. But my words seemed to comfort the lad, if only infinitesimally.

Victor wiped his nose on his sleeve and regarded me in silence. While I awaited a response I studied his silhouette. That unruly head of hair perched above his sticklike body made him resemble a much-abused mop.

"I wanted only to get to know her, to show her who I am," he said. "But I never got the chance. If I were given the chance now, I don't think I would take it."

I tried to look understanding and sympathetic. I slowly nodded.

"Am I a fool?" he asked.

"Not in the least," I said. "Everyone treads this path at some time. You are just unluckier than most because you fell in love with ... well, a tart."

He hung his head, slowly shaking it at his fatuity.

"What was it you wanted?" he asked.

"To apologize," I said. "And to ask a question."

"What?"

"Crowley said you gave him a book, a copy of *Ordo Ab Chao*. I was hoping you could tell me how you acquired it."

Victor looked up. The darkness could not hide his puzzlement.

"Why?" he asked. "What does that have to do with anything?"

"I'm trying to trace its origin," I said. "So far you're the only person I've found who might be able to provide me a lead. Can you tell me where you got it?"

He was silent. I suspected he was considering the situation, recognizing it as a way to strike back at me for Euphemia, and judging whether spiting me would alleviate any of his pain. Fortunately, he was not a vindictive person.

"It was given to me by someone in Germany, a man named August Wende. I met him in Munich, at a coffee house on Schellingstrasse. Is that helpful to you?"

"Very helpful," I said. "Thank you."

He nodded and went back to staring at the sidewalk.

"I suppose I am ruined now," he said. "I don't think I will ever love again."

Once I had the information I needed, I wanted nothing more than to exit the scene, to leave Victor alone to deliver his soliloquy, and to put as much distance between Crowley and me as possible. But suddenly I recognized an opportunity, one which I could manipulate according to my choosing. Crowley was clearly infatuated with Victor; and Victor, by my reckoning, was in some vague way drawn to Crowley. Perhaps he had never acted upon those taboo feelings, but I was certain I detected the propensity. If Crowley made an advance, I was sure Victor would reciprocate, or at least tolerate it for a time.

My dilemma, however, was this: I had the ability to strike back at Crowley, to punish him for his exploitation of others, by poisoning Victor against him. The selfish part of me wanted to put lies into Victor's head, to rob Crowley of the boy he so clearly desired. But the selfless part of me objected. It insisted Victor had been through enough, and ironically, like it or not, Crowley was the one person who could rescue him from his current misery. It was quite a predicament, and not one I enjoyed.

I stood over him in silence, weighing my options. I had no idea what decision I would make until I spoke.

"Go to him, Victor," I said. "Crowley will help you get through this."

Victor looked up at me as if dumbfounded. But slowly an understanding shown in his eyes, and he stood up. I again extended a hand, and this time he accepted it.

"Oh, and if you don't mind, please give him this," I said, producing the forgotten letter from his wife.

He accepted it without question. He then nodded and mournfully walked back toward Crowley's apartment.

I, on the other hand, turned and ran in the opposite direction, not stopping until I found a hackney cab to carry me back to the hotel. I never wanted to see, hear, or think of Aleister Crowley again.

I arrived back at the hotel just prior to midnight and was met by my companions. As I approached I saw them pacing in the lobby. After the ordeal I had just been through their concern warmed my heart. My eyes went straight to Ms Alexander, and I chastised myself for my earlier heresy. Yes, Euphemia Lamb had been alluring, but she did not compare to our Russian princess. Ms Alexander was perfection. No one could replace her, and there would never be another like her.

As I entered they all rushed forward. For a moment I thought Ms Alexander might embrace me, and I imagined it so vividly that I thought it might be a precognition. But at the last moment she drew up, allowing Dietrich to embrace me instead. He grabbed me by both arms like a long lost son.

"I'm so sorry for leaving you like that," he said, but he did not need to say it. The look of relief on his face said it all, that he had done nothing but worry since we parted company. "I would have remained, but since we needed him to cooperate, I obeyed. I tell you, it was the most difficult decision I've had to make in years."

"No need to apologize," I said. "You did the right thing."

"What happened?" Irish asked.

"Nothing of consequence," I said. "More of Crowley's mind games. But in the end he answered my questions, and he introduced me to a young man who provided our first real lead."

"A lead?" Dietrich exclaimed. "What is it?"

"The name of someone closer to the source of *Ordo Ab Chao*. How soon can we secure passage to Munich?"

"Tomorrow, I should think," Dietrich replied, eyeing me appraisingly.

He stepped away to inquire with the concierge, leaving me with Irish and our lady.

"We are all much relieved to have you back safe and sound," she said.

"Thank you."

"We were quite worried," she said. "As lovely as Paris is, it too has its dangers."

"Oh, I was never in any danger," I said.

"Nevertheless, we should take this as a lesson learned. I think in the future we must be more careful, perhaps take measures to ensure no one gets separated again."

I smiled at the thought of never being separated from her. As I entertained the notion, Dietrich returned.

"Good news," he said. "There is a daily train to Luxembourg. From there we should have no difficulty reaching Munich."

"So we can depart tomorrow," I said. "That is good news. I think I'd like to put Paris behind me."

Dietrich shot me a knowing look and laughed nervously.

"Would you excuse us for a moment?" he said to Irish and Ms Alexander.

He grabbed me by the arm and steered me to a corner of the lobby. I shot Ms Alexander a mock frantic look, and I was pleased to see she had to suppress her amusement.

"All right, tell me," he insisted. "What happened with Crowley?"

"Nothing," I said hastily.

He looked at me in silence. Meanwhile my attention strayed back to Ms Alexander, whom I hoped to get to myself for a few minutes of conversation before bed. When I again glanced at Dietrich, a look of horror crossed his face.

"Dear God," he hissed. "He didn't…"

It took me a second to interpret his meaning.

"No!"

"Did he try his *sex magick* on you?"

I opened my mouth to reply and hesitated. It had been an exceedingly strange evening. Perhaps I *had* fallen under one of Crowley's carnal spells. But regardless, I could not confess to it.

"Again, no!" I said with a nervous laugh.

"No, of course not," Dietrich said, looking relieved. "Forgive me. And again, I apologize for leaving you back there."

"No harm done," I said.

I looked past him to see Irish and Ms Alexander heading toward the stairs. My hope of getting her to myself waned.

"I promise you it will never happen again," he said. "We'll take measures to ensure it."

"That's fine," I said impatiently, watching as Ms Alexander ascended. "From now on we'll all stick together."

"Exactly!" Dietrich said, clapping me on the shoulder. "Now, I think we should call it a night."

I watched over his shoulder as she passed out of sight.

"Yes," I sighed. "It's time to call it a night after all."

12: A SHOCKING REVELATION

Our train ride the following morning was, in a word, depressing. We awoke that day to an unrelenting deluge that lasted the entire morning. The sky was a mass of grey, as heavy and oppressive as a sheet of lead. Our trip would have otherwise been a pleasant experience. Beneath the sun I imagined the countryside, a patchwork of farmland and forests, to be pastoral and quaint. Instead we were treated to an endless landscape of weeping skies and soggy vegetation riddled with distant and forlorn cottages.

The trip to Munich took an entire day to complete. Along the way the train stopped to unload and receive passengers in several towns, but only two were notable. The first was Luxembourg. As we pulled into the station the rain abated, and the sheet of water covering the window fractured into a hundred tiny drops, offering a clearer view. I observed what appeared to be a quaint little city, but it was unfortunately upstaged by the chaos occurring immediately around us. The train station, or what little was left of it, was in the process of being demolished to make way for a newer one. An inspection of a nearby sign revealed a sketch of the impressive building to come, but it would be several years before the structure was complete. It made an impression on me that such an historic location was not excused from the demands for progress.

The disarray of debris and those hauling it away could be momentarily put out of mind by standing on the north end of the platform and turning one's back on the demolition, which we all did. Then we were able to better appreciate the simple beauty of Luxembourg. It appeared to be built around a rocky hill, at the top of which sat a medieval fortification. Ms Alexander, who had visited the city at some time in her life, held forth with commentary on the few sights visible from that vantage.

"See the twin spires?" she asked, pointing with one delicate gloved hand while using the other to hold her hat atop her head. "They belong to the

Notre-Dame Cathedral. The exterior is somewhat plain compared to others I have seen, such as the *Notre Dame de Paris*, or Saint Isaac's in Saint Petersburg, but the interior is beautiful. It is a shame we are unable to visit it."

We all stared at the vista above the trees and rooftops. Dietrich inclined his head to get a better look through his glasses, but Irish was completely uninterested and took the opportunity to roll a cigarette. I, however, was more struck by the postcard image before my eyes than the distant fortifications and steeples. In the foreground stood Ms Alexander, her back to me in such a way that only a hint of her profile was visible, one hand atop her head, the other extended, pointing with an almost childlike innocence and enthusiasm, at the spires in the background. In that moment, and not for the first time, I wished a photographer were present to capture it. That moment, and others like it, would remain fixed in my mind.

The second major stop along the way was Stuttgart. As we raced toward it, I had fallen asleep with my head propped against the window of our car. I was roused by the sound of Dietrich coughing to clear his throat. I opened my eyes to find him sitting opposite me, cleaning his glasses with a handkerchief. A glance out the window showed us to be on a bridge, crossing a considerable body of water.

"The River Moselle," he said. "We are now in Germany."

I leaned back and crossed my arms intending to doze off again, but before I closed my eyes I noticed a wistful look on our captain's face. Suddenly I recalled the story he had related to me on our ocean voyage, and I realized this was the first time since his mother had fled home that a member of the Dietrich family had returned to these lands. Of course this was Bavaria, not Prussia, but it still had an effect on him. I wanted to acknowledge it, to show I understood the significance of the moment, but as he stared out the window his eyes showed he was far away, so I let him be.

By midafternoon we arrived in Stuttgart, an expansive city which I presume has its own fine history, though the city itself is not what made the stop memorable. In the short time we had before the train moved on, Ms Alexander coaxed us from the station to the street. There she again regaled us with her knowledge of the sights, none of which could be seen due to the close press of buildings.

"I believe we are facing south," she said, spinning around to get her bearings. "Just a few blocks from here is the university, and south of that is Stiftskirche, a Protestant cathedral of sorts. It is interesting, but rather common compared to the grandeur of others."

I noticed in her manner a waning alacrity, perhaps because the church was both obscured and truly unspectacular. But it seemed to me that her enthusiasm ebbed not because of any architectural shortcomings, but at the mention of *Protestant*. At that moment I detected in her some ecclesiastical bias which roused my suspicion only because I had been raised a Protestant. But the issue for me was neither here nor there. I had abandoned my upbringing decades ago, lumping religion and its complexities into the category of the Absurd, though I kept this fact to myself. But to appear attentive and polite I turned my head in the general direction she indicated and nodded.

As she looked thoughtfully in each direction trying to recall other obscured attractions, the train announced its imminent departure with an ear-splitting shriek from its whistle, and we hurried back into the station for the continuation of our journey.

It was approaching dinnertime when we arrived in Munich. In spite of the late hour the sun was still high in the sky, making possible a survey of the city. As we approached the station I looked east to see a variety of taller buildings, which no doubt marked the city's heart. In every other direction, as far as I could see, the land was covered with rooftops, interrupted here and there by spires and steeples. Irish nodded out the window at the hundreds—nay, thousands—of houses within view.

"Finding this Wende might not be easy," he remarked astutely.

Dietrich followed his gaze.

"Leave that to me," he said.

I was glad to leave it to him, since I had no clue where to begin. Irish also nodded, though he did not look convinced.

We had traveled three hundred miles in one day, a miraculous feat even for such modern times. Still, various parts of my anatomy were prepared to revolt. My companions must have felt the same, because as soon as we set our feet on the platform we each let out a sigh of relief and stretched to get the blood flowing again. I heard a symphony of popping sounds to my right and witnessed Irish go through a series of motions that cracked every joint between his neck and knuckles. Dietrich, on the other hand, hobbled along with a palm planted in the small of his back, massaging the feeling back into it. Even Ms Alexander, whose poise and posture were perpetual and immaculate, closed her eyes and tilted her head from side to side to relieve stiffness in her swanlike neck. She then placed a hand over her mouth, yawned, and pointed to a pair of distant towers topped with bulbous turquoise domes.

"The Frauenkirche," she said. "The Cathedral of Our Blessed Lady."

Her eyes lit up again momentarily. Apparently this cathedral, which by her reaction I presumed to be Roman Catholic, appealed to her Orthodox sensibilities. But any zeal was short lived as another yawn drove off further commentary.

We walked slowly into the station, allowing the crowd to precede us. By the time it had dissipated Dietrich had already secured our luggage, found an attendant to cart our trunks, and secured two coaches to transport us to a hotel.

"I had some difficulty communicating with the attendant," he said, looking perplexed. "After spending so much of my life in America, I began to think of German as a single language. But in Bavaria, and probably throughout the south, they speak a different dialect."

I had always thought of Germans as homogenous, at least as far as the language was concerned. It had never occurred to me that a person raised in the north would speak a different kind of German than one from the south.

"Is that going to be a problem?" Irish asked.

"Not at all," Ms Alexander chimed in. "Mr Dietrich, if you ever need assistance, do not hesitate to ask."

"Ah!" Dietrich exclaimed. "Of course. I know you speak German, but it did not occur to me that you might understand the southern dialect. I will gladly accept any assistance."

Ms Alexander smiled and nodded.

"It will be my pleasure," she said. "Besides, so far I have not contributed anything of substance to our endeavor. It is time I earned my keep."

We looked at her with expressions of dismay and collectively shook our heads in vehement disagreement.

"Nonsense," Dietrich said. "It was you after all that coaxed the needed information from Mrs Crowley."

"Precisely," I said. "If you're measuring worth by what we've each contributed, we may as well send Irish packing. After all, what's he done so far?"

I had meant it only to make a point, to demonstrate that no one had yet been put to the test. Irish was obviously capable of handling any matters that required brute strength. So far we had been fortunate and not needed him to exercise his talents. But my companions took it as a joke at Irish's expense, and the ox shot me a questioning look.

"Are you saying I'm not pulling my weight?" he said.

"Not at all—"

"That was very rude," Ms Alexander interjected. "We might ask you the same question."

"What?"

"We might ask what helpful thing you have done in service of our mission," she said.

I hesitated. For an instant I became defensive, and I opened my mouth to inform them of the details of my personal sacrifice with Crowley. Then I realized it would do me more harm than good.

"Forgive me," I said. "It was a poor attempt at humor."

"Please give more thought to your words in the future," Ms Alexander said.

"Of course."

As far as I was concerned the matter was closed. Ms Alexander was mollified, but Irish still wore a dismayed expression. I expected I would have to pull him aside later and provide a more substantial apology. But in the meantime Dietrich brought us back to the business at hand.

"As for our accommodations," he said, getting us back on track, "the attendant recommends we stay at the Hotel Bayerischer Hof."

Everyone looked to our resident expert on European travel to see if the name met with her satisfaction, and judging by her smile it did. As the coaches wove toward the hotel my eyes came to rest on yet another magnificent spire rising above the city. This one was intricately carved with gothic details, and ornamented with all manner of statues ranging from kings to commoners.

"What's that?" I asked.

"That is the town square," Ms Alexander said. "It is called the Marienplatz."

At the same moment music reached our ears.

"Oh! The carillon," she exclaimed. "Look at that tower there and you will see a show!"

I peered out the window and saw the statues had become animated. They rotated slowly in place on an invisible disc, which itself revolved so the figures moved in and out of sight to the music of the bells.

"Yes, that's quite a show," I said.

Actually I was thoroughly unimpressed, as the so-called show was rather lackluster. To Renaissance audiences perhaps it was once considered magical, a miraculous feat of technological ingenuity. But by modern standards—and certainly by Vaudevillian—it was worthy of only a halfhearted glance.

However, witnessing the expression of joy and wonder that lit Ms Alexander's face, I was glad to be there at that moment. She was all the show I needed.

"Now, to work," Dietrich said, wiping the corners of his mouth with a cloth napkin. We were seated in the hotel's restaurant and had just enjoyed a hearty German breakfast of bread, butter, jam, ham, soft-boiled eggs, and coffee. Ms Alexander had satiated herself with a single egg, and Dietrich had wisely drawn the line after a slice of ham and two rolls. I, on the other hand, had overindulged. I had sampled everything and now wanted nothing more than to return to bed and allow digestion to catch up with my appetite. In contrast, Irish was a bottomless pit. He continued to consume everything edible within reach.

"So far we have been quite fortunate, I think," Dietrich said. "While the end of our mission is nowhere in sight, we've been steered to where we are now, without much difficulty or sacrifice. But we are now far removed from our references. Starting today, I think our mission becomes more difficult."

"Why's that?" Irish said around an entire roll he had stuffed into his mouth.

"So far we've met with friendly, or at least non-hostile, persons who directed us to our next contact. But I think our luck ran out with Aleister Crowley. Would you agree, Mr Grey?"

"Yes," I said. "Crowley answered our questions, but he did so on his own terms, and the information was not easily acquired."

"We are now at a point of diminishing returns," Dietrich said. "There comes a time when an investigator crosses an invisible line, when he has separated the useful information from the misleading, and he is at last on the right track."

An expression of puzzlement came across Irish's face, as if he were engaged with a great calculus.

"If we're on the right track, what are the diminishing returns?" he asked.

"It is a paradox," Dietrich explained. "The closer we get to the truth, the less those with useful information will want to cooperate, because of fear of reprisal, or because they simply don't want to get involved."

"Or because they *are* involved," I said.

"Yes," Ms Alexander said, "but I think his point is that we have no more references or introductions to smooth our way, which means those we interview will be less inclined to help us."

"Correct," Dietrich said. "You must keep in mind that the people we encounter will not be naturally inclined to assist. We must be cautious in how we proceed."

Everyone nodded in agreement.

"There is another point I should mention," Dietrich continued. "It may seem like paranoia, but it is still worth consideration."

He leaned forward, and we followed his lead.

"There is yet another reason for caution," he said in a lowered voice. "At this moment we sit only a stone's throw from Ingolstadt, the birthplace of Adam Weishaupt and his Illuminati."

It was an obvious truth, but one I had somehow overlooked. I glanced at the other patrons dining around us. They all seemed normal enough. There were several tables occupied by couples conversing in low tones. I thought I discerned words in both French and Italian. There were also two long tables against opposite walls lined with Bavarian gentlemen, men of hearty stock with red cheeks and bushy moustaches who frequently wore smiles and broke into laughter. But everyone present, native and foreign, seemed benign. Dietrich continued in a hushed tone.

"If President Roosevelt is correct, and the Illuminati have evolved into a universal threat, they must by now be scattered around the globe. But the one place I would expect them to have great numbers is here in Germany. We can never be sure, outside our fellowship, who is friend or foe. Not only must we be cautious, we must use all our wits, especially in seeking this August Wende."

"How shall we proceed?" Ms Alexander asked.

"We will divide," Dietrich said. "Since Ms Alexander and I speak the local language, we will each lead a team. Mr Irish will come with me, and Mr Grey will accompany the lady."

For me, the Illuminati instantly became a secondary concern.

"Each team will make its own discreet inquiries as to the whereabouts of Herr Wende," Dietrich said. "Ms Alexander, I recommend you begin with official channels, such as the town records, if you can gain access to them."

"What of you and Mr Irish?" she asked. "Where will you go?"

"We will pursue a riskier path," he said. "We will begin making inquiries at the location of the *Ordo Ab Chao* connection, the coffee house on Ludwigstrasse, where the boy, Victor, associated with Wende."

Dietrich's path did sound risky by my thinking. To walk blindly into a coffeehouse and start asking questions about a mysterious cult was to invite trouble, or at least suspicion. But he was taking Irish with him, who was perhaps the greatest deterrent to aggression on the continent, so I put it out of my mind.

Before we parted, Dietrich suddenly grabbed me by the arm.

"Be careful," he said emphatically. "Watch over her. Here, put this in your pocket."

To my surprise he reached under his coat, produced a pistol, and inconspicuously pressed it into my hand. It was a compact revolver that could be easily concealed.

"Have you been carrying this all along?" I asked, astonished.

"Yes," he said. "One can never be too careful. Do you know how to use it?"

I had never fired a pistol in my life, but it seemed simple enough.

"Well, yes," I said. "It's not very complicated."

"Good," Dietrich replied. "Be careful with it, too!"

Although I had the good fortune of accompanying Ms Alexander—of being assigned her knight-protector, providing me the chance to spend a day basking in her warm glow, breathing her intoxicating scent—the day proceeded excruciatingly slow. Her charms notwithstanding, I had to constantly battle the tedium of standing idly by as she spoke to local officials, or paged through dusty old ledgers and documents, all in a language I did not understand. And to make matters worse, I could do nothing to help move us along any faster.

She decided to begin at the town hall, which she called the *Rathaus*. (I did not ask for an explanation of the term, but I smiled at the literal English interpretation.) Unfortunately for us, we soon discovered that Munich possessed not one, but two, town halls, one old and one new. They were both conveniently located on the town square, but inconveniently they were both still in use, which meant we now had two locations to explore.

"I suppose I shall begin at the *Neue Rathaus*," she said. "It has served as the main hall for more than thirty years. Hopefully my guess is correct, and the records we seek have already been moved there."

No matter how much we may have hoped for a stroke of luck, it turned out not to be the case. We approached the new town hall, which coincidentally bore the large spire containing the carillon we had seen from our carriage the night before. As we stepped through the doors we were immediately set upon by a handful of clerks. At first I thought they intended to boot us from the place, that they had somehow recognized us as foreigners who meant only to rape their records for our own nefarious purposes. But they drew up before Ms Alexander, their faces all filled with smiles.

"What's happening?" I asked.

A rather officious man in a black suit and sporting a walrus moustache stepped forward, clicked his heels together, and executed a half bow while spouting something in his incomprehensible tongue. Ms Alexander replied equally incomprehensibly; and so the exchange continued for several minutes, the two sharing words, smiles, and occasional laughter. At length the walrus turned and indicated a nearby vacant desk, and as he escorted us to it the other clerks scattered.

"They are being most helpful," she explained as the walrus pulled out her chair. "This gentlemen has dispatched the others to bring us the necessary documents."

"Documents?" I asked, momentarily encouraged. "So, they will tell us where to find Wende?"

"Perhaps," she said. "But do not get too excited. Look."

The errant clerks were already returning, and to my dismay I noticed that each carried a dishearteningly tall stack of books.

"Oh, no," I said.

"It appears we have our work cut out for us," Ms Alexander said with a sigh.

As the clerks piled the books on the desk, I reflected ruefully on her use of *we*. I could do nothing more than spectate, which meant *we* would be there a long time.

Shortly after noon Ms Alexander stood and stretched her limbs. I had been drifting in and out of consciousness beside her for the last three hours, which was not altogether unpleasant. Her proximity influenced my waking dreams in the most arousing fashion. But the second I sensed her moving I came instantly awake.

"Any luck?" I asked.

"No, regrettably," she said. "I found no mention of a Wende family line."

She looked across the room toward the walrus and slightly inclined her chin. In an instant he was at her side. After a brief exchange he again summoned his clerks, who swept in and carried the books away to their respective shelves. He then acquired a pen and paper, and in a loping script began to scrawl out a message.

"A significant number of records are still stored in the old town hall," Ms Alexander explained. "We may find what we seek there. This gentleman is writing us a letter of reference."

The walrus gave the note to Ms Alexander. She thanked him, to which he responded with a lengthy reciprocation that had all the appearance of leading to a marriage proposal. I sighed and bounced on my toes impatiently until she took the cue. Finally, she thanked him and led me out the door.

"He was very friendly, but I fear the lack of variety in his work has starved him for conversation," she said. "As for you, you must be more patient. Your demeanor back there bordered on petulant. You may not be able to speak the language, but your manners speak just as loudly."

I registered her words, but the scolding did not bother me much because I was thinking of lunch.

We dined at a nearby café and were back at work by one o'clock. We had made our way a little further down the square, toward the east end, and entered the old town hall. Inside we were met by another assembly of courteous clerks who accepted the walrus's letter with broad smiles. They too led us to a desk, though this one was much older with little varnish remaining. The clerks then scattered to the four winds to fetch the requisite records. They returned with stacks of even more depressing scale than before, and I slouched in a chair while Ms Alexander busied herself with her research.

The sun was low in the sky before we departed. She had devoted herself to investigation for almost five uninterrupted hours with no sign of success. As light drained from the room and the clerks performed their closing duties, suddenly I heard a quiet gasp, and she urgently gestured for pen and paper.

"What is it?" I asked, passing the items to her. "A lead?"

"Possibly," she said as she wrote down the information, the excitement evident in her face. "All day long and no trace of anyone by the name of Wende, and suddenly here, mention of a property sale in 1899."

At that moment the clerks began to coalesce around us, their faces full of sympathy and apology. I could tell they had come to kick us out for the night. But Ms Alexander had the information she needed, which brought broad smiles to their faces. She thanked them all as they escorted us to the door.

Outside she turned to me and held up the scrap of paper.

"We should go there at once," she said.

I regarded the darkening sky.

"It's getting late," I said. "The others will be expecting us."

But she would not be dissuaded.

"I have traveled thousands of miles to be here, and so far I have been of

163

little service. Now, after an entire day of reading through old records, I hold a possible clue. It must be investigated. Would you deprive me of this opportunity to contribute something?"

"No," I said. "But wouldn't it be wiser to wait until tomorrow?"

She locked her eyes on mine and gave me a look that was both chastising and pleading.

I should not have let her beauty or spirit conquer my judgment, but I did. I gave in to the thrill of the idea, the two of us on an adventure alone.

"Very well," I said. "I'll hail a cab."

We had no idea where the address would lead us, but still the cab ride was longer than I expected. The further we rode, the darker the sky became; and the darker the sky, the more ominous Munich began to appear. This was due to a combination of lengthening shadows and venturing into the unknown. I began to grow concerned. However, I balked at asserting myself over her and turning us around. As Ms Alexander's assigned protector, I was not about to show any fear, especially when she was so determined to demonstrate her usefulness.

We spoke little during the cab ride, mainly because she was so intent on the change of scenery outside the windows. The streets gradually narrowed, and multi-storied buildings encroached on us. People on the streets became as shades, hostile spirits who eyed our cab with interest. We passed several pubs and heard the rambling melody of drunken song, and in the same vicinity witnessed a variety of outrageous alleyway spectacles: fisticuffs, vomiting, and other bodily evacuations. Instinct began to scream at me, warning me that we should turn around and come back during the day, but I willfully ignored common sense for brave appearance.

When the cab came to a halt, the darkness was so complete we could barely see anything out the windows. But we climbed out all the same, and Ms Alexander exchanged words with the driver.

"He cannot find the exact address," she said, "but he thinks it is somewhere along this street."

"Then let's have a look," I said, trying to sound resolute in spite of my misgivings.

We began making our way down the street. Apartments loomed over us on both sides. If any lights were on within, they were shuttered against the night.

"What are we looking for?" I asked.

She was so intent on her search that she did not reply. She began walking quickly down the street, doing her best to read building numbers in the darkness. Though she wore heels, she moved with surprising speed. All I could do was follow.

She walked to the end of the block, and not finding what she sought she crossed to the next. Here my apprehension grew, but a look over my shoulder told me our cab was not too far distant. I could still see the ember of our driver's cigar burning in the night, and I was foolishly reassured.

The second block, however, offered us no assistance. Here, Ms Alexander paused for a moment in thought, and I could sense her frustration. I was about to make another inquiry when she turned and continued to the next block. As we crossed the street I looked back in dismay. At that distance no trace of our cab was visible.

I was about to point this out when I realized my companion had got away from me, outpacing me by another ten steps. I hurried to catch her, and I was about to hiss at her through the darkness when she suddenly stopped to gaze up at a building on our right.

"Is this it?" I asked.

"I think so," she said quietly.

We inspected the building, but in the darkness I could see nothing of interest. It was one of many dark monoliths lining the street.

Here, her hesitancy told me she finally was facing the reality of the situation. She may very well have found the residence of August Wende, which was itself an appreciable accomplishment. But to take the next step, to knock on his door and confront him, was another matter entirely. At mention of *Ordo Ab Chao* or Illuminati, he was likely to shut his door in our faces, or worse. What then?

As she looked up at the many dark windows staring down at us, she took two small steps back. I did not need to see the delicate features of her face to read her crestfallen expression.

"Discovering his home is achievement enough, I think," I said.

She turned to me, and I could sense her appreciation.

"Investigation is more difficult than I thought," she admitted. "How does one approach a stranger and ask if he knows anything about a plot to rule the world?"

I chuckled.

"I'm afraid I don't know, either," I said. "But I agree that it's a tricky business, and not something we should rush into. We should inform the others, and let Dietrich decide how to proceed."

"You are right," she said. "I should not have brought us all the way out here. It was impetuous."

"Don't fret," I said. "I too was caught up in the excitement."

With a last glance at the building we turned and made our way back. Our cab was totally obscured by darkness. I could only hope the driver was still waiting. As we walked I used the cover of darkness to steal a few glances at her. Though her features were hidden, I could admire her slender shape, her graceful movements. She was no less exquisite in shadow than in light.

It was perhaps because of my distraction that I did not notice until too late a pair of figures shambling out of an alley. I heard Ms Alexander gasp, and I looked up to find two shadowy men a scant ten yards away. Inexplicably the hair stood up on the back of my neck, and I had to resist the urge to stop in my tracks.

The strangers—a pair of drunkards judging by their beery scent—drew up in front of us. One said something in such slurred German that even Ms Alexander had difficulty understanding him. But she deciphered it and offered a curt response.

"What do they want?" I asked.

"Nothing," she said, attempting to sidestep the matter.

Upon hearing us converse in a foreign tongue, one of them interrupted.

"*Ah, Engländer?*" he said.

"*Amerikaner,*" Ms Alexander replied stiffly.

The two men seemed surprised but unmoved. They exchanged meaningful looks and an instant later advanced on us. We instinctively stepped back, hoping for a way to find a peaceful conclusion, but in the process we foolishly let them corral us into the alley. At the same time they spoke in low threatening tones. I do not know what they said, but it sounded hostile and came too quickly for Ms Alexander to translate.

Suddenly both men stepped toward me, their arms outstretched to grab me. As I stepped back to escape their grasp I felt something heavy against my right side, and I remembered the pistol Dietrich had given me. It had been irritating me all day, an uncomfortable weight in my coat pocket, but I had finally become accustomed to it and put it out of my mind. Now it thudded against my hip and I remembered. I tried to retrieve it, but it fit so snugly in my pocket that it did not want to come loose. In my struggle to free it I gave it a yank, which did the trick—but it also sent the gun flying from my hands. As it clattered against the ground I scrambled to retrieve it, but with a speed belying his drunkenness one of them snatched it up.

It all happened so fast there was no time to cry out. Ms Alexander, who of course knew nothing of the pistol, had watched in complete bafflement as I struggled with my coat. It was not until the drunk held the pistol in his wavering hand that she realized what it was.

Time froze as we stared down the barrel of the gun. Briefly, each party stared at the other in a state of shock over this new development, though our antagonists recovered more quickly. Within seconds they adjusted to their good fortune, and the man brandishing the gun backed us further into the alley. The closeness of that space brought Ms Alexander near to me, almost shoulder to shoulder. I was about to enact a desperate plan that involved me breaking away and running for help, but then events accelerated.

In the darker recess of the alley I could see little of our captors. They were so shrouded in shadow that all I could make out for certain was the glint of moonlight on gunmetal. But there was no shortage of sound to gauge their positions. They both breathed heavily, polluting the air between us with besotted breath. Ms Alexander raised a hand to her face to shield herself from the reek.

Now that they had us in the alley, they stood in silence for a time as if at a loss of what to do. Initially, they had probably intended to do nothing more than rob us, but the gun gave them unanticipated power and control. As these implications sank in for everyone, I finally decided to act. I produced my billfold and offered it in an outstretched hand. The unarmed hooligan snatched it away, removed the few bills it contained, and stuffed them into a pocket. The two then had an exchange in low voices. I felt Ms Alexander draw closer to me.

I was about to request a translation when the man with the gun again spoke. Ms Alexander responded in a calm voice, her words seeming to give the man pause. But his hesitation was short-lived. Both men scoffed, and the unarmed hooligan stepped forward and reached for her.

Without thinking I placed myself between them, which earned outcries from both men, followed by a punch to the face that made me see stars. When my vision cleared I discovered I was lying on my back in the filth of the alley.

"Prometheus, don't!" she cried.

It was a moot imperative, because before I could get up, a foot came down on my chest, pinning me to the ground. She then repeated a German phrase several times, apparently calming them down.

"Do nothing," she said to me. "I will be fine, and this will be over in a moment."

I could not believe my ears; nor could I stomach what I thought she was implying. But I had little choice. I was pinned down and helpless.

The man with the gun stepped forward. Ms Alexander retreated several steps until her back pressed against a wall. As the man came closer, she spoke what sounded like a warning. The vagabond's only response was a sneer as he reached for her.

What happened next literally occurred in a flash. I saw her assailant with his free hand reach for her throat, which lit a fire in me. In spite of her assurances I began to struggle, causing the man pinning me to apply more of his weight. I coughed as the air was crushed from me. In an effort to breathe I grabbed his foot and wrestled against it, but to no avail. Thus we were both distracted when the alley echoed with rending cloth, and for a split second was filled with blinding light. In that instant I saw everything in perfect detail—my assailant with his foot upon my chest; the man with the gun, one hand groping for the lady; and Ms Alexander, pressed back against the wall, eyes closed against the light. Then all was dark again, followed immediately by a thud.

As we all rubbed the stars from our eyes, my assailant removed his foot from my chest and spun around to investigate. I too rolled onto one side to catch a breath, and to find out what had happened. Though I had heard no shot, I was almost sick with fear that Ms Alexander had been gunned down.

But to our shared surprise we found instead his partner lying insensible on the ground, and Ms Alexander now holding the gun.

She brandished it and shouted something at the unarmed man, who hesitated long enough to do a double-take before turning on his heels, abandoning his friend, and bolting away into the night.

"Are you all right?" she asked, leaning over me.

"Yes," I said, climbing to my feet. "The question is, are you?"

"I am fine," she said, clutching her blouse together where it had been torn. "Come, we must leave at once."

And without another word she quickly strode from the alley and back toward our cab. I scrambled after her, looking around for indications of more trouble, but there was no sign of pursuit. As we hurried back, it finally sank in that she was still clutching her torn dress. I offered her my coat.

I was relieved to find the cab still waiting. The driver and horse each looked bored, the former hunched over and leaning on an elbow, the latter shuffling its hooves. As we approached, Ms Alexander drew the coat closed around her, concealing from the driver's prying eyes that anything unusual had transpired. Once inside, the cab spun around and headed back to our hotel.

We rode in silence for a time. Ms Alexander stared out the window, still clutching the coat closed around her. I presumed she was too shocked by the ordeal to speak. I confess that I was still shaken, at least until we had put some distance between us and the scene of the crime.

"What happened back there?" I asked finally.

She did not respond at once. She continued to stare out the window, collecting her thoughts.

"We were robbed," she said. "They were not satisfied with the money you had, so they decided to search me."

"It didn't look much like searching to me!" I said.

She tensed, and I realized that speaking of it only made her relive the indignity. I cursed myself for my insensitivity, but I still had questions.

"But what else happened?" I asked. "One moment they had us, then there was a flash, and then …"

I did not understand enough to summarize it any further.

"Mr Grey," she said. "I have something very confidential to tell you."

I became instantly curious.

"What?"

She opened her mouth, then shut it again. She seemed tormented, as if she were working up the courage to confess some crime.

"I suffer from a strange and dangerous condition," she said.

"What?" I asked.

Again she hesitated before taking the plunge.

"I am electrified," she said. "The flash you witnessed came from me."

I stared at her in disbelief.

"I'm sorry, you're what?"

"Electrified," she said patiently. "My body generates electricity. When conditions are right, the charge is released. When that happens, I can deliver a considerable shock."

I looked at her in disbelief. It seemed preposterous, but she was entirely serious.

"What do you mean?" I said. "Like an eel?"

She did not immediately respond. I could not read her face in the dark, but I gathered that likening her to an eel was less than flattering.

"I suppose that is the only comparison," she said with a sigh. "So yes, if it helps you understand, consider me like an eel."

"I don't believe it," I said.

She straightened. If the eel comparison had not offended her, questioning her integrity did the trick. She removed one of her gloves and offered me her hand.

"Do you wish another demonstration?" she said.

A thrill went through me. Since I had first laid eyes on her I had desired to take her hand in mine. Suddenly the overdue opportunity was before me, and electrocution or not, I was not going to pass it up. I reached out and grasped her hand.

She must not have seriously expected me to take the risk, because just before I grabbed her she gasped. As soon as I touched her, however, I was convinced she had spoken truth. Every muscle instantly and violently went into spasms of pain, and I was thrown to the far side of the cab. She immediately withdrew her hand and it was over. I opened my eyes to a veil of fading stars.

"Are you all right?" she asked.

"I think so," I managed.

I sat up and stared at her in wonder. It was true, every word. She had delivered a shock that incapacitated me, if only for a few seconds.

"How?" I said. It was all I could muster.

"I do not know," she replied, "nor does anyone else. So far no doctor has offered a medical explanation, or a cure. That is why I came to America, to seek the advice of Mr Tesla."

"Tesla?"

"Yes," she continued. "In lieu of a medical cure, I hoped for a scientific one. Mr Tesla's work with electricity, along with his impeccable reputation, gave me hope. Unfortunately, he was unable to offer more than mitigation."

She turned her glove inside out and offered it for examination. A smooth, almost paper-thin elastic material, perforated at regular intervals with small holes, had been stitched into it.

"What's this?"

"Rubber," she said. "To avoid accidental shocks."

"And the holes?"

"They allow the skin to breathe," she said. "Mr Tesla also taught me about grounding, which is a method of using the earth to draw off the charge. Unfortunately, grounding proved unreliable because he could not determine how fast, and how much, electricity my body can produce. I still perform the grounding process several times a day, but only as an extra precaution."

Suddenly it all made sense. Her standoffishness was not a product of phobia or conceit, but a cautionary necessity. She could unintentionally shock anyone who came in contact with her. It explained her Victorian standards of dress, which served to reduce her exposed skin and to avoid accidental shocks. I now fully understood why she avoided crowds, and why she was reticent to touch, or be touched.

"Is there hope for a cure?" I said, handing back her glove.

"There is always hope," she replied with a sad smile. "But I no longer expect to find a cure. This," she said, wiggling her fingers back into her glove, "will be a lifetime practice. By this means I am able to avoid seriously injuring anyone around me, or worse..."

Her words hung in the air. I wondered just how bad a shock she could deliver, but fearing to touch on some tragic incident in her past I dared not ask.

We fell silent again. The evening had given me a lot to think about. Still, in spite of recent developments I remembered something else significant.

"You called me Prometheus earlier," I said.

"Pardon?" she said.

"Back in the alley, you called me Prometheus," I said. "It was a first. Please feel free to continue."

"I do not think it would be appropriate," she said. "I would have to be on the same terms with our companions, which I am not."

I sighed.

"Then again," she said, "tonight's circumstances have changed things. If you like, I will call you Prometheus when we are alone. Will that satisfy you?"

"Yes!" I exclaimed.

She laughed, and it was like music to my ears. I bit my tongue and waited, expecting—praying—she would reciprocate by extending to me a similar invitation. But it was not forthcoming. I guess it was her way of letting me know that whatever she called me, it held no hidden meaning, that she remained Ms Alexander.

It left me a bit mystified, but I managed to soon forget it. Her declaration that she would use my name *in private* suggested that we would have more privacy, and that was a wonderful thought. Of course I was unsure how to proceed, now that I knew she might accidentally fry me like an egg, but I brushed such cynical thoughts aside for the time being.

As we neared the hotel she roused me from my thoughts.

"I would like to keep everything that happened tonight just between us," she said. "At least for now. I do not wish to answer any more questions at the moment."

I nodded. Between her disappointment at not finding Wende, the incident in the alley, and revealing what I presumed to be her greatest secret, she had been through a lot. As we came to a stop in front of the hotel, I spied Dietrich and Irish in the lobby awaiting our overdue return. I thought of her torn dress.

"There they are," I said. "Keep my coat for now."

She thanked me, and together we went forward to face our companions.

13: WENDING OUR WAY

Owing to the late hour Ms Alexander and I managed to defer any questions until the following day. As we had entered the hotel lobby, our companions had rushed forward with concern. Dietrich scolded us mildly for making him worry, but then noticed my coat wrapped around Ms Alexander's shoulders and, thinking her ill, dismissed us for the night.

The following day we met at the breakfast table and discussed what each team had discovered. As we dined, Dietrich cast sidelong glances at the other patrons until confident no one was eavesdropping.

"From your late night exploration I take it you found something," he said.

Unsure of what to divulge, I looked to Ms Alexander.

"Not much," she said. "After a day of searching for some clue, all we found was an address that may or may not be Wende's. Last night we located it, but that is all."

"That's just as well," Dietrich said, "You would not have found August Wende there."

"Oh?" Ms Alexander said. "What makes you so sure?"

Dietrich took a sip of coffee.

"Because Wende is in jail," he said.

Ms Alexander and I looked at him in amazement.

"Are you sure?" I asked.

"Oh, I'm quite sure," Dietrich replied.

"How do you know?" Ms Alexander asked.

"I visited him there yesterday," Dietrich said.

He went on to explain the events of the previous day as they had transpired for Irish and himself. They spent much of the day inquiring at shops and coffee houses along Schellingstrasse, but they came up empty-handed. So they broadened their search to new avenues. Eventually they happened across a police station, and on a whim Dietrich decided to inquire within. When he informed the desk sergeant he was trying to locate a man named August Wende, the sergeant unexpectedly stood and indicated he should follow. At first Dietrich thought the man was leading him to a records room, or to another office that could help. Instead, the sergeant unlocked a heavy iron door and led him into the jail. Dietrich began to wonder what he had gotten himself into. His thoughts returned to Irish, whom he had left outside, ostensibly for a smoke, but really to avoid unwanted suspicion from the police. But his trepidation turned out to be unwarranted. They stopped in front of an occupied cell, the sergeant told Dietrich he had five minutes, and without further explanation walked away.

Inside the cell a man sat in a wooden chair and languidly smoked a cigarette. At a glance he was thin and distinguished, not the sort one expected to find in jail. His greying hair was immaculately combed so that not a strand stood out of place. On his face he wore a thin moustache and an amused expression. And though he was in his shirtsleeves he looked nonetheless dignified.

"It was Wende?" Ms Alexander asked.

"Yes," Dietrich replied.

When Dietrich first appeared at the door to the cell, Wende had eyed him curiously. Wende, however, seemed more preoccupied with his cigarette than the stranger who had come to visit. He exhaled a stream of acrid blue smoke as natural as a rushing stream. Both men watched it flow around the bars of the cell.

"August Wende?"

"Yes?"

"My name is Meyer Dietrich, from America."

"Really?" Wende said, sounding cordial. "Then allow me to welcome you to Bavaria, Herr Dietrich. What brings you to Munich?"

"Frankly, it's you," Dietrich replied.

Wende paused to again draw upon his cigarette, narrowing his eyes and exhaling another cloud.

"How curious," he said. "Go on."

Poor at guile, Dietrich made no pretense. He stated the facts as they were, that he sought information about the *Ordo Ab Chao*, and that an acquaintance of Wende's (whom he wisely did not name) had referred us to him.

"Youthful indiscretions," Wende said, shaking his head. Even without a name, he seemed to know who had dropped his. He wore an expression more of nostalgia than regret. For a while he stared wistfully into space. Then he smiled and let an uncomfortable silence stretch out between them.

For his part, Dietrich knew to hold his tongue. He knew enough about interrogation to let Wende bear the burden of filling the awkward silence. Normally, regardless of guilt, people would feel compelled to talk, to say anything to fill the silence. Most continued to proclaim innocence, but the weak-willed or guilt-ridden sometimes broke under imagined or self-imposed pressures.

Wende, it turned out, was not that type. He looked not at all concerned, only amused as he gazed patiently back at our captain. With the tables turned on him, it was Dietrich who suddenly felt the urge to speak. He became anxious that his time with Wende was ticking away. The sergeant would soon return, and their time would be terminated. Fearing he may not get another chance like the one at hand, he cracked.

"Truthfully, I am not interested in the book," he confessed. "I am more interested in the Order itself."

Wende gave him an appraising look, but still he said nothing.

"Specifically," Dietrich said in a low voice, "I seek information on the man known as Brother Iscariot."

If Wende was at all surprised he maintained his composure. He sat in silence, his eyes probing Dietrich, the cigarette burning closer to his fingers. At length he tapped the ash into a tin cup.

"So the trail leads to me?" he said, amused. "Tell me, why are you interested in such things?"

"I cannot say," Dietrich replied. "I will say only that I have been retained, and leave it at that."

In spite of his collected manner, Wende's curiosity had been roused.

"Why should I help you?" he asked.

Dietrich was caught off guard. He had so fortuitously stumbled upon Wende that he had not considered his position or what he could offer. Then an idea came to him.

"Perhaps I could help your current situation," he said, gesturing to the bars separating them.

Wende raised an eyebrow.

"You're a lawyer?"

"No," Dietrich replied. "But I have some experience with the law."

This appeared to make an impression.

"And *you* wish to help *me*?" Wende said.

"Perhaps," Dietrich said, trying not to sound too eager. His heart began to race at the prospect of getting answers. "If it will encourage cooperation."

Wende scrutinized him for several seconds, then swiftly extinguished his cigarette in the tin cup.

"Then listen carefully," he said, suddenly sounding urgent and conspiratorial. "Your time here is almost up. You must memorize what I have to say."

"Remembering your words will not be a problem," Dietrich assured him.

"I have been falsely accused," Wende explained, his words coming quickly. "There is evidence that will clear me, but the police do not—cannot—know of it."

Dietrich opened his mouth to speak, but Wende held up a hand.

"Listen only!" he insisted. "The police are not to be trusted. I need a neutral party to covertly retrieve this evidence, to ensure it finds its way into the proper hands. If you desire my help you must do this for me."

"Do what?" Dietrich asked.

"There is an apothecary on Ludwigstrasse. He records all his transactions in a ledger. There is a notation in the book that will exonerate me. Get the ledger and take it to my lawyer, Ehrlichmann, in his office on Königsplatz. He will use it to clear me. When I am free, I will give you the information you seek. Where are you staying?"

"The Bayerischer Hof," Dietrich stammered. "But I don't understand. Why don't you trust the police?"

At that moment the door opened. The sergeant barked something and impatiently motioned for Dietrich to follow him out.

Wende suppressed a grin.

"We have our differences," he said. "Shall we leave it at that?"

Ms Alexander and I sat amazed at his story. Irish had already heard it and was unmoved.

"That brings us to our current predicament," Dietrich said, crossing his arms. "Wende will help us if we aid him. Now we must decide if we want to."

"Don't we?" Irish said. "We've come all this way. If he has answers, we need them."

"True," Dietrich said with a nod. "But after meeting the man, I do not trust him."

"Rightly so," I said. "But in this case we are fortunate enough to have a bargaining chip. Wende needs our help. We may not have the opportunity of such leverage again. We should exploit our advantage."

"If we help Wende," Ms Alexander said, "what assurance do we have that he will still assist us?"

We all took a moment to consider it.

"I see no way around it," I said. "What choice do we have? Wende is our only lead. If we dismiss him, we'll be back to square one."

Dietrich looked grim, but he nodded slowly.

"He's right," he said. "We must pursue this to its conclusion, or we risk missing something vital."

We fell silent again, absorbed in thought. Dietrich continued to frown as if displeased with his own logic. Ms Alexander looked at him thoughtfully.

"Something else is bothering you," she said. "Something other than the integrity of August Wende."

Dietrich looked at her mournfully.

"Yes," he said. "There is another factor I have not mentioned."

Still he was reluctant to speak. Ms Alexander was somehow able to read him.

"You have a moral objection to it?" she guessed. "You said Wende claimed he was falsely accused, but you have not mentioned any crime. Why is he in jail?"

"Suspicion of murder," Dietrich replied.

After his jailhouse interview, Dietrich had inquired about Wende's incarceration from the desk sergeant, who revealed that Wende was a suspect in the death of a local policeman.

Collectively, our eyebrows raised.

"Why?" Ms Alexander asked.

"I did not get those details," Dietrich said. "But this suggests Wende could be of the worst sort."

All fell silent, conflicted by the thought that Wende, our only link to our goal, might be a menace to society. All but Irish, anyway.

"I've no problem with it," the giant said with a shrug. "Isn't our mission more important?"

"Yes," Dietrich said. "But I am unable to shake the feeling that we are being tricked. I believe we will come to regret helping August Wende."

"Perhaps," I said. "But what choice do we have?"

"I agree," Ms Alexander said. "Whatever Wende turns out to be, he is a nefarious character. I do not enjoy getting mixed up with him, but our mission demands it."

Dietrich nodded, but he was lost in thought. As I watched him I appreciated his dilemma—he must again subordinate his morale and professional objections to the greater purpose.

"So be it," he said. "But I have a request. Since we must recover this evidence covertly, by which I assume Wende meant *illegally*, I ask that you excuse me from the task."

"Done," I said, looking to Irish. "I think we can manage."

"And one more thing," Dietrich continued. "I ask that Ms Alexander be excluded. If something should go wrong, I could not bear the thought of the lady being apprehended."

"Thank you," she said, "but I am quite capable of taking care of myself."

After the shocking example I had witnessed the night before, nothing could be more true. However, I agreed with Dietrich. I would sooner see the world burn than any harm come to her.

"He's right," I said. "There's no need for all to run the risk. Besides, I think we can handle this."

"This is nothing," Irish said with a nod. "Don't worry yourselves about it."

Ms Alexander started to object, but Dietrich cut her off.

"Thank you, gentlemen. In that case, after breakfast we shall leave you to it."

Irish and I nodded and went about finishing our meals. As we ate a mood descended on our table. Dietrich, still wrestling with his demons, frowned at his plate, while Ms Alexander pouted and stared out the window. Clearly she was not pleased at being overruled.

Irish and I waited until evening for our mission. Since Wende had insisted the work be done in secret, it seemed only natural to wait for darkness. While we waited at the hotel, Dietrich and Ms Alexander did some sight-seeing, or more accurately some reconnaissance, to locate the apothecary. At dusk we met in the lobby and they provided us with directions and intelligence.

"The shop is little more than half a mile north of here," Dietrich said. "An old couple owns it. They live upstairs, so you must be stealthy."

"Naturally," I said.

Dietrich stifled a sigh of exasperation at my tone, but then he held out a hand.

"Good luck."

We shook hands, and as we parted Ms Alexander stepped up. She too looked unhappy and annoyed.

"After your encounter with Mr Crowley I thought we had learned our lesson about separating," she said. She looked at me, but it was clear her words were meant for all, especially Dietrich. "But everyone has made up their minds. I only hope we are not repeating the same mistake."

Dietrich stiffened but did not take the bait. Having said her piece she forced a smile.

"The shop has a large front window bearing the word *Apotheke*," she said.

She spelled it out to ensure we would know it, and Irish and I repeated it to commit it to memory. When she was convinced she gave a quick nod.

"This kind of intrigue is new to me," she said. "There is little I can tell you besides good luck and be careful."

There was a firmness in her tone that sounded almost motherly, but then her expression softened. As she looked me in the eyes I held her gaze. It was a fleeting look, one which happened so quickly the others would not have perceived it. But in that instant her eyes betrayed her and I understood the depth of her concern. There was something between us. But she said nothing else, and not wanting to ruin the moment with awkward chatter, I nodded and hurried away with Irish in tow.

Irish and I made our way casually down the street. In spite of the dishonest work ahead he was completely at ease. I, on the other hand, experienced a growing unease, which perplexed me since in my life I had done far worse than stealing ledgers. But I felt nervous just the same.

Within minutes we found our target, a small storefront making up the ground floor of a narrow two-story building, with a plate glass window bearing the word *Apotheke*. As the sun set we paused on the sidewalk across the street to survey the scene. Through the window we spied movement, followed a moment later by the extinguishing of lights.

"They're still up and about," Irish observed. "We'll have to wait."

I sighed. I wanted only to get the job done and to put it behind us. He continued to glare at the storefront as if it were a foe, and I began to feel conspicuous. We had stopped in the middle of a narrow sidewalk causing passersby to flow around us.

"We should get off the street," I said, looking around for some cover.

He broke off his glare.

"And go where?"

I then noticed a disturbance further down the block. I watched as men entered into a small, well-lit establishment that echoed with sounds of laughter and conversation.

"There," I said, walking toward it. "Care for a drink?"

Before he could reply I was several steps ahead. Without looking at him I could sense his disapproval, a strange sensation to pick up from a man who had led a life far more raucous and questionable than mine. But he dutifully followed and held his tongue, and soon we were inside and seated at a corner table with large mugs of beer before us.

"This is a mistake," he said, longingly eyeing the brew in front of him. "It's best to wait until our work is done."

I did not hesitate to take a large draught from mine.

"Don't be a wet blanket," I said. "It's just to pass the time and blend in. Would you rather spend the next hour standing across the street from the very place we intend to rob?"

My reasoning was sound, but in truth I wanted something to steady my nerves. I was almost done with my first mug by the time Irish raised his to his lips.

The next hour passed slowly enough that we both enjoyed several more mugs. I did not set out to get drunk; in fact it was the furthest thing from my mind. But the beer was plentiful and strong. We drained mug after mug of that fabulous Bavarian brew just to pass the time, and before I knew it Irish was swimming in front of me.

In retrospect, Irish was correct. It was unwise to indulge prior to a burglary. Drunkenness crept up on me so unexpectedly that by the time I realized my condition it was far too late. Irish was less affected owing to his size, but he still leaned heavily on the table. But the strangest thing was that even though we kept a low profile, we somehow drew the attention of all the locals. They gathered around and slapped us on our backs, laughing jovially as if we had entertained them with some joke—an impossibility since neither of us spoke a word of German. When I finally looked at my watch and realized we had passed almost two hours, I caught Irish's eye.

"We should go," I said.

I could barely hear myself over the shouts and laughter, but Irish must have heard me, because he stood, announced he had to "take a leak", and headed for a dark corridor at the back of the pub. I registered these events only dimly, as I suddenly began to feel very tired. I propped my head on my hands and closed my eyes, to rest for only a moment. But when I opened them again my head was on the table, my face buried in my arms. I had no idea how much time had passed, but it felt as if Irish had been gone for an inordinate amount of time. Since he had not returned I decided to go find him.

I staggered in the direction I had last seen him. I numbly felt thuds upon my back and strong grips on my arms as I worked my way through the crowd, and more than one cheerful patron tried to push a mug into my hands. But I deflected them all and continued toward the corridor. I worked my way down it using a wall to keep steady. As I progressed I smelled clean air, and once my eyes adjusted I discovered an open door at the far end, swaying gently on its hinges. Something about it disturbed me, but I needed to find Irish, so I lurched forward into the night air.

I found myself in a small fenced lot wedged between the pub and a garbage-strewn alley. The lot held a small, poorly constructed shed, which judging by its reek served as an outhouse. The door to the shed stood open, and though all was blackness inside, enough moonlight seeped through the planks to show that Irish was not within.

I wondered about my friend's whereabouts. As improbable as it seemed, I began to worry that Irish might have come to some harm. As I puzzled over what to do next, I was suddenly baffled by an explosion of stars before my eyes.

I instinctively knew I had been struck, but due to my intoxication I felt little pain. I tried to turn around to see who had hit me, but something stopped me. When the stars cleared I discovered the problem: I could not turn around because I was lying on the ground.

I was not on the ground long, however, because next I felt hands grabbing me by the lapels, hoisting me up and forcing me back. My back met with something hard, followed quickly by my head. As I struggled to come to terms with what was happening, a snarling face materialized just inches from mine, a face I in no way recognized. It belonged to a large man, not as large as Irish, but large enough to be of concern. Whoever he was, his breath was almost as offensive as the vapors from the outhouse at my back. I began to writhe in an effort to escape, but he had an iron grip—and judging by the cold, stinging pressure at my throat, a knife.

Desperate for some explanation I tried to focus on the man's face. I thought that if I could identify him it might offer some understanding. He was dark haired and unshaven, with a scar carved into the whiskers on one cheek, attesting to a habit of violence. But none of these features conjured any memories. I was sure I had never encountered him before. Finally I gave up—literally—and threw my hands up in the air.

The man's scowl did not falter, but after my hands went up I detected the slightest relief of pressure at my throat. He hissed something in his own language. Noting the confusion in my eyes, he brought his face close to mine and repeated himself in English.

"You seek illumination?" he asked in a heavy German accent. He wore a twisted grin, clearly pleased with his double entendre.

His face was so close that his breath wound its way up my nostrils like putrid tendrils. I must have reacted with an expression of disgust, because the knife was applied with renewed vigor. I felt a sting at my throat, followed by a tickling sensation as a trickle of blood ran down my neck.

"Why do you seek the Illuminati?" he asked more plainly.

I stared back in shock, in response to the threat, and in surprise at mention of the order.

"Why?" he demanded.

But it was useless. Even sober I could not have thought clearly with a knife at my throat. I dropped my arms and simply stared back at him, which did nothing to improve his mood. His mood, however, suddenly ceased to matter.

His face was so close to mine that it filled my vision. As I stared into his dark eyes I gradually became aware of someone else nearby, a presence more felt than seen. My assailant sensed it, too. I watched as his expression changed from anger to surprise. He turned to investigate, but by then it was too late.

A pair of mighty hands seized him by the shoulders and practically lifted him off the ground. In the instant that he was held before me flailing, I saw in his face the fear of what was to come. In those final seconds of his life he opened his mouth to scream, but before sound could escape him he was hurled headlong into the bricks of the pub. His flight ended with a sickening sound, a sort of wet thud, and he collapsed in a lifeless heap.

I felt my neck fearing an artery might have been inadvertently opened in the excitement. I found only a superficial cut that had already begun to crust over. As I examined the smear of blood on my fingers, a shadow loomed up and blew smoke in my face.

"Who the hell was that?" Irish asked around a cigarette.

"No idea, but apparently an Illuminati agent. Where have you been, by the way?"

"Having a walk and a smoke," he said, tossing his head toward the alley.

He lit a match and held it up to my face, then moved it around to inspect my neck.

"You'll be all right, but we can't go back in there," he said, glancing at the pub. He then looked at the crumpled body against the wall. "Damn. We gotta do something about him now."

"Why not leave him?" I asked.

"No," he said, shaking his head. "Too easily tied to us. People will remember we were here. We've got to get rid of him, and fast before someone else comes along."

"What do you suggest?"

I meant it as sarcasm, but Irish missed or ignored it. He scanned our surroundings but found no quick solution. He ran a hand beneath his flat cap and scratched his head.

"I guess there's only one way," he said. "I'll take care of this. You get the ledger."

I hesitated. I did not want to burglarize the place alone. Then I considered that my lumbering companion would only complicate what should be a stealthy operation, and that between the two tasks at hand, I would rather retrieve a book than dispose of a body.

"Very well," I said, straightening my coat and tie. "How do I look?"

"Well enough for the job ahead," he said. He turned and effortlessly hoisted the body onto a shoulder. "But looks don't matter since the idea is not to be seen, so make sure you're not."

"Touché," I said. "I'll see you back at the hotel."

He nodded and disappeared into the alley.

So the task that had been intended for the two of us now fell squarely on me. It was not a difficult one, especially for the likes of New York's infamous Ghost. Still, in spite of his size I would have felt better having Irish along. After all, he had now saved my life twice, and each time with such ease that he made beating men into pulp seem a simple affair. If nothing else, he could have stood watch outside. But circumstances had changed, so I took a deep breath and moved on.

Few people were on the streets by then. As I approached I inspected the apothecary's shop and upper level windows for lights. I was relieved to find every window dark and vacant. I crossed the street and disappeared among the shadows of the alley. I moved slowly, with one hand touching the nearest wall and the other extended before me, to avoid any noisy collisions. As I made my way down the alley, I stepped in a pile of soggy garbage that was followed by a number of skittering sounds. An involuntary chill ran down my spine at the thought of rats around my ankles. It spurred me on.

I made my way to the back of the building and again found myself in a small, moonlit lot facing a door. I made quick work of the lock with an improvised pick crafted from one of Ms Alexander's hairpins. Seconds later I was inside.

The interior was impenetrably black. I had hoped for some light from the front window, but it seemed I had entered a windowless office at the rear of the shop. I was dismayed at navigating a pitch black and unfamiliar room, but I was not deterred. I reassured myself that it was little more than an inconvenience for such an accomplished burglar, and I waded into the darkness.

I fanned my arms out and slowly ventured into the room, trying to map its perimeter and contents in my head. I could tell the room was small by the sound of my shuffling feet echoing off the walls. It was a little reassuring to know I did not have much to search. But even in that small, dark room, it turned out not to be as easy as I had hoped. My body chose that moment to remind me I was inebriated. Lost in total darkness my equilibrium began to fail me, and without something to fix my eyes upon, I could not tell if I was standing straight or about to topple over. Several times I staggered but managed to catch myself on something unseen—a table, a chair—but the final time I reached into space and found nothing. I fell to the hardwood floor with a sonorous thud.

As I climbed to my feet silently cursing myself, I became aware of sounds coming from above. First I heard muffled voices, followed by the creaking of floorboards, then footsteps on a staircase. At that point I should have fled. I should have thrown caution aside and stumbled through the darkness in search of the door. Instead I inexplicably froze like a quail, unsure of what to do. As the footsteps descended toward me I finally roused from petrification, but I only managed one step before I was suddenly blinded. Someone unseen had switched on an electric bulb suspended from the ceiling.

I shielded my eyes and continued forward, convinced that if I could get to the door I would get away. But before I reached it I heard exclamations of German outrage. Hands grabbed at my arms and shoulders and pulled me back. In order to avoid toppling over I spun around and fell directly into the arms of a stout, red faced gentleman in striped pajamas.

As I stumbled into his arms we both momentarily froze. Briefly, we stared at one another's shocked faces. Then his look of shock transformed back into one of moral outrage. Before I could react, his arms moved from my lapels to my back, securing me in an inescapable bear hug.

Held fast, I could do nothing other than stare into his face and wonder about his intent. But a second later it became clear. He began calling out, raising his head and yelling something incomprehensible at the ceiling. When I heard another pair of feet on the floorboards above, it all became clear. He meant to hold on to me until his wife called for the police.

Upon this realization I began to writhe, struggling to break free. But in spite of his age, the old druggist was still a large, strong man. He tightened his arms and lifted me bodily off the ground so that my toes barely skimmed it.

This hefting had two effects. First, it achieved my captor's goal of immobilizing me; second, it put unwelcome pressure on my already weak stomach, making the situation become especially problematic for me. Where I had moments earlier sought to escape the scene, I now only sought to relieve my internal churning. But I was caught in a paradox: the more he squeezed, the more I struggled; and the more I struggled, the more he squeezed. Soon I felt something rising up inside me, and I clenched my eyes against rushing discomfort. A moment later I felt a wave of relief, and I opened my eyes to find the utterly horrified countenance of my captor, covered in a putrid glaze.

He released me at once. I dropped to my feet and staggered backward, wiping my mouth on my sleeve. He stood aghast, half bent at the waist, arms outstretched at his sides. I took advantage of his mortification. I quickly looked around the room and cried out when I spotted a desk on which rested a very ledger-like book. I swept it up, dodged around the frozen man, and darted out the back door.

The remainder of that strange evening passed uneventfully. I hurried back to the hotel, occasionally stopping to retch, or to lean my head against the cool iron of lampposts. In spite of the spectacle, at that late hour no one harassed me. Thankfully, I did not cross paths with any policemen. When I finally arrived at the hotel, I went straight to Dietrich's room and knocked on the door.

"Thank goodness," he said with a sigh. "I knew you could handle this business, but I worried just the same. Is that it, then?"

I nodded and handed him the notebook, which he opened on the spot and inspected. He nodded approvingly.

"Yes, this has to be the one," he said. Then he looked up at me and his smile faded. "You don't look well."

"I'll be fine, but I need some rest, if you'll excuse me."

Without another word I turned, walked back to my room, and collapsed into bed to sleep it off.

I awoke the following day to knocking at my door. I had been fast asleep and completely unaware that it was already midmorning. Through a part in the curtains, a shaft of light streamed in and projected from the floor like a spear. A glimpse at it made my head hurt. Mustering all my strength I climbed from bed and opened the door to find Dietrich.

"It's almost noon," he said. "Are you all right?"

"I'm fine, or I will be," I replied.

He nodded absently, looking me up and down.

"In truth, you don't look any better," he said. "So I won't keep you except to say the deed is done. I took the ledger round to Wende's lawyer, that Ehrlichmann fellow, this morning. Wende must have gotten word to him, because he seemed to be expecting it."

"Good," I said, trying to sound unenthusiastic.

"With the evidence, he said Wende should be out by tomorrow. Still, I plan to visit Wende this afternoon to inform him of our success. Perhaps I can get some preview to the information he has for us."

"Wonderful," I said, inching the door closed.

"I'll let you recuperate," he said. "If you need anything, don't hesitate."

I thanked him and quickly closed the door.

When I awoke for the second time it was again to knocking. The light between the curtains had taken on a dusky glow. I shambled to the door. By then I felt somewhat better, if still sluggish. I stuck my head out to find Irish.

"You okay?" he asked. "I heard you got the book."

"Yes," I said. "It was dicey, but I managed."

"Good," he replied. "Dietrich's been bugging me for details all day."

"What did you tell him?"

"Nothing yet," he said, scratching his head and looking up and down the hall. "I keep putting him off. Should I tell him about the guy in the alley?"

"No, let's keep it a secret for now," I said. I did not want to explain what happened behind the pub, especially since it would lead to discussion of our presence in the pub. "What of your mission?"

"Done," Irish said. "I dumped the body in the canal."

I took a moment to reflect on this point. The police would soon find a dead body floating in the city's central canal. Unless someone saw Irish disposing of the body, there was nothing that could tie us to it. Still, the thought of police looking for the perpetrator made me uneasy. We needed to leave Munich, and soon.

"That's that, then," I said. "Let's hope Dietrich gets what we need from Wende so we can put this city behind us."

Irish grunted in agreement.

"What should I tell Dietrich?" he asked.

"Just tell him everything went as planned, and I'll give him a full account tomorrow."

I closed the door in his face and returned to bed—only to be roused a third time only minutes later. I expected to open the door and find Dietrich, back to pester me for details. To my pleasant surprise it was Ms Alexander.

"It is past time for dinner," she said. "Are you well enough to join us?"

I started to accept her invitation. Then I caught myself. I was feeling much better, but I was not ready to answer Dietrich's inevitable questions.

"Getting better," I admitted. "But I think it would be best if I skipped dinner tonight and let this thing run its course."

She nodded, though I was pleased to note some disappointment in her face.

"I do not like that we have gone an entire day without seeing you," she said. "If you need company, I would be happy to read to you."

I almost agreed, just to have her near. But then I looked over my shoulder at the room in disarray, and I caught a whiff of myself.

"Thank you, but maybe another time."

She stared at me a moment longer before forcing a smile.

"Of course," she said. "I, or *we*, only want you to be well. If you need more rest then I will look for you at breakfast tomorrow."

I thanked her and she bid me goodnight. I then crawled back into bed and slept like the dead.

The following day I awoke renewed. I quickly cleaned up, dressed, and made my way downstairs in search of a much needed meal. I went straight to the hotel restaurant to find my friends sitting quietly at a table in a secluded corner of the room. As I approached they looked up. Ms Alexander and Irish looked anxious. Dietrich looked downright despondent.

"Is something wrong?" I asked, taking a seat. "Why the long faces?"

A silence followed. Ms Alexander and Irish cast glances at Dietrich, who sat holding a folded newspaper in his lap. He broke the silence with a deep sigh.

"Wende has been released," he said.

"That's good news, isn't it?" I asked.

"One would think so," he replied. "But there are two problems. First, he has disappeared."

"What do you mean?"

"Yesterday I went to speak to him," he said. "By the time I arrived he was already gone."

"That may not be a problem," I said. "He knows where to find us. And if he doesn't show up, Ms Alexander found an address for him. We can pay him a visit."

Dietrich nodded but did not seem optimistic.

"Is there something else?" I asked.

He frowned and stared at his hands. At length it was Ms Alexander who answered.

"Today's paper contained an article on Wende," she said. "It seems our worst fears about Wende were correct."

"What do you mean?"

"That Wende is a murderer," Dietrich said, "and we just played a pivotal role in setting him free."

He took the newspaper from his lap and read aloud:

> Police released August Wende yesterday after his arrest for suspicion of murder. Wende was suspected of killing Wilhelm Brücker, a policeman investigating the suspect's involvement in a similar case in Ingolstadt. Neighbors of Brücker identified Wende as a visitor the day before the officer's body was found. A doctor who examined the body determined Brücker had been poisoned with mercuric bichloride, a medically controlled substance.

When he finished, he dropped the paper on the table.

"So," I said, slowly putting it together, "we gave Wende the only evidence tying him to the poison."

Dietrich nodded.

"After you gave me the ledger, I searched it for Wende's name," he said. "I found a note of sale for mercuric bichloride, but lacking a chemist's knowledge I did not know its uses, or that it could be lethal. I foolishly gave the book away without delving further. It was the integral piece of evidence that would have sent Wende to the gallows."

"We were duped," I said.

"Yes," Dietrich replied, removing his glasses and rubbing his eyes with thumb and forefinger. "He knew, better than I, anyone seeking Iscariot would be desperate. And we were—I was—desperate. I was determined to make some headway."

"I understand how you must feel," I said. "But deep down, we knew this might turn out to be the case. We chose to put our mission above all else."

Dietrich's hands migrated to his forehead and massaged his skull.

"Yes," he said, "but I was a fool. I convinced myself that Wende might be innocent, to justify our decision to help him. Deep down I knew it was a mistake."

We sat quietly for a moment while Dietrich mentally flagellated himself.

"What's done is done," Irish eventually chimed in. "Now we need to find Wende and get the information he promised."

"Wende has disappeared," Dietrich said, sighing hopelessly. "I do not think we will see him again."

"Let's at least check out his address," I said.

He looked at me with tired, red-rimmed eyes. He clearly thought it was pointless, but he knew he could not argue against the logic of it.

"It will not hurt to check," Ms Alexander said reassuringly. "There is always hope."

He smiled ruefully.

"All right," he said. "We will pay Herr Wende a visit."

We wasted no time. We hailed a cab and returned to the address Ms Alexander and I had discovered two days before. When we came to a stop in front of Wende's residence, I barely recognized the place. Daylight had transformed the neighborhood entirely. I spotted the alley where we were accosted. It was unremarkable and lacked any sense of foreboding. It was hard to believe it was the location of the same nightmarish event burned into my memory.

Irish and I climbed out of the cab, and it was only when we looked back that we realized our companions were not following. Dietrich remained inside, staring forlornly out the window, while Ms Alexander attempted to console him.

Irish and I entered the building, climbed the stairs, and located Wende's apartment. Irish hammered several times, giving anyone inside more than fair chance to respond. When no answer came, I fished in my pocket for the hairpin I had used to get into the apothecary. But before I could find it Irish hurled his shoulder against the door and it burst asunder.

The apartment was modestly furnished and very orderly; in fact it was so spare it did not look lived in at all. Aside from the furnishings there was no clutter, not even the slightest trace of everyday accumulation: no mail or newspapers on the tables, no pictures on the walls, no photographs on the mantle, not even a bowl of wax fruit on the dining room table. Irish and I separated to wander through the place, meeting up again in the foyer with expressions of puzzlement. We then shrugged at one another and returned to our companions.

Dietrich did not say a word in response to our report, not even an "I told you so." He looked so distant I wondered if he had heard us at all. It was strange to see him in such a state. As our captain he had managed to keep us motivated and on task. He was the experienced investigator, the man with the plan to see our mission through. If this single setback affected him so profoundly, if it meant he had given up, I feared the rest of us had no hope for success. I admit that for all my cleverness I did not possess the insight to find Iscariot, or to unveil, much less destroy, the Illuminati. And Irish—he was our muscle, but nothing else. Ms Alexander, though keen and well-traveled, lacked the necessary training and experience to lead us to conclusion. As much as I hated to admit it, without Dietrich we were lost.

No one spoke of it, but we all recognized it. The feeling was palpable, apparent in our collective mood as we rode back to the hotel. Ms Alexander's prim exuberance and optimism had vanished. Irish stared dumbly at the passing scenery.

When we arrived, everyone went their separate ways. Irish wandered off down the street, his meaty paws stuffed into his pockets, his head hung in whatever passed for thought. Ms Alexander stepped down from the cab and met my eyes. I could see she was of the same mind, that she too had fallen into a contemplative mood. I did not try to engage her. And poor Dietrich— he was so distraught, he slowly climbed the stairs to his room as if the gallows awaited him there. He then secluded himself in his room and did not come out for the next two days.

Thus far on our mission we had experienced some unusual twists, and encountered a variety of characters ranging from royalty to reprobate. Such diversity notwithstanding, the next two days numbered among the strangest of our adventure. Over the past several weeks I had grown accustomed to the persistent company of my companions. Now, I was suddenly bereft of it. For the next two days it was almost as if we tried to avoid one another, each of us pursuing separate schedules and dining in solitude. It was as if Dietrich's mood had affected us all.

I rarely saw Irish, though I sometimes heard him coming and going from his room. He stayed out most of the day, returning well after midnight.

I tried to cross paths with my lady, to bask in her light and banish the funk Dietrich had brought down upon us, but we failed to connect. Dietrich's Doom (as I had begun to think of it) worked to confound me. I only saw her in passing, never close enough to start up a conversation, and my strange mood made me reticent to knock at her door.

And of course there was the man himself, Meyer Dietrich, the crucible of our erstwhile hopelessness and despair. He locked himself in his room and did not once leave. In my comings and goings I noted trays of untouched food left by his door. He clearly was not eating, instead allowing his guilt to consume him.

Then, just as suddenly as that strange bout of despondency had engulfed us, it was gone. On the third day I was startled awake by frantic knocking at my door. It was so sudden and unexpected I thought the hotel was on fire. I leapt to my feet and flung open the door to find a ghastly looking man I almost did not recognize as Dietrich. His hair and clothes were disheveled, and after only two days of fasting he already looked sallow and gaunt. But in spite of his haggard appearance, he was positively ecstatic.

"Prometheus, you won't believe what has happened!"

I stared at him in wonder and awaited an explanation. Instead he began rapping on the doors of our companions. When they finally stuck their heads out, he motioned to us all.

"Follow me!" he said, turning on his heel and heading downstairs. "We must talk at once."

We were all startled, but we obeyed. We followed him downstairs to the restaurant and commandeered our usual table. When a waiter approached to take our order, Dietrich quickly shooed him away.

"Something incredible has occurred," he said excitedly.

"What?" Ms Alexander said, looking concerned for his sanity.

Dietrich grinned maniacally.

"August Wende," he replied. "He was here!"

For two days Dietrich had been holed up in his room, lying prostrate on the bed, too distraught to eat or sleep. The realization that he had returned a murderer to society made him physically ill. He could not forgive himself. From the moment we returned from Wende's apartment, he had lain in his room in darkness, praying for the release that comes with sleep, or death.

But his mind—his greatest asset—would not allow him rest. No matter how he tried to calm himself, it continued to grind on, a self-sustaining engine of logic and shame. It endlessly replayed all the incidents since his arrival in Munich, fixating on every error and misstep.

For Dietrich those days were like a living nightmare. He tried everything to distract himself. He ordered food that he could not bring himself to eat. He had a bottle of brandy delivered, which on an empty stomach only made him queasy. Finally, the morning of the third day, desperation drove him to try a walk to tire himself out. Though he loathed the idea of going out, he shrugged into his coat and went downstairs. He was almost to the door when someone called out his name.

"*Mein Gott*, Herr Dietrich, you look a fright!"

The voice was one he had never expected to hear again. He turned, and to his combined shock and dismay found August Wende sitting in the lobby. Wende appeared at ease, reclining in a generously upholstered chair, a cigarette perched between the fingers of his right hand. In his smart, dark suit he looked very distinguished, even dashing.

Dietrich froze, unsure if it was an apparition. He walked over to Wende slowly, as if fearing Wende might dissipate, and took a seat across from him. They stared at one another in silence as Dietrich tried to master his sleep-deprived mind. Wende gazed at him in brazen delight.

"You used me," Dietrich said at last.

"Guilty," Wende said. "I was desperate. You appeared in my time of need, and you were clearly in need yourself. I would have been a fool to pass up such opportunity. I would ask your forgiveness, but I can tell by your face I wouldn't get it. So I will simply offer my thanks. Whether you welcome me is up to you."

Dietrich resisted the uncouth urge to spit in his face. In spite of his contempt, he had many questions for Wende. He felt a desperate need to get to know the man, to get a better idea of the person he had released upon society. But as much as he wanted those answers, he feared what he might learn.

"Why are you here?" he asked instead.

Wende apparently had been waiting for this question. He tried to suppress a grin.

"Because I am a man of my word," he said. "In my business, reputation is everything."

"So you are an honorable murderer," Dietrich said quietly. "How comforting."

Wende's mirth briefly flickered.

"You did me a great favor," he said. "And though my appreciation means nothing to you, I would uphold my end of the bargain. When you came to me you had questions, and if you can bear my despicable company for a short time, I am prepared to answer them."

In spite of Wende's insistence that he was a man of his word, Dietrich still did not trust him. But since Wende had against all likelihood returned, Dietrich played along.

"Tell me all that you know about the Illuminati," he said.

Wende's expression again flickered, his eyes darting left and right to see if anyone had overheard.

"I would not toss out that name so indiscriminately, if I were you," Wende said. "Whatever has led you to this point, you would be wise not to pursue it."

Wende paused, and the two stared at each other in silence. When Dietrich did not flinch, he went on.

"I can see *I* will not be able to dissuade you. Very well. Several years ago in Berlin, I was involved with a crowd who sought to establish a new fraternal order that they themselves could rule. At the time it seemed a good idea to enlist with them, to make new connections in what they assured me would someday be a global enterprise. I enlisted with the hope of being awarded a high-ranking position as the brotherhood grew. As time passed, however, I began to comprehend they were not so much interested in creating a new order as in resurrecting an old one."

He shot Dietrich a knowing look. Dietrich nodded in acknowledgment.

"When I learned this I hesitated, because that name carries with it certain implications. Being associated with it invites danger. But curiosity got the better of me, and I joined."

"Tell me more of these founders," Dietrich said.

Wende eyed him shrewdly.

"Theodor Reuss was chief among them—"

"Is he the one called Iscariot?"

"Don't leap to conclusions, Herr Dietrich," Wende chuckled. "Please, let me finish. The order's rebirth cannot be attributed to a single man. Reuss had two partners, Doctor Karl Kellner and Leopold Engel. They were two very different men. Kellner was a successful industrialist, bookish but ambitious. Engel was a charismatic actor and spiritualist, liked by all and favored by Reuss. Engel ingratiated himself with Reuss by supporting his vision of growing the order worldwide. This was in stark contrast to Kellner's vision, which was more academic. All Kellner wished to do was collect and hoard esoteric knowledge. He believed this would give the new order a mystical edge over their competition. But Reuss and Engel believed they should continue to expand. They dismissed Kellner's goal, which only infuriated him, though he kept it hidden from them. Realizing he would never have any effect within the order as long as Reuss and Engel stood united, he worked to cause a rift between them. At the height of Engel's popularity, Kellner began whispering in Reuss's ear. He led Reuss to believe that Engel intended to supplant him. The gambit worked. To protect his position, Reuss expelled Engel from the order in 1903."

"Reuss, Kellner, Engel," Dietrich said. "Which is Iscariot?"

Wende shook his head and sighed.

"None of them went by that name," he said. "But on occasion I heard them mention it. One might know."

"I must seek them out," Dietrich said.

"You misunderstand," Wende said. "I literally mean that one might know. Reuss? Perhaps. I think he now resides in London, still struggling to hold the

191

rabble together. A group of Irregular Masons really is an impossible beast to tame...."

For a moment Wende seemed wistful. Dietrich coughed and brought him back.

"If I were you I would not waste time on Reuss. He revived the order because he craved power, but he hadn't the slightest clue how to wield it. He was a charlatan."

"Kellner, then?"

"No," Wende replied, looking amused. "The good doctor died three years ago. I believe he ate something that disagreed with him."

"I don't suppose it was mercuric bichloride," Dietrich said dryly.

Wende inhaled on his cigarette and shot him a wink. Dietrich resisted the urge to throttle him.

"As for Leopold Engel," Wende continued, "he is still alive and well. If you have questions, he would be most likely to answer them. After his expulsion he departed the order with some bitterness."

"Where is he now?" Dietrich inquired.

"Saint Petersburg," Wende replied. "I think he moved there to care for his father."

Dietrich almost deflated. Saint Petersburg was very far from Munich. He rallied himself by taking a new angle.

"During your time in the order you heard Iscariot mentioned," he said. "What did you hear?"

Wende hesitated. Dietrich sensed he had asked a salient question. Suddenly Wende stood up.

"I think for now I have answered enough of your questions," he said with a smile. "I have other business to attend. I must be going."

Dietrich quickly arose and stepped in his path. Wende gave him a chastising look

"Really, Herr Dietrich? Must it come to this?"

Though weakened from lack of sleep and sustenance, Dietrich suddenly burned with righteous indignation. He had not expected to see Wende again, and now that the man stood before him, he did not want to let him go. If he had been armed with his revolver, he would have pulled it on the spot.

They stared at one another in silence. Finally, Dietrich mastered himself, accepting that he could do nothing without endangering the mission. He stepped aside, and a satisfied grin spread across Wende's face. Then Wende donned his hat and strolled out into the street.

At the conclusion of Dietrich's tale we all sat stunned. Irish frowned and leaned back in his chair. Ms Alexander was more subtle. She folded her hands in her lap and stared fixedly at the slender vase at the center of our table. It contained a quartet of lilies, two freshly cut, two wilting. Dietrich, on the other hand, looked at us expectantly. It was plain he had decided to take Wende's reappearance as a good omen.

"Wende's return is truly unexpected," Ms Alexander said at last, "but am I to understand you are willing to take him at his word?"

Dietrich deflated a little.

"You have a point," he admitted. "But given our situation, what other course do we have? Wende was the reason we came to Munich, and now he has provided us direction."

"Or a fiction to throw us off track," Ms Alexander said. "Forgive me for seeming contrary, but after being so expertly tricked, I am reluctant to act on any of his information."

Dietrich opened his mouth but paused. His eyes showed he was unwavering in his position. I anticipated an argument, but his next words were a surprise.

"As you know, I possess considerable intellect," he said. "It is so great, in fact, that it has consumed much of my life. The consequence is that I have long neglected other aspects. I am fifty-one years old. I have not wed. I have no children. I have a great many professional acquaintances, but I cannot name anyone I would call a true friend."

Ms Alexander's look softened.

"Do not pity me," he continued. "That is not my intent. I mention these things only to illustrate a point. When we arrived, I mistakenly placed my trust in the wrong man, putting us and our endeavor at risk. But that error began a wholly remarkable chain of events. I sank into an abyss of shame and self-loathing. That is where I have been for the past two days, at the bottom of that pit, wishing I could take back my mistakes. Miraculously, something good has come from it—the return of instinct. I was so enslaved by intellect that I ignored what instinct was telling me. Had I listened to it, I would not have fallen for Wende's scheme. But that's in the past. I am now focused on the future, and the successful conclusion to our mission."

We looked at one another, not quite sure of his point.

"Sorry if I seem dense," I said, "but what are you trying to say?"

He looked imploringly at us. His gaze met Ms Alexander's.

"I am saying that although August Wende is unquestionably despicable, and that only fools would take him at his word, on this singular occasion my instincts tell me differently. I do not *know* if Wende spoke the truth, but I *believe* he did."

We looked at him skeptically. It was a moving speech to be sure, but hardly enough to convince us to go on another wild goose chase. I was searching for gentle words to point out these facts when Ms Alexander spoke up.

"You ask much of us, Mr Dietrich," she said, "especially since my mind and instinct tell me differently. Are you so sure of this feeling that you are willing to risk everything?"

His red-rimmed eyes looked like they might spill over with tears.

"My dear, I have never been more certain of anything in my life."

She regarded him in silence, during which I continued searching for the right thing to say that would divert us from his absurd proposal. No one had bothered to ask me, but I had the distinct feeling that if we acted on Wende's information it would lead to tragedy. However, I could not bring myself to say it, especially with Dietrich in such a fragile state. Then Ms Alexander put the issue to rest.

"All right," she said with a sigh. "You are our captain. I do not trust August Wende, but I have faith in you. Tell us how you wish to proceed."

Irish and I sat amazed. He looked to me to inject some rationality, but I could summon no words. If Ms Alexander noticed our dismay, she did not acknowledge it. Instead, she kept her gaze fixed on Dietrich, who looked as if he had been relieved of a great burden.

"Wende said we should try Leopold Engel," he said. "We will go to Saint Petersburg."

14: CALAMITY

Upon hearing that our next destination was Saint Petersburg, the most beautiful city of her native homeland, Ms Alexander quickly overcame any reservations about Dietrich's newfound instinct. But she did not openly reveal her joy. Rather, she conducted herself perfectly, with only the slightest widening of her eyes at the mention of the Russian capital. For the short time we remained at our table that morning she was unusually silent, though looking at her I perceived a new radiance, so noticeable to my eyes that at first I thought it might be an effect of her peculiar condition.

We now had a destination, but that did not hasten our departure from Munich. After two restless nights Dietrich had to recuperate, to regain his wits, strength, and health. With new purpose his appetite returned, at least of sufficient proportion that he managed to down some bread and bratwurst for breakfast before locking himself in his room for hibernation. When he emerged a day later, he was himself again: all business and ready to lead us to our doom, if necessary. He busied himself with a variety of errands, including sending a wire to Cross, to inform him of our next destination. He sent a cryptic message about our latest adventure, omitting the embarrassing details of our being hoodwinked. He then made our travel arrangements, picking out particular trains and stops along the way (Prague, Dresden, Berlin) that would lead us eventually to the port city of Lübeck, where we would abandon the iron horse in favor of an iron leviathan, a steamer that would carry us across the Baltic to Saint Petersburg.

Until Dietrich awoke, Irish and I judged it best to stay indoors and out of sight. After our recent misadventures we thought it best to make ourselves scarce and stay off Munich's streets. By then the police probably had been informed of a foreign burglar with a weak stomach working the area, and rather than tempt Fate I chose to remain inconspicuous. Irish did not need me to explain the logic behind my decision. We were of the same mind and no explanation was required. When I produced a deck of cards and asked him if he fancied a game of poker, he immediately took me up on it, and from there it grew into an all-day tournament. We met with Ms Alexander for meals, and once I dared to escort her to the post office to mail a letter (I was tempted to ask to whom, but she did not offer, so I did not press). But aside from those brief interruptions, Irish and I spent the remainder of our time dueling at cards.

It was during this time that Irish began to act rather strangely. It was a subtle change that I did not at once pick up on, but looking back it should have been as clear as crystal to me. No matter how clear it may have been, I never would have guessed to what it would lead.

Ever since we had set out from New York, Fate had often paired us together, almost as if to encourage a friendship. For indeed Irish and I were much alike, sharing the same predisposition toward good food, drink, and company. Unlike Dietrich and Ms Alexander, who were restrained by propriety and would never allow themselves the freedom to indulge in the moment, Irish and I were more down to earth, it's salt, you might say. Neither of us was afraid to skirt the boundary of impropriety if it meant we would have a laugh doing it. Though we did not speak of it, we both realized it, and that unspoken bond made us like brothers.

As brothers, we got along so well that I never expected we would encounter a conflict of interests, nor did I imagine trouble arising from a convergence of the same. But on that day I gradually became aware that Irish was not exactly the brother-in-arms I had supposed him to be.

"You and the lady seem rather close," he said, dealing out another hand.

"I suppose," I said. "I think sometimes our mission can be difficult for her, being the only woman along. I do my best to take her mind off it."

"You must be doing a good job," he said, inspecting his cards. "She looks happy."

"Especially after hearing we're going to Saint Petersburg," I said. "That certainly pleased her. She's been glowing ever since."

"Yeah," Irish admitted. "It's hard for a man to take his eyes off her."

"Agreed!" I said wholeheartedly. "She's the most beautiful creature I've ever laid eyes on, and I've known plenty in my time."

He glanced at me over his cards.

"I had no idea you were such a ladies' man."

"A gentleman doesn't speak of such matters," I said with a wink.

Irish stared blankly at his cards for a while.

"Sometimes when I look at her," he said in a distant voice, "it's all I can do not to grab her."

While I empathized with his desire, I found the honesty of his statement disturbing. But I dismissed it as another of his uncouth behaviors. Then I recalled her electrical propensity and I chuckled.

"That would be a mistake," I said.

I looked up to find him glaring at me, looking hurt, as if I had said something cruel.

"What?" I said.

He said nothing. He looked stunned, like a bully who has received his first punch in the face, and from the scrawniest kid in the schoolyard. I was about to press him when he sobered. The next thing I knew he was all in, pushing his few remaining coins into the center of the table. I had to concentrate to keep from laughing, as he really was no match for me at cards. I saw his bet and leaned back in my chair.

"Call," I said.

We laid down our cards. I laughed when I discovered he had been bluffing with nothing more than queen high. I shook my head and displayed three jacks. I raked my winnings toward me.

"I guess she's all yours," he said.

He sat staring sadly at his lost money for a moment. Then without a word he left, not even tossing out so much as a *goodnight*. As I added up my winnings, I dismissed his petulance as the chagrin of a sore loser. I did not attach any further significance to his taciturn mood, but in the coming days it would become clear that I was not the only one in our party who had set his sights on Ms Alexander.

We departed Munich after a stay that felt like an eternity. On our way to the train station I was most anxious, expecting at any moment to feel hands clamp down on my shoulders, to be identified as the notorious vomiting vagabond, and to be hauled off to jail. I had learned from experience that such tragedies occur when least expected. Most would dismiss it as superstition, but based on previous arrests it was for me a twice-proven fact. So as we journeyed from the hotel to the train station, I was never more paranoid and vigilant. The Tombs had been frightening enough. I did not want to explore the German equivalent. It was not until Munich's spires had dwindled in the distance, and the windows were filled with the patchwork of the German countryside, that I finally felt at ease.

The trip to Berlin would take most of the day, and after the excitement we experienced in Munich I was almost looking forward to a long, dull train ride, alternately napping and chatting with Ms Alexander about whatever subject tickled her fancy. After recovering from his guilt-induced funk Dietrich seemed almost chipper, and I even looked forward to conversation with him. Strangely, it was my boon companion, Irish, whose company I enjoyed the least. For most of the trip he either napped—his chin on his chest, tree-trunk arms crossed, and his flat cap pulled down over his eyes—or he stared morosely out the window, only responding with a grunt to any question asked. By the afternoon I began to wonder about him. He was obviously in a mood, and I wanted to know why. But I held back, not wanting to embarrass him in front of the others. Knowing Irish, he would not have liked being questioned about his emotional state.

Shortly after brunch the train made its first notable stop in Prague. The tracks led us south of the city and crossed the Vltava River before looping back around to the north and west, depositing us at the main station in the center of Old Town, as it was called. As we made the loop, Ms Alexander had suddenly come alive. It seemed her proximity to even the least of landmarks awoke the tour guide in her.

"There," she said, pointing at a series of spires miles to the north. "That is the Prague Castle, the home of Bohemian royalty, though it passed into the hands of the Hapsburgs centuries ago. Within its walls is Saint Vitus Cathedral, a very magnificent church." She then drew our attention across the river to the northeast. "And over there, that castle that predates the royal seat."

As the train curved around northward she continued to point out sites of interest, mainly old churches and cathedrals which, viewed from miles away on a moving train, were not at all interesting. I smiled politely and gazed out the window in their direction, but I did not really see them.

The jaunt from Prague to Dresden was the shortest leg of the day's journey. Compared to the remainder of our trip it was a pleasantly tranquil period. When we pulled into the Dresden station, we took the usual stroll along the platform and feigned interest in Ms Alexander's cultural lessons. We then wandered into the station and found a small café and took lunch. Afterward we stood on the platform idly chatting while awaiting the conductor's invitation to return. Still, Irish remained aloof. I approached him to inquire about his mood, but just then the train whistle sounded and we were called back aboard.

We were less than two hours from Berlin when the conductor announced the dining car had opened for supper. Suddenly everyone was bustling in the aisle and heading toward the rear of the train. We waited a few minutes for the aisle to clear in order to give Ms Alexander the space she desired (or more so needed). When we arose, Irish remained slumped in his seat.

"You're not joining us?" Dietrich asked.

"I'm not hungry," he replied.

This struck us as strange, and definitely unprecedented. But we could do nothing more than wonder and move on. We left our taciturn companion gazing out the window, but even as we departed Ms Alexander shot him curious glances over her shoulder.

It was unsurprising then that Irish's mood became a topic of conversation over supper. Ms Alexander wondered aloud about what could be bothering him, in response to which Dietrich and I shrugged. I attempted to find something more interesting to discuss, even going so far as to point out distant towns and landscapes, hoping to draw my lady into a lesson on geography or history. But she did not take the bait. Instead she became pensive as she washed tiny bites of bread down with sips of tea. When the entrée arrived she pecked at her food without much appetite. Dietrich and I were midway through our meal when she excused herself from the table.

It was not difficult to read her thoughts, so clearly did they play across her features. Though Dietrich, Irish and I were many years her senior, she was at times like a mother to us all. Not that we thought of her in a matronly way, but her natural instinct for caring drove her to think of us as her wards. And as long as someone under her care was distraught, she was compelled to get to the bottom of it.

She made her way back to our car, but when she reached our seats, Irish was gone. She looked around perplexed. The car was not even a quarter occupied, but even before her eyes completed a sweep she knew he was not present. As she stood wondering, she noticed a man seated nearby watching her with interest. He was well-dressed with a stern face, his hands crossed atop a silver-handled walking stick.

She looked away, annoyed by his rude behavior, and continued her search. Since she had come from the rear of the train and had not seen our giant friend, she thought he must be further forward. She therefore headed to the next car.

As she reached the door she noticed another man sitting beside it, and at the sight of him she almost gasped. He was short and dressed in shabby clothes, with small, dark eyes that gleamed with the intensity of a badger's. But his most notable feature, the one that made her gasp, was not his feral eyes, but his grotesquely large shoulders. As she gawked at the hunchback she realized she was the one now being rude, and she hurried through the door.

She found herself in a cargo car among a maze of crates and traveling cases stacked head high. If Irish was somewhere within, she would have to look for him. She began weaving her way among towers of luggage, tentatively looking around each corner for our companion. However she found nothing but more cargo, haphazardly stacked throughout. She was about to give up when she caught a whiff of smoke, the acrid yet unmistakable odor of a cigarette. As she turned in place trying to locate the source, she heard the door behind her open and close.

Although she was most interested in pursuing the smoke and locating Irish, the latter event commanded her attention. She suspected an attendant, likely the conductor, had come to scold her for venturing where she had no business. She turned to see who had entered, but the luggage was stacked too high to get a clear view. Since she knew she was caught, she decided it was better not to press on. No need to involve Irish in her mistake. She turned back toward the passenger car, and as she rounded a stack of crates she let out a tiny scream.

She stood face to face not with the conductor, but with the hunchback she had seen only moments before. More precisely, she looked down at him, because he was a foot shorter than she. But now that he stood before her, she realized he was not a hunchback after all. The grotesque shoulders remained, but there was no slouching beneath their burden. Now they looked more powerful than misshapen.

The unwelcome surprise sent her back a step. She staggered before catching herself on a stack of crates and regaining her balance. As she straightened and waited for her heart to descend from her throat, the man studied her with the curious stupidity of an animal. She began to wonder if he was an imbecile, but before she could reach a conclusion she was half unconscious with pain.

It happened so unexpectedly that all she could do was wonder at it. In the blink of an eye, the man lowered his head and launched himself at her, burying a swollen shoulder into her midriff. The force of the assault stole her breath and lifted her into the air. She collided with cargo, first her body, then her head. She saw stars, followed by an encroaching darkness. For a moment the pain receded and she felt like she was floating, perhaps even dreaming. Still, she knew she was in danger and became desperately afraid. Somewhere inside her a small voice said to hang on, that to live she only needed touch her assailant. The solution was so simple it momentarily reassured her, until she remembered she would have to first remove her gloves.

In her half-conscious state even this simple act became a challenge. As she came awake she discovered she had been emptied of breath and filled with nausea. She tried to command her hands, but they involuntarily grasped at her stomach. She closed her eyes and focused on breathing, hoping this would help her regain control. When she could breathe again she opened them to find not one, but two men standing over her. If she had not been so distraught she would have been shocked by the realization that the second man was the stern-looking one from the passenger car, the one with the walking stick.

Both men gazed down at her curiously as she grappled with her pain. While her immediate thoughts were of survival, in the back of her mind she marveled that there were men who made sport of such punishment. Then, in a moment of association, her thoughts returned to Irish. He must be near. She could call out to him, if her lungs would allow it.

The gentleman said something to his misshapen friend, and the little beast grabbed her by the shoulders and seated her on a steamer trunk. Her body complained and continued in its attempt to fold over. The villainous gentleman then addressed her, but the situation was too riotous to focus on his words. Fear, pain, noise, confusion—these made it impossible for her to comprehend him. She was distantly aware he had mentioned the Illuminati, which was enough to make her realize her danger. She knew she must put aside her pain and control herself. With her hands hidden beneath her breast, she began to tug at her gloves.

The man repeated himself with greater insistence. When she still said nothing, he scowled, grasped his walking stick in two hands, and pulled them apart. Ms Alexander watched as a long silver blade was drawn out just inches from her face. Suddenly her blood ran cold. She struggled with her gloves more frantically, but the rubber lining made them difficult to remove, especially inconspicuously.

As she wrestled with her hands, the hunchback grabbed her by the hair and pulled her head back, exposing the curve of her neck. It was only when her head was so roughly jerked back that she realized the scene before her had changed. The two villains still occupied the foreground, but the background of the baggage gar was suddenly replaced by a wall of brown tweed.

Oddly, considering he was a man of action, Irish did not immediately execute his sworn duty. Instead he spent several seconds staring down in disbelief, his eyes locked with our lady's. In unprecedented fashion, the bottom dropped from his stomach and dizziness crept into his head. As he absently reached out a hand to steady himself, his mighty paw alighted on the knife-wielding gentleman's shoulder. This earned a startled cry that went unnoticed by Irish until the hunchback, suddenly called to action, turned, leapt, and struck him on the chin.

If Irish's mind was still in turmoil, his body—after a lifetime of brutality—was quite capable of acting on its own. It did not require his conscious approval to go into action. It registered he had taken one on the chin and reflexively went to work, operating of its own natural and violent volition, made all the more horrific by a slowly growing rage.

His right hand clamped down on the gentleman's shoulder like a vice, causing the man to shrink in pain until he stood no taller than his deformed companion. At the same time Irish's left hand found the hunchback's coat and latched onto it. He did not notice or care that the man reigned blows upon him, bloodying his face in the process. All he cared about was keeping a hand on the man, so he would know where to find him when his turn came.

But first things first—the man with the knife posed the greatest threat and had to be dealt with swiftly. As the villain aimed the blade at Irish's heart, Irish hurled him repeatedly against a stack of crates until his face was bloodied and his eyes dazed. He then tossed him aside, allowing him to slump into a pile against a wall of the car.

He now turned his full attention to the hunchback, who in spite of events had not ceased his assault. If this had been a prizefighting match, Irish would have been duly impressed by his opponent's determination.

The hunchback degenerated into a snarling, savage beast, hurling himself at Irish with such ferocity that he broke free and was on the giant's back before Irish's slow-but-deadly hands could stop him. Once there, the little beast wrapped his arms around Irish's neck, using the strength in his distorted shoulders in an attempt to choke the life from him.

Even as Irish turned a shade of purple, he managed to pummel the man's face until blood ran freely. But in spite of the blows, the little beast did not loosen his grip. Irish then repeatedly hurled himself backwards into anything concrete—crates, shelves, walls—until the man's grip slackened. When he felt it go loose, he reached behind his head, grabbed hold of the man by hair and collar, and threw him off.

The hunchback landed in an explosion of luggage, sending it tumbling down around him. Before Irish could make a move, the man scrambled back to his feet. As he did, his hand alighted on his partner's blade, and like lightning he launched himself through the air.

As they collided, the knife sank deep into Irish's left shoulder. He grimaced but otherwise ignored it, instead taking advantage of his adversary's close proximity. He landed a blow that sent the hunchback to the floor dazed, then descended upon him, hammering him so relentlessly the man's face was reduced to pulp.

Then, as casually as I scrawl these words, Irish walked to the car's loading door, flung it open, and tossed each man out. The hunchback was beyond resisting and went with no more objection than a sack of potatoes. His partner, however, was more vocal. When the car filled with wind and noise, he awoke in time to watch his sidekick being thrown out. As the same massive hands reached for him, he began to kick and scream. A moment later he was hurtling through the air into a trackside copse of trees. Finally, to punctuate the battle, Irish plucked the knife from his shoulder, and tossed it out, too.

As these events transpired, Ms Alexander had been mostly quiet. There were times when she wanted to scream, but she found her breath lacking. By the conclusion of the brawl her breath had returned, and perceiving Irish's intent she cried out to stop him from throwing the men from the train. She was thinking clearly enough to realize they might offer some useful information. But Irish never heard her. Her words were swallowed up in the roar of the wind and the train.

His work complete, Irish stood staring blindly out the door for a moment, letting the wind wash over him. Cooled, he turned to find Ms Alexander standing before him, her eyes full of concern and appreciation. It affected him in a way neither of them expected—before she could object, he took her in his arms and crushed her to him. It came as such a surprise that she was helpless to stop it. But no matter how surprising it was, it did not prepare her for what he did next.

As she looked up at his brutish face he suddenly closed his eyes and planted his lips on hers. Had his eyes been open he might have noted the look of astonishment, objection, and warning on her face, and he might have reconsidered, or at least paused. But he was still in the grip of primal emotion, and, frankly, nothing short of electrocution would have deterred him.

As chance would have it, Dietrich and I were there to see it. When we returned to our seats and found our friends absent, it naturally aroused our suspicion. We set out to find them, and our timing was perfect. Just as we entered the baggage car we witnessed the shocking event. As Irish lowered his massive head toward hers, we both gasped—Dietrich at the scandal, and I at the danger.

No sooner did Irish's lips meet Ms Alexander's than we were dazzled by a flash of light. When our vision returned we saw that Irish had gone rigid. He stood frozen for a moment, like a statue, before toppling over, perilously close to the open cargo door. Dietrich and I leapt into action, bounding forward to save him from rolling out. I grabbed hold of him while Dietrich closed the door. It was while I held him that I noticed Irish's many injuries. His face was cut and his left shoulder was soaked, and a quick glance around the car showed it to be in gruesome disarray. During the battle he had smeared blood on almost every surface.

"What happened?" Dietrich demanded.

As Ms Alexander recounted events, Dietrich attempted to staunch Irish's wound with a handkerchief.

"And what was that flash?" Dietrich asked.

Ms Alexander and I glanced at one another. There was no point in attempting to hide her condition any longer. Dietrich may not have understood what he had seen, but the image of it was forever burned into his perfect memory. Nothing we could say would convince him he had imagined it. And of course Irish, once he got his wits back, would also want an explanation. So Ms Alexander, in as concise a manner as possible, explained the effects of her condition.

Dietrich listened as he applied pressure to Irish's wound, showing no surprise or emotion in reaction to the strange news. As she spoke, Irish came around, and listened to her story with a dazed expression. At the conclusion, Dietrich looked at her over his spectacles.

"Good Lord," he said. "Like an eel?"

I had expected a more conscientious response from such a scrupulous gentleman, but Ms Alexander dismissed the *faux pas*. Meanwhile Irish propped himself against a wall and stared into the distance. No one mentioned the near-fatal kiss. Instead, we pretended it had not occurred, at least for the moment.

"What now?" I asked, more from a need to fill the awkward silence than from fear of being discovered by the conductor.

Dietrich looked at the bloody mayhem around us.

"We can't be linked to this," he said. "The authorities will have questions. Even if we avoid arrest, our mission will be compromised."

He inspected Irish with a discouraged expression. Irish looked as disheveled as the contents of the car. The handkerchief had absorbed its capacity of blood, but thankfully the bleeding had slowed. Still, the numerous stains on his clothes were impossible to hide. Dietrich looked at me.

"Sort through these bags and find his trunk," he said. "We must get him fresh clothes." He looked to Ms Alexander. "You should do your best to clean up and return to your seat. Once we're done we will join you."

She ran her hands down her dress to smooth it and looked at Dietrich for approval. Dietrich was momentarily taken aback, then lightly touched his face. Where Ms Alexander's cheek had pressed against Irish she wore a grisly rouge. She quickly recovered a kerchief of her own, dabbed it on her tongue, and wiped away the stain.

It took me a few minutes to locate Irish's bag among the clutter, but I finally hauled his from beneath a pile of suitcases and upended trunks. By then our lady had departed, so Dietrich and I were not shy about stripping Irish down. Dietrich fashioned a bandage from strips of Irish's ruined shirt, and soon we had him dressed in clean clothes. During it all Irish stared at the floor like an idiot child.

The shrill sound of the train whistle filled the air.

"Quickly now!" Dietrich exclaimed, wrestling Irish's arms into a fresh tweed coat. "We're approaching Berlin. We must decide how to proceed."

Although his words suggested a solution was needed, his expression told me he had already arrived at one, though he was reticent to voice it.

"Well?" I asked.

He frowned but said nothing. Sensing his stare, Irish finally roused from his stupor. He looked at Dietrich, whose eyes suddenly became sympathetic. They somehow seemed to understand one another without speaking a word. Irish rolled his eyes and sighed.

"Fine," he said. "Where do we meet?"

"The Palast Hotel," Dietrich replied hoarsely.

"Got any money? I may need it."

"Of course," Dietrich said. He quickly removed his wallet and passed Irish a handful of marks. "That should suffice. Good luck, and be careful."

Irish stuffed the marks into his pocket, slid open the cargo door, and stepped into the doorway. Suddenly I understood what he was about to do.

"Wait!" I said, but my words were drowned out by another shriek of the whistle.

I stepped forward and extended a hand to stop him, but at the same moment he leapt. I hurried to the door to look after him, but some tree branches whisked by and almost took off my head. I never managed to lay eyes on him, to know if he had survived the jump.

Considering Irish's unusual physique and talents, I naturally presumed he had survived. It seemed inconceivable that such a sturdy creature would be seriously injured (or worse) by jumping from a moving train. If Dietrich or I—or, God forbid, Ms Alexander—had attempted the same maneuver, I suspect the consequences would have proven dire. But for Irish such an action seemed well within his ability, as if leaping from vehicular transportation was something he could do on a regular basis. His nonchalant acceptance of the situation only reinforced this notion. Nevertheless, as we made our way back to the passenger car and took our seats by Ms Alexander, I could not stop worrying about him.

As we slid into our seats, our lady gave us a quizzical look.

"Where is Mr Irish?" she asked.

"He will meet us at our destination," Dietrich replied.

He clearly did not want to speak further on the matter, at least for the moment, but Ms Alexander only became more perplexed. She looked at me for some clue. I attempted a reassuring smile, but my facial contortions did nothing to alleviate her concern.

"Is he to remain in the baggage car?" she asked.

Dietrich shifted in his seat.

"No, he has taken a different route."

She stared at him in confusion. Then she glanced out the window and a look of realization lit her face. Foreseeing her reaction, I was already leaning forward to avert an unwanted exclamation. She caught herself and lowered her voice to a whisper.

"He is no longer on the train?"

Dietrich nodded almost imperceptibly, but his tight-lipped manner made clear he was unwilling to discuss it further while surrounded by strangers. Ms Alexander sat back and alternated her glares between us, not at all pleased with how we had handled the matter.

"You let him do this?" she said to me.

"Don't worry," I said. "We gave him money."

I thought this news would reassure her, but it only seemed to irritate her more. She turned away and stared out the window until we were on the outskirts of Berlin. Then Dietrich broke the silence.

"We will arrive shortly," he said. "Our tickets take us as far as the Alexanderplatz station, but we cannot risk staying aboard. We must get off at the first stop, the Schlesischer station, abandoning the train and our luggage. We must move with haste and get into the city before the conductor discovers the mess in the baggage car. Once he sees it, he is sure to summon the police."

Normally I would have been put out by such news, because replacing a wardrobe is a considerable nuisance. But if leaving behind my suitcase was the price of avoiding the police then I was all for it. I imagined it would be good news for Ms Alexander, as most women enjoy shopping abroad, returning home in the latest fashions to the envy of all. But the news did nothing to cheer her up. She continued to stare out her window, watching the countryside give way to low-lying buildings that quickly multiplied and crowded in on one another. A few minutes later the track swung out to the east, and from the west-facing windows we caught sight of Berlin. The track then gradually curved back around to the west and we lost sight of the city until minutes later its buildings raced by our windows.

As the train pulled into Schlesischer station—a monolithic tunnel of steel and glass—a feeling of dread came over me. My mind suddenly returned to the scene of my latest arrest, in which I had walked heedlessly into the hands of the police. As impossible as it was that the authorities would be lying in wait for us, I experienced the same sensation now.

I began to perspire uncontrollably, a fact I hoped would go unnoticed. Then I felt a tickling sensation start at my right temple and work its way down my cheek. As I searched my pockets for a handkerchief, I felt Dietrich's piercing gaze.

"Are you all right?"

I replied with a vigorous nod, and a wave of the hand to say it was a trifle. Dietrich nodded slowly, but he looked unconvinced.

"Stay calm," he said. "We will disembark and walk purposefully toward the station exit. Once we clear the station we will be fine."

I nodded. I glanced at Ms Alexander to see how she was holding up, and I was disappointed to find her as composed as ever.

The train came to a halt and the passengers immediately crowded into the aisle. As usual we were forced to wait on our lady's behalf, remaining in our seats until the crowd had thinned. While we waited the air in the car grew stale, and I felt my temperature rising. And as I grew hotter I began to itch uncontrollably, causing me to fidget almost convulsively. My friends looked at me in amazement as I worked a finger under my collar and did my best to loosen it. Just as I thought I could take no more, the car finally emptied. By the time I set foot on the platform I was myself again, though considerably damper.

I was the first one to gain freedom from the car, and as I stood on the platform I noticed in horror that the cargo car had already been opened, and porters were climbing into it. I froze and watched as the first bags were unloaded. The porters were working diligently and did not appear to have yet noticed any irregularity. As I turned to point this out, however, I heard a startled cry. A porter emerged examining his crimson-stained palms. Dietrich and Ms Alexander also noticed, and together we hurried in the opposite direction. As we made our way to the street we passed a pair of policemen hurrying toward the train.

When we exited to the street, relief washed over me. I knew we were safe, but we continued to walk, to put the station as far behind us as possible, until Dietrich managed to flag down a cab. Once inside, conversation resumed.

"When can we expect to hear from him?" Ms Alexander demanded.

"I don't know," Dietrich said. "By my estimation we were ten miles from the city. Perhaps some time tomorrow."

"Ten miles," Ms Alexander repeated, as if to emphasize the foolishness of the decision.

Dietrich forced a smile.

"Presuming he survived the leap," I said.

Dietrich's smile became a scowl.

"Yes," he said. "But he is sturdy. I'm sure he is fine."

Ms Alexander, however, did not seem reassured.

"I pray you are right," she said. "I hope that a large and formidable-looking man, wounded and disheveled, who speaks not a word of German, who wanders in along the tracks, does not draw undue suspicion."

Since she was the last person one expected to employ sarcasm, it took Dietrich a moment to recognize it. Once he worked it out, he turned toward the window to escape her scorn, and remained that way until we arrived at our hotel.

Our travel to the hotel turned out to be more of a trial than expected. It was no more than three miles from Schlesischer station, but at that early evening hour Berlin's streets were full of all manner of traffic that impeded our progress. A trip that should have taken less than thirty minutes took twice that. When we finally arrived at the Palast Hotel we practically leapt from the carriage.

While Dietrich picked through his pockets in search of payment for our fare — an embarrassing scene because he had given all his marks to Irish — Ms Alexander headed straight for the lobby, and I paused on the sidewalk to take in my surroundings. The Palast Hotel occupied the corner of an expansive block, which looked out across Potsdamer Platz, a convergence of broad avenues that in spite of its breadth was nonetheless choked with pedestrians, coaches, and streetcars. It put me in mind of New York, which for the first time seemed impossibly far away. It was a depressing thought, and one I was thankful to have interrupted.

"Forgive me," Dietrich said. "I'm coming up short. Do you have money for the fare?"

I dug into my pockets and came up with enough to cover it without a tip. The cabbie accepted it with a frown, then snapped the reigns and blended back into the vehicular current.

We entered the hotel and found Ms Alexander seated on a sofa, her hands crossed in her lap, the very picture of perturbed patience. I sat with her in silence while Dietrich hurriedly checked us in. As he handed us our keys he spoke, meeting Ms Alexander's eyes as little as possible.

"The business with Mr Irish aside," he said, "we must once again exercise great caution. It is strange that new troubles greet us at every destination."

I began to comment, to point out that no matter how resourceful Cross considered us, we were in fact novices in matters of intrigue. Looking back it was simple enough to see the trail of mistakes we had left along our way, and to recognize that in many cases it was luck that had guided us aright. But such criticism would do nothing to improve anyone's mood so I bit my tongue.

Without any baggage we had no need to visit our rooms. Instead we decided to have an awkwardly quiet dinner before retiring.

It was our first dinner-cum-meeting with a member *in absentia*, and though Irish had more often been a spectator than a contributor, we had all become accustomed to his presence: the heavy breathing, the insatiable appetite, the open-mouthed chewing. And of course there was the bulk of him, which reassured us and served as a natural ward against danger. Suddenly, all those aspects were gone, and a gaping hole was left in our circle. I attempted to distract us from his plight with idle chatter, and to drive out the image so indelibly burned into my mind of the brute intimately embracing Ms Alexander. But my observations earned me nothing more than obligatory grunts and nods. Finally, as we poked disinterestedly at our desserts, Dietrich chimed in.

"We are all worried for Mr Irish. But as I said, he should catch up to us by tomorrow." He looked at our lady. "In spite of your misgivings, which, mind you, I acknowledge as prudent concerns, Mr Irish is most capable."

Ms Alexander blushed, then sighed.

"Forgive me if I seemed upset," she said. "Many unexpected events occurred today. I have given the matter more thought, and I understand your decision to separate. We were all in danger of being embroiled in a serious legal matter. Separating from Mr Irish was the logical choice, and I admire you for making so difficult a decision."

Dietrich, who was normally somewhat rigid, visibly relaxed.

"Thank you," he said. "You are most gracious."

She offered a meager smile to show the matter was now closed. Nevertheless, the silence at our table persisted and followed us back to our rooms.

The following day we waited anxiously for some sign of Irish. We shared a pensive breakfast together in the hotel restaurant. Afterwards Dietrich went in search of a telegraph office to wire Cross, and I took advantage of the rare occasion of having Ms Alexander to myself. To distract her from her worries I recommended we do some shopping to replace our abandoned wardrobes. She accepted, but not with the enthusiasm I had anticipated.

We spent the morning taking inventory of the shops along Potsdamer Platz, finding several dress shops in which she disinterestedly browsed. As she perused her options I watched her. She wandered slowly among racks and mannequins, showing little emotion other than a slight frown at those fashions she disliked. In the end she purchased three dresses, more out of need than desire. While we waited for her items to be wrapped, she suddenly adopted a far-away stare.

"I am to blame, Prometheus," she said.

"Pardon?"

"I am to blame for this situation," she said. "If I had not gone into the baggage car, there would have been no combat, injuries, or deaths, and our company would still be together."

"Nonsense," I said. "Irish lives for fighting. His injuries will soon heal, and those villains on the train got what they deserved, especially after what they did to you."

She gave me a funny look, hopeful but skeptical.

"As for Irish," I continued, "we may be separated from our friend, but he will soon return."

This appeared to reassure her, or perhaps she was only being polite. She smiled weakly, but even her weakest smile made me feel as if warmed by the sun. I took it as a victory. Still, I could see she needed further reassurance.

"Something about that business on the train bothers me," I said. "Clearly the Illuminati are aware that we seek them. But when did they find out? When did we tip our hand?"

Her expression of worry was replaced with one of concentration.

"It could have happened at any point along the way," she mused. "Think of the characters we have encountered so far, all in service to one secret association or another. Who knows where their allegiances lay?"

I nodded.

"Men like Crowley and Wende are inherently untrustworthy," I agreed. "A wicked occultist and an assassin. They have no reason to protect our anonymity. I wouldn't be surprised if Illuminati agents were watching us even now."

The thought took both of us by surprise. We looked cautiously around, but the only others in the shop were the proprietor and his seamstress. When our eyes met again we laughed nervously at our shared paranoia.

"There have been others who have played smaller, but no less threatening roles," I pointed out. "What about the men we encountered in the alley in Munich? A chance encounter, or were they out to get us?"

She colored and looked away. I pressed on, intent on proving my point.

"And let's not forget the man who attacked me in Munich."

She gave me a perplexed look.

"I do not recall that report," she said.

I stared at her, both confused and amused that she would forget. A split-second later it came to me—she had forgotten nothing. Rather, Irish and I had never reported the incident. Wende had disappeared, Dietrich had descended into melancholia, and the matter had been forgotten.

"I have a confession," I said hesitantly.

"What?" Ms Alexander said in a tone full of dread.

As I recounted the ordeal a look of disapproval crossed her face. My plan to distract her from the plight of Irish was working to perfection.

"We must tell Mr Dietrich," she said.

I opened my mouth to dispute, but a look from her silenced any disagreement.

"Of course," I said sheepishly.

"Unfathomable," Dietrich said.

For several minutes it was the only word he said—repeatedly—as he fumed over the *foolish recklessness* and the *reckless foolishness* of Irish and me.

It was lunchtime, and we were in the restaurant of the Palast Hotel. After my accidental revelation I had managed to convince Ms Alexander to hold off until our midday meeting. She had agreed, but only after leveling a glare that made me feel like a child who was futilely attempting to postpone punishment, vainly hoping the transgression would be forgotten. When she sighed, rolled her eyes, and shook her head, I knew I had won. But when we returned to the hotel and sat down to await our captain, we sat in silence. That's how we remained until a bell tolled noon and Dietrich came down for lunch.

The conversation that followed—though it was more of a one-sided account delivered by Ms Alexander—had fascinated Dietrich up to the point of my drunkenness. Then his expression had gradually darkened until he was scowling and shaking his head. If I had not known him for a perfect gentleman, I would not have been surprised to receive a thorough belt-lashing at the conclusion. In truth, I had resigned myself to some sort of reprimand, most likely in the form of a withering rebuke. But I consoled myself with the facts that I had completely distracted Ms Alexander from her feelings of guilt, and I had acted as the catalyst of a vital, if belated, detail. These victories were naturally overlooked by my companions, which, in a strange way, only made them sweeter.

"Did Mr Irish know of this?" Dietrich asked.

I stuffed a piece of bred in my mouth and raised a finger to buy time. I did not want to drag Irish into this quagmire, so I searched for a way to extricate him from the story. But since he had obviously been my partner that night, I could not think of a way out for him.

"Yes. In fact it was Irish who disposed of the body."

That bit of the story, which to me had seemed self-evident, took them both by surprise.

"*What* body?" they hissed.

My companions stared at me in slack-jawed wonder as I explained how the assault, and its resolution, transpired.

"While I retrieved the ledger, Irish disposed of the body in the canal," I said finally. "But there's no need to be concerned on that account. Everything worked out fine."

But no matter how finely I portrayed the result, Dietrich saw it differently. He looked like he might have a seizure, or perhaps even explode. His jaw and hands worked in unison, rhythmically clenching with the shaking of his head. Even Ms Alexander, who was no less annoyed, was taken aback by the display. Dietrich sat back in his seat, crossed his arms, uncrossed them, stood, raised a finger, opened his mouth, closed it again, dropped his arm, reseated himself, leaned forward on the table, and stared into his plate.

"Unfathomable," he muttered.

I could only nod in agreement, as it had been a remarkable series of events. But in spite of the trouble I found myself in, I felt relieved that everything had finally come to light. The fact that we were known by the Illuminati, and that henceforth would be in mortal danger every minute of the day, was indeed unfathomable. But it was clear my friends were having difficulty getting past my transgression, still gripped as they were by disappointment over my failure to report the incident. Therefore, sensing this was a matter not soon forgotten, I sought to further distance Irish from myself, hoping to spare him.

But alas, who should come through yonder door at that particular moment, as if delivered by Fate to stand trial for his complicity? O, Fortuna! Why dost thou so mock and revile Mr Irish? What could he have possibly done to deserve this?

Dietrich was the first to spot him. While his outraged expression did not disappear, a slight widening of his eyes clued us in. Ms Alexander was next to notice him, and the moment she did her expression softened noticeably. I was sitting with my back to the door and was last to see him. I looked over my shoulder just as he strolled into the restaurant. He was less disheveled than expected. He had his sleeves rolled above his large, sunburned forearms; his shirt was stained beneath his arms; his pants and shoes were covered in dust from his trek along the tracks; and he casually carried his jacket over one shoulder, the wounded one, carefully hiding the bloodstains that had seeped through his makeshift bandage. As he approached our table he slowed, like an animal sensing a trap.

"What?" he said in greeting.

Dietrich arose and placed his hands on his sides.

"Welcome back," he said. "We're relieved to see you are well. Now, would you like to tell us your version of what happened in Munich?"

Irish stared at him dumbly. Then, slowly, understanding crept into his eyes. But friend that he was, he held the line.

"What are you talking about?" he said.

Dietrich bristled.

"I am speaking of an altercation, apparently minor in the combined estimations of you and Mr Grey, that culminated with the disposal of certain remains in a canal."

Irish furrowed his brow as he worked his way through Dietrich's words. He soon found his way, but he remained mute, invoking his right against self-incrimination.

If he thought, or hoped, his silence might conclude the matter, he was sorely mistaken. Dietrich, still fuming with righteous indignation, stormed out of the restaurant and upstairs to his room. A moment later Ms Alexander rose, shook her head at both of us in disappointment, and followed. I stood as she left the table. After a few steps she turned.

"I am glad that you are safe, Mr Irish."

Her words were sincere, but her demeanor was cold and had much more effect than any rebuke she might have given. Then she went on her way.

We watched until she passed from sight, staring after her for several seconds besides. I sighed and was about to offer my friend words of welcome when he gave me a look that caused me to take a step back. I smiled sheepishly. He half raised his free hand, and I winced expecting a blow. When none came I opened my eyes and noticed his upturned palm.

"What the hell?" he said.

Apparently it was rhetorical, because before I could answer he threw his hand in the air and walked away.

Fearing further and unified admonishment, I avoided my companions for the rest of the day. After lunch I went up to sulk in my room. I drew a chair up by my window and spent the afternoon staring at the ever-changing scene below, wishing I spoke a modicum of German that I might find someone in that ancient city with whom I could converse. I sat with one elbow propped upon the windowsill to support my chin. Eventually I tired of the vista and drifted off, still sitting in that same position. I would not have thought myself capable of sleeping while propped up, but either Time hastened or I dozed at the window for longer than expected, because I awoke to find the sun in descent. While I slept it had maneuvered around to the west and now lit my room, bathing me in evening's crimson rays.

I stood and stretched my limbs. As I crossed the room I thought I heard someone in the hallway outside my door. Curious, I walked quietly over and put my ear against it. I heard the voices of a man and a woman whom I identified as Dietrich and Ms Alexander.

"What are you doing?" Dietrich said.

"I am getting Mr Grey for dinner," the lady replied. "Do you object?"

"I'm still angry with him and Irish for their collusion," he said. "I'd be satisfied if I didn't see them again tonight."

"Are you so angry you cannot sit at the same table and share a meal?" Ms Alexander asked. She said it innocently, but I detected her sarcasm.

A pause followed, which revealed the depth of his dismay. Finally he relented and said, "Fine," but his voice made clear that he was only playing along to please her.

By then I had already decided that if I was not wanted at the table, I had no intention of subjecting myself to Dietrich's silent scorn. I would remain in my room for now and later get supper on my own. Then Ms Alexander rapped on my door, and it was like thunder in my ear.

Startled, I leapt back onto some creaking floorboards and winced, certain I had given myself away. A long silence followed in which I held my breath. Eventually I heard my lady say, "It looks like you get your wish," and they moved on.

I sat in my room and moped for another hour, succumbing to my own unjustified indignation. By then I was getting hungry, but I was determined to avoid Dietrich for the rest of the evening. As a result I began to think childish thoughts, the most ridiculous—and absurdly appealing—of which involved going out by a window. The more I thought about it, the more it amused me. Since my anger had been roused I had some pent up angst, and scaling down a building seemed like just the thing to burn off some energy and adrenaline.

But as I shrugged into my coat I reconsidered. The spectacle of a man scaling down a five-story building would draw unwanted attention from the street, and, if my companions heard of it, additional scorn. But finally I gave in, self-assured I could find a way that would avoid attention.

I exited my room and wandered the hallway, following it as it conformed to the perimeter of the building. Soon I discovered a window at the end of a hallway overlooking an alley. I looked once over my shoulder to ensure no one was watching, then opened the window, crawled out onto the ledge, and closed it behind me.

By New York standards the alley was broad, on the order of ten feet wide, and the opposite wall was almost identical to the one against my back. Neither building had many features from that angle, because the architects had designed the alley walls to be simple—both contained a spare number of windows and drain pipes. But those that existed were more than sufficient for a skilled acrobat to make the climb down. Looking to my right I spied a pipe that would serve my purpose. Without further ado I leapt from my ledge, grabbed it, and began sliding down.

The thrill of the climb made me laugh to myself, and for the twenty-or-so seconds of the ordeal I almost forgot all my problems. Then, as I passed by a third-story window, I happened to glance in and find myself face-to-face with a woman. She was standing in the hallway and leaning against the sash as she smoked a cigarette. I only briefly registered that she wore a black dress and white apron—a maid's uniform—before she saw me and screamed.

Her scream startled me. I felt like I had been caught in the act of something far worse than that which I was actually doing. The urge to flee was incontrovertible. I loosened my grip to speed my descent down the pipe, and in my haste I scraped every last knuckle against the brick wall, leaving a trail of blood the rest of the way down. As soon as my feet hit the ground I took a step back to examine my injuries. Then I heard the window above being flung open, and I took off running. As I ran I glanced back over my shoulder to see the maid leaning out the window, staring at me in disbelief.

After that I wandered Berlin's streets for several hours. I sacrificed a handkerchief, rending it in two to form bandages for my raw knuckles. They looked truly horrific, like half-minced meat, and I wrapped them more to hide than to heal. Even wrapped they seemed to shout for attention, bleeding through the linen in bright red blotches. Finally I shoved them into my coat pockets and kept them there. As painful as they were, once hidden from sight I was able to forget them fairly quickly.

I feared returning to the hotel because of what might be happening as a result of my shenanigans. I imagined the maid telling the police a story involving a man—half spider, half voyeur—fitting my vague description, clinging to a wall outside a third-story window, hoping for an eyeful. For my own safety I stayed away. For dinner I bought some spitted meat from a sidewalk vendor at the edge of a park. Afterwards I kept walking, following the sidewalk until, sometime later, it deposited me back at Potsdamer Platz.

By then the day was in its death throes. The sky had deepened to a purplish-black, and streetlights had begun twinkling into life. Since it was my first Berlin outing I did not have my bearings, and I did not immediately realize that after wandering countless blocks I had completed a full circle. As I looked skyward I saw the sign of the Palast Hotel directly ahead. I then heard a snort to my right, and my eyes fell to a bench along the sidewalk. There sat a massive shadow with a burning ember between its teeth.

"There you are!" Irish exclaimed. "Want to find a brothel?"

15: A BRUTE'S TALE

Much to the chagrin of Irish, we would neither visit a brothel, nor find ourselves in fevered trans-lingual negotiations with Berlin's back-alley wenches that evening. When I sat down to join him, I had not wholly dismissed the idea of engaging a few molls for some life-affirming diversions. But after we got to talking it quickly became apparent, at least to me, that no such adventure would occur that night.

I sat beside him on the bench and stared across the boulevard at the façades facing us. Windows had begun to light up and decorate the evening. My eyes involuntarily strayed to the upper tiers as silhouettes moved back and forth.

"You skipped dinner," Irish said.

"Given my recent ebb in popularity, it seemed wise," I said.

From the periphery of my vision I saw him inspecting me.

"What the hell happened to you?" he said, gesturing at my poorly bandaged knuckles. Then, with what sounded much like admiration in his voice: "Did you get into a scrape?"

"In a manner of speaking," I said.

"Illuminati?" he muttered.

"No, nothing like that."

He nodded slowly and gave me an appraising look. He then grinned, looking at me like a proud father whose son had uncharacteristically stood up to a bully. While I enjoyed this newfound respect I could not mislead him.

"It was an accident," I said, leaving it at that.

"Huh," he said. "If anyone asks, you should say it happened in a fight. Women like scars. At least that's what they tell me."

I imagined the kind of women Irish frequented would like scars, or so they would claim, as long as there was money in it for them. I was about to feel him out on the subject when I sensed he had become pensive. I looked at his face and could tell an uncharacteristic mood had descended on him. His distracted stare revealed that something strange was going on behind his eyes, some sort of previously unimagined self-examination. Since Irish was not the sort to willingly reveal anything about himself, I saw in this an opportunity for my own enlightenment. If ever there were a time to delve, it was now.

And my judgment proved correct. With little prompting I managed to get the sullen beast talking, or at least trying to, for he had difficulty recalling his own life. When pressed for details about his childhood, Irish's brow would furrow and he would get lost in thought. At first I attributed this to a general slow-wittedness, but I soon realized he genuinely could not recollect more than a handful of early memories. The cause behind this dearth of memory is anyone's guess: an inherent and underlying stolidity, perhaps too many blows to the head, or maybe it was willful forgetfulness. As he spoke, however, I formed, from the scraps he recalled, an impression of his life that was none too happy.

You may be wondering why I have bothered to present his fractured narrative in the pages that follow. The answer is simple: because even a surly and murderous soul is capable of self-sacrifice, heroism, and redemption, and in the aftermath of a great deed deserves to be remembered.

Circa 1861, Irish's earliest memory: sitting on a rough stone floor between two pair of booted feet, manly voices engaged in conversation above. The tones began to sour and rise in volume. It made him anxious, but before he could look up a dark shadow streaked across the floor, bridging the gap between them. He heard a startled cry, and a man—one for whom he had some undefined visceral attachment—collapsed to the floor. The child gripped the soiled, sticky shirt before him and pulled himself up on the warm body to take in the scene.

He was startled by a high-pitched cry and fleeting movement. Someone rushed toward him but was violently intercepted. A billowing skirt brushed his cheek, washing him in a fragrant breeze. Another heap then appeared on the floor near him, this one softer and with an assuaging scent. The child queried in a warbling tone, and, unanswered, began to crawl toward it. Suddenly someone grabbed him around the waist. He was hoisted before a top-hatted, black-bearded countenance. Dark eyes stared into his. Eventually the man placed him against his chest, cradling and shushing him.

He awoke as he was handed off to another, an unfamiliar man who was less consoling. His new bearer was old, fat, and redolent with a sickly-sweet smell. The man wore a shoddy black suit that, to the child, felt unpleasant all over. He recoiled from whatever part of the man he touched—his clammy skin, the bristles on his cheeks, his scratchy wool coat. The men briefly exchanged words before the blackbeard departed. Then the child was carried into a dark house. He did not understand the man's mutterings as they went, but they frightened him.

Every feeding was a trial. He resisted the spoonfuls of grey pudding, leading to angry mutterings and exclamations from whomever happened to be feeding him. But in each instance the utensil was forcibly worked into his mouth, and all he could do was wince and complain at the combined taste of mush, tears, and mucus. No matter how bad it tasted, hunger always overcame him, and by the end of the feeding it did not seem as bad as it had at the beginning.

William, as he came to understand was his name, grew accustomed to, but unaccepting of, several faces: the old, fat, prickly man; the fat lady; the thin lady; the big dirty man. He did not know why, but it was the last with whom he felt an unexpected kinship. It was a strange sensation because, unlike the Others—his distinction for the other adults in the place—the big dirty man did absolutely nothing for him: never held him, never fed him, never even spoke to him. But sometimes when William looked up he noticed the big dirty man looking around at the children. (Yes, there were many other's like William, though most were much bigger.) Occasionally the man's eyes would meet his and regard him with disinterest. This was the most pleasant and hospitable expression William had seen in a long time, and he developed a liking for the man.

The other children called the man Guy, so William did the same. Guy went about the place—a drafty stone building with four wings surrounding a cobblestone square—doing chores that left dirt, soot, sawdust, paint, and other dark smears on his hands, face, and clothes. Sometimes the Others talked to Guy like he was one of the children. William noticed that after such incidents Guy became quiet and angry, and if children got in his path Guy was likely to yell at them, or knock them out of his way with the back of his hand. William learned to stay away from Guy when he was in those bitter moods.

He learned the place he lived was called an orphanage. He learned this not from the Others, or from any of his fellow orphans. Instead he learned it from a priest who occasionally visited. Eventually he gathered that the name of the orphanage was *St. Oliver Plunkett's Home for Boys*, which was usually abbreviated to St. Oliver Plunkett's. He figured this out because it was the precursor to each of his daily reprimands.

Here at St. Oliver Plunkett's we always—, or, *Here at St. Oliver Plunkett's we never*—.

Gradually he began to understand there was a much larger world beyond the walls of St. Oliver Plunkett's. He learned, from looking out the few windows to which he had access, that there were other people and buildings outside. He pieced together that the orphanage was one of many, many buildings in a city called New York, and New York was only one of many, many cities in the world. This made an impression on him. He began to wonder what else lay beyond the four wings and the cobblestone square to which he was confined.

He made some friends among the boys, or at least he thought of them as friends since they always gravitated toward one another in the square. There were four of them, and William was the youngest of the bunch. He did not ask their names, nor did they ask his. They just started circling one another, and soon it turned into a raucous game of tag. It was great fun, until their voices carried in through the open windows facing the square, and the face of an Other would appear and yell at them to be quiet. They would stop running and calm down, but soon they would be at it again. After several iterations of running, yelling, and being yelled at, one of the Others always stormed into the square, grabbed whichever two boys happened to be closest, and hauled them away.

William knew what happened next, because he had been grabbed on several occasions. The Other took them to the common room and made them bend over a bunk, side-by-side. Pants were yanked down and a long, thin reed was briskly applied to their collocated bottoms. It was unbearably painful, so thankfully the Other usually limited the strokes to five, not because they were satisfied, but because by then the boys were on the floor howling in pain.

William also found himself drawn to Guy. If Guy was within sight and in a tolerant mood, the lad would sidle up and watch him at his work. Eventually, whether Guy was driving a nail or mopping the floor, he would notice William and nod. A couple times Guy even smiled. And once, a profound day in William's early life, Guy even spoke to him. He was sitting on a doorstep that led into the square, idly smoking a pipe while the children played. William wandered over to him. Guy eyed him with only the faintest curiosity.

"What's your name?"

"William."

"William what?"

The question surprised him. He had never considered that he might be anything more than a William.

"Never mind, kid," Guy said. "William, eh? Sounds like a goddamned Lord or something. How about I call you Bill from now on?"

It was less a question than a declaration, but William did not mind. Any acknowledgement from Guy made him feel good about himself.

Thereafter he was proudly known by most as Bill, the exception being the cold, often cruel, collective of the Others. As for them, Bill eventually absorbed their names, too: Mr Mercer, Ms Boone (the fat one), Ms Sneed (the skinny one). These became important to remember, because soon he was forced to begin a daily ritual that he did not entirely comprehend.

One day Ms Sneed instructed him to rise and follow the routine of the older boys. He found their early morning tasks were really no different than his, until he had finished a bowl of watery oatmeal for breakfast. Then Ms Sneed herded the older boys into a room lined with benches and tables, and they all sat in perfect stillness and silence facing the same direction. After a short time Ms Boone came in and proceeded to lecture them for hours on end in a variety of subjects completely incomprehensible to Bill's young mind. In spite of his boredom and discomfort, Bill knew to sit quietly, to stare forward, and to move as little as possible during the lessons. Children who fidgeted drew Ms Boone's attention, and that was never a good thing.

One day one of Bill's friends, a boy named Trip, was approached by an older boy in the square. The older boy pushed Trip around for a few minutes while saying cruel things. Both Bill and Trip stood dumbfounded, neither understanding why it was happening. Eventually the larger boy pushed Trip down, and kept pushing him down every time Trip tried to get up. When Trip looked like he was ready to cry, the older boy laughed and walked away. This scenario repeated itself almost daily, alternating between Trip and Bill's other friends, Jack and Robert. Each time it made Bill angry, but he was too scared to do anything—scared of the older boys, and scared of the whipping he would get if caught fighting. Both the encounters, and the thought of them, made knots in his stomach that lasted for hours.

One day during a confrontation he noticed Guy on the far side of the square, sitting on a doorstep and smoking his pipe, watching but not intervening. Afterwards Guy motioned him over.

"You gonna take that from those little bastards?"

"They're older," Bill said, as if it explained his inaction.

Guy puffed on his pipe. Smoke trickled upward from the corner of his mouth.

"You know why they don't pick on you?"

Bill shrugged. He suspected his time was coming.

"Because you're the big one," Guy said.

Though he was younger than his friends, Bill had experienced a growth spurt. He had noticed he was now taller than them, but he had never thought of himself as *bigger* than any of the older boys.

"You're the one they're scared of," Guy said. "Those bullies are pushing your friends around to scare the lot of you, but mainly you. And they're gonna keep doing it until you fight back."

Bill felt a small thrill.

"What should I do?"

Guy used the stem of his pipe to point, in turn, at Bill's face and belly.

"Hit them here and here."

The next time the older boys gathered around Bill and his friends, he did not wait for them to choose a victim. As soon as they stepped within reach, Bill launched a punch straight into a boy's eye. At first he was shocked at his own action and felt only fear. But when the boy fell to the ground crying, he started to feel better. He then put his fist into another boy's gut and sent him to the ground, too. When the third boy reared back to strike, Bill was a second ahead of him. He planted his fist squarely in the boy's nose and watched a gush of red coat the boy's upper lip. The appearance of blood both frightened and exhilarated him. He also knew it meant he was in trouble.

The ruckus got the attention of Mr Mercer, who stormed out, grabbed Bill by the ear, and hauled him to the common room. Bill got twice the usual number of lashes, but he was feeling so good about his victory, and he was so sure Guy would approve, he did not even care.

Bill silently followed the routine every day. Sometimes his friends, usually Trip, whispered and laughed during class. The teacher would either give them a warning or smack the backs of their hands with a ruler. One day Trip got caught four times, and since repeated use of the ruler had failed to curb his misbehavior, Ms Boone dragged him out of the room and gave him the reed. When Trip returned to his seat his face was red and tear streaked, but his expression was defiant. He nodded once at Bill, and Bill at once understood. Trip held out. He may have been whipped, but it did nothing to break his spirit. An unspoken understanding passed between them: they had a secret pact to resist. Through their defiance they would show they could not be broken.

Five days a week they endured the classes, but there was no respite on the weekends. Saturdays were dedicated to chores. Children were forced to spend much of the day sweeping, mopping, dusting, washing windows, helping in the kitchen, emptying outhouse buckets, et cetera. Sunday was much like the other five days, except instead of the Others holding them prisoner in class it was the priest's turn. He would arrive in the morning and subject them to lectures no less tedious than those delivered by Ms Boone. The difference was that the priest had kinder eyes and a kinder voice, and instead of introducing them to numbers and letters, he endeavored to introduce them to God. Most of the boys handled the introduction respectfully, or at least pretended to, but for Bill it was simply another boring lecture. He looked forward to the moments of lengthy prayer and supplication so he could close his eyes and rest without getting whipped by the Others for sleeping.

After the service the priest, Father Michael, mingled with the boys in the square. Everywhere Father Michael went, one of the Others shadowed him, glaring at the children over his shoulder as a warning not to complain. Trip had complained to the priest once and later got lashed for it.

Eventually Father Michael would leave and the boys would be allowed to entertain themselves in the square. One day after the priest departed, Bill spotted Guy sitting on the usual stoop and wandered over.

"Morning, Bill," Guy said. "Have you been a good Irish Catholic boy? Did you say your prayers and repent of your sins?"

There was something in Guy's tone that revealed he did not think much of church, and Bill was inclined to agree with him. It was boring and tedious. But he got stuck on some of Guy's words.

"What's Irish Catholic?" he asked.

Guy tilted his head and frowned.

"You are, lad. As is this place." Guy waved his hands at the walls surrounding them. "And all your little friends, too."

Bill thought on this but failed to make sense of it. Guy noted his confusion.

"Irish is what you *are*. It means you hail from Ireland, or your folks or their folks did, anyway. Ireland is a place on the other side of the world, full of people as shat upon as we are."

"What about Catholic?"

Guy considered it for a moment, then waved a hand dismissively.

"That bit's not as important as the Irish part, of which you should be goddamned proud. You remember that now, okay?"

Much later, perhaps a year or more, the boys Bill had beaten up came back for more. By then most of Bill's friends had disappeared. The one named Robert actually went home with a couple brought round by the priest, never to return. A few months later Jack developed a fever and a hacking cough and died a week later. Then one night Trip used a chair to shatter a window, which he then climbed through and ran away. Bill no longer had anyone he was close with, so when the bullies approached, he knew they were coming for him.

Oddly, this did not much disturb him, even when he noticed one of them carrying the broken-off leg of a stool. He knew the odds were against him, that the beating was unavoidable, but instead of dread he felt strangely self-assured. As the boys strolled up to him, others started to gather in their wake to watch. As the crowd gathered, Bill stared the bullies in the eye. Suddenly the boys seemed hesitant, as if they had not considered the implications of their actions until that moment.

In the awkward stillness Bill thought of Guy, and he did what he thought would make Guy proud. He shook his head and rolled his eyes to show his impatience, then landed a blow on a boy's jaw. That was the jolt the others needed. They leapt into action, jumping on him and dragging him to the ground. Bill tossed out a few punches, but in the end he just curled up and let the boys rain blows on him. The beating hurt, but not near as much as he imagined. Getting whipped by the Others was actually a lot worse.

He stayed in a ball until the boys ran out of steam. When the blows ceased and the bullies stepped back, looking down at him with a mixture of shock and satisfaction, Bill slowly climbed to his feet, wiped his bloodied face on his sleeve, and with a mischievous grin beat the holy hell out of them.

During a visit Father Michael noticed the black eyes and split lips on the boys. Ms Sneed cast a damning finger Bill's way.

"It's that one's handiwork," she said.

Father Michael raised an eyebrow and suggested Bill's aggression might be put to a more useful and constructive purpose. Ms Sneed was both uncomprehending and lacking in authority, so the priest took the idea to the warden and headmaster. Mr Mercer was at first unwilling. But Father Michael was persistent, and Mr Mercer always had difficulty saying no to a priest. In the end Father Michael won, and when he departed he had Bill in tow.

That was the first time Bill had ever been allowed outside the orphanage. Until then his knowledge of the outside world had been limited to what the Others had told him during school, which amounted to a mish-mash of historical facts that Bill saw no reason to absorb. Now, faced with the outside world, Bill felt almost overwhelmed. He did not get to see much of it, but as they walked he glanced down several streets and noted they all were lined with an endless variety of shops and buildings, and that the streets themselves curved and dwindled into the distance, suggesting a scale he had not previously imagined.

So this is the city, he thought. *This is New York*. He saw incomprehensible numbers of people coming and going, and children running freely along sidewalks and in the streets. He wondered how they were different from him, and why they possessed such freedom.

The walk with Father Michael was brief, so brief in fact that Bill was disappointed when they began to climb the steps to a large structure of hewn grey stone. Until then Bill assumed Father Michael lived far away, because the priest only visited once a week. He never would have guessed the priest lived and worked no more than three blocks away.

Father Michael led him into the church. At first sight of the sanctuary Bill experienced a feeling of dread. The rows of pews reminded him too much of the classroom at the orphanage, and he feared he was in store for a personal sermon. But Father Michael strolled down the aisle and led him through a door into a small office. There he deposited a Bible and some other personal items on a desk, hung his coat on a rack, and continued on. They exited a door in the back of the church, and the priest navigated through a maze of alleyways, sidestepping piled garbage and fetid puddles, until he came to a door. They entered and Bill was struck by a wall of thick, stale air. They pursued a dark hallway and emerged finally into a room containing something resembling a low, roped-off wooden stage.

The stage was surrounded by a handful of men who obscured Bill's view, but Father Michael guided him to an open spot and the two looked on. Bill was surprised to find two bare-chested men wearing what looked like swollen and stained leather mittens. They appeared to be in a scuffle, but they were doing more dancing than punching. Then one took a swing at the other, which led to a brief and exciting exchange of blows before both withdrew and began circling one another again. This went on for several minutes until another man stepped between them and put a stop to it, followed by laughter and a smattering of applause from the onlookers. The fight seemed to be over.

"What do you think?" Father Michael asked.

Bill shrugged.

"For the Irish, being able to fight is important," the priest said. "Throughout our history we've often had to defend ourselves against those stronger than us."

Bill had no notion of Irish history, but given his trials he could relate.

"But we must weigh our earthly love of the fight with God's law. Do you think Christ would approve of you beating up those boys?"

Bill shook his head, but only because he knew it was what the priest expected. Father Michael smiled.

"I have an offer for you, William. It's good for a lad to learn to fight, but it's also important to show compassion and forbearance to our fellow man. The compromise is here." Father Michael gestured at the boxing ring. "Here, two men can exercise their skills and afterward walk away as Christian brothers. Sometimes men come here with disputes, disagreements they can't work out in words, and they settle their differences in this ring. It's not the way I would prefer, but it's better than brawling in the streets. My offer to you, William, is this. I'll teach you about fighting if you'll promise to keep what you learn in this ring. Do we have a deal?"

"Sure," Bill said with a shrug.

"All right," the priest said, looking very pleased. He looked toward an older man who was busy unwrapping strips of cloth from the hands of one of the fighters. "Sean! I have a new student for you."

Several factors helped Bill honor his half-hearted agreement with Father Michael. After single-handedly defeating three bullies he became the undisputed boss of the yard. And once everyone knew the priest was teaching him to be a *better* fighter, no one wanted to provoke him. Most significantly, he had reached adolescence, and his body was rapidly changing in startling ways. He rarely consulted a mirror, mostly because the ones in the bathrooms at the orphanage were broken, and the Others refused to replace them. But he happened to catch a glimpse of himself in a mirror at the gym, and he was startled at what he saw. It was as if overnight he had grown as tall as Mr Mercer, his shoulders had swelled to the width of the doorways, and his fists had become veritable mallets.

Guy was noticeably impressed when he learned the priest was teaching Bill to box, and he encouraged Bill to make the most of it. He was so interested, in fact, that he told Bill he would stop by the gym and watch him fight the following Sunday. Guy's interest in him made an impression. For the next week Bill could think of little else.

The following Sunday, after the orphanage service, Father Michael collected Bill and they left for the gym. As the priest forced Bill's hands into the puffy leather gloves, Bill scanned the gym for Guy, but he saw no trace of him. Once the gloves were tied, he was almost reticent to get into the ring, as if doing so would eliminate any chance that Guy would show. But Father Michael, Sean, and the rest were impatient and chided him until he climbed through the ropes.

In the ring he found himself standing across from a young man who was obviously several years older. Suddenly Bill felt small, even though he was taller and heavier than his adversary. Then he recalled what Guy had taught him, that he was actually the big one, and his confidence began to grow. Bill's mind returned to Guy, and he was so preoccupied that he did not realize the fight had begun until a blow landed on his chin. That managed to wake him, and over the next minute and a half Bill beat the pulp out of his opponent. When the round ended Sean stepped in to wave him off, but Bill was so inexplicably angry that he continued to beat the young man down. It was not until Father Michael jumped into the ring and interposed himself that Bill finally paused.

"Enough!" the priest shouted.

Bill retreated to the furthest corner of the ring and cooled off as Father Michael and the referee saw to the unconscious boy. Afterward, Father Michael had words for Bill as they walked back to the orphanage.

"You've got a smoldering fire in you," the priest said. "It can be a good thing when turned to a purpose, but it can be a curse if you let it consume you. After what I saw today, I wonder if putting you in the ring was a wise choice. You've already got plenty of fight in you, more than any man I know. I don't think you need any encouragement to bring it out."

They continued on in silence. As they approached St. Oliver Plunkett's, Bill slowed his pace. Father Michael stopped and looked at him. The priest frowned and sighed.

"Relax, lad," he said. "God has blessed me with wisdom and insight. Now I have a better understanding of our situation. My mistake was thinking you needed to learn to fight. What you really need to learn is control, of both fists and spirit. Your fists I'll leave to Sean, but I'm uniquely qualified to help in the spiritual department."

Bill's disappointment with Guy took the form of quiet anger. The next time they crossed paths was in the square. Guy took up his usual smoking spot on the stoop, but Bill ignored him and pretended not to notice. He thought that was a good way to make his displeasure known. But a few sidelong glances showed that Guy was unaffected by the cold shoulder treatment. In fact, Guy was oblivious to it, not once looking Bill's way.

The boxing lessons became a steadfast part of Bill's weekly routine. On occasion he got carried away, and Father Michael had to leap into the ring and stop him. But contrary to the priest's belief, Bill's ruthlessness was not due to a smoldering anger. When Bill stepped into the ring, all emotion melted away. He had a singular focus, and every blow, delivered or received, only sharpened it.

In spite of the occasional need to intervene in the boy's fights, Father Michael saw Bill's progress as a triumph. He was confident the boy had rounded a bend.

Bill's body continued to grow and develop. Stubble broke out on his face and grew so wantonly that Mr Mercer forced him to shave three times a week. Bill realized he was becoming a man, though he was not sure what that meant. He wanted to talk to someone about it, but none of his peers at the orphanage were any smarter on the subject. He considered Father Michael, but he quickly dismissed the idea, because all the priest's talks ended on the weary topics of compassion and forbearance. He suspected Guy had the answers, but ever since Guy had let him down, he had avoided him due to a mixture of anger and embarrassment. So he forced himself to concentrate on the priest's watchwords, hoping that somehow the mysteries of manhood would become apparent.

One night, out of the blue, he awoke to prodding and rolled over to find Guy only inches from his nose. Guy had a mischievous look in his eyes, a wicked grin on his face, and breath that made Bill recoil. He shushed Bill and motioned for him to follow.

Though it was strange and unexpected, Bill got up, dressed, and followed Guy out a back door. Once outside, Guy rummaged behind a slowly decomposing stack of wooden crates and produced a tall bottle. He uncorked it with his teeth, took a long draught, and handed it to Bill.

The acrid scent made Bill turn up his nose, but sensing it was a test, he forced himself to drink. He stifled a cough as the whiskey burned its way down, mapping his esophagus and stomach. Guy was pleased, and together they strolled through the dark city streets taking turns at the bottle.

By the time the bottle was empty, Bill felt wonderfully relaxed. As if on cue, Guy turned into a doorway and climbed a narrow stair. Bill followed and found himself in a musty room furnished with old abused sofas. A woman of similar age and girth as Ms Boone appeared, wearing a dark dress that revealed a commanding view of her prodigious cleavage. Guy passed her a handful of coins.

"Evening, ma'am," he said, removing his hat and smoothing his dirty, unkempt hair. "We seek some nocturnal entertainment. While I can't be absolute, I suspect this is my young friend's first time. So be gentle with him, if you don't mind."

The woman looked Bill up and down, clearly impressed by the size of him, and skeptical that gentleness was necessary. Then she turned and headed toward a curtain. She drew it back to reveal a hallway, and Guy shoved Bill after her. As he followed her down the dark passage, Bill looked over his shoulder at his smirking and swaying companion. Guy grinned and gave him a salute.

Bill reluctantly followed the fat woman down the hall until she stopped at a door. She knocked once and opened it, not really giving whoever was inside a chance to respond. There was a girl inside, dressed in nothing but a corset and torn stockings, laying on a soiled mattress, and reading a dime novel.

"You've got company," the woman said. Then to Bill: "This is Jezebel. She'll take care of you."

The girl sighed, marked her page, and stood to greet Bill. When he stepped into the room, her eyes widened and she took a step back, but the fat woman shot her a look and she quickly mastered herself. The madame then left them to their business.

The girl took a minute to warm him up, hanging on him and whispering suggestively in his ear. Bill's thoughts briefly returned to Father Michael and his sermons on morality, but the slender, perfumed girl rubbing against him effortlessly drove them away. She soon worked Bill out of his clothes, guided him to the bed, and pulled him down to her. Bill had no idea what he was supposed to do, but Jezebel guided him through it, whispering words of arousing encouragement as she writhed beneath him. Afterwards, as they lay naked on the bed, Jezebel rolled away and onto her side, and Bill drifted off to sleep.

Once again he awoke to prodding. He opened his eyes to find Guy silhouetted against a window full of pre-dawn sky, poking at him with a booted toe.

"Get up," Guy said, sounding not at all as friendly as he had the night before. "We gotta get you back before anyone notices, or it'll be my arse."

Bill slowly rolled onto one elbow and rubbed his eyes, trying to recollect his whereabouts.

"Get up, goddammit!" Guy said, this time with a sharp kick to Bill's arm.

"I ain't losing my job over you, so get moving!"

In his grumpy, half-wakened state, Bill was irked and had to resist punching Guy in the face. He rose, scrambled into his clothes, and hurried for the door. As he went, he glanced back toward Jezebel. He caught a brief glimpse as she turned her head away and pretended to be asleep.

A week later Bill worked up the nerve to ask Guy when he could visit Jezebel again. Guy smiled and shook his head.

"I don't think you'll be able to see her again," he said, "but there's plenty of others who'd love to make your acquaintance."

Bill was disappointed about Jezebel, but he took encouragement from the implication that Guy would take him out again to meet others.

One day as everyone was being herded into the classroom, Ms Sneed diverted Bill to a small office where he found Mr Mercer and Father Michael. The choleric headmaster directed him to a seat, shuffled through some papers, and addressed him without looking at him.

"William Irish, you were delivered into the care of Saint Oliver Plunkett's in November of 1861. Since you arrived with no pedigree, we assigned the date of your arrival, November second, as your date of birth."

Bill stared at him blankly. He was both surprised and satisfied at the utterance of his last name, which no one had ever bothered to tell him. It struck him as a name Guy would be proud of. Mr Mercer sighed impatiently.

"Today is the second of November, 1876. By our reckoning you are aged fifteen years."

The headmaster looked at him expectantly. Bill wordlessly returned his gaze. Mr Mercer bristled.

"This means," he continued, "that you are now considered *of age* by our standards, and that you are to be released into the world. We at St. Oliver Plunkett's have invested much time and expense toward your care and education over the years, so you should be well-prepared for whatever the future holds."

Finally, Bill understood what was happening, but he was too surprised to believe it. Mr Mercer again became perturbed, his jowls quivering with impatience.

"It is customary for a young man in your position to be thankful, to express his gratitude for the years of hard work the staff at St. Oliver Plunkett's has invested in you."

Bill considered ignoring the statement, but he did not want to give the priest cause for a lecture. He muttered an empty *thank-you* that only made Mr Mercer more livid. Father Michael then intervened.

"This is a momentous occasion that some find daunting, because they are so accustomed to being looked after," the priest said. "The prospect of heading out on one's own, especially into such a large and ominous city, can be unnerving. That's why I'm here, William. I'll help you find work and a place to live so you can get by on your own. No need to worry, son. Everything will be fine."

Father Michael found Bill a job as a stevedore. The docks were an endlessly busy place visited by ships from all over the world. When they arrived it was the job of Bill (and a hundred others) to unload the cargo and place it on wagons to be hauled away. The labor was difficult for most, but Bill's size and strength made him apt at it.

In the course of such work there were often injuries, and even some deaths, which sometimes scared off a dozen workers or more. But most were like him, hard-luck cases with no other prospects. They learned to quickly put tragedy behind them and carry on.

Bill did not find the work overly difficult, but it was tedious, and he disliked the crusty foreman who threatened the workers if they paused longer than it took to tie a shoelace. The only good part of the job was that it made him stronger and harder, valuable qualities when stepping into the ring.

He still went to the gym every Sunday and fought with anyone who was man enough to get into the ring with him. Most took one look at him and declined, but now and then a cocky bastard would come along and take up the challenge. None of Bill's bouts ever lasted more than a couple minutes, and they usually lasted that long only because he liked to absorb a few punches before knocking his opponents out cold.

Father Michael still came by on most Sundays to watch him fight. Sometimes he told Bill how proud he was of him, of the man he had become. Bill never quite understood the compliment, because he saw himself as just another longshoreman.

Bill continued to grow into an adult, and the combination of growth and hard work turned him into something of a monster. By eighteen, he dwarfed most men and had become a bit frightening in appearance. The weekly beatings he subjected himself to had not improved his looks. He had suffered several broken noses over the years, and, as if in response to his eyes being so repeatedly struck, his bony brow seemed to have grown outward to protect them. When he looked in the mirror he saw an ogre, but it did not bother him much. When he felt lonely he would find a brothel, buy a girl for the night, and forget himself, usually terrifying her in the process. Once the transaction was complete, he would depart knowing he would not be welcomed back. No woman, whore nor otherwise, would consent to see him again.

One day Father Michael convinced him to come to dinner, to meet a young woman he thought might interest Bill. Bill agreed, looking outwardly reluctant, but feeling inwardly hopeful and desperate. When he met her, he was impressed by her, but he saw in her eyes the feeling was not mutual. After an awkwardly quiet meal they went their separate ways. Bill knew it went badly, and his feelings were confirmed when Father Michael never spoke of it again. It was as if it had never happened.

Bill passed almost a decade in this fashion.

One day Bill was in the ring sparring when a door to the street opened and light flooded in. He noticed a silhouette in the doorway for an instant before the door closed and the figure was lost in shadow. It was only a brief distraction, and Bill gave it no further thought because he was busy letting a braggart punch him in the face. A few minutes later he became bored and took the man out with three rapid punches, two to the belly and an uppercut, that almost launched the man out of the ring.

Afterwards, as he dabbed the blood off his face with a filthy towel, he spied someone standing ringside, leaning on the ropes. He performed a double-take because the man looked very familiar. When the man smirked and winked at him, he realized it was Guy. Bill awkwardly approached him and they moved off to one side to talk. As Bill unwrapped his hands, Guy took long draughts from a flask.

"Christ Almighty, look at you!" Guy exclaimed. "You're a goddamned monster! You laid waste to that bastard with only three punches. And he was no pansy, either. I know that one, seen him in the bars, a big talker. Always on and on about how rough he is, and threatening to beat down anyone who looks at him cross-eyed. But by God, you laid him out. Amazing! Where'd you learn to fight like that, lad?"

Bill stared back at him, half amazed and half amused by Guy's forgetfulness.

They went to a bar and Guy bought them some rounds. At first it was just catching-up talk. Bill told him the meager details of his life at the docks, and Guy complained about his continued position at the orphanage. Guy did most of the talking, rambling from one subject to another with ease. They passed several hours and emptied a bottle of whiskey before Guy got around to making his offer.

"Listen, the way you beat that son-of-a-bitch earlier. You've got talent, lad, and you're wasting it in that goddamned gym. I know a way you can make some money—good money—with those skills. If you're interested."

Bill nodded. Guy told him of some places where men gathered to fight for money. He called it prizefighting. Given Bill's ability, Guy said it was a sure thing. Easy money. It sounded so easy, Bill could think of no reason not to try it.

They met again the following evening and Guy took him on a back alley excursion. They came to a door, and after a knock and a few words from Guy they were allowed inside. Within was a raucous gambling house, replete with a variety of card games, craps, and roulette, all arranged at tables around the outskirts of a large room. At the center stood a ring in which two men were using bare fists to beat each other to a pulp.

Soon the fight ended with one man bleeding on the floor, and the call went out for any takers. Guy jumped up and nominated Bill, and everyone in the room turned his way. There was a moment of silence as the crowd looked him over, then the room exploded with voices as wagers were hastily made. Bill removed his coat and shirt and climbed into the ring. Before the fight began, Guy told him to play it just like at the gym, to let his opponent get a few shots before unleashing hell. Bill nodded.

The fight began and Bill did as he was told. He let the man pound on him for several minutes, occasionally throwing a half-hearted punch that his opponent easily dodged. As he was being punched in the face he was peripherally aware of the jeers, of comments that he was too slow and stupid to win. He caught a glimpse of Guy taking mock offense at these insults and redoubling all his wagers, and then he grasped the strategy. He continued circling the ring and taking a beating until Guy caught his eye and nodded. Bill waited until the man's elbows drifted apart exposing his midsection. He then delivered a rapid one-two punch to the gut, followed by an uppercut that sent the man into the air. By the time he landed he was out cold. A stupefied silence fell over the crowd.

They quickly left the gambling house and found a vacant alley where Guy counted out the money and handed Bill his share. Bill noticed Guy's share seemed larger than his, but he was happy to make anything and did not complain.

A new routine was established. Every week Guy went in search of new bars and gambling houses where fights were held—places where he and Bill were not known—and every week Bill showed up, clobbered his opponents, and they left considerably better off than when they came in. For the first time in Bill's life, things were looking up.

One would expect the longevity of such a grift to be brief, but Guy was clever and knew how to work each new crowd.

"My friend here packs a wallop, but he's awful slow. Still, what are friends for? My money's on him!"

That was usually enough to hoodwink most, especially those who had already downed a few. Besides, the crowd had come to gamble, so they seldom needed much cajoling.

As for Bill's opponents, one would think they would get a look at him and smarten up. But something strange happens to men in dens of vice. If they are not already drunk and brimming with false confidence, they are stone sober and full of foolish pride. The former is usually more of a threat to himself than his opponent, and the latter is so determined to prove he is the better man that he would leap into the ring against a lion. So Guy's part of the business, running the con, was easy considering so many naturally fell into those categories.

Their luck held out for a couple years before they had searched out and exploited every ring in the city, departing a good deal wealthier each time. But after every fight Bill stupidly followed Guy to a bar or a brothel, and by the next day their profit was gone.

At that point they suddenly faced a two-headed beast of a predicament. First, Bill's reputation had spread far and wide, well beyond their ability to outpace it unless they headed somewhere remote. In New York everyone was wise to their game, and no one would take Guy's bets anymore. Second, and more serious, was that Bill had accidentally killed three men in the ring. Now, no one would fight him.

Bill's first victim was a fellow who went by the name Big Jim Dandy, the self-proclaimed Gentleman of Prizefighting. Big Jim was bigger than average, but he did not look particularly big to Bill. And he was certainly a dandy, because he would show up to the ring in a top-notch suit, hair oiled and moustache waxed. He would then make a great show of removing his fine garments and jewelry, alternating between courteous small talk with the audience and making jokes at Bill's expense. The crowd loved him, especially compared to the morose behemoth sitting in the opposite corner. At the end of the second round Bill delivered a blow that drove bone shards into his brain and left him flopping on the ground like a fish out of water.

The second victim was a large, pale man with golden locks as long as a woman's. The referee introduced him as Mjölnir. Bill supposed it was a Viking name, because before the fight Mjölnir's manager made a great show of braiding the man's hair like a little girl's. But any similarity between Mjölnir and females ended there, because Mjölnir was well-muscled and a good fighter. He lasted three rounds before Bill shattered his ribs and he coughed up blood. It was not until a few days later that word of Mjölnir's death reached Bill. The mighty and ostensible Norseman had died from a punctured lung.

After Bill's second casualty, rumors began to circulate of a big Irish fellow who was certain death to anyone fool enough to get into the ring with him. Prizefighting fans and aficionados, always on the lookout for the next sensation, must have thought Bill was The One. They took it upon themselves to invent for him a moniker that became instantly and inextricably attached. The first Bill knew of it was when he showed up for his next fight and the announcer introduced him as Black Irish.

He managed nine more fights (all wins, of course) before his third casualty: a large Negro with the eyes and nostrils of an angry bull, which was perhaps why he was called Mad Bull Johnston. Coincidentally, he also happened to be as large as a bull, which meant he was still a bit smaller than Bill. But the size difference did not seem to bother Mad Bull in the least. From the moment he stepped into the ring he glared at Bill with such unadorned hate that those ringside wondered if there were a secret grudge between the two.

Mad Bull's furious intensity intrigued Bill, and he let the Negro land a few blows to see if it was an act. He quickly discovered Mad Bull was much stronger, and madder, than anyone else he had fought, and he decided not to give away any further injuries. He and Mad Bull squared off and went at each other for seven rounds, which was unheard of with Bill. By then both men's faces were unrecognizable, and their hands swollen from pounding each other's stony skulls. Then, out of weariness or confusion, Mad Bull dropped his guard and Bill struck him on the side of the head. Through his fist Bill felt (and imagined he heard) something snap, like the breaking of a broomstick over one's knee. The crowd erupted as Mad Bull crumpled to the floor. Never before had any in attendance seen such a wonderfully brutal match. It was not until minutes later, when the crowd around Bill thinned, that anyone realized Mad Bull was still on the floor, dead from a broken neck.

So their predicament was a very real one, more so for Guy than for Bill, who still worked days at the docks. As long as he could lift cargo, Bill had a future, albeit a bleak one. But Guy had nothing.

Since their reunion, Guy's livelihood had centered on Bill's willingness to climb into the ring and take a beating. Guy had made those beatings his life's work, and the prospect of his grifting career abruptly coming to an end was an idea he could not abide. The money was one thing—perhaps the most substantial thing—but Guy refused to let such an opportunity slip away. He had worked under the yoke of the splenetic staff at St. Oliver Plunkett's for two decades, and he refused to go back now. (In fact, he could not go back— Guy had quit the orphanage and made his departure irrevocable by breaking into the headmaster's office, stealing anything of value, and defecating on the man's desk.)

So it was understandable, if not forgivable, that Guy bent his feverish, scheming mind to a new plan. He told Bill not to worry, he had it all figured out. Everything would be fine.

At the next fight—which took almost three months to arrange—Bill was sitting in his corner on a rickety stool that looked as if it might collapse under his weight at any moment. He was waiting on the announcer to call him and his opponent, an Italian who did not speak a word of English, to the center of the ring. But the announcer did not seem to be in a hurry, even if the crowd was getting impatient. He occasionally walked to the middle of the ring, cast a furtive glance at Bill, and strolled back to the ropes to converse with members of the crowd. The behavior was odd, but Bill gave it no thought and continued to scan the crowd for Guy.

Guy finally appeared, carrying a length of rope in one hand. He motioned

Bill to his feet, tied the rope around his waist, and told him to turn around. Bill followed his instructions in baffled confusion until Guy wrenched one of his massive arms behind his back and began to tie it off.

"Look here," Guy hissed. "It's the only way I could get anyone to fight you. You gotta fight this guy with one arm tied back."

At first Bill thought it was a joke, but as Guy secured his left arm he went dumb with incredulity. As soon as Guy completed the knot, he jumped out of the ring before Bill could say a word. At that moment the announcer, suddenly satisfied, called the two men to him and began the fight. Bill was in such a state of shock over the situation, instead of quitting on the spot, he defaulted to playing the hand he had been dealt.

It made for a good show, watching the wily Italian dance around while jabbing at Bill's nose and ribs. He managed to open a few cuts on Bill's face that got the crowd howling that Black Irish had finally met his match. But if Bill appeared slow and ungainly to the crowd, it was not because he had been handicapped. Yes, it was an awkward way to fight, but it was not really slowing him down. He was slow because he was not really thinking about the fight at all. Instead he was ruminating over the fact that Guy had made this absurd arrangement without telling him.

He made a few circles around the ring, absently swinging at the Italian until he happened to connect. His fist was almost the size of the Italian's head, so even a glancing blow was enough to make the man see stars. The Italian staggered to his corner and collapsed, and more than thirty seconds passed before he was clear-headed enough to stand on his own. Bill won, Guy collected their winnings, and they left. As they made their way to the nearest brothel, Guy acted as if nothing were out of the ordinary. Bill finally voiced his displeasure with Guy's new arrangement.

"I did what I had to," the old grifter exclaimed. "It was the only way to get you a match. And look—it paid off! We're back in business. You think about that before you judge me, you ungrateful shite."

At the brothel they went their separate ways. Bill did not see or hear from Guy for another month after that. Then the old drunk turned up, acting as if nothing had ever happened, to inform Bill of his next match.

Guy was an adroit shyster, and by placing more and more demands on Bill he managed to keep them in sporadic business for a few more years. With Bill handicapped other fighters were more willing to get into the ring with him, but since his defenses were halved he began receiving more injuries. Still, Guy was relentless. If he went to the trouble to arrange a fight, then goddammit, Bill had better get in there and hold up his end of the deal.

"This is a business," Guy frequently pointed out. "You gotta do your part, or we're through."

In the end Bill always conceded, though he was not sure why.

Guy drew it out as long as he could, but even with one arm Bill continued to win. Soon, reducing him to one arm was not deemed enough, and in addition to having one arm bound he was expected to fight two men simultaneously. When that did not slow him down, Guy arranged a bout in which Bill was mercifully allowed to use both hands, but he had to fight four men at once. By then, rules and regulations had ceased to matter. Eventually his opponents were allowed to grab chairs or jump into the ring with clubs. It was then that Bill realized they had left the prizefighting circuit far behind, that he had entered the frighteningly absurd underground realm of gladiatorial freak shows.

Remarkably, Bill somehow took this with aplomb. He told himself he was doing it for Guy, and those outlandish bouts would lead to a better life for the both of them. Over time, however, his injuries began to mount, and he began to lose those dubious matches. (No man, not even one as stout as Black Irish, could repeatedly come out on top of ten men with axe handles.) On those nights he would amble back to his corner to find it empty, with Guy nowhere to be seen.

For reasons he could not understand, Bill was willing to accept far more from Guy than from any person on Earth. But Guy spurning him cut deep, deeper than it should, and he began to wonder if their partnership was worth it.

Then without warning, Guy disappeared for six months, during which Bill was mildly content to work at the docks. Longshoreman work paid poorly, but with Guy gone he stopped squandering all his money on liquor and prostitutes. (Those vices remained intact but were regulated.) For the first time in his life, Bill, then aged 40, had squirreled away some savings—the unprecedented sum of three hundred dollars. It was not much, but to him it seemed like the wealth of a pharaoh.

Guy unexpectedly, but nonetheless predictably, returned. When he knocked on Bill's door he was excited, so excited he seemed to have forgotten all his previous disappointments.

"Fortune smiles on us!" he exclaimed, as if no bad feelings had passed between them. "I've got you another fight. Now, hold on! It's not what you think. It's not one of those bouts like before. No hands are tied, no one has any weapons, and it's one man against another. No unfair odds. It's a straight-up fight, just like old times, only better. It's a title fight, lad! Bare-knuckles champ of the underworld, with a thousand dollars to the winner! Seems the challenger dropped out, and they're looking for someone to take on the current champ, a fellow called Locomotive Jones. Oh, he's a tough one from what I hear, but that makes no difference. I know my Bill, and you'll lay him to waste. The only catch is, I need some money to buy you in, you know, some good faith money to guarantee you'll show, plus a few dollars to make

234

wagers. I'm all out, lad, as broke as a whore in a convent. The last few months have been cruel to your old pal Guy, but let's not get into that now. So, partner, what do you say?"

Bill experienced a nagging sensation in the back of his mind. He had the distinct feeling he should say no, that he should put fighting, gambling, and crazy schemes behind and settle to the task of making a normal life. But then he looked at Guy and saw a poor rendition of the man he remembered. He recalled his earliest memories of Guy back at St. Oliver Plunkett's. In his mind he pictured the lanky, hot-headed, swaggering mentor he had so admired as a boy. Now, Guy was old: his dark hair was thin on top and streaked with grey, his chin covered by a patchwork of multi-colored stubble, his sagging shoulders and potbelly apparent even under his shabby long coat. And of course there was the permeating reek of whiskey and sweat, Guy's perennial cologne.

In spite of the revolting spectacle Guy had become, Bill suddenly realized the old drunk was the only constant in his life, the only one who kept coming back, for better or worse. He could not abandon him yet.

Bill nodded and Guy became ecstatic.

"So, lad, how much money do you have? Your old Guy is going to need a stout wallet to make his bets."

Against his better judgment, Bill retrieved his savings from a whole knocked in the plaster wall of his tenement room. At first Guy was almost touched and looked as if he might weep, but he quickly transformed his emotion into a maniacal laugh and danced a gleeful jig that Bill found oddly reassuring. He had not seen Guy this hopeful in years, and he convinced himself that this time Guy was on the level, that this time would be different.

Two weeks later Bill found himself in the ring opposite Locomotive Jones, or "Loco" as he was known by the crowd. He was a formidable-looking man who almost looked like a younger version of Bill. He was built much the same: broad-shouldered, well-muscled, and stout. But he was shorter by almost a foot, which strangely made him seem all the more dangerous, as if condensing such strength in a smaller form made it all the more explosive.

When Bill looked into Loco's eyes he perceived the same confidence and detachment he had always felt in the ring. For the first time in his fighting career he experienced a flicker of self-doubt. It was a new sensation for him, both curious and worrisome. Guy, who was standing just outside the ring, clapped him on the back.

"Locomotive my arse," he muttered. "Keep in mind, lad, if he's a locomotive, you're a goddamned mountain. Crush the bastard!"

The fight began and the two men approached one another. As they circled, Bill thought back to his many fights, his countless wins, the rare but humiliating losses. He recalled the worst beatings he had received, and how they did not seem to hurt as much as the lash when he was a child. Now, however, he had the feeling the punishment he was about to endure would be worse than any he had yet known.

Much to his chagrin, his instincts proved correct. In the first round he discovered Locomotive's power rivaled his own. They traded punches, and Locomotive shook off the effects with disquieting ease. In return he delivered numerous punches to Bill's face and head. The blows jarred Bill, but his overly-thick skull absorbed the worst of it. When Locomotive delivered several rapid blows to his ribs, Bill retreated with a lingering pain. He spent the rest of the round protecting his side and throwing cautious jabs.

Rounds two and three followed suit. During these Bill landed a few good punches, most notably a blow to Locomotive's jaw that briefly dazed him and sent him to one knee. But overall the rounds belonged to the younger man, who took advantage of the fact that Bill was protecting his body by making Bill's face look resemble a Christmas ham.

By then the crowd had reached a fevered pitch of excitement. The noise was deafening, a combination of cheers, jeers, and wagers being renegotiated as bets were doubled and tripled. But Bill was only marginally aware of it. His swollen eyes gave him a narrow field of view that was wholly focused on his adversary. The din of the hall was reduced to a muffled but persistent roar in his cauliflowered ears.

In round four Locomotive reigned, mauling Bill so badly that half the ring floor was a-smear with Bill's blood. For his part, Bill never landed more than a glancing blow.

It all came to an unexpected end in round five. Bill was still letting Locomotive pummel his face to keep the man's thunderous blows away from his ribs. Occasionally he tossed ineffectual jabs that were easily batted away. However, he could tell that Locomotive's detachment was giving away to frustration. Locomotive was wondering how the hell this old-timer was holding out, why he would not drop. Bill saw him bare his teeth with each swing, putting all he had into every blow. Still, Bill's tree-trunk legs refused to buckle.

Locomotive became angry and impatient, and the next time they were in close he drove his shoulder into Bill's side. Bill's ribs felt as if they had caught fire. If his face had not resembled a lumpy tomato, the crowd would have witnessed a rare thing—Bill wincing in agony. But his features were so misshapen that it looked more like a mocking grin. Locomotive finally came unhinged.

He dove into Bill's midsection, trying to knock him down. The charge forced Bill back into the ropes, which collapsed under him. As Bill sprawled backward into the crowd he was taken aback, never before having seen that kind of reckless determination in an opponent. As the fighters collapsed to the floor, Bill rolled on his good side to protect his ribs, but that also had the effect of leaving his injured ribs exposed. Locomotive clambered to his feet and proceeded to kick at them.

Bill was introduced to a degree of pain he had not previously imagined. At first he was only startled by it, as if the pain had leaped out and shouted *boo!* But a split second later his side erupted in flames that took his breath away. He tried to roll away, but the crowd was pressed in around him to witness his downfall. All he could do was press a mighty arm against his side to protect against Locomotive's boots. After a half dozen blows something took hold of him, a growing anger that quickly rivaled the pain, and he managed a punch to Locomotive's groin that brought the man to his knees.

It took Bill a moment to get to his feet and locate Locomotive among the throng, but when he did he found his adversary defenseless, doubled over with both hands in his crotch. Then Bill casually gripped the man's chin, angled it just so, and with no thought of pain or injury to himself delivered a Herculean uppercut that launched Locomotive backward into the mob.

The crowd erupted and pressed forward to clap Bill on the back. By now they had forgotten their wagers and were simply thankful of having been in attendance to witness such a titanic spectacle. But Bill, still in the grip of a primal rage, swatted them aside like flies and made his way toward Locomotive. When he located him, he distantly noted the man's jaw was askew, obviously broken, and that his eyes seemed to be looking in opposite directions.

Locomotive was done, but Bill was not. He knelt down beside his foe, as casually as a gardener about to pluck a pernicious weed, and delivered a *coup de grâce* that stove in the man's skull.

The crowd went silent. Bill rose, a bloody hulk. The crowd parted to make way for him as he lumbered back to the ring. As his rage ebbed he looked around for Guy but saw no trace of him. He picked the announcer out of the crowd and shambled toward him to inquire about the prize money.

"That was collected by the old fellow in your corner," the man said, wilting beneath Bill's gaze. "He left only moments ago. I took him to be your manager ... wasn't he?"

News of the death of Locomotive Jones at the hands of Black Irish spread by word of mouth. While many reporters had been in attendance that night, no respectable paper would publish an article documenting the gruesome and illegal event. The only acknowledgment from the press came in the form of an obituary when Locomotive's bloated corpse was found stinking up a drunkards' alley. The papers chalked it up as one of the city's numerous unsolvable crimes.

For his part, Bill did not worry about police knocking on his door. Since the fight had been illegal, no one in attendance would ever admit to it.

He went back to the docks. It took him a few weeks to heal up enough to return to work, but even hurt he could still lift more than most able-bodied men. The foreman, who by then had heard the terrible rumors of Black Irish, allowed him to return with no questions asked.

Two years later Bill was on his way home and stopped at a gin house. He took a seat at the bar and ordered a drink. As he was draining the glass he glanced to his left. Through the gloom he saw a man slouched across the bar, an empty whiskey bottle in one hand. It was an all-too-common sight in such establishments, but there was something familiar about this particular lump of humanity. It was Guy.

Bill froze in disbelief. Guy had always been as reliable as a bad penny to turn up again. But after he had made off with the prize money, Bill was certain the old shyster had disappeared from his life forever. But to his disbelief, there Guy sat, or rather sprawled.

As Bill stood staring at him, Guy roused, tried to take a drink from his empty bottle, and groggily looked up at him.

"Bless my soul ... Billy boy, is that you? Hell if it ain't! Black Irish in the flesh. How the hell you been, lad? Let me get a look at you. Damn! Still as big as a goddamned mountain! You always were a good Irish lad, Bill. Like a son to me. Say, you wouldn't mind buying your old pal a few drinks, would you? Sit down here beside me. We'll tie one on together and catch up. Just like old times, eh? How's that sound? Say, have I ever told you how proud I am of you?"

Guy then fell irretrievably silent, and Bill departed shortly thereafter. It was not until later, when the barkeeper tried to rouse Guy from his drunken torpor, that he discovered the old grifter had suffocated from a collapsed windpipe, his throat stamped with the imprint of a mighty fist.

By the time my companion had completed his tale, every light save the sputtering streetlamps had been extinguished. As he uttered his last words I marveled at his altogether sad and shocking history, and especially at his murderous liberation from a lifelong and cancerous father figure.

The account left me speechless. After such a lengthy and revealing tale I felt drained, depressed, and unsure of how to respond. So we sat together in silence for a while, staring at the empty street before us, until Irish rummaged through his pockets and produced a cigarette. He struck a match, which in the stillness sounded to me as clear as a gunshot. He relished his smoke in silence, and when it had burned half way down he nodded in my direction.

"So, you gonna tell me what happened to your hands?"

At that late (or by then, early) hour I did not want to launch into another story. All I wanted was to go back to my room and collapse in bed, to allow sleep to descend on me and wash away the melancholy mood.

I stood and shook my head as I peeled the soiled rags from my scabrous knuckles. I gave him a wink as I raised my fists, bobbed back and forth, and lunged at an invisible opponent. He looked at me quizzically, as if I were performing some mysterious tribal dance. I decided I would rather leave him thinking I had been in a brawl than reveal the truth. Without another word I gave him a salute, turned on my heel, and marched back to our hotel.

16: REUNION

The morning following Irish's all-night narrative, I slept in until noon. Irish must have done the same, because he showed up for lunch red-eyed and solemn. As we sat down there were only three issues that concerned me. The first was obvious—the reproach of my companions over the Munich debacle. I feared that once I stood before the collective, it would lead to further lectures or reprimands. To my surprise, nothing of the sort occurred. Conversation was awkward but civil. No questions were asked, nor were any recriminations leveled at Irish and me. We had, it appeared, been forgiven.

My second fear was that I might encounter the maid who had seen me climbing down the hotel exterior. I did not need the added complication of being identified as a Peeping Tom, especially in the presence of Ms Alexander. But my anxiety on this point was unwarranted. No member of the hotel staff accosted me for the remainder of our stay at the Palast Hotel.

My third concern, the only one I could not leave behind when we departed Berlin, was over the relationship between Irish and Ms Alexander. No one spoke of his inappropriate advance on the train, but I could not shake the feeling that some new dynamic had evolved after their electrifying embrace.

The following day we departed on the next leg of our journey. Dietrich had, as usual, coordinated with Cross by wire to secure money and make all the arrangements. We would take the train to Lübeck, and there board a ship for a two-day voyage to the Jewel of the Russias, Saint Petersburg.

When we set out Ms Alexander was positively vibrant. The thought of seeing her homeland made her glow. It was as if every atom of her exquisite being was excited, giving her an almost visible aura. At first it gladdened my heart, but then I began to wonder if it was perhaps a reaction linked to her strange condition. Erring on the side of caution I discreetly kept my distance.

The train ride to Lübeck took the entire day, and for its entirety we stayed together. We had finally learned a lesson from our previous encounters: our enemy preferred to target stragglers. We also had realized our enemy might appear as anyone, patrician or plebian. I spent much of the day watching the other passengers, looking for some hint of ill intent in their eyes.

We made stops in a dozen small towns along the way, none of which made any impression on me. They all looked perfectly quaint, and I could easily imagine a painter of pastorals capturing them on canvas. But for me they were nothing more than hindrances, obstacles set in our way to prolong our journey. Fortunately, most stops were short, lasting only long enough to allow a swift exchange of passengers. But in the late afternoon, when the train pulled into Hamburg—its spires and red brick and façades mirrored impressively in the waters of the Elbe—our journey came to a standstill. Hamburg was a major stop, and for at least an hour we waited as passengers and cargo were exchanged.

By early evening we were again underway. Then the sprint to Lübeck was so brief that by the time we left the dinner car, the train was sounding its whistle to announce its approach. Fifteen minutes later we were on the platform collecting our bags.

As we made our way to a cab, Ms Alexander provided the obligatory narration: Lübeck, or at least the heart of it, was an island unto itself, rather like Manhattan by my thinking. At the southern end of the city the Elbe River divided, rejoining itself as the Trave River scant miles to the north. The city had been erected on the encircled land, and with the passage of time had rapidly spread across the canals, into the countryside, and along the river toward the sea. As we rode she pointed out the spires of the Marienkirche and Saint Peter's clock tower, among other sites of interest. By then I was tired, and all vistas had become repetitive to me. I could not muster any enthusiasm, but I forced a polite smile and feigned interest.

We passed the night in a hotel overlooking the eastern canal, just to the north of the Holstentor, the city gate. It too was wonderfully scenic, the sort of place I imagined would be perfect for a private walk with Ms Alexander. But after a day of travel I wanted only rest. As soon as Dietrich checked us in I headed for my room.

As I closed my door behind me I listened for the same from my companions. After all three were safely inside I seated myself on the balcony beneath a late evening sun. I much desired an aperitif, but I refrained. Instead I closed my eyes and concentrated on the sensation of the sun's dying rays on my face.

I drifted off for a short time. When I awoke the sun had disappeared, leaving the sky in shades of blue and purple. I stood to go inside and paused to again take in the view. I watched as a skiff made its way along the canal. It passed beneath a small stone bridge several hundred yards to the north. My eye strayed to the span itself, studying the architecture and the traffic upon it. As I stared, some motion alongside the canal caught my eye. At first I took it for a cab ambling along the sidewalk, but when that did not seem right I looked more closely. Finally I discerned it was a couple, a man and woman—an exceptionally large, ox-like brute wearing a flat cap, accompanied by the most angelic creature that ever walked the Earth.

My accidental discovery of Irish's secret rendezvous with Ms Alexander drove away all traces of fatigue. I marked their path, watching them stroll casually along the canal. They stopped at the little stone bridge and walked out onto it, watching the skiff head out to sea. There they remained for a few minutes before retracing their steps. At the foot of the bridge I expected they would make a turn that would bring them back to the hotel. To my chagrin they continued in a straight path, moving perpendicular to the canal and around a corner, disappearing from my sight.

For several minutes I tensely watched the spot where I had lost them, hoping they would step into view. But they did not appear. Frustrated, I collapsed into the chair. I could not imagine what business warranted such privacy. If I had seen any other pairing—Irish and Dietrich, or Dietrich and the lady—I would have thought nothing of it, but the pairing of Irish and Ms Alexander was incomprehensible. It so defied explanation that I began to question what I had seen.

It did not take me long to decide I must have been mistaken, that it was a trick of the light or mind. Or, barring that, a case of mistaken identity. Irish was exceptional, but he could not be the only ogre in the world. And—though I could hardly believe it, or believe I was *thinking* it—the same went for Ms Alexander. She was arguably *sui generis*, but it was not inconceivable that somewhere in the world another woman might somehow resemble her. But no matter how I rationalized it, a part of me remained skeptical, and moments later I set out to determine if they were indeed together.

To set my mind at ease, all I needed to know was if they were in their rooms. I donned my coat, went to Ms Alexander's door, and knocked loudly. If she answered I would simply invite her for a stroll of our own. When no answer came I attacked Irish's door, hammering with my fist so that it shook the walls of the corridor. There was no reply. Dejected, I began to retreat when a door suddenly opened. I spun around to find Dietrich in his shirtsleeves.

"Good God, man," he said. "Is that you banging?"

I apologized and quickly slipped back into my room. I pressed my ear against the door until I heard Dietrich shut himself inside. I took off my coat and hurled it across the room. There was no mistaking it. Irish and Ms Alexander were together.

I laid awake long into the night. I took some consolation in the fact that any amorous expression was impossible, and on several levels. First, Ms Alexander was too proper. She would never allow another advance like the one on the train. Second, even if they desired one another—and here I paused to reiterate to myself the implausibility—any contact with her would result in searing pain.

Then I remembered her explanation of grounding electricity. If both were willing, she might be able to discharge herself for a brief time, perhaps long enough for intimate contact...

"No!" I screamed, coming awake and sitting up in bed. I realized I had been in a half-sleeping state for some time. I was still dressed; even my shoes were still on. I then realized that in my torpor I unconsciously had been working out how a man might succeed at getting close to Ms Alexander. And to my simultaneous delight and dismay—delight because of the possibilities it offered; dismay because Irish may have beaten me to it—I knew how it might be achieved.

But the thought that, at that very moment, *my friend* might be manhandling *my lady* made me furious with jealousy. I felt betrayed by Irish, spurned by Ms Alexander, and ostracized by the lot of them. (I do not know how Dietrich got mixed up in it, but suddenly I considered him as guilty as the rest.)

As I laid there alternating between loathing and self-pity, a knock came at my door. At first I thought I had imagined it, because it was late and my mind was out of sorts. When the door shook again, I climbed to my feet, fumbled for the knob, and opened it to find.

"You all right in there?" he asked. He was in his undershirt and his feet were bare. His eyes looked bleary, as if he too had just awoken.

"I'm fine," I said testily.

"I thought I heard yelling," he said.

I stared back at him defiantly. Eventually he grunted, turned, and lumbered back to his room. I watched as he went, closed my door in unison with his, then felt my way to the bed and collapsed.

In the morning I blindly pawed the bedside table until I found my pocket watch, and saw that it was almost eight o'clock—the time Dietrich had instructed us to be ready to depart. I cursed and leapt from bed. I had only enough time for a mad dash around the room to splash some water on my face, get dressed, and grab my valise as I ran out the door. I stepped into the lobby just as the bells of Saint Mary's and Saint Peter's began to toll.

Dietrich was checking his watch as I strolled up. When he saw me he grinned and stuffed it back into a vest pocket.

"Excellent," he said. "Everyone is present and punctual. A superb start to the day."

He then shepherded us outside and into an awaiting cab. Inside, I feigned disinterest in them all, but I glanced at Irish and Ms Alexander to read their moods. In Irish's eyes I found no more intelligence than that of a crocodile. When I searched Ms Alexander's, I sought some hint of change, some flicker of guilt. She simply smiled. I chose to interpret it as jubilance over setting sail for her homeland.

When our cab came to a stop, we were on the opposite side of the isle of Lübeck. We climbed out to find ourselves face-to-stern with our vessel. I gazed up at large and unfamiliar letters emblazoned across her posterior.

СПУТНИК

"What does it say?" I asked.

"*Sputnik,*" Ms Alexander said, her smile widening. "It means traveling companion. A wonderful name for a ship, is it not?"

A porter approached and inspected our tickets, collected our bags, and escorted us aboard. The ship was small compared to the *Minnetonka*, but given the Atlantic's rough waters, the length of the voyage, and the number of passengers, this made sense.

Dietrich won some points with me when we reached our rooms. He had secured quarters for us on the upper deck instead of condemning us to the steerage accommodations. This small gesture made me feel more appreciated for the service I was doing the world.

By midmorning we were coursing through the icy blueness of the Baltic. We spent some time strolling on deck, enjoying the invigorating sea breeze. After our first circuit of the ship Dietrich had had enough of cold air and excused himself. Indeed, I too was ready to retreat from the bitterness of the wind. I would have followed Dietrich had I not been suspicious of leaving Irish and Ms Alexander alone together. Instead of retreating to the warmth of my cabin, I made a second and third circuit with them. I was practically freezing by the time Irish decided to go indoors, but I stuffed my hands in my pockets and fought on.

For her part, Ms Alexander was also cold, as evinced by the rosiness of her cheeks and nose. But in spite of her delicate frame she was somehow able to endure the cold better than I, perhaps owing to her Russian origin.

As I contemplated her Slavic upbringing, she looked at me and smiled. Under any other circumstances that would have been enough to warm me, but my suit coat was not enough to resist the wind. As I looked at the cheer in her face, I realized she had no intention of heading indoors, which made my next decision easier than expected. I continued with her for a few more steps before excusing myself and darting for the nearest hatch.

Ms Alexander strolled the deck for the better part of the day. She enjoyed the dichotomy in climate—the cold wind, the smell of the sea, and the warmth of the sun shining down. And she was not alone. Many of the passengers hailed from that part of the world, and they too were as comfortable as she in those conditions. Consequently, as she strolled along she had many opportunities to greet other passengers, to examine the fashion of other women's dresses, to watch children racing around the deck at play. She stopped along the port side of the ship and lounged against the rail.

Everything about the situation put her at ease. The mere knowledge of the ship's direction, and the growing proximity to her homeland, thrilled her. Given her elation one can therefore understand why she allowed herself a moment of indiscretion, when a distinguished-looking gentleman in a topcoat and Homburg stopped at the rail nearby.

At first she did not notice, so casually did he wander up and gaze out at the endless sea. Then a pair of children began to run in circles in their vicinity, and they both turned to watch and laugh at the spectacle. When the children ran off, they regarded one another for the first time. The man nodded courteously, and Ms Alexander acknowledged him with a tight-lipped smile. The stranger then returned his attention to the sea, and by all appearances took no further interest in her. From that moment, however, she remained keenly aware of him.

Since adolescence she had known that she was attractive. The number of boys who had unsuccessfully tried to slip under the watchful eye of her sentinel and servant, Irena, underscored this fact. But she had learned something about boys, and by extension men, from watching their futile efforts. As a result, she knew when she was being stalked. So she was not fooled by the gentleman's outward disinterest in her. His lingering presence betrayed what was actually on his mind.

After a minute of standing there—during which he idly placed his left hand upon the rail to reveal no wedding band—she risked another look. He was considerably older than her, even older than her traveling companions. From what hair was visible beneath his Homburg she noted a preponderance of grey, an effect that had not yet infiltrated his thin moustache. As he squinted into the wind she noted the wrinkles in the corners of his eyes. She estimated him to be in his late fifties. She wrinkled her nose as she calculated their difference in age, especially into future years, rhetorically wondering if a man and woman from different generations could make a happy couple. Then she rolled her eyes and stifled a laugh, chastising herself for so foolish an indulgence.

Still, if the gentleman chose to engage her in small talk, she would not mind. She remained at the rail, staring out to sea, occasionally turning to look fore and aft. Once she even disengaged from the rail, wandered away a few steps, then returned to a spot a foot closer to the man, giving him both a hint and chance at conversation. To her disappointment he made no attempt, nor did he once look her way.

Annoyed, she began to think she had misread the situation, that she had underestimated him, or worse, vainly overestimated her own appeal. She absently bit her lip as she considered it. She was about to hurry away in self-reproach when she heard him speak, against all probability, in English.

I must down to the seas again, to the lonely sea and the sky,
And all I ask is a tall ship and a star to steer her by,
And the wheel's kick and the wind's song and the white sail's shaking,
And a grey mist on the sea's face, and a grey dawn breaking.

She stared at him in wonder. He had spoken the words as if to himself, his attention on the horizon, yet his words were clearly meant for her. After such a profound overture she was forced to reassess the situation. She could not help but be impressed. Of the few men she had allowed to get close enough to attempt conversation, none had ever delivered so imaginative a preface.

"Is that verse your own?" she said.

"No," he said with a smile. "Just something I once read."

He turned to face her, looking around at the others on deck. "I find it hard to believe that such a beautiful young woman would be here alone."

She smiled, both flattered and relieved to know she had not misread the situation after all.

"I am actually traveling with several others," she explained. "But they are from warmer climes and have gone indoors to escape the wind."

As she regarded him, she noticed for the first time that he bore a lacquered wooden box, about the size of a tall hatbox, which he had set down on the deck by his feet. The lid, which was fastened with a heavy brass clasp, bore a handle on top like a suitcase. She wondered about it but resisted the urge to inquire. The man, however, noted her curiosity. He lifted the box, unlatched the lid, and invited her to look inside. She took a few timid steps forward.

The interior of the box was padded and lined with felt, and within those protective confines sat a strange scientific device. It consisted of two metallic rings that intersected perpendicularly at their poles, forming a sort of spherical skeleton. Another ring, notched with degrees, formed the skeleton's equator. An axis ran vertically between the sphere's poles, and midway along its length, centered within the equator, was a strange-looking brass cube, a mechanical device composed of many small gears.

"What is it?" she asked.

"A navigational device," he said. "A new invention, courtesy of some clever gentlemen I met in Kiel."

"Oh," Ms Alexander said. "How does it work?"

"It is quite exceptional," he explained. "Once informed with a coordinate system, it will know where it is located. One can then give it another set of coordinates, and it will find its way to them. Integrated with a steering device, it will, in theory, independently guide a vessel—land, sea, or air—to practically any point on the surface of the Earth."

"Are you suggesting," she began, "that this device might be used in some sort of air-craft?"

"Yes," the stranger said, shooting her a knowing smile.

"What vehicle would use such a thing?" she asked.

The man grinned as he resealed the box, but he did not reply. Instead he gazed at Ms Alexander with raised his eyebrows, suggesting she might already know the answer.

She knew of experiments in flight. She had heard of a pair of Americans who had, on more than one occasion and against all likelihood, managed to pilot makeshift air-craft over a distance of twenty miles. Aside from these breakthroughs, she had not heard of any air vehicle that was considered reliable.

"An airship?" she guessed.

The man chuckled.

"A possibility," he said, "but that is not the destiny of this device. It is meant for a very different experiment, one that will change the world and usher in a new age."

He said those last words almost mischievously. Ms Alexander was even more intrigued.

"What sort of experiment?" she asked eagerly.

The man's eyes gleamed. He shook his head and laughed quietly to himself.

"It was a pleasure to meet you, Miss…?"

"Alexander."

"A distinct pleasure, Ms Alexander," he said. "I've said all I can. You will understand soon enough. Now, if you will excuse me."

And without further ado he walked away. Ms Alexander was so stunned by this sudden rudeness that she did not realize until he was beyond earshot that she had never learned his name.

At the dinner table that evening she related the curious encounter to us, placing more emphasis on the device than on the man. We all listened to her description of the item, but before she had the chance to identify its purpose, Dietrich chimed in.

"A gyrocompass," he said. "I've heard of it. Superior to the standard compass commonly used for navigation, and a great boon to navigators of all sorts."

Ms Alexander was a little disappointed that Dietrich had stolen her thunder. After a sigh she went on to describe in detail what a strange and riveting invention it was, and how she wished we all could see it. She scanned the dining room for the stranger but did not see him.

"If I encounter him again I will arrange a viewing for you," she said. But for the remaining eighteen hours of our voyage she did not see him, and no one thought or made mention of the stranger or his world-changing device again.

We arrived in the port of Saint Petersburg in the late afternoon. We disembarked and Dietrich guided us through customs with the help of Ms Alexander's translation. As we went through the process, Ms Alexander seemed strangely distracted. At the time I dismissed it, thinking she was simply excited to be back on her native soil.

We made our way to the street, and Dietrich began examining the line of cabs and coaches to choose one to take us into the city. As Irish and I stood idly by, I noticed an impressive-looking black coach pull up to the rear of the line. It was large and polished to an unusually high sheen, and the driver wore a grey wool coat and high black boots that lent him the appearance of a military man. It was clearly meant for someone of importance, perhaps a member of government, or even someone of royalty. I began to search the crowd to see what noble figure might have been traveling incognito among us, but I saw no one warranting such stately transport. Before I could give the matter further thought, Dietrich beckoned us to board a coach and we were off.

Saint Petersburg bumped right up against the harbor, so the moment we crossed the Neva River we were immersed in the city. I had little time to take in any sights, but my first impression was that the city was perhaps the most interesting in Europe. The architecture was a strange mix of eastern and western influences. Where much of Western Europe was gothic, Saint Petersburg was a peculiar mix of Baroque and Neoclassical, with an occasional splash of the Medieval.

On this singular occasion I had to make these observations on my own because Ms Alexander offered no narrative. After she had taken so many opportunities throughout our travels to educate us, I had expected her to deliver an endless exaltation of the achievements of the Russian Empire. Instead she was completely silent. Dietrich and Irish must have noticed it, too, because more than once they looked at her expectantly as we passed by an impressive building or statue. But not a word escaped her lips until our coach took an unexpected turn.

I should have suspected something was amiss from the beginning, and I certainly should have taken more notice of her anxious fascination with whatever was following us. When she had climbed into the coach, she had taken up a seat facing the rear, and from the moment we set off she seemed more interested in the traffic behind us than in the city. Several times she craned her neck to get a better look, once even sticking her head out the window. When she brought it back inside she looked startled.

"Is something wrong?" Dietrich inquired.

Before she could reply we suddenly heard the clattering of hooves on flagstones, and men on horseback appeared in the windows on either side. As they overtook us I noticed they wore grey wool coats and black boots, and they were armed with rifles slung on their backs and sabers dangling at their sides. They passed by our windows and began shouting. Suddenly we were thrown to one side as the coach took a sharp turn.

Dietrich became irritated rather than worried. He had interpreted the wrong turn as our driver's countermeasure to being cut off by the horsemen, who were probably on an urgent military errand. But when it soon happened again—another right turn that meant we were now backtracking along a different path—his expression changed to one of concern.

"What the devil?" he said, banging his fist on the ceiling. As if that were the international signal to come to a calamitous halt, the driver suddenly reigned in the horses so violently that one would think we were about to go off a cliff.

Dietrich struggled to get out the door to berate the driver, but Ms Alexander made a strange and shocking announcement that froze us in place.

"Gentlemen," she said with urgency, "I am not sure what is about to happen, but I assure you we are in no danger. Please let me to do the talking, and do as I say."

We stared at her in wonder. As we did we heard a clamor behind us—the unmistakable sound of another coach coming to a quick stop, followed by many voices and footsteps coming our way.

Suddenly a bayonet appeared in my window, inches away from the tip of my nose. A soldier began issuing incomprehensible, yet unmistakable, commands, and I quickly raised my hands to the window to show I was unarmed and compliant. My companions followed my example. Soon we were all standing side by side, our backs against a stone wall, facing four soldiers pointing rifles.

I quickly took in the scene. Our coach had been diverted along a back road to a small, empty plaza, surrounded on three sides by a six-foot retaining wall. At the head of our coach stood the horses of the cavalrymen, dutifully awaiting the return of their masters. Our driver still sat atop the coach looking confused and afraid. Clearly he was as shocked as we were, and I could see in his face a growing suspicion about us. My eyes then swept to the rear to find a large black coach—none other than the one that had caught my attention back at the harbor. Beside it an imperious-looking officer sat on his horse, his hand resting on a pistol at his belt.

I had no idea what was happening, but given the situation I had the nauseating feeling we were about to be executed by firing squad, or worse, skewered cruelly at the ends of bayonets. I began to think about survival. I was especially defenseless. Irish had his lethal brawn, Ms Alexander her electricity, and presumably Dietrich had his revolver beneath his coat. I, on the other hand, had nothing. I began looking for possible escape routes. The soldiers had us covered, but if Irish launched at them, during the confusion I might be able to escape by clambering over the wall behind us. Given my natural athleticism I estimated I could manage it within seconds.

As I peripherally inspected the wall, I noticed movement to my right. Irish had slowly inched forward, planning some sort of defense. The officer, who until that moment seemed to be having a conversation with someone in the black coach, noticed and barked an order. Instantly three of the four bayonets—and the rifles to which they were attached—came to bear on Irish.

"*Nyet!*" Ms Alexander cried, stepping forward and placing herself between them. She then launched into what I expected to be an impassioned plea for our safety, but by her tone it sounded more like a stern lecture. As she spoke I watched the soldiers' eyes dart uncertainly between her and the officer. A tense silence followed that was finally interrupted by a harsh voice from black coach.

"*Kapitan Petrovskiy!*"

It immediately caught the officer's attention, and he looked to a curtained window only feet away. He sidled his mount nearer and quietly conversed with the man inside. He then barked another order at his troops, and a moment later the soldiers shouldered their rifles and climbed back onto their mounts. The officer then opened the door of the black coach and indicated with a hand that we should enter.

We looked at Ms Alexander for guidance.

"As I said," she explained, "all is well."

We were still off balance with no idea what was happening, but now Ms Alexander seemed so at ease that we automatically followed her instruction. We filed into the coach, much relieved to have escaped a firing squad. Inside the coach, however, we faced another unpleasant surprise.

A strange man awaited us therein. He reminded me at once of a sinister Medieval wizard. He had wild, almost threatening eyes. His hair was long, dark, and lank, and looked almost as unkempt as his long, wiry beard. He wore a dark frock, grey breeches, and high black boots whose care been thoroughly neglected.

Then driver of the black coach cracked the reigns and we began to move, almost at a gallop. As the coach careened through the streets, the man looked each of us slowly up and down. He did not seem too interested in Dietrich, but he was noticeably impressed by Irish's size. When he came to Ms Alexander, he gazed upon her for an indecent amount of time, his eyes obscenely traveling the length of her before favoring her with a slight bow of the head. Finally, he came to me, and his expression was so wolfish that I half expected him to pounce and begin devouring me. An involuntary shiver ran through me as I suffered an image of him, his beard soaked in blood and his eyes burning with cannibalistic glee.

It was during his silent appraisal of me that Ms Alexander spoke up. He inclined his head toward her, but his eyes lingered on me. The two then began a conversation, in Russian, that left the rest of us completely in the dark. As we watched, the madman pressed a palm against his chest and nodded to her in lieu of a bow.

"This is Father Grigori," she said as an introduction. "He has been sent to collect us. He apologizes for any alarm the soldiers may have caused, and he asks that we excuse their behavior. They were told only to secure us and given no other details. He assures that we have nothing to fear, that we are entirely safe."

We nodded at Father Grigori to show we understood, but we were still mystified. All we could do was wait until Ms Alexander was ready to provide an explanation, since she was now in control.

As we traveled she continued to converse with the priest. At length he must have said something witty, because she covered her mouth and laughed. This put me a bit more at ease. Where the priest's reassurances had done little to assuage my concern, Ms Alexander's magical laughter succeeded.

As the Russians conversed in their native tongue, I became bored and pushed a curtain aside a few inches to take in the sights. We were following a city road that paralleled a river embankment, heading in an easterly direction. I watched numerous boats drift by. Moments later a small isle drifted into view, its perimeter lined with a great stone wall, and beyond it a towering spire. I swept the curtain back to show the others, and instantly Father Grigori erupted in a litany of unmistakable maledictions, casting a damning finger in my direction.

"Prometheus, close the curtain!" Ms Alexander exclaimed. "We are supposed to be incognito!"

I did not understand the need for such subterfuge. While my reputation often preceded me, I was quite sure no one in Saint Petersburg would recognize me. But I heeded their demands and let the curtain fall back into place. The priest was mollified, but his gaze lingered on me for an uncomfortable amount of time.

Moments later the coach careened to the right as we made a sharp turn without slowing. I did not understand why we were driving at such a rapid pace. It made me wonder if we were being pursued. Considering the priest's outrage over the curtain, I resisted sticking my head out to look behind us. The urge was purged from me a moment later when we came to an abrupt halt.

We exited the coach and found ourselves on the central path of a most beautiful and immaculate park. The path was ensconced by trees and vegetation, and though the city lay only a few hundred paces in any direction, it was completely obscured—or more significantly, we were obscured from it. The path was lined with marble statues of both historical and mythological figures, men and women in scant clothing, frozen in various moments of repose and contemplation. Interspersed among these were benches, though a glance up and down the path showed none were occupied. I then realized we were not in a park but a private garden.

As soon as Father Grigori stepped from the coach, Captain Petrovskiy dismounted and issued an order to his men, who immediately scattered. The cavalrymen headed along the path in the direction we had come, and our coachmen took up positions along the path before and behind us, eyeing the trees and bushes as they went. As I watched them, I spied a figure making his way toward us along the path. When he came within speaking distance the sentries saluted him.

The man strode toward us purposefully. The garden canopy was thick, but even in that subdued light his red tunic blazed like fire, and the gold embossing on his epaulets glowed. He wore grey trousers and high boots, polished to such a sheen that I could see my reflection in them. And as he neared, I was able to make out his features—a kind face with tired eyes, a full beard, and a moustache that stretched beyond the perimeter of his face.

He strode up, and Father Grigori shouted something indecipherable and executed a bow. Ms Alexander curtsied and said:

"Gentlemen, I present to you Tsar Nicholas the Second, Emperor and Autocrat of all the Russias."

Since Dietrich and I had encountered royalty before, one would expect we might have reacted to the Tsar's presence with more aplomb. I am sorry to report we failed. We acted as awkwardly and foolishly as we did in the presence of Prince Arthur, if not more so. We looked at one another and tried to recall how we had extracted ourselves from our first royal ambush, reverting to our accustomed awkward bows and obsequious sputterings. Irish, however, took the introduction casually, not to mention rudely. He had the good sense to pull the cap from his head, but aside from that he looked the Tsar up and down as if he were a passerby on the street. To the Tsar's credit, he pretended not to notice.

The Tsar's smile grew as he approached. He strode purposefully into our group, bypassing the rest of us and heading straight to Ms Alexander. They looked as if they might embrace, but at the last moment the Tsar stopped and took a step back to get a look at her. I noticed how their eyes shined at one another, and I wondered if my affections for the lady had been unwittingly trumped from the beginning. Briefly, I felt as if one of the Tsar's men had run me through with a bayonet after all. The two spoke for a moment before turning toward us.

"Gentlemen," Tsar Nicholas said in almost perfect English. "Welcome to Saint Petersburg, the jewel of the Russias. Thank you for taking such good care of my cousin, and for returning her to us safely. It is my distinct honor to have you as my guests for as long as you care to stay."

My jaw dropped, as did Dietrich's. Irish merely snorted.

"The Tsar is your *cousin*?" Dietrich said quietly.

Ms Alexander blushed, and so did I as I recalled my behavior so far. It was one thing to make a fool of oneself in front of a beautiful and intelligent woman, but it was another to make a fool of oneself in front of a woman who was altogether more. And Ms Alexander was definitely *altogether more*.

The Tsar was exceptionally kind and gracious to us considering our lowly status. In America, we have the luxury of never having to bow before another man, not even the President, and Nicholas seemed to understand this. As Ms Alexander made introductions, he approached each of us with an outstretched hand.

"This is Mr Dietrich, an investigator and the leader of our expedition," she said. This sparked a brief exchange on the fascinating nature of criminal investigation. I noted that Nicholas did not inquire further about our so-called expedition.

"This is Mr Irish," she said next, leading the Tsar to stand in the shadow of our companion. "He is charged with our overall protection."

The Tsar extended a hand that was subsequently engulfed by one of Irish's. He commented on Irish's great size and strength, pointing out that our friend's stature rivaled even Peter the Great. Irish had not the slightest idea who Peter the Great was, but he said thanks and nodded appreciatively.

"And finally," Ms Alexander said, "this is Mr Grey."

I expected a more colorful introduction, but when no words came I grabbed the Tsar's hand to dispel the awkwardness.

"A great honor to meet you, Your Imperial Highness," I said.

"The pleasure is mine," he said. "But such ceremony is unnecessary, as Katya will attest."

"Katya?" I said.

Nicholas nodded.

"Yes," he said, looking at Ms Alexander affectionately. "She has always been little Katya to me."

"Katya," I said to myself, relishing the word. Ms Alexander shot me the briefest of glances.

"Pardon me, Your Imperial Majesty," Dietrich said, earning a mildly irked look from the Tsar for his refusal to break with protocol. "If you are cousins, how exactly you are related? While she has proven remarkable in every way conceivable, I never once dreamed we were traveling in the presence of royalty."

The Tsar opened his mouth to respond but hesitated.

"Do not worry," Ms Alexander chimed in, "because there is nothing royal about me. It is a very distant relation, fourth or fifth cousins, or something along those lines. It is so mundane that it is not worth the time it would take to explain. Suffice it to say we are related, that as youngsters we had occasion to know one another, and that we have ever since considered ourselves closer in love than in blood."

Dietrich was slow to take the hint. He furrowed his brow and began to form another question, but I elbowed him in the arm to stop him from prying. Either our lady was telling the truth, and it was a genuinely uninteresting story, or she simply did not want to discuss it.

"You are probably wondering about the strange reception at your arrival," Nicholas said. "I apologize for the unconventional nature of it. Of late there have been many plots by malcontents against the government, its officials, and my family. I have taken to moving about with a degree of secrecy, but I insist upon far more secrecy and safety for those important to me. I arranged for my men to waylay you, and to deliver you here. I understand from Katya that the confrontation was tense for a moment. I am sorry if it alarmed you. I am relieved no violence erupted during the confusion."

"As are we," Dietrich replied. "But if I may ask, how did you know of our arrival?"

Dietrich asked the question innocently enough, but I could tell he was wondering if we had been under the scrutiny of Russian spies; and if so, for how long. Nicholas grinned almost sheepishly—a surprising look for a monarch—and again deferred to Ms Alexander.

"That was my doing," she explained. "Once I knew our destination was Saint Petersburg, I wired ahead to inform him, so he could make arrangements to receive us. I knew there would be—," and here she paused to pick her words, "—security concerns."

Dietrich smiled and nodded, seemingly appeased. But I wondered at her meaning, unsure if she meant the Tsar's security or ours.

The Tsar pointed north along the gravel path.

"There is a summer house at the end of the garden which is yours for as long as you desire to stay. You will find it already prepared." Here he looked over his shoulder and spoke to Father Grigori, who had stood aside so silently that I had forgotten he was there. The grim priest nodded in affirmation. "The house and garden are at your disposal. I will have guards posted at the gates to ensure your privacy and safety. Do not let their presence alarm you. The people may be restless, but you are in no danger. The guards are merely a precaution. For my part I will retire to the Summer Palace, just across the canal, for the evening. Tomorrow I depart on state business. I ask that Katya join me in the Palace tonight that we may take some time to catch up. I hope you will not object if I steal her away for one night."

We shook our heads and blathered obsequiously, "Of course not, Your Highness."

Nicholas perceived that we had business to conclude before he absconded with our lady. He graciously stepped aside and spoke in confidential tones with Father Grigori while we gathered around her. Before any of us could speak, she launched into an apology directed mostly at Dietrich.

"Forgive me for not confiding in you before now. Please believe that I remain committed to our endeavor, and to you. But I am also loyal to my family. If I had not taken secret measures to inform Nicholas of our arrival, it would have been impossible to meet him. As you can imagine, he is a potent ally, especially while we pursue our business here."

255

"Of course," Dietrich said reassuringly. "It came as a shock, but I see the sense and purpose of it now."

"Thank you," she replied.

She then turned and walked toward Nicholas, who broke off his conversation with the priest. He called out to the guards, who returned to the coach.

"My men will take you to the summer house," he said. "Make yourselves at home. The house is usually vacant, but the staff should already have arrived. Instruct them on your needs and have a good evening. I will return Katya to you in the morning."

Nicholas turned and offered an arm to Ms Alexander, who reached for it before stopping herself and laughing. Nicholas shared the laugh as they walked south along the lane, the disturbing priest following discreetly behind. Dietrich, Irish, and I then climbed back into the coach and headed in the opposite direction.

The house was located in a northern corner of the Summer Garden. The name implied a small house maintained as a second residence for a family on holiday, but as with all things owned by royalty it was far more. The house was a small mansion containing fourteen rooms, any one of which could serve as an entire apartment in New York. It was a two-story brick structure perched on the edge of the garden and overlooking a canal that separated it from the rest of the city.

The staff, which consisted of a single old man and his wife, greeted us upon arrival with grim smiles. As we approached they nodded and said something in Russian, but when we offered no response they automatically switched to German. This earned a warm response from Dietrich. Once inside they showed us to our rooms, which were much more elegantly decorated than any I had ever seen. The old couple escorted us back downstairs to a dining room where they served a substantial dinner. As we sat around the table, I took the opportunity to discuss Ms Alexander.

"It's curious that in all our conversations she never mentioned her family, especially that she's related, however distantly, to the Russian emperor. Such an omission cannot be so easily explained away."

"Yes," Dietrich admitted. "I don't understand why she would hide it. I appreciate the Tsar's situation, but I fail to see what harm would have come from telling us."

"Maybe she thought we'd treat her differently," Irish said, with rare insight.

"Maybe," I said. "But did her explanation of their relation strike anyone else as suspicious? She brushed the topic aside as if it were boring. I find nothing boring about the fact that she might have royal blood running in her veins."

"I understand your perspective," Dietrich said. "But a woman's mind is like a maze. The path you think will lead you to its conclusion inevitably gets you more lost than before."

Irish chuckled in agreement.

"Whatever the case," he continued, "she did not want to discuss it. It is not germane to our mission, so I suggest we drop it. If Ms Alexander wishes to disclose that part of her life, she will do so at a time, and on terms, of her choosing."

I grudgingly agreed. Needling her about it would only irritate her, and I preferred to be in her favor. Still, I resolved to get to the bottom of it sooner or later, one way or another.

When the old couple finally brought our food we were all so hungry, our appetites so aroused after the afternoon's excitement, that we attacked the various dishes set before us. About midway through our entrée (some sort of boiled beef) Dietrich had a clever idea and invited the old couple to join us. At first they firmly declined, but after a short conversation Dietrich convinced them there was nothing royal or official about us. Finally the couple relaxed somewhat, and within a few minutes they had seated themselves at the table. They became so disarmed, in fact, that by the time we had consumed the leathery meat they served, the old man had disappeared to the kitchen and returned with a bottle of wine not previously offered. He then set to pouring glasses for everyone, offering a toast in German.

Our conversation began as small talk, but eventually we learned some practical, and some quite useful, information. We first inquired about the grounds and learned that a canal surrounded the whole garden like a moat, making it accessible only by a series of guarded bridges. Furthermore, even if someone were to cross the canal they would have to climb over a wrought-iron fence and contend with the guards. So the garden, which was designed as a playground for the Tsar's family, was very much *safe*. He then went on to explain that the Summer Palace was situated across a canal to the south, and that our lady was no more than half a mile away, and many times *safer*.

All these reassurances about our safety piqued my curiosity. Since our arrival we had been given several hints that the country was not entirely stable. When I inquired about these points, the couple's cheerful mood faded. They looked at one another nervously, and the old man tried to explain. At first it only confused Dietrich, owing to a loss in translation. After another exchange he got no clearer answer, so he gave us his interpretation.

"There is much turmoil in the country, far more than is visible on the surface. Much of it is due to the Bolsheviks, who, if you are not informed, are revolutionaries, trying to stir up the common people against the Tsar."

"Do they pose a danger to us?" I asked. If there were to be a revolution, the last place I wanted to be found was lounging in a mansion in the Tsar's Summer Garden.

He waved a hand dismissively and continued to converse with the couple about news of the realm.

"In addition to Bolsheviks, there are rumors of strange occurrences in the east," he said at length. "Apparently a contingent of soldiers in Siberia recently vanished without explanation."

I nodded, my interest waning. I was less concerned with distant military mysteries than I was with the possibility, however unlikely, that Bolsheviks might sneak into the garden with ill intent. As long as such a threat was not imminent I was mollified.

Dietrich continued to talk with the old couple, occasionally providing us with brief summaries of what he had learned. I feigned interest as long as I could. Irish finally ate his fill of boiled meat and pirogi, and we retired to our rooms and left Dietrich talking with the old couple well into the night.

17: THE MAD MONK

All reiterations of our safety notwithstanding, I slept restlessly that night. Perhaps it was because of sounds I occasionally heard outside, sometimes in the form of footsteps, other times like hushed voices. They were probably the sounds of our guards on patrol, doing what they could to keep themselves awake in the dead of night. But those sounds wafted on the air like smoke, found their way in through my window, and invaded my dreams. More than once I started awake from the feeling that a bloodthirsty Bolshevik was creeping towards me. In each nightmarish reenactment I saw a shape silhouetted against the moonlit window, hands outstretched, preparing to throttle me. In the pivotal moment the figure would lunge forward from the shadows, his face suddenly illuminated to reveal a wild-eyed proletariat grinning with diabolical glee. The only way to dispel him was to come awake with a start.

Or perhaps my restlessness was simply because Ms Alexander was separated from us for the first time since we had undertaken our mission. She may have been secure in a palace surrounded by guards, but that did nothing to reassure me of her inviolability. Though I was ill-equipped and ill-prepared to protect her, I still preferred to have her close at hand.

When I finally drifted off to restful sleep it was almost dawn, and shortly thereafter Dietrich knocked on my door and summoned me downstairs in haste. I did not understand the reason for his urgency, but remembering my horrific dreams I feared they were perhaps an omen. I dressed and hurried after him, expecting bad news. As I exited the house, I found all my companions standing around Tsar Nicholas.

"Good morning," he said, as I joined them. "I hope you are well rested."

As Dietrich expressed his gratitude for the hospitality, I took in the scene. The Tsar stood before a dark coach similar to the one we had arrived in the day before. Beside him stood Ms Alexander, and behind them loomed the cavalry officer, Captain Petrovskiy, and the unnerving figure of Father Grigori.

"I must depart immediately," the Tsar said. "But I wanted a brief word before I go. Katya and I talked long into the night, about family matters and her travels. Eventually we came to the reason you are here, your *mission* as she calls it."

Our eyes shot to Ms Alexander. Nicholas raised a hand to calm us.

"Do not be alarmed," he said. "It was necessary that Katya inform me, but she has not betrayed you. I support you in this undertaking. Since your search has led you here, I insist that you take one of my men as a guide. Katya may have grown up here, but she has been away far too long to find her way around, and to know where dangers may lay."

In spite of our misgivings, we were hardly in a position to decline.

"Thank you," Dietrich said, forcing a smile.

Nicholas then turned to the men standing behind him. The captain snapped to attention. While I questioned Ms Alexander's wisdom over entrusting the Tsar with our secrets, I felt somewhat reassured to know Captain Petrovskiy—with his forbidding military manner, gleaming sabre, and pistol at his side—would be accompanying us to ward off Bolshevik assassins. But my assumption was incorrect.

The Tsar motioned with a hand and the priest stepped forward.

"You have already met Father Grigori," Nicholas said. "In recent years he has become a close confidant of my family. His uncanny spiritual ability has proven useful in times of dire need, and on occasion I have asked him to perform other discreet services. He is reliable. He will be your guide."

An awkward pause followed as we gazed at the priest. Dietrich cleared his throat and forced himself into motion, extending a hand. The priest accepted it, pressing his left hand to his chest as they shook.

"*Grigori Yefimovich Rasputin,*" he said in his slurred tongue.

Father Grigori, or Rasputin as we called him for simplicity, came around to each of us in turn, shaking hands and staring with his wild eyes into our souls. When he came to Irish, unlike most men he did not seem swayed by my friend's size. In fact, quite the opposite occurred—it was Irish who looked a little uneasy. When the priest got to me he seemed to grip my hand and stare into my eyes more fervently than the others, mumbling something beneath his breath that only the two of us could hear, and only he could understand. When I cocked my head to show I had not understood, he broke off and made his way over to the Tsar and Ms Alexander. He tried to take her hand, but the Tsar stepped between them. For a moment Rasputin's face darkened, and I thought he might dive at Nicholas and sink his teeth into the man's throat. A brief exchange followed in which Nicholas appeared to provide some explanation—or warning—to the priest. Gradually, the savage look on Rasputin's face faded to one of perplexity. In the end he satisfied himself with a deep bow before Ms Alexander, his eyes lewdly traveling over her.

Following this final introduction, the Tsar took Ms Alexander off to one side. I watched fascinated as she removed a glove from one hand, gripped an iron-ringed wheel of the coach, then hesitantly embraced Nicholas in a hug.

Eureka! I thought. This was the grounding she had spoken of—my dreamt solution to our union appeared to work! If she could manage a hug before her body recharged, I wondered what else might be accomplished.

The Tsar eventually tore himself away and said a few more words, which I missed due to my preoccupation. He then climbed into his coach and was spirited away, his cavalrymen in tow, on whatever affair of state demanded his hasty and secret transport. The rest of us watched Ms Alexander as she stood in the lane and waved farewell to him, in spite of the fact that he could not see her through the coach's impenetrable black curtains.

Our first order of business in Saint Petersburg, Dietrich announced, was to locate Leopold Engel. He spoke it in an annoyed but resigned tone. It was clear he was not entirely pleased with the situation, neither with the Tsar's knowledge of our mission, nor having Rasputin assigned to us. But he would not rebuke Ms Alexander publicly, and probably not at all now that he knew of her connections.

We resigned to the dining room of the mansion, and Dietrich stood at the head of the table. The meeting went a bit slow because everything he said had to be translated by Ms Alexander for Rasputin, and vice versa. Additionally, before Dietrich could adequately address the business at hand, Rasputin demanded a thorough account of events that had brought us to Saint Petersburg, the retelling and translating of which took more than half an hour. At first Dietrich was so irritated he looked like he might suffer a stroke, but by the end, when Rasputin had almost every piece of intelligence we had uncovered to date, Dietrich was so weary he would have told the priest anything just to advance the meeting. By then lunchtime was approaching, Irish was almost asleep in his chair, and Dietrich rubbed his temples as if battling a paroxysmal headache. When the elderly couple intruded with a cart bearing our meal, and Rasputin leapt up to get at it, I thought Dietrich might walk out. Instead he threw up his hands and collapsed in his chair. A few minutes later he straightened and joined us for refreshment.

The meal was brief, though in that time Rasputin managed to drink more wine than even I deemed constructive. He was on his sixth glass when the dishes were cleared away and the old couple wheeled their squeaky cart back into the kitchen.

"Finally to business," Dietrich said. "Ms Alexander, please explain to Rasputin that we are seeking Leopold Engel, that we believe he is in Saint Petersburg, possibly staying with his father. If the priest is truly to act as our guide, ask him how we can find the man."

Ms Alexander translated. When she finished, Rasputin blinked once slowly, almost drowsily, before replying.

"He will make inquiries," she said. "He said he knows of a man called Engel who is the concertmaster of the Imperial Russian Theater. He also said that for the past several months the man has been in poor health. He does not know if this gentleman has a son, but he will find out."

Dietrich nodded and forced an appreciative smile. Rasputin stood, drained a seventh glass of wine, and departed. Aside from his brief stolidity he showed no sign of drunkenness. At his departure Dietrich sighed as if relieved. It was apparent he had his doubts about the priest's efficacy.

Ms Alexander said nothing on the subject, but I had noted her growing anxiety as Rasputin downed each successive glass. Her eyes also revealed that she was questioning the role of our volatile guide, and her decision to confide the details of our endeavor to the Tsar.

There was nothing to be done for it, however, at least for the time being. Rasputin was off to perform his errand. He would question his contacts, and likely harass an innocent and bedridden old concertmaster in the process.

With Nicholas gone, Ms Alexander moved into the summer house with us. The house had a surplus of rooms, and she moved into the largest one upstairs. The old couple set her up in a resplendent bedroom befitting a princess, a baroque chamber at the end of the upstairs hall, set apart from the rest of us as if she were indeed royalty.

As we awaited the return of Rasputin, we passed the time as best we could. Dietrich was restless, and since he had nothing to read (everything was in Russian) he spent the afternoon performing an extensive wandering of the garden, leaving no inch unexplored. Irish was content to sit in a chair propped against the house exterior, rolling and smoking innumerable cigarettes, drifting off when the tedium became too much.

Ms Alexander spent much of her time sequestered in her room, doing *what* I have no idea. I had not seen her behave so reclusively since our Berlin doldrums. I presumed her solitude was due to embarrassment. After all, she was solely responsible for giving away our secrets to Nicholas and saddling us with the lunatic priest. I was relieved when she emerged in time for supper, and we dined together as usual.

Afterwards she seemed intent on an evening stroll through the garden. I followed close behind, thinking I would join her. However, Irish had left the table unusually early, and when I stepped outside I was disappointed to find they had already linked up and begun down the garden path. Fearing the planting of any seeds between them, I hurried along in pursuit, joining them for a long and slow walk that lasted until sunset. During our walk Irish shot me a few meaningful glances, but when I pretended not to notice he eventually gave up.

It was after ten o'clock when Rasputin finally returned. Everyone had said goodnight and scattered to their rooms when we heard a commotion of voices downstairs. We each appeared in the upstairs hallway looking questioningly at one another, wondering if we should investigate. As we made our way downstairs, Irish in the lead, the voices became louder. We hurried on to the dining room to find Rasputin in a shouting match with the old caretakers.

"What's happening?" Ms Alexander demanded.

The old couple would say nothing, but the woman gestured at Rasputin who sneered in response. Ms Alexander did not understand, but I immediately realized the priest was sloshed. However, the situation was defused when Rasputin collapsed into a chair and began speaking conversationally to her as if the old couple were not in the room at all. They hovered for a minute, wondering if their part was done, then quietly retreated to their quarters.

Ms Alexander spoke with the priest at length before providing an explanation.

"He says he made several inquiries today," she explained. "He sent word to his underworld contacts—I did not ask what *that* means. Later he paid a visit to the Imperial Theater and learned the concertmaster, Karl Engel, is suffering from a slow consumption. Father Grigori learned this from the maestro's apprentice, who also revealed that Engel's son, Leopold, is tending him. When asked for details about the son, the apprentice said only that the man is an accomplished actor and mystic."

She said the last word with some distaste.

"A mystic?" I thought aloud.

"Does he know where Leopold is?" Dietrich asked.

"Yes," she said. "He will take us there first thing in the morning."

Dietrich nodded, looking surprised at the ease with which we had performed the task. Rasputin was questionable, but he had exceeded expectations.

We headed back to our rooms. As it happened I was the last, and as I left the room I glanced over my shoulder at Rasputin, plastered and recumbent in the dining room chair. He acknowledged me with a nod of the head, a rapacious grin, and a wink of an eye. It sent a chill down my spine. If Irish had not blocked the staircase above, I would have raced back to my room, bolted my door, and prayed for deliverance from the Russian devil.

The next morning we rose, grabbed a quick bite from a buffet the old couple had set out, and prepared to set off in search of Leopold Engel. We had only one problem preventing our departure: Rasputin was nowhere to be seen.

As we were eating, Irish had commented on the priest's absence. We thought nothing of it since he had not taken up residence in the summer house. When we heard a coach pull up outside, we presumed Rasputin had arrived. But when we stepped outside he was nowhere in sight. Irish opened the door to the coach only to find it empty. Dietrich began to fume.

"This priest will be the death of me," he muttered.

We stared at one another for a moment before Dietrich recommended we fan out around the house in search of him. I made a quick circuit and encountered a guard, but no priest. The guard, however, realized that we were looking for someone and inquired. Once Ms Alexander explained the situation, the guard smiled knowingly and pointed down the lane.

"He said Father Grigori never left last night, that he came outside before sunup and wandered off into the garden," she said. "He was drinking from a bottle, and last seen near the statue of Pomona."

We walked down the lane in search of Pomona. Soon we spotted her, a bare-breasted goddess immortalized in white marble. We stopped beneath the statue and awkwardly looked at Ms Alexander, who blushed as she spoke.

"According to the guard, he found Father Grigori here..."

Irish laughed out loud. Dietrich closed his eyes and shook his head. We all looked upon a disgraced Pomona, grubby handprints visible on her pallid, immaculately rendered breasts and exposed thighs.

As we stood gawking, I heard a gentle snoring among the bushes. I proceeded into the shrubs immediately behind the statue and spied an empty wine bottle, and a pair of booted feet.

"Found him!" I called out. I knelt down to rouse Rasputin and was met by such vile vapors, it was as if he had been eating sulfur. I gagged and retreated.

The sound made the priest stir. As I stood back drinking in fresh air, he came fully awake, climbed to his feet, and stared at me from beneath ragged locks.

He said something, an animal sound more than speech, and glared at me as if awaiting a response. When he realized none was forthcoming, he staggered out of the bushes and into the lane.

We congregated in the shadow of Pomona's humiliation. I noticed many eyes darting between Rasputin and the statue, but he did not seem to notice or care. He stretched out a hand and grabbed one of Pomona's bare feet to stabilize himself, idly scratching himself with the other. Ms Alexander looked away. Rasputin then straightened, wiped his grimy face on a sleeve, and nodded to show he was ready for the task at hand.

The coach rattled through the streets of Saint Petersburg for half an hour before it came to a much welcomed stop. Rasputin pulled back a curtain, took in the scene, and climbed out. We followed him and found ourselves standing in the middle of a block of modest townhomes. Before we could stop him, Rasputin picked out a building, strode to the door, and knocked.

Suddenly we all came to our senses. We had been so distracted by the morning's events that we had not discussed a plan, or a pretense for our visit. I looked at Dietrich, and to my amazement he simply shrugged. He seemed to have uncharacteristically come to terms with the unpredictability of our guide. When I looked at Rasputin, I understood: his hair and beard were wild and peppered with bits of compost from his garden slumber; his tunic was stained and disheveled; and his boots were disgracefully tarnished. Nothing about him was inconspicuous. I gave up any delusion of subtlety.

We crowded onto the doorstep, and thankfully, before the door opened, Ms Alexander edged her way to the front. We did not want Rasputin to represent us. To his credit, however, the priest offered one helpful last-minute tidbit.

"Ah!" Ms Alexander exclaimed. "He says that Engel speaks English."

"Finally, we can follow a conversation," Irish said.

The door opened to reveal a stout gentleman of perhaps fifty, in his shirtsleeves and holding a folded newspaper. He was balding and wore a robust mustache-and-mutton chop affair, a style that in America had passed from vogue decades prior, but which seemed oddly fitting here. In spite of his prodigious whiskers he had a friendly face, even if it looked troubled when he took in the motley crew assembled at his door.

"Good morning," Ms Alexander said. "We are seeking Mr Leopold Engel. Is this the correct residence?"

"I am Leopold Engel," he said, looking surprised. He swept his gaze across us. "You are English?"

"Americans," she replied, "though I am in fact from Saint Petersburg."

"Ah," Engel replied, staring at us in wonder. It took him a moment to decide how to react to such a strange troupe. For a moment I thought we would have to interrogate him at his door, but Ms Alexander was so disarming in beauty and grace that a moment later he invited us inside.

He led us down a narrow hallway and around a corner into a small sitting room, where he invited everyone to make themselves comfortable. The room was furnished with a sofa, and opposite that, a tea table accompanied by two wooden chairs, framed by a picture window. After the briefest of introductions, Engel seated himself on the sofa next to Ms Alexander. Dietrich and I took the two chairs at the tea table, leaving Irish and Rasputin to stand.

"So your friends are from America," Engel said, easing into conversation.

"Yes," Ms Alexander confirmed.

Engel took a few seconds to examine us.

"I sense you are tourists, and that you have come for a divining."

"A divining?" Dietrich said.

"Yes," Engel replied. "Divination is my specialty. I sense that you are seeking something, or perhaps someone, and that you require my assistance."

Dietrich stared at him. As the seconds ticked by I thought our captain was at a loss of how to proceed. Then Engel gestured at the pictures hanging on the walls as if they contained some explanation. We turned our heads to get a better look. They were all photographs, each depicting Engel in a moment of concentration. In each image Engel stood or sat in a domestic setting—on a sofa, at a table, at a writing desk—accompanied by another subject. His subjects, however, looked gauzy. They were clearly people but they lacked distinction, as if they were somehow less substantial. As I looked closely at one—an image of Engel sitting across a tea table from a round-faced woman he identified as the spirit of Madame Blavatsky—I realized the woman was insubstantial, that though she sat in the chair, its lines were visible *through* her.

"Are they ghosts?" Irish asked.

"Spirits," Engel said. "Some deceased, others of a more supernatural cast."

Ms Alexander seemed in awe.

"How can such a thing be possible?" she asked.

Engel smiled and shrugged.

"There is a nuance of the modern photographic apparatus that enables it to capture glimpses into the spirit world," he said. "I am no scientist. I cannot describe it. I only know that it is a genuine phenomenon."

I was impressed. I could only imagine how much more lucrative my former mystic endeavors would have proven if I had possessed such evidence, even if it were trumped up. A glance at Ms Alexander and Irish revealed they were also impressed, though both looked a bit unnerved by the photos, as if they proved (or disproved) some deep-seated belief. The only ones unaffected by Engel's proofs were Dietrich and Rasputin. Though he tried to play along, Dietrich's expression was clearly skeptical, and Rasputin, excommunicated by our English conversation, simply sneered at Engel's spirit photography.

"Remarkable," Dietrich said unenthusiastically. But in spite of his disbelief I saw a gleam in his eye. "Your presumption about us is correct. Your reputation precedes you. We are here for a divining."

"Excellent!" Engel exclaimed. "But before we begin, we should discuss my fee."

Dietrich waved the matter aside.

"Money is no object."

Engel grinned, clapped his hands together, and rubbed them vigorously.

"In that case, let's proceed!" he said. He crossed to the picture window and drew the curtains, casting a pall over the room. "I will act as the crucible for the spirit world. But first I must know if there is a particular spirit with whom you wish to commune, and what you wish to learn."

A moment of silence followed in which I thought we had again stumbled, but Dietrich spoke up.

"For the spirit, we have no preference," Dietrich said.

"Very well," Engel replied. "In that case I will ask whatever spirits are manifest. And the information you seek?"

"We wish to know everything there is to know about a man called Brother Iscariot," he said evenly.

If Dietrich's intention was to provoke a response from Engel, he failed utterly. Engel merely rubbed his chin and looked contemplative for a moment.

"Brother Iscariot," he repeated. "This man is living?"

"I was hoping you might answer that for us," Dietrich said.

"And you have no other information, not his real name, just an alias?" Engel asked.

"I am afraid not," Dietrich said.

Engel thought for a moment.

"I will be honest," he said. "Without more information I do not expect results. But I will put it to the spirits, and we will see what they have to say."

Dietrich nodded, making clear he had expected nothing less.

Engel placed both hands on the table, closed his eyes, and became quiet. At first he breathed deeply, becoming noticeably relaxed. Then stillness followed for several minutes, during which everyone watched him intently. The air began to thicken, and Engel began to twitch as if small spasms were firing at random places throughout his body. I watched him raptly. If he was a fraud, he knew how to put on a good show.

When he spoke his throat was hoarse.

"I am now in contact with the realm of the spirits," he said. "I am among them, and they are among us, crowded densely around us, more than I have witnessed at any other sitting." Here he wrinkled his brow curiously to accentuate his performance. "It is strange that so many would gather. They have taken a keen interest in you. They say you are pursuing an urgent matter, and they wish to see the outcome."

Engel paused, probably waiting for one of us to speak, to offer a clue that would tell him if he was on the right track. But Dietrich shot us a look that said no one should say a word.

"Yes," Engel said at length. "They are very interested in you, and in your *endeavor*." The way he emphasized the word hinted that he (or the spirits) somehow knew of it. Irish shifted in place, his face revealing he was taken by the performance. "While we have the attention of so many, I will ask the question: O, spirits! Essences of mystery! These in whom you have taken such avid interest come before you seeking answers. They seek one known only as Brother Iscariot. Do you know this person? Can you offer any clue to his true identity or whereabouts?"

Engel slightly inclined his head this way and that, as if harkening to a discussion of many voices. His face went through numerous reflections of confusion and interest as he took in all the spirits had to say. Then, keeping his eyes closed, he provided a summary.

"They say you walk a dangerous path, that if you pursue this mysterious stranger you will meet with nothing but anguish, despair, and death. But they will say nothing more as they do not wish to influence mortal affairs."

Dietrich nodded expectantly.

"And what of his location? Can the spirits not help us with that, either?"

Engel furrowed his brow.

"No," he replied. "I am afraid the spirits do not know, or will not tell."

"Very well," Dietrich said. "What can you tell us about the Illuminati?"

"The Illuminati?" Engel said, as if the word were unfamiliar to him. "I will inquire among the spirits."

"Never mind the spirits," Dietrich said. "I am speaking to *you*, Herr Engel."

Engel did not move for several seconds. He kept his eyes closed as if still preoccupied with his mediation. Then, slowly, he opened them and looked at Dietrich.

"Me?" he said, sounding confused. Perspiration stood out on his brow, though it could have been due to the stuffiness in the room.

"Ten years ago, you were involved in a plan to resurrect the Illuminati," Dietrich said matter-of-factly. "Your partners in this were Theodor Reuss and Doctor Karl Kellner."

Engel froze. As the seconds ticked by, his face began to color. He scanned our faces again, licking his lips.

"You're not police," he said bitterly. "Who are you?"

"You have our names already," Dietrich said. "That is all you need to know about us."

Engel weighed his options.

"It's clear you are not here for a reading," he said, straightening. "And if you are not the police then I must ask you to leave."

"No," Dietrich replied.

Engel looked at him incredulously.

"No?"

"We have traveled a thousand miles to see you," Dietrich said. "We will remain, and you will answer our questions."

I tried to hide my surprise. I had never heard Dietrich sound so resolute. When we started out he had been so concerned with propriety and the surreptitious collection of information, this kind of declaration had been unimaginable. Something had brought about a change in his character.

Engel narrowed his eyes and examined us all again. His gaze lingered on Irish, who noticed and gave him a suggestive smirk.

"Someone spoke to you," he said, rubbing his hands on his knees. "Whoever it was, he should not have."

"If it matters, it was August Wende," Dietrich replied. "Use that information as you wish. He means nothing to us. I am only concerned with Brother Iscariot and the Illuminati."

Another shock! It was uncharacteristic of Dietrich to give out information so flippantly. But of course he had a personal score to settle. If dropping Wende's name would lead to the villain's untimely end, it would suit Dietrich just fine.

At the mention of Wende, Engel briefly lost his composure, becoming pale and jittery.

"You spoke to Wende?" he said

"Yes," Dietrich said, noting Engel's restlessness.

"And he sent you to *me*?"

"Correct," Dietrich replied, a bit impatiently.

Engel's color slowly began to return. He stared at the floor, his eyes darting back and forth as he licked his lips. But then it was his turn to surprise us.

"Very well," he said, suddenly and inexplicably agreeable. "What do you want to know?"

In retrospect, Engel was too easily trumped, and too willing to answer our questions. Deep down we all recognized it. But given his situation—outnumbered and surrounded in his own parlor, interrogated by an impassive inquisitor, glared at by a maniacal monk, and grinned at by a beast whose walnut-sized knuckles cracked like logs popping in a fire—his expedient surrender seemed more a wise recourse than a clever stratagem. Indeed, in his place I would have done the same, only sooner. In the end, however, it was not the veracity of his tale that we should have questioned, but his motivation for telling it.

"Tell us of your role, past and present, in the Illuminati," Dietrich said.

Engel sighed, sagged, and launched into his tale.

"In 1880 Reuss made his first attempt to resurrect the order, but it failed. I do not know why. I think the manner in which the Illuminati embraced chaos appealed to his sensibilities. He was an anarchist at heart, you know."

"I did not," Dietrich replied. "But the methods laid out in *Ordo Ab Chao* demonstrate an embrace of anarchy, with a goal more sinister than anarchy itself."

"You are familiar with their bible, then?" Engel said. "Good. That means I will have less to explain."

Dietrich gazed at him stoically.

"As I was saying, Reuss carried an interest in the Illuminati since at least 1880, but nothing came of it until 1888 when we met in Berlin. We met at a party after his performance in *The Magic Flute*. We were introduced, and I was surprised to discover he knew of me from my work."

"Your work?" Dietrich said.

"Theoretical writings on naturopathic healing, hypnotism, mysticism, and the occult," Engel said. "Soon we found ourselves seated in a corner of the room, away from the crowd, discussing our mutual fascination with mysteries of the universe. It was during this conversation that he confided in me his interest in recreating the Illuminati. I had heard of the sect, but I knew little about it. The mystery of it intrigued me. We struck up a friendship and correspondence, and when I returned to Dresden he continued to write me as if I were his protégé. At first I was only intellectually curious, but as the years passed I began to understand what a powerful organization the order would become. I then stated an interest in becoming an Illumined leader. Reuss instructed me to organize a chapter in Dresden, and I set about recruiting members. By 1897, the Dresden Lodge was in operation."

"What was the purpose of the Lodge," Dietrich said.

"To recruit as many of the irregular Masonic lodges as possible," Engel said. "There are many unsanctioned lodges that persist in spite of being shunned by regular Masons. Some flourish and expand, others atrophy and die. Reuss and I set out to harness the dormant power that lay in the unsanctioned brotherhoods. We knew if we could rally them, we would have an order to rival the ancient and revered Masons themselves!"

In spite of his predicament, Engel temporarily got caught up reliving his glory days as an Illuminati conspirator. In that moment I had an insight: so many of the men wrapped up in this conspiracy business had an unhealthy fixation on the Masons. Once spurned, it was as if they had made it their secret ambition to outdo the ancient fraternity, to collect all of Freemasonry's pariahs under one banner and create something to make the Masons—nay, the world—pay for their rejection and humiliation. If I had not already witnessed men dying in service to this idea, I would have written it off as petty jealousy and bitterness.

Engel mastered himself before he got too carried away. He coughed into his fist, cleared his throat, and continued.

"Ruess and I pursued the task from two angles. He created a lodge in Berlin while I worked in Dresden. Once each had absorbed an appreciable number of irregular lodges, we merged administratively. I then stepped aside and Reuss took over as Grand Master."

"And then?" Dietrich probed.

"Then," Engel said with a sigh, "Reuss turned out to be the wrong man for the job."

"Explain," Dietrich insisted. "Why was Theodor Reuss the wrong man?"

"Reuss turned out to be more of a dilettante than I had imagined," Engel said, "and more a *slave to* than a *master of* his own aspirations. Here enters the betrayer and provocateur, Doctor Kellner. He was bookish and fascinated by Masonic knowledge. He was also wealthy, which gave him leverage to influence and lure Reuss away from our original plan. Kellner urged him to take up a new project, to invest his energies into constructing a Masonic library, to serve as a repository for mysteries and secrets. He whispered in Reuss' ear until he had won him over, and perceiving me as a threat to his goal, he convinced Reuss to ostracize me. Reuss summoned me to his office in Berlin on the pretense of discussing business and summarily dismissed me. He then sent word throughout our network that I had been excommunicated. There ended my association with the Illuminati. When August Wende found out, he was furious. He went into such a rage, I thought he might kill *me*."

We all froze and stared at him as if he had just casually uttered the most profane word imaginable.

"Wende?" Dietrich asked, looking suddenly apprehensive. "How does he fit into this?"

"He was our courier," Engel explained. "It was Wende who delivered direction to Reuss from Brother Iscariot."

"You had communication with Iscariot?" Dietrich said, almost in a whisper. Suddenly he was sitting on the edge of his chair. "And this through Wende?"

"Of course," Engel replied, as if this should have been evident from the beginning. Then understanding came over his face. "I presumed you already knew."

We stared at him. Dietrich's glare had taken on a strange, piercing quality that was not there before. Engel noted his rapt attention and continued.

"Reuss was not our prime mover. Where his 1880 attempt to re-establish the order was self-inspired, his second attempt was at the behest of the man known only to us as Brother Iscariot. Word arrived in the form of an unanticipated letter, delivered by August Wende. In it Iscariot identified himself as Weishaupt's heir and successor, and he laid out the plan to unite the irregular Masons. To demonstrate his veracity, an account was opened in Reuss' name at the Bank of Berlin, in the amount of ten thousand marks to cover our starting expenses."

"Do you know Iscariot's identity?" Dietrich asked.

I cringed. He sounded unflatteringly desperate. But Engel looked at him regretfully and shook his head.

"I'm afraid not," he said.

"What of Wende?" Dietrich asked.

Engel mulled it over.

"I suppose Wende could have been the architect. We only knew him as an intermediary, but it could have been a ruse. I never considered it before."

"No, no!" Dietrich said impatiently. "Granted, that is an intriguing concept, but it is not what I meant. What interaction did you have with him?"

"Wende was itinerant," Engel explained. "He would arrive with money to fund our efforts, along with direction on what lodges, or people, we should attempt to enlist."

"People?" Dietrich asked.

"Yes, there was a variety. Financiers, industrialists, scientists, inventors.

271

The latter became more the trend in the final years."

"How else was Wende involved?"

"Well," Engel went on, "while in Berlin he would attend our meetings, but only as a silent partner. He claimed he was there only to deliver his message, to observe how things were going, and to report back to his master. His visits occurred perhaps once a month and lasted only a few days."

"Do you know anything else about Wende?" Dietrich inquired. "Anything at all?"

Engel looked uncomfortable, as if the questions had taken a turn he had not expected.

"Yes. After interacting with him for several years I learned, through happenstance, of his skirmishes with the authorities. Trouble seemed to follow him. There were suspicious deaths in his wake. He was frequently arrested, but always released. When I was expelled, I was secretly relieved that I would no longer have any interaction with him."

Dietrich ruminated for a moment. During the pause I noticed Rasputin. He stared at Engel as if he hung on every word, in spite of the fact that he spoke no English.

"Presuming Iscariot is neither Reuss nor Wende," Dietrich continued, "have you any other ideas about his identity or whereabouts?"

"No," Engel said. "Wende guarded that information carefully."

Dietrich looked disappointed. Then, after what I would have sworn was a pause for dramatic effect, Engel's eyes lit up.

"On second thought," he said, "there was one occasion in which I may have learned more than I was intended to know."

"Go on," Dietrich said eagerly.

"Wende traveled extensively, so this could very well be a false lead. But once, after attending a Berlin meeting, I happened across him again in the telegraph office. I found myself in the same queue, though I did not realize it until I heard his voice ahead of me. As he spoke with the man at the counter, I heard him say the word *Véles*."

"Véles?" Dietrich repeated, furrowing his brow. He searched his immaculate memory but came up short. He turned to the rest of us, his eyes alighting on Ms Alexander. She responded with a mystified look and a shake of the head.

We entered another period of thoughtful silence as Dietrich's mind explored possibilities and connections. During this time I noticed motion in the corner of my eye, and I turned to find Rasputin visibly agitated. Before he had only sneered at the proceedings. Now, he suddenly appeared righteously indignant. He took everyone by surprise when he stepped forward to tower over Engel.

"*Véles?*" he demanded.

"*Da!*" Engel replied, his eyes wide.

"*Kult Vélesa?*" Rasputin asked, his voice rising in volume.

"*Ya ne znayu!*" Engel said, shaking his head.

We looked to Ms Alexander for translation, but she too was surprised and fascinated by the scene. Rasputin became still more animated.

"*Shto ti znayesh o Vélesi?*"

"*Nichevo!*" Engel exclaimed, shaking his head vigorously.

And so the Russian conversation played out, with Rasputin supplanting Dietrich as our interrogator. The intensity and furor with which the priest spoke was so unexpected and frightening that no one dared interrupt. Rasputin's voice continued to rise in volume and emotion. He began to shake a fist in the air over Engel, whether in emphasis or threat I could not be sure.

As Rasputin yelled, Engel receded into his chair, as if by slouching down he could put a safe distance between them. A look of growing fear was in Engel's eyes. Rasputin was half bent in his tirade, his face near Engel's as he roared and pelted him with spittle.

"*Yaznychnik! Idolopoklonnik! Dissident!*"

At every accusation Engel frantically shook his head and cried out, "*Nyet!*"

Eventually Dietrich overcame his amazement and called out to Ms Alexander. She started as if from a trance, stood, and demanded Rasputin explain himself. The priest spun on her with fist raised. In a motion that belied his size Irish came between them. By the look in Rasputin's eyes, Irish only angered him more. But he quickly mastered himself. He lowered his hand, though none of the rage left his eyes. He then sidestepped Irish and addressed Ms Alexander in a level but stern voice.

"He accuses this man of being in league with pagans," she exclaimed, "of working secretly against the church and the Tsar!"

Dietrich shook his head in confusion.

"What does this have to do with our business here?"

Ms Alexander shrugged. As one we turned to Engel, who was watching Rasputin nervously.

"It seems he has the answers you now seek," Engel said, nodding at the priest.

Dietrich looked in puzzlement at Rasputin, who had reverted to his dark but silent intensity.

"Father Grigori?" Dietrich said.

"Yes," Engel replied. "He will tell you all he knows, I am sure." Engel closed his eyes, inclined his face to the ceiling, and was quiet for a moment. His eyelids flickered and his mouth dropped open. I thought he might be suffering heart failure from the excitement. Before I could raise the idea, he spoke in a strange, far-off voice.

"The monk knows and will send you there, to the place called Véles, named after the god of its people, and there you will find the answers you seek." Engel opened his eyes and looked at us each in turn. "You will also find despair. You will know death, disease, and fire. You will be forsaken, and only in the end will you understand your folly."

Silence followed. Anxiety gripped me as Engel's eyes, and the final words of his prophecy, all seemed directed at me. I stood transfixed, the words echoing in my mind. I was only peripherally aware of Rasputin exchanging words with Ms Alexander. Then the monk spoke, and his harsh voice brought me back to my senses like a dreamer being shaken awake. As he spoke, he made motions with his hands in the air: the gesture of a cross, as if he were placing a blessing upon us. But the way in which he executed the maneuver made it look deformed, more like an X. When he finished he glared at Engel.

"Father Grigori says heed not the unholy vision of this man," our lady explained, "for his words are a blasphemy. God has spoken to him and assured him our task is holy, noble, and just. We will prevail."

Engel shot an indignant look at the priest. Rasputin returned it with far greater effect. After such an unexpected series of events, no one seemed to know what to do next. Dietrich again took charge.

"Thank you for your assistance, Herr Engel," he said quietly. "Before we depart, I will reward you with a bit of information that might please you. I take from your story that you cared little for Doctor Kellner."

"Not especially," Engel said hoarsely.

"Not a week ago I encountered August Wende, and during our conversation he informed me that Kellner is dead."

"I heard as much," Engel said. "Heart failure, if memory serves."

Dietrich smiled grimly.

"Wende did not tell me the entire story, nor did he reveal the cause. But he implied that Kellner met an untimely and unnatural end. So if Kellner slighted you, and you wished for revenge, know that he received his come-uppance."

Engel looked conflicted.

"Thank you," he said hesitantly.

Dietrich made his way to the front door and we followed. We climbed into the coach and set out for the Summer Garden. With the exception of Rasputin, who gazed tranquilly at Ms Alexander most of the way, everyone stared quietly into space, still assimilating the morning's events

We arrived at the mansion by noon and found the old caretakers had assembled a hearty lunch for us in the dining room. Rasputin disappeared to the kitchen and no one objected. As we ate, a laconic pall hovered over us. The old couple, who stood by dutifully and solemnly, exchanged curious glances as we ate. When we finished, they cleared the table as quietly as we had eaten and retreated to the kitchen.

"I think we have much to talk about," Dietrich said.

"Yes," Ms Alexander agreed. "Shall I begin?"

Dietrich nodded.

"Last night I visited with my cousin. After dinner we retired to his library and talked late into the night. He told me much news, but it was of Russia that we spoke at length. The empire is suffering from many problems. Famine, sickness, border disputes, Bolshevik uprisings. They all weigh heavily on Nicholas, and he is going to great pains to manage everything. But for all these problems he confided in me something stranger still, something more disturbing which he has kept secret. At first I dismissed it because it seemed so absurd, but after our interview today I have a growing suspicion these events are somehow connected."

"What events?" Dietrich asked.

"When Father Grigori reacted so vehemently at mention if Véles, it all came together for me. Nicholas said that just months ago something strange happened in Siberia. There were rumors of strange events in the Urals, of mysterious disappearances that suggested foul play, and of armed men coming and going in remote places. Nicholas believed Bolsheviks might be secretly assembling an army. He dispatched scouts to investigate."

"What did they find?" Dietrich asked.

"No one knows," Ms Alexander replied. "The scouts ventured into the mountains and were not heard from again."

"They went in search of Bolsheviks," Dietrich mused. "Perhaps they found them."

"Perhaps," Ms Alexander said. "But the scouts were last seen departing Bogoslovsk, a town at the feet of the Urals. They were en route to a village in the mountains, a place called Véles."

"Fascinating!" Dietrich said. "What else can you tell us?"

"Nothing, unfortunately," she said. "But here I think we should inquire of Father Grigori. He hinted at much during his exchange with Leopold Engel, more than I could comprehend. I think it is time we heard what he knows on the subject."

She stepped to the kitchen door and called out to the priest. We heard a grunt in response, and a moment later he entered with a bottle of wine in one hand and a thick hunk of bread in the other. As he chewed, crumbs dislodged from his mangy beard and fell to the floor.

She bade him to sit at the table and tell all that he knew. Rasputin frowned, washed the mouthful down with a swig from his bottle, and told us of his experience with Véles.

All we wanted to know was what Rasputin knew of the place, but apparently the knowledge was so inextricably woven into the larger fabric of his life, he could not tell us anything without first telling us about himself.

He grew up in a small village about fifty miles outside of Ekaterinburg. As a boy he discovered he had the supernatural gift of second sight, the ability to see and know things that were hidden. On numerous occasions he helped his family and neighbors find things that had been lost or stolen. He considered his ability a gift from God, but he was troubled that such divine sight could not penetrate the unknown. No matter how long or hard he concentrated on spiritual matters, he came up with more questions than answers. This troubled him greatly and became an obsession.

At the age of eighteen he joined a monastery, thinking the solitude and devotion would help him crack secrets previously denied him. After several months with the monks, however, he knew he was going about it all wrong. It was then that he heard a voice speak to him, telling him to abandon the monastery and become a priest. Without hesitation he left the monks behind and began wandering the countryside, searching for a new teacher.

Eventually he came across a ramshackle hut in the middle of nowhere, outside of which sat a mangy old man, wearing a tattered and filthy robe, smoking a pipe. Rasputin stayed with him overnight and learned that his host was a holy man, a hermit who had devoted the last forty years of his life to learning the mysteries of the universe. Rasputin knew at once God had led him to this man, and he beseeched the old man to teach him. The hermit agreed.

Rasputin spent almost a year under the tutelage of the old man, having long discussions about God's will and the unknown. His teacher had a profound impact on him, so much that Rasputin modeled himself after the man, growing out his own hair and beard.

Eventually Rasputin felt compelled to heed his calling. After all, the voice had commanded him to become a priest, not a hermit, and priests worked among the people. With regret he left his beloved teacher behind and resumed his travels. Over several years he ranged far and wide, venturing to distant and diverse lands, searching for enlightenment in exotic locations like Greece and Jerusalem. But eventually the voice led him back home.

Rasputin spent the next twenty years wandering the Russian countryside, visiting towns and villages to spread the word of God. His pilgrimage took him into the Ural Mountains, into villages so remote they had gone untouched by progress. In those places Christianity was little more than a rumor. He spent much time with those people, preaching and using his gift to dazzle by finding lost items and wayward cows. In his wake every village was converted.

The farther Rasputin wandered into the mountains, however, the stranger the towns became, and the more curiously resistant the people seemed to his ideas. One day, after a formally hospitable but awkward stay in a village where the inhabitants only feigned interest in his talk of a Christian God, Rasputin found himself on what seemed an endless mountain road. For three days he walked and saw no sign of habitation. He ran out of food and water, and began to think he might die among the rocks when he finally spotted a sign of life: a strange stone carving alongside the road. He could not make it out— perhaps it was a poor rendition of a tree—but it had an unmistakable serpentine quality to it. Whatever it was, it meant a village had to be near, and he hurried down the road to find it.

A few miles away he found it: a gathering of fifty or so wooden buildings that were surprisingly modern for their remote location. In fact, the village more resembled a town, with a main thoroughfare lined by shops. Rasputin thanked God for delivering him to safety. He imagined his work would be easier in a placed that exhibited some signs of modernity. At the same time he was puzzled that such a place had no apparent church, yet he was hopeful that they would be receptive to his message.

The people were suspicious but polite toward him. After he helped a man find his lost hammer, and healed another's ailing goat, they warmed up to him quickly. When it was time to perform the task for which he had been called, to spread the word of God, the villagers balked, whispering and shooting him dark looks. As the whisperings grew to a murmur, Rasputin finally learned that they were heathens, that they had a god of their own—a pagan god of old—and they were not in the market for another.

A perennial stranger to tact and diplomacy, Rasputin then climbed atop a wagon in the square and launched into a fiery sermon, denouncing their beliefs and rebuking them for their unholy ways. The situation only got worse from there. People began to shout at him. Women covered the ears of their children and led them away. And the men took up axes, pitchforks, and shovels and chased him out of town.

Rasputin fled for his life. About a mile outside of town his pursuers turned back, choosing to let him get lost and die in the wild. Miraculously, Rasputin wandered through the mountains for three days without sustenance. He then came across a traveled road where he fainted. He was discovered hours later and shown kindness by some farmers returning from a market. They loaded him into their cart and took him back to their town in the valley. As they lifted him from the cart he awoke, and he was much relieved to look up and see the Holy Cross erected atop a church. He knew then he was safe. The town was called Bogoslovsk, and its people took him in. When he told them of his ordeal, they all adopted dark looks, shook their heads, and spat three times over their shoulders.

"That is the village of Véles," they said. "They are all ungodly pagans. No priest in his right mind should go there!"

"That was in 1901," Ms Alexander said. "Father Grigori has not returned to that region since. He says the people of Véles adhere to eldritch beliefs that have no place in the modern world, that they are not civilized like us."

I raised an eyebrow at the thought of Rasputin being *like us*. I leaned toward Irish to make a joke, but Ms Alexander knew me too well. She shot me a look that kept me quiet.

"So when Father Grigori heard Engel speak of Véles," she continued, "it roused his fear and suspicion. He was prepared to haul Engel straight before the Tsar, to have him account for himself and reveal all he knows."

"I see," Dietrich said. "Yet there is still a connection to be made. You are suggesting this village of Véles is somehow central to the mysteries of Wende, Iscariot, and the Tsar's missing scouts. What is the connection?"

"I do not know," she said. "But I cannot believe it is just coincidence."

"It's strange," Irish said. "We've never heard of Véles before. Then in the span of a day we hear it from the Tsar, Engel, and the priest. Could it be a real clue?"

Dietrich frowned. He stood and stared out the window into the garden, his hands clasped behind his back.

"We came here to see what information we could get from Engel," he said at last. "He provided a surplus. I am especially interested to learn that Wende is more integral than I had guessed. But I must concede the only genuine lead we brought back from our meeting is this place called Véles."

He turned toward us, his eyes lingering on the priest.

"Can Father Grigori find this village again?"

Ms Alexander spoke to Rasputin. The monk scowled as if this was the greatest of impositions. He replied with only a few words, but in a tone that sounded almost amicable.

"He says that if he returns to Bogoslovsk he would be able to retrace his steps," she said.

"Good," Dietrich said, sounding satisfied. "Then we have our plan, at least for the moment."

Then Rasputin looked to the ceiling and spoke as if to himself.

"But it is a long journey," Ms Alexander translated, "approximately fifteen-hundred miles to Ekaterinburg, then another two-hundred and fifty to Bogoslovsk. These we can accomplish by train."

"That will take several days, I moaned, "even by train."

"Four or five days, depending on the schedule," Ms Alexander said. "But the accommodations of the Trans-Siberian Railway will make it tolerable."

I brightened.

"From Bogoslovsk," she continued, "we will have to secure some other means of transportation to reach Véles. But Father Grigori said one more thing."

We looked at her inquisitively.

"By the time we arrive in Ekaterinburg, he predicts he will have to return here on urgent business."

We were perplexed, but not dismayed

"Predicts?" Dietrich said, sounding skeptical. "So be it. From Ekaterinburg we will make do without him."

Sensing his part was done, Rasputin upturned the wine bottle to illustrate its emptiness and disappeared into the kitchen in search of another.

"Does anyone else find it odd that a priest drinks so much?" I said.

Ms Alexander pursed her lips, making it obvious she had an opinion on the matter but was reticent to speak. No one else commented. Dietrich placed his hands on the table and leaned heavily upon it.

"I'll make arrangements for Ekaterinburg and Bogoslovsk," he said. He sounded weary, as if all this travel was taking its toll on him. "I recommend everyone take the opportunity to enjoy the garden while we can. We will be on trains for several days to come."

I took Dietrich's advice to heart and spent most of our remaining time making slow, repeated circuits of the Summer Garden. I had company during a good many of those rounds. At first Ms Alexander joined me, keeping pace for almost a half dozen orbits. That was both a blissful and troubling time for me. As strange as it may seem, I had very little to say. Normally I would have said or done anything to win a smile, to hear the magical sound of her laughter, but it was as if my wit had abandoned me. I was still too vexed by the private friendship she had struck up with Irish, a relationship from which Dietrich and I—but more importantly I—had been excluded. Until recently I had thought she and I shared something special, that we were silently but immutably endeared to one another. But ever since Irish had ignorantly risked his life for a kiss, the chemistry within our group had changed. It was as if he had become her unacknowledged favorite.

As if to drive this point home, as we completed a circuit she suddenly looked up and exclaimed, "Oh, there is Mr Irish!" She then broke away from me as if I were a wisp of a memory. I watched as she strode merrily toward him, and as he grinned stupidly in greeting.

Wounded, I hurried on before they could invite me to join them—or worse, exclude me. As I continued my circuits, I caught occasional glimpses of them through the trees, and I was unsurprised, but nonetheless hurt, to see them strolling casually among the statues. They walked slowly, stopping in front of each marble figure for several minutes while Ms Alexander educated the brute on who the figures were and what they represented. As pedantic as she could be, and as tedious as I found such instruction, I would have given anything to stand in Irish's place.

At that time I came across Dietrich, who was strolling in the opposite direction. When he saw me he reversed course and joined me. At first we engaged in small talk, about the peace and beauty of the garden, Saint Petersburg's weather and the like. As he rattled on, I thought to myself about the evolution of our relationship during our adventure. When we met we had found each other insufferable. Now, we were like old colleagues.

It seemed absurd, but in the span of a few months I realized how much I had changed. Not long ago my thoughts had been wholly absorbed with Houdini's betrayal. Now, my seething hatred of the man had become an afterthought. I had never maintained any true friendships, but now I found myself wondering if I would still be close to my companions post-endeavor.

Before I met Ms Alexander I had carnally known, though never loved, numerous women. Now, she was practically all I could think about.

My reverie, however, was soon shattered. Dietrich inevitably turned the conversation to business. He regaled me with the tedious details of our impending travel, of our mission and the challenges ahead. I quickly became bored with him and subtly quickened my pace. In a matter of minutes he began to get winded, eventually lapsing into a coughing fit that forced him to retire to the house. I watched him go with some fondness, though at that moment I was glad to be rid of him.

By late afternoon, I was on what felt like my hundredth round when I was suddenly joined by Irish, who had come to fetch me for supper. He found me on the path at the opposite end, so we had a long walk back.

One thing I liked about Irish was his simplicity. If there were no dire need to communicate, he was content to be silent, sufficiently comforted by wordless companionship. On the other hand, if I felt the need to speak— which, admittedly, I often did—he was an attentive audience. On this occasion, however, he disappointed me by forcing a conversation I had no interest in pursuing.

"You've been in a mood lately," he said.

"Have I?"

"There's no need pretending," he said. "Everyone's picked up on it, even if they won't say."

I knew exactly what he was talking about, but I gave no hint of acknowledgement.

"You're a pal," he said, "but even I've got to admit, you've been acting like a selfish child."

I regarded him coldly. If he had not already saved my life twice in as many months, I would have given him a piece of my mind. Still, I gave in to petulance.

"In that case, I must ask your forgiveness," I said, sparing no sarcasm. "In fact, as soon as we get back, I will prostrate myself before you all, and beg your collective pardon."

He glared at me from beneath his flat cap, the bill of which only barely extended beyond the promontory of bone making up his primeval brow. I would have quailed had I not felt so indignant.

"What's got into you?" he demanded.

"As if you don't know," I muttered.

His look changed from one of annoyance to stupefaction.

"I don't," he insisted.

Now it was my turn to glare at him, and I did my level best to make him feel as anxious and inadequate as he, albeit unwittingly, made me. Here was my chance. Though he chose to pretend ignorance, he had opened the door on the awkward issue that lay between us: Ms Alexander.

By pressing the issue he was inviting attack, maybe in an effort to assuage his guilt for stealing her affection. He was giving me a chance to wound him in the only way I could, to cut him to the quick with spiteful wit. I almost took him up on it. I opened my mouth to say something cruel, but I caught myself at the last moment. As much as I wanted to lash out at him for coming between the lady and me, I knew nothing good would come of it. I knew I would only alienate myself from the one member of our company whom I considered a true friend.

I reconsidered and searched for some response that would sound appeasing but still carry a hint of derision, some double entendre that would evade his intellectual grasp but find purchase in his psyche, spread like a cancer, and over time wreak untold damage. But before I could come up with anything, my conscience intervened.

If Irish and Ms Alexander were meant to be together, there was little I could do to stop it. Lashing out at either of them would only deprive me of both. Perhaps, I thought, it was best to handle the situation like a man, to take Irish by the hand and congratulate him on his victory, to wish him the best and assume the role of unrequited lover. I finally decided that was the best thing to do, to clear the air between us, to rescue an endangered friendship, to surrender for the sake of their mutual happiness. The more I thought about it, the more strangely appealing the prospect became. My heart swelled with the pride of self-sacrifice.

I turned to him to deliver my overdue response and suddenly realized we were approaching the mansion. Given the distance to the front door—maybe thirty paces—I would not have enough time to adequately express myself. I was about to stop in my tracks when the door opened. There stood Ms Alexander and Dietrich, smiling warmly and beckoning us inside.

I panicked. I knew the time was at hand, that I must seize the moment and speak to Irish while I had the nerve. If I delayed, my passion would cool, I would bite my tongue, and the matter would remain a constant barrier between us.

I slowed to buy time, to give myself a chance to find the proper words, and to speak to him confidentially. I presumed he would do the same, that he would match me and stay by my side. But a glance at his face revealed I had waited too long. Where moments before his expression had been one of puzzlement, it was now one of irritation. He shook his head and quickened his pace, arriving at the house ten paces ahead of me. I watched as he joined our friends, the three of them forming a tableau that I mournfully admitted looked complete without me. As they filed into the house, the door swung closed. When I reached it I paused, my hand lightly resting on the knob. I swallowed dryly, took a deep breath for strength, and followed them inside.

When we arose the next day, we found none other than the Tsar awaiting us outside. This time he stood before two large coaches, one plain and black, the other ostentatious and white, the latter clearly his own regal conveyance. Behind him, hovering like an evil specter, was Rasputin. The priest wore a fresh tunic but looked as disheveled as ever.

"I hope you have enjoyed your stay," Nicholas said. "Father Grigori came to me last night and explained everything. I understand you are setting out today for Ekaterinburg, and that your business may be linked to our secret troubles in Siberia." He focused on Ms Alexander, and his glowing regard for her transfigured into growing concern. "This news disturbs me. There is an urgent mystery to be solved there, but it is surrounded with dangers that no one fully comprehends. Father Grigori has elaborated to me about his previous encounters with remote tribes in the Urals. If his suspicions are correct, that one of these tribes is responsible for the disappearance of my scouts, then I am at pains to allow you to go there."

He gazed with almost fatherly concern into Ms Alexander's eyes before lapsing into Russian and exchanging quiet words. The only discernible word to my ears was his endearment of her, calling her Katya. The sound of it made my heart ache. I would have traded everything to be able to speak to her in such intimate tones, to call her by that name. Their private conversation lasted no more than a minute. By the Tsar's worried expression I knew she had not been dissuaded.

"Father Grigori says he will travel with you as far as he can," the Tsar said, "but he foresees circumstances that will require him to take leave before reaching your final destination."

Dietrich smirked. Nicholas noticed and nodded.

"Strange though it seems, I have come to trust his premonitions," the Tsar said. "He has performed services for my family that I can only begin to repay, and he has asked nothing more than the opportunity to continue aiding us in times of need. Do not let his appearance or manner mislead you."

The Tsar spoke with such sincerity that he almost convinced me. But as he spoke I glanced at Rasputin, who absently and inappropriately scratched himself, and I had to resist the urge to chuckle. If the Tsar of all the Russias held Rasputin in such high esteem, the empire truly was in trouble.

We took our turns thanking the Tsar for his kindness and hospitality. Ms Alexander went first, of course, and almost forgot herself and embraced him. At the last moment she stopped and blushed. She removed a glove from one hand and gripped one of the royal carriage's iron struts. After only a second she released it, tugged the glove back onto her tiny hand, and hugged the Tsar goodbye. Both looked like they might shed tears, but they went their separate ways before any fell.

We took that as a sign our stay in the Summer Garden was at an end. We climbed into the darkness of our coach with Rasputin. From outside we heard the sounds of Nicholas' coach pulling away. As the sound dwindled and our own coach began to move, I heard a sniffle and looked at Ms Alexander. With the curtains drawn it was too dark to see her face clearly, but I could see her white-gloved hands dabbing at her cheeks to catch her tears.

18: THE TRANS-SIBERIAN

I will be brief in my recollections of traveling across half of Russia. Actually, after returning home and consulting a map (I had known little of Russia's geography at the time), our journey took us only a third of its distance—a sobering revelation considering the countless miles, the depressing landscape, and the endless hours spent upon the Trans-Siberian Railway. Once I realized how little of Russia's expanse we had actually covered, I was thankful our mission had not taken us any further. God forbid had we been trapped on that train until the end of the line, to the far-eastern port of Vladivostok. I think I would have gone stark-raving mad from the tedium, murdered everyone on board, dressed myself in their skins, and thrown myself under the wheels before we reached the end.

We arrived at the Saint Petersburg station and boarded a train for Moscow. Our entire first day was spent aboard that train, which was no less tolerable than any I had ridden back in America. When I commented to this effect, Ms Alexander admitted that until the Trans-Siberian had been undertaken, the western trains that crisscrossed the European part of the continent had been far superior. As the Empire had made physical claim of its eastern lands, however, the Tsar strived for more homogeneity in travel standards. The Trans-Siberian was ostensibly the solution meant to cater to the whims of the more urbane Euro-Russians, not to mention it was needed to move the military back and forth across that endless expanse.

We stayed the night in the newly constructed Hotel Moscow. While the building lacked the history and lineage of the Tsar's Summer House, the rooms of the hotel were almost palatial. I complimented Dietrich on his fine selection, and I relished the experience since we would be living on a train for days to come. That night Ms Alexander employed her connections and procured tickets to a ballet at the Bolshoi Theater. I was impressed by the size and decoration of the building, and by the quality of the production. Though the performance was flawless, I became bored with it and spent my time examining the walls and balconies, wondering what it would be like to scale them.

The next morning we made our way back to the station to board the Trans-Siberian. We were disappointed to discover we had missed the latest *Train de Luxe*, a more spacious and luxurious conveyance. Instead our passage was on a *Train d'Etat*, a government train made up of an engine and five long cars: one First Class, two Second Class, a dining car, and one for baggage. As we approached the train, Rasputin separated from us and headed toward the Second Class cars. A feeling of dread came over me at the thought that we too might be traveling in such quarters. I was relieved when Dietrich steered us toward the First Class car, though my elation was short-lived. Once inside I was dismayed by the arrangements. As on our trip across the Atlantic, Ms Alexander and Irish rated compartments to themselves—she due to a woman's need for privacy, he owing to his intrusive size—while I won the honor of sharing a cramped compartment with Dietrich. As we sidled into the tiny space, he looked at me apologetically.

"It's all that was available," he said.

We would be sharing a space about eight feet long and six feet wide, but with furniture it was reduced to six by four. Along the wall were two bunk beds, and under the window was a small table and chair. Once we got our bags stowed there was a little more room, but the only way we could both be comfortable in that space was if someone was in a bunk. My bunk, the top one, folded up against the wall to make a divan of the lower. Technically, one of us could sit on the divan while the other sat at the table. Still, the two were in almost intimate proximity.

The train got moving and I stepped into the corridor to watch as we departed the station. When I returned our cabin had magically doubled in size. Dietrich had discovered the wall separating us from Irish could be folded back, and we were now like three peas in a pod, all sharing one living space. Under other circumstances I would have frowned on such conditions (one roommate was more than enough), but the increased area afforded by the combined quarters suddenly seemed spacious, and I welcomed it.

For the next four days life progressed as if I were in Limbo. Initially, the train pressed forward at a rapid speed. Its pace was so unexpected that it lulled me into a false sense of our progress. At any moment I expected to see the Ural Mountains looming up before us, a sure sign that Ekaterinburg was just around the corner. This sensation was only reinforced by the train's tireless drive, only pausing briefly a few times a day for water, fuel, and a few passengers. But after each successive day of watching the landscape race by—interrupted only by the wretched plight of serfs, the repetition of meals, the occasional desperate conversation, morning and afternoon naps, and nighttime slumber—I began to think I had perhaps died in my sleep and was unwittingly serving time in Purgatory.

The idea took root in my mind, especially when I saw no outward evidence that others were similarly vexed. Irish was content to lounge in his bunk, his cap pulled down over his eyes, for most of the day. Ms Alexander handled the journey with aplomb, as if this were the sort of thing she did all the time. (And in retrospect, given her previous travels, perhaps it was.) But if anyone could relate to my distress I thought it would be Dietrich, whose hungry mind demanded preoccupation. But the pantologist never appeared anxious. Without anything to read—the books and newspapers in the dining car were in Russian—he spent much of his time jotting notes in a small leather-bound notebook he had procured somewhere along the way. He would scribble for a few minutes at a time, pause to gaze thoughtfully out the window, then scribble some more. I had no idea what he was writing, and he offered no explanation. If I inquired, which I did several times, he only shot me the briefest grin, waved a hand dismissively, and mumbled something that was drowned out by the nose of the train. After several such responses I gave up and left him to his business.

By the end of our second day aboard the express I had made casual observations of most of our fellow passengers. Since there was only one dining car it became as busy at mealtimes as a kicked anthill. Examining the variety of characters that paraded through became the highlight of each day.

Since the train was moving from west to east, most of the passengers were genuine Russians, which is to say Slavs. Most had pale complexions, except for the more rustic individuals in Second Class. Many of them were farmers, as evinced by their tanned arms and faces, their simple dress, and their poor manners. They were heading east to the incalculable expanse of Siberia, to begin new and, ostensibly, more prosperous lives than they had enjoyed on European soil.

Among the Second Classers were several priests, easily identifiable by their grey-streaked beards, their smock-like habits, and the heavy wooden crosses that depended from their long beaded necklaces. Each possessed an air of piety that Rasputin entirely lacked. I was amazed when I spotted them grouped together at a dining table, their rapt attention focused on Rasputin as he related some story or teaching to them. It was unseemly that these other men should hold him in such esteem. He did not fit into any crowd, and among that gaggle of holy men he seemed even more out of place. But there he sat, speaking to them as if he were Christ upon the mount, and they his disciples.

At least three quarters of the passengers were made up of simple folk. The remainder were more refined and to my liking, though none of them approached the refinement of Ms Alexander. All she needed to do was enter a car and all heads would turn her way. Even the holy men stared at her longer than was proper, and they were duly impressed when she acknowledged Rasputin with a thin-lipped smile and a nod.

Still, there were other notable and interesting people on board. There was a Spanish correspondent who was riding the Express to its termination, documenting everything about his journey for a travelogue to be published upon return. There were two Frenchmen traveling together, partners in a race around the world that started and ended in Paris. Apparently it was part of a gentlemen's wager in which they had pitted themselves against another two-man team. Both parties had set out from Paris at the same time, but traveling in opposite directions. What this difference proved I have no idea, but the outcome was that the losing party would pay the living expenses of the winners for an entire year. This, combined with the superior style and quality of the men's garments, suggested to me they were dilettantes with more time and money than they knew how to spend. They were inseparable, and appeared to dote on one another like newlyweds, but that is neither here nor there.

The most notable passenger among this upper crust was unquestionably a young German girl of perhaps eighteen. She was traveling with her husband—they were genuine newlyweds—a man perhaps fifteen years her senior. The girl was young and pretty, but she fascinated me because of her anxiety and wide-eyed innocence. Whenever she was near I could not help stealing glances.

Ms Alexander introduced her to me over lunch one day. It was approaching noon, and to get a jump on the Second Class crowd I went to the dining car early. I found the two talking privately at a table for four. Since the lunch mob would soon invade and rob them of privacy, and since it would be awkward to sit down a few feet away and pretend I had not seen them, I stepped up to their table and took a seat. The girl looked at me as if I were a cruel stepfather, her eyes filled with weepy protest. It was then I realized she was unhappy about something, and that Ms Alexander had been consoling her.

"Mr Grey," Ms Alexander said stiffly. Her eyes said much more, specifically that I was intruding. At that instant, however, a dozen Second Classers filed into the car. When she saw them she realized what I had already determined. Her eyes softened, if only slightly, and her tone became more tolerant. "Would you care to join us?"

A ridiculous statement since I was already seated, but I thanked her for the invitation and played along. She introduced the girl as Mrs Lena Something-or-other. Seeing that she needed cheering up, I stood and half bowed.

"Prometheus Grey, at your service."

Lena—my, she was so innocent!—was so distracted by my theatrical behavior that she seemed to forget her woes, an advantage I pressed home as lunch progressed. Ms Alexander, who had been the girl's erstwhile confidante, was reduced to a mere interpreter as I fired away question after question, leaving her little space in which to inject her opinions. From our conversation I learned that Lena's marriage had been one of convenience, that it had been more or less arranged, that she had no real love for her new husband, but that

288

she had felt pressured to go through with it for the sake of her family, whose business interests were in decline. Now, she was being dragged to the middle of nowhere—Irkutsk—by her husband to set up a new business. Her future was bleak: she would spend the rest of her days taking care of a man she hardly knew, and probably would never see her family again.

It was a sad story, one in which I had the sense not to meddle any further. Instead I decided to distract her from her woes. As we spoke, I performed minor acts of magic, trifles of prestidigitation I had picked up before dedicating myself to escape, that made the girl forget her troubles. Simple sleights of hand, such as producing endless cloth napkins form my cuffs, or extracting silverware from my mouth as if it had been lodged there without my knowing. By the end of lunch, I had the girl laughing so gaily she had forgotten her tragic destiny. Her eyes hungrily begged for more. It was then that I took my leave. It was an old performer's trick: leave them desiring more, whether they will get it or not.

Over the next several days I kept an eye out for Lena, and if she happened to be in the vicinity I tried to cross her path. It did not matter if she obligatorily hung on the arm of her humdrum husband. All I wanted was to be seen by her, because each time her eyes lit up in a way I knew her husband would never enjoy. No matter how intimate they might become, I had infiltrated a place in her he would never know. This secret knowledge gave me a feeling of significance, an emotion that recently had dwindled like a shadow in the light of Irish's burgeoning relationship with Ms Alexander.

On that subject, the conclusion drawn after my fateful stroll with Irish in the Summer Garden proved to be correct. After that night the urge to acknowledge and overcome the issue quickly faded and never returned. I cannot explain it. One moment I had been prepared to bare my soul and to wish them the best; the next, the feeling was gone. Thinking back, it seemed more like a dream than an actual inclination. From that moment on, I had no impulse to engage him on the topic.

I have until now neglected the stops we made along the way, if only because they offered little more than brief diversions. At some stations little girls in bonnets rushed out to meet us bearing fresh milk in reclaimed liquor bottles. The milk was sweet, better than any I could recall drinking elsewhere, or perhaps it just seemed so refreshing after so many days on the train with only water, tea, and liquor. At other times we found actual restaurants built into the larger stations, boasting long tables covered with white tablecloths and lined with ornate high-backed chairs, as decorous as any found in the dining rooms of New York's aristocracy.

Appearances aside, the restaurants had their own dark secrets. For instance, laundering seemed to be a foreign concept. After one meal I wandered back inside and saw the waiters refolding soiled cloth napkins for the next crowd.

Such unclean practices aside, the meals, though served in an abrupt manner, were satisfying and consisted of never-ending loaves of fresh bread, veal, and hearty soups. After each stop I climbed aboard the train with a full belly, which made drifting off for frequent naps an easy task.

Aside from the milk, the food, and an assortment of interesting-looking characters loitering around the stations, the stops were nothing more than brief-but-welcomed interruptions in our monotonous journey.

Astonishingly, it was Rasputin to whom I grew closest in the dusk of our Trans-Siberian odyssey. Numerous days of eastward travel and repetitive napping had thrown off my body's clock. The result was that by the fourth night of travel I could not sleep. I laid in my bunk until midnight with my eyes closed, as if by sheer stubbornness I could make myself unconscious, but my body would have none of it. Finally, I surrendered to wakefulness, dressed, and slipped from the compartment to wander the narrow corridors of the train.

The passages offered no distraction whatsoever. The night was black and our position remote, and neither lights nor landscape were visible. Looking out the windows was as entertaining as staring into a well. So I continued on, making my way through the Second Class cars, resisting the urge to draw back the curtains and peek in on the snoring farmers. I moved on to the dining car expecting it to be empty, but instead I found another solitary passenger, perhaps the last person I wanted to encounter.

Rasputin sat lounging at a table on which sat two glasses and an open, but untouched, bottle of vodka. When I entered he was absently stroking his wild beard, staring into the blackness beyond the windows as if it were no hindrance to his vision whatsoever. When the door closed behind me, he turned, grinned, and gestured for me to join him. It was an eerie moment. I had half a mind to flee back to my cabin, but then curiosity overcame fear. I had the unmistakable feeling he had been waiting there for me.

I sat down across from him, watching him warily. It did not matter that he was the Tsar's man, or that he was (supposedly) incontrovertibly on our side. I feared him all the same. He fixed his gaze on me and continued to stroke his beard. After an uncomfortable time, during which my eyes darted to everything in the car except the priest, Rasputin leaned forward, took the bottle, and filled both glasses. He then pushed one gently toward me. I was not in the mood for it, but I accepted to keep the situation convivial. I had no intention of actually draining the glass. I knew it would undo, or at least lead to the undoing, of even a stalwart bacchanalian such as I. But to appease him I took a small draught and sat back to see what would happen next.

Rasputin drained half his glass in one long gulp, placed it on the table, and leaned back in his chair with a sigh. He shot me another grin, eyeing me like a fox eyes an injured hare. Feeling obligated to hold up my end, I smiled and nodded in return. He responded with a slur of Russian syllables that ended so ambiguously I could not tell if it was meant as a statement or question. I smiled and nodded before seeking refuge in my drink. I had no idea what he was expecting, but my response seemed to please him. He chuckled, which was both encouraging and unsettling. I considered attempting to excuse myself, but then he spoke again, this time at length.

Whatever he said must have been didactic, because he became more animated as he spoke. Since I had no clue what he was saying, I passed the time by slowly draining my glass, which he repeatedly refilled. He carried on in this manner for a long time, perhaps an hour, talking as if I were a part of the conversation. When at last he felt he had made his point, he finished with what must have been a joke, because he laughed loudly and hoarsely and sank deeper into his chair. He then nodded and waved a hand as if to indicate it was my turn.

"Well, I have no idea what this is all about," I said, raising my glass to him. "I'm just making the best of a very unusual situation. The very idea of you and I sharing drinks and carrying on a pointless dialogue is quite possibly the most absurd thing I can imagine."

I shot him a grin that he acknowledged with a conspiratorial wink.

"But since we are here and you expect me to say something, God only knows *what* I might add, I will do my best to appear courteous, and I will find something to ramble about at length."

This must have pleased him, because he raised his glass as if in a toast.

"Come to think of it, I do have something I'd like to say. Recently I've had many things on my mind, and some of them I simply can't discuss with my companions. To begin, what the hell am I doing in the middle of Russia? Just months ago I was enjoying the modest life of a well-to-do burglar, living comfortably off the spare change of New York's elite. How is it that I'm now here? You're supposedly a holy man with visions and such, so perhaps you can explain it to me!"

At this we both laughed, and I refilled our glasses. But Rasputin did not interject. He slouched with both hands clasping the glass at his chest, listening patiently as I carried on.

And on I carried. I do not recall the full scope of things I said that night, but I am quite sure I told him about every extraordinary detail, every outlandish twist and turn our mission had taken thus far. I spoke of Cross, President Roosevelt, our secret commission, the Illuminati, the Masons, Tesla, Ms Alexander and her secret condition. I told him what I had learned of the pasts of Dietrich and Irish, and how I was hopelessly infatuated with Ms Alexander, though I pretended not to be.

And Rasputin endured it all with the patience of, well, a priest. He sat in silence, solemnly nodding at regular intervals as if to say he understood my every word, my every point, and my incredulity over everything that had happened up to, and including, that moment.

"So now we come to it," I said, leaning heavily on the table. By then the vodka had taken its toll. "What does this all mean? Is this part of some larger plan? Some divine comedy? I never wanted any of this, and yet circumstances grow more preposterous every day. I'm an entertainer, an escape artist, not a hero. But I can only conclude that someone up there," I indicated the ceiling with my eyes, "has something in store for me, has chosen me for whatever reason to perform some earth-shaking feat, some miracle, the substance and criteria of which I haven't even the slightest inkling!"

By those last words I was sitting upright, my excitement momentarily outstripping the effects of the alcohol. But no sooner had I punctuated that sentence before the energy drained out of me and I collapsed back in my chair.

Rasputin continued to nod as if he understood. He drained his glass and set it on the table. I looked at him swimming before me and somehow discerned a flicker of his eyes. I turned my head toward the window and noticed the Stygian darkness had given way to the dull greyness of morning. At that moment the priest laughed out loud, stood, clapped me on the shoulder, and retreated into the Second Class compartment. I hesitated, wondering if he meant for me to follow. I could not have been more than five seconds behind him, but as I passed through the two Second Class cars he was nowhere to be seen. Confused, and by then exhausted, I staggered back to my shared cabin, collapsed into my bunk, and slept until we arrived in Ekaterinburg the next day.

I awoke to the sound of the train whistle announcing our approach to Ekaterinburg. We were no more than ten miles out when the shrill sound invaded my slumber and brought me to my feet, but the distance afforded me sufficient time to splash some water on my face and put on a clean shirt. Dietrich and Irish were absent, so I took advantage of the extra space to stretch my limbs and shake off my weariness. As I shuffled about the space they both returned to collect their bags.

Dusk had settled on Ekaterinburg as the train pulled into the station, and except for a smattering of silhouetted domes and spires—I had expected more from a city named after Catherine the Great—it made little impression on me. Surely the growing darkness affected my view and my mood, but I suspect it was also an effect of desensitization after so much travel. I had seen so much in the past few months that even the most beautiful European architecture now garnered from me little more than a yawn. Besides, after so many days on the train, the only thing I wanted was to get off it. When we gathered around Dietrich on the platform and he revealed we would be boarding another train to take us north the next morning, I groaned.

"Must we leave so soon?" I said. "I'm sure Ms Alexander would appreciate some leisure time in the city."

She gave me a funny look indicating I was correct, and that she questioned my motive for suggesting it. But Dietrich squashed any such hope before it could take hold.

"I would like nothing more," he said, "but we are getting close to our objective and must remain focused."

I skulked along behind them as we made for the street. Before we had taken ten steps Dietrich halted and counted heads.

"Where is Father Grigori?"

We looked around and quickly found him, for even in a busy train station Rasputin stood out like a sore thumb. He was further down the platform by the Second Class car, bidding farewell to the priests he had met on the train. Once again he held center stage among them, speaking in a determined tone and waving a finger to make his point, as if before their parting he were bequeathing to them a few final words of wisdom. Then the train whistle emitted an ear-splitting shriek, and the holy men disengaged themselves and climbed back aboard. Rasputin made his way toward us, the crowd on the platform parting before him like the Red Sea.

As we stood there a man separated from the crowd and approached us. He wore the uniform of the Imperial Army, but he was armed only with a letter. He strode purposefully toward us as if he knew us by sight, offering his hand with a Russian greeting. Dietrich awkwardly accepted it, but looked at Ms Alexander for assistance.

"He is Lieutenant Gorlov," she said. "He received orders originating from the Tsar himself, instructing him to find us and deliver this telegram."

The lieutenant then side-stepped us all and presented the letter to Rasputin. But the priest did not accept it. Instead he spoke a few words and waved a hand dismissively. Rebuffed, the lieutenant did not know how to respond. He froze, his expression a mirror of the thoughts going through his head: the Tsar's letter had been rejected. What was more important, duty to the Tsar, or respect for a holy man? As he pondered this conundrum, Rasputin's attention drifted elsewhere, and he wandered away into the crowd. The soldier, bound by his duty to the Tsar, began to get impatient. Thankfully, Ms Alexander intervened.

She held out a hand for the letter. At first the soldier was hesitant to hand it over, but after looking upon her heavenly visage, he realized she had his best interests at heart. He handed it to her, and she read aloud.

"*To Father Grigori Rasputin. Urgent family matter requiring your presence. Please return at once—Tsar Nicholas.*"

"Why did he refuse it?" Dietrich asked.

"He said he already knew what it contained," Ms Alexander replied.

We raised our eyebrows, remembering the monk's prediction that he would be recalled by the Tsar and unable to accompany us beyond Ekaterinburg. We looked at one another in wonder before our eyes again sought Rasputin. We found him standing before a ticket booth, already securing passage back to Saint Petersburg.

That was the last we saw of Rasputin. After purchasing his ticket on a train that would not leave until the following day, he returned to us and said his goodbyes. Since we were staying the night in Ekaterinburg I presumed he would remain with us. I do not know why he chose to part company then and there. His eyes drifted over the city to the darkening sky as if he were heeding a call—to where I do not know, though given his habits I could make an educated guess. Then with a nod he bid us an almost disinterested farewell. His eyes lingered on me for a time, and I saw traces of a grin at the corners of his mouth. When he departed I think I was the only one who felt regret, thinking back on our preposterous conversation on the train, and how he seemed, in spite of the language barrier, to understand me perfectly.

Rasputin's sudden disappearance left us without a guide—not an insurmountable obstacle, but one for which we had no ready plan. But Tsar Nicholas had taken this into account. After a brief exchange with the lingering lieutenant, Ms Alexander delivered some pleasant news.

"Lieutenant Gorlov is replacing Father Grigori as our guide. He will travel with us to Bogoslovsk, and from there assist in locating this mysterious village of Véles."

"Ah," Dietrich said, looking pleasantly surprised. "If he is the Tsar's man then I trust him implicitly."

This turn of luck, of having a skilled soldier join our ranks, was welcome news to most. While Irish could certainly take care of any rough business we might face, it did not hurt to have another able-bodied man along. Lieutenant Gorlov also made a more socially suitable guide than Rasputin, to be sure. But deep down I suspected the monk was capable of works none of us had yet imagined. I believed what the practical lieutenant might achieve with force, Rasputin could achieve with nothing more than a flicker of his maniacal eyes. So it was with a trifling grudge that I shook the young officer's hand and welcomed him aboard.

The lieutenant led us to a pair of coaches in front of the station. After a lengthy ride we came to a stop outside a high stone wall interrupted by an iron gate. At first I was hopeful, anticipating a night in another stately residence like that of the Tsar's Summer Garden. But as a pair of soldiers pulled the gates open, the iron hinges groaning in rusty protest, I knew no well-tended royal playground lay ahead.

We entered a large square lined on three sides by low, unadorned stone buildings. I realized at once we were in some sort of compound, and a moment later my heart sank as I realized it was a military garrison. As we came to a halt a pair of soldiers exited from one of the barracks, collected our luggage, and led us inside. He took us through a large common room with rows of empty beds, and into a rear room that was spartanly furnished, boasting only a small table with four chairs. Here he lit a lamp and stood with hands clasped behind his back until we had all filed in.

"This room is the common area for officers," Ms Alexander translated. "There is a bedroom across the hall where the commander would reside, but as this barracks is empty the lieutenant has prepared it for me. You, gentlemen, are welcome to any beds in the common area."

Dietrich was gracious, managing to smile and nod even though the accommodations were poor.

"Are there no hotels in Ekaterinburg?" I asked.

"The Tsar has sent instructions that we are to be looked after," Ms Alexander explained. "The lieutenant is only doing what he must to ensure our safety."

"Please express our gratitude," Dietrich interjected, derailing further protest. "It is already getting late, and tomorrow we must leave early. These accommodations will be fine for tonight. I suggest we all get some rest."

His words were suddenly punctuated by a series of creaks and groans as Irish collapsed on a rickety bunk. Ms Alexander took this as a cue, and after few words with the lieutenant she excused herself to her private room—a room in which, owing to a glimpse I managed before she closed the door, her only luxury would be privacy itself.

I suffered another sleepless night in the barracks, owing largely to the snores of Irish and the complaints of his bedsprings. And on the rare occasion that he made no sound, I was treated to brief coughing fits from Dietrich—violent episodes that would come from nowhere and last frustratingly long, as if he were a man saved from drowning who now struggled to expel brine from his lungs.

It was then that I realized these sounds had accompanied me for the last five days aboard the Trans-Siberian. During our trip they had been much less intrusive, commingled as they were with the many sounds of the train. Here, on the outskirts of the city in the stillness of an empty barracks, the stirrings of my companions were as intrusive as a lunatic minstrel. So, between temporal episodes of sleep I wiled away the night by staring at the unadorned ceiling, pursuing flights of fancy, all of which invariably led to scenes of Ms Alexander in all manner of compromising situations.

When morning came and the barracks door swung open to reveal an alert Lieutenant Gorlov, in a uniform complete with saber and pistol, I rolled over and pulled the covers over my head. I was exhausted. But as my comrades roused themselves and went about their morning business—snorting, coughing, dressing, washing—I slowly came to my senses. Just as Dietrich's patience with my perceived laziness was reaching its climax, I rolled out of bed and staggered to the lavatory. An hour later we were on a small train struggling to climb the slopes of the Urals.

19: BOGOSLOVSK

Bogoslovsk was a small town along the rails, approximately two-hundred and fifty miles north of Ekaterinburg. When Dietrich delivered this news I presumed another day of tedious travel and moderate leisure lay ahead. I could not have been more wrong. The iron road to Bogoslovsk was of narrower gauge than the Trans-Siberian, which meant a smaller train and cramped quarters. The cars were of considerably less luxury than those of the Trans-Siberian's exiguous *Train d'Etat*. In fact, they were strictly utilitarian, possessing little more than narrow and poorly cushioned seats that were already crowded.

The moment we entered the car I sensed Ms Alexander's anxiety, but there was nothing we could do to give her more space. We shuffled along the aisle until we found five seats in the vicinity of one another, which we quickly claimed before other travelers could seize them. Dietrich, Irish, and Ms Alexander managed to sit together, with the lady snuggled safely between them. This relegated me to sit two rows back, wedged between the lieutenant and a large, doughy woman who smelled of sweat and onions. As my shoulder met hers she eyed me with annoyance. She mumbled something to herself and I got a whiff of her putrid breath. I shrank away as much as I could, maybe a quarter of an inch, which she promptly puffed herself up to claim.

All hope of rest evaporated as the train jerked into motion and we got underway. Not only was I crushed uncomfortably between two strange Russians, but every time a moment of slumber seemed imminent, the woman would shift in her seat and jar me awake. Or worse, she would yawn, cough, or mutter something in my direction, and her mephitic exhalations would invade my nostrils and bring me instantly awake.

Lieutenant Gorlov was little better company. He seemed to suffer from some gastrointestinal dispute that repeatedly asserted itself throughout the day. No less than twice an hour a hot, creeping, disgraceful pungency would coalesce in our row causing everyone to look our way. Invariably the accusing eyes would focus in on me, the obvious foreigner. I noted with quiet outrage that the lieutenant would follow suit, glancing at me with a roll of the eyes, wordlessly sidestepping responsibility for his own embarrassing effluence. But by midday it had occurred with such frequency I became accustomed to those hateful glares, and my outrage had given way to amusement. Thereafter I met every accusing eye with an arrogant wink. I put aside my anger with the lieutenant, for which I would later be thankful. He would soon enough pay for his sins.

The journey dragged on from morning until night, and as noon approached we discovered another folly. As everyone's stomachs began to grumble, all the aboriginals reached into coats, bundles, and handbags to produce morsels of food. As we Westerners looked around in confusion and wondered when the conductor would announce the opening of the dining car, they munched contentedly on meager bits of bread and cheese. When Ms Alexander finally inquired about our meal, the lieutenant explained the train was indeed utilitarian, its only utility being as a mode of transport. The line served one singular purpose: to move cargo and people (in that order) back and forth from the mineral-rich slopes of the Urals.

We had made the mistake of securing passage on an industrial vehicle. No expense or care was given to making the trip pleasant—a point driven home when I went in search of the lavatory and found only a sort of closet containing a reeking pot through which one could see the tracks racing by below. After completing my transaction I opened the door and recoiled from the sight and smell of my neighbor, the bovine woman against whom my left shoulder had been pressed for several hours. She scowled as if our meeting was an unpleasant surprise. I straightened and held my breath as I squeezed past her ungainly bulk into the corridor.

As she sealed herself into the closet I made my way back to my seat, but instead of choosing my previous spot in the middle of the row I took her window seat. This had two significant advantages: it allowed me to open the window and breathe fresh air, and I was able to prop myself against the wall for the rest of the journey and get some rest. By the time she returned I was half asleep, or at least I pretended to be. Only a dead man could have slept through her rowdy displeasure as she huffed, puffed, cursed, jostled, and threw elbows while squeezing in beside me.

But with my head propped against the open window and the wind carrying away the foulness of my neighbors, I finally managed to sink into an impenetrable slumber that lasted until we reached our destination.

I awoke with a start. A hand was grasping my shoulder and shaking me roughly. At first I thought it was part of an unsettling dream, a nightmare in which I had been buried alive beneath a heap of dead Russians. What had killed them, or more importantly how I ended up beneath them, was apparently inconsequential, as no explanation was provided. Still, within the context of the dream, I somehow knew my companions were working diligently to free me, even though they made no appearance. Somehow I knew the hand on my shoulder was part of their rescue effort. I supposed it belonged to Irish, that he had thrust a mighty arm after me in an attempt to pluck me out. As the hand struggled to get a firm hold, I began to awaken.

I opened heavy lids and shook the sleep from my head to find not Irish but Lieutenant Gorlov manhandling me. I instinctively threw up my arms to ward him off, and as I did I realized I was the center of attention. The eyes of every Siberian bumpkin in the car were upon me. In that moment I realized the train had come to a stop. A quick scan of the car revealed my companions were gone. Like a lost child I looked out the window in search of them, but a light had been turned on in the car and night had fallen outside. The windows had become dark mirrors, and all I could see was my own wild-eyed and haggard reflection.

I experienced a moment of panic, but the insistent hand of the lieutenant brought me back to my senses. As I climbed to my feet the train lurched, almost toppling me into the laps of several peasants. Lieutenant Gorlov's urgency suddenly became clear: the train was resuming its journey after a stop, and we did not want to be on it.

I scrambled behind him as we made our way toward the door, each of us roughly colliding with random legs and shoulders that occupied the aisle. When we finally leapt from the car we had only a few feet of platform to spare, a fact that became clear only after several seconds of standing in almost complete darkness. As the train pulled away it took all light with it, leaving us in a pitch black netherworld. At length my eyes adjusted to darkness and moonlight, and I made out the silhouettes of my friends. Relieved, I finally began to wonder about where we were, and why the station was so dark. As if sensing my question, Dietrich piped up.

"Bogoslovsk," he said, taking a few tentative steps along the platform. He placed his hands on his hips and spun around. "Where the devil is everyone?"

As Ms Alexander conversed with the lieutenant, the rest of us peered into the darkness. We stood on a long wooden platform, that much was clear. But the rest of the station was literally lacking—it was nowhere to be found. When arriving at a train station, one has certain reasonable expectations. One expects the bustle of baggage handlers, conductors and engineers, all set against the backdrop of the station itself, some sort of structure to act as ticket office and shelter. But all of these features were void from the terminal at Bogoslovsk. We were left standing on an otherwise empty wooden platform that was bereft of a station house or any attendants. Furthermore, a scan of the area, or what little we could see of it in the dark, showed we were nowhere near any town. Aside from the fact that rails had been laid and a platform constructed, the only hint that any sort of habitation was nearby was a dirt road that wound away into the trees.

"The lieutenant is as baffled as we are," Ms Alexander said after a brief exchange. "Someone from town should have heard the train whistle and come out to meet us. But the town is less than a mile away along that road, and it is an easy journey on level ground. Perhaps we should walk."

"This is ridiculous," I said. "What time is it?"

Dietrich pulled his watch from his vest. Irish struck a match.

"Half past ten," Dietrich said. Even in the dark I could sense his irritation. But no matter how unconscionable it might be to leave visitors standing on a platform in the middle of the night, no amount of indignation would bring us any closer to a hotel. With an exasperated sigh he made his way toward the road.

As we descended the stairs we heard a rhythmic racket approaching—the sounds of hooves and wheels—and a few seconds later a light bobbed into view between the trees. It was a lantern affixed to a weatherworn coach.

"It's about time," Dietrich muttered.

As the coach pulled up before us, the driver reigned in the horses so roughly that they reared and cried out. But the last thing on the driver's mind was the comfort of the horses. Paying them no heed, he hoisted the lantern above our heads to see our faces. As he did I was able to take in and read his. He was a gaunt old man with a scraggily white beard, wearing simple clothes and a look of worry on his face that eliminated the need for an apology. Still, he spoke to us insistently, waving an arm to indicate we should climb aboard immediately.

The urgency with which he behaved was excessive, as if he thought haste might make us forget he had been late. As far as we were concerned, we were so pleased to see him that all was forgiven. I watched as Ms Alexander tried to convey this to him, but he would have none of it. The more she tried to reassure him, the more frantically he gesticulated for us to climb aboard.

"I do not understand why he is so bothered," Ms Alexander remarked. "But let's do as he says, and quickly before he becomes more agitated."

We climbed aboard, and the driver snapped the reigns before we could find our seats.

The journey was brief. In a matter of minutes we broke free of the trees on either side and were shuttling across open fields toward a cluster of low, dark geometries: the town of Bogoslovsk. As we trundled along we passed rows of houses, small boxlike structures that were little more than cabins— the unmistakable habitations of Siberian clodhoppers. As we passed by I caught glimpses of figures in lamplit windows, faces of simple folk who briefly revealed themselves to get a look at us. After a nervous glance they let their ragged curtains fall back into place, swallowing their homes in darkness.

The driver took us to a two-story structure near the center of town, a building that turned out to be the only inn. (Bogoslovsk was not the sort of place that drew tourists.) As soon as the wagon came to a halt, the driver hurried us toward the door. Before we could knock or lay hand on the knob, the door burst open and eager hands sprang forward and pulled us inside.

We found ourselves facing a distraught old couple in their night clothes. The old man appeared to be self-conscious of this fact and was in the process of donning a shabby wool coat even as he pawed at me. Meanwhile his wife, wrapped in a flannel robe, her head covered in a kerchief that only partially contained her wiry hair, clamped onto Dietrich's arm as if at any moment he might drift away. As soon as we were all inside, our hosts slammed and bolted the door as if the hounds of Hell were making a charge against it.

Lieutenant Gorlov chose that moment to assert his authority. Stepping forward he insisted upon an explanation for their behavior, which the old innkeeper was reticent to provide. The only explanation he offered was that we were in dangerous territory, that it was unsafe to be out past sunset, and that he thanked God nothing had happened to us before his man had rescued us from the platform. Then, before another word could be said, he ushered us toward a counter on one side of the room, nodding obsequiously as he went. He stepped behind the counter and produced a worn ledger, followed by a pen and ink bottle. Dietrich stepped forward and signed the near empty registry. As he performed this formality, the old man's eyes darted back and forth between us appraisingly.

The moment Dietrich set down the pen the old man—his name was Botkin—leapt out from behind the counter and led the way upstairs, turning every few steps to ensure he had not lost any of us. He led us down a narrow and musty hallway containing six doors, five of which he opened along the way. At the end of the hallway he turned and gestured for us to pick our rooms. Experience had taught me to take a room as far as possible from Irish to escape his thunderous snoring, so I hurried past my companions toward the far end of the hall. As the rest made their choices, Lieutenant Gorlov, still vexed by the proprietor's strange behavior, again pestered the man for explanations. But the old man again brushed him aside with a few words, wished us good night, muttered a prayer over us, and hurried back downstairs.

"What was that about?" I asked.

"He told the lieutenant all questions are best left until morning," Ms Alexander replied.

Aside from Lieutenant Gorlov, no one else was in the mood to argue or to pursue the matter. We bid each other goodnight and retreated to our rooms. I quickly fell asleep, worn out from another day of travel. It did not matter in the least that I had slept untold hours on the train. Within moments I was dead to the world.

I slept well, at least until some unknown hour when I suddenly and inexplicably sat bolt upright in bed. At first I thought I had been dreaming, and in my dream something loud and violent had occurred. But as I sat trying to separate dream from reality, I had no recollection whatsoever of any nightmare. As I mulled it over I began to believe that in my sleep I *had* heard something, a sound so jarring it had brought me awake. Suddenly worried and curious, I decided to investigate. I had no idea what I was investigating, but I thought a quick look around would be wise. After all, we were on a dangerous mission, and strange enemies had appeared unexpectedly in the past. So, making as little noise as possible, I arose, pulled on my trousers, and made my way to the window.

My room was at the end of the house, but due to the house's angle I knew I would be able to see a portion of the square on which it sat. The window, however, had not been cleaned for ages, and all I could do was confirm that it was still night time. Then, as I was pulling my nose away from the dirty glass, I caught a glimpse of something moving out in the street. I thought I saw a figure step from the shadows of one building to another, and disappear. Again I pressed my face to the window but saw nothing more.

An uncontrollable chill ran down my back as I imagined Illuminati assassins slowly closing in on us. My first thought was to fetch Dietrich's revolver, but it was locked in his room with him, and I did not want to wake him up unless I was sure we were in danger. Next, I thought of Irish. He was arguably more deadly than anyone with a pistol, and protecting us was his job. But I hesitated to seek his help, mainly because we had been on the outs since Saint Petersburg. Plus, the thought of waking him made me feel inept and foolish. I was a man, after all—physically less than him, but no less capable. He might tower over me, but he did not own the patent on courage. So I steeled myself and headed for the door.

I wanted to make as little sound as possible, so I did not bother with shoes. I opened my door, cringing as it squeaked, and froze to listen. After a full minute of holding my breath in anticipation of some telltale sign of a stalker, I continued into the hall. I left my door ajar to avoid further commotion, and to give myself easy access should the need arise to flee back to safety.

The hallway was windowless and pitch black. I let my right hand brush the wall as I walked to provide some sort of bearing. When my toes found empty space I knew I had come to the staircase, which, if memory served, consisted of sixteen steps. The first eight would follow a path straight down before the staircase made a corner and descended the final eight to the parlor.

The staircase presented several problems. First, like everything else in that shoddy, rustic hotel, it squeaked. I knew that the moment I set foot on it I might as well burst into song, because that is how much warning I would instantly give anyone below. Second, since the stairs rounded a corner I was unable to get any look below before descending. For all I knew a madman could be standing just around the corner with a large axe raised above his head. Finally, presuming the axe-wielding maniac scenario was nothing more than imagination, even if I made it down the first eight stairs and rounded the corner without betraying myself, I would be completely exposed to attacks of all sorts—gunshot, knifing, bludgeoning, skewering by crossbow—as I attempted to creep down the remaining eight.

(Though thought of a crossbow may seem anachronistic, it was actually easily explained. During my touring days with the Mangle Brothers there had been a dark-skinned man among us who went by the name of Karloff. He was of average height, muscular, but unusually thin. He had piercing eyes, a sliver of moustache, and a beard waxed to such a point he could have used it to spear fruit. He was a weapons-master, proficient with every martial weapon imaginable. His act involved hurling, launching, or firing the full gamut of his arsenal—darts, knives, spears, arrows—at a beautiful young girl strapped to a large spinning target. One of his many weapons was the crossbow, which he used to place a bolt—horrifyingly yet impressively—at the apex of the triangular space between her thighs. Of the strange and myriad acts recruited by the Mangle Brothers, it was the only one I could never bear to watch.)

The crossbow-induced memory faded, and I realized I had descended the first eight stairs and was standing at the corner. If I had made any noise during my descent I had been completely oblivious to it. All that was left was the moment of Truth, to test my courage by rounding the corner and facing a possible room full of assassins. I drew a deep breath and stepped around the corner.

From my perch I could see most of the room, palely lit by moonlight filtering through the windows. I was relieved to find nothing out of the ordinary, and I breathed a thank you to Fate as I turned to retrace my steps to my room. Then I heard an ambiguous sound, a rustling of sorts, the unmistakable sigh of movement. My heart began to beat in double-time. From where I stood I could not see the corner of the room masked by the stairway wall to my right. Whatever I had heard, it came from that obscured quarter.

Another chill ran down my spine, causing me to shiver briefly but violently. Against all reason I moved forward, the step beneath my foot whining like an alley cat in heat. I cringed and froze, waiting for a reaction. But nothing happened. So I took another step. More creaking, but still no reaction from anyone below. And so it went for every step—creak, freeze, cringe, pause, listen—until I finally set foot upon the worn rug at the foot of the staircase.

The sight that met me was not frightening but still unexpected. As I peered into the shadows I made out a figure in the farthest corner opposite the front door. It was a man, seated in a cushioned chair, his chin on his chest as he snored softly. As I stared at him he resolved into the proprietor, Botkin, still clad in his wool coat overtop his pajamas. I was about to awaken the old fool when something caught my eye. Across his lap lay the unmistakable shape of a rifle.

The realization shocked me and gave me pause, not for fear of being shot, but rather because I could not fathom why the old man would be standing guard over the door. The idea leapt into my head that he was another of the Tsar's men, another unlikely ally like Rasputin, assigned to aid and watch over us. But in the next instant I shook my head at the absurdity of it. This old codger, running an inn in the middle of Siberia, could not possibly be connected to the Tsar. So the question remained.

As I pondered his possible reasons, I wondered if the door lacked a lock, and I stepped up and gave the knob a little twist. I was relieved to find it locked, but the sound it made—a tiny, barely audible *click*—had an instant effect on Botkin. It was as if someone had thrown a firecracker at his feet. He snorted, leapt from his chair, and began waving the rifle around wildly in search of a target. I raised my arms above my head to show I was no threat as he sighted in on me. But then his head cleared and he recognized me for what I was, a foolish investigator prowling around at night, and the rifle was quickly lowered. He shook his head at me reproachfully before shooing me back upstairs.

So like a mischievous boy caught up after his bedtime, I returned to my room, undressed, and climbed back into bed. But I was still high on the adrenaline rush of fear, and still puzzling over the circumstances. It was a long time before body or mind allowed me to fall back to sleep.

The next morning at breakfast all was explained, even if it seemed like a bunch of superstitious nonsense. We made our way downstairs, but Lieutenant Gorlov was noticeably absent. As I looked around for him, Dietrich took notice.

"The lieutenant rose early to arrange our travel," he said.

We sat around a small table that had been set beneath the parlor windows, and I confided in my colleagues about my nighttime adventure. My description of the old man and his rifle piqued everyone's interest, and renewed our collective curiosity about the innkeeper's mysterious behavior the night before. But Dietrich seized on another bit of my story.

"And what of the shadowy figure?" he asked.

I gazed at him dumbly.

"The one you saw from your bedroom?" he offered. "The one that led you downstairs in the first place?"

"Ah," I said. "It was probably nothing. Or if it was something, at least nothing came of it. As you can see, we're all alive and well."

My explanation did not fully satisfy him, but then the Botkins wheeled in a cart from the kitchen bearing a variety of dry, bland foods that in those parts must have passed for breakfast. We unenthusiastically helped ourselves. As we ate, Botkin's wife wheeled the cart back into the kitchen. The old man, however, hovered nearby, orbiting us like a planet, slowly and equidistantly, watching us keenly for the first sign that we were done. When at last Irish swabbed down his plate with the final crust of bread, Dietrich signaled the man with a nod. The Botkins then swept in to clear the table. They carried the dishes through a doorway, and by the din that followed they must have thrown the lot into a corner. Before we knew it they were back at our side, looking at us expectantly.

We smiled at them awkwardly until Dietrich cleared his throat, prompting Ms Alexander. A brief exchange followed.

"First," she said, "they are pleased to have us as guests. Apparently the town sees few visitors."

I glanced out the window at the simple houses, the dusty streets, and the few old men haunting them. Beyond that my eyes fell on a grey bulk with a spine of smokestacks, a factory of some sort. Even in daylight it was no more than a distant shadow. I was not surprised I had not noticed it the night before.

"Hardly surprising," I muttered.

Dietrich followed my gaze out the window.

"What is that?" he asked.

Ms Alexander inquired.

"A refinery," she said. "The town was once a stopping point for copper mined in the mountains, but the region has become too dangerous."

Dietrich looked puzzled.

"Why?"

Ms Alexander again conversed with our hosts, this time at length, and with no shortage of pantomime on the old couple's behalf. As the old man spoke he looked like he might fall to his knees and tear at his remaining wisps of hair. Meanwhile his wife practically buried her face against his arm, gnawing at his sweater. As the dialogue progressed I could tell Ms Alexander was as taken aback by their words as the rest of us were by their behavior. In spite of their antics, she maintained her poise and gave the couple her undivided attention, here and there asking questions or prompting for more details. Eventually she smiled and turned to us.

"Forgive me" she said. "I have been trying to make sense of what they have been saying. Apparently it is dangerous to be out after dark, or to wander too far from town."

"We gathered that," I mumbled.

"Why?" Dietrich asked.

"Wolves, bears and the like," I offered. "After all, we are in the middle of nowhere."

Irish nodded to affirm that this made perfect sense. Dietrich, however, was less quick to jump to conclusions. He ignored us and leveled his gaze at Ms Alexander, who seemed hesitant to explain.

"What's the matter?" he asked.

Ms Alexander's eyes darted between us and the floor. She looked almost embarrassed.

"It is not wolves or bears they fear," she explained. "Those can be dealt with. They speak of something different, of the Tsar of these lands."

Dietrich leaned across the table.

"They fear Nicholas?" he whispered.

"No," she replied. "They fear Tsar Koschei, also known as Koschei the Deathless."

At mention of the name Koschei the innkeeper's wife gasped, tightly clasped both hands together, and began biting her knuckles like a squirrel trying to crack a resilient nut. And her husband looked no less distraught, though he had sufficient sense to resist hysterics. He spent the next few seconds in a silent struggle as he tried to wrest the woman's hands from her mouth before she gnawed them to the bone. Once the innkeeper had his wife's hands firmly in his, whispering and shushing her as if she were an imbecilic child, we returned our attention to Ms Alexander, eager to find out who this mysterious second Tsar might be.

"Tsar Koschei?" Dietrich wondered aloud. "Who is he, a pretender to the throne?"

"Nothing like that," Ms Alexander said. "Koschei was a wicked sorcerer of ancient times, who is rumored to have hidden his soul so that his body could not die."

We stared at her dumbfounded.

"Koschei is a creature of legend and folklore," she explained. "He is not someone in whom civilized people believe. However, I do not think I need remind you of where we are, that the nearest city is hundreds of miles away. In places like this, old beliefs still hold."

Dietrich opened his mouth to comment, but Ms Alexander cut him off.

"When strange and unexplainable events occur, my rustic kinsmen, lacking the experience and education you and I take for granted, turn to superstition for explanation."

"I still don't understand," Dietrich said, shaking his head. "What events are you talking about?"

"Over the past year the town has been plagued by disappearances," Ms Alexander replied. "These must be the same incidents Nicholas told me about. On several occasions those who traveled the western road, or wandered too far into the hills between here and the mountains, vanished mysteriously. This has earned the area a dangerous reputation. No one willingly uses the road, or hunts or farms among those hills, for fear that they too will be taken."

"By Koschei," Irish said.

Ms Alexander nodded.

Dietrich was frozen in an expression of incredulity, but when he spoke he did so with unanticipated tact.

"An interesting bit of folklore," he said, forcing a smile. "I should like to hear more about this Koschei. But look! The good lieutenant returns."

Before anyone could react we heard the sound of horses, and Dietrich leapt up and strode out the door. The Botkins, who did not consider the matter closed, followed us outside.

As we stepped onto the porch we found a coach awaiting us, drawn by two horses and piloted by none other than our lieutenant. As soon as he pulled up, he began to berate the Botkins, who looked both indignant and horrified.

"What now?" Dietrich said.

"The lieutenant tried to hire the coach, but when he told the coachman we intend to go to Véles, the man refused to take us because the road is too dangerous."

"Why is he yelling at them?" Irish asked, indicating the Botkins.

"The coachman works for them," she said. "The lieutenant is angry with them for letting their superstitions get in our way."

We watched for a minute until the argument began to wind down.

"Apparently the lieutenant intends to take us himself," Ms Alexander continued. "He stole the coach from the coachman."

"How do you know?" Irish said.

Ms Alexander nodded down the street. We turned to see the old driver hobbling toward us, shaking a fist in the air and hurling incomprehensible curses. When the lieutenant noticed, he turned in his seat and fired back some verbal abuses of his own, probably berating the old man for his foolish beliefs and wild beard. As the coachman strolled up, the Botkins felt compelled to intervene on his behalf. The lieutenant then turned his annoyance against them, which inevitably dragged Ms Alexander into the fray as arbiter. Dietrich, Irish, and I could only stand by and watch.

It made for good entertainment, even though I could not understand a word of it. It reminded me of a scene a painter might capture, a slice of rural Russian life: the lieutenant atop the coach, red faced from yelling, his arms thrown wide in a plea for sanity; the slighted coachmen standing below, yelling back with fist raised; the Botkins, innocent bystanders, being drawn to the conflict; and in the center of it all the exquisite and cultured Ms Alexander, her white dress aglow in the sunlight, her arms outstretched in a plaintive gesture of peace.

Soon enough it was over. The old man braced himself against the coach wheel, panting as if he had run a marathon. The lieutenant sat in his seat with his back turned to the coach's rightful owner. And the Botkins detached themselves and again stood to one side. Ms Alexander had worked out a deal to appease all parties.

"We will rent the coach with the understanding that it must be returned," she explained. "It is the only one in town, and it is that man's livelihood."

Now it was the Botkins' turn, for during the dispute they had finally pieced together that we were going to Véles. They approached Ms Alexander with hands extended so that she had to retreat behind Irish to avoid giving them a life-altering shock. Instead Dietrich absorbed the imploring presses of those wrinkled palms.

"They warn us against going there," Ms Alexander offered from behind Irish, "because the road is dangerous and the people are strange."

"We are aware of their unorthodox beliefs," Dietrich said. "We will be fine. Gentlemen, please collect our bags so we can get underway."

"We're leaving now?" I groaned.

"Do you have some other business here?" Dietrich replied.

Further discussion was curtailed as Dietrich was busy disengaging himself from the Botkins' groping hands. Meanwhile my companions and I fetched our bags and climbed aboard the coach. We politely waved as the lieutenant got us underway, but the Botkins only stared back at us, their faces full of grief, as if we had foolishly climbed aboard a coach to Hell.

According to Lieutenant Gorlov, the western road terminated at our destination, so finding the town would pose no problem. The road, which was really no more than a dirt trail worn into the earth by traffic back when it was considered safe, snaked its way through distant hills toward the grey slabs of the Urals beyond.

It took us all day to complete our journey. The road was a long and lonely stretch with little variation in scenery, just endless hills to the left and right. Occasionally we saw a derelict cart or wagon alongside the road, as if it had been abandoned in haste. Some were disabled and looked as if they had been subjected to violence. Who, or what, might have damaged them was not clear, but we managed to reach our destination without molestation.

Late in the day the gentle rocking of the vehicle caused me to drift off. I must have slept for a few hours, because the next thing I knew I felt a heavy hand on my shoulder.

"Koschei?" I said.

"Don't be an idiot," Irish said. "There's no Koschei."

"I know," I said defensively, rubbing the sleep from my eyes. "What, then?"

"Véles," he said. "We're here."

20: VÉLES

After hearing so many strange and foreboding things about Véles, I was disappointed when I finally laid eyes on it. On the surface the town did not live up to expectations. It looked so ordinary that at first I thought it was a joke, that Irish was putting me on. The street was orderly and lined with weatherworn clapboard shops and houses. People walked between them wearing traditional peasant clothing, looking no different than the inhabitants of Bogoslovsk. I don't know what I had been expecting—maybe mud huts, spears, and a tribe that wore bones through their noses—but what I saw left me deflated.

In fact, the only difference in scenery between Bogoslovsk and Véles was that the Urals now loomed over us.

"It is beautiful," Ms Alexander said as she climbed from the coach and took in the scenery.

"Yes," Dietrich said. He curiously examined passersby, and was met with equally suspicious looks in return.

"Not a very friendly place," Irish said.

"So it would seem," Dietrich agreed.

"*Dobriy dyen,*" Ms Alexander said to a woman and a girl as they passed near us. The woman, who looked like a spry grandmother, and who fell squarely into the group that would have benefitted from a hairbrush, frowned and gave an obligatory nod but said nothing. The girl with her, a fetching young brunette who couldn't have been more than sixteen, looked at us in wonder as they passed. Her reaction was understandable, for we were an unusual bunch. I did not give it a second thought until, a few paces later, the young wench stole a glance over her shoulder at us. I happened to look her way at that precise moment and our eyes met. I nodded and gave her a polite smile. She coyly reciprocated before her matron jerked her by the arm and spun her back around.

After the lieutenant had found the livery and stabled the horses, we began our search for room and board. In any other place such a task would go without comment, but in Véles it proved difficult because, to the man, they were reluctant to speak to us. Ms Alexander tried repeatedly to get the attention of passersby to ask for assistance, but even she had no success. The people shot her dark looks, or continued walking and shaking their heads as if she were speaking a language they did not understand. After the third stranger had spurned her, Lieutenant Gorlov became irate. As a middle-aged woman carrying a basket of bread tried to skirt us, he grabbed her by the arm and demanded, in the name of the Tsar, that she direct us to lodging and food. The woman shrank before him, more surprised than frightened, but her eyes remained defiant. She did not say a word, but she pointed across the street at a nondescript two-story building.

"We're off to a good start," Irish scoffed.

We entered the establishment and found it to be spare: wood paneled walls, unfinished floorboards with no rug, and except for an upholstered sofa against one wall and some burlap curtains hanging in the windows, everything else was carved or assembled from wood. The frontier lifestyle of Véles drove home the uneasy feeling that the town was remote, and that we were for the first time beyond any assistance. If we encountered trouble, not even the Tsar could help us.

As we entered the establishment a man stepped out from a back room to greet us, but he almost froze when he laid eyes on us. Ms Alexander did her level best to be courteous, but even she failed to crack his icy demeanor. She expressed our need for rooms for the night, earning a confused look from him. But even as he stared suspiciously, he reached under the counter and produced a ledger. Dietrich stepped forward, and as he signed the man finally spoke. He said no more than ten words, but Ms Alexander gave him ten times that in reply. As she spoke his eyes grew narrower, and his brow became more furrowed.

"He wants to know why we are here, and how long we intend to stay," she said.

"What did you tell him?" Dietrich asked.

"I told him we are on holiday touring the Urals, and that we will be here several days, maybe longer."

The look on the proprietor's face revealed that he did not believe a word of it, and even if he did, he would rather go bankrupt than tolerate us to stay under his roof for more than one night. His behavior could not have been more opposite from that of an innkeeper. I had spent nights in jail with guards who were more hospitable.

"He doesn't seem to care for our business," I said. "Are you sure we should stay?"

"To be honest," Dietrich muttered, "I am not sure about anything in this place."

Meanwhile Ms Alexander continued to speak with him, getting little more from him than grunts and shakes of the head.

"He says the dinner hour has passed," she said. "He has no meal for us."

At that moment Lieutenant Gorlov intervened. I had been peripherally aware of a growing tension in him—a restless shifting of weight, crossing and uncrossing of the arms, sighs of exasperation. Finally his patience expired, and in full military fashion he leapt into the fray. I would not have been surprised if he had let out a battle cry, drawn his saber, and waved it over the man's head. Without warning he stepped forward and, in a tone he must have used many times to dress down undisciplined soldiers, laid into the man.

The innkeeper took a step back, half raising an arm as if to deflect a blow. But as the tirade continued, the man rebounded. By the end he was his old, supercilious self again. The berating, however, at least set him in motion. With an unwavering scowl he hastily scratched something into his ledger and then, grumbling to himself, went about setting a table by the front windows. We seated ourselves while the lieutenant stood to one side supervising, as if the man might try to bolt at any second. Soon our cantankerous host brought out milk, bread, and cheese to placate us while he hustled up an unanticipated entrée. When he disappeared into the kitchen, followed by the clamor of pots and pans being angrily handled, the lieutenant shot one last look at the kitchen door and took a seat.

"Well done," Irish said.

In spite of the language barrier the lieutenant understood perfectly. He acknowledged with a nod, tweaked his moustache, and offered a few words. We looked to our lady for explanation.

"He said the man clearly did not know with whom he was dealing."

"I should say not," I chimed in. "I think he'll remember the good lieutenant for many years to come. I hope you don't find yourself here on honeymoon!"

I laughed and clapped the lieutenant on the back, getting in return a polite but confused grin. He looked at Ms Alexander inquisitively, but she replied only with a quick shake of her head.

"What's with everyone acting so strange?" Irish said, staring back at the people on the street.

We turned and looked out the window. Where we were sitting, we were in plain sight of those on the street. All who passed slowed to get a look at us. Word already seemed to have spread that strangers were in town, because people were almost gaggling across the street to stare.

"They must not get many visitors," Dietrich said.

"Based on the welcome we received, I'm not surprised," I said.

"Their notoriety as pagans probably keeps many away," Dietrich added.

Ms Alexander nodded in agreement, and we all tensed for what she would have to say on the subject. She surprised us, however, by saying nothing.

"They better move along," Irish muttered. "They're getting on my nerves."

With no translation, Lieutenant Gorlov acted in a way that again suggested he and Irish understood each other perfectly. Without a word he placed a hand on his saber and glared with such vehemence at those loitering outside that they immediately began to disperse.

"This place is disturbing," Ms Alexander said. "The people act so strange. Even if they are not connected to our mission, they certainly behave as if they are guilty of *something*."

At that moment the kitchen door swung open and our host returned bearing a cutting board loaded with more bread and cheese, and some sliced red meat. To show his displeasure he practically dropped it on the table, causing the foods to leap into the air. He then took a step back, pulled a stained dish towel from his back pocket, and wiped his hands distastefully. Ms Alexander thanked him. He ignored her and did not wait to be further bothered. He disappeared into the kitchen and left us to serve ourselves.

Most of our meal was spent glancing out the window. After the lieutenant's glare, no other passersby stopped to stare at us like animals in a zoo. But in the growing gloom we caught glimpses of small congregations across the street, little groups of individuals who clustered together for a few seconds to exchange a few words and point at the inn as if to say, "That's where they are, all right!" By the time we were done eating, everything outside had fallen into shadow, and the nosy people of Véles were reduced to dark, gossipy silhouettes.

As we left the table I happened to glance up and notice some movement in the street. In the darkness I had to stare intently to be sure I was not imagining it. Soon I was able to make out a strange procession marching into town, a long line of men—maybe fifty, maybe a hundred. In the gloom I could not be sure of anything except that there were a lot of them. From their rough shapes and weary postures I could tell they were laborers, clad in overalls and dungarees, heads hung low after a long day of toil. A few carried lanterns to light their way, which shed enough light to reveal their clothes were filthy.

Dietrich noticed as well, but he said nothing as they filed by. His eyes, however, showed they had piqued his interest. When our host returned to gather up his serving board, Dietrich engaged him on the subject.

"Where are those men coming from?" Dietrich asked.

The man's reply was accompanied by a sneer.

"The mines, of course," Ms Alexander said.

"The mines," Dietrich repeated. "I thought the mines had closed due to the dangers along the road."

Ms Alexander explained, and the man's sneer quickly faded. His eyes darted around, and he colored as if caught in a lie. When he spoke he did so quickly, then turned and marched upstairs before Ms Alexander could manage another word.

"He said he does not know," she said, rising from the table. "He also said it is time he showed us our rooms."

We followed him upstairs to our quarters, stopping to collect our bags that he had intentionally ignored. At the top of the stairs he waved down the hall to indicate we had our choice. I chose a room near the stairs and went inside. It was unsurprisingly simple, with nothing more than a bed and a small table with a kerosene lamp. It had a window overlooking the street, which I thought would be pleasant until I glanced out to find a host of shadows milling about and staring back at me. I caught my breath and stepped back, colliding unexpectedly with Dietrich. He glanced past me out the window.

"They are fascinated by us," he said.

"Apparently," I replied. "Though I don't know why. I don't think we'd get this much attention on an island of starving cannibals."

"A grim comparison," he said. "Let's hope we fare better."

"One can always hope," I said with a nervous chuckle.

He straightened and paused, staring back at the specters in the street. The closeness of the room suddenly became oppressive, and I was made uncomfortable by his presence.

"Did you want something?"

"Yes, actually," he said. "I have a task for you."

I experienced a moment of thrill and dread.

"For me?"

"Yes. Only you."

"What is it?"

He nodded toward the window.

"Those men we saw, the miners. I want you to follow them tomorrow, to see where they go."

"You don't think they're going to a mine?" I asked.

"On the contrary," he said. "It would not surprise me if they were. But the refinery in Bogoslovsk is closed. What are they mining, and for what purpose?"

"Okay," I said hesitantly. "I don't understand how this is tied to our mission."

"Nor do I," he admitted. "It may be nothing, but it's clear the people are involved in something they don't want outsiders to know about."

I paused and bit my lip, not sure if I wanted to voice my next concern. Dietrich noticed my trepidation.

"What's wrong?" he asked.

"What about this Koschei business?" I said.

He looked at me as if I were joking. When I did not laugh he forced himself to become serious.

"You've touched on another piece of the puzzle," he said. "This Koschei nonsense is too convenient. It's almost as if someone created it specifically to discourage people from coming here. I'm sure you will be fine."

I nodded, though I was unconvinced. He turned to go.

"By the way," I said, "why is this task solely for me?"

"You're the best man for the job," he said with a shrug. "We need someone who can do it without being detected."

I thought about it and admitted he was right. Irish was too large to sneak, Lieutenant Gorlov was not privy to the details of our endeavor, and placing Ms Alexander in harm's way was out of the question. I was about to ask him why he had factored himself out of the equation when he slapped a handkerchief over his mouth and coughed violently, shaking from the exertion.

"That's gotten worse lately," I said.

He nodded as he gathered his breath.

"Very well," I said. "Is there anything else?"

He looked at me questioningly.

"Is there anything in particular I'm to look for, or to do?"

"*Look* for everything, and *do* nothing," he said.

"I'm your man," I said, gripping his arms in a brotherly fashion.

He smiled in response, though it looked more like a grimace. He then disengaged from me and went back to his room. As I was closing the door Ms Alexander opened hers and stepped into the hallway. She gave me a quizzical look.

"Is something happening?" she asked.

"No," I said. "We were just talking. Nothing to worry your pretty head over."

She was not convinced. She began to say something else. I closed the door to avoid further questions, and to give her something to think about.

The following morning—if such a word applies to such wee, dark hours—I thankfully awoke before sunup. Without an alarm I had feared I would oversleep, but when I awoke at five to the call of nature, I forced myself to get dressed and ready for my mission. I shrugged into my coat as I descended the stairs, grumbling to myself about missing breakfast. I considered stepping into the kitchen and grabbing something to hold me over until I returned, but as I approached the kitchen door I heard a floorboard creak from somewhere in the house. To avoid prying eyes and ears, I lightly hurried to the door and slipped outside.

The air was cool and bracing, and it served to rouse my senses. I felt instantly and completely alert as if I had dived into a cool, clear lake. Once outside, however, I realized the darkness was not as complete as I had thought. The sky had already transformed from black velvet to slate grey, offering sufficient light to be spotted by anyone out and about. I suddenly felt exposed and hurried toward the edge of town, casting glances over my shoulder to ensure I was not seen. At town's edge I continued past the last buildings for perhaps a hundred paces before stepping off the road and into the brush. There I crouched down and waited anxiously. After twenty minutes with no sign of traffic I decided to get more comfortable. I was in the process of seating myself on the damp earth and leaning back against a tree when the first hints of voices reached my ears.

I climbed back to my feet and hid behind a throng of wild bushes. The sound of two men talking was unmistakable. Then they were joined by a third, and moments later a fourth, all mumbling in the gravelly tones of early morning. Over the next ten minutes they talked and smoked while waiting for everyone to arrive. When they finally set off I sank to the ground to avoid detection, held my breath, and watched as they passed.

As expected, they were common men who made their way in the world with hard, crude labor. They were broad of brow and limb, and even from my concealed spot I could spot thick calluses on their large hands. Most were unshaven, and all looked as dirty and haggard as they had the night before. Most appeared to have risen and dressed in the same filthy clothes they had worn the day prior.

I counted as they trudged past and came to ninety-three. So, I was expected to spy upon almost a hundred strong, able-bodied, naturally suspicious men, with whom—if they caught me—I would be completely unable to communicate. Suddenly the risk slapped me in the face, and for a moment I was too afraid to move. I had the urge to press my face against the dirt, to stay put, perhaps take a nap and report back to Dietrich some lie about how they spent the day tilling fields. But as I watched them disappear down the road, another unexpected urge gripped me. Before I could question it, I leapt from the bushes and chased after them.

I spent the next hour in a constant state of panic as I tried to stalk them without being detected. I remained in the brush as much as possible, but there were times when I encountered a tangle and had to go along the road for a time, walking in plain sight. Those were the most frightening moments, because it would only take one idle glance backward for someone to spot me. Then Dietrich's plan, and likely our lives, would come to an abrupt end. It was then that I realized everything hinged on me, that my success or failure would determine our fate. I became anxious, even more than I already was, as I crept from tree to tree. It was more responsibility than I desired. But as the day grew on I realized there was nothing for it. I had the best chance of successfully spying, so I had better do a good job and not get caught.

Fate took pity on me that day, and I went completely unnoticed. The men were either so rutted in habit, or so focused and duty bound, that not one ever took so much as a casual glance around. Like soulless golems they marched onward to their bleak calling.

By my estimate I followed them five miles, weaving in and out of brush-covered hills toward a wall of mammoth grey mountains. For the last half mile our path followed a decline, and soon the brush on both sides of the road was replaced with walls of rock. We were on a narrow road carved into the feet of the mountains, in what looked like a manmade gorge. Since there was no place to hide I was forced to take the open road, becoming totally exposed. As a precaution I hung back further, using the curves in the road and the rock walls themselves to hide behind.

I continued along the road as long as I dared, which was not much further. The road descended very quickly for perhaps one hundred and fifty paces before it rounded a bend and opened into a small basin. The rock walls fell away so suddenly I had to leap backwards to seek cover. In the process I lost my footing on loose gravel and caused some discernible scraping sounds that caught the attention of one of the men at the rear. As I groped a wall for stabilization, I saw his head begin to turn. At that moment my fingers found some purchase and I hauled myself back. The combined strength of my arms and legs launched my light frame quickly around the corner, and I pressed myself against the rock, held my breath, and waited. After thirty seconds passed and no one rounded the corner to investigate, I carefully peeked out and took in the scene.

The basin itself had been a product of nature, though Man had turned it into a quarry. It was several hundred feet in diameter and surrounded by rock walls that had been scored and graded. Along the walls were numerous cave mouths—yawning black tunnels laid with rail tracks that lolled on the ground like tongues. In the middle of the basin the tracks joined and led away to a deeper recess of the gorge that I could not see. Interspersed throughout the unoccupied spaces were large piles of spoil—heaps of rock and dirt taller than me—and several wooden shacks, around which were piled a variety of tools and equipment of the mining trade.

As I took this in I realized the number of men I had been following had decreased. Only half were now visible, and I surmised the rest had continued along the tracks to some other distant station. In an effort to prove myself a competent and obedient spy, I began looking for a way to follow them. I picked a path between piles of debris that, if I were quick, would allow me to get past the workers unnoticed. As I examined the route I realized it would be a difficult feat. The piles were large and numerous, but they were separated by spaces of up to fifty feet. If I attempted it, I would have to dash across loose gravel and many open spaces to get to the other side of the basin. It was not an impossible feat, but definitely a risky one. But I could see no way around it, so I watched the men intently, waiting for the right moment. Fortunately an opportunity did not immediately present itself, for if it had, I would have hurried on and missed the exceedingly strange preparations of the miners.

They had congregated around the shacks and started assembling their equipment for the work ahead. Mostly this meant tossing a variety of picks, shovels, sledgehammers, and chisels into the rusting iron push carts sitting on the tracks. Before anyone entered the mine, however, they split again. A few continued to gather tools while the rest made for the sheds and disappeared inside. While everyone was distracted, I took advantage of the moment and began sneaking across the yard, careful to avoid the eyes of the few men loading the equipment. I managed to avoid detection as I rushed behind several spoil piles, and soon reached the heap nearest the bend where the tracks disappeared. I was about to make a final break for it, to round the bend to see what lay beyond, when the door to the nearest shack swung open, and out stepped a monster.

It was not an actual monster, but it was so alien to my eyes that at first I took it for one. It was of course a miner, but he was hidden from head to toe in a suit that looked like something out of a nightmare. He was covered in thick, boiled leather that had been scuffed, scarred, and singed by his trade. He wore a coat, pants, gloves, and boots made of the stuff, and he moved so stiffly he resembled the walking dead. The most frightening aspect of his get-up, however, was his mask. His head was entirely covered with a frightful shroud of the same material. It had been stitched together along seams resembling horrible scars, and in place of eyes were large, black, soulless lenses.

The sight of him froze me in place for a moment. I managed to duck behind a pile of earth just as several others followed him out, all wearing the same strange outfits. At the same time the doors to other shacks swung open, and similar monstrosities issued from them as well.

I watched in fascination as they all shambled toward the tunnels. I noticed that during this time the other men had not been idle. They had maneuvered the carts along the tracks, staged them at the entrances, and affixed lanterns to them. As the suited men approached, the rest stood back, watching as they split into groups of four, leaned heavily upon the carts, and rolled them into the mines.

I watched until the last group wheeled their cart into the darkness. Then, while the men outside were preoccupied, I darted across fifty feet of open terrain and around the bend before they saw me.

It was a reckless maneuver, but I had no alternative. As I rounded the bend I half expected to run headlong into someone coming back my way, but thankfully it did not occur. The way was clear. From there I took it slowly, being as quiet as possible and giving my racing heart a chance to catch up.

I found myself in another narrow, winding gorge of sheer stone walls. Despite my misgivings, I followed it until it widened, several hundred feet later. Here the walls were not manmade, but the natural, craggy faces of the mountains, neither barren nor impossibly steep. They were covered in trees and brush, and the slope, while steep enough to be considered a wall by most, would be easy for one such as me to climb. But before I could give it further thought, I heard the sound of men approaching, and I instinctively began to scramble up the slope and into the bushes at the top. I made it just in time, too, for no sooner had I dived into the brush than a pair of men rounded the corner heading back toward the quarry.

Having narrowly avoided detection, I took a moment to collect myself. I rolled onto my back and lay among the thistles, gathering my wits in preparation for my next run of excitement. As I laid staring up at the sky I laughed quietly. I had known all along I was on an adventure, but it was not until then that I had felt like an adventurer. In spite of the danger, and the fact that I was not meant for this line of work, I felt light-hearted, almost invincible—something about the thrill of almost being caught, I supposed.

The sensation was short-lived. Within moments the feeling ebbed and I was myself again, an entertainer out of his element. My chuckles faded and I was left with the sounds of the wild: stirring leaves, buzzing insects, birdsong, and the faint sound of running water.

Water! The sound called to me. I realized I had had nothing to drink all morning. I peered through the bushes to get the lay of the land, scanning the terrain for the source, but I could not find it.

My reconnaissance showed I was on a natural shelf, no more than four feet wide at its broadest point, that followed the face of the mountain, both forward and back the way I had come. I had not noticed it before because I had been so focused on following the miners into the basin, and I was not familiar with the terrain. It had never occurred to me to look up and around for a ledge to follow. It was the perfect place from which to spy. I began working my way forward, both in search of water and to get a look at the valley beyond.

I moved along the shelf in a crouch, keeping myself hidden behind brush as much as possible. As I progressed the ledge began to incline, and soon I was up much higher than I had intended. Here the brush thinned and I was more exposed than I preferred, but the altitude allowed me to take in all I needed to see.

First, I found the source of the water. Not far from where I crouched a narrow stream rushed down the mountainside. As I traced it I found, perhaps a hundred feet below, a wooden trough positioned to receive the flow. The trough, however, was only the beginning.

My curiosity piqued, I crept closer to the edge to get a better look below. Almost directly below my vantage point the trough, and the rails from the mine, terminated at a platform, the surface of which was made of an iron grate. The first thought that came to mind was the device was used to sift through excavated minerals, rather like panning for gold. But the iron grate was much too large and coarse for such work.

As I wondered about it I heard distant sounds that drew my attention—the sharp *plink* of metal striking stone, the sonorous *thud* of metal on wood, the high-pitched *ting* of metal on metal—unmistakable manmade sounds hinting that a great work was under way nearby. I crept further along the ledge, which continued to rise as I went. Several hundred feet later, and perhaps fifty feet higher, I came to a spot that allowed me to look out over the valley beyond.

318

The valley was a large bowl that I estimated at a mile in diameter, completely ringed by rocky slopes. Unlike the rest of the region, it was barren. A smattering of blackened tree trunks stood in a few places, but the rest—the vast majority—had been knocked down, scorched, and lay in a massive jumble like spilled toothpicks. Paths had been cleared through them for traffic, but no other effort had been made to clear or dispose of them. As far as natural terrain was concerned, the rest of the valley was nothing but rock, dust, and ash. But there were two features of manmade terrain that offered immediate points of interest.

The first was an ancient stone structure erected on a ridge overlooking the valley from the West. It was large enough to spot from a distance, but still modest in size and design. At the time I mistook it for a medieval castle and gave no thought to the fact that it was by itself in the middle of Siberia.

The other, and far more significant, point of interest stood in the center of the valley. Erupting from the floor was a great silver spire, like a sword sprung from the earth, reaching several hundred feet into the sky; and surrounding it a skeletal frame, an immense latticework of timber and metal. As I peered at it I had no idea what to make of it, but I decided the latticework must be scaffolding, because I could faintly detect movement on it. Men were at work there, which I thought explained the sounds that had drawn my attention. But as I crawled closer to the edge, the valley floor opened up, and I found the real source of the noise.

Beneath the spire stood a makeshift town: a dense collection of shacks, shanties, and tents that teemed with activity. Among the structures moved many men, all involved in diverse labors—chopping wood, feeding fires, sawing, hammering, forging, shaping—and those were just the activities I thought I recognized. There were other things going on, the most interesting of which was centered round a shrouded structure set off to one side that vented what looked like steam. All these efforts created a rising cloud of smog over the camp that, in the stillness of the valley air, hung there like an amorphous demonic presence. But as strange as those myriad labors were, it was clear they were all in service to the silver spire.

I reeled in wonder. The sights before me resembled something out of Medieval fantasy—a town enslaved by an evil wizard who ruled from somewhere within his arcane tower.

"Koschei!" I whispered. Perhaps there was some truth to local superstition, and a sorcerer was controlling these people, forcing them to do his bidding. In the next moment I chided myself for such foolishness—or I would have, had my attention not been drawn by the ringing of a bell.

As I tried to figure out where it was coming from, everyone in the valley camp began hurrying in my direction. I became paranoid, thinking someone had seen me. Suddenly I felt exposed. I pressed my face in the dirt and began worming back along the ledge the way I had come.

I crawled on my belly for maybe a hundred feet, but once I reached the brush, I got into a crouch and hurried along. By then I could tell the bell was sounding from the direction of the mines. The first men from the camp scurried into the ravine below, and I pressed myself against the wall to void being seen.

As I reached the mining area my curiosity overcame my fear. I had reasoned that if someone had detected me, they would have already made some overt attempt to apprehend or kill me. Instead of fleeing I got on my belly and crawled to the edge to see what the disturbance was about.

The mining pit was all commotion. The bell continued to toll, making it easy to find. It was one of several mounted atop posts just outside the tunnels. The rope that controlled it ran away into the nearest tunnel, and someone deep within was pulling on it relentlessly. As the bell tolled, the miners in the horrific leather suits spilled out of the tunnel like angry ants. They stumbled into the light, and others grabbed them by the arms and dragged them aside, making way for those behind.

While this went on, the crowd from the valley gathered with much yelling and excitement, but as they rushed into the quarry they drew up, not desiring to get any closer to the action. Instead, they began to form a ring around the edge, constantly jockeying for position to better watch the spectacle.

The bell ceased ringing, and no one exited the tunnel for a long time. When the last two men exited carrying a third—his arms over their shoulders, the front of his protective suit scorched and smoldering—I imagined some mining-related calamity had occurred, and that the excitement was over. But it had only begun.

Six men in leather suits stepped forward, picked up a thick rope from the ground, and began hauling it in. As it became taught, I saw the other end disappeared into the vacated tunnel. It took them some time to retrieve the burden. They switched out with others no less than four times before they finally hauled it into the light. What they pulled from the tunnel appeared to be nothing more than a mining cart full of earth and rocks.

I do not know what I was expecting, but I was at first disappointed. As the cart rolled out onto the tracks, everyone began to fall back as if it were cursed. I then noticed a strange effect surrounding it, a distortion of light and form like one sees when staring at something above a flame. Then I realized that whatever the cart contained was hellishly hot.

At least some of the men appeared to have anticipated this, because they at once formed a bucket brigade to douse the contents. And none too soon, I might add, for the sides of the cart had begun to glow, like iron left too long in a fire. The buckets were emptied into the cart, which soon filled up but threatened to boil away every drop into steam. The water did little, if anything, to quench the heat, but it appeared to retard the heating of the cart itself. And this turned out to be the goal: to stop the cart from collapsing into a heap of slag before the men could move in with poles and begin nudging it along the tracks.

The crowd fled down the gorge before the cart, and I stealthily paralleled them from above. As they reached the next station they again spread out in a ring formation and waited. Eventually the miners pushed the cart into sight with their poles and maneuvered it to the iron grate. Once there, they wedged their poles beneath it and levered it over onto its side, spilling much of the contents onto the grate. Those parts that did not spill out were then worked out using the poles. As they scraped rocks and dirt onto the grate I struggled to identify the source of the heat, but I could not see anything clearly through the rippling air.

As the miners struggled to empty the cart, a pair of wagons arrived. The first was operated by a lone driver, drawn by a team of four horses, and transported a large iron pot resembling a cauldron. The second was, at a glance, unremarkable. It was smaller, drawn by one horse, and bore only two men: a thuggish-looking driver, and another who, in this environment, looked completely out of place. I am no judge of age, but he looked to be an older man, perhaps a little older than Dietrich. Even though he wore a scruffy wool coat, his hair and clothes were neat and clean, making apparent that he was not the typical man of Véles. Before the smaller wagon came to a stop, he leapt down and began issuing orders, commanding the miners and onlookers both.

At his direction a lever was pulled and the stream diverted. Water filled the troughs and raced down to empty upon the grate. As water coursed over the contents a great steam rose up, completely obscuring my view. Through the cloud I caught glimpses of men working with poles, poking and cajoling whatever lay upon the grate. This went on for some time, until the gentleman gave instructions for the water to stop. The cloud of steam began to disappear, and as it dissipated I was able to better make out what rested atop the grate.

If the purpose of the water had been to cool the thing then it had failed, for waves of heat continued to radiate from it. In fact, the heat seemed more intense than before, because now all the insulating material had been rinsed away, leaving only the thing itself. And that thing—that unquenchable, unearthly object—was a rock.

At first I thought my eyes, or the distorted air, had deceived me. But as I watched them prodding it with metal poles I saw it from all angles. It was indeed nothing more than a rock, not much larger than a pumpkin. It had a strange color—a deep, earthy crimson that seemed to be its natural hue rather than a reflection of its temperature—but otherwise it was unremarkable. I would not have given it a second thought if not for the heat it radiated.

As I watched a leather-suited man with a great set of tongs hesitantly approached it, while two others hurried to the large wagon, removed the lid from the cauldron, fell back, and waited. The man with the tongs had to get closer to the object than anyone else had so far dared, and his hesitancy revealed that he had his doubts. And understandably so, for even as he inched forward in his great leather suit, I watched it blacken and crack. Finally he mustered the courage to grab the thing with the tongs, and holding it as far ahead of himself as possible, he hurried to the cauldron and dropped it in. A hiss issued forth followed by a pillar of steam, but then the lid was thrown over it and everyone seemed to relax as if the situation was under control.

The gentleman, however, was not at ease. He shouted at the driver, who spurred the horses away toward the camp. As the wagon rattled away, everyone hurried after it. Apparently there was more to see, but I balked at venturing into the valley since I could not pass for a local. The rest of the show would have to remain a mystery. But that was of little concern to me, because I already had plenty to report.

I was about to start working my way down when I realized a few had not yet departed, the gentleman among them. Two men approached him bearing a leather-suited miner between them. By the horrible scorching on his suit I surmised this was the man I had seen carried from the tunnel. At the gentleman's behest they laid the victim on the ground and removed his mask. Even from that distance I heard the gasps, but the men blocked my view so I did not witness the horror. Judging by their reactions I could imagine it, which was more than enough. A moment later the gentleman stood, shook his head, pulled a pistol from his belt, and shot the injured man three times in the chest. The others then lifted the corpse into the back of the remaining wagon and headed back toward the camp.

The journey back to town was long and hot, even with my coat removed. I had used it to bundle up an object of interest, a strange item I would have been at pains to explain had I met anyone along the road. But the road appeared to serve only the miners, because for the hour it took me to return I did not encounter another soul.

It was mid-afternoon by the time I reached Véles. I strolled casually into town as if nothing was amiss. That, however, did not stop the locals from eyeing me suspiciously. I nodded at them in greeting, which only seemed to enflame their obvious distrust. One gaunt woman even wrapped a protective arm around her daughter, pulling her closer as if my very proximity might result in her deflowering.

I reached the hotel and quickly passed through the parlor. Our surly host was standing desultorily behind his counter. I gave him a cursory nod, not bothering to look for a response, and headed upstairs. The sound of my ascent alerted my companions, and as soon as I stepped into the hallway their doors opened.

"At last!" Dietrich exclaimed, grabbing me by the arms. "We had begun to worry. What did you find?"

I explained everything—the mine, the suited men, the spire, the infernal ore. They hung on my every word. Dietrich found it all incredibly fascinating. In fact, when I finished he made me run through it all again, not because he had missed any detail (for that was quite impossible), but because he wanted to see if I would remember any details I had failed to mention. When I finished, he thoughtfully stroked his beard and glanced at the coat beneath my arm.

"What do you have there?" he said.

"Ah! I almost forgot about it."

I unrolled my coat and pulled out a blackened object the size of a human head. Ms Alexander had expected nothing like it and let out a small cry.

"What the hell is that?" Irish said.

"A mask," I explained. "All the miners wore them. This one came off the poor soul I mentioned, the one who died."

I held it aloft, turning it left and right so they could take in the details. Ms Alexander took a step back, but Irish found it so interesting that he took it from me to examine for himself. Dietrich, the one person I thought would find the evidence most intriguing, forgot about it instantly.

"Think, Prometheus," he said. "Is there any other detail that might benefit us?"

I could think of nothing else, and at that point I did not want to. I was dying of thirst and hunger.

"I'm afraid not," I said.

He was dissatisfied with my response. He opened his mouth to ask another question, but I cut him off.

"Is there anything left of lunch?"

Ms Alexander cast a final look of distaste at the mask in Irish's hands.

"You have done an outstanding job today," she said. "Let's speak to the proprietor and see what he can find."

She smiled at me in a way I had not seen in some time. Even without her smile I would have enthusiastically agreed. To sit alone with her was more reward than I had hoped for. We headed downstairs, leaving Dietrich and Irish in contemplation.

We enjoyed a pleasant lunch together in spite of the innkeeper's reluctance to serve us. He made little effort to accommodate us and brought out more of the same food we had eaten the night before.

As I ate I was my usual self, prepared with witticisms at every turn. When Ms Alexander first sat down she was still in a serious, business-like mood. But my humor soon distracted her from the perplexities of our mission, and from the mysteries I had brought back from the mines. Afterward I tried to lure her along for a stroll, but after a glance out the window at the inhospitable townsfolk, she decided against it and returned to her room.

The sun had been out all morning, but now an endless blanket of clouds had crept in and turned everything grey. The air tickled my nose and I knew rain was in store, but the sky showed no imminent signs. Lunch had refreshed me. In spite of my morning exertions, I felt a need to be active, so I pressed on.

I nodded in a friendly way at all who passed, most of whom were women since practically all able-bodied men were at the mines. I had always fared well with the fairer sex, probably due to my knack for entertaining. This propensity normally extended to my most casual meetings, and even those I had just met were inevitably drawn into conversation. But on the streets of Véles my smiles were met with suspicion. Here and there I got a nod in return, but no smiles or friendly Russian greetings. I did not let it deter me. When I realized it was hopeless, I added a mischievous wink into the mix. That grabbed the attention of more than a few women—all old hags, regrettably—who noticed and did a double take.

The town was small, so my stroll was brief. I had no desire to wander beyond what passed here for civilization. When I reached the last houses I turned around and slowly worked my way back. About midway I stopped to stare at some raw, flayed creatures hanging in a butchers' window. I got the feeling I was being watched, and looking up I saw a lovely peasant girl eyeing me from another shop down. I would have thought nothing of it, but her dark, untamed hair and flirtatious smile caught my eye. Then I recognized her—I had passed her on the street twice since our arrival, each time accompanying her cronish matron. Now, however, she was alone. I smiled in return and pretended to stare into the shop window.

I did not wonder at her interest. It was expected, if not predictable. After all, I was fit and not without physical charm. My clothes and grooming made me stand out in sharp contrast to local men. I am certain she saw me as something spectacular and exotic, rather the way a pigeon must consider a peacock.

As I inspected the grisly meats in the window, I was peripherally aware of her. She may have been a Russian hillbilly, but she was comely and lithe. From the corner of my eye I noticed her look my way repeatedly, almost exaggerating her motions as if to draw my attention. I held back a smile and pretended not to notice. After a minute she seemed to give up on me. She turned and began to walk away. I did the same, walking slowly behind her, keeping my eyes on the windows to avoid any appearance of impropriety.

Not twenty feet later she shot a mock-casual glance over her shoulder. Our eyes met. She smiled and abruptly turned away—a time-honored tactic that must come naturally to females. Like any man, I was then effectively hooked. She picked up her pace as if she might bolt. As she stepped lightly along the sidewalk, I had to abandon pretense of window-shopping to keep up.

She now moved with such purpose that I began to think she was trying to lose me. I was about to cut my pace and let her go when she rounded a corner, glancing at me before disappearing. If I had begun to doubt her interest, the look I saw in her eyes banished all doubt. Her message could not have been clearer if she had spoken.

I rounded the corner to find myself in an alley. I hesitated, suddenly remembering where I was and the business that had brought me there. The thought danced across my mind that it might be a trap, that she might be luring me to my doom. But the alley was clear to the end, with an open space not far beyond. It did not look foreboding, and no one assailed me. Then I caught a glimpse of her hair flitting in the breeze beyond. I put caution aside and hurried on.

As I cleared the alley I found myself in a small yard. It was strung with clotheslines from which the maudlin garments of peasants swayed in the breeze. I quickly ducked through them and came to a dark line of trees divided by a small dirt path. Again I hesitated. A flit of motion caught my eye and I advanced to get a clear view of her. I spotted her on the path as she paused to give me another wanton look. As I stepped toward her, she suddenly laughed, turned, and broke into a run. I followed.

As we ran the trees became dense, and more branches spread across the way. I tried to swat them aside, but several times my coat snagged on barbs and slowed me. Eventually I managed to gain on her so that we were no more than thirty feet apart. Running in her wake, her scent carried back to me. I had imagined her smelling of perfume, which was ridiculous because she was too simple to afford it. Instead she was redolent as tilled earth, mixed with the whispered sweetness of wildflowers. It was nothing like any feminine scent I had encountered. The combination confused my senses. It was more natural, primitive—dare I say it—animal. It had an unexpected effect on me, spurring me on.

No matter how great my arousal, it was no match for the chase she gave. I may have been fit, but I had long since forgone any exercises of endurance. I raced after her for perhaps a quarter of a mile before my legs felt like rubber and my heart like it would leap from my mouth. Meanwhile she sprinted ahead of me like a playful doe. I began to slow, soon decelerating to a walk as I gasped for breath.

Moments later we cleared the wood. As suddenly as stepping through a doorway I found myself in a large clearing. It was ringed by a dark wall of trees, and in its midst stood a tall, bald hill. I watched as the girl skipped lightly toward it and began to climb. I halted to catch my breath, but she shot me another of her mischievous looks and I forced myself on.

I staggered to the foot of the hill and began to climb. By then she had reached the top and had disappeared from sight. I pulled out a handkerchief and mopped my brow. As I climbed I felt a growing fatigue, almost as if I could feel myself aging. Accompanying this sensation was the growing idea that I had made an error, that I should not have followed her. But I was beyond the point of return.

I crested the hill and found the girl dancing, as gaily as a nymph, around a strange and massive object, a crude statue or totem of rough grey stone. It looked ancient. Much of its finer details had eroded, and the rest was covered in lichen. Still, its form was clear. It represented a cross between a serpent and a ram—head and body of serpent, but with horns. It reared up eight feet tall and seemed to glare balefully down at me.

I was transfixed. I moved my mouth in a silent oath. Then I heard a deep rumbling from above, and I noticed dark clouds had gathered overhead. A peal of thunder shook the ground, and I jumped. I heard a giggle, and my eyes returned to earth to find the girl.

She was half hidden behind the statue, leaning around it just enough to see me. As I wondered at her she stepped out from behind the pillar, and I almost fell over from shock. She had shed her blouse and stood before me naked from the waist up. I was again transfixed, this time by her modest breasts. I froze as she walked slowly toward me.

The wind whipped up around us and I felt the first light drops of rain on my face. Still I could not move. Lightning flashed, lighting the girl's exquisite shape, burning the image into my mind. Thunder followed, but I was only vaguely aware. By then the girl had stepped within reach, moved in with a tilt of her head, and inclined her lips toward mine.

This dreamlike scenario was suddenly interrupted by a startling tirade that sent a chill through me. An incessant and shrill voice, like fingernails on a chalkboard, began shrieking in a language I could not understand. I spun around to find a furious crone wrapped in shawl cresting the top of the hill. As she approached, she shook her skeletal fist in the air. At once I recognized her as the girl's keeper. I stared at her in shock as the rain fell more heavily.

Then instinct took over and I ran. Even if I had had my wits about me, there was not much else I could do. I did not speak their language, and even if I had, there was no innocent explanation. As I ran downhill I stumbled and rolled most of its length. At the bottom I climbed to my feet and sped for the wooded path. As I ran I hazarded a glance back and saw another sight I will never forget: the old woman, still cursing and shaking her fists, the sound of her anger barely audible over the storm; and the girl, still bare-breasted, watching as I ran, her shoulders glistening in the rain.

Unsurprisingly, I kept the incident to myself, because I did not know how to explain any part of it. I probably could have told Irish. He at least would have understood the girl's allure. But Dietrich would have found it beneath reproach, and Ms Alexander—I do not like to think how it would have darkened her opinion of me. No, there was no way to inform them without disgracing myself.

I spent the rest of the evening in fear—fear that at any moment the inn doors would fly open to reveal the old woman ahead of a lynch mob. That would have been the worst possible scenario, to be accused of molestation in front of everyone, with Ms Alexander, our only multi-lingual member, forced to act as translator and arbiter.

At the same time I felt I should tell them about the idolatrous shrine hidden in the woods. I sensed it was a part of the puzzle, though I could not fit it with any other pieces. I supposed Dietrich would be able to make short work of it, or at least file the knowledge away until such a time as it became relevant. But it was too dangerous. If I described it to them they would want to investigate, and I feared that if we went back we might cross paths with the old shrew and her half-naked kin. So I kept it to myself.

In retrospect, it was probably a mistake. There is no way to be conclusive, of course, but there is the possibility that, had I confided in my friends, they would have understood and forgiven me. They also might have had some special insight, or foreseen the trouble that lay ahead.

On second thought, no. Nothing would have prepared us for what happened next.

They came for us while we slept.

I had returned to my room early after dinner. I collapsed on my bed without undressing, and it was not long past dark when I drifted off. I thought, or dreamed, that I heard a knock at my door, but my mind was so mired in sleep that I did not bother to investigate. Instead I rolled onto one side, faced away from the door, and drifted deeper into sleep. There is no way to tell how long I rested that way, but my next conscious thought was to wonder who was manhandling me. A hand as rough as sandpaper had clamped over my mouth, and strong hands had secured my arms behind my back. In this way I was lifted out of bed, shoved out of my room and down the hall.

I was too tired and surprised to think clearly. In the darkness I could not identify my captors. Given my earlier mischief, I expected they were a lynch mob. In any case, they had me, and I offered no resistance. As they maneuvered me down the stairs, however, I managed a glance back and saw many other shadows in the hall. The door across from mine—Ms Alexander's—stood open, and at that very moment I saw two men rush in. I heard a faint rustling sound, followed by her startled voice. Then there came a flash that lit the hallway, followed by a figure who half-flew backwards into the corridor, crashed against the wall, and collapsed to the floor.

The realization that Ms Alexander had just been attacked brought me to my senses. I planted my feet and pushed back against those who held me, halting our progress along the stairs. I sank my teeth into hand over my mouth, and its owner cried out in pain. The hand withdrew and I cried out.

"Help! They're here! They have me!"

The hour must not have been as late as I thought, because another door immediately swung open. Lamplight brightened the hallway, and out leapt Lieutenant Gorlov. He was still in uniform, minus his coat, and he had his saber in hand. In an instant he surveyed dark figures lined up before him and charged in.

The corridor was too narrow for wide slashing movements, so he instead thrust repeatedly as he advanced. I watched as his blade quickly pierced the torsos of two men, who groaned and collapsed where they stood. By then the other attackers—I cannot be sure how many—had begun to retreat and cry out in alarm. The lieutenant pressed his advantage. He made a charge that enabled him to run a man through to the hilt. This brave but reckless move proved his undoing. Before he expired, the skewered man pulled a pistol from his belt, pressed it against the lieutenant's chest, and fired. The fateful rounds blossomed out his back. Just like that, Lieutenant Gorlov was dead.

To this point I had managed to defeat the best efforts of the men restraining me, but now one got a foot in front of mine and gave me a shove, causing me to trip. They did this without releasing my arms, causing me to tumble forward without actually falling. In this way they hauled me downstairs. I began to scream—nothing sensible, just noise to warn the others—but my captors clubbed me over the head and all went black. The last thing I saw before passing out was another host of adversaries rushing up the stairs.

I do not think I was ever wholly unconscious. My vision gave way to darkness, but I vaguely remember noises and the rough treatment of my handlers. However I can neither recount nor make sense of anything that happened for some time thereafter.

When I finally regained my senses I thought all was well, for I was staring into the eyes of Ms Alexander. But then I knew something, or several things, were wrong. The back of my head throbbed, and I was lying face down on something rough—the road. As my vision cleared, I realized Ms Alexander was in a similar position, no more than six feet away. Her hair was mussed more than I had never seen it, and her eyes were wide and brimming with tears.

"Prometheus!" she whispered.

I was about to respond when I noticed something peculiar that robbed me of words. Suddenly, I understood why she was face down on the ground. Standing over her was a man holding pole of perhaps eight feet in length. At the end of the pole was a sort of noose, the tension of which he controlled by pulling on the slack, and the noose itself was wrapped tightly around my lady's swanlike neck. The brute was using the device to both keep her at a distance, and to pin her to the ground.

Someone barked an order in Russian. A pair of heavy boots came between us, blocking her from view, and I looked up into the bore of a rifle. I nodded and pressed my face back into the dirt. I then heard a hacking cough behind me and rolled my head to find Dietrich prostrate on my other side. As he coughed he stirred up small clouds of dust that drifted into my face. It caused me to cough, too, but with nothing compared to the violence of his fit. In fact he went on so long, becoming so red-faced and winded, that several of our captors began to gather around him to see what was the matter. Rather than do anything to alleviate his condition, one thug remedied it by rolling him on his side and kicking him in the stomach. Robbed of breath, Dietrich's coughing devolved into a quiet gasping. Our captors must have found this tolerable, because they did not harm him again.

As we lay helpless, I became aware of a dull and distant clamor. I looked in the direction of the noise and discerned the sound came from somewhere inside the inn. I heard a variety of distinguishable noises: tumbling furniture, breaking glass, cries of desperation and agony. As I craned my head upward for a better look, there came a loud shattering, followed by a man falling from a second floor window. He hit the ground near us and landed on his neck. After that he did not move.

The clamor inside continued. No one else was hurled from the windows, but whatever was happening in Irish's room, it was going badly for his adversaries. The man who had pointed the rifle in my face barked more orders. I heard boots scrambling on the road nearby, followed by another handful of men with clubs rushing inside. The din continued for several more minutes, but gradually the crashing sounds were replaced with excited and exhausted voices. Finally, no less than eight men exited bearing Irish, whom they had hog-tied.

They carried him into the road along with the rest of us and dropped him as if he were a sack of potatoes. He struck the ground hard, his chest and face absorbing the brunt of it. The sound alone made me wince. He raised his head, twisting it wildly in an attempt to find his captors. His face was a bloody mess, but he did not notice or care. He was entirely focused on a round of verbal attacks. He let fly a torrent of such violent, insulting, and horrific obscenities that I balk at repeating them here.

Even though our captors knew only Russian, Irish must have adequately conveyed his message. The man with the rifle walked over to him, inverted the weapon, and struck him in the face with the stock. There was a sickening *crack* as it struck my friend's skull. Like a dazed bull our protector shook it off and resumed his tirade. Not to be outdone, the man struck him again, with more weight behind it. The second blow met his jaw and had more effect. Again Irish shook his head to clear it, then rebelliously spat a mouthful of blood and broken teeth on his tormentor's shoes. When he resumed his invective, it was noticeably less inspired and coherent. After the third blow, which by the sound broke his jaw, Irish finally abandoned his temerity and put his face in the dirt. I watched him lying there, face down in a pool of blood—that was the moment I knew we were doomed.

Once they had us subdued, our captors were in no hurry to deal with us. They ensured we were securely trussed, placed guards over us, and stood about chatting in a most casual manner. As they did, townsfolk gathered to gawk at us. From what I saw in their faces, they were neither sympathetic nor surprised. They had been in on it.

A muffled clamor came from inside the inn as if someone was ransacking it. Eventually a man came out carrying something. He approached the one with the rifle, and they both looked at it in silence. They stood directly over me, and I could not crane my neck enough to see what so interested them. I did not have to wonder long. A moment later I heard a thud and turned my head to find myself staring into the empty lenses of a blackened miner's mask.

Eventually I heard the sound of horses. A train of wagons pulled up, and each of us was hoisted into a separate one. Dietrich and I, owing to our slight frames, were tossed in with little effort, but Ms Alexander and Irish posed more of a problem. Our captors already knew of our lady's strange defenses, and when it came time to move her, she was dragged up by her neck at the end of the noose-pole and prodded into the back of a wagon. Since no one dared ride in the back with her, her pole-bearer climbed up next to the driver and sat facing backward to ensure she remained snared and in his control.

In the case of Irish, though he was bound he still gave them pause. When the men of Véles had assaulted him, he must have put up a terrible fight. Thirteen bodies were lined up on the sidewalk in front of the inn. By my count, Ms Alexander had possibly electrocuted one to death, and the lieutenant had claimed three before he fell. Assuming the lieutenant was among them, that meant Irish had killed at least eight men with his bare hands. But soon the man in charge yelled at his men, and half a dozen came forward and lifted the giant into the back of a wagon.

Once our captors had us loaded, the wagons began the long trip to the valley of the spire. It was a painful journey, even more than it had been on foot. The wagon rocked and bounced on that rough road, and since I was face down with my hands bound behind me, my ribs took the worst beating. By the time we arrived I was all bruised and battered.

I had no way of marking our progress until rock walls rose up on either side, and we began the descent into the quarry. From my position I could not see over the wagon walls, but I imagined passing by the mines, and through the area of the grate and trough system. When the rock walls fell away, I knew we had entered the valley of the spire.

Rather than heading toward the tower, or the camp at its feet, I felt the wagon veer to the west and continue on that path for several minutes. When it reached the mountains hemming in the valley it began a steep climb, cutting back several times before we reached the top. It then followed a short path through a large stone gateway, and I realized we were being taken to the ancient castle-like structure I had seen during my reconnaissance.

The wagons stopped in the courtyard, we were hauled out, and I got a look at our surroundings. It was a simple structure, not much more than a stone wall surrounding a courtyard that contained a large building. I counted the windows (which I noticed were hollow and without glass) and determined the structure contained three levels. The doors, however, were intact and new, as evinced by the quality of the planks that composed them.

Our captors cut our feet loose and herded us toward the building. We made a foreboding procession—my guards and I in the lead; Dietrich next; Ms Alexander, throttled and forced along at the end of a pole; and Irish, a rifle pressed to his back, and four other armed men close behind.

They led us through a large door into a long room, lit by torches and lanterns along the walls, and containing simple wooden chairs and tables. The furniture and arrangement reminded me at once of a barracks, and I imagined the men of Véles resting and eating meals here. The architecture, however, suggested it had been designed for a different purpose. At the far end of the room was a stone dais, and there were cutaways spaced evenly in the walls where statues and artifacts might have once been on display. The room was unmistakably a sanctuary.

Several doors and stairways led from the room, but our captors were only interested in one. They prodded us into a pitch black doorway to our right and up a winding stair. We emerged in the hallway on the third level. Several doors lay ahead of us, and beneath one of them escaped a sliver of light. Our captors steered us toward it and pushed us inside.

The room was spacious and lavishly decorated compared to what we had so far seen. It was well lit by tall lamps standing in each corner. Curtains covered the hollow windows, and a broad oriental rug had been thrown across the floor. On one side stood a small table with two chairs, and on the other a writing desk, framed by large, well-stocked bookcases.

Our captors entered behind us and lined us up in the center of the room, keeping rifles held at the ready. The noose was removed from Ms Alexander's neck and the pole retracted. As she massaged her slender throat, the men stood back and flanked the door.

Dietrich looked left and right to take stock of us.

"Is everyone all right?" he said.

Ms Alexander and I nodded. Then as one we looked to Irish. I was unsure if he could speak. His jaw was swollen, and his face was a mess of lacerations and bruises, but among these his eyes shown clear. He met our gazes and nodded.

"What now?" I said, eyeing the guards. "Are they going to kill us?"

"I cannot say," Dietrich said as he studied them. "If so, they are in no hurry. But I think not. If they meant to kill us, they would have done so already."

As we wondered at our fate, we heard footsteps approaching. We held our breath and straightened in preparation for whatever came next. The footsteps grew louder and were accompanied by voices. Then two men walked in. The first was just another commoner, but the second captured everyone's attention. He was a distinguished-looking gentleman of respectable age, with perfectly parted hair and piercing eyes. He wore a shoddy wool coat, but beneath it dark, clean clothing that was completely out of place. He breezed in with a grin on his face as if just called from a dinner party. Upon seeing us he drew up, broadened his smile, and opened his arms as if in welcome. Half of our party recognized him immediately.

"Wende!" Dietrich exclaimed.

"So good to see you again, Herr Dietrich!" Wende replied.

"This is August Wende?" Ms Alexander gasped. "He is the man I met on the ship to Saint Petersburg!"

"Yes, it was I," Wende confirmed, devilishly stroking his chin. "I could not resist approaching you, knowing what I did of your mission, and your destination."

"What do you know of our mission?" I said haughtily.

A light came on in Dietrich's eyes.

"He knows because he is the enemy we seek," Dietrich said grimly. "He led us to Engel. Engel led us to Véles, and now we are here, at his mercy."

"Bravo!" Wende said. "You are a clever man, Herr Dietrich. I knew you would work everything out eventually."

"But Engel was a fraud," I objected. "He knew little of use, and he recalled Véles only with difficulty. How could you be certain he would guide us here?"

The same look of awful comprehension crept into Ms Alexander's expression. Wende rubbed his hands together, deriving great satisfaction as he watched us work it out.

"They were in collusion," she said quietly. "It was an act."

"We believed Engel had been excommunicated," Dietrich said gravely. "But he is still in your employ, is he not?"

"On that point you miss the mark," Wende said. "Engel is no longer affiliated with us, but he is still sworn to secrecy. If I had not contacted him before you arrived, he would have divulged nothing, for he knows the consequences would be dire."

"But if you wanted us here, why send agents against us?" Ms Alexander said. "Why involve Engel at all? Why not just direct us to Véles?"

"So many questions!" Wende said delightedly. "In order: I sent no agents against you. If you were attacked, it was at the direction of some ambitious Illuminati official, not by my direction. As for Herr Engel, I needed you to visit him to give me time to conclude my business and arrive before you. As you have guessed, you were close on my heels."

"In Lübeck," Dietrich said.

"Yes," Wende replied. "I had to pick up an item there. Fate then placed us on the same ship to Saint Petersburg, where I risked an interlude with this lovely creature. Of course I had observed her in Munich and knew her to be one of you, which is what made toying with her so irresistible."

Ms Alexander colored.

"I'm afraid my interest in you was a ruse," Wende said in mock apology. "You are exquisite, without a doubt, but your charms have no effect on me. My interest in you was pure thrill, like standing on the tracks of an approaching train. I could not help but flirt with disaster. A flaw in my character, I suppose."

"On the ship you went out of your way to show me a strange device," Ms Alexander recalled. "What was it?"

"Ah!" Wende exclaimed. "How wonderful of you to remember. That would give away too much, too soon. Let's save some surprises for later."

"Later?" I said. "You're not going to kill us?"

"Let's not get ahead of ourselves," Wende replied.

A silence followed. I looked to Dietrich, but he was too busy glaring at his nemesis, too busy seething.

"So," I said, "you are the infamous Brother Iscariot, author of *Ordo Ab Chao*, and leader of the Illuminati?"

If it was possible to improve Wende's mood, I had done it.

"Now, there is a surprise ready for revelation!" he exclaimed. "Among my brothers, I am called Brother Tantalus."

"Then who is Iscariot?" Dietrich said, finally roused.

Shuffling footsteps approached from the hall. Wende stepped aside and a moment later a man entered—an elderly gentleman hunched in his old age. The top of his head was smooth, and wisps of snowy hair stood out over his ears. He wore a trimmed beard, spectacles, and a simple tweed suit. He stopped in the doorway and smiled at us with kind eyes. We stared back in amazement.

"Allow me to introduce myself," the old man said in a German accent. "I am Doctor Franz-Jakob Drechsler, but I think you know me by another name. I am also called Brother Iscariot."

21: THE DOCTOR

Doctor Franz-Jakob Drechsler stood smiling at us in a warm, grandfatherly way. He looked so harmless and congenial, I half expected him to shake us by the hands and give each of us a nickel. Instead, he clasped his hands behind his back and looked at each of us in turn.

"This is most unexpected," he said, though he did not seem the least bit put out.

"On the contrary," Dietrich said. "It seems you were expecting us."

The little old man looked at him as if he were a child who had made a surprisingly keen observation. I half expected him to reward Dietrich with a piece of candy. He chuckled and shook his head.

"You are correct," he said. "Brother Tantalus informed me you were en route. I was referring merely to your knowledge of us. We expended much effort to keep ourselves hidden over the years. I expected our work to be complete before anyone found this place."

He paused to look each of us up and down.

"Who are you?" he asked.

We remained silent. I looked to Dietrich, and he gave me a look of warning. Doctor Drechsler chuckled.

"Ah!" he said. "I suppose I should not expect cooperation. Very well. I shall tell you what I already know."

He took a step toward us.

"You, sir, are Meyer Dietrich, the leader of this inauspicious troupe. From what Brother Tantalus tells me, you have some association with the law. I do not know your brute's name, but my men tell me he is incredibly dangerous, and looking at him I do not doubt it! As for the young lady, I do not know her identity, but I know she is singular in her propensity to emit electricity, powerful enough to kill. One of my men died from her touch. That is a remarkable ability, and one I will have to get to the bottom of, time

335

permitting."

At last his eyes fell on me. He wrinkled his brow.

"You I know nothing about," he said. "But that will change in time."

He took a moment to stand back and smile at us.

"Furthermore, I know you are from America, and it is this point that now presses on my mind. What's more, you were traveling with an officer of the Imperial Army, which is a very strange association. It makes me wonder if you are working for the Tsar. Is this the case?"

He gazed at us, awaiting a response. Again I glanced at Dietrich, who shot me a look that said to remain silent. But suddenly I had an idea.

"Yes," I answered.

Everyone in the room reacted. My companions looked at me as if I had sprouted horns. The Doctor's eyebrows almost leapt off his head.

"Incredible!" he said. "So the Tsar knows. He has found us."

I nodded, though I had no idea what he was talking about. I could feel my companions boring holes into me with their eyes. I avoided looking at them.

Doctor Drechsler lowered his head in thought and stayed that way for some time. I began to think the little old man had fallen asleep on his feet. At length he raised his head and sighed.

"Then we must strike with all haste," he said, turning to Wende. "How soon can you be ready?"

The smile Wende had thus far maintained quickly faded. Somehow the news I had invented had complicated matters for him. I took it as a personal victory.

"A few days," he said in a needlessly low voice, because we all could hear.

The Doctor frowned. Another victory, I thought.

"Begin at once," he said. "Let our man at Bogoslovsk know, and post spies to watch the trains. We must know the instant the Tsar's men arrive."

Wende nodded and quickly departed. The Doctor shook his head and stared at the ground.

"Unfortunate," he said. "But there is still a chance our work will come to fruition."

"Your work?" Dietrich asked.

The Doctor looked up at him, incredulous.

"Do you jest, Mr Dietrich?"

Dietrich, inexperienced dissembler that he was, shrugged in response. The Doctor took a moment to search all our faces again, lingering on mine. I unflinchingly returned his gaze, watching as his narrow eyes brightened in response to some internal conclusion.

"Can it be?" he said. "Could you have come all this way to find me, yet understand nothing about my work?"

His mood improved and he smiled. He went on to stroke his beard and to chuckle to himself. I wanted desperately for Dietrich to say something—anything—that would rob him of his mirth. But he just stared at him dumbly.

"Not to worry," the Doctor said. "There is still enough time to educate you. I would very much like to begin tonight, but other business demands my attention. For now, take some rest. Tomorrow will be a busy day."

The Doctor exited, leaving us to wonder what he had planned. Before we could ponder it, our captors herded us from the room and escorted us to our accommodations.

They drove us back downstairs, across the sanctuary, and into another dark doorway containing a spiral stair carved into the natural rock. We made several circles as we descended, finally emerging into a torch-lit room piled with sacks, crates, and barrels. They borrowed torches from the walls and led us to another dark doorway where we descended further into the earth. By then I had lost all bearing and sense of depth, but I knew we were deep in the mountain. As we went I tried simply to remember the way we had come.

At the bottom of the stair we entered a tunnel in which no effort had been made to provide any light. It was pitch-black, and had our captors not grabbed torches on the way down, we would have been completely blind. At the bottom of the stairs, corridors branched left and right, and here we were separated. I was forced down the passage to the left.

After a few minutes we passed in rapid succession several recesses on either side—little more than alcoves—covered with iron bars. My captors threw me into one so roughly that I bounced off the back wall. As I recovered they secured the door with a lock and chain, then departed, taking all light with them.

Once they were out of earshot I made quick work of the ropes that still bound my hands, wriggling until they loosened and slipped from my wrists. At the same time I heard footsteps approaching, and I cowered in the back of my cell to hide the fact that I had so quickly freed myself from the bonds. For this reason I did not see who they shut into the next cell. I heard another crash of iron, another chain being looped through the bars, and then they left me in darkness again. When their footsteps had faded, I pressed my face against the bars and called out.

"Hello?"

I heard a stirring and a muffled cough. I expected to hear Dietrich's voice in reply. I was thrilled to hear another.

"Prometheus!" Ms Alexander said hoarsely. "Is that you?"

"Yes!" I exclaimed. "I'm here. Everything is going to be all right. Are you hurt?"

"It's nothing I won't survive," she said. "But I cannot say the same for our friends. Mr Irish, at least, is badly hurt."

"Don't worry about him," I said. "He's hard as nails. He'll be fine. We should concentrate on finding a way out of here."

"But we must work to save them, too," she insisted.

"Of course," I hissed. "But for now we can do nothing for them. We must take strength and solace from one another, and bide our time until an opportunity presents itself."

A pause followed, but she finally came around to the logic in my plan.

"All right," she whispered back. "Though we do not have much time. They have something terrible planned, and from their talk it sounds like it will happen within days."

I crouched at the bars of my cell. In spite of the circumstances, I could not help feeling a little elated at having Ms Alexander to myself, even if we were separated by several feet of solid stone.

"Prometheus?"

"Yes?" I said eagerly.

"Are you afraid?"

"Not at all," I said, using my hands to examine the lock and chain securing the door. They would be easy to defeat, if only I had a simple tool. But my makeshift pick had been in my coat pocket, and my coat was probably still hanging on the chair in my room at the inn. Still, the lock was not complicated, and I guessed I could probably coax it open by banging it a certain way against the bars, causing the internal mechanism to release. It would be a noisy and experimental business, but it was very possible.

Then another thought began to form in my head. I was confident in my ability to escape, but I had less faith in my companions. They were not trained in these matters, nor were they particularly stealthy. Perhaps Ms Alexander, with her young, lithe form, would be able to keep pace with me, but even that was a stretch. During escape, every extra person riding my coattails would compound the likelihood of capture. When the time came, Dietrich, with his insufferable cough, and Irish, due to his sheer bulk, would be liabilities. But these were grim thoughts I was not ready to entertain.

Ms Alexander did not speak for a long time. I thought she had fallen asleep. I seated myself on the cold rock floor and leaned against the wall. I had begun to drift off when she spoke again.

"Prometheus?"

"Yes?"

"I am frightened," she confessed.

"Don't be," I said.

"I cannot help it," she said. Another pause, then: "In our journeys we have maintained a professional distance, but now I would feel better if you would call me by my name."

I held my breath. Her name held for me a forbidden yet magical quality that made me hesitate to say it aloud. To speak it had until that moment been almost taboo—a seeming necessity to maintain propriety—which made uttering it all the more thrilling.

"Of course," I said, closing my eyes and savoring every syllable. "Katherine."

"No," she said.

"No?"

"I mean, please call me Katya."

I could not believe my ears. She had invited me to use her familiar name—a name previously reserved for her closest friends and relatives. I marveled at this turn of events and tried to interpret the meaning. In the end I concluded it could only be an admission of her unspoken passion, a hint that deep down she felt just as I had since our first meeting.

"Katya," I whispered. The effect it had on me was pure elation, nothing less than rapture.

"Thank you," she whispered.

I closed my eyes and immersed myself in the moment, reliving it again and again. All fell silent, and I imagined I heard the soft sound of her breathing, as if she slept against my shoulder. Soon I drifted off, whispering it to myself.

Katya.

Katya.

Katya.

In the void of the dungeon I lost all track of time. I awoke to the sound of a key turning in the lock, and I felt as if I had only just drifted off. I wearily staggered to my feet to prepare for whatever might come next. To my relief my jailers only waved revolvers at me, motioning for me to step out. I obeyed and they guided me back along the tunnel. As we went I glanced left and right into every cell we passed, hoping to discover the exact locations of my remaining companions, but they were empty.

We reached the stairs that led up to the storeroom, and as they shoved me up them I heard an unmistakable hacking cough further down the tunnel, along a part we had not walked. In my mind I marked Dietrich's location, but Irish eluded me. If he were anywhere nearby, he did not make a sound.

I did not have long to dwell on my friends, because the guards quickly ushered me upstairs to the Doctor's study. As they pushed me into the room I noted a change. The table and chairs had been repositioned on the Oriental rug in the center of the room. Two trays rested upon the table. The first I noticed instantly, because it held two cups and a teapot, curls of steam rising from its snout. I did not identify the contents of the second until I was forcibly seated in one of the chairs. The second tray held a variety of unanticipated instruments: a few small green glass vials, a length of galvanized rubber, a glass tube roughly the size of an index finger, and what looked to be a series of needles of differing gauges. As I puzzled over them the guards took up positions immediately behind me. A moment later Doctor Drechsler entered the room, positioned his chair immediately in front of mine, and sat down so close our knees practically touched.

"Good morning," he said. "You had little time to rest. I hope you slept."

I stifled a yawn and shrugged. The Doctor watched me keenly.

"What is your name?" he asked.

I hesitated, wondering if Dietrich would approve. The Doctor shook his head.

"Surely there can be no harm in telling me your name," he said. "If you don't give me a name, what shall I call you?"

I decided there was no harm in it.

"Prometheus Grey."

His eyes flashed briefly behind his spectacles. For a moment I thought he might have heard of me.

"A pleasure to meet you, Mr Grey," he said. "Now that introductions are out of the way, I would like to have a conversation. I should inform you that the manner in which we proceed depends entirely on you."

He glanced at the two trays on the table. He reached for the teapot, filled a cup with the steaming liquid, and sipped. The fragrance began to revive me.

"We can proceed with discussion in a pleasant and gentlemanly fashion," he explained, "in which case I will offer you a cup of tea."

He replaced the teapot and reached for the second tray. He gathered the green vial, the glass tube, and a needle.

"Or," he said, affixing the needle to the glass tube to create a syringe, "if you choose not to cooperate—or to lie—there is a less civil path we can take."

I watched in horrified fascination as he completed the assembly, inserted the needle into the green vial, and filled the syringe with a clear liquid. He then held it up so I got a good look at it.

"What is it?" I asked.

"Morphine," he said quietly.

I had never been subjected to it, but I knew of its effects. Delivered subcutaneously it would render me insensible, making me more likely to talk. I hesitated, wondering if I possessed the constitution to withstand it. Then I heard Dietrich's voice in my head, chastising me for such foolishness.

"That won't be necessary," I said. "I'll take the tea."

"I am glad," the Doctor said with a smile.

He replaced the syringe on the table and poured a second cup of tea. I sipped from it and quickly felt invigorated. The Doctor leaned back in his chair.

"Let's start at the beginning," he said.

I awaited his first question, but he patiently returned my gaze. Then it occurred to me: it would be better to take him on a path of my choosing rather than let him guide me with questions. So I started at the beginning—the very beginning. I told him about my childhood, forced to tag along with my father in his desperate attempt to expand his dry goods business across the Midwest. I chose to overlook the details of my life that taught me all manners of escape, carefully detouring around the learning of skills that might

340

save my life. Instead I focused on aspects of magic and mysticism. By the time I spoke of Houdini's betrayal, unmasking me as a spiritual charlatan, the threads were woven together so seamlessly that even I almost believed this new version of my life.

The Doctor listened to it all good-naturedly, nodding and smiling at details here and there. After an hour of my rambling he placed our cups on the table and invited me for a stroll. As I arose from my chair I placed a hand on the table and palmed one of the heavier needles from the medical tray. I then fell in alongside him. Two guards accompanied us, never more than a few feet away, with pistols trained on me.

"Thank you for that intimate look into your life," he said as we descended the stairs and stepped into the courtyard. "I have heard of this Houdini before. I had no idea he was such a rascal."

"Oh, he's the worst sort," I confirmed.

"Now, I would like to hear about what brought you here," he said.

Again, I knew better than to tell him the whole truth. I chose instead to tell him half-truths, to use just enough facts to keep myself on track, but to disguise important details so he would get no useful intelligence. I told how Dietrich had rescued me from jail, and how we had collected the others. I omitted Cross, the President, and our secret commission, instead portraying Dietrich as the ringleader. I confessed we had discovered his sinister plans laid out in *Ordo Ab Chao*, and that we had set out to stop him. At mention of the book he looked wistful.

"Ah," he said. "It has been a long time since I thought about that work."

I was perplexed by his choice of words.

"A long time?" I asked. "Isn't it your plan for the Illuminati to rule the world?"

"It is the Illuminati plan," he said, "but I abandoned it years ago."

"You're not their leader?" I asked.

"Heavens, no," he said. "They are nothing more than a greedy rabble. My work has a singular and greater purpose."

This took me by surprise. I became quiet as I puzzled over it. If he was not the leader of the Illuminati, our mission truly had been pointless. I silently chastised Cross for sending us on a wild goose chase, and myself for falling for it.

The Doctor could tell I was crestfallen. He allowed me a moment to process the information before resuming his questions.

"Are there others?" he asked.

"Others?"

"Yes," he said. "Do you have an affiliation? Or is it just you and your companions?"

I decided we stood a better chance of survival if he thought we were part of a larger scheme.

"Oh, yes, there are many others," I said. "Mostly back in America."

"And the name of your organization?" the Doctor asked.

The question took me by surprise.

"Name?"

"Yes," he said. "What is it called?"

Cross had not bothered to christen us, and I had never given it any thought. To make my story believable, I felt compelled to give him something more mysterious.

"We're known as The Order," I said.

"The Order?" he said with disappointment. "That's all?"

My mind flew back to the house at Corona Park, to the weather-beaten sign above the door, and the silhouette painted on it.

"Of the Albatross," I added hastily.

"Albatross?" he repeated, his look of disappointment replaced with one of intrigue. "Fascinating! I've never heard of it."

"We're very secretive," I said.

"And your connection to the Tsar?"

"Our lady is distantly related to him," I answered truthfully.

He bowed his head in thought as we walked. We crossed the courtyard and passed through the open gate. Outside the stone walls, we came to a stop on the path that zigzagged its way down the mountain. The Doctor stood with his hands clasped behind him and appeared in deep thought. I looked out over the valley at the silver spire, and wondered at its purpose.

"You stay in the castle, correct?" I said.

"Hmm?" he said, turning slowly to face me. "It's actually an old monastery. As you can imagine, Christian monks did not enjoy much success in these parts." He had a chuckle over it and looked to me expecting the same. When I gave him nothing he went on. "Yes, I conduct my work here. Why?"

"Then what's the purpose of the tower?" I asked.

He looked at me with the same incredulous look he had given Dietrich the night before. I shrugged to show I had no idea what he expected from me. He tilted his head to one side and examined me for a time.

"You honestly don't understand, do you?" he said, shaking his head. "Your troupe, and your presence here, continues to astound me."

I looked away at the valley, wondering what I was missing.

"I will show you," he said happily. "When I am done, I will want a full account of the Order of the Albatross."

I nodded. I had no idea what else I might tell him, but I decided to worry about it later. It was less important than finding out the secrets of the tower and the rest of the operations I had witnessed.

The Doctor summoned a wagon and we climbed into it. He sat beside the driver, while my guards and I piled in the back. The wagon followed the steep path down to the valley floor and made its way among the fallen and blackened trees. The tower was only about half a mile away, and we made the journey in only a few minutes. During our ride the Doctor was silent. As we neared the edge of the camp he turned to me.

"The camp entirely supports our work," he said. "From carpentry to metal-working to chemistry, it is all done here in the shadow of," and here he winked, "*the tower.*"

We came to a halt, climbed out of the wagon, and took a path into the heart of the camp. The path was narrow, crowded on both sides by tents and shacks like an Arab market. The din of industry—mostly the hammering and grinding of metals—grew too loud for conversation.

The Doctor wove his way among the shacks to the base of the tower itself. At that proximity I noticed several peculiarities. There was no door at ground level. It lacked a foundation, nor was it set into the ground. Instead it sat wholly upon the surface, and due to its great height and narrowness it seemed to teeter above us. The scaffolding, I realized, also served to help hold it erect.

The Doctor ascended a plank that served as a ramp and clambered up into the scaffolding. It was a steep climb, and I marveled at the old man's spryness. I followed, zigzagging back and forth along the planks as we climbed higher and higher. Finally we came to a stop outside a door, or a hatch, perhaps a hundred feet above the ground. Still, we had climbed to only a third of the tower's height. The Doctor took a moment to catch his breath, then directed my attention to the camp below.

"As I said, with few exceptions all of the items we need for our work are produced here," he said proudly, pointing at the steaming tents. "The metal work, et cetera, is significant but mundane. I wager our operation over there is something you have never seen."

I glanced at the tents he indicated, from which issued many vapors.

"Those house our regenerative cooling process," he said significantly. "We achieve this through vacuum flasks, first developed by a Scot, of all people, a decade ago. We are using the process to manufacture liquid oxygen."

I nodded and feigned interest, not really understanding his chemistry jargon. The Doctor seemed to think he had made his point and now directed my attention to the rock walls circling the valley.

"The mountains here are unique," he said. "They provide us the minerals required for our work. By keeping our operation within these walls we have maintained secrecy, at least until your arrival." He touched the exterior of the tower. "You can imagine the suspicions we would raise if we had such large quantities of steel delivered."

"I witnessed your mining operation the other day," I said. "I saw the burning rock that was extracted. It certainly was not a component of steel."

The Doctor brightened.

"Ah! That makes explanation much easier. We completed mining the requisite iron a year ago. Since then, we have searched exclusively for the element you saw."

"What is it?" I asked.

The Doctor paused for effect.

"Red Mercury."

"Never heard of it," I said. "Sounds sinister."

"Indeed it is!" he exclaimed. "This valley was once green and full of life. A mishap with Red Mercury—our first attempt at harnessing it to an explosive device—destroyed everything here."

I gazed out over the burnt trees and fields of ash.

"Fortunately we were working with a very small amount, and the mountains served to contain the blast," the Doctor said. "Otherwise the devastation would have been far greater."

I shook my head in amazement.

"What can you possibly want with it?" I asked.

He raised a finger as if I had asked the pivotal question. He turned toward the tower, approached the hatch, and climbed inside. I followed, dogged by a single guard. Inside I found myself on a narrow metal stair that ascended along the outer wall, spiraling up to the top. We began to climb. Occasionally we passed small windows, like portholes on a ship, which had been cut to illuminate the way. But much of our ascent was executed in stifling heat and darkness.

As we climbed I wondered what madman had designed such a thing. As far as I could tell there was nothing more to it than a staircase to the top. At no point did I see or feel any openings along the way. This defied reason, because the diameter of the thing was huge, at least fifty feet by my reckoning, which meant *something* lay at its core.

"The theory came from a schoolteacher, believe it or not," the Doctor announced as we climbed. "A Russian gentleman by the name of Tsiolkovsky. However, the structural design is my own."

Eventually we reached the top and emerged into a small, tight chamber. It was only large enough to admit the three of us, and even then we had to crouch to accommodate walls that curved sharply inward to form a cone at the top. Into the walls were cut four small portholes for illumination, each ninety degrees from its neighbors, but together they admitted sufficient light to see that an apparatus stood in the middle of the space. It stood waist high and was sealed in a large metal cylinder with a removable glass dome on top. The Doctor opened the dome, leaned on the edge of the cylinder as if staring into a well, and invited me to do the same. As my eyes adjusted I saw an odd device made of interconnected metal rings, with a clockwork mechanism at its center.

"Our latest acquisition, courtesy of a gentleman in Kiel," he said. "A gyrocompass, for navigation."

I nodded and stifled a yawn. The climb had been too long, the spaces too cramped and hot. After all that effort I had expected more than a scientific geegaw. By then all I wanted to do was get back into the open. Three bodies crammed into that tight space seemed to suck up all the air and make the temperature soar. The Doctor noticed, too, and after mopping his brow with a handkerchief, he led us back the way we had come. When we were back outside on the scaffolding, he turned to me.

"There you have it," he said, using his handkerchief on his bald pate. "You have witnessed every aspect of our work. What do you think now?"

I wiped my brow on my sleeve and shrugged.

"It's the most insane and ridiculous contraption I have ever seen," I said matter-of-factly. "What's it supposed to do?"

He stared at me in a way that made me feel idiotic.

"It is a rocket, Mr Grey," he said.

I looked back at the thing and tried to imagine it. My vision was filled by only that part before my eyes, which was a tiny fraction of it.

"You expect this thing to fly?" I scoffed. "What on Earth could power such a thing?"

He sighed and pointed to the steam-wreathed tents below.

"Liquid oxygen," he said.

I shook my head. He continued to speak as if such words should make sense to me. I decided to let it go and focus instead on his madness.

"Okay," I said. "Suppose you somehow get this monstrosity off the ground. What's the purpose? Are you going to the moon?"

He closed his eyes and shook his head.

"No," he said patiently. "It is not meant to carry men. Its purpose is to deliver the Red Mercury."

"Deliver it where?"

"Wherever we choose," he said. "But for now, Saint Petersburg will do."

I paused to allow his plans to form before my eyes. They did not.

"What will that achieve?" I asked.

"This," he said, indicating the devastation of the valley.

His meaning slowly materialized in my mind. I was horrified as I imagined that waste of ash reproduced in the Russian capital.

"Why in God's name would you incinerate Saint Petersburg?" I finally managed.

"The empire is perilously unstable," he said. "It is ready for collapse. With the Tsar removed it will fall to anarchy, taking the rest of Europe with it. Slowly, perhaps, but inevitably."

I marveled at how casually he spoke of such things—razing a city, murdering a million souls, plunging Europe into conflict.

"But why?" I demanded.

He regarded me impassively.

"It is my calling," he replied.

We rode back to the monastery with the sun beating down on our backs. As we went I noticed the Doctor appeared more hunched than before. Though spry for his age, apparently our excursion had taken its toll. By the time we reached the gate he had either forgotten about his inquiry into the Order of the Albatross, or he no longer cared. Either was fine by me since I had no idea how I would answer questions about an imaginary organization. Once the guards had sealed me back into my cell and departed, Katya called to me.

"Prometheus, are you all right?" she whispered.

"Yes, I'm fine."

"Where did they take you? What happened?"

I recounted my stroll with the Doctor, and the revelation of his absurd and preposterous scheme. I was openly skeptical about the sanity of both, which I thought would lighten the mood. But to my chagrin she found no humor in it.

"Prometheus," she said gravely, "if the rocket works then I fear he is correct. Russia will fall. Since the death of—of Nicholas' father, Alexander— the empire has grown increasingly unstable. Nicholas struggles to keep everything under control, and to hide our troubles so we do not appear weak in the eyes of the world. But the people know the truth and are becoming restless, even rebellious. "

Her validation of the Doctor's prediction made my heart sink. But in the next moment I laughed.

"Not to worry," I said. "I've inspected this so-called rocket up close. It's enormous. There's no way it will fly."

She said nothing. I sat back against the wall and extracted the needle I had so assiduously palmed and hidden inside my cuff. As I stroked it to get a feel for its dimensions, she spoke up.

"We must stop him," she said. There was a desperate edge to her voice I had not heard before.

"Really, Katya," I said reassuringly. "There's no need to worry."

But she would not be moved on this point.

"No," she said. "We cannot let this happen. Promise me you will not let this happen!"

Her desperation affected me as powerfully as if she were clinging to my leg.

"I promise," I said.

My words quieted her for a time, and I went back to idly rolling the pilfered needle between two fingers. It would suffice as a pick. I began to think of escape. Sooner or later I would have to attempt it, but timing was everything—and the time was not yet right.

"Have you tried the lock?" she said.

"What?"

"Have you tried the lock yet?" she repeated. "You are a master of escape, are you not?"

I felt as if she had read my mind. I quickly hid the needle back in my cuff as if she might at any moment walk around the corner and catch me with it.

"Yes, I am a master of escape," I said. "But no, I have not tried the lock. I have no tools."

At the time the words came naturally, and I had no inkling why I had lied. Looking back, however, I must have realized that revealing my ability to escape would have precipitated an insistence that we do so at once, and that was out of the question. There was still so much more to learn, not the least of which were the locations and conditions of our friends. The news that I was unable to free myself, or anyone else, must have depressed her. She became quiet and we did not speak again for a long time.

I made the mistake of falling asleep again, so that when I awoke I had no sense of time. I might have slept for ten minutes or ten hours. There was no way to tell in that underworld. I awoke to the sound of approaching footsteps, and a moment later two guards had my cell open and were shoving me along the tunnel.

They again delivered me to the Doctor's study. The scene was much the same as before. A tray containing a teapot and two steaming cups sat on the table. But this time the other, more foreboding tray was absent.

The Doctor was in mid sip when we entered. He placed his cup on the table, stood, and smiled.

"Welcome back, Mr Grey," he said. "I hope you will forgive my earlier abruptness. At my age such exertion takes a lot out of me."

"Think nothing of it," I said, taking a seat and sipping from the cup prepared for me.

"But I have not forgotten our agreement," he said. "I revealed the most intimate aspects of our operation to you, and in return you owe me an account of your Order. I would like to hear it now."

The tea revived me once again. I felt agile, both physically and mentally.

"May I ask, Doctor, how old you in fact are?" I said.

He eyed me while taking another sip.

"Ninety-nine this year," he said.

"Impossible!" I exclaimed. "You don't look a day over seventy!"

And I meant every word. Judging by his appearance, and his ability to climb to the top of his rocket, his body was decades behind in decrepitude. He grinned and shrugged.

"Now and then God gives some of us more time than others, perhaps because we play a central role in some larger plan."

"I see," I said, detecting an opening. "You believe in God, then?"

"Of course!" he cried. "In my youth I was a student of divinity, after all."

"You don't say."

347

"Yes. It was not until later, after my master's death, that I began to study the sciences."

"Your master?" I inquired.

"Brother Spartacus," he replied with a nod. "Adam Weishaupt."

It took a moment for the name to sink in.

"Not the same Weishaupt who founded the Illuminati?"

"The very same," he confirmed.

"Amazing!" I cried. "How did you come to know him?"

The Doctor leaned back in his chair and gazed at me through his spectacles.

"That is a long story," he said wistfully.

No matter how long it might be, and no matter how troubled he was by the apocryphal yet enigmatic Order of the Albatross, his story was one which, once solicited, he could not resist telling. Besides, I think he might have been a touch senile, which made distracting him all the easier.

I did not learn the details of Franz-Jakob Drechsler's childhood, aside from the facts that he was born in 1809 and grew up in the town of Gotha. Instead, he began with the point mentioned above: his initial calling to become a man of the cloth.

At sixteen, Franz-Jakob was called—according to him—by none other than God Himself. It would be the first of several such callings, or Revelations, peppered throughout his lifetime (which is all the more reason to believe the man was completely insane). Prior to this calling, he had labored under the idea he would follow in his father's footsteps and become an influential banker. That changed in his final year of school when he had a vision.

It was really more of a dream than a vision, because he was asleep when it came to him, but that did not diminish its potency. It affected him no less than if he had been strolling along and had come across a burning but talkative bush. In his dream he was disembodied, a spirit floating among the clouds, looking down upon the world. As he floated, he became aware of an accompanying presence, guiding and holding him aloft. He knew it was some divine being and supposed it was an angel, because whenever he looked in its direction it shone with a blinding brightness. It was not until the being spoke to him that he realized he was accompanied by God.

"There is a great work that must be done," God said. "Many are called but few are chosen. Will you be one of the many, or the chosen?"

"I will do your great work, Lord," he replied. "What would you have me do?"

They flew on for a while until, looking down, Franz-Jakob began to recognize the terrain below as his homeland. They flew east from his hometown, and in seconds they traveled a hundred miles. When they descended he recognized the town below as Leipzig, and the school beneath them as the university.

"Go there and learn," God said. "In time you will come to know My divine plan."

In the next moment his dream became a nightmare, as God vanished and he began plummeting toward the ground. The experience was made still more nightmarish because, though certain he would soon strike the ground and perish, the ground continued to recede, trapping him in that most prolonged and dreadful moment when one anticipates his demise. When he awoke screaming and drenched with sweat, he was both relieved and terrified. As he sat in bed with his chest heaving, the relief soon faded, but the terror remained, convincing him the dream had been more than a trick of the mind. He arose that morning a different man than the night before. He had been chosen to do something great, though he knew not yet what. He had faith, however, that everything would soon be revealed.

Franz-Jakob's plan did not please his father, who, in spite of his faith, saw in Divinity little chance for upward mobility, and no lucrative opportunity. But Franz-Jakob would not be dissuaded. His father grudgingly paid the bills to sustain his divine studies.

University for Franz-Jakob was nothing remarkable. He made several acquaintances but no real friends, as he felt compelled to spend his time in his studies. He had not the slightest inkling why he must study, especially when he had spoken to God directly. If this knowledge were integral to His plan, could it not be bestowed upon him as if by magic? But alas, no one chosen by God had ever had an easy time of it, and he could find no reason why he should be any different.

His father had not entirely given up on his son. Whenever Franz-Jakob visited home, his elder would drop frequent hints that there was always a position open for him at the bank. But Franz-Jakob sidestepped them all. Finally, in desperation, his father played his final card.

"I would like you to accompany me to a meeting tomorrow night," he said after dinner one summer's eve.

Franz-Jakob deftly extricated himself by pointing out that he had a sheaf of Biblical verse to translate from Latin to German, and the task would consume his evenings for some time. His father was no fool. No matter how polite Franz-Jakob might be, the older gentleman perceived his son had no interest in financial or fraternal associations. To avoid further awkward invitations, Franz-Jakob hastily retreated to his room, leaving his father to pine over his empty chair.

As chance would have it, Franz-Jakob would have his second revelation that same night. While dueling with a particularly complicated verse, he placed his head on the desk intending to take a short break. He must have drifted off, because the next thing he knew he was standing in the center aisle of the local church, the very one he had attended as a boy. Standing before him was the most amazing creature he had ever seen—a ram as large as a horse, with six horns and six eyes.

"Do you know me?" it asked.

"Yes," Franz-Jakob replied. "You are the one true God."

"You are wise," the ram said. "I have come to deliver your next instruction."

"What is it, master?"

The ram blinked several of its many eyes.

"Honor thy father," it said simply.

Franz-Jakob considered this. As he did the ram suddenly burst into flames and was instantly consumed.

He awoke with a start. He had long awaited further direction. Now that he had received it, he knew exactly what he must do. He marched downstairs and found his father alone in the study.

"I would like to accompany you to your meeting tomorrow night," he said.

The next night Franz-Jakob set aside his studies and accompanied his father to the prescribed meeting. He was surprised, however, when en route to the bank they took a wrong turn. He did not believe for a moment that his father had lost his sense of direction, and he inquired about their true destination. His father touched him on the shoulder and smiled.

"Patience," he said.

At length they came to a large and venerable-looking house sandwiched between others of its kind. They approached the door, knocked, and were admitted by an elderly gentleman wearing a suit, a heavy gold medallion around his neck, and a decorative blue, gold-fringed apron about his waist.

"And who is this?" the old doorman asked, though the look in his eyes revealed he already knew the answer.

"This is my son," his father replied. "He is here for introductions."

The old man nodded and invited them inside. Franz-Jakob followed his father through a dark paneled foyer to a large closet, where another man stood waiting with an apron folded over one arm.

"Good to see you, Brother," he said.

"Likewise, Brother," his father replied. He took the accoutrements and donned them.

They proceeded to a large den, around which was arranged many sofas and chairs in which numerous men—most of them more than twice Franz-Jakob's age—reclined and smoked pipes and cigars. As they entered, all conversation seemed to die, and the men stood and turned to face them. His father then took him around and introduced him to them, one by one. Franz-Jakob politely greeted them one after the other, trying to hide his perplexity. He knew these men were not all in the bank's employ.

After twenty minutes of socializing, a man announced the meeting was about to begin. Franz-Jakob's father took him aside.

"You must excuse us," he said. "Make yourself comfortable. I will be back for you within the hour."

Everyone exited the room and disappeared into a deeper recess of the house, leaving Franz-Jakob alone and wondering about the point of his visit. He had expected to suffer through mind-numbingly dull discussion of interest rates, or the value of the mark compared to the franc or pound. He had never expected his father would abandon him in an empty study. Angry and confused, he sat in a chair and moped. An hour later the hallway resounded with footsteps and conversation, and the gentlemen flooded back into the room.

He spotted his father and approached him, intending to express his desire to leave at once. His father, however, was in discussion with an ancient white-haired gentleman. As he moved toward them, both men sensed his presence and turned to face him. Before he could say a word, his father spoke.

"Here is my son now," he said, extending a hand. "He is a student of divinity at Leipzig, though I hope after tonight he might expand his horizons."

Franz-Jakob forced a smile and extended a hand.

"Franz-Jakob," his father said, "allow me to introduce a very important man—Herr Adam Weishaupt."

As they walked home along dark cobblestone streets, his father was clearly pleased. He was so happy, in fact, that Franz-Jakob regretted what he was about to say.

"Father, what was the point of that? I learned nothing of banking or business. If your goal was to interest me in another trade, introducing me to a room full of your colleagues did not accomplish it."

His father looked surprised, but it did little to affect his mood.

"Son, life has taught me two things," he said. "No great work can be performed without wealth, and wealth extends beyond money. There is a larger wealth that comes from knowledge and associations. In that regard, I have given you a leg up. Tonight you met many of the wealthiest men in Bavaria, with connections throughout Europe. Their resources are vast, and if you proceed smartly, they will be at your disposal."

They walked the rest of the way home in silence, causing his father's mood to be somewhat deflated. His father probably thought he had failed, that his son's silence indicated disinterest in such affairs. But Franz-Jakob was so preoccupied with the implications of his father's revelation—and how the wealth of Europe might be put in service of God's plan for him—that his mind was racing. By the time they reached home, Franz-Jakob had come to a decision.

"Father, I see the wisdom in your words. I must learn more. I would be thankful if I could attend more of your meetings."

His father was so overwhelmed that he embraced his son on the doorstep, his tears darkening his son's shoulder.

His divinity studies abandoned, Franz-Jakob took a simple accounting position at his father's bank. He found the work extraordinarily tedious, but he gained insight into the arcane workings of finance; he learned the identities and businesses of the bank's richest patrons; and now living again in Gotha, once a week he accompanied his father to his fraternal meetings. These he found more fascinating than the rest, if only due to the power commanded by its members. Sponsored by his father he applied for membership, and after a strange but symbolic initiation involving a blindfold, blood drawn from a palm, and blasphemous oaths that weeks before would have sent him into a liturgical frenzy, he was initiated into the Illuminati under the hand of none other than Herr Weishaupt, and re-christened Brother Iscariot.

"Weishaupt's position and status were honorary," the Doctor explained. "I did not know it at the time, but the only reason he attended that particular Lodge was due to a fear for his life. Still, the members held him in high esteem. I gathered it was a great honor to have him preside over the ceremony. Thereafter we became very close in a short time, and I learned the details of his life and pursuits. Sadly, less than a year later he would be dead."

Before Weishaupt died, however, he revealed much of his life and his grand scheme. He confided how, years earlier, the Bavarian government had intercepted some of his documents, labeled the Order of Illuminati heretical and seditious, and passed a law banning its existence. Almost overnight he had become an outlaw and fugitive.

"Fearing imprisonment, or worse, he fled his homeland for the Duchy of Saxe-Gotha-Altenburg," the Doctor said. "There he found refuge in the service of none other than Duke Ernest II, which gave him sufficient political protection to continue his work."

On the topic of Weishaupt's work, the Doctor painted a fascinating, yet disturbing, landscape.

"He envisioned ensnaring the world in the same way one might cast a net over a globe. Pseudo-secret societies of the elite already existed everywhere. Weishaupt's genius was recognizing that if he could unite them, or influence them, he could effectively control the world. It was always his vision, but not because he hungered for power. Rather, he recognized Mankind is mostly made up of sheep, stupidly grazing and awaiting a shepherd. He feared that if he did not seize the opportunity to rule, someone less scrupulous would."

In addition to revealing his life's work, Weishaupt did Franz-Jakob two more unanticipated favors. First, he publicly took him under his wing. During social hour at the Lodge he would seek out Franz-Jakob, press a glass of brandy into his hands, and they would sit down in an out-of-the-way spot to discuss everything from history to philosophy to law. Franz-Jakob found him remarkably intelligent and capable of speaking on a diverse range of subjects, but the one subject for which he had little tolerance was religion.

"In this area we could not have been more opposite," the Doctor said with a chuckle. "For Herr Weishaupt, faith did not enter into the equation. Religion was another tool with which we could manipulate those who held to it. I imagine it was both humorous and perplexing to those who saw us thus engaged, the devout atheist with his arm around the former divinity student."

The second gift Weishaupt bestowed upon Franz-Jakob was his status. In the years he had been attending the Lodge at Gotha, no one had seen him take to anyone like he took to Franz-Jakob. Everyone wondered at the meaning of it. By the time of his death, the meaning was clear. On his deathbed he asked to speak to only one Brother.

"It was I," the Doctor said with a wistful smile. "He had nothing important or insightful to say. Really all I did was sit quietly with him for a few minutes holding his hand. But the import of it, to be summoned to the deathbed of the father of the Illuminati, spoke volumes. It was no less than a coronation. By the time I left his room, word had spread to every Illumined Brother in the city, and within days of that it had spread to every corner of the continent. I began receiving congratulatory letters from people I had never heard of, in languages I had not studied, from all across Europe."

In one fell swoop Franz-Jakob inherited all the powerful associations Adam Weishaupt had accumulated over a lifetime. His father could not have been more proud.

It was shortly after Weishaupt's death that Franz-Jakob had his third revelation. He had just come home from a Lodge gathering at which the post-meeting discussion had centered on the passing of Weishaupt. To take the edge from their collective grief, the Brothers had spent several hours sipping brandy and reminiscing over the loss of such an esteemed member. Oddly, Franz-Jakob had been more of a spectator than participant in those conversations, sipping from his ever-full glass as others related what they knew, or thought they knew, of the great man. He listened to them late into the night. At the conclusion they parted company and staggered home.

That night Franz-Jakob felt a great tremor in the earth and hurried outside to investigate. In the middle of the street stood an enormous figure, so enormous he feared it might step forward and crush him. It stood over fifty feet tall, and, in spite of its frightening appearance, he instinctively knew it was another Heavenly incarnation. Before him stood a beast with the head of a ram, the torso and arms of a man, and the legs and feet of a goat. It stood erect like a man, and with every shift of its mighty hooves the earth trembled.

Franz-Jakob knelt before the creature and looked up into its strange eyes.

"Do you know me, Franz-Jakob?" the creature asked.

"Yes, Lord," he replied.

"I have your next instruction," it said. "But first I will bestow upon you secret knowledge."

"I am your humble servant," Franz-Jakob said.

"I am the God of all, of the heavens and the earth, of water and fire, of life, death, and judgment. I am known everywhere and by many names. As you see me now I am called Baphomet. Does this form displease you?"

Franz-Jakob glanced up at the horrible beast, hesitating only for a second.

"No, master."

"You are wise," Baphomet replied. "Such wisdom deserves reward. I have already transferred to you Adam Weishaupt's power. Now you must further prepare yourself, and the world, for my will."

"Thy will be done," Franz-Jakob replied.

"Study in the ways of science," Baphomet said.

"Science?" Franz-Jakob repeated.

"Yes," Baphomet replied. "As you tower above insects, I tower above you, but one thousand times more. From your position you see only what is before you. From my height I see all, from the beginning to the end, and the end is near. Science will make this possible, and you will make it come to pass. You will be my herald, the usher of the apocalypse, preparing the world for my glorious arrival."

Franz-Jakob felt a chill at these words.

"The apocalypse?"

"Yes," Baphomet proclaimed. "For the world to end, I must be present. In this you will be as instrumental as was Judas to Christ. Do you think, Brother Iscariot, your namesake was not part of my plan? Do you think for his self-sacrifice I forsook him? Have no fear, Franz-Jakob. I will remember you always for your service. I will reserve a special place for you in my kingdom."

Franz-Jakob obediently bowed his head.

"I will do as you say."

When he again opened his eyes it was morning. From where he lay he could see out his bedroom window. The sky was blanketed by storm clouds, and the house trembled from nearby thunder.

In 1833 Franz-Jakob returned to university to study science. Since his instruction had been vague, he was unsure of what field to pursue. He finally settled on physics and chemistry because they seemed most likely to yield apocalyptic results. But try as he might he was not at heart a scientist. He could not envision himself discovering or theorizing anything that would change the world, much less end it. He learned a few interesting facts about explosives and corrosives, but ultimately the subject was too sterile. After his second year he abandoned physics and chemistry for biology and medicine. He spent the next two years either buried in books, crushing herbs with a mortar and pestle, or disassembling the freshly departed dregs of society.

When it came to biology he discovered that he enjoyed the thrill of dissection, of exploring dark innards, poking and prodding at things not meant to be seen. The high point of his studies was the time he performed, albeit illegally, a vivisection. The patient, or victim, was a drunk who had lain in a nearby street until a carriage sped by and clipped his skull, crushing a good portion of it. The poor soul miraculously survived, though he was insensible. When the man was delivered to the university, Franz-Jakob happened to be the only medical student on hand. He assured the police the man would soon die, and he dismissed them with the promise he would summon a priest and see the remains properly disposed. After they left, he sealed himself up with the lingering wretch and methodically disassembled him, all the while taking great care to keep him alive as long as possible.

Such excitement notwithstanding, he had no interest in healing and knew he was not meant to become a medical practitioner. He abandoned university in 1837 and returned to his father's bank. His father had passed away a year before, but the patina Weishaupt left upon him impressed the bank's managers. Though he had been away four years, upon his return the officers sagely placed him in charge of investments, where he used his fraternal status to earn the bank—and himself—immense wealth.

"For forty years I lost my way," the Doctor admitted. "Or so I thought. I abandoned science and devoted myself to building a fortune, and I excelled at it. Over time I thought less and less about my revelations, the apocalypse, and my role in it all. Eventually, like an adult who looks back on his childhood belief in Father Christmas, it became inconceivable to me that I had ever believed such things to be true."

During that time, however, he never totally abandoned science, or the Illuminati. He remained an amateur, a scientific enthusiast, and stayed abreast of scientific achievements, clipping them from newspapers or trade journals. He would slip the articles into an envelope and place them in a desk drawer for future reference. Somehow this little habit made him feel as if his years at school had not gone to waste.

As for the Illuminati, he could never abandon them. Too many people around the world looked to him for guidance; so many, in fact, that his free time was filled with correspondence, essays, et cetera, to distant Brothers he would never meet face to face. He was so consumed with his business and his work that he never married, or even considered it. He judged his life to be complete all the same, because without his Illumined disciples and their influential acquaintances, his fortune would have been a fraction of what it became.

"I became a millionaire," he said wistfully. "Without realizing it I had replaced Baphomet with Mammon."

If he ever wondered what a normal family life might be like, such fancies evaporated when he met August Wende.

Franz-Jakob—by that point in his life referred to almost exclusively as Doctor Drechsler, in spite of the fact that he never earned the title—met Wende at a lodge meeting in 1881. One night during the social hour the Doctor looked up to find a saturnine man sitting alone and scrutinizing the crowd. He was handsome in his way, even charismatic, though no one else took notice of him. His invisibility appeared to amuse him, and he smirked to himself as he languidly smoked a cigarette. When he smiled there was a slyness in his eyes that hinted at dark ambition in his heart. Until that moment the Doctor had never considered taking a protégé, but suddenly the idea struck him as an overdue imperative.

"Long did I watch him through the crowd, and he was completely unaware," Doctor Drechsler said. "My eyes were drawn to him like a work of art. I did not understand why I found him so compelling, but I would soon come to realize it was his nascent exuberance, his aura. He burned with an inner fire, and it singled him out from the others who, like me, had become wealthy, old, and complacent."

He introduced himself to Wende that evening, but he left it at that. He did not take Wende under his wing just yet. Even though he knew in his heart Wende possessed the spark to re-ignite their collective ambition, he could not rush into naming an heir, as it were, especially if the man were to inherit his status and control of the brotherhood.

"I was seventy-two at the time and had no idea how many years I had left," he said. "I knew it was time I took a protégé, but I had to proceed carefully else risk losing the faith of my brothers."

So, just as Weishaupt had courted him, the Doctor spent more and more time with Wende at their weekly meetings, and learned much about the fire burning in him.

The Doctor learned that Wende descended from royalty, that he was the illegitimate result of an infidelity committed by Duke Ernst I, of Saxe-Coburg-Gotha. Circa 1840, the good Duke had sewn his final seed in a common woman who foolishly thought succumbing to him would help her climb the social ladder. The joke, however, was on her, because he died shortly thereafter, leaving her with child. August Wende was born in 1841, a descendant of royalty he would never know, and which would never recognize him.

Wende grew up as a commoner, though all his life he knew he was different—better—than the rest. But since he was a bastard and his mother a chambermaid, he could not reconcile his suspicions with reality. It was not until 1859, when he was eighteen years old, that he learned the truth. His mother was on her deathbed and finally revealed everything: the identity of his father; that semi-royal blood ran in his veins; that he had two half-brothers who enjoyed lives of privilege; and that he had as much right to those privileges as they. Then she died.

Wende left his mother's bedside a changed man. He grieved over the loss, but at the same time he felt liberated by the truth. He also felt compelled to reach out to his pseudo-siblings. Since they were the only family he had left in the world, he wrote to them. One of them, named Ernst after his philandering father, had inherited his namesake's title as Duke of Saxe-Coburg-Gotha. From Ernst he received a skeptical missive that nonetheless wished him well in life. Crestfallen, he picked up pen and paper and tried again with his only remaining relative, Albert.

"None other than Queen Victoria's husband, Prince Consort of the United Kingdom," the Doctor said, shaking his head. "August believed that his letter would never reach the prince, and if it did, he believed it would be dismissed as a hoax. But this time he was mistaken. The potential for scandal and embarrassment to the Royal Family carried his letter right to the top, into the Prince's very hands."

One would then expect a reply, or perhaps an invitation, to discuss their tenuous familial bond. Instead the Prince sent some men round to visit him. As Wende was entering his apartment one evening, four men stepped suddenly up behind him, ushered him roughly inside, and threw him into a chair for interrogation. Judging by their treatment and their insulting questions, Wende knew he would neither be meeting Albert nor further corresponding with him. And at the end of the interview his hunch proved correct. Before departing, those fine gentlemen explained that if he continued to harass the Prince, or anyone else in the Royal Family, he would be dealt with harshly.

"This, it turned out, was the secret fire in him," the Doctor explained. "His ambition was fueled by the insult received from his half-brothers, and his desire for retribution. Spurned by one brother and threatened by the other, he thereafter harbored a sincere disdain for them, and for royalty in general. Toppling such regimes became his life's work."

Since Albert had roused his ire, Wende began laying plans for the Prince's demise. He took a small apartment in London and found work in the office of a chemist, not far from Buckingham Palace. During his off hours he would pick an inconspicuous spot near the palace gate and mark the comings and goings of the staff. Of these he identified several young men such as himself, whom he thought he might turn to his purpose. He pursued each in turn, and due to a misinterpretation on his part was rejected by most. Finally he hit the mark with a young man who worked in the kitchen, a servant who, in spite of his comparatively fortunate position over the rest of London's dregs, nonetheless seethed at the thought of spending his life in service to those who ruled only by virtue of birth. Once this key discovery had been made, the rest was simple.

Wende, though untutored in diabolical machinations, possessed a mind predisposed to Machiavellian scheming. He courted the kitchen-boy, earned his trust and his love, and nurtured his resentment. Within six weeks the boy was ready to do Wende's sinister bidding.

"Though brilliant, August was still a novice," the Doctor said. "He used his position in the chemist's office to acquire arsenic, which, if the Royal Family had been the least bit suspicious, could easily have been detected. But luck favored August. He instructed his companion to introduce it to the Prince's food. As mere kitchen help, however, the boy was unable to routinely get near the Prince's meals, so the poisoning process was prolonged."

For two years Wende manipulated the lad, bedding him and whispering empty promises into his ear. And for two years the boy continued to pepper the Prince's meals whenever given the opportunity. The result was a long and painful decline for the Prince that delighted Wende. When the Prince was misdiagnosed by the royal physician as having typhus, and finally died in the winter of 1861, Wende's mission was finally complete. He concluded his scheme by cutting his lover's throat while he slept, and catching the next train back to Gotha.

"This was the résumé August boldly presented at our first meeting," the Doctor said. "Or at least part of it. He told me of many other wicked deeds he had committed over the years, but I will not waste time on those. I will say only that he enjoyed a prolific career of subversion even before he found us."

Wende discovered the Illuminati after many years of searching. Through his dark dealings he had encountered numerous secret societies, so he of course had heard of the Illuminati. And when he came across one of the Doctor's writings—none other than *Ordo Ab Chao*—he knew he had found a brotherhood that fit with his ambitions. All he needed was to find and convince them to accept him. That, however, proved more difficult than expected.

"It took August more than a decade to find us. During that time he traveled much of Europe, living as a professional assassin—poisons became his specialty, you know—ferreting out lodges, Masonic and otherwise, until he happened upon the one true lodge—ours—that fateful night."

Shortly thereafter he was inducted into the Illuminati as Brother Tantalus. The Doctor chose the name for him because Wende possessed the mad desire to carve up the world to suit his purposes, the same way his mythic namesake dismembered his son and served him to the gods.

"August's arrival marked the beginning of a new era," the Doctor said significantly. "For the Illuminati, and especially for me."

Forty-four years had passed since the Doctor's last revelation, and since then his faith had cooled. But the arrival of August Wende was like a breath of air on the embers of a dying fire. Whereas the senior members of the Illuminati were content to bask in their wealth, Wende's vision resurrected the Doctor's desire to do something truly noteworthy, to reshape the world. Wende had his own ideas, namely to destroy the undeserving royalty of Europe. This excited the Doctor, and he would have thrown his weight behind it, if not for two timely coincidences.

First, the brotherhood objected. Over the last century they had insinuated themselves into the existing governmental apparatus like tapeworms in a dog. Their continued and ever-growing wealth was symbiotically linked to the health of the very organism they claimed to detest. When pressed to attack the host, they sided with it rather than the Doctor and his upstart protégé. This, it turned out, was the beginning of the end of the Illuminati as the world understood them.

Second, and most significantly, the Doctor's spiritual rekindling was followed by his fourth revelation. He found himself standing in a broad basin blanketed in fog, overlooked by grey mountains and sky. Looking up he discovered he stood once again before Baphomet, half-shrouded in the mist.

"Do you remember me, Franz-Jakob?" Baphomet said, gazing down at him. The creature almost seemed to hover above the fog.

The Doctor knelt before it and lowered his head.

"Yes, my Lord."

Baphomet regarded him for a long time in silence.

"Why do you not look upon me?" it asked.

"Because I am ashamed," the Doctor confessed. "Many years have passed since I stood before you. In that time I lost faith and abandoned you. I have failed you and proven myself unworthy."

The great beast made a guttural sound akin to a chuckle.

"Franz-Jakob, did I not tell you at our last meeting that I see all ends? Nothing you have done was unforeseen. On the contrary, you have proven yourself worthy at every step."

In spite of the praise, the Doctor could not bring himself to look up.

"How can that be," he said, "when I stopped serving your purpose long ago, and served only my own?"

"You have never ceased to serve me, no matter what you might think," Baphomet replied, with all the warmth of a loving parent. "Do you not see how the threads will now be woven together?"

The Doctor thought for a moment.

"No, Lord," he said.

"Then I will enlighten you," Baphomet said. "I commanded that you should honor your father, and you obeyed. He led you to the Illumined Brotherhood. The brotherhood earned you status, and you became exceedingly wealthy. I commanded that you should learn science. You pursued all disciplines, gaining a wealth of knowledge that will be required for the coming apocalypse. With your limited understanding you have done everything I asked, Franz-Jakob. Why, then, should I be displeased?"

Still the Doctor hesitated, his eyes affixed on the ground. In spite of Baphomet's words, his shame was simply too great.

"I know you better than you know yourself," Baphomet said. "And knowing your mind I led unto you August Wende, to revive your belief and conviction in the grand scheme, and in the work ahead."

Hearing this, the Doctor half raised his head.

"And now I have come to bestow upon you another revelation."

As Baphomet spoke, the Doctor heard a stirring in the mist, as if something were sliding across the earth. But whatever moved was hidden from sight.

"What is your instruction, Lord?" the Doctor asked humbly.

"My final word to you is this," the beast replied. The stirring in the mist grew louder. "I told you long ago I am known by many names. Now I reveal unto you another, a name so ancient and secret that few remember it. It is this name that will lead you to your destiny, to a place where you must delve to accomplish our great work. Raise your eyes now, Franz-Jakob, and look upon your god."

The Doctor raised his chin and opened his eyes to find the creature hovering before him. The great beast emerged from the mist and grew to a still greater height. As it reared before him, the Doctor realized for the first time it had changed in appearance. From the waist down it now appeared as a giant serpent, its mighty coils grating against the rock as it slithered over the earth. Once it reached its full height and stood swaying above him, the beast spoke.

"I am Véles, god of the underworld and lord of death," it said. "Go now and prepare the world for my coming."

Given these clues, the Doctor thought ushering in the apocalypse would be a simple matter, and that Véles himself (or whatever the god preferred to be called next) would arrive in short order. But when his inquiries about Véles earned him only shrugs, baffled looks, and dead ends, it quickly became apparent his faith would continue to be tested.

The Doctor began with old-fashioned research and investigation. Supported by his immense wealth and Wende's unswerving dedication, the two spent the next several years scouring the libraries of Europe's most venerable institutions, and picking the brains of the most wizened scholars. However, they could find no trace of a place called Véles. It was as if the place did not exist, or every reference to it had been burned, and everyone in the world had been sworn to secrecy.

Finally in 1898, out of desperation he dispatched Wende to Russia to seek out the place. Wende succeeded, but only after three years of hunting and questioning. He began in Saint Petersburg and worked his way east, seeking out every academic and old-timer who might possess some hint. Still he found no clues. It was not until he reached Ekaterinburg in 1901 that fortune favored him. As he sat in the train station awaiting the next train, a wretched-looking and malodorous priest happened to sit near him. Repulsed, he was about to move to another location when the holy man grabbed him by the wrist and smiled.

"I have a story that will amaze you," the priest said.

Wende grimaced at the contact. His thoughts leapt to the vial of Prussic acid in his vest pocket, and how he might acquaint the dirty priest with it. But before he could express his disinterest or physically disengage, the priest launched into his tale.

Wende only pretended to listen to most of it. He spent most of his time glancing around for a means of escape, and cringing at the uncommon strength and dirty fingernails of the hand that so firmly held him in place. It was not until the priest uttered the final sentence of his yarn that Wende finally paid attention.

"They told me I had trespassed on the village of Véles," the priest said, "and that no man of God who cared for his life should ever go there."

Wende was thunderstruck. He could not believe what he had just heard. Before he could speak, the priest suddenly released him, stood, and began to walk away.

"Wait!" Wende cried. "This place—Véles—where is it?"

The priest looked back at him as if bored. He regarded Wende for a moment, scratched his crotch, and shrugged.

"Bogoslovsk, then west," he said.

The priest then turned and disappeared into the crowd.

When the telegraph arrived bearing the simple message "Ekaterinburg," the Doctor made travel arrangements for a train the very next day. Ten days later he arrived, embraced Wende like the prodigal son, and the two boarded another train for a small industrial town to the north called Bogoslovsk. From there they hired a wagon west and arrived in Véles by nightfall.

For the Doctor it was like a visit to the Holy Land. Finally he had discovered the place his god had intended him to find. Wende escorted him through the town, and he smiled and warmly greeted all who passed. The people looked at him strangely, but when he explained he was a follower of their ancient pagan god they welcomed him. And when Wende led him down a lonely forest lane that opened into a clearing, occupied by a single hill, atop which stood an ancient stone statue of a creature—half-ram, half-serpent—the Doctor fell to his knees and wept.

"It was as if a burden had been lifted from me," he explained. "No matter how strong one's faith, when a god appears and speaks, you cannot help but wonder if you are going mad. In that moment I knew for certain I was sane, and my resolve became like iron."

The locals showed him their mining operations. Recalling Véles's command to *delve for truth*, the Doctor instinctively knew the answer lay hidden under the earth. He used his fortune to improve their equipment, and they doubled their output. It was this investment in industry that led to the unearthing of Red Mercury. Upon discovering the strange element and witnessing its volatility, he set about experimenting with it. When his first test resulted in the destruction of the valley, he understood Red Mercury was the key to the apocalypse Véles had prophesied. Once he understood its power, the rest fell into place: he needed a device that would enable him to detonate the element from a great distance. His scientific knowledge suggested guided rocketry was the solution, but no one had yet attempted such a feat. Using his vast resources he began to collect and refine the knowledge and equipment that would make it possible.

"By the summer of 1905 we were in full swing," the Doctor explained. "Three years later, here we are, ready to finally complete our work. And here you are, just in time to witness it. How fascinating that everything should be so perfectly timed. Truly, we all play roles in Véles' grand design!"

"Really?" I said, raising an eyebrow. "How do my companions and I fit into all this?"

The Doctor's mirth over the mysterious workings of Véles flickered for a moment, but then he bounced back.

"I honestly do not know," he said brightly. "But I am eager to find out, as you must be."

As I stared dubiously at him, the door to his chamber opened and Wende stepped in.

"Is this one cooperating?" he asked with a wicked grin.

"Yes," the Doctor replied. "We have been having a very agreeable conversation. Mr Grey makes a wonderful audience."

"Audience?" Wende said. He looked between the Doctor and me. "Has he told you anything about his Order?"

Here the Doctor looked confused for a moment, and his smile faded. Slowly his expression became one of embarrassment and anger. He shook his head, realizing his folly.

Wende sighed and nodded to the guards, who roughly seized me from the chair and shoved me out of the room. As I went through the door I looked back to see the Doctor hanging his head in senile shame, and Wende with a reassuring hand on his shoulder.

"It is all right," he said soothingly. "He is a clever one. Next time we shall try a different tack."

22: THE GRAND DUCHESS

After my chat with Doctor Drechsler I was thrown back into my cell, presumably so the doddering old fool could gather his wits for my next interrogation. But even as the guards hurled me to the floor of my cell I chuckled over my victory, amused that I had so easily avoided the decrepit villain's questions. The guards' steps had barely faded before Katya was pressed against the bars of her cell.

"Prometheus, are you all right? What happened?"

I gleefully recounted the scene for her, displaying both my wit and the Doctor's lack thereof. Perhaps I was too jovial in the retelling. At the end I did not receive the praise I had expected.

"I am glad you are well, and that you outsmarted him," she said. "But you sound almost as if you are enjoying this."

"Don't be silly," I said. "This is serious business. Still, I can't help but be amused by every aspect of this operation. Granted, I learned much about the Doctor and Wende today. They are menaces, to be sure. But with each passing day I gain confidence in our ability to emerge triumphant."

As I spoke I felt in my cuff to ensure the needle was still concealed there. It was safe and sound. As if on cue, Katya suddenly changed the subject.

"I am glad to hear such optimism," she said. "We must get out and warn Nicholas as soon as possible. Have you had any success with the lock to your cell?"

"Not yet," I said, leaning against the wall and pondering it. She was correct. If I, or we, were going to make a break for it, we would have to do it soon. While I was confident I could distract the Doctor, I was much less confident that I could toy with Wende. And after my last tea-time interrogation, I had the feeling Wende would get involved in my next session. The thought gave me pause.

"You must keep at it," Katya insisted. "Please, keep at it."

"Absolutely," I said, idly running my fingers over the rust-covered lock.

She must have thought I had devoted my attention to it because she did not speak further. Instead I heard her moving in her cell as if pacing. Eventually I heard the rustle of her skirts as she seated herself on the floor and became quiet. I did the same, propped against the wall by the door, staring into the darkness and wondering when I should make my move. The timing did not yet feel right.

I awoke with a start to the sound of metal grating on metal. I had fallen asleep by the door, and when I heard the metallic sounds I jumped. I expected rough hands to drag me from my cell, but it was not my cell that had been opened. I heard a scuffling of feet in the corridor, and pressing my face to the bars I saw two guards standing back before the open door to Katya's cell. This time they did not attempt to lasso her with the noose-on-a-stick. Instead, they stood back from her by several arm lengths, and with pistols motioned her out. As she emerged they backed away to keep their distance, then motioned for her to proceed down the corridor.

"No!" I gasped. "Katya!"

If she heard me she did not reply. She continued to bravely march toward her fate.

I was beside myself. I began pacing and biting my nails with worry. Within minutes I had convinced myself that now was the time to escape my cell after all. I produced the needle and had the lock open in seconds, closing the door behind me in hope that my absence would go unnoticed.

After my earlier visits to the Doctor's office, I had no difficulty finding it again. The only challenge was passing through the monastery's common areas unnoticed. This was only difficult when I encountered the sanctuary, which was occupied by two men drinking at a water barrel. But I only had to wait a few minutes before they departed. I then passed through the room unthreatened and quickly came to the Doctor's door.

The door was closed, but upon close inspection I discovered it contained a rather large keyhole through which I could see an appreciable swath of the room.

The scene was similar to what I had experienced. The Doctor sat in his chair opposite Katya, flanked by his pistol-wielding minions. The tea table separated them and bore two silver trays, one promising hospitality, the other torture. But something struck me as different. It was not until I noticed Katya flexing a delicate wrist that I understood. The Doctor was sitting perilously close to her, so close in fact that all she needed do was reach out and give him the shock of his life. In anticipation of this he had arranged for her to be bound to the chair, with lengths of heavy rope around her wrists and ankles.

I could not help but rile at the rough treatment of so fine a creature. But before I could dwell on it further, I caught wind of their conversation and bent all my will toward hearing it.

"Herr Doctor, neither your tea nor your drug concerns me," Katya said defiantly. "I do not intend to cooperate with the enemy of Mankind."

I expected to see the Doctor cringe at such withering words. To my surprise and horror, he nodded and smiled.

"From you, my dear, I expected as much," he said quietly.

From within his coat he produced a pair of long rubber gloves, so long they almost reached his elbows. Once he had wiggled his hands into them, he carefully maneuvered the syringe between his thick fingers, fired a thread of quicksilver into the air, and then plunged the needle into Katya's slender arm. The suddenness of it surprised Katya, and in spite of her defiance a small squeal escaped her. Watching, I felt mildly nauseated by the haste and recklessness of it.

The Doctor withdrew the needle and sat back to observe the effects. In less than a minute Katya began to descend into somnolence. I watched as her eyelids grew heavy and her chin drooped toward her breast. Satisfied, the Doctor nodded to the guards, who rapidly began to advance toward me.

Since they had remained during my interrogations, I had not considered they might be dismissed now. I urgently backed away from the door and fled in search of a place to hide. Fortunately for me this level must have been almost exclusively used by the Doctor, because there was no other traffic in the corridor. I ran down the hall to the next room and opened the door. It was a reckless move, but given the circumstances I had no choice. I had to attempt to hide or I would be caught. If bursting into an unknown room resulted in capture, my situation would be no different.

I entered and was relieved to find it empty. Since I was preoccupied with avoiding the Doctor's men, I paid little heed to my surroundings. But vaguely I recollected seeing some strange furnishings: a high table, several cabinets containing multi-colored bottles, and a variety of strange gleaming tools hanging from hooks on the wall. Before I could give it any thought, the guards descended the stairs, and I hurried back to the Doctor's keyhole.

The Doctor sat in silence studying Katya, gauging the effects of the drug on her. When he seemed satisfied, he blinked slowly and spoke.

"Let's start at the beginning," he said. "What is your name?"

Katya looked up and attempted to focus.

"Ekaterine," she said, her native accent becoming more pronounced.

"Ekaterine?" the Doctor prompted.

Katya's chin again fell to her breast, but a moment later she straightened and leveled her distant eyes.

"Ekaterine Alexandrovna Romanov," she said.

Since I had known her only as Katherine Alexander, I was slightly surprised to hear her claim a different name. Otherwise it had no effect on me. But I noted a distinct change in the Doctor's face. His smile faded and his brow furrowed. He leaned forward in his chair to study her more closely.

"Ekaterine Alexandrovna Romanov?" he repeated. "This must be coincidence. You cannot be so closely related to the Tsar."

Katya's eyes closed. She nodded almost imperceptibly.

"My brother."

I could not believe my ears, nor could the Doctor believe his. His expression grew more troubled still, and he leaned further out from his chair.

"Impossible," he scoffed. "There is no Ekaterine among the royal family."

The hint of a dreamy smile crossed Katya's face.

"I am … a secret," she said. "I have hidden all my life."

The Doctor's self-assured smile flickered. He stared at her in silence, looking as if he might fall from the edge of his chair. I too was so fascinated by the words spilling from those perfect lips. I pressed my face against the lock.

"Really?" he said. "Tell me more."

What follows is the account I heard through the door. Given Katya's drugged state I cannot vouch for its veracity. Who can definitively say she was not lost in some morphine-dream, that the whole tale was not a fiction? For my part, however, once I heard her confess her identity, everything about her made sense, and I knew it to be true: she was a genuine Russian princess, a young woman who was nothing less than a Grand Duchess of the Empire.

Ekaterine, or Katya, was born in 1885, the final child of Tsar Alexander III and Maria Feodorovna. It was a dangerous period for the Russian Royal Family (though in retrospect their whole dynasty was plagued with tragedy). Four years earlier, Katya's grandfather, Alexander II, had died in a bomb blast engineered by revolutionaries, and only four years into her father's reign he had already narrowly survived more than a dozen assassination attempts. So when the devout husband and family man heard of his wife's unexpected pregnancy, he was both joyous and vexed. He had already relocated his family from the Winter Palace in Saint Petersburg to the one at Gatchina—a home that more resembled a fort than a royal palace—specifically to offer more protection. But the child in Maria's womb made her more precious still. While the Russian people loved the Tsarina—more than the Tsar, in fact—in the primal darkness of Alexander's mind he could imagine how tempting it might be to a maniacal dissident to pre-empt the birth of another Romanov.

"Please, let's keep this one secret, and you stay out of the public eye," he said. While it came as a request, he spoke with a firmness that told Maria it was not open to debate. "I could not bear to lose you or any child, not even the one you carry now. For the next nine months, let's keep you safe within these walls, and the news to ourselves."

In spite of the expansive palace and grounds of Gatchina—the palace contained no less than nine hundred rooms and was surrounded by ramparts, moats, sentry boxes and barriers—Maria did not see how she could possibly remain hidden for nine months, nor how her pregnancy could be hidden from the people. But Alexander, who on matters of family and security could be as mentally immovable as he was physically indomitable, would not budge. So Maria surrendered to his will and prepared herself for a long stint at home.

The first six months passed slowly and the pregnancy proceeded normally. In fact, Maria found being relieved of noble expectations rather refreshing. Surrounded by her five surviving children, and accompanied by her soon to be sixth, she could not complain. But in her seventh month something went amiss, and she began to experience erratic and inexplicable seizures. This greatly concerned Alexander, and he was graver still when her fits confounded the family physician. Unable to diagnose the cause, the doctor fell back upon the reactionary advice of his trade and confined her to bed for the remainder of the pregnancy. Bed rest did nothing to abate the seizures, but as the doctor explained, at least in bed there was no need to worry about Maria falling and injuring herself or the child.

Aside from seizures, the pregnancy went without incident. But Katya's birth was complicated. While extracting her from the womb, the doctor's hands went inexplicably numb, and a servant had to take over under his direction. Together they managed to bring Katya into this world and place her in her mother's waiting arms. When a few minutes later Maria felt as if she might be having another seizure, Alexander proudly seized is new daughter. But he, too, became strangely afflicted. After a few minutes his arms began to tingle. He almost dropped her before hastily passing her to a servant, who wisely swaddled her and placed her in a basinet. When the doctor at first observed this phenomenon, he thought nothing of it. But when, after treating Maria and returning to the child, he received a mild jolt, he knew something was amiss.

"The child continues to shock me," he said. At first this unnaturally recurring charge disturbed him, but as far as he could tell Katya was fine and quite peaceful for a newborn. To be sure she was well, he stayed with her late into the night, every half hour or so checking her, and every time receiving a shock. After perhaps thirty of these incidents, and seeing no distress in the child, he finally pieced it together.

"I think the empress's seizures will not return," he said.

"Really?" Alexander asked eagerly. "Why?"

"Because I am almost certain they were caused by the child," he said. "Your daughter has a propensity I cannot explain. The child has the unnatural ability to generate electricity, rather like an eel. It was the development of this ability in the womb, the expression of electricity, that affected the mother."

The doctor was correct. Maria experienced no further seizures, and Katya seemed no worse for the electricity her tiny body produced.

Still, the problem was neither easily dismissed nor resolved. Before the doctor had packed his bag and left the room, Alexander and Maria, possessing the foresight of royalty, recognized the complexities of the situation. They had a new daughter whom they loved, but who would be impossible to reveal to the world for fear she would be seen as a freak. It was fortuitous they had chosen to keep the pregnancy secret. The controversy it would create for the Royal Family, and the spectacle for which Katya would be taken, were reason enough to keep her hidden from the public, at least for a time. But Alexander, the stalwart family man, took it one inconceivable step further.

"The children must not know," he said.

Maria looked at him confused.

"Our children?" she said incredulously.

Alexander nodded.

"The older ones can keep a secret," he said. "Nicholas at least we can confide in, and George. But the rest should not be told."

Maria almost laughed.

"How on earth do you expect to hide it from them?"

Alexander glanced at her and looked away. There was something in his manner that Maria found disconcerting.

"What are you thinking?" she said hesitantly.

Alexander motioned to the nursemaid and servants.

"Move the nursery to the furthest corner," he said. "And move your quarters as well. You will need to be close to her."

With his last words he looked down at little Katya and leaned upon her basinet.

"Alex, what are you doing?" Maria demanded.

Alexander closed his eyes and hung his head over his daughter.

"I will not deprive the children of their new sister," he said. "We will tell them Ekaterine has arrived. But we will say she is ill and must be kept separate from them for a while. In time we will come up with a solution, or, God willing, perhaps the situation will resolve itself."

"You cannot be serious!" Maria protested. "You would banish your own daughter to obscurity in another wing of the house?"

"We must keep everything about her secret for now," he explained. "Until we can think of a better way to proceed, this is how it must be."

Maria's protests failed to move him on the matter. He explained that she would be able to visit Katya at will, that he was not attempting to separate the mother and child. He even agreed to allow Nicholas to visit the nursery. But he drew the line there for the time being. In the end Maria surrendered to his will and grudgingly agreed to adhere to his absurd plan.

For the first years of her life Katya was a challenge to care for. Quickly the servants discovered that if she shocked someone, it would take her little body a few minutes to recharge. So they devised a system to fairly determine whose turn it was to touch her and draw off the charge. That person would then touch her tiny hand and jump back while the others would swoop in for the requisite diaper changing, bathing, clothing, or feeding. This became the practice even when the parents visited. If Maria or Alexander wanted to hold their daughter, a willing servant first took the brunt of it.

Due to her remote nursery and the procedures required to be near her, Katya knew only her father, mother, and a handful of servants for the first two years of her life. As Alexander promised, Nicholas and George were taken into the fold and informed of their sister's strange condition. They too visited the nursery, but with less frequency. Both boys were by then in their late teens and too preoccupied with studies and girls to take much notice of a new sister. But on those occasions that they did seek out "the lost nursery" as they called it, they were warm and friendly to little Katya. Naturally, both made an impression on her, Nicholas because he was the eldest, and George because he was delightfully charismatic. Katya got to know her other siblings too, but they continued to believe she suffered from some malady that required them to keep their distance.

As Katya grew and her condition showed no sign of abatement, the rest of the children were eventually granted more access to her. Xenia, her eldest sister, was quiet and shy, but nonetheless fascinated by her littlest sister. When the two were first introduced, Alexander had to physically restrain Xenia from running over and hugging her. Michael, the next brother after George, and Olga, until Katya's arrival the energetic "baby" of the family, were similarly entranced, but less curious. They were satisfied to stand back and talk to their sister as if she were a new child on a playground. But these were only first reactions. Over time all the children came to love her, to pity her, and upon the order of their father, to keep little Katya a secret.

Amazingly, Alexander managed to maintain Katya's quarantine until she was three without significant resistance from the Empress. Until then Maria was happy to know her husband loved his daughter, and that her banishment to the far side of the palace was not an attempt to hide an embarrassing member of the family. In fact the opposite was true—whenever Alexander was not abroad on business, he made visiting Katya an integral part of his daily schedule. No one could claim he did not love the girl for he practically doted on her, lavishing upon her all sorts of gifts and luxuries that had been denied the other children. (He had always maintained a Spartan upbringing would make them more resilient.) But when Katya turned three, Maria finally cornered him.

"Is Katya to forever be hidden?" she said. "She is already old enough that introducing her to the nation is going to be awkward. We will have to give some explanation why she has never before been revealed. What will you say?"

Alexander sat in thought for a long time.

"We will tell them nothing," he replied. "Because we cannot reveal her."

Maria was taken aback.

"What are you saying?" she demanded.

Alexander slouched and sighed. Instantly she knew he had made this decision long ago, and that he had dreaded this moment.

"Katya is a Romanov," he said patiently. "As royalty, she is not her own person. If we introduce her to society as a princess, she becomes a prize to other nations, nations with princes that wish to establish ties with Russia. We cannot allow a marriage of that sort to occur."

Maria shook her head in disbelief.

"Alex, she is only three years old!"

"I know," he said morosely. "I am thinking of the future. To avoid embarrassing her, and making her into an oddity in front of the nation and the world, we must continue to hide her, and to love her all the more for the unique trials she will face."

"We do not know her condition will persist," Maria argued. "It could pass with time."

But Alexander was again immovable. Nothing Maria said would convince him otherwise. She would have defied him if she had not loved him and known he had only the best intentions. All she could do was, in her private moments, kneel and pray for a future different than the one her husband predicted. No less than three times a day she found an empty room and entreated God Almighty to grant poor Katya a normal life.

In spite of her condition and exile to the farthest corner of the palace, Katya's life was not terribly different from those of her brothers and sisters, just lonelier. She had access to much of the palace, but as a child she longed for other children to play with. Her servants did their best to entertain her, and she was happy to play games with them, but they were not half as fun as her brothers and sisters appeared to be.

By the time she was five she understood that she was different, and that she could hurt someone with even an accidental touch. Once she understood this, she was invited to join the family at meals, and mealtimes became her favorite parts of the day. The food was good, but she savored each meal purely for the company it offered.

By the age of six she was disciplined enough to receive her tutors, who kept her busy with studies and other activities. She received the same tutelage as her siblings, but she excelled at languages. By the time she was eight she could speak, in addition to Russian, passable French, German, and English.

Over the years she was allowed to roam the expansive palace, which strangely frightened her with its endless array of furnished but otherwise unoccupied rooms. She was also allowed to roam the grounds as long as she did not advertise her existence. (It was, of course, the servants' job to ensure she was not exposed to public eyes.) She was even allowed to play outside with the others, to run and play with them while keeping two arm-lengths away. She liked to go on walks or ride bicycles with Nicholas and George, or race the tomboyish Xenia, or accompany Michael and Olga on long hikes through the woods. But most of all she enjoyed any time spent with her father, who was so busy ruling an empire that the few minutes a day she got to spend with him were each indelibly burned into her memory. When he died in 1894, nine-year-old Katya was heartbroken.

But for all the pain Alexander's death caused the family, Maria saw in it finally the opportunity to set Katya free. She summoned her daughter and her servants to her and informed them of her will.

"Your brother Nicholas will take your father's place as Tsar," Maria explained. "But your father's passing also brings a strange gift for you, my dear. It was his protective nature that kept you hidden away all these years. Of all the children, you were his brightest jewel, and because of your condition he could not bear the thought of adding to your troubles. I loved him and so respected his wishes, but I never whole-heartedly agreed with him. You are growing into a beautiful and brilliant little lady, and I would not deny you the world, or the world you."

Maria looked into the eyes of each of Katya's servants, one at a time, until she found the quality she sought. It was a look of inquisitiveness matched only by concern for what might happen next, and what it would mean for Katya. The woman was Irena, a middle-aged servant who had dedicated the last nine years to ensure the safety, care, and upbringing of a special Grand Duchess.

"You, Irena, will take Katya away from here. I am setting her free of this place, and of the family."

"Take her where?" Irena stammered.

"Anywhere she desires," Maria replied. "She excels at French. Perhaps begin in Paris. It will do wonders for her appreciation of other cultures."

Katya was too surprised to object. It was an opportunity she had never been offered. Even when the family had taken holidays she had usually remained home, to avoid both questions about her identity and the more frightening possibility of inadvertently electrocuting someone. To suddenly be offered such adventure made her happy, frightened, and sad at the same time. Tears welled in her eyes.

"But Mama, I don't want to leave you," she said.

Maria resisted the hazardous urge to dry them.

"Dearest, go with Irena and see the world," Maria said soothingly. "You have been kept at home too long. Go see all the things you have only read of in books. Do not let attachment to family keep you here. We all love you deeply, but we will still be here when you return."

Katya nodded, and though tears spilled down her cheeks, she felt a flutter of excitement in her heart.

At nine years old, Katya, with Irena acting as her guardian, set out to see the world. She followed her mother's suggestion and visited Paris first, but she found it so beautiful and magical that she did not want to leave. And with the wealth of her family backing her, she and Irena encountered no obstacles. They rented a large apartment overlooking the *Avenue des Champs-Élysées*, and they arranged a variety of tutors to educate her on the finer points of French and Parisian culture.

Though she made Paris her new home, she did not confine herself to it. With Irena acting as her shield, the two traveled Europe extensively. Germany and England, two nations where she could converse fluently, were of course on the itinerary. Between them there was hardly a country, province, or city that they did not visit. Before she was a teenager, Katya was already as worldly and experienced as anyone else in her family.

As she grew, Irena's job of protecting her only became more difficult. Even before Katya blossomed into a young woman, Irena recognized the beauty the girl would become. By the time Katya was fifteen, deterring would-be suitors became for Irena an almost full-time occupation. She had to be alert and quick on her feet to intercept the many young men who had designs on her ward. If she detected anyone moving in Katya's direction, she would shoot a withering scowl, stopping them dead in their tracks. For the few who went undeterred, she would bodily block them before they could utter a greeting.

Irena turned out to be a tireless sentinel. To Katya, however, it was clear Irena acted more out of desire to protect her from others than to protect others from electrocution.

Katya's electricity became more of a problem as she grew older. Living with and protecting the girl as Irena did, it was impossible to avoid mishaps. On occasion they would brush against one another at home or on the street, and Irena would receive a shock. It was an occupational hazard to which Irena had grown accustomed, and for her it was a small price to pay for the girl she thought of as her own daughter.

While Irena expected occasional jolts, she was keenly aware that over the years they had intensified. When Katya was six, Irena could absorb them several times a day, almost nonchalantly. When Katya was ten, however, her electricity had increased so that Irena could stand it no more than once a day. After each incident she would sit rubbing the affected area like a burn from a stove. By the time Katya was fifteen, Irena had learned to give her a wide berth, because the intensity of the jolt might knock her down or unconscious. This naturally made every venture into the city a trial, because Irena had to walk perilously close by Katya's side in order to quickly react to anyone who dared approach.

The combined effects of Irena's responsibilities and the physical demands they placed on her aged the poor woman prematurely. When she and Katya had departed Gatchina, Irena had been, and looked, in her mid-thirties. After six years of watching over adolescent Katya, she became gaunt, her face became lined from so much scowling, and her hair turned a dark and unflattering shade of grey.

In spite of it all, she became only more formidable, which ultimately worked to her advantage. For the rest of her time with Katya, Irena looked so stern and frightening that her mere presence sufficed to ward off all how-do-you-dos.

But Irena's protection could not last forever, and both women knew it. Besides, Katya had not given up hope for a cure. Over the years they had discreetly met with some of Europe's best doctors, none of whom had the slightest clue how to treat Katya. After so many disappointments, Katya had resigned herself to a life of solitude, accepting that she would never have a husband or children.

Then in the summer of 1906, Irena discovered an article in the newspaper about a man who could work wonders with electricity, who commanded it as authoritatively as Moses commanded the Red Sea. With hope in their hearts the women packed their bags and traveled to America in search of a man named Tesla.

"You met Tesla?" the Doctor asked. "As an amateur scientist I have wanted to meet the man for years, but my calling prevented it. I take it he found no cure."

"No," Katya said.

The Doctor sat back in his chair, raised his eyebrows, and sighed.

"Thank you for so thorough an account," he said. "I no longer doubt you, though I am amazed by your story. I am still surprised to have encountered you here, and under these circumstances. But now I would like to discuss a different matter. I would like you to tell me all you know about the Order of the Albatross."

My heart froze. Suddenly the folly of my mental joust with the Doctor slapped me in the face. Since I had fabricated The Order, Katya would know nothing of it. I cursed myself for not taking it into consideration, and for not taking advantage of our solitude to inform her about the details of my interrogation. I pressed my cheek against the door harder still, desperate to hear how she might respond. At that moment footsteps in the corridor informed me that someone was coming my way, and they were coming from the direction opposite the stairs. Apparently the upper floor was not as empty as it seemed.

I was cut off and left with no choice but to hurry in the opposite direction. I fled down the stairs and across the sanctuary. There I watched as a man descended the stairs, seated himself at a table, and began to slowly carve slices out of an apple with a dirty pocketknife. I badly wanted to get back to hear what Katya was saying, but there was nothing I could do. Instead I made my way down through the cellar and into the subterranean tunnels. At the crossroads to my cell I paused. Since I was already roaming about, I decided it was time I made contact with my other companions. I chose the opposite passage and went in search of their cells.

They were not hard to find. Their cells were perhaps fifty paces away, down the opposite tunnel, marked by a guttering torch. Dietrich was easy enough to locate. All I had to do was follow the sound of his incessant cough.

"Dietrich!" I exclaimed.

He climbed to his feet and leaned against the bars of his cell. For a moment, he forgot his rebellious lungs.

"Prometheus!" he managed between gasps. "Thank God! How did you escape? Never mind that now, can you get us out?"

"Us?" I said. "Is Irish near?"

He pointed further down the tunnel.

"There," he said.

I stepped back to get a look, but Dietrich grabbed me through the bars.

"Wait! Aren't you going to free me?"

I looked up and down the tunnel before answering.

"Not yet," I said. "The time isn't right. I don't even know if I'll be able to get back to Katya—"

"Katya?" Dietrich said.

"Ms Alexander," I explained.

"Ah! She is safe, then?"

"She is alive, but her safety is up in the air at the moment."

Even in the dark I could feel his eyes boring into me.

"What do you mean?"

"She is being interrogated by the Doctor," I said. "She has been drugged."

"The fiend!" Dietrich hissed. "We must rescue her at once."

"No, no," I said in an attempt to calm him. "They drugged her, but she is otherwise fine. Besides, I can't free you now because we don't have a plan. If we go running blindly into the monastery they will only catch us again."

"What do you propose?" Dietrich demanded. "We cannot wait forever."

"Let me check on Irish," I said, disentangling myself from his clutches and hurrying away before he could seize me again.

The door to Irish's cell was sealed with a simple chain and padlock. It posed me no challenge at all, yet it imprisoned the mightiest man in the world. I peered inside and saw only blackness.

"Irish?" I hissed.

I was answered with sounds of slow movement, of a hulk raising itself from the floor and lumbering toward me. I sensed his presence at the door before my eyes adjusted enough to make out his swollen head. His face was bruised horribly, and the side of his jaw where he had been struck was so battered it looked like it might burst. He leaned upon the bars and said nothing.

"Are you all right?" I asked. "Can you speak?"

He grunted in response, but then he muttered something that was so slurred it took me a moment to interpret.

"Shome eshcape artisht you are," he said. "About time you turned up."

"I'm going to get you out of here," I said. "But not yet. I have to find a way out, and I have to free Kat—Ms Alexander."

He sighed, nodded, and muttered something else that sounded like "Hurry the hell up." He then turned and lumbered back into the darkness of his cell.

I retraced my steps and passed Dietrich in the process.

"What is the plan?" he said, desperately trying to grab me by the sleeve.

"I told you, I have to find a way out, then free Ms Alexander," I said irritably. "Now I must find my way back before my absence is noticed."

It was a lie—I had no intention of returning to my cell yet—and I felt bad for it. But I did not have time to argue with him. I dodged his flailing arms, ignored his repeated hissings of my name, and crept back upstairs. To my relief, the sanctuary was again empty, and I hurried back to the Doctor's door. Peeking through the keyhole I noticed the scene had changed—Wende now stood at the Doctor's side. I pressed my ear to the door in time to hear their final words.

"And the Tsar?" the Doctor asked. "What does he know?"

"Nothing," Katya said, her speech slurred. "He has heard strange rumors, and he wonders what happened to the soldiers he sent. But he knows nothing."

The Doctor glanced at Wende.

"It seems we were played for fools," Wende said dryly.

The Doctor considered it.

"Perhaps, but it cost us nothing. At most it has been a mild inconvenience, and the result is we are now ahead of schedule. There can be no harm in that."

Wende nodded but still looked annoyed.

"Shall we stay on schedule for tomorrow, then?"

"Yes," the Doctor said. "Véles has waited long enough for this moment. Let's not stall simply because we are early."

"Very well," Wended replied. "What time?"

"Noon will suffice," the Doctor said. "It will give me time to conclude my business with the young lady."

Both regarded Katya. The Doctor sadly smiled at her, but Wende smirked in a way that gave me chills. Then the Doctor slipped his hands back into his rubber gloves and picked up a syringe.

"I'll give her something to bring her around," he said.

I realized they were about to take Katya back to her cell, and I raced back to mine, picked the lock, and shut myself inside. Several minutes later Wende returned with Katya and locked her up. When he had gone I hurried to my bars.

"Katya!" I said desperately. "Are you all right? Speak to me!"

She was slow to respond. After calling her name repeatedly, I heard her shuffle to the bars of her cell.

"Prometheus," she said weakly.

"Thank God you're okay," I said. "What happened?"

"He drugged me," she said. "He asked me questions. I fear I gave away too much."

"What did he ask?"

"He asked …"

She trailed off. When she spoke again she suddenly sounded more lucid.

"He asked about an Order of the Albatross," she said. "I have no idea what he was talking about. Do you?"

"No," I said. I did not mean to mislead her. I was more interested in finding out what lay ahead, and I did not want to get mired in explaining myself to her. "What do they plan next?"

"The rocket," she said. "I think they will attempt to launch it tomorrow."

"And what of you?" I said, attempting to lead her to the point that most interested me. "Are they done with you?"

"No," she replied. "The Doctor has some plan for me, but he did not elaborate. Whatever it is, I will find out tomorrow."

We did not speak more. I thought about telling her I had found our friends, but I knew it would only lead to desperate pleading for immediate escape.

"Let's rest now," I whispered, as if her ear were only inches away. I fancied I could almost smell the fragrance of her hair. She must have heard because she retreated into her cell, and I heard the rustling of her dress as she collapsed on the cold, hard stone.

After half an hour of sitting in the dark my ears had become attuned to the stillness, so much that from my cell I could hear the steady breathing of Katya in slumber. I then produced the needle from my cuff and opened the lock to my cell. The sound it made as I unlatched it seemed like a clamor in that stillness, and I froze expecting Katya to inquire. But she did not stir in the least, so I again sealed up my cell and began my exploration of the tunnels.

This time I set out in the direction that led past my cell, traveling away from the stairs and deeper into the earth. I had neither been that way nor observed anyone come from it, and I expected to find a dead end. Still, I pressed on, tiptoeing and feeling my way.

Unlike the other tunnels it was utterly black. There were no lamps or torches anywhere along the way, which only added to my belief that no one ever came this way. Meeting no resistance I continued, if only to confirm my belief that it was a dead end. And thank heavens I continued, because I could not have been more wrong.

For a long time I shuffled blindly onward and came across nothing. The tunnel went on so long that I began to question the wisdom in following it. For all I knew, it could end in a subterranean cavern, or plunge into a bottomless pit. Either reason would explain why it was abandoned. I was about to turn back when my hands met a rocky wall, which, from the feeling of it, was natural stone.

It seemed to be a dead end after all, and I sighed and leaned heavily against it. Suddenly, it began to rumble and move. I leapt back in shock, but not before a large stone tumbled down against my foot and pinned it. I yelped, more from surprise than pain. I was not hurt, just temporarily immobilized. As I choked on dust and struggled to free my leg, I felt a breeze on my face. It came from somewhere ahead, somewhere past the rocks that had just collapsed. I worked my foot free and stared into the darkness ahead, which had taken on a greyish hue. I pressed on, the air becoming noticeably fresher as I went. A moment later I detected a dull glow ahead, and as I rounded a bend a disc of bright light appeared ahead. I rushed forward.

I emerged from what, on the outside, looked like an old mining tunnel. I stepped into the dying light. The sun was almost behind the mountains, but much of the valley was still illuminated. I received a full view of the rocket, and the shadowed town at its feet. I looked south and spied the crevice that served as the valley's only entrance. From where I stood it was no more than half a mile away, but it looked much further.

I had no idea how we might traverse the open space without being caught. If we escaped at night the darkness would cover us, but greater problems then arose. If we made it to the crevice and beyond, what then? Would we find horses, or were we expected to walk? Would we be able to skirt the town of Véles, undetected and unmolested? If so, where would we go? Bogoslovsk was at least twenty miles away. Dietrich was ill, Irish was injured, and Katya was drugged. We would never make it.

Escape was more problematic than I had at first thought. If we hoped to succeed, much more thought would have to go into it. I followed the tunnel back to my cell and quietly locked myself in. I laid down on the floor and stared into the darkness, wondering how I would pull of an escape of this magnitude, and with so much dead weight.

23: ZENITH

"Prometheus!"

I awoke and stumbled to the door of my cell.

"Yes?"

"There is something I must tell you," Katya said. "I may have little time, so please listen carefully."

"All right."

She paused to work up her nerve.

"Today," she said, "I fear I might meet my end. You, Mr Dietrich and Mr Irish are my only true friends. If something happens to me, I would like you to know the truth about me."

"Yes?" I said eagerly.

"I have misled you," she said. "I am not who you think I am."

"What do you mean?" I said, playing along.

"There is a secret I have carried all my life. I do not want to take it to my grave without someone knowing the truth." She took a deep breath. "My name is not Katherine Alexander."

"No?" I said.

"My name is Ekaterine Alexandrovna Romanov. My father was Tsar Alexander III. Nicholas is not a distant cousin. He is my brother."

"Are you saying you're royalty? A princess?"

"Yes," she replied with a sigh.

"Oh, I've known that for some time," I said casually.

Incredulous silence followed.

"How on earth could you know?" she asked.

"My dear, you underestimate me," I said, grinning to myself. "Since the day I laid eyes on you, I knew you were extraordinary. I didn't peg you as an actual princess, but once I learned how close you were to Nicholas, everything fell into place."

"But that does not explain…" she trailed off, flustered. "Do the others know?"

"Hardly!" I scoffed. "For all Dietrich's mental prowess, he never picked up on the clues as I did. And Irish? Ha! He can barely count sticks."

She became quiet for a time, no doubt retracing our journey and wondering what clues she had let slip. It was hardly the time or place to jest with her, but I accepted the situation for what it was—an opportunity to further mystify and impress.

The moment was quickly ruined by the sound of footsteps, followed by the appearance of two guards. They again brandished pistols, which they leveled at Katya as they removed her from her cell. Before they marched her away, she spoke to me over her shoulder.

"Remember who I am," she said desperately. "If I do not return, please do everything in your power to save my family!"

Then she and her captors disappeared down the tunnel.

This time I did not call after her melodramatically, for I had another plan in mind. I removed the needle from my cuff and was soon out of my cell. Again I made my way upstairs, and again fortune favored me by removing all obstacles. I went straight to the Doctor's office and was surprised to find it empty. As I stood in the doorway wondering, the guards suddenly exited the next room down the hall. It happened so unexpectedly I barely had time to dive into the Doctor's office and conceal myself. But they did not detect me. They continued downstairs on some other errand. Once they had disappeared, I hurried down the corridor to the door from which they had come.

I pressed my eye to the keyhole, vaguely recalling the room's furnishings from when I had briefly hidden there the day before. At the time the room's contents had not impressed me, but now as I studied the scene a queasiness came over me. I suddenly realized it was meant to be a medical room, an operating theater. Katya lay upon the high table, secured by shackles at her wrists and ankles. The Doctor stood to one side with his back turned, busying himself with the preparation of a syringe. He then wriggled his hands into rubber gloves, took up the syringe, and approached the table.

"Good morning, princess," he said with a smile. "Do you remember what today is?"

Katya searched his face and shook her head.

"Unsurprising since you were heavily drugged," he reflected. "I will refresh your memory. Today is an auspicious occasion, for today Brother Tantalus and I will strike a blow against the largest, most precarious empire on Earth. Your empire."

"You speak of your rocket," Katya said.

"Yes."

She tried to laugh.

"What is so amusing?"

"I have it on good authority the thing will never leave the ground," she said.

The Doctor's brow furrowed, but his smile did not diminish.

"Really?" he said. But if Katya's claim gave him even the tiniest cause for doubt, he neither showed it nor pursued the topic. Instead he changed the subject.

"Today is special for still another reason," he said.

"Why?" Katya asked.

The Doctor leaned upon the table and brought his face closer to hers.

"You suffer from the most fascinating condition," he said. "Your body produces electricity, and I cannot stop thinking about it. I should not be so intrigued, for you are not the only creature capable of such a feat. Does the eel not possess the same quality? Yet of the millions of people in the world, you alone possess this unique ability. As a man of science I cannot let this opportunity pass."

She tensed as he pressed the needle into her arm and emptied the syringe. Within seconds the morphine began to take hold.

"What are you going to do?" she murmured.

The Doctor set the syringe aside.

"Surgery," he said calmly. "Vivisection."

He selected a small but lethal gleaming instrument from a tray. He looked down at Katya almost regretfully.

"You should know this is a decision I did not make easily," he said at length. "I was up most of the night fretting over it. I am not too old to appreciate your beauty, or to see in you the daughter I might have had. As a man, I am loathe to perform the task ahead."

"Then why?" It was all Katya could muster in her drugged state.

"Because in the end, it does not matter," the Doctor said, shaking his head sadly. "Today we cross the threshold of the apocalypse. Véles will soon claim the Earth, and nothing that has come before will matter. Not you, not me, not the terrible thing I am about to do. It will all be forgotten, as if it never happened."

"Madness," Katya murmured.

The Doctor sighed and pulled at the cloth of her blouse. He slipped the knife into the fabric and began slicing it up the middle. I froze, transfixed by her perfect, porcelain breasts, and by the horror he intended. As he worked at her clothes, the sound of rending fabric caused Katya to open her eyes.

"Will it hurt?" she asked.

The Doctor spread the two halves of her torn blouse aside and placed the gleaming instrument against her midriff.

"That, my dear, will be for you to tell me," he said.

Even before I had witnessed the scene in the Doctor's room I had decided the time had come to act. I had known in my heart that when the precise moment arrived I would leap into action. I did not know when the moment would be, or what I would do, but when I saw the Doctor lowering the scalpel toward Katya, every atom suddenly screamed and I went into motion.

Without a thought for myself I burst into the room. Katya remained immobile, eyes closed, too adrift in morphine to know what was happening. The Doctor, however, started, pulling the scalpel away from Katya's bare breast and staring at me in wonder.

Once inside I too froze, wondering what to do next. I had never considered myself a man of action, so a method to resolve the situation did not naturally come to me. I stood there, bouncing on my toes, hands fluttering nervously. My pause gave the Doctor time to collect himself.

"Mr Grey!" he said. "What are you doing here? How did you get out of your cage?"

I noticed a wooden chair against the wall by the door. I seized it, upended it, and raised it over my head.

"Get away from her!" I demanded.

The Doctor looked down at Katya as if he was suddenly surprised to see her.

"Get away or I'll bash your head in!" I cried.

He took two steps back from the table.

"What are you doing, Mr Grey?"

The table, and Katya, lay between us. I edged toward it, trying not to be mesmerized by her nakedness.

"I'm saving her from a madman," I said. "And a monster."

"Are you?" he said. "I don't think you've thought this through."

I edged closer and raised the chair higher, causing him to take still another step back.

"Desperate times call for desperate measures," I said.

"You are desperate, I'll grant you that," he said with a chuckle. "But my point is this. Where do you go from here? My men stand between you and freedom. You are burdened with an unconscious woman, armed only with a chair. Will you carry her? You will have to put down that fearsome chair to do it. How far do you think you will get?"

"Enough of your nonsense!" I shouted. "Release her!"

He regarded me for a moment, not moving a muscle. I was beginning to think I would have to strike him. I was working up the nerve to do it when he stepped forward.

"Very well," he said with a shrug.

He went around to each of Katya's wrists and ankles and released the manacles that secured her to the table. As he worked, Katya neither moved nor made a sound.

"She better be all right," I warned, "for your sake."

The Doctor stared at me. He was as intrigued to find out my next move as

I was. Then his jaw dropped, and he seemed to stare blindly past me and into the distance. The scalpel fell from his hand and clattered to the floor. I lowered the chair and stared at him. For a moment I thought he was experiencing a stroke, but then he suddenly became animated again, looking around as if surprised.

"Remarkable!" he said.

"What?" I half raised the chair to show I still meant business.

He looked at me wide-eyed and stroked his beard.

"A revelation!" he said. "Véles just appeared, in this very room, and spoke to me. Did you not hear him? Did you not see?"

I shook my head. The little old madman appeared to have finally lost what remained of his sanity. No change at all had occurred in the room. It had only been in his addled brain. But he was convinced of it nonetheless. His face lit up like a bulb, grinning from ear to ear. He then began to move toward me.

"Tut, tut, Mr Grey," he said, tugging off the rubber gloves and dropping them to the floor. "Véles has shown me how this will end. The game is up."

"What are you talking about?" I said, taking a step back. "Any closer and I'll crack your skull!"

The crazy old fool continued to approach. I raised the chair higher, and he stopped and looked at me with amusement.

"I have seen the outcome of this standoff," he said. "You will not harm me. Indeed, you cannot harm me, for Véles is on my side. You will put down the chair and surrender, so that I may continue my work."

I froze. My shoulders burned from the exertion of holding the chair above my head. I knew I would not be able to maintain that position much longer. I began to feel as if the situation were out of my control. All I had to do to was strike, but looking into the rheumy eyes of that shriveled lunatic, I could not bring myself to do it. As mad and dangerous as he was, I could not bludgeon to death a helpless centenarian.

As I gazed into his eyes he nodded, and suddenly my arms gave out. Though I willed otherwise, the chair steadily sank below my head. I struggled to raise it again, but my strength was spent. The chair fell to the ground, and the Doctor gave me that familiar sad smile.

"Very good, Mr Grey. Very good."

In that moment I was both frightened and ashamed. In spite of the flame I had felt moments before, I now felt completely impotent. I had failed Katya, my friends, my country, and the world. I had held the enemy's life in my hands, and I had spared it. My limbs felt as if they had turned to lead. I sank to my knees before him.

He looked down at me for some time, smiling and saying nothing. I realized then that I was his, to dispose of as he saw fit, but more likely to transform. He would make me a disciple, a believer of the madness behind his eyes. He would convert me to Véles, or whatever it was he worshipped, and I would stand by his side and face the apocalypse. It was insanity. The most disturbing part was I knew it, but to deny the outcome would have been a lie. I, too, saw it as clearly as a vision. It was inevitable.

He reached out a hand. I was both thrilled and sickened at the prospect of this new beginning. His touch would be an evil benediction, ushering me into the fold. I was terrified. I closed my eyes hoping to ease the transition.

Seconds passed. I had expected to feel the soft, withered flesh of his hand caress my cheek, but it did not come. I opened my eyes to find him frozen before me, his trembling hand only inches away. I looked up into his face to find not his warm smile, but a horrific grimace—eyes clenched shut, teeth bared. He was clearly in great pain. I leapt to my feet, and then I understood. Splayed on both sides of his balding head were five thin, pallid fingers.

I stepped back in awe, and just in time, too, because the hands released him. He collapsed to the floor in a lifeless heap, leaving Katya standing before me. Without the Doctor to support her, she staggered back against the table. She was deathly pale and seemed almost asleep on her feet.

"Katya!" I cried, rushing to her side and wrapping an arm around her waist. I did it without thinking, and only as I maneuvered her toward a chair did I realize the significance of the moment. I was touching her without being electrocuted! But I did not have time to dwell on it. I guided her to the chair and kneeled before her.

"Katya! Can you hear me?"

Her eyes fluttered open and struggled to find mine.

"Is it time to go?" she said weakly.

My resolve returned, rejuvenated.

"Yes," I replied.

Before Katya became an electrified rag doll, I had an idea. I grabbed the rubber gloves the Doctor had discarded and put them on. I then scooped her up in my arms and made my way back to her cell. As I carried her down to the dungeon, she fell into a deep slumber, not even awakening when I laid her on the cold floor of her cell.

With the Doctor dead we needed to flee at once, but I first needed to free Dietrich and Irish. I removed the gloves and hurried to the area where they were being held. As soon as I stepped up to Dietrich's cell, he scrambled to the door.

"The Doctor is dead," I said, working the lock open.

"How?" he asked.

"Katya!" I said, shaking my head in amazement.

He tried to follow with another question, but his cough would not allow it. By the time I got his door open, he was back in control.

"Quickly now!" he rasped.

We hurried to Irish's cell, and again I made short work of the lock. Irish, who had been asleep on the floor, climbed to his feet and lumbered out.

I took a step back and looked at them. Even in the gloom I could tell they were in awful condition. Dietrich looked thin and haggard, as if a few days captivity had aged him ten years. And Irish, in addition to his swollen jaw, was covered in scrapes and bruises, mementos of his heroic battle against our captors. But in spite of their poor condition, there was a gleam in their eyes that said they were ready for anything.

"Have you found a way out?" Dietrich asked.

"Yes," I said. "And it's a way no one else knows. We should be able to escape these tunnels without contention."

"Perfect!" Dietrich said. "What of Ms Alexander?"

"Follow me!" I said.

We set off through the tunnels and soon came to Katya's cell. I flung open the door and we crowded around her. Dietrich and Irish stared down at her torn clothing. Only then did I realized that in the excitement I had done nothing to cover her.

"What happened?" Dietrich asked, horrified. "Is she all right?"

"She's drugged, that's all," I said. "Morphine, I think."

Dietrich reached out to touch her face, but I caught him by the wrist at the last minute.

"What are you doing?" I said.

"Of course," he said, realizing his folly.

"I have these!" I said, producing the rubber gloves. I then put them on before anyone could take them from me. I bent close, caressing Katya's face and speaking her name. Slowly she came around. She struggled to open her eyes. When they focused, she favored us with a dreamy smile.

"Gentlemen," she said weakly. "It is so good to see you!"

"And you, my dear," Dietrich said. "Can you walk?"

I helped her sit up, and she took stock of herself. In a distracted way she noticed her bisected blouse, which she demurely pulled closed and kept secured with one hand.

"I think so," she said.

I helped her to her feet. Her balance was as tenuous as a newborn calf. She tottered and Irish flinched, prepared to catch her. But since I had the gloves, I took her securely by the arm and held her at my side. Dietrich nodded.

"Prometheus, lead us out of here!" he said.

Aside from the inherent risk in guiding an electrified lady through a series of pitch black tunnels, we encountered no problems. We proceeded slowly, more due to Katya's condition than to the darkness and terrain. Soon the darkness gave way to greyness, and we spotted the disc of light ahead. I exhaled a sigh of relief at the sight of it, because I had expected at any moment to hear sounds of pursuit. We came to a halt just inside the opening to get a look at what lay ahead.

Outside it was early morning. The sun half peeked over the eastern ridge of the mountains. We gazed out over the scorched landscape, our eyes drawn to the valley's only feature: the rocket. We gazed in silent wonder until Dietrich turned to us and sighed.

"Iscariot is dead," he said. "We accomplished the objective of our mission, but we still must contend with this."

"What do you mean?" I said. "Let's get out of here before it's too late."

I tried to step toward the exit, but Katya did not move.

"No," she said. "The Doctor is dead, but his work continues without him. That weapon must be destroyed."

I marveled at them.

"What?" I exclaimed. "There are a hundred men out there. And look at the size of that thing! If it works, how can we stop it? Irish, help me talk some sense into them."

But to my utter disappointment, he too shook his head.

"Musht be shtopped," he mumbled.

I had been outvoted. I was preparing to throw a tantrum when I had one more idea.

"What about her?" I said, indicating Katya. "She's in no condition to storm the valley, or to sneak among the enemy and sabotage that thing."

Dietrich looked at her and hung his head. After a short pause he spoke.

"You are correct," he said. "We cannot accomplish this with Ms Alexander in such a state. Therefore you will escape with her, and we will take care of the rocket."

I deflated. My plan had been to take Katya and my friends away from that accursed placed. I had not anticipated such heroics from them. I opened my mouth to argue, but no words came. Dietrich's plan was irrefutable.

"Mr Irish," he said. "Are you with me?"

Irish nodded.

"Then we have our plan," he said. "You will make your escape, and we will follow, if we are able."

"Good luck," I said, extending my hand.

Dietrich accepted it. I then grabbed Irish by an arm and squeezed.

"Be careful," I said with all sincerity.

He grunted in response.

"God be with you both," Katya said. Suddenly she looked paler than before and leaned more heavily on me.

Dietrich and Irish nodded at us, then stepped out into the light.

We watched for a few moments as they ran across the waste of ash. It was difficult to tear my eyes away from them, but finally I managed. I squeezed Katya's arm.

"Are you ready?"

She nodded, yet her eyes were fixed on our friends.

We exited the cave and began working our way around to the crevice that served as the valley's only entrance and egress. We moved slowly, hugging the feet of the mountains, using felled trees and rocks for concealment whenever possible.

Though the valley was little more than a mile in diameter, the curvature of the basin forced us to travel further than our friends. They needed only charge straight across its floor to reach their goal, while our path followed a long arc.

We moved painfully slowly, and I felt terribly exposed. It seemed inconceivable that no one would notice, but miraculously our luck held. As we approached the crevice I thanked Lady Fate for watching over me yet again. But as Katya and I inched toward escape and safety, a much more daring and profound story was unfolding in the shadow of the Doctor's apocalyptic weapon.

Dietrich and Irish made what felt like a mad dash toward the rocket, but due to their respective conditions, it was in fact little more than a steady jog. When they had set out, they had been so determined and full of adrenaline that they expected to reach the rocket in less than a minute. Before they were half way, however, their strength began to fail, and Dietrich became terribly winded. That was the most frightening time for them, as they tried to hurry across that vast space without being noticed and picked off by riflemen. But if anyone noticed them, no one raised an alarm. They must have been mistaken for a tardy pair of disciples, hustling to do their part for the ensuing apocalypse.

After an excruciating and breathless five minutes, they reached the outskirts of the shantytown and pressed themselves against the side of a poorly constructed shack. They both stood panting for another few minutes until they caught their breath. Then Dietrich began to cough. He doubled over as Irish peeked around the corner.

"Going to give ush away," he muttered.

Dietrich nodded and pressed a fist to his mouth, clenching his jaw shut and turning red in the face. A moment later he mastered himself.

"Sorry," he said hoarsely.

They each hazarded a look around the corner and took in the scene. Everywhere men were busy at work, on the ground and in the scaffolding. Much of the activity was as indecipherable to Irish as ants swarming around an anthill, but Dietrich was able to make some sense of it.

"They appear to be making final preparations," he said. "The launch must be soon..."

Dietrich's words trailed off, causing Irish to look at him expectantly. Irish then realized Dietrich had become preoccupied. Dietrich's full attention was fixed on something in the shantytown. Curious, Irish followed his gaze.

The scene was busy, almost chaotic, with men hauling tools and the like to wagons as they prepared to vacate the area. Then he noticed someone standing above the hustle and bustle, perched in the back of a wagon to oversee it all.

"Wende!" Dietrich hissed.

August Wende directed the men's many efforts. Most of his attention was directed at those scampering around him, but now and then he would glance up at the men in the scaffolding, cup his hands around his mouth, and shout some instruction.

Dietrich withdrew from the corner and leaned against the wall of the shack.

"How could I have forgotten him?" he said, scolding himself. "He is the other half of this insane conspiracy. The Doctor may be dead, but Wende will carry on his work. As long as he lives, the threat persists."

Irish studied him and nodded.

"Sho we kill him," he muttered.

"Yes, but how?" Dietrich said. "He is surrounded. How can we possibly get to him?"

At that moment Dietrich's lungs again constricted, launching him into an unprecedented coughing fit. Maybe it was all the excitement, or maybe the motes of ash in the air had aggravated his condition. Whatever the cause, he coughed with such violence that spittle sprayed from his mouth. He desperately tried to bring it under control by flinging an arm across his face, but it did little to stifle the noise. When he pulled it away to gasp for breath, his sleeve was flecked with blood. His lungs were in open rebellion and determined to draw attention—and this time they succeeded.

As Irish steadied him by one arm, a man rounded the corner. Irish, who thought Dietrich might collapse on the spot, was so preoccupied that he did not notice the onlooker until the man cried out in alarm. Without hesitation Irish punched him in the throat and the man crumpled, silenced for good. But it was too late. As Dietrich regained control of himself they heard cries in response to the alarm.

In that moment Irish took command. He bent over the fallen man and wrestled something from his belt. When he stood, he pressed a revolver into Dietrich's hands. He then grabbed him by the arms, gave him a shake, and looked him in the eyes.

"Kill Wende," he said simply. Then he turned and dashed toward the rocket.

As soon as Irish cleared the shack and stepped into the open, voices rose in dismay and footsteps began to fall. Even before Dietrich got a clear view, he knew the entire camp must be giving chase, and a glance around the corner confirmed it. Realizing his chance, he hurried to the opposite corner of the shack and tried to work his way closer to Wende without being seen.

Since the shacks stood so close together, he was able to move among them quite easily without being detected, especially since everyone's attention was on Irish. Within seconds he was able to move close enough to get Wende into an acceptable pistol range. As he peeked around the corner of another shack, he found Wende in the same place as before, standing in the back of the wagon, wearing a mixed expression fury and disbelief as he barked orders and gestured frantically at Irish.

Dietrich knew he must take advantage of the distraction Irish had provided, and he stepped into the open. He strode forward another half dozen steps to ensure he would not miss. Wende was so preoccupied, he did not even notice as Dietrich, a mere fifty feet away, came to a halt, took careful aim, and pulled the trigger.

But that day Fate toyed with Meyer Dietrich. At the crucial moment, another cough surged up and threw him off. He fired, but the shot struck the wagon just below Wende's knee. Wende started and looked around wildly in search of the source. When his eyes fell on Dietrich, who was in the process of trying to squeeze off another shot, his jaw dropped. And in the next instant, Wende dropped, too. Another bullet whizzed by him as he leapt to the ground and fled.

Dietrich gave chase. As he cleared the immediate shacks he glanced to his left and watched the backs of five score men in hot pursuit of Irish. Only a few stragglers noticed him and paused, torn between whom to chase. Dietrich helped them decide by making a wild shot in their direction—but he scored a lucky hit that took off a man's left ear. The man fell to the ground screaming, cupping the side of his bloody head. The others decided to chase Irish instead.

This interruption took only seconds to resolve, but it was enough time for Wende to almost double the distance between them. Cursing, Dietrich drove on, giving chase as Wende dodged among the shacks. As he ran, his lungs felt strangely well, perhaps a result of the extra oxygen flowing through them. It almost made him feel young and vibrant, as if he might be able to run Wende down. But at the same time the rest of his body began to fatigue. His legs, still weary from the run across the valley, felt like rubber. Several times he stumbled and thought he would crash face first to the ground, but each time he managed to regain his balance and press on.

They emerged from the shantytown and into the fields of ash, and Dietrich was heartened to note the distance between them had stabilized. Wende no longer seemed to be getting away, though he did not appear to be getting any closer. Given the pace at which he was exhausting himself, Dietrich accepted the distance and was thankful that he was still holding on.

Now clear of the camp, Dietrich was able to see far enough ahead to identify Wende's goal. In the distance stood a lump of a structure that looked like little more than a hut. As they neared it, however, he noticed it was a stone shelter; and as they drew nearer still, he noticed to his left, perhaps a hundred yards off, a taut cable running along the ground between the shelter and the rocket. In the depths of his immaculate memory he logged it, but he had no time to puzzle over it.

Wende came within a hundred yards of the shelter, and Dietrich suddenly realized his danger. There was no way to tell what was inside. If Wende reached it he would be protected against further shots, and gain access to any weapons stored within. If he were to get his hands on a rifle, Dietrich would be easy prey. Faced with this deadly possibility, Dietrich drew up and again took aim. His chest was heaving, which made aiming like trying to shoot from a ship in a storm. But he gave it his level best, holding his breath and squeezing the trigger.

The revolver leapt in his hand, and to his amazement Wende stumbled, fell, and rolled. He could not tell where the round had struck, but he was so relieved to have hit his target he did not care. He urged his weary body on, even as Wende half raised himself and scrambled into the shelter.

Dietrich reached it only seconds behind him, but he nonetheless drew up outside the door. He noted with satisfaction the trail of blood leading inside. Still, he hesitated. Wende had entered with enough time to arm himself, if any weapons were to be had. So he paused in a vain attempt to catch his breath. At that moment he heard distant shots and frantically tried to identify their location, but he could see no one. Fearing that someone might be shooting at him, and realizing that every stalled moment gave Wende more time to prepare, he summoned every bit of strength and courage and charged inside.

The shelter was small, no larger than fifteen feet square, and dark, the only light entering through the doorway and a small aperture that served as a window facing the valley. As far as Dietrich could tell, the space appeared empty, apart from Wende and himself. But this was a peripheral observation and not the first thing he noticed upon entering. The first thing he noticed was that he stood in a pool of blood. Apparently Wende had collapsed just inside the door, rested there momentarily as his life seeped out of him. On the far side of the murky puddle began a long smear, as if Wende had dragged some part of himself through it.

Tracing the vile trail he quickly found Wende. He raised his pistol in anticipation of some violence or trickery, but aside from gasping in pain Wende did not move. He merely stood there, his left hand holding a bloody wound where the bullet had passed through his belly. With the other hand he leaned heavily on some prop, which in the shadows Dietrich took for a walking stick, or maybe a cudgel.

The two men regarded each other. Dietrich knew he should fire and end the wicked man. Considering all the evil Wende had done in his life, he was long overdue for termination. But Dietrich hesitated—he felt he had missed something, some clue that now caused Wende to crack a smile.

"Well done, Herr Dietrich," Wende said, wincing as he spoke. "You have me."

Dietrich did not reply. Sensing misdirection, he drew back the hammer on the revolver.

"This madness stops today," he said.

"Does it?"

"Yes," Dietrich affirmed. "The Doctor is dead, and now I have you."

Wende's smile flickered.

"Dead?" he said, skeptically. "How?"

"The lady," Dietrich said. "Electrocution."

Wende's smile faded.

"Damn you!" he said bitterly.

Dietrich was not one to gloat, but he had to fight back a satisfied smile at seeing Wende so deeply wounded.

"I suspect you will learn about damnation much sooner than I," he replied.

Wende's grin slowly returned, this time with alarming sincerity.

"Then allow me to catch you up."

Wende shifted his weight, suddenly tilting to one side. As he moved there came the sound of metal on metal, of gears clenching together against some resistance. Suddenly Dietrich realized his folly—the prop upon which Wende had leaned was a lever.

In desperation he fired. The round pierced Wende's chest. He coughed once, spraying blood from his mouth, and collapsed.

Dietrich looked down in awe at what he had done. He had never taken a life before. He felt simultaneously elated and ashamed. But before he could sort himself out he was distracted by the sound of thunder—persistent thunder—that shook the earth and sounded as if it were rending the sky in twain. It was so powerful it threw him off balance. Clinging to the wall for support, he lifted himself up to the small window, looked out, and saw the valley engulfed in rising smoke and flame.

"Dear God, no!" he screamed, but his voice was swallowed by the roar of Armageddon.

When Irish bolted for the rocket he had no particular plan in mind. It did not matter that it towered over him, or that its metal skin was impervious to his mightiest blows, or that at any moment it might belch flames that would engulf him, or even explode. Like a hero of myth he charged forward to do battle with it, his victory a surety, his personal well-being an afterthought.

He had covered no more than thirty yards when they spotted him. He heard a cry and looked up to see men in the rigging pointing and yelling. Their cries drew the attention of those on the ground, and en masse the mob converged from both above and below. The men in the rigging began to descend to intercept him, and those on the ground hurried to catch up. But they did not have to hurry too much. Irish was large and strong, but he was also injured and slow. If he could get his hands on a man, that man was as good as dead; but he was too old, heavy, and ungainly to make a good sprint. By the time he reached the scaffolding, his enemies from above were prepared to meet him, and their cohorts on the ground were not far behind.

They came with whatever weapons they had at hand—hammers, knives, lengths of pipe or chain. Fortunately the planks leading up into the scaffolding were only a few feet wide, so they could only come at him one at a time. But they threw themselves at him with such abandon that he could not help but be impressed at their confidence. It brought a cruel smile to his face as he absorbed the first bludgeoning pipe with a meaty forearm, then seized his antagonist by the shirt and hurled him into a support beam. The man met it face first and went down. Seeing his friend so expediently dispatched, the next man in line hesitated. But it was more than enough time for Irish to deliver a combination of punches that left him flattened.

This cleared the way into the scaffolding, and Irish scrambled up a plank that led to the next tier, laughing as he went. As his head emerged someone tried to crack his skull with a sledgehammer, which he just avoided by happenstance. By the time his attacker had drawn back for a second blow, Irish had climbed up and squared off. As the man swung the hammer, Irish rushed in, caught the handle in his left hand and the man's throat in his right. He then lifted him bodily off the ground and charged into the queue beyond, driving three men over the edge. They all tumbled ten feet to the ground below and landed in a heap. Before they could get up, Irish gleefully hurled their friend down on top of them.

He made the second tier with no resistance, though he could hear the clatter of footsteps not far above as others rushed to meet him. At that moment he looked down and noted the mob on the ground. The crowd had reached the base and men were filing up the plank behind him. He urgently moved on.

He came face to face with the men above. The first wielded a knife and threw himself helter-skelter at Irish in a desperate attempt to skewer him. Irish had just climbed up and was not yet prepared when the knife came down. The man gave a war cry as he drove the blade forward, sinking it into the meaty muscle between Irish's chest and left shoulder. The man got a surprised look on his face, as if he had not really expected to land such a blow, and then he erred by releasing it. He must have expected Irish to fall, but Irish only grimaced and plucked it out. The man was so horrified that he stood perfectly still as Irish raised the knife and drove it down through his collarbone.

The brutality of the attack gave pause to those beyond. They turned to retreat, but too many of their fellows from above had piled up behind them. Irish did not hesitate to press this advantage. He waded into them, taking their desperate blows as he hurled them left and right, casting them down to shatter on the ground, or in the crossbeams below. He dispatched at least half a dozen this way, but the truth is he had stopped counting. Victory and success—they were all he cared about. Nothing else mattered, not his life, and certainly not the paltry lives of the fodder that served the Doctor.

On he went, climbing two tiers higher and with similar results. By the time he was fifty feet up, the men from the ground had finally caught up to him. He turned, claimed his space, and fought them for it tooth and nail. It was a horrific yet comical scene: men lined up along the planks all the way to the ground, all waiting their turn to die. And Irish obliged them. He tossed at least a dozen to their bone-crushing demise before the rest realized their folly and pushed back against those behind them.

At first Irish laughed at them, because finally they appeared to have learned their lesson—they did not stand a chance against him. Then a nearby beam suddenly shattered with a resounding *crack*, sending a hail of splinters into his face. As he brushed them away, two more beams exploded. Then he realized the sounds were not coming from the beams, but from rifles below.

He may have been nigh unstoppable in melee, but when it came to guns even Irish was no match. Bullets are small harrowing things that burrowed into organs and leave seeping holes. His only defense against them was to take cover.

He backed away from the edge and pressed himself against the steel skin of the rocket, and in the process discovered a hatch. As he wrestled it open, three more bullets punched through the plank he stood on and ricocheted around him. Without delay he dove inside and sealed the hatch behind him.

He found himself in a narrow stairwell that wound up along the interior wall of the rocket. With the hatch closed the darkness inside seemed almost total, at least until his eyes adjusted and he detected a faint light from above. He climbed the stairs toward it. As he climbed, bullets continued to *ping* against the hatch behind him. No more than ten steps later he discovered the light source was a small porthole, sealed with glass so thick it distorted the view beyond. He paused to glance through it before continuing his ascent. Then the unexpected occurred.

From somewhere deep within the contraption he heard the whine of straining metal, like a heavy door on a rusty hinge, and before he could guess at what it meant, everything around him began to violently rumble and shake. The sound quickly became deafening, so ear-splitting he thought his head might explode. He wanted nothing more than to curl up in a ball and cover his ears. At that moment he collapsed, not from pain or fear, but from gravity.

The rocket began to climb. At first it was an almost gentle upward movement like an elevator, noticeable but not alarming. Then it rapidly accelerated and pressed him bodily against the stairs, practically pinning him. Like a drowning rat he felt the primal urge to climb higher, and hand over hand he began to haul himself up in defiance of the forces working against him. But the further he went, the heavier he felt. Soon he could no longer raise his arms from the floor. Then his crawl was reduced to a pathetic worm-like slide along the surface, moving onward and upward, his most colossal expenditures gaining him no more than inches.

He remained determined and continued to squirm upward. Before entering the hatch, he had not got his bearings—he had not realized he was half way to the top—so he had no idea how much further he had to climb. But he refused to give up, to die pressed against those iron steps. He summoned inhuman reserves and carried on.

When he finally reached the top of the stairs he sprawled on the floor, pinned by the rocket's momentum. His mind was in disarray, but he noted he was in a tight conical chamber lit by four portholes. In spite of his predicament, he desired to climb up and look outside, to confirm that he was in fact hurtling through the air. But even if he could reach one, he knew what he would see: wisps of cloud racing by, and the earth far below. He let gravity attempt to crush him against the steel floor as he wondered what it would be like to see it with his own eyes.

The portholes offered enough light to see a sort of cylinder in the middle of the chamber. Instinctively, he crawled toward it, and as he did he noticed the top was covered with a small glass dome. Even with no knowledge of rocket engineering, Irish understood it must contain something of importance. Just as the head contains the brain, he reasoned that whatever was commanding the rocket must be inside. With Herculean effort he raised his arms, gripped the cylinder, and pulled himself up to his knees. The rocket had begun to pitch over, and he was able to rest his chest against the cylinder for stability as he worked the glass dome open. The dome was hinged to the cylinder, but when he threw it open the hinge gave way. The dome fell to the floor and shattered, but the shards of glass did not scatter. Instead they stuck in place as if glued. Irish then pulled himself higher until his eyes broke the horizon of the container, and he gazed down at the thinking parts within.

The cortex was a series of metallic wheels within wheels surrounding a boxlike mechanical device. Irish grinned to himself, though gravity tugged at his face and turned it into a grimace. He knew he had found the weak spot, the behemoth's brain. Without hesitation he shrugged an arm over the edge and into the basin until his fingers found bits he could firmly grasp. Then he began to pull with all his might. As delicate as the pieces looked, the device was unexpectedly resilient and did not want to budge. But as his hand interfered with its operation, he felt the great beast shudder. Confident in his plan, he shrugged his other arm into the leviathan's brainpan, grabbed another handful of steel, and pulled.

To his surprise, the mental machinery came free, and both Irish and it collapsed, instantly immobilized. With his back pressed against the floor he could feel the beast's confusion, lurching one way and then another as it tried to cope with its sudden lack of direction. Aimlessly it searched for a destination, and after a while it seemed to randomly pick one. It began to tilt to one side until Irish was certain it was moving parallel to the earth, yet the forces pressing against him continued to hold him fast to the floor.

In that moment fear and joy combined to create a sense of euphoria. He began to laugh. His part was done, and very soon he would be, too. And he accepted it. Rather than lament his sad life and misfortunes, he chose to spend his last moments dwelling on his companions below, each fighting to survive. His heart went out to them. He wished them luck in their endeavors, long lives, and a lasting happiness he had never really known. Then he closed his eyes, mumbled a poorly-worded prayer recalled from childhood, and waited for the end.

I know what you are thinking, Dear Reader, for if our places were reversed I would be thinking the same. How, you ask, can I know what happened to Irish when I was fleeing the valley with Katya? My answer is simple. You will recall my early pledge, that I intended to record the truth and embellish only where necessary. Here, necessity intervened.

It is impossible to know how Irish spent his last moments, but consider the alternative: had I not taken the liberty, the world would never know the service he performed. I could not in good conscience allow my friend, or his sacrifice, to be forgotten. I therefore maintain that this is what happened, and that it simply could not have happened in any other way.

Compared with the trials of our companions, Katya and I met with considerably better luck. We made our way around the western edge of the bowl, trying our best to keep a low profile. We moved slowly due to her condition, but the further we went the more she shed the effects of the morphine. By the time we were half way between the monastery and the crevice, she had enough strength to support herself, but she still tightly gripped my gloved hand.

It was around that time that we began to hear distant gunshots. We turned our heads toward the rocket, but it was too far to make anything out. We pressed on, often glancing over our shoulders in hopes that we might discern some news of our friends.

Several minutes later we reached the crevice without incident or hint of detection. But before we entered it a mighty roar echoed around the valley and shook the earth. We turned to see the most amazing and horrific sight imaginable. The rocket was belching inexhaustible flame against the ground, causing a cloud of smoke and ash to billow out in every direction. We covered our ears, but the sound was so deafening our hands did little to muffle the noise. Then slowly—impossibly—that massive steel spire began to rise into the air. We watched as it climbed higher and higher, gaining momentum as it went.

We stood in awe, watching and not speaking a word. When at last the thing climbed to an altitude at which its engine was no longer deafening, we lowered our hands from our ears. I glanced at Katya, and though her face was expressionless, tears streamed down her porcelain cheeks. Suddenly she dropped to her knees. I stepped forward to catch her, then realized she had not fallen. She closed her eyes, bowed her head, clasped her hands together over her breast, and began to pray in her native tongue. She was a portrait of innocence and purity, and if there had not been a technological marvel racing toward the heavens, I would not have been able to take my eyes from her.

At length she stopped speaking, but she did not rise. Instead she sat back and looked forlornly up at the sky. To see her so tortured broke my heart, and I wanted nothing more than to take her in my arms and whisper reassurances to her.

Before I could give it further thought, she gasped and rose to her feet. I followed her gaze and traced the path of smoke to an incalculable height. It had attained such altitude, the rocket itself had vanished. All that was visible was the unquenchable flame that propelled it. As we watched, it appeared to pitch over to one side, turning in the direction of the sun. Another glance at Katya revealed more tears, but she was smiling.

"Are you all right?" I said.

She nodded without looking at me.

"I am fine," she said. "It is a miracle."

"I'll say," I said. "I guess the Doctor was right. His mad invention worked after all."

She looked at me in an amused yet puzzled way.

"No, Prometheus. Look—it is flying to the east."

"Yes, so?"

"Saint Petersburg is west," she said, wiping her tears on the back of a hand. "Nicholas—my family, my people—are saved."

"Ah!" I said, feeling a bit foolish. But she was too happy to give my slow wit further thought.

"Now I worry for the rest," she said. "I pray that it falls to earth somewhere remote and does not harm a soul."

"That would be ideal," I said, nodding.

"And I pray that our friends return to us unharmed," she said.

"It looks like that prayer has been answered," I said.

She followed my gaze toward the eastern wall of the bowl, and we watched as a thin, ash-covered figure staggered in our direction, one fist pressed over his mouth.

"Mr Dietrich!" she cried. She would have run to him had I not grabbed her by the hand and held her back.

Dietrich made his way slowly. He did not notice us until he was within a few hundred yards. Then he made a feeble wave.

Katya had to restrain herself, so badly did she want to leap forward and help him.

"Are you injured? Are you well?" she said, noting the blood on his sleeves.

"It's nothing," Dietrich said. "I'm fine. I only hope that damned machine doesn't harm anyone else."

Katya suddenly seemed more optimistic than before.

"I have faith that all will be well," she said.

"What of the others?" I said.

"Others?"

"The enemy," I said. "All those men working on the rocket. Are we safe?"

"Quite," Dietrich said. "The flame was like an inferno. To the last man, they were incinerated."

"And what of Mr Irish?" Katya inquired, glancing around the valley as if she expected to see him lumbering toward us.

Dietrich lowered his eyes and shook his head. We stared at him pleadingly, as if doing so might change the grim news. Tears began to well in Katya's eyes, and my heart again felt so heavy that I almost sank to the ground. But then Dietrich, our stalwart captain, rallied us.

"We must go," he said. "It is a long way back, and we are not yet out of danger."

The journey back to Véles was excruciatingly slow, mostly owing to Katya's condition. She was well enough to make the trek, but under any other circumstances we would have forbidden it.

By the time the town came into view it was past noon. Before anyone noticed us, we left the road and paralleled it within the trees. In this way we managed to approach town and get a look around without being detected.

Since it was the middle of the day the streets were busy. Women and children came and went, and here and there a shopkeeper swept the sidewalk as if unaware, or unconcerned, that only a few miles away a horrific event had occurred. Dietrich pulled the pistol from his belt and handed it to me.

"It has only one round left. Don't fire unless you must."

I did not know how one bullet was supposed to save us, but without another option I played along and nodded.

We left the trees and entered town along the road. We must have made a peculiar sight, two men and a lady, all dressed in fine clothing that was ragged and stained, hobbling into town on sore feet. But the spectacle of us worked to our advantage. Once the people laid eyes on us they froze as if they did not know what to think.

"Remember," Dietrich said in a low tone, "these are the friends, wives, and children of the men who captured us. Do not let your guard down."

He led us to the stable where the departed lieutenant had stored our horses and coach.

"Wait here and keep watch," he said. He and Katya then disappeared inside.

I stood at the door eyeing the many onlookers we had attracted. Slowly a crowd began to assemble, inching toward us with suspicious looks on their faces. I restrained myself until they were within twenty feet. Then I brandished the revolver, waving it in a wide arc to show I was not beyond shooting any one of them. This was enough to make them halt, but they did not retreat. Though they were mostly women and children, they did not seem afraid of death. Instead they glared at me like predators, waiting for me to drop my guard.

Then the stable door opened, and Dietrich led our horses out by the reins, the coach in tow. When he saw the crowd and their dark looks, he paused.

"They won't disperse!" I hissed.

"They worship Véles," he said. "A god of death and destruction. They are not afraid to die."

"Then let's get the hell out of here," I said.

I looked back to see Katya watching from within the coach, and with a nod I signaled Dietrich to join her. I then climbed atop the coach and with a cry slapped the reins against the horses' flanks. The beasts whinnied in protest and took off. The crowd split before us and we sped out of town at a full gallop.

About a mile out of town I looked back to make sure no one was following us. Reassured, I slowed the horses to a trot so as not to fatigue them. We had at least twenty miles to cover to Bogoslovsk, and I wanted to ensure the beasts would take us nonstop. But it was not the horses that turned out to be the problem. About midway the rear axle suddenly broke, rendering the vehicle useless. Dietrich crawled beneath to inspect the damage and emerged scowling.

"The heathens never intended to let us leave," he said. "The axle was filed half through. I'm amazed we made it this far."

"Can it be repaired?" Katya asked.

Dietrich sighed and shook his head.

"What now?" I asked.

"We unharness the horses," he replied. "There are two, so two of us will have to pair."

"I cannot ride," Katya pointed out. "I might hurt one of you, or the beast itself."

Dietrich deflated a little, but quickly rebounded.

"Then we walk," he said.

We freed the horses, which for a time stood around wondering what was happening. Gradually they accepted their newfound freedom. Then their homing instincts kicked in and they began to trot ahead of us toward Bogoslovsk.

Once again Katya suffered the most. She had already covered five miles in her uncomfortable shoes that morning, and now she was expected to repeat the trial. We had hoped the rest she got in the coach would rejuvenate her, but we had not gone a mile before she began to wince at every step. So the journey that should have placed us in Bogoslovsk by supper was extended, and due to frequent stops night fell upon us with miles to go.

No one spoke, but I sensed the darkness made us all uneasy. Even Katya hobbled along at a quickened pace. When at last I made out dim lights in the distance, I started to feel safe, perhaps prematurely.

Suddenly something rushed at us out of the darkness. At first I thought it was an animal, maybe a wolf, but as it charged I realized it was running on two legs. It had a strange shape that in the gloom seemed to shift and change. I wanted to turn and run, but I was too startled. As I stared at it, I heard my companions cry out. I was too mesmerized to comprehend their words. I sensed Katya and Dietrich falling behind me on either side, and I watched as the creature slightly adjusted its charge to come at me. As it approached it raised its arms, and I saw that each ended in three long, thin claws. It was clear the thing intended to shred me, or run me through.

Then I remembered the revolver, and in one swift motion I pulled it from my belt and fired. I did not have time to aim, and I feared I had missed. But to the surprise of all, the creature collapsed and rolled onto its back, making horrible gurgling sounds. Katya and Dietrich then returned to my side, and we inspected the oddity.

What in the dark had seemed like a feral monstrosity turned out to be nothing more than a hoax, albeit a deadly one. As we inspected it we quickly discovered it was a man, perchance shot through the throat. He was wrapped in sackcloth and furs, and his beard and hair were wild. In his hands he clutched the sawn-off prongs of pitchforks. He was either some deranged madman from the hills, or he was meant to frighten the locals and discourage travel along the road.

"I think we just met Koschei the Deathless," Dietrich said grimly. "Only he is not so deathless after all."

24: THE HONORABLE THING

The town of Bogoslovsk welcomed us with open arms, so pleased and amazed were they to see we had survived our travels along the Koschei road, and our time among the thralls of Véles. They inquired about our large friend. Katya choked back her tears and explained he had continued his travels without us. I applauded her quick thinking. There was no reason to inform or involve them in our adventures. They also asked if we had seen the strange event in the sky, to which we replied that we had not.

The following day Dietrich summoned the town elders for a brief meeting. They were happy to oblige since they so seldom received strangers. He told them of our encounter the night before, and that they would no longer be plagued by so-called Koschei. To allay their skepticism he told them where to find the body, and a group of men with hunting rifles and axes went to see for themselves. After that we took no interest in the matter and prepared for the noon train to Ekaterinburg. It was not until we were climbing into a wagon that the group returned with grim looks on their faces. They had spent the entire morning searching the area outside of town and found nothing. We were puzzled by the news, but as the train would soon carry us far from that place, we left the matter behind.

In Ekaterinburg we took the time to visit the garrison where we had stayed the night. We informed the men of Lieutenant Gorlov's company of his death. Though our endeavor had concluded, we still judged it best to keep it secret. We blamed his demise on a tragic accident and a moment of heroism, claiming he had died saving a child from the wheels of a runaway carriage. At least that way his men would remember him for his sacrifice.

From Ekaterinburg we caught the Trans-Siberian back to Saint Petersburg. I think I adequately portrayed the monotony of the journey earlier, so I will not relive it here. I will only say that as tortuous as it was coming, it was worse going back. All our thoughts dwelled on the empty fourth seat in the lounge, in the dining car, et cetera. Also of note: by our third day aboard train Dietrich became a recluse. His lungs pained him so badly that he purchased private quarters and shut himself in them for the remainder of the trip.

In Saint Petersburg still greater tragedy befell us. We were welcomed by the Tsar, with whom Katya disappeared and presumably told everything. We stayed there only one night, with Dietrich and I back in the guesthouse in the Summer Garden. It was awfully depressing, what with Katya's absence and Dietrich's condition growing worse. He had refused the Tsar's doctor without explanation, and when I tried to question him he shook his head and retreated to his room to waste away. So I did not pursue it. But as bad off as he was, that was not the tragedy.

"I am remaining here," Katya told us at breakfast. "Nicholas is concerned the Doctor, and Véles, may have other adherents. He asked that I remain and advise him in the matter."

Dietrich stared at her across his untouched plate, nodded and smiled. I, on the other hand, could think of no worse news.

"But we still have to report to Cross," I argued. "It's our duty."

Katya wrung her hands in her lap and stared at them uncomfortably.

"The two of you are more than capable of making our report. Each of you did far more than me. Besides, I have not spent time with my family in almost a decade. Now that our mission is over I am afforded the opportunity. Surely you would not deprive me of that."

She had me. I would not deprive her of anything she asked.

"You will return to America, won't you?" I said.

"Perhaps, in time," she said, forcing a smile.

The day of our departure she came to the harbor to see us off. As she stood primly upon the dock, the wind whipping her dress around her shapely figure, the sun lighting her golden hair, I had to restrain myself from embracing her, though at that moment the thought of dying in her arms for the price of a kiss seemed entirely worthwhile. But since physical expression was impossible, we only looked awkwardly at one another across four feet of empty space. Finally, words having failed us, I turned and followed Dietrich as he struggled up the gangplank.

"Make him see a doctor," she said in a low voice behind me.

"I will," I said, looking back at her one last time. "You'll write, won't you?"

"I will," she replied.

We retraced our route almost exactly, landing in Lübeck a day later. Dietrich had again secluded himself in his cabin, not even emerging for meals, so I did not see him until it came time to disembark. By then he looked pale and drawn, and I wondered if he would make it to shore without keeling over. Amazingly he did, and we climbed aboard the first train for Berlin. It was during that time, sitting beside him as he filled a handkerchief with crimson expectorant, that I finally lost patience.

"This is ridiculous," I cried. "You're obviously dying. You must see a doctor."

To my surprise he acquiesced.

"There is a sanitarium in Baden," he offered.

We made for Baden, which was well known throughout Europe for its hot springs. This gave me hope for my stubborn companion, as I imagined the pure spring waters would serve as a panacea for his condition. But by the time we arrived he was in no condition to wade into the magical waters and breathe deep their curative vapors. Instead he went straight to a private room where he was waited on by doctors and nurses. When I was finally allowed to see him, he looked like a man already deceased.

"I suffer from consumption," he said weakly. "It will be the end of me."

"Nonsense," I said, looking around the place. The room was quite lavish for a sanitarium. "You'll get well, and we'll return to New York."

He made a pathetic attempt at a smile.

"No," he said. "I'm done. I don't think I'll ever make it back. It is fitting that I stay here, so close to the land where I was born. But you must go. Report to Cross and inform him of our victory. And promise me you will inform Prince Arthur. I gave him my word, and I would not be remembered a liar."

I did not want to leave him behind, and I tried to argue. But for one so feeble, he was adamant. He would remain in Baden unless by some miracle he were cured, in which case he promised he would return to New York and look me up. I did not believe a word of it. But since my only alternative was to sit by his bedside and watch him waste away, I finally agreed. I boarded a train to Brussels the next day.

I passed through a variety of lands without noticing them, so consumed were my thoughts with all the tragedies of late. We had gone so far and accomplished so much, and then in a matter of days I had lost all my friends. My thoughts dwelled mostly on Katya, wondering what she was at that moment doing, if she missed me as much as I missed her, and if so, whether she had begun to write to me yet. In the event that she had, I did not want to be remiss. In Brussels I purchased a series of ten beautiful leatherbound notebooks and began feverishly filling one with thoughts of her.

I crossed the channel in some massive black hulk that, to me, looked like all the rest. I never bothered to remember its name. In London, my attention was so devoted to capturing thoughts of Katya in my notebook that my time there came and went. I barely remembered to send Cross a telegram in preparation for my arrival.

> Evil vanquished. Due New York 13 July. Full report upon arrival. --Grey

That was my last act ashore. That afternoon I departed from Southampton aboard another behemoth plowing the waves toward New York. It was not until several hours later that I realized I had forgotten to provide a report to Prince Arthur. But with the Doctor dead and the Illuminati defunct, informing him would have been little more than a formality, so I put it aside.

The day before my arrival I remembered Cross would be expecting a full report. Only through supreme effort of will did I manage to pull my conscious mind away from Katya long enough to scribble out some notes. When I was done I had a report of three pages, which I tore from one exquisite notebook and folded neatly in preparation for Cross's sweaty hands.

I arrived in New York harbor precisely on schedule. Returning home so uplifted me that I set aside my journal—already three quarters full—and stood on deck as we entered the harbor. The sight of Lady Liberty and my city beyond brought a tear to my eye.

We docked and began to disembark. As I descended the gangplank I spied Cross nearby. He looked very pleased with himself. When he met my eyes, however, his smile flickered, and by the time I reached the dock he looked downright distraught.

"Welcome back," he said. "Where are the others?"

I explained Irish's sacrifice, Katya's decision to remain in Russia, and Dietrich's tragic illness. On the subject of Dietrich, I commented, "He could be dead by now for all I know."

This visibly agitated him.

"But we need him here," he insisted, as if I could produce Dietrich from thin air. "We require his account of what happened."

"Not to worry," I said. "I have a full report."

I produced the papers. He shuffled through them incredulously.

"Three pages?" he said. "You were abroad for months!"

"Six pages," I replied. "I wrote on the backs."

He did not bother to flip them over.

"This is a travesty," he said. "We require Mr Dietrich. Only his account will be perfect in every detail."

I shrugged, not sure what else to tell him. He continued to bluster about how the plan was now ruined, and that Dietrich had been the linchpin. I quickly became bored and began to scan the faces of the crowd. As my eyes danced across them I noticed a pair of eyes fixed on me. They belonged to a woman—dark haired, fair complexion, plain of feature and simple in dress, but otherwise not without her charms. Her expression was a mask of anxiety.

"Well, I can't solve it here and now," Cross said finally. "I must get back to the office. Where did you say you left him?"

"Who?" I asked.

"Meyer Dietrich!" Cross exclaimed. "Where did you leave him?"

"Baden," I said. "In a sanitarium."

"Vague, but it's a start," he replied, bristling with exasperation. "Here."

He pressed some bills into my hand.

"For a cab. I must go."

He turned and began to walk away.

"That's it?" I asked. "What about my stipend?"

He sighed and held out a small card. He let it go before I had a hold on it. I spent a few seconds clapping at it like an idiot child trying to catch a butterfly.

"You'll find an account created in your name," he said. "It already contains the first installment. On behalf of the President and the nation, thank you for your work. Your services are no longer required. Good luck to you."

His words could not have sounded more insincere, but as long as my stipend was secure I did not care. Cross was done with me, and I with him. "Good riddance," I said as he climbed into a cab and rode away.

As I turned to look for a porter to fetch my luggage, I again noticed the young woman staring at me from afar. I was not particularly in the mood to make her acquaintance, but I had learned from experience to take advantage of such opportunities when they presented themselves. I straightened my coat and was about to approach her when she began walking toward me.

As she neared I got the distinct impression I had seen her someplace before—maybe even met her—but try as I might I could not place her.

405

She strode up to me and stopped, anxiously fidgeting with a handkerchief.

"Welcome back, Mr Grey."

"Thank you," I said, smiling. "It's good to be back."

She looked at me expectantly, and I returned her gaze. The silence between us became awkward. Then it struck me like lightning.

"Abigail!" I exclaimed. She was none other than the young housemaid from the residence at Corona Park. When I cried out her name she brightened, though she still looked strangely uneasy. I thanked her for coming out to welcome me back. I then turned to go in search of my luggage, but she grabbed my arm.

"Mr Grey, we need to talk," she said.

I was a bit taken aback by her forwardness, but her insistence intrigued me.

"About?"

She looked at me pleadingly for a moment, then scanned the crowd around us to make sure no one would overhear.

"I'm pregnant," she said softly.

I had not known what to expect, but that declaration was beyond anything I had anticipated.

"Congratulations!" I cried, and I gave her a hug to express my joy on her behalf. But as I disengaged her smile faded. Then I was at a loss, for I could not understand how my remark could have brought her down. She went back to rending her handkerchief and glancing around nervously.

"What's wrong?" I asked.

She sighed and looked timidly into my eyes.

"It's yours," she said.

"Mine?"

"Ours," she clarified.

"Our what?"

"Our child," she said. "Don't you remember? The night before you left on your trip?"

I was speechless. As I stared at her in disbelief, my own anxiety began to grow.

"Impossible," I said.

"It's true," she insisted. "I have not been with another man. Only you. And because of it, Jonas has abandoned me."

"Who?" I said.

"Jonas," she said, tears welling in her eyes. "He was my fiancé. Don't you remember? Now he refuses to see me. There is nothing I can do to get him back. So I must look to the future, and to you to help take care of our child."

She prompted me with a look. It was my turn to speak, but I had no response.

"I need to know your intentions," she said, dabbing at her eyes. "What will you do for me and the child?"

I opened my mouth but no words came. I found it hard to believe the child was mine. I began to think I was being fooled into taking responsibility for some other man's deed. Without another word I handed her the cab fare Cross had given me, turned, and hurried away into the crowd.

I quickly set my life in order. The stipend was enough to return to my adopted home, my beloved Brooklyn, where I took an apartment overlooking the turgid waters of the Upper Bay. With money left to spare I did not require additional employment, and after so remarkable a journey and such heroic demonstrations, I felt I had earned some time off. I chose to spend the next month or two relaxing, gathering my thoughts, and making plans for whatever would happen next. I knew I would soon become restless, so I entertained thoughts of returning to show business. I could perhaps reinvent myself under a pseudonym and escape the patina left on my reputation by Houdini's betrayal. The thought excited me, and I opened one of my beloved notebooks and began making notes for new tricks and escapes.

But to my chagrin I quickly ran out of steam. I had not filled half a page before my thoughts returned to Katya. As if my pen had a mind of its own, it began to scrawl out thoughts of her. It was then that I admitted to myself that I was hopelessly in love with her, and lost without her. I then lapsed into a depression and did not leave my apartment for three weeks, except to fetch meals that I picked at but never ate.

As I sat in solitude, occasionally my mind wandered from Katya to my lost friends. Irish was gone forever, and I had no clue if Dietrich were living or dead. It was during one of those moments that I recalled my final meeting with Cross, and his words bubbled up in my mind. He had said the plan had been ruined, that Dietrich had been the linchpin. The comment perplexed me. Dietrich had been our captain, and he had possessed a perfect memory, but I did not understand why or how that made him more valuable than the rest of us. In fact, I would have argued Katya, our moral compass, was far more valuable to our endeavor. However, his comment stuck in my head and haunted me, until one evening I decided to get to the bottom of it.

I remembered well enough how to find the house at Corona Park. As I strolled up I noticed no effort had been made to improve the place during my absence. I rang the bell and was met by a round faced, red cheeked matron whose smile faded the instant she laid eyes on me. She took a moment to look me up and down in mute disgust.

"She's in back," Mrs McMurtey said. "You can wait outside while I get her."

It took me by surprise. She almost closed the door in my face before I stopped her.

"No!" I exclaimed. "I'm not here to see Abigail. I'm here to see Cross."

She opened the door the approximate width of her girth and eyed me.

"He's not here," she said.

"When do you expect him?"

"I don't," she said haughtily. "He rarely comes here anymore, and when he does it's unannounced."

"Well, is he in the city?" I asked.

"I wouldn't know," she said obstinately. "I'm not informed on his comings and goings. You can leave a note if you like. I'll give it to him when I see him."

"No," I said. "That won't do at all. I need to speak with him immediately. It's urgent."

She placed a beefy hand on a well-insulated hip.

"More urgent than an unwed mother and a fatherless child?"

My shoulders sagged.

"Please, let's not get into that," I said.

At that moment a call came from within.

"Who's at the door, Mrs McMurtey? Do you need help with anything?"

I cringed at the sound of Abigail's voice. Mrs McMurtey closed the door a few inches and spoke over her shoulder.

"No, dear. It's nothing I can't handle."

She then turned to me, more displeased than before.

"You've made her sick with worry. You've done enough harm here, now go away."

I stuck my foot in the door before she could close it.

"Not until you tell me where I can find Cross," I insisted.

She quickly glanced over her shoulder. Her faced turned a shade redder.

"You listen to me," she hissed. "You get out of here before you upset this girl any further!"

I stood my ground.

"Not until you tell me where to find him!"

The stout woman pursed her lips as if torn between expletives.

"Where does he live?" I demanded. I was certain she knew more than she was letting on. Servants always do.

"I can't tell you that," she said with finality.

"What about his work?" I said. "Where does it take him?"

She shook her head and opened her mouth to deny me, but then she froze. By her expression I could tell I had found a chink in her armor. I insinuated myself a few more inches into the opening.

"Yes?"

"You might find him at his office," she said.

"Office?" I said. "I thought this was his office."

"Not anymore," she said. "He works most days at the lodge."

"Lodge?" I said.

"Yes," she replied. "The Mason's lodge, at the corner of Sixth and Twenty-third."

As I processed the information, she seized the opportunity to expel me.

"Now get away from here before Abigail notices you, or so help me, I'll call the police!"

With a shove she removed me from the doorway and shut the door before I could regain my ground. But that was well enough, because now I knew where to find Cross.

I took a cab to Twenty-third Street and got out a few blocks down. I then strolled casually toward the building, trying as I went to work out what Cross could be up to, and what I would say when I confronted him. Before long the building came into sight, a large, five-story brick structure with gables. I slowed my stroll to give myself more time to work things out, but I came up with nothing. Cross was obviously a Mason—a fact he had not bothered to reveal when discoursing on how the Illuminati had grown from Freemasonry. Instinct told me it was a significant point, but I could not make sense of it. So instead of trying to puzzle through it, I decided to put Cross on the spot, to make him do the explaining.

I walked resolutely to the door. I turned the knob and found the door to be unlocked, so I bypassed the bell and marched inside.

I found myself in a darkly paneled foyer, empty except for several coat racks and a pair of empty benches. I moved on. The foyer opened into a larger antechamber beneath a large chandelier. Here I was presented with several doors on the ground floor, and a winding staircase that led to the upper levels and a balcony overlooking the room. I was instantly drawn to a pair of heavy wooden doors. I boldly strode forward and flung them open.

The room beyond was not what I had expected. It was one of those rooms that seems to defy the confines of the house it occupies. It was large, many times larger than my whole apartment, and mostly empty. Dim lamps burned along the walls. Chairs were lined up beneath them, but they were unoccupied. On the far side of the room, and directly opposite me, was a platform containing three desks, and seated behind them were three men. Two of them were older gentlemen whom I neither recognized nor cared to meet. The third, and central, man was Cross.

The fury of my entrance immediately drew their attention. They looked surprised, but not alarmed. They remained seated and watched me as I strode to the middle of the chamber.

"So, Mr Cross is a Mason!" I exclaimed theatrically.

"Mr Grey?" he said, rising to his feet. As he did I noticed he wore the traditional Masonic raiment, a medallion and the apron. "What are you doing here?"

"Looking for you," I said. "You owe me an explanation."

He looked at his elder companions, who glanced at him from beneath bristly white eyebrows.

"What explanation do I owe?" he said.

I waved my arms at the walls around us.

"This for a start," I said. "I'd like to know why you didn't tell us you were a Mason when you recruited us."

"It was not germane to the conversation," he said.

"Not germane?" I cried. "On behalf of the President you recruited us to eliminate a threat spawned by the Masons, and now I find out you belong to that very fraternity! How do you explain that?"

He gazed at me in silence before looking again to the solemn old men at his sides. They looked at each other before nodding in response. Cross then sighed and turned to me.

"Very well," he said with sarcasm, "since you have so adeptly uncovered our involvement, I will tell you the truth."

"Finally!" I cried, my voice echoing around the hall.

"Though I doubt you'll like it," he continued. "The truth is, you never held a secret commission, and the President has no knowledge of you. That was pure fabrication meant to prey on pride, loyalty, duty to society, what have you. And, as we hoped, it worked. You each stepped forward for your own reasons."

"But why us?" I demanded.

"As I said when we first met, you each possessed unique qualities that would contribute to accomplishing the mission. And accomplish it you did, in a far more spectacular manner than I thought you capable of."

He picked up a newspaper clipping from the desk and held it out. I cautiously stepped forward and snatched it from him.

"I can't read this," I said. "It's in Russian."

Cross grinned.

"It tells of a phenomenal explosion over Siberia that laid waste to thirty square miles," he said. He held up another handful of papers. It was my report. "It was your rocket, Mr Grey."

I shuddered to think of such devastation, but I did not let it distract me.

"But what was the purpose of it all?" I said.

"To take action and responsibility," Cross replied. "For more than a century Freemasonry has been haunted by the specter of the Illuminati. We do not claim them, and yet they grew from us. When Weishaupt died, the Masons thought the threat perished with him. We did not know he had taken a protégé, this Doctor Drechsler, until the man published his thesis. For decades we tried to seek him out, but to no avail. Finally, we decided to try a different approach, to employ a small group of outsiders, uniquely talented individuals, to see if they would succeed where we failed."

I grudgingly accepted his logic, but I still was not mollified.

"What of Dietrich?" I said. "Why was he so important?"

"Because we needed to know everything you learned," Cross said, "about the Illuminati, the cult of Véles, Red Mercury, the rocket. The Doctor managed to create a device of the future, a weapon of inconceivable reach and destruction. In order to ensure such a thing is never again constructed, we needed to know *everything*."

He tossed the pages of my report on the desk as if they were refuse.

"Instead, we know nothing," he continued in disgust. "All of those details are lost, glossed over in a single paragraph of this worthless banality you call a report."

His criticism of my work wounded me—I thought my report had been quite thorough—but I was determined not to let him know it.

"Well, you'll have to get by with what I've given you," I said. "Dietrich can't help you."

"We're looking into that," Cross said smugly.

His arrogance infuriated me, more so than being exploited. Still, he had to be held accountable for using us.

"You lied to us from the beginning," I said. "It was a fool's errand."

"And yet you succeeded," he replied. "In a matter of months you achieved that which thousands of Masons have failed at for a century. You thwarted Mankind's greatest enemy, and you saved hundreds of thousands of lives. Who else on Earth can claim such accomplishment?"

His words found their mark. I could not help feel some pride for my role. But the thought that we had been duped still rankled.

"Perhaps," I said. "But that doesn't justify your manipulation of us. It insults the memory of Irish, and the integrity of us all. That I will not tolerate."

Cross arched an eyebrow.

"What do you intend to do?" he asked.

My mind cast about, trying to think of some way to hold him and the Masons accountable. I thought of buying a gun and returning to take revenge, but that was too extreme. I considered telling the authorities how we had been misled, but even if they believed me (which they would not), what accusation could I make? Cross had lied and manipulated us— immoral, but hardly a crime. If investigated, I would be culpable for the crimes committed in pursuit of our goal, and I had no desire to be extradited and thrown into a foreign prison. No, it was in my best interest not to get the authorities involved. But another idea came to mind.

"I'll write about it," I said. "I'll capture all the details you so jealously covet and publish them for the world. Then everyone will know of the threat, of our success, and of our sacrifices. More importantly, they will know of you, and how you used innocents to achieve your ends."

Cross glared at me. By the way he worked his jaw, I thought I had him.

"There are two flaws in your plan," he said at length. "First, no one will ever believe you, at least no one of consequence."

He had a point, but I was not prepared to concede.

"And second?"

"Doing so would violate the terms of our agreement," he said, a grin forming at the corners of his mouth. "You will recall your stipend is conditional upon success and secrecy. Success has come and gone, but the requirement for secrecy persists. If you write anything beyond this report, the money is forfeit."

There he had me. I had not agreed to the mission for want of adventure, or because it was the right thing to do. I had agreed because, innocence aside, I was a criminal facing imprisonment, or death; I was destitute with no prospects; and the offer had come at the right place and time. I hung my head. All my ammunition was spent. I stood there a few seconds more, battling humiliation, before I turned and walked away. As I passed through the chamber doors, Cross called out.

"Good luck in life, Mr Grey. Remember your oath. To ensure you stay true to your word, we'll be watching."

I wandered home in a stupor. I was so filled with rage I could not think straight. The image of Cross standing above me, chastising me as if he were my master, and wielding power over me as if I were his slave, seared my mind like fresh welts from a lash. If in my lifetime I would be able to forget it, the day would not come soon enough. Uncontrollable tears welled in my eyes.

As I set foot on the steps to my apartment, however, a change came over me. Call it obstinateness or righteous indignation, take your pick, but as I climbed the stairs I decided to act. I would not live out my life as his thrall or according to his rules. I would not live in fear of losing my pension. I would do the honorable thing, putting integrity and the memory of my friends above all else. And I would spite Cross if it was the last thing I did. I hurried up the steps, sealed myself in my apartment, lit a single lamp, and drew the curtains. My privacy complete, I retrieved my notebooks. I selected one which I had not yet violated, opened to its first virginal page, and began putting down the account that you, Dear Reader, have just read.

It has taken me much longer to complete than I anticipated. When I first set pen to paper, I presumed I would be done within a month. When a month came, I deferred to three; at three months, I fell back to a year. Nine years later, I have finally finished the task, and not without grim satisfaction.

During the past nine years little of significance has transpired in the life of Yours Truly, but much has happened in the world at large. War plagues Europe and millions have perished, which makes me question the legitimacy of our victory. What is worse? To slowly murder millions in a prolonged war, or to incinerate them in a fiery flash? I am victim of a dark irony, because I would much rather perish from the Doctor's weapon than be riddled with bullets or choked on mustard gas. No matter how desperately we try to save Mankind, there is no shortage of men willing to commit unspeakable crimes, to see the world burn, to do their part to usher in the apocalypse. The sad and terrible truth is that Man is his own worst enemy. A bleak perspective, but one I cannot deny.

But enough doom and gloom! For now my story comes to a close, and on a hopeful note. My account complete, I am setting out this very week for Saint Petersburg. The trip is costing me a fortune, as it is ill-advised, and in some ways illegal. The war in Europe rages on with no end in sight. Travel there is discouraged, and in some cases forbidden. Therefore I have made arrangements with some less-than-reputable personages to reach my destination. Though I am not seeking adventure, there may be some in store for me yet.

I have not seen Katya since we parted in 1908, but I have thought of little else since then. We have corresponded on occasion, but in recent years I have heard nothing from her. At first I feared the worst, that the violence of the war might have found her, or that some unwashed Bolshevik may have found his way into the Winter Palace and done her harm. But in my heart I know Nicholas will have kept her safe, which is why her silence is so perplexing. Whatever the case, I have decided to get to the bottom of it. I have also decided I am long overdue to confess my love. Surely she already knows, but I am too old to play games anymore. I plan to make my intentions clear. I want her, even if I cannot touch her.

I am considerably greyer than when we parted, whereas she will still be comparatively young, in her mid-thirties by now. I hope she will not be put off by my inevitable venerability. For my part, I still have my charms, and I will not hesitate to use them to overcome our discrepancy in years.

I do not know what will become of this manuscript, or if anything will ever come from it. I can only hope that whatever happens, it causes some consternation for Cross and his kind. I have a few days left before I depart. I suppose I should find it a keeper.

Prometheus Grey
18 February, 1917

25: REPORT ON EVENTS AT THE IPATIEV HOUSE

To the Ural Regional Soviet

As directed, here is my account of events leading up to the execution. The Romanov family and their attendants were delivered to me on April 30, 1918, at the house of Ipatiev in Ekaterinburg. To be specific, I received Nicholas, his wife Alexandra Fyodorovna, and their children, Olga, Tatiana, Maria, Anastasia, and Alexander. Also, I received a number of servants who remained devoted to the family. They were Dr Botkin, the family physician; Pavel, his assistant; Anna, a maid; Ivan, a chef; and an attendant called Alexei. All were routinely kept in the house and only occasionally let into the yard for sunlight or exercise. They were under constant guard, though there seemed little need because Nicholas clearly did not intend to escape of his own accord. He looked old and haggard. He would not have put his family at risk in this way.

For two months the Romanovs lived in captivity in Ekaterinburg with no consequence. Their daily routine involved rising, bathing, baking bread for their meals, mending clothing (theirs and those of their guards), making minor repairs to the estate, and chopping wood. The only member of the family who did not assist was the Tsarevich Alexander because he was always too sickly. The attendants of the family kept themselves busy with the duties of their trade. The doctor performed weekly checks of each captive's health, but most of his time was spent looking after the boy. The maid stayed close to the Tsarina and her daughters, helping them with their chores because they were poor at them. None of the women had experience performing any of the simple tasks assigned. The handmaid ensured they learned the necessary skills and completed them adequately. The chef was required to feed both the family and my men. This occupied much of his day, because as soon as one meal was complete he would have to begin cleaning dishes and preparing the next. The Tsar's footman always stayed nearby and did most of the work assigned to the Tsar. Nicholas attempted all his tasks, but he had grown thin and weak and he always let his man take over for him.

It was after their first month in my charge that I realized the strange behavior of the doctor's assistant, the man called Pavel. He was an older man who followed the doctor around, but he had no skills and performed no medical function I could ascertain. When I questioned the doctor about him, he assured me the man was indispensable, even though he could not explain to me the man's purpose. But since the prisoners came to us from Tobolsk, where they were in the charge of another, I accepted them all on good faith. I believed they were all associated with the Tsar's family, and that they all belonged in captivity. I continued to watch Pavel, but I took no action to remove him.

Pavel spoke little, and understood less. On several occasions I watched as the doctor would give him some instruction, but Pavel would stand staring at him as if he had not heard a word. The doctor would have to repeat himself several times to get his assistant's attention. But even when he had it, Pavel seemed slow to understand. I began to think I finally understood Pavel's problem. He was an idiot, which explained why a man of his age would be reduced to such a menial position and given only the simplest of tasks. I almost felt sorry for him, because I saw in his eyes sufficient intelligence to recognize he had been reduced to the life of a halfwit. But Pavel remained happy in spite of his captivity. He appeared to enjoy following the doctor on his visits, especially when they spent time with the Tsar's children. Pavel particularly enjoyed the company of the young women, who had become quite sorrowful. In spite of his idiocy, Pavel somewhere had learned a selection of magical tricks, and he would try to cheer up the young ones by making small items disappear into thin air only to reappear from behind their ears. The tricks worked on some better than others. Maria and young Alexei were often entertained, but the rest only smiled politely. This seemed to make Pavel work harder, and sometimes he would spend half an hour performing tricks just to get a laugh. He sometimes involved my men in his performances, pulling items from their coats that belonged to someone else. Olga, the oldest girl, was the hardest to win over. Pavel never gave up until he got a quiet laugh from her. He had a talent for acting foolish. I began to think he was less of an idiot than I had thought, but he still seemed too idiotic to pose a danger.

In the final days the girl Olga became sadder, almost as if she sensed the end was near. I noticed Pavel spending more time around her, trying desperately to cheer her up. But even from my position at the window, as I watched them standing in the yard I could tell Olga forced herself to smile to humor him. To his credit, Pavel seemed to understand this, and after a few tricks he would stop bothering her.

One morning, the 15th of July, I heard noises outside and went to investigate. I was angered to find my men carrying planks of wood and tools into the yard. I demanded an explanation. They said the wood and tools were for Pavel, that he had promised to do a magnificent trick for them, but to perform it he required a cabinet. I did not reveal it, but I was most angry because they had collected the wood I had ordered to make coffins, should the need arise. When my men asked why I was so angry with them, I did not tell them the real reason. I only reminded them that they must request permission before indulging the prisoners. But from what they described to me, I could imagine no harm coming from it. So I granted them permission to let Pavel build a cabinet.

During the day of the 15th I frequently glanced out the window to check Pavel's progress, and I learned he possessed a skill other than his magic tricks. He was a surprisingly accomplished carpenter. He spent most of the day constructing his cabinet, which was large enough for a man of his stature to stand in. By nightfall a large but unadorned wardrobe stood in the middle of the yard. Pavel promised everyone he would perform his trick the following day. We left the cabinet in the yard during the night.

The next day after breakfast the family and their servants went about their chores. Around midmorning my men allowed them to take a break, and the Tsarevich asked if Pavel would perform his trick. I allowed it, and Pavel agreed. We all went into the yard and he made a show of walking around the cabinet and knocking on it to show it was real. He then invited Olga to inspect it. She did not look as if she wanted to take part, but she did as he asked. Then the other young ones came forward and did the same, opening the doors and knocking on all the walls. Finally the inspection was complete and everyone stepped back. Pavel circled the cabinet three more times, grinning and knocking. He then opened the doors, climbed in, and shut himself up inside. We waited for several minutes before we began to wonder at the purpose of the trick. We called out to him to find out if we had missed something he had intended us to see, but he did not answer. We waited another minute before I ordered one of my men to open it. He approached it cautiously, as if he expected the doors to fly open and Pavel to surprise him, but nothing happened. He flung open the doors to reveal it was empty. Everyone laughed and applauded because we thought we had finally grasped the trick. But as our cheers died down, nothing else happened. Pavel did not emerge from the cabinet, nor did he suddenly appear from some other location. I ordered my men to search for him, and they went through every room in the house and over every inch of the yard. I then suspected there was a hidden compartment in the cabinet that we had overlooked. I ordered my men to search it completely. They grabbed it and knocked it over and inspected every plank and nail, but the construction appeared plain. There was no secret compartment to be found.

Angered at the treachery I ordered the prisoners back inside and the premises searched again. A second search delivered nothing different. Furious, I realized my next duty was to inform my superiors that a prisoner had escaped. I went inside to write a letter. I sat at a desk facing a window, through which I could keep an eye on the cabinet. Every time I glanced up I expected to see Pavel creeping out to complete his escape. But he never appeared. I quickly completed my letter and with great shame and humiliation dispatched it.

As I awaited instruction from the Regional Soviet my men began to act strangely. Those on watch in the yard took up positions as far from the cabinet as possible. When I asked them why they were acting so strangely, they said the cabinet was evil, that it was the Devil's work, that maybe Pavel was himself the Devil. Upon hearing such nonsense I struck one man and knocked him down, berating him for his foolish superstition. But my actions did nothing to dispel the fear in the others. To put them at ease I had them douse the cabinet in kerosene and burn it. As it burned we all watched in terror and fascination, expecting to see the burning body of Pavel topple out. But the cabinet burned without incident.

Late in the evening I received a reply to my message. The Regional Soviet feared the escaped prisoner intended to deliver intelligence to the Tsar's supporters, that they would attempt to rescue the family and return the Tsar to power. To eliminate the possibility I was to execute the family at once. Upon reading the order I was horrified and could not bring myself to do it. I stayed at my desk late into the night struggling with it, but finally I admitted the necessity to protect all the Bolsheviks had achieved. In the early hours of July 17th I ordered the prisoners be awakened, dressed, and taken to the basement. My men performed this task. Nicholas, his family, and their attendants were left in the basement for half an hour while I instructed my men on the task ahead, and they prepared their ammunition and bayonets. We then returned to the basement and I announced they were to be executed. Upon hearing the words the women gasped and Nicholas stepped forward to plead, and at that moment I gave the order. The first volley did not kill everyone, and subsequent volleys were fired. But to our shock some still lived. We then realized jewels, remnants of the royal fortune, had been sewn into their clothing, and that our bullets had ricocheted off them. To complete the task my men drew bayonets and pistols. The survivors were then stabbed, or shot in the head.

It is with great regret that I complete this report. No trace of Pavel was ever found. I am responsible for his escape, but I submit that neither I nor my men were at fault, that circumstances were strange, and that we performed to the best of our ability. I ask that the Soviet take our loyal service into consideration when reviewing this case for negligence or misconduct.

Yakov Yurovsky
Bolshevik Secret Police
20 July, 1918

ACKNOWLEDGMENTS

Due to the proliferation of conspiracy theories, getting a scholarly and concise history of Freemasonry is extremely difficult. Much of what I learned of Freemasonry's history, of its tenuous links to the Illuminati, and of the individuals who sought to revive it, came from a variety of essays courtesy of The Grand Lodge of British Columbia and Yukon. (http://freemasonry.bcy.ca)

Part of Nikola Tesla's dialogue was culled from the scientist's own words that appeared in a New York Times article dated March 27, 1904, entitled "Cloudborn Electric Wavelets to Encircle the Globe: This is Nicola Tesla's Latest Dream, and the Long Island Hamlet of Wardenclyffe Marvels Thereat".

The character of Aleister Crowley, and the scene at his residence, were inspired by an event depicted in Do What Thou Wilt: A Life of Aleister Crowley, by Lawrence Sutin, Macmillan Books, 2002.

The poetic verse in Chapter 16 is taken from "Sea-Fever" by John Masefield, published in 1902.

Details of the Turn-of-the-Century Russian rail system and the experience of traveling the Trans-Siberian Railway were derived from the incredible travelogues of Burton Holmes. (http://archive.org/details/burtonholmestrav01holm)

ABOUT THE AUTHOR

J. Clark Hallvin is a graduate of the University of Central Florida's Master's program in Creative Writing. He is married, has two children, and calls no place in particular home.

≫«◇»«◇»«

To request author interviews, promotional support and other information, please direct all correspondence to contact@macguffinbooks.com.